I0652697

The Stench of Space
Or
How the Satanic Cow Saved The Universe From Itself

Keevy McAlavy

Music, Lyrics and Characterizations of The Clergy
By Craig Cawlfield and Topher Cawlfield

Published by Acne Press
an imprint of Barthan and Folgui Heavy Industries
www.etherplanet.com/barthan

ISBN 978-0-9883431-2-2
PI-th Printing December 2012

3.14159265358979323846264338327950288419716939937510582097494459230781640628620809

WARNING!

This warning label is not to be removed from this book even under duress or threat of life. This warning is here to warn and not to be taken off. Anyone caught tampering with or removing this warning will be reported to the Warning Watchers Association, a division of the Mattress Police.

Preface

These three paragraphs are the only serious ones in the whole book so you'd better pay attention. I originally wrote the Adventures of Rogicphil Suflipinic over twenty years ago and it had no ending; it just stopped. So I wrote a sequel, that was slightly more funny but had an ending. I knew readers liked having endings to their stories, so shortly before finishing the sequel I came up with one. It wasn't just an ending to the story but the entire universe as well. That way I wouldn't have to worry about writing a threequel.

This past year I thought about the books again and remembered that we're living in the future now, with print on demand sevices, so I dusted off the old computer files and sent them off to be printed. But they turned out to be 450 pages for volume one and 407 pages for volumn two. I knew that would be too much for even my most gracious friends to pretend to read so I contrived to condense them down into one book. That's the book you have in your hand or computing device right now. In the process I combined all the desparate story lines into more manageble chunks and completely threw out entire chapters.

If you seriously want to see what you're missing I have some printed copies of the original volumes left or you can download the pdf files from my website etherplanet.com/barthan.

Now back to your regularly scheduled idiocy.

Unacknowledgments

Ordinarily this section at the beginning of a book acknowledges people who helped in the creation of the book. I will do that later, in an unprinted format. Instead I would like to use this paragraph to unacknowledge people who hindered in the making of this book; you know who you are.

Guide to Pronunciation

Due to the many requests we hereby provide an idiot's guide to pronouncing terms within the Big Idiot Universe (no long affiliated with the Banana Universe).

Rogicphil (raw – GIK – fill)
Suflipinic (suu – FLIP – uh – nik)

Neblorkgodinzorbobgit (neh-bul LORK gho-din-zur-bob-git)

Table of Contents

Timeline

1987 Clergy's Adventure
1997 Greyson Sofecstat is born
1999 Clergy strike it rich
2001 Builds Clergy street on island
2010 Completes the Clergy Building on island
2021 Clergy Island officially becomes nation of Rufasonia
2027 Spyman time travels
2061 Space Navy and Space Marines enacted
2073 Last Clergy member dies of old age at 113
2089 Wormholes invented/discovered*
2096 First Extra Solar Star System explored
2115 First Terran Colony started on Barnards IV
2168 Plutoman is born
2192 Space-Bo is born
2208 Plutoman is stranded on Pluto
2227 Space-Bo and Plutoman time travel
2255 Terra is overthrown as capital of its empire by the Coco-Cola Planet
2256 First colony declares independence (Pepsi Planet)
2263 100th Terran Colony founded
2281 Space-Bo is sucked into another dimension and is never seen again
2324 Plutoman succeeds in blowing up Earth and himself
2413 Holovision goes out of style
2445 First Grand Galactic War is started between the Coco-Cola Planet
      Empire and the Pepsi Planet Empire
2475 GGII is started because no one remembered how the first one ended
2479 GGII ends when midgets blow-up both planets
2500 New Years celebration kills fourteen trillion in drunken spacecraft pilot
      accidents
2534 New Capital of dwindling empire is named: The Royal Crown Planet
2586 Empire crumbles and anarchy reigns
2593 Anarchy goes out of style
3955 Apes protest inhumane treatment of movie cliches
8661 X-day finally arrives but no one notices since the Earth had already
      been destroyed and long forgotten
10191 Special showing of Dune the Movie on Arakis
13163 Age of Dullness Begins
15429 Age of Dullness ends when see-thru miniskirts come back into style
23454 Second Age of Dullness Begins
74005 Third Age of Dullness Begins
80808 Name of Milky Way changed to Soggy Place Galaxy
97149 Deo 7 colonized
100702 Superlative Industries Spacescraper is completed
101999 Raul Rall Beta colonized
102678 Rogicphil is born
102701 Rogicphil becomes the Gladerunner
?????? The Universe Ends!

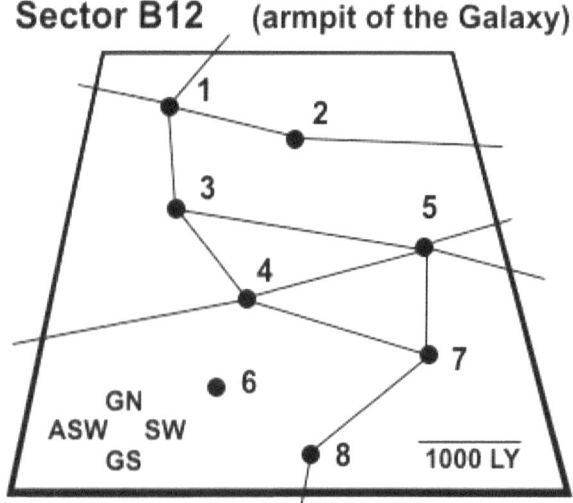

Sector B12 (armpit of the Galaxy)

Thin lines represent wormholes

1. Roganivar IV   (z-12)
2. Hespuets II   (z+14)
3. Danville   (z-3)
4. Rall Raul Beta (z-7)
5. Trigurard   (z-7)
6. Moorgnad IV   (doesn't exist)
7. Deo 7   (z+3)
8. Splas Toorg   (z-4)

GN - Galactic North, GS - Galactic South
ASW - Anti Spinward, SW - Spinward

Note: There are many maps showing the continents and cities of most of the inhabited worlds in this sector but mostly they're too boring and don't help much in the understanding of the story line. If you're really really interested the author has graciously offered to send you copies upon request.

Rogicphil Suflipinic

The Funky Chicken

Conrad Bovastein

Prolog: The Cow

The grass tasted good that morning, not too much mildew. A few crickets spiced it up a bit. Farmer Brown's cow, Besey, was enjoying the dew covered grass on the fifty hectare spread that was the farm. Besey had a whole ten hectare field all to herself; Farmer Brown couldn't afford another cow.

Despite it being early winter, that morning was relatively warm and proceeding along fine until Farmer Brown's dog choked on a dog biscuit, developed laryngitis trying to cough it up, and had to be taken to the veterinarian. Of course Besey didn't know about what happened to the dog and could care less about the stupid beast even if she did.

Besey was working her way over to the west corner of the field when, with a low rumble, a crack developed in the grass issuing red smoke. The crack grew into a hole and more red smoke came out. Besey turned her massive body around to see what was happening. Four metal rods emerged from the smoke, slowly rising from the hole. The rods were positioned to form a square. Crossbars appeared turning the square into a box. After the smoke cleared two figures emerged from the elevator onto the damp field. They were clad in red jump suits with little horns and each carried a pitch fork.

The shorter and fatter of the two had a clipboard in hand. The tall skinny looking one had a tiny mustache just under his nose and one eye that wandered around while his other stared blankly at the field.

Fatty, as Besey thought of him, looked at his list grumbling, "This is the place, Jake. Farmer Brown, UPC code number 529-ZX-123-BITS."

Jake just grunted.

Besey watched as they searched the farmhouse. They returned cursing, "Why ain't he here Jake? The form says he should be here." Fatty poked Jake in the eye when he just shrugged. "What are we going to do Jake? We need to make our quota today. If the Bossman gets mad with us again he'll bust our ranks. And then we won't get to wear these neat insulated suits anymore. And you know what that means."

"What about that cow?" Jake said unmoving.

"It means trouble. What are we going to do Jake? We need a soul to make our quota."

"That cow," Jake said a little annoyed.

Fatty poked Jake's eye again. "Idiot. We need a soul, not jokes."

Jake rubbed his eye.

"Come on, Jake. Think!"

"The cow," he said covering his eyes with one hand and pointing at Besey with the other."

"See no evil, huh? Well, what about your eyelids? They're evil too."

"What about that cows soul?" Jake said one more time.

"What cow?" He looked around the field, "You mean that ugly Holstein over there?"

Besey watched as Fatty walked up to her and made a thorough

examination of her teeth. "Not too bad. Needs a few cavities filled though, but I guess she'll do." She saw that growing look of evil in his eyes and tried to bolt for the barn. Too late did she realize that she was under his hypnotic powers, or maybe it was the injection he gave her while she was distracted by his goofy eyes.

As Besey watched, the field disappeared in a cloud of red smoke. She knew she'd never see her field or taste her dew covered grass again. It was the end. Goodbye, cruel farm, she cried. Oh well, maybe they severed alfalfa salad at the Fire and Brimstone Cafe.

*   *   *

Besey awoke up to find herself in some sort of a cave. She'd never been inside a cave before and therefore concluded she couldn't possibly be inside something she didn't know the name of. So the concept of a cave must be a random fluctuation in her brain. Brain? She never knew she had a brain. The thought had never crossed her mind before. The fact she now knew things she shouldn't have known made her apprehensive. She would have to analyze the situation thoroughly later, after she dealt with the problem of getting out of the cave.

She was enclosed in a single stall build into the rough cave wall, almost like the stall in Farmer Brown's Barn, blast his hide. Several humans in red clothes were walking around in the large cave, examining machines and tubes and things.

One of these humans came up to her carrying a fishbowl under one arm. She knew what a fishbowl was even when at the farm; she had had a friend named Herman who was a fish and had lived in a fishbowl. On nice days Farmer Brown would bring Herman out to the pasture to soak up the sun. She use to spend hours talking to him about what the Farmer's house looked like on the inside. But Herman was tired of the farm and wanted to move to the city. He and Besey had concocted a plan to run away. She would have carried Herman and his bowl on her back. But Brown must have learned of their plan for he killed Herman in cold blood then fed him to Boris, his ugly dog. This made Besey very upset and angry and from that point on she would only give him sour milk. Some day Brown would pay for his cruelty

"This is the last time old girl, then you'll be one of us," the human said and plopped the fishbowl over her head. He connected some tubes to the fishbowl and then joined the tubes to a black box sitting on a cart just outside the stall. Suddenly she felt an explosion in her head. The pain was like a white hot branding iron on her brain. Her memories slowly faded off into oblivion.

Then a mesmeric voice spoke to her, "You are now a member of H.E.L.L. an elite intelligence organization created for the preservation of evil, and other minor semi-goods. You will be a loyal member from this day on, you will obey your superior officers, you will..." The voice droned on into the black recesses of her mind. It was then she realized that rather than this being the end, this would only be the beginning. The beginning of her rein of terror upon all humans who dared keep farm animals. Yes, with the power of H.E.L.L. behind her, she would at last have revenge upon Farmer Brown.

Chapter 1: The Search Party

102701 A.D.
After what died? That question had been asked for thousands of years but nobody knew exactly what had died 102,701 years in the past. For that matter why was a year that long anyway? 365 days is too uneven a number for a Galactic time system. It is true, Rombolinzium, atomic number 365, has a half-life of 2.7 seconds, and that each standard day is 27 hours long. The top scientists in the galaxy had thought the solution was finally found until somebody pointed out that 102,701 years ago Rombolinzium didn't exist. So it has been left one of the great mysteries of the universe along with how teflon can stick to a pan if nothing sticks to teflon.

  — Excerpt from Barlow's Galactic Almanac

Rogicphil Suflipinic put down the Almanac he had been flipping through and tried the Flax-9000 Galactic Edition newspaper again. He had printed it out during the flight. The version he had picked back at the spaceport on Roganivar IV, his homeworld, had too many local interest stories for his taste and he'd shoved it down the recycler at his first chance. He was only interested in the big story. The story of the century that would rewrite all the history books in the galaxy. That would be cool.

But there wasn't anything galactically significant in this version either. The masthead slogan read: **Flax-9000 the only newspaper with the power to move you**. Amatures, he thought.

Not able to shake off the anxiety, he looked out the shuttlecraft window. Far below, covered by wispy clouds he could see the smooth dark surface of the ground. Perfect for bowling alleys. The main continent was directly below with its many seas huddled in the center and mountain ranges rising up in a ring around them. It was around sundown at the capital city, also named Danville, and he watched the terminator line slowly creep to the west.

He'd come a long way to the planet Danville for his present assignment. Back on Roganivar IV he and his editor had a bit of a personality clash and so he had been sent to an entirely different star system. Danville and Roganivar IV were just one wormhole jump from each other in galactic sector B12 but it was his first time out of the system and his homeworld seemed very far away indeed.

"Thank you for traveling on Lugietorp Spaceways," a crackling voice said over the intercom, "We will be landing on Danville presently. Stewardesses prepare for a lively arrival." He knew what that meant and so pulled his feet in as far from the center aisle as possible. Soon a series of bowling balls were cruising down the aisle, back and forth to keep any potentially unruly passengers in line.

Half an hour later the shuttle was fighting the spaceport ground traffic to the terminal. A smaller private shuttle was moving into an open gate but Suflipinic's shuttle fired up its engines and roared into the spot cutting off the smaller craft. He looked out the window at the other shuttle. Its pilot was making rude gestures at his shuttle.

Rogicphil was met at the terminal by a large husky man with a graying beard. "You must be the replacement reporter," he growled, "You're late. Follow me."

Rogicphil followed him past the designated self immolation area into the terminal main lobby. The man got a pack of flamers from a stupid vending machine that thanked but warned him not to operate flamethrowers while flaming.

"Got any luggage?" the man growled as he zapped his flamer to life.

"It's all up here," Rogicphil said tapping his head. "The greatest story the galaxy's ever read."

The man looked at Rogicphil funny but didn't say anything. He led him to the curb were his ground sedan picked them up. It had just rained and the early evening air was crisp and cool.

"Name's Rickerson," the gray beared man said after they were on their way. He had the car in manual mode and enjoyed swirving around all the boring automated traffic. He made a sharp right hand turn and barreled down a way too narrow street. "As this is the only scene I'll be in," he mentioned jovially, "it doesn't matter what I say right now."

"Is it me or are Danville's streets a bit cramped?" Rogicphil asked noting the orange sparks shooting off the sedan as it scraped the buildings on either side of the alleyway.

Rickerson looked at him sideways and chuckled a little. "Nah, just the interesting ones. That's the way I like it." A set of headlights were coming directly at them now and he floored the accelerator, zooming the sedan faster towards disaster.

"Name's Suflipinic. Raw-GIK-fill Suu-FLIP-uh-nik."

"Weird name."

"Weird life."

"So I've heard," Rickerson said suddenly swirving hard to the left and down another super narrow street, thereby barely missing the other oncoming car. He dropped Rogicphil off at a sleazy cheap hotel on the bad side of town.

The sedan's passenger door wouldn't open because the building was in the way so Rogicphil had to crawl out the sunroof. "Nice to meet you, uh..." he said poking his head back down into the car.

"Rickerson," the man said, "And don't forget, swallow your pride and eat the damn pie."

"What?"

But Rogicphil didn't get an answer as the car suddenly sped away, flipping him over end to end. He landed on his butt on the wet pavement. "Ouch."

*   *   *

"Top Government Officials Taking Bribes? You call that a headline? I'm not even moderately impressed with this story, uh mister.." the editor looked up at him questioningly.

"Suflipinic, Rogicphil," the reporter said.

"Suplufinic, right. I've got to write that down. Well, despite it appearing in the travel and leisure section, it's got some top government officials in an official uproar." The editor shook her head in dismay. She was sitting in the same receptionist like desk he had seen her in when he first walked in a month ago.

"Don't worry about," he said, "They get over it. They always do."

She was beginning to regret offering him the job. His reputation was terrible but she owed his former editor a favor. "No where does it say who was doing the bribing," she complained, looking at the story again.

Rogicphil didn't tell her that it was he who had bribed the officials for the story. Instead he said, "I'll rout them out first thing next week."

"Uh huh."

"Hey I see your new name plate arrived," he said admiring the shiny new desk ornament. It proclaimed "Ms. Editor in Chief (not the receptionist)." It was in large over sized block letters and rested at the end of her desk. It was a present Rogicphil had bought for her with his first paycheck.

"This is almost as bad as that story you wrote about stolen spaceport luggage." She pulled her glasses down to the end of her nose so she could look directly at Rogicphil. "But all those officials, officially uproaring want you to put that story on the back burner for now. They.... I've got another assignment for you."

He had stolen the luggage himself, saying that a band of hooligans were roaming the sewers under the spaceport, only coming out at night to pilfer the place. It had been a slow day and he had been in need of a story. Danville just didn't generate enough real stories to keep a newspaper going. Besides the non-profit Hospital for the Recently Alright was more than happy for the donation of designer clothing.

"Another assignment?" He perked up seeing the gleam in her eyes. "Is this the big galactic story I've heard about that's been brewing for a while?" He looked closer. No, that was the sleep inhibitor she was hooked on.

"With travel involved," she said with a smile and pushed her glasses back up on her nose. Due to ancient medical advances no one had needed glasses for tens of thousand of year but some people were just plain conservative and refused to give them up. Eyewear support groups can be found on every major planet in the galaxy. I know dear reader what you are thinking at this time that this is really stupid, but for 99% of the human race's existence, clothing hasn't been necessary and yet people still wear it. So in retrospect there really isn't anything wrong with wearing something you don't need, like glasses, or boots on your head.

Rogicphil pondered this for a moment. "Do you go to a support group?" he asked abruptly.

"Hey, my drug problem is none of your business."

"I am a reporter. It's my job to know."

"Yeah, well, about once a week."

"Now what's this about another assignment?"

She pressed a button on her desk and a pre-recorded hologram of the government official he'd been bribing appeared. "As a good citizen of Danville, as I'm sure you are too, I'm a firm believer in the Manifest Bowling Destiny. We all know the true spirit of bowling is in the heart and not the wrist. We need more bowling alleys not to keep kids off the streets but to teach them the true meaning of gambling. We need more bowling alleys not simply to replace our current out-of-date facilities but also to promote growth and bolster our re-election campaign. Uh I mean economy. You can edit that out can't you? Thanks. As a good citizen..." The hologram began to loop and she cut it off.

"Bowling alleys? Is that what this assignment is about?"

"Partly." She fished out a clipping from under a pile of papers, "Read this."

Rogicphil took the clipping. It read:

SEARCH PARTY DISAPPEARS
Last week the search party looking for Dr. Gronblec's Survey Team mysteriously disappeared themselves. They were searching the barren western continent for signs of Dr. Gronblec's ill fated team that are believed dead. The famous Dr. Gronblec failed to report, last month, on the progress of his team to find suitable locations for future bowling alleys...

Rogicphil scratched his head. "Where's the sexy part? What about the existentialist angle?" This most definitely was not the big story. He saw the editor's disapproving look. "I mean it's fantastic that, I get such an opportunity to help out the cause of uh, the bowling alley shortage because..."

"Listen Sufluffinic, you're not stupid, you know as well as anybody that bowling alleys is just code for... well you know." She paused to let him ponder. "I want you out there finding out what's going on. These 'bowling alleys' are important." She made the quotation sign with her fingers as she said it. "You're one of my best 'reporters', Suplifinic, so I know you'll get to 'the bottom' of 'it'."

Rogicphil blinked at each quotation, then said, "Didn't Gronblec have a locator beacon with him so he could be picked up later?"

"Yes, but it keeps giving messed up 'readings'." She handed him a packet. "This contains maps and a 'travel voucher' to get you there. You can get whatever else you need from the 'supply room'."

He took the packet and sat down on the edge of her desk. "You can count on me, uh, 'chief'." He made his own quotation sign as he took a sip of her RC cola. Ignoring her glare he then said, "But I'm going to need some 'men'."

She took the cola away from him and set it out of his reach saying, "Quit fooling around. You can get nineteen pre-approved people for three weeks, that's all that payroll can handle, and no other reporters. We can't afford to be short staffed when... uh I mean we need them here because uh... you'll be gone and no one will be able to cover all these wonderful stories that have suddenly started popping up soon after you arrived."

"Awesome."

"Report in weekly as I don't want to waste my time paying you when you're 'dead'."

14

"I'm glad you're, concerned...?"

In the supply room Rogicphil found some old camping gear and stuffed it into a duffel bag. He also grabbed a wad of counterfeit money to bribe the unemployment center officials with.

He was about to exit the building when the editor stopped him. "Suplifinic," she called behind him, "Don't 'screw' up!"

At the unemployment center he waltzed in wearing a dark blue pleaded pin-striped turtle-necked oversized suit (one of the few things he hadn't dumped into the Hospital rag bin) that was presently in fashion on Danville. He personally thought it was ugly but he needed to look good if he was to bribe the officials.

He made his way past lines of 'welfare' people to a window labeled 'Highering'.

"I think your sign is misspelled," he told the red and blue stripe skinned lady behind the window.

Suddenly machinery came to life, metals arms swung down from the ceiling grabbing his arms while clamps held his legs fast. The arms then pulled up, stretching him up to eye level with the lady. "What did you say?" she asked.

"I-I guess it was spelled right. Ouch this hurts."

"Of course it hurts. It's called unemployment. It effects three and a half percent of our population, an unprecedented amount in this day and age, and it gets worse." She stomped on a foot pedal stretching him even farther.

Rogicphil's back cracked. "Oh, hey. Wowza."

"Welfare is only a temporary solution. You need to develop job skills."

"Right. Uh, what if I wanted to uh, hire someone?"

"You want Hiring, next window down."

"Okay, I'd really like to do that." His eyes pleaded with her.

"What!?" she barked.

"It would be easier if I wasn't strung up like this."

She gave him an evil look, "You getting smart with me?"

He could tell when they were about to give him the run around. If he went to the other window the lady there would tell him to come back to this window and then back and forth he would be going between the two windows not getting anywhere. Running in place was preferable to being stretched like this however. "Ut-oh, look at that, my brand new crisp fifty Jeedude bill is hanging out of my pocket. Could you help me with it?"

"Sure," the lady took it out and stuffed it under her armpit. "Now you were saying something about hiring people?" she said releasing the Highering mechanism.

"Yeah," he said rubbing his sore wrists.

"Next window."

"Thanks." At the next window he met the same lady.

"Okay, what did you have in mind?"

"Nineteen people to be exact. Different fields of expertise."

In the course of an hour he collected a motley band. They consisted of three geologists fired from the University of Danville for using a lead to gold transmuting machine for other than purely scientific goals, one cook just released from Scitzoward #5, two mercenaries claiming that their beautiful and

15

lovely prisoner Avania "The Mauler" Ivlegsky over powered them in a break out, one accountant who couldn't pay his long distance phone bill, one barber that "accidentally" slit the throat of a leading politician suspected of being a drug informant, two ditzy archeologists that couldn't seem to keep their minds on their jobs, one bartender prone to starting bar brawls, three barmaids thought to have extorted extremely high tips from patrons, one hovertruck driver who threatened to kill Rogicphil if he wasn't hired, two nurses that each had married the same five men (coincidentally also archeologists), and one blind piano player that claimed he could see in the dark. He had also tried to hire a one armed fisherman but he only ran off and drowned himself in the sea as soon as he got out of the unemployment center.

Rogicphil chartered a transport VTOL (Greymule Spaceways were temporarily out to lunch) to drop them off at the exact spot Dr. Gronblec was to have begun his survey. It was a rock strewn beach with no vegetation. The air was chilly and the water frigid. Spring was only in the very early stages on the barren western continent. As soon as the VTOL was out of sight the archeologists started to complain.

He climbed a low rise west beyond the beach. As far as he could see it was flat plains covered in low yellow grass. The overcast sky ripped open and began to drizzle when he returned to the group. The cook had a porto-stove unpacked and the others huddled around it for warmth. A cold gust of wind made the archaeologist-nurses whimper and huddle closer.

*   *   *

What was he thinking! Rogicphil gave himself a mental kick in the butt as he paced back and forth on the beach. His team had been wandering up and down the bleak coastline for six days, finding only some nice pieces of driftwood that the blind piano player used to hit people with every time he wanted something from them.

Even if he could solve Dr Gronblec's disappearace, it wouldn't be the great story that would catipult him to reporter's fame, let alone the big story he knew was brewing out there somewhere.

Rogicphil consulted with his second in command, the barber, about what they should do.

"Well, I'm no tactician," the barber was saying, "But maybe we should split up into teams."

"Brilliant idea, Buz." Rogicphil divided the main group up into smaller groups, two of six and one of seven. For his team he choose the barber, the piano player, the two archeologist-nurses, the hovertruck driver, and the accountant. Then he sent the other teams off in opposite directions along the coast while he and his smaller team trekked inland.

"Meet back here in three days time," he told the other teams as they departed, "If you find anything just wait where you are and the others will come and get you."

"Uh, uh, uh if, if, uh," the cook stuttered, "What if, uh if?"

"Spill the beans, Bob."

The cook dropped the pan he'd been heating. "What if we get attacked?

16

I've heard there's all kinds of weird things out here that would eat a man alive, without even bothering to cook him, you know."

"I understand what you're saying. And that's why I use," and he pulled a green can out of his trenchcoat, "Bug-Off * brand insect repellant and non-stick cooking oil, guaranteed to repel biting insects, lawyers, or any other pesky vermin you find in your home... and it won't leave a radioactive signature on your carpet." His voice grew quieter and quicker, "caution some users of Bug-Off may experience occasional bouts of explosive diarrhea. Illegal in some sectors."

The cook suddenly felt sick, "Uh Rogicphil I'll see you later." Hunched over in abdominal discomfort, he packed up his portostove, and ran off into the ocean waves.

That night as his group sat around a campfire, actually a small grass fire that the piano player had started when he tried to light a flamer, Rogicphil wrote his first report. The cook had floated out to sea taking all the portostoves with him so the group was forced into using small brush fires to keep themselves warm.

By the flames leaping up from the yellowed grass, Rogicphil wrote:

```
SECOND SEARCH PARTY MARRED BY COOK'S DEMISE
```

```
The search party searching for the search party that was
looking for the famed Dr. Gronblec's sexy survey team, lost
over half of its members today, quite suddenly and for
unknown yet violent reasons including the team's buff
dietitian Robert Doldinee who was killed by a rare land
attack from a shark. The remaining members say they will
continue their search for the bikini swimsuit clad surveyors
despite of the 'setbacks' including loss of all
communications equipment. Blimpton and Squeeler, the
law firm that finances the team when asked said, "When it
comes to bikini clad surveyors we're behind them all the
way."
```

Rogicphil wondered if he had put enough sexual innuendo into the piece. He still wasn't sure about the level of subliminal propaganda that was deemed in good taste on this planet.

In the morning they began to trek inland again. Around noon, right about the time when they were going to stop for lunch anyway, the accountant ran smack dab into an invisible barrier. Upon inspection they decided it was too long to walk around so they helped each other over.

The nurses' high heels dug into Rogicphil's head as he helped them over. On the other side they found another invisible barrier about three meters from the first one running parallel to it. It was still too long to walk around and they were too lazy to climb over again so they all milled about waiting for Rogicphil to do something.

"Looks kinda like a track for some sorta maglev train," the barber speculated.

"Well, when does the next train get here?" the infrablond nurse asked.

The hovertruck driver leaned over to the accountant and whispered,

"Why aren't infrablonds allowed to vote?"

"Huh?"

"Because every time they go into the voting booth they start to take their clothes off."

"What do you think it is Rog?" Buz asked.

"I don't know yet," he was looking around the sparse fields through the invisible barrier.

"Whut ju lookin' fo?" The piano player asked, tapping Rogicphil on the shoulder with a piece of driftwood.

"Any cities that these walls might lead to."

"How'ud ju know any hah? You cain't see thoo waals."

"I can if they're invisible."

"Invisbal?" the man said indignantly.

"I'm sorry, I forgot you couldn't see."

"Invisbal! Shee man, watchu tryin' ta pull, honky cracka? Ev' tangs invisbal ta me."

"No really, mister musician," the infrablond nurse said trying to comfort him, "It's like really not there, I'm mean it's like, there, but it's not.... there. You know?"

"Git away fum me you ho." He swung wildly with his driftwood. She screamed and jumped into Rogicphil's arms.

"Which way do you think we should go, Slick?" Rogicphil asked the piano player trying to pull the nurse's arms from his body.

"Duh only way da trains goin, foo," he said pointing his arm one way down the track while looking the other direction.

Half of the team looked where Slick was pointing and other half looked where he was facing. The later group was perplexed to see a group of people floating in the distance who oddly enough seemed to be growing larger by the minute.

"Ah donz wanna get runned over. Hep me up," Slick ordered as he tapped his stick on the invisible wall.

Rogicphil personally helped the blind piano player over since no one else seemed to care. They all somehow managed to get over the second invisible barrier just before the invisible train blew by. It screeched to a halt a moment later. The visible passengers lurched forward as it came to a stop.

With a hiss, an invisible door slid open, allowing Slick through into the funky train. He talked to the conductor for a moment then motioned the others to follow him onboard.

Stumbling around and not sure how to proceed, the rest of the group scampered up some invisible steps and into the invisible machine. Soon they were off, cruising through the barren countryside.

Rogiphil thought it very odd how he could see the ground zooming by below his feet. The floor felt very firm to his feet, if not his eyes. He felt like asking Slick about the invisible nature of their conveyance but thought better of it.

They assumed they were in a standard passenger compartment since it consisted of a bunch of bored looking people sitting in neat little rows all facing the same direction. They didn't seem to notice the train was invisible and most just kept their eyes closed.

Rogicphil leaned over to a sleeping passenger and asked, "Hey, what's up with all the invisibility around here?"

"Huh?" the passenger grumbled waking up, said "Can't you read? It's posted in every compartment," and went back to sleep.

"Fulla mae," Slick said striding down the aisle toward the rear with confidence and swinging his stick over his shoulder. He began to whistle an old song.

All this invisibility had to have something to do with Dr. Gronblec's disappearance. Rogicphil felt it in his bones as he and the rest of his team followed the blind piano player. Things were getting more interesting by the minute but not interesting enough. He needed to figure out a way to read those invisible signs. At least that would keep him from getting bored.

A couple of passenger cars later they found themselves in the party compartment. They knew it was the party car since Slick said so. The only other indicator they had was the standup piano and a group of passengers sitting in the wrong direction.

Slick instinctively knew where the piano was and it greeted him like a long lost lover. The tune he had been whistling turned into a full blues melody with the piano hammering out the funky chords.

Rogicphil recognized the song and sang the melody while the others, excluding the accountant who thought it was all rather stupid, joined in on the chorus:

I was walkin' down the street
With a loaded forty-five, singin'
Do wa diddy, diddy, dum diddy do.

I met a politician
Said he's glad to be alive, singin'
Do wa diddy, diddy, dum diddy do.

I broke three noses and
Cracked his spine, singin'
Do was diddy, diddy, dum diddy do.

Cop tried to bust me but
I'd already done my time, singin'
Do wa diddy, diddy, dum diddy do.

As the they danced Rogicphil pick-pocketing some lipstick out of one of the archeologist / nurse's purse. He felt along the walls above the doorway into the compartment where he hoped an embossed sign would be. He found it and smeared the infrared lipstick all over it. Doh! He still couldn't see it.

Looking around for inspiration he spied an ash tray on top of the piano. Without asking permission, he grabbed a small handful of ash and flamer butts and smeared it all over the infrared lipstick coated sign. Squinting fiercely this is what he read: **Minotaur Express.** *Please note, due to continued bad* *relations with Danville central authority the Overhanded Bowling League and Colony will enforce a permanent ban on all optical wavelengths emitted from objects larger than stand up pianos.*

Ah, that was it. The Overhanded Bowling League (OBL) he had learned, in his short time planetside, was an ostracized subculture on Danville that refused to bowl underhand. For that alone they were banned from all legal bowling establishments. So this is how they survived. Nice.

While most of the team was partying down, Eugene the accountant sat in the corner with an insurance adjuster talking shop. When the noise became too much for them, they retired to the bowling car to continue their exciting conversation.

"Hole dawn," Slick said bracing himself.

Suddenly the train came to a screeching halt. Everyone that ignored the piano player's warning was thrown forward into the invisible bulkhead, and that meant everyone except the piano player himself.

Rogicphil regained his balance and looked forward trying to see what the problem was. Far ahead, in the car they had originally gotten onboard in, was a commotion of some sort. Passengers were fleeing left and right as a group of mean looking octagenarian troglodytes rumbled aboard.

"Train robbery!" shouted Rogicphil with glee. Maybe this assignment would turn out to be interesting after all.

Soon the train started up again and the party resumed, ignoring what Rogicphil hoped was an imminent threat approaching from the front of the train. Presently the door into their car burst open and a scrawny old guy in rags moseyed in. He took one look at the party crew and burst into laughter. It was more of a cackle than a laugh and he slapped his knee in time with the beat. He had a long shaggy gray beard that jiggled as he laughed. He waddled a bit being bent over and bow legged.

Mack, already angry because Slick didn't want to play his Metal Church songs, accosted the old man. "Okay you, stop right there. Come over here and fight like a man."

The man laughed even harder at that. "Ah havn't herd thet song fer a hunert yeres," and he busted out laughing so hard he fell to his knees.

"Get up you. You can't beg for mercy yet." Mack slowly approached.

The old man had just about spent his laughter when he looked up at Mack and flew into another fit. He laughed until he fell over and knocked himself unconscious. Mack took the opportunity to tie him up and gag him.

Rogicphil splashed a handful of bottled water in the old man's face. His eyes opened. He looked right at Rogicphil. "What'er yu lookin' et, boy?"

"A crazy old man."

"Da yu know who ah am?"

"A crazy old man."

"Ah said, Da yu know who ah am?"

"A crazy old man."

"Yu'er jus singin' ma song."

"You mean that hymn?"

"Hymn?" he got angry real quick, "Thet ther song taint no hymn. It's ma song. Damn rhat ah'm Buckshot. Don't yu fergit it neither." The man spoke with righteousness in his voice.

"Okay Mack, untie him. He can't hurt anyone." Then quietly he whispered to the old guy out of the corner of his mouth, "There's fifty jeedudes in it for you if you make it look good."

"Ah'll show yu,"Buckshot barked, stood up and raised his fists. "All rhat boy, come on." He began to do a little jig with his feet.

Rogicphil gave him a shove and a wink. The man toppled over landing on his rear end. "Hey, yu can't do thet." the man stood up. He stepped closer. Then suddenly charged. Rogicphil pretended to stare out the side of the train, rubbing his chin. With a smooth side step he let the man charge past, right into the piano. Slick deftly avoided the flailing old fellow then went back to his baby after the old man swaggered a bit then fell over.

"Well, that was a dirty trick," the infrablond nurse said miffed. She rushed over to the old man.

"Buz," Rogicphil called the barber over. "Shave his beard off. Maybe it will bring him back to a civilized state."

"My idea exactly." The barber already had his number four buzzer in hand and was ready to do his duty for God and planet.

But old man Buckshot had other ideas. He leapt up surprisingly quick and gave Rogicphil a solid slug in the face.

Buz jumped on the old man trying to shave his beard off. They twirled around for a few moments with wild hairs, from any number of bystanders who were unlucky enough to be in the path of Buz's number four, flying around.

Finally Buz wrestled him to the floor and attempted a proper cut and shave, which would have been the current "plowed field" style. And by current standards not bad looking. But Buckshot was too squirmy and wouldn't let Buz get a good buzz in on him.

"You will look much better with all that useless hair cut off," the infrablond said trying to be helpful.

Buckshot gave Buz a good wallop on the side of his head and broke free. He had bits and pieces of his beard shaved off and his hair was even more mangled than before. The old man felt his chin. His face grew very grave and he scrunched up one eye in an evil glare.

"Thet dos it," he said. Putting two fingers to his mouth he gave a loud whistle. All of a sudden a dozen or more menacing humanoid octogenarians appeared from the next car over.

"Git 'em." Buckshot shouted.

It was useless to fight, the party was outnumbered by the troglodyle like old people who looked like they'd spent many harsh winter's out in the barren plains surrounding them. Rogicphil's team, along with the rest of the partygoers were blindfolded and forced to sit still. They traveled on for what seemed like three days, eight hours, fourteen minutes, and thirty seconds, through the caverns on a decending path.

Soon after the troglodytes arrival the train made a gentle turn downward and decended underground into a labrynthian like cave system. Of course, most of the passengers didn't notice this since they were either blindfolded, bored or didn't care.

"Hey buckshot," Rogicphil called to the old man, "This is turning out to be a pretty boring train robbery. When are you going to starting looting?"

"Ah aint no danged train robber, ya igit. Ah mah freedome fitter see."

"Huh?"

Buckshot proceeded to tell Rogicphil his life story, (Soon to be a major holovision event! Check local listings! The ideas appeared fully formed in Rogicphil's head.) and how he'd been a loyal monk for the Galactic Church back at the founding of the Minotaur mission on this part of Danville. Over the years he'd seen the OBL take over his tiny settlement and replace the church's bingo parlors with fancy new ones from Lugietorp Prime. He and his fellow monks had been run out of business and fled into the wilderness where they had wandering aimlessly for decades until accidentally coming across the invisible train just a short while ago. Now their plan was to retake the Minotaur colony and restore the Galactic Church bingo parlor to its rightful place.

"Have you ever seen this man?" Rogicphil asked holding out a holopic of Dr. Gronblec. "I think he might have fallen in with the wrong sort of people around here."

Buckshot snatched the pic out of his hand, glarred at it a moment then ripped it to shreds saying, "Bawling alleys, smallin alleys. Dant go en tawk tah mae bout no dang blasted bawling alleys."

Just then the train pulled into the Minotaur station and all the other old men / troglodytes / freedom fighters whooped and hollered so loud Rogicphil thankfully couldn't hear the rest of Buckshot's tirade against bowling alleys.

His team all pulled their blindfolds off and eagerly stepped off the train, happy to stretch their legs. They were expecting to see the Minotaur colony but all they got was a big empty cavern full of smoldering piles of burning garbage.

"Ah dang it! Space Marines!" Buckshot cursed and threw down his straw hat.

"I guess they couldn't figure out how to make the trash heaps invisible," Rogicphil surmised.

Mack walked over to one of the heaps and kicked it with his boot. "This looks like laser scorchmarks."

"Space Marines couldn't have wiped out the colony," Eugene added, "It's underground. How would they have flown in here?"

Rogicphil found a clue next to the closest ash pile. It was a red business card. "HELL's Bingo Parlor," he announced reading it aloud.

"Naw, it's Space Marines. Ah nude it, fore it happened." Buckshot squinted his beady little eyes at Rogicphil. "And you done un told em warz it wuz. Git 'em agin!"

It was still useless to fight. The party was still outnumbered by the former monks turned rebels. They were reblindfolded and forced to sit still while the old men setup a makeshift bingo parlor.

Buckshot revealed to them his knowledge of strange men in red jumpsuits he'd seen snooping around the barren wasteland lately. He wanted to know what they were up to but Rogicphil's team was just as clueless. Of course, Buckshot didn't believe them and all their mumbo jumbo about bowling alleys and several times Rogicphil overheard grumblings from him about danged Space Marines. He ignored the skuttlebutt all as none of made sense in context of an easily digestible storyline.

They hung out all night and in the morning Buz gave Rogicphil and old fashioned lathered shave.

"So what brings you here, Rog?" the barber asked.

"Do you mean here on this boulder getting shaved, or in this burnt out underground secret bowling colony?"

"Neither. I meant why did you come to Danville? I heard you're originally from Roganivar IV."

"Yeah, those Roganivarians. They're a bunch of idiots. Danville's a much better place to launch a career. How did you know I came from there?"

"I'm a barber. I know these things. I read all the newspapers in the sector including the Roganivar Daily Digress..."

Rogicphil cut him short by saying, "Stop right there buz. That paper prints nothing but lies. Let's not talk about it okay?" He wondered how much Buz knew about his activities back on Roganivar IV.

"Okay. I'll keep the rumors to a minimum. Don't you worry about that Rog. Besides I hear the insurance adjustor that Eugene's been talking to lately knows who really wiped out the Minotaur colony."

"Insurance adjustor? Of course, I should have see it sooner."

"Seen what?"

"Think Buz. Why would an insurance adjustor travel all the way out here? He knew the place was going to get wiped out and he's here to investigate the claim. I bet he knows something about the disappearance of Gronblec too."

"If that's true you'd better get going. I just saw him slip past the guards and sneak off into the caves."

Rogicphil jumped up half shaved saying, "thanks Buz," tipped him a five jeedude note and scurried off after the insurance adjustor.

Down a series of green glowing tunnels, he found the squirrely little fellow next to a calm undergrand pool of water.

The pool had a purplish green tint to it. Something he hadn't seen in these caves before. He sniffed at it. It had a funny smell that tingled his nose. It tingled a bit too much, actually, and made him want to sneeze. But he managed to contain himself and boldly approached the insurance adjustor.

The adjustor was taking samples of the pool water and when he saw Rogicphil, made a run for it.

"Hey wait!" Rogicphil called out running after the shadowy figure, "I just want to bribe a few answers out of you." He was almost on him when his nose begain to itch again. He tried to contain it, but the pressure continued to build up inside his nose and he had to stop his chase.

With a rush he sneezed the biggest sneeze he could ever remember.

AHHHHHCHEWWooooooooooo! echoed throughout the cavern.

The insurance adjustor ignored the loud echo and scurried around a stagmite, disappearing from view.

Rogicphil shook his head and was about to start running again when he was stopped by the sound of a distant low rumble. It grew louder. It sounded like a cave in. Rogicphil ran a few more paces then stopped. Cave in? he thought. Cave In!

Without hesitation he dove right into the shimmering pool. There was a strong current below the surface and he let it carry him. He couldn't see through the purple haze that glowed all around him.

Swimming up he searched for air but only found rock. He was now in an underground river. No telling how far it went before entering another pool. He was running out of air. Rather than try to breath that purple muck he banged his head on the rock wall, in an attempt to knock himself out. Better to die quick than face drowning, was what he assumed would be his last thoughts. He didn't regret anything he'd done back on Roganivar IV but he sure wished he could have been part of the big story. Fortunately the rock cracked under his head butt and the surging water swifted him into a chamber beyond.

As the water rushed in he was carried through and then up a fast rising column of purple water. Up fissures and tiny passageways he was jetted, getting scraped up along the way. Eventually he realized, he was flying horizontally through the stale cave air. The water had shot him up into a high roofed cavern. A stalactite passed by so he grabbed it after the force of the water subsided. He slid down it, landing on the cave floor, which was rapidly rising with purple water.

He found a nearby ledge to sit on, exhusted. He figured he only had a few minutes left before the water would overtake him. He wondered briefly what was happening back at Minotaur and if the cave in was affected them too.

No sooner had he sat down than the entire cave floor fell away. Now it was simply a gurgling pool of purple water fifty meters down. He could see down that far because of all the glowing purple slime that covered everything in the cave. It was much brighter than the glowing green stuff that had covered the walls back at Minotaur. It fact he could even use his hands as flashlights since they were now covered with the stuff too.

Just then somebody tapped him on the shoulder. Startled, Rogicphil jumped up and spun around. A tall brown haired youth stood before him. He had a pair of boots in his hand.

"Hey mister, wanna buy some boots?"

Rogicphil relaxed. It wasn't a caveman. "How much?"

"Twelve jeedudes."

"Okay." With a shrug Rogicphil pulled out a soggy twelve jeedude bill. "Why are you selling them? What about your feet? Wont they get cold?"

"I can't stand them anymore." The youth looked greedily at the money. He grabbed it, dropped the boots, and hooted. Jumping up and down he ran away yelling, "I'm free, I'm free, free at last, I am free at last."

"Weird guy," Rogicphil shrugged picking up the boots. They were pure black with a blue stripe running down the side of each one. He threw his old ones over the edge and was about to put on the newer, shinier boots when he noticed an anxious buzz in the air. Almost as if hundreds of minor supreme beings were holding their breaths in anticipation but took bunches of little gulps instead. Weird.

He slipped the boots on. There, that felt better, and they were the right size too.

"ROGICPHIL SUFLIPINIC!"

He looked slowly to his left...Nobody there....He looked slowly to his right.. Nobody there. He shook his head. Some drops of purple water came out his left ear. That purple stuff must be causing him to hear things. He shrugged and adjusted the boot straps.

"ROGICPHIL SUFLIPINIC!" The voice was loud but not shouting and filled his ears, but soft too and without all the echos you would have expected from someone talking that loudly inside a cave.

He looked slowly to his left...Still nobody there. Hmmmm. He scratched his head then said, "What?"

"GET UP!"

"Is that you, Marge?"

"NO, NOW GET UP."

"Okay," he agreed and stood up, "How do you know..."

"I KNOW EVERYTHING."

"Then what's the cube root of..."

"SHUT-UP!"

"Okay..."

"YOU REALLY NEED TO HELP YOUR FRIENDS BACK THERE IN THE CAVE-IN BUT IT WILL HAVE TO WAIT. I HAVE AN IMPORTANT MISSION FOR YOU, GLADERUNNER."

"I thought you knew everything. My name..."

"WAS ROGICPHIL SUFLIPINIC. IT NOW IS GLADERUNNER. GOT IT?"

"Yeah, it's a cool name, Gladerunner. What's it mean?"

"A MATTER OF GREAT CONCERN IS IMMINENT. THE SATANIC COW IS ATTEMPTING TO DESTROY DEO-7. YOU AND YOUR TEAM MUST STOP IT OR THE GALAXY AS YOU KNOW IT WILL NO LONGER EXIST."

"Huh? You mean Deo-7 the galaxy's largest producer of deodorant? I couldn't care less if that stinking rot hole was blown off the face of the universe unless...."

"TRUST ME."

Wonderful, every great fiasco the galaxy had known had begun with those two words, and Rogicphil knew this would be no exception. Unfortunately, as far as big stories went, this one was just too implausible. He could never win it seemed.

* bugoff

Editor's note: The author was in financial trouble during the period this section was written and resorted to selling out in order to feed his family and domestic staff.

Chapter 2: Galactic Beatniks

2227 A.D.

A figure was flying through space. Tumbling and turning he whizzed through space on the outskirts of the Sol system. The space suit was of standard military issue but now of surplus vintage. Although not too long before the owner would have been wearing a space marine issued battlesuit. He enjoyed the fact that his legal name was banned by the Society for the Prevention of Social Indecency, but to his friends and enemies alike was simply called Space-Bo.

    Just hours before he had tried to jump start his rocket engines by personally crawling up the nozzles and manually overriding the computer lock that prevented the engines from firing in the first place. The computer readout had indicated that the main drives would melt and quite possible explode if they weren't allowed to cool down, but Space-Bo had desparately needed them to run just a little while longer. His mistake was that he attempted to eat lunch while working. When his crewmate in the control room heard him choking on an olive he thought Space-Bo said to fire up the engines.

    Now 200,000 kilometers from his used junkyard special, twice rebuilt by hand spaceship, he finally came to. "Hey, I swallowed the olive! I can breath now, Moe. Moe?" He thought it was bit strange that he wasn't in the engine nozzle anymore. He looked around for the airlock. Hey, were did his spaceship go? It was just there a minute ago. He looked all around but saw no sign of the ship. He hadn't even paid off the third mortgage on it yet.

    Oh no, granny! What would happen to her space farm if the back taxes weren't paid on time? He needed to get back to his ship right away. He quickly rummaged through the contents of his various pockets and found the mini distress beacon. Whew! If he'd lost that he'd be a goner for sure. And granny too to boot.

    He broke the seal by smashing the device against his visor plate then peeled back the child proof coating to reveal an expiration date two decades old. Oh no. With nothing to loose he pressed the red activation button and its little green led lights began to weakly blink. It would have to be enough. Moe would pick up the signal on the ship's emergency radio and hurry back to pick him up. Think about grandma, Moe, he thought to himself.

    He waited and waited but the ship didn't return. Soon he grew tired of looking at the same empty space over and over so he dozed off.

    Sometime later he awoke to find himself in a standard orbit around Sol IX, AKA, Pluto. Pluto! What the heck was he doing way out here? He had been racing to get to the courthouse on Triton, Neptune's Favorite Moon ™, when the computer had locked out the engines. No wonder Moe hadn't found him yet. It was looking around the wrong planet.

    He became so interested by the otherwise completely dull view of Pluto and its moon that he didn't notice the strange ship sneaking up behind him. If he had noticed he might have tried to thumb a ride on the worn out old space liner.

It had him in it's tractor beams before he could do anything about it, as if he could do anything about it floating around in the void of space without much more on him than several pockets full of useless trinkets.

He had been about to greet his rescuers with the traditional space marine salute of kicking each other in the groin when he realized they'd pumped knock out gas into the little complementary oxygen canisters that were velcroed to a welcome basket just inside the airlock.

He strained to breath and open his eyes at the same time. It sure was harder than it looked but he somehow managed. The snout of a beagle greeted him. Its bad breath smelt of penguins. It was hard to breathe, he now noticed, because the dog was sitting on his chest. The dog licked his face, sending more bad breath into his nostrils.

"Hi yah, puppy," Space-Bo said licking right back at the dog's face. He couldn't pet the dog since heavy duty straps held him firmly to some form of a platform. His head wasn't bound so he was able to look around the strange and complicated room. He could recognize its type anywhere throughout the system. It was the brig.

"Attention prisoner!" a raspy voice echoed all around him.

The dog jumped to the floor and looked around excitedly then it jumped back on top of Space-Bo and put it's paws over his mouth so he couldn't speak. No one else was in the room.

"I don't believe in ghosts," Space-Bo informed the disembodied voice.

"Yoooou idiot!" the voice scolded, "I'm talking to you through the ship's PA system."

"Oh. You ever go to a costume party dressed as a PA system?"

The raspy voice ignored the comment and continued giving him the standard speech. It told him that he was now a prisoner of the Plutonium Liberation Front for the Revolutionary Jyhad faction of Pluto. And furthermore, he was going to be executed in the morning by the old tried and true space pirate method of walking out the airlock (with no suit on). His dead body would then be retrieved, and sent back to Terra with a note demanding the release of 14,000 PENGUINs* trapped in ZOOs** around the planet.

Space-Bo wasn't paying any attention to the voice, he was looking around the brig. It was a standard spaceship brig with scalpels, needles and medical things lying about. Lying about? Aha, with a spurt of brilliance, Space-Bo realized the ship was equipped with artificial gravity. He gave himself an imaginary pat on the back for his deduction.

"Okay you raspy voice, I demand bread and circuses!" he yelled at no one in particular. The dog barked at him now to shut up. "Oops, I mean bread and water."

When the raspy voice didn't say anything else he tried to reason with the dog. "Nice doggie, I'll give you a twin-key if you untie me."

The dog whimpered, ran and hid in a cabinet marked 'Bioharzard Waste Only'.

Frustrated, Space-Bo just lay there a while trying to remember how to count to pi. It wasn't bery long before he heard some flapping coming from somewhere. He turned his head toward the door and saw a parrot fly into the room. It landed on a surgical cart that was close to his head.

27

"Squawk! Captain says, make him talk." The parrot's breath was better than the dog's. "Squawk! Make him talk. Alk, alk, alk. Rhymes with squawk."

"That's much better," Space-Bo smiled. "First I'll have biscuits and space gravy- the green kind. I can't stand the red variety. It makes me belch. With a side of scrambled pterodactyl egg. And your finest pirate booze to wash it all down."

"You idiot. Captain says you're an idiot." The bird carefully examined the various implements on the surgical cart it was standing on. It picked out a rather nasty looking one with three hooks and a corkscrew and held it up menacingly with one of its feet. "Ready to talk, squawk?"

The dog leaped out of the waste cabinet and jumped on Space-Bo growling at the bird. It barked a few times but the bird just ignored him.

"It's okay puppy," Space-Bo said trying to sooth the doggie, "That's just what he uses to scramble the egg with." He turned back the bird who was staring right at him. "Can you make it quick, huh? I need to get back to Triton right away? You see granny is going to loose her space farm and the back taxes have to be paid in person at the steps to the court house and....EEEoooh! Watch were you point that thing. You could put somebodies eye out with that."

"Tell us. Or granny's next! Squawk."

Space-Bo laughed. "You're funny. I like you guys. You're all right."

"Don't take his side, Bagidol. Squawk, squawk. Remember whose side you are on."

It took several more sharp pokes in various unmentionable places for the situation to fully realize itself inside Space-Bo's thick head. The dog continued to bark at the parrot but did little else to defend his new friend.

"Okay, that's enough." Space-Bo broke the bond on his left arm and reached out, snatching the pointy thing away from the parrot. "I'm going to report you to the pirate captain for this."

"Rrrrah!" the dog barked in agreement.

The parrot dropped the impliment and flew out the room.

With his left arm now free, Space-Bo was now able to pet the dog.

His relief was short lived as the parrot soon returned holding a specialty built laser pistol in it's beak. It didn't bother with a warning but just started randomly shooting at the ex space-marine.

Laserfire! Now that was something he knew how to handle. Space-Bo quickly jumped up on the gurney and into a karate stance he once saw on holovision. The straps that thought they had been securely holding him down were suddenly shredded and strewn on the sterile floor.

The dog ran for cover.

"Okay, you lilly livered space freaks. Which one of you wants to give up first?" he boldly demanded of the two animals.

The bird continued to wild shoot it's laser pistol to no avail.

Space-Bo looked down at the dog and was shocked to see a little laser pistol firmly in its mouth. "You too, puppy?"

The dog whimpered but motioned towards the door with the pistol. Space-Bo could tell it meant business, so he put his hands up and casually followed the bird out the doorway. The parrot zapped him with a low stun in the butt in order to direct him down the hall. Space-Bo took off running while rubbing his backside. Somewhere in another dimension, little green men giggled.

Please note, an interesting side tangent to our story has been summarily deleted by the editor so that we may continue the story without further delay.

A CRASH accompanied his entrance into the food prep bay. He landed on his back but managed not to cry out. No one attacked him so Space-Bo stood up and dusted himself off. Looking around he found a kitchen knife rack, and selected the biggest one he could find, a gleaming blade, 45 centimeters in length. He examined it thoroughly then stuffed it into his belt.

There was an intercom panel on the wall near the main swoosh door. Maybe he could reason with the captain, or at least threaten him a bit. "Captain, this is Space-Bo. I want to talk about your unconditional surrender." He decided he should sound in control.

There was silence for a few minutes then the PA system kicked in. The raspy voice came crackling over the worn out speakers. "Yooouuuuuu, are in no position to demand surrender from me!"

"Oh yeah? Well, if you were a captain worth his pirate sweat you would have already located me on your scanners."

"You already gave away your location when you activated the intercom in the lower deck passenger galley."

"I'm not falling that that old trick again."

"Yoouuuu think I'm so stupid not to notice the bombs you planted on the shipboard scanners, set to go off when I try to scan for you?"

Space-Bo was perplexed. He hadn't thought of planting bombs. "That's good idea," he thought out loud into the intercom. "So call your animal freaks off or I'll trigger the detonators by remote control," he lied.

"Yoooouuuuu, are an idiot. You're surrounded. Give up now, and I'll go easy on you with the mind probe."

"Not until you correct the impedance on your sound system. It sounds terrible, or is that just your voice?"

"Take him!" the scratchy voice shouted.

"Squawk! Give it up." The parrot's voice suddenly said behind him.

Space-Bo whirled around and landed in a fighting crouch. "Alright, come and get me," he tossed the kitchen knife back and forth between his hands.

"Bagidol," the parrot squawked, "Get him."

The dog emerged from around a sandwich preparation counter, the laser gripped tightly in its jaws. It closed it eyes and fired a beam that narrowly skimmed Space-Bo's hair and sent some pans clattering to the floor.

"Squawk! That was just a warning shot. Surrender now. Now, now, now."

Space-Bo's mind raced. He realized it was in neutral, wasting gas, so he shifted it to low then quickly into high gear. He'd been trained to fight peace protestors in the Space Marines, not animal freaks.

With a jolt, a plan seeped into his brain from some idea hidden amongst the cobwebs in the dark recesses of his mind. If he could shove the parrot into the microwave (the door of which had been left carelessly open) the dog would be distracted for an moment allowing just enough time for Space-Bo to cross the alps into Geneva where he could meet Khan Raht a... no that wasn't right.

...Allowing him just enough time to knock the dog's legs out from under it then get the laser away from it quickly. That sounded better.

The plan might have worked to if he hadn't spent so much time figuring it out. We will never know because at that exact moment something began materializing in the air right before his eyes. A shape took form. Limbs popped out. A head came into focus.

The parrot and the dog were just as shocked as Space-Bo was, when suddenly there stood between them a meter and half tall chicken like humanoid.

Before the Dawn of Time:

If it was before time began how could it be before, you may ask. You don't need an answer. Just accept it as is. In fact, you must accept it because as a gullible reader you must faithfully believe everything you read unless of course what you read tells you that it is false. But sometimes you are lied to anyway without any explanation. This might be one of those times. You'll never know. You're just a gullible reader, right?

This is the first and probably the only time you will get a direct injection of material to which this book is dependent (I haven't got to the rest of it so how am I supposed to know whether I'll be nice or not), but anyway in the chaos that spawned this universe (the universe that I just made up for you to believe in) there were several "Original" entities created. The first and foremost were the Quasars, beings whose energy was so great they couldn't get within a thousand light years of any self-respecting piece of matter without vaporizing it right out of its Higg's field. The Quasars committed their unimaginably vast intelligence on creating a cosmic order. They created lesser beings to create the actual Laws that would govern the universe. In turn these lesser beings created the first life forms on which these laws could be tested. Special gifts were given to those lesser beings that found small errors in the Laws. But that is another story all together (it might be dealt with in the sequel to this book, then again it might not).

One of the "Original" entities was a being that became known as Destiny. Destiny was the only "Original" entity that would directly interfere with the lesser creations which had begun to appear quite haphazardly and without reason on small pieces of matter in orbit around some poorly built stars. That is, except for the last and most unknown of all the "Original" entities.

This lone being had no say in whether or not it interfered with the lifeforms because by some strange or mixed up probability factor in the primeval soup of the universe before the dawn of time, it was created in the form of a living creature, albeit a twisted and messed up creature but a living creature none the less. Like all "Original" entities this weird creature was totally immortal, meaning until time shut down operations and closed up shop in our universe, it would retain its existence and its so called soul regardless of whatever may happen. Unfortunately, being in a physical body, not only could it be dismantled but also robbed of its will to live. It is said the need to want to survive is a useless one and that this strange and mixed up individual did away with its will to survive as soon as it learned it couldn't die like all the other life forms it had first befriended (it needs to be mentioned here that this entity, being created in a finite physical form lacked the vast intelligence that typifies the rest of the "Original" entities).

When the creature noticed all of its lifeform friends had suddenly died off, it tried to chop its head off. Unfortunately for the poor creature its head promptly reconnected itself to the body where it belonged. Frustrated the creature ingested some highly volatile substances. It was blasted to smithereens, of course, but the individual particles knew where they were and slowly rejoined one another. The body reformed without a scratch. This made the creature furious and soon drove it completely insane. But insanity grew tiresome after a few million years so it cut it out. It is said to roam the universe now, in search of some way to finally and once and for all, get itself killed.

You as gullible readers in this universe are warned to not associate with this creature, it is very dangerous and presents a threat to the welfare of the universe as a whole. The creature in question has gone by so many names that only a few really mean anything anymore. The others have become senseless profanity all throughout the universe. The most common of these are: Diggel Diffel Wantaka-Bleeurp which means the One who is truly Insane; and Blarfnurumple, the meaning of which is lost beneath 200 billion tons of aluminum scrap on the planet Debarnus in the Reglekon galaxy. But perhaps the most well known name, and the one the creature itself prefers, is based on the resemblance it has with a Terran (Sol III) farm animal: the chicken. The creature has the head of one of these animals and the shape of a basic humanoid covered in grayish-white feathers. (A Terran baseball team, the San Dimengo Patres, made him their mascot because of this). The creature's name in the first language it learned sounds like Neblelezgodenzorbobgit, but usually pronounced Funky Chicken.

Back on Plutoman's starcruiser, the chicken let out a fierce war cry and plowed right into Space-Bo. They crashed into a pile of cooking pots making a horrible din.

"What's going on down there?" the raspy voice on the intercom shouted.

"Squawk! It's a giant bird," the parrot said.

"Get rid of it, I'll bust...." there was a pause, "Damn it! How did they find me? Emergency stations everyone. I'm taking us out of here." With that the ship gave a great lurch. Everything was thrown into the rearward bulkhead. A jumbled mass of bodies, pot, pans, and food preparation devices were thrown back and forth as the ship maneuvered, while the gravity stabilizers fought to keep the rapid accelerations to a minimum.

Somehow the parrot and dog made it to the hallway and disappeared. Space-Bo watched them go, cursing to himself. Wait a minute, he was their would be prisoner, not the other way around. He should be glad they left him alone, but, on the other hand, a few incompetent enemies is better than no friends at all.

The weird chicken like humanoid managed to stand up and brush itself off. "Pardon me," it said in a deep mellow voice then proceeded to attempt to smash itself into the rear bulkhead every time the ship accelerated. After a while the chicken gave up and walked out.

31

Space-Bo was still flailing around in the pile of pots and pans, unable even to stand up. A large pot came flying at him and nailed him on the head. BOOOONNNNNG!

When he came to, the ship had stopped maneuvering. He climbed out of the pile of pots and pans and slowly found his way to the door and stumbled out into the hallway. The bridge is usually near the front and top of a spaceship so he started off in that direction.

Soon he heard voices when he neared the bridge.

"...lucky the Nepto One wormhole is open on Saturdays," the deep soothing voice of the crazy chicken was saying.

"Well, it'll be a few minutes before those deranged insurance adjusters catch up," the captain growled. "You'd think that Greymule Spaceways would be happy to get rid of an old heap like this. But noooooo, they had to file an insurance claim."

Space-Bo couldn't see much through the slightly opened swish door except for the forward viewscreen and it was stuck on a video game screen saver. He wondered what that raspy voiced and paranoid captain was up to.

"By the time they catch up, we'll be long gone," the captain continued, "There's the wormhole now."

Space-Bo was wondering how they had gotten to the Nepto One wormhole. It was in orbit around Neptune. Then he remembered that this year was the first time in over 200 years that Pluto's orbit crossed that of Neptune. It was just a short hop between the planets now. He gave himself an imaginary pat on the back for being so smart. He smiled to himself and smoothed his hair back with his hand, accidentally bumping the swish door's open button with his elbow. The door swished all the way open and he stumbled onto the bridge.

Those on the bridge instantly spun around. His smile melted at the sight of a laser pistol not only in the crazy dog's mouth but also in the chicken's and the captain's.

The captain! Thought of laser guns fled Space-Bo's mind like a thousand little Japanese people from Clodzilla, when he saw the malformed man. He suddenly realized he'd never seen the captain face to face and in that same instant wished it had stayed that way. If Space-Bo thought he was among freaks before, he'd have to redefine the word for the captain, who resembled the little alien from a cartoon show he liked to watch back at the marine base, between quelling riots and stomping protestors.

The captain's body best resembled a series of black cardboard tubes connected to form legs, arms, and a torso. A spherical head topped it off with two blue patches around each eye. He wore a little green jumpsuit that, fit his 120 centimeter short body, like a glove.

"Oh, its only you," the chicken gave the laser back to the captain then turned around to stare out the viewscreen. The excellent blue swirls of Neptune now filled the screen. The dog did the same.

"Yooouuuuuu," his raspy voice found Space-Bo's ears, "Are once again my prisoner. Tie yourself up, I've got more important business to attend to right now beside babysitting prisoners." He turned to the parrot and said, "See if you can fix that voice synthesizer in bank 19."

Space-Bo watched the parrot get to work repairing some circuitry near

32

the computer console as he tied himself up. The sight of the captain had taken him off guard so he figured he'd play along with him until he could come up with another plan. He quickly tied his hands to his feet with some utility rope he carried around with him. The thought of making some weak knots, so he could easily get out, never crossed his mind, he was an expert knotsmith and would never insult the profession by deliberately tying poor knots.

He found that if he sat down and rolled onto his back he could watch the ship's progress all the while remaining firmly tied up. The parrot was still at work soldering the circuit board, while the dog happily licked his face, and the captain and the strange chicken character were discussing something over at the lone acceleration chair. Again, he wondered what the captain was up to.

If they went through the Nereid Public Access Wormhole designated Nepto One, they could end up at any of the 250 other wormhole locations through out the Terran Confederation. He had always wanted to go exploring out of the Sol system, but he couldn't afford it, but now was his chance.

The plan formed slowly in his mind. It percolated down, drip by drip, into his consciousness. He would wait until they were safely through the hole then commandeer the ship and go exploring. Good plan except for one thing. He was leaving his two buddies back on his ship thinking he was dead. Well, he'd just mail them a postcard to join him and that would be that.

"Hey captain," he shouted trying to sound authoritarian.

"Be quite," the captain scolded him and went back talking to the chicken.

"Hey, I'm talking to you."

"Don't ever call me, you, you understand. I am the King, Emperor, and sole inhabitant of Pluto. I worked my butt off for thirty years making it the iceball it is today, so don't ever call me 'you'. You can call me Plutonius Magnificentcia."

"Okay Plutoman, I want to know where you're taking me."

"First I'll take you to..." he leaned close to the chicken and whispered, "What's the name of that planet again? Oh, right." He raised the volume of his voice once more to badger Space-Bo. "Epsilon Zendrady, home of the tallest chorus line girls in the Confederation, to be tortured. Then I will incinerate you in the lowest slag pits on the Pepsi Planet for twenty years. After that, I'll make you roam the wastes of Dartanuboo as a monk for a week. And then..."

"Cool."

"Cool?"

"Yeah, sounds like fun. It's been real boring around here lately. Besides I've always want to go to Dartanuboo."

The chicken spoke again, "Don't worry about him, we can always sell him to slave trader when we get to Zendrady."

"Oh yeah," Plutoman perked up, "I forgot about the slave traders." He turned to the parrot, "You ready, Pauli?"

"Squawk! Finished, done. Ready, ready."

Plutoman went over to the console and pushed a red button. "Heeeeeeelloooooo computer. Are you there?"

A bland androgynous voice said, "Hello.I.Am.Here."

"So, what do you think of your new voice?"

"It.Is.Too.Sexy."

"Whatever. Set a course through the wormhole for Epsilon Zendrady."

"Sorry.Insufficient.Funds."

Plutoman pounded the console, "What are you talking about? Insufficient funds. I don't pay you, you're my slave."

"Not.Me..The.Wormhole."

"Oh, well how much do they charge?"

"Too.Much."

"Any ideas of how to rip them off?"

"I.Do.Not.Know."

Plutoman pounded the console in the same manner that caused the computer to loose its voice in the first place. "I'll smash yooouuuu, you stupid computer if it's the last thing I do. Months of planning down the tubes."

"Excuse me," the chicken said, "but how does one, in this aeon, pay for a wormhole crossing?"

"Huh?" Plutoman didn't like it when other people thought of things to ask his computer.

The computer answered, "A.Toll.Booth.Orbiting.With.The.Wormhole."

"And what happens if the payment isn't the right amount?"

"The.Wormhole.Shunts.You.To.The.Center.Of.A.Red.Giant.Star.Some where.In.The.Constellation.Gemini."

"Hmmm, has anyone every tried ramming the toll booth into the wormhole?"

"That's it!" shouted Plutoman, "That's how we'll get through. I'm glad I thought of the idea. Computer, plot a course to ram us and the booth through the wormhole and onto Zendrady."

"Okay..It.Is.Your.Ship."

They moved closer towards Neptune's moon Nereid, floating blandly in space. Suddenly a black shimmering appeared before them, the wormhole. Somewhere in orbit around the moon was the Nepto One Space Station in charge of everything.

"Attention unidentified ship #XJ7-3045," a signal came in over the radio, "State your destination and deposit correct change in the toll booth. Coordinates will follow."

"Got 'em?" Plutoman asked the computer.

"Homing.In.On.It.Right.Now.Captain."

"You are veering off course unidentified ship #XJ7-3045, please adjust course to match approved vectors."

The tiny toll booth floated there helplessly with a stupid grin on its face. The collection bin was the mouth and two tiny microwave dishes above it made the eyes.

"Now the idea is," the chicken said, "That they don't want to loose all the money in the toll booth and so will let us through to a place they know the exact location of."

"But what if they don't care about the toll booth?"

"Oh well."

There was a tiny crunching sound as the ship impacted with the booth. Stars swung by as the computer adjusted course to make a run for the wormhole.

Several Pitfighter ships came around the limb of Nereid and were accelerating to intercept.

"You are in violation of Space Law and Statues governing the wrongful appropriation of stellar property. Stop your vessel and surrender yourselves immediately."

"Oh yeah?" Plutoman answered, "Kiss my mass!"

If had popcorn, Space-Bo would have been munching away right then. This was so exciting! If the wormhole authority didn't care about the tollbooth then the entire ship would be sent into the core of a nearby star. If they did care, the ship would be sent to a deep space penal colony. Ooo, he couldn't wait to find out what happened next.

The wormhole, looking like a shimmering piece of pantyhose hung out to dry in space, engulfed them. Time and Space were turned inside out like a pair of pants in the laundry, at least that's how Space-Bo thought of the experience. Hey, wait a second, Space-Bo thought. He suddenly realized he wasn't watching a holovision program. He was on the ship himself and not an innocent bywatcher. Whatever terrible fate fell upon the ship and its crew, would fall on him as well.

*   *   *

Profanity the likes of which Space-Bo hadn't heard since he was in middle school erupted on the bridge. They had survived the wormhole transit and he would have thought the reaction would have been more jovial and up beat.

"Those tree branch snorting, bean poled, polyhedral, hypocritical, ptarmigan smelling, puss leeches," Plutoman was shouting at the transmat controlled vending machine in the corner. Whenever the machine detected an inhabited planet within its transmat range it would wirelessly negotiate a vending license to sell to the crew whatever wares and sundries the planet might have. The transmat would then teleport the goods into itself once an agreement had been reached. But in this case once the Zendradies saw how short the prospective patron was, they laughed and refused all service.

Epsilon Zendrady, homeworld of the tallest (at that time) chorus line girls in the known universe, was slowing coming into view on the main screen. It was a small planet, second out of eight planets that orbited the tiny star Epsilon Boggie. It was named that because when it was first discovered, the Space Scouts thought it was an alien attack battle cruiser trying to flee. No actual alien vessels were ever detected before or since. All the inhabitants, not just the chorus line girls were extremely tall, due to the planet's weak gravity.

Space-Bo tried to sit up to see the viewscreen. He caught the edge of the planet, just a small orange sliver with strange blue clouds. But it was enough to tell him they were really out of the Sol system.

"Refused to sell me crappy pies because I'm too short?" Plutoman was jumping up and down, kicking and screaming at the damned vending machine.

The chicken wasn't that amused. "Something went terribly wrong back there. We weren't supposed to have actually come out here, to our destination, you understand."

"The righteous will be vindicated at last!"

"Fortunately, we've only got two minutes, at the most, before those Pitfighters come screaming out of the wormhole behind us and blow us to bits. But if you're into that kind of thing it's okay by me, I don't mind. Really."

"Revenge is a dish best served out of a microwave. Slow roasted and plump with rage. Mine enemies will rue the day they ever offered me a post on Pluto. Damned be the pitfighters. Down with the Zendradies! Terrans go home!"

The chicken scratched its plumage. "Your enemies huh? Are they diabolical?"

"Fiendish!"

"Are they unrelenting?"

"Like a middle aged woman with a 2 for 1 coupon at Z-mart."

"If captured, would they torture us endlessly before gassing us to death?"

"You know it." Plutoman looked up at the chicken with his beady eyes. "What do you have in mind?"

"Is there a super secret chamber on board that is rated for up to level four spy beams?"

"Why yes," he said becoming more cheerful, "Right this way." And he led the chicken into a small room off to one side.

Even though he was thoroughly tied up, Space-Bo tried to put his ear next to the door to see if he could hear anything.

"Message.Coming.In." the computer voice said.

"Uh, on screen computer," Space-Bo ordered. Hee, hee, he thought, they can't hear me from in there.

A gristled old man in an absolutely gaudy uniform stood there. "This is Lord High Admiral Kopchifs of the Sol Nepto One Space Task Force. We are looking for a spaceship that hijacked a tollbooth then gained illegal entry to this system. You haven't seen anyone suspicious around here have you?"

"Uh, no not really." Space-Bo tried to lean forward to get a better view, "Do you have any idea what they look like?"

The Admiral went to reach for a mug shot but got his arm snagged in the forest of medals that plastered his chest four centimeters deep to the point where the color of his uniform underneath wasn't discernible. But then again, with that many medals it didn't matter what color the uniform was. The sleeve ripped but he managed to get the picture in view. It was a mug shot of Plutoman. "This thing is armed and dangerous. If you have any information don't hesitate to call."

"Okay."

"By the way. Why are you tied up like that?"

"Oh it's nothing, just hijacked by some space pirates that's all."

"Well, don't hesitate. Lord High Admiral Kopchifs out." The screen reverted to a view of the tiny blue Zendrady moon.

Suddenly the door swooshed aside and Plutoman stepped on Space-Bo's head entering the control room. With far more grace, the chicken kicked Space-Bo out of his way as he entered.

The captain was rubbing his hands together in anticipation. "Set course for 519-9331. On my mark." Nothing happened. "Computer are you listening to me?"

"No.I.Am.Not." it said.

"Ah got you. If you aren't listening to me, how come you answered?"

"Force.Of.Habit?Random.Circuit.Glitch?"

The chicken spoke. "I think the computer is still offended by that remark you made to the Zendradian."

"Then I'll set the course myself." Plutoman typed numbers into the console. That done, he opened a drawer underneath the keyboard. Inside was a steering wheel. He took it out and over to his command chair where it fit into a slot between two pedals that were within his reach. Gripping it tightly he pumped the pedals up and down with his feet.

The engines started to rev up. Space-Bo could feel their rumblings as he lay on the floor. All of a sudden the ship dived toward the planet at full power.

That crazy Plutoman was going to ram the planet! Space-Bo freaked out by curling up into a fetal ball, holding his hands over his ears and humming to himself as loud as he could. He was trapped on a kamikaze spaceship with a Homicidal captain about to be one with the Cosmos, simply because the planet was insulting. All was lost. Space-Bo knew he should never have listened to his mother all those years ago when she said the school bus wouldn't hurt him. He'd been down-living that moment all his life.

When Space-Bo opened his eyes again he found himself in assault shuttle Beta sitting behind the Funky Chicken who was in the co-pilot's seat. Plutoman and his freak pets were there too. It was an older style surplus assault shuttle capable of carrying a dozen space marines. Space-Bo was familiar with it from the days he was a space cadet.

The engines came to life. The shuttle blasted out of the bay heading for the orange planet below. He watched Plutoman at the controls.

There were several blips on the radar screen rapidly approaching. A little red warning light identified them as enemy craft. Plutoman moved the control sticks maneuvering around them. The screen showed the shuttle firing. One, two, three, of the blips disappeared.

Space-Bo looked out the viewport but only saw fluffy blue clouds sailing smoothly by. "Must be difficult getting them with all these clouds around."

"What clouds? I don't see any clouds." Plutoman kept his eyes glued to the radar screen. More blips were coming up behind them.

"Those clouds right there, out the window." He pointed out the viewport.

"No, no, yoouuuuu idiot. This is just a video game." Plutoman kept blasting down the blips. After ten games he set the autopilot into landing mode. The shuttle broke through the clouds and made a smooth landing.

"Too bad about your starcruiser huh? That was a might fine ship."

"Don't patronize me, you Terran scum. You know as well as I do that death plunge was just a distraction to let us land."

Space-Bo could see throngs of rioters outside on the landing strip. They had signs and were picketing up and down the strip. Well, that certainly looked familiar. He suddenly felt the urge to go down there and stomp on some protester's squishy heads. "What are they protesting?"

The Funky Chicken looked out the window. "Oh that. Don't worry about it, we'll be gone before the bombing starts." He helped Plutoman into a flak jacket.

"Bombing?" Space-Bo's eyes lit up. "They've got bombs?"

"No, but the police do, so be quite." Plutoman opened the hatch.

Without a second thought Space-Bo burst his bonds and dived out the hatch. He hit the ground in a roll. Jumping to his feet he ran down the asphalt strip. His XJ6 Heavy Duty Kill-Em-All Big Knife was back on his spaceship somewhere near Pluto (or Triton) but the kitchen knife he had taken from the galley took its place in his hand as he ran straight for the rioters.

The people threw down their signs and ran when they saw him coming. By the time he got there no one was left. Disappointed, he picked up a sign. It said: UNFAIR! SHORT PEOPLE NEED TO USE THE TOILET TOO!

"Hey," he shouted at the fleeing protestors, "What are you protesting? I won't stomp you, honest."

The Funky Chicken and Plutoman were standing outside the shuttle in flak suits yelling at Space-Bo to come back. But he ignored them and continued trying to figure out what the sign meant. They gave up and went off elsewhere.

A huge airtruck flew overhead not ten meters above Space-Bo's head. Somebody must have left a window open because a small squashed oval box fell out. Space-Bo held out his hand to catch it, but that was before he noticed it was painted in the distinct bright happy face yellow of a Megabuster brand dirty-no-good-lowdown-nuke-your-best-friend's-grandmother bomb. The best (er worst) antipersonnel weapon you could buy! As a marine he had tried to keep a few in his pockets at all times.

Well, Space-Bo didn't take kindly to being on the other end of the boot for once. So he positioned himself in a batting stance. He swung the sign, like a minor league baseball player, right at the bomb. (He might have made a good baseball player too, if they used footballs instead of baseballs.) If the bomb had been the shape of a baseball it would have landed on the pavement destroying everything within a twenty meter radius. But since the Megabuster dirty-no-good-lowdown-nuke-your-best-friend's-grandmother bomb was shaped like a football Space-Bo was able to hit it cleanly and with all his strength. If it was a football though, the hit would have been a home run, that is if they used footballs in baseball and protest signs instead of bats. However, the bomb being what it was, decided not to be a football or a baseball, but a bomb instead and exploded upon contact.

Space-Bo was left staggering around all charred up, sooty black and mumbling. "No mama, I didn't drink daddy's tomato juice."

The distopic police airtruck circled around him once then landed a couple dozen meters away. Inside the truck two distopic cops looked out the window.

"Hey, that protester does a good impression of a frosted mini-wheat," one of them said.

"I'm just glad there's someone left to stomp on," the other replied.

"Let's get him."

"I hate short people."

"Me too." The first cop hopped out of the truck, his laser drawn. The second followed. They stood there watching Space-Bo wander up to them.

"Okay you," the first cop said, "Give up now, or we roast you."

Space-Bo wandered over. He looked up at them standing over him at just under two and a half meters tall. "Hi, got any wheat germ?" He said feeling a strange sense of deja vu only in reverse.

"That confirms it," the second Zendrady cop said to the first, "he's too short for his own good. Let's arrest him, try him, and then summarily execute him on the spot."

"I don't know, there's that great concert showing tonight. Let's kill him now and say he was blown up by the bomb."

"Aw come on. It'll be more fun this way."

"Okay, you tie him up and I'll go get the judge's gown."

"Hey," Space-Bo said not realizing the danger he was in (and for that matter not really caring), "Why are you trying to blow up all those people? Did they rob a bank or kidnap a little kid's prize winning pet goat or something?"

"Hey shrimp!" The first cop stooped over to get a good look at him, "Are you going to give it up or do we roast you?"

"You mean like a celebrity roast?"

"No, I mean like a chuck roast."

"Don't know any Chuck, but I've known several Charles'."

"Zap him!" But before the second Zendrady got a chance Space-Bo leapt up into the air and smacked the cops' two distopianly fat heads together.

He flipped over their rebounding heads, landed in a ball, and accidentally rolled up into the airtruck. Without hesitation Space-Bo quickly shut the hatch behind him.

Wham! Crunch! The first cop got his hand smashed in the door, then fumbling with his laser managed to shoot himself in the ear while his partner laughed. It's now time to save the damsels in distress, thought Space-Bo, but he didn't know of any damsels in distress. Don't forget about dear ole granny, some small part of his mind reminded him, but he ignored it since that wasn't the kind of damsel is was interested in at the moment. Hmm, compromise, he thought. Damsels rhymes with manuals which starts with man- which coincidentally also starts Manitoba where logically he should expect to find his damsels. Hmmmmm.....

The crowd of fleeing rioters had stopped, turned around and were now cheering when they saw that the cops were locked out of their distopian airtruck and were pounding on the hatch trying to get in.

He put a microphone to his mouth, "Take a number, I'll be right with you." Morons, he thought, as he reved the engine and then boosted off the ground. The airtruck was off balance because one of the cops was still hanging on to the side where his hand was wedged in the doorjam.

Space-Bo bent over to tickle the long finger tips protruding into the cab and accidentally took out some rioters with the swinging body of the cop. The rioters now decided it was a good idea to flee again. "Oops."

The truck was sent wobbling through the air with Space-Bo frantically trying to regain control, as if he ever had it. An overhead loop and half twist brought them to bare on the landing strip's terminal building. Seconds before impact Space-Bo popped the sunroof and gracefully dived out. The airtruck, still dragging the cop along, entered the building like it was melted margarine. Space-Bo managed to make the cold, hard, concrete exterior look like frozen playdough when he crashed on it.

*   *   *

An ugly tall cop was walking on the ceiling. He was heading for Space-Bo who tried to walk over to him so he could break him like a twig in his powerful hands, but his feet wouldn't move. Drab. The ugly tall cop walked up to him.

"I bet you thought that was a pretty funny stunt you pulled back there, huh?" The cop said when he noticed Space-Bo eyeing him maliciously. "What're you lookin' at, dweeb?"

"I like your boots." Space-Bo couldn't figure out how they could make magboots strong enough to walk on ceilings. He tried to look casual but his arms kept flapping into his head.

"My boots? You like my boots?"

"Yes, they're very nice, but no matter how much I like them, I wouldn't want to be in them right now." He remembered that line from a movie he'd seen once.

"And what's that suppose to mean, Dork?"

Space-Bo couldn't remember what the guy said next in the movie so he improvised. "No that doesn't mean dork. Duh. What it's suppose to mean is, well, you see those mag boots have a tendency to stop working when you least expect it."

"Huh?" The cop leaned closer.

In the movie, the hero had a tennis racket and was attacking the bad guy in the nice boots. "You got a tennis racket I could borrow? I want this to be authentic."

"What do you want it for? Shrimps aren't allowed to play tennis, unless they're the ball. Too bad there isn't enough time before the judge gets here or I'd let you lick my boots clean."

Space-Bo grabbed the guy's head between his shackled hands and rammed it into his own hard head.

Whop! The cop fell to the ceiling unconscious. A robot wizzed up, also on the ceiling, picked up (down) the knocked out cop, then sped away. This place sure a had a fascination with sticking things to the ceiling.

In a short while the the other cop came in. His hand was one big ball of bandages, his left foot was in a cast, and he leaned on a crutch with his good arm, all on the ceiling. An obviously fake judges robe hung about his shoulders. "I'm here to try you, find you guilty, and then execute you on the spot. How do you plead?"

"I like your boots." It worked once....

"You short people are all alike. Guilty."

"I'm not short. In fact I'm damn huge." It was true. Space-Bo was 198 centimeters tall. On Terra he could tower over all, save basketball players, but alas, on Epsilon Zendrady he was short.

"Yeah, sure. I'd ask you to play space poker but short people don't make much money these days, ha, ha. But I'm not here to laugh at you."

How could that cop laugh like that and not fall off the ceiling? Baffling. Space-Bo's brain hurt. His face felt swollen with the effort.

"While we're waiting for my comrade to get here I thought I'd amuse you with some jokes. "Did you hear about the short guy who wanted to play football?"

Space-Bo shrugged easily. Too easily.

"The coach passed him over. Ha, ha. I love that joke."

Space-Bo felt like he was going to throw up.

"Or what about the short guy who wanted to join the illegal drug club? No? They wouldn't let him join because he wasn't high enough. Ha, ha, get it?"

The pressure in Space-Bo's head was building.

"Ooo-ooo. Why did the short guy cross the road?"

Space-Bo dispensed with the formality of the boot remark and went straight to the head bashing part. He bent low, grabbed the cop's head, and yanked down until it hit the floor. Bong! And the body fell to the ceiling. How!? Why did everything here keep thinking that up was down and down up? He was sure there wasn't any wires connecting them to the ceiling. And there went his arms flapping him in the head again.

The robot came by again with a grumble. It whisked the body away across the ceiling like it had the first time. How utterly strange.

He stood there unable to move his feet no matter how hard he tried. Well obviously the bolts locking him to the floor had something to do with it. An idea percolated down from that hidden space above the cobwebs of his mind. It was a good idea too, that he was certain of, but didn't know what it had to do with his not being able to move or why the cops liked the ceiling so much. This was the idea: call people collect saying the government owed them a thousand dollars in back taxes then hang up before they could get the address to write to and bill them fifty cents for each call. No, that wasn't it.

Space-Bo scratched his head, oh yeah, the real idea was: open up a Happy Hindu Hamburger Hut in India then claim it as a business loss when the place is trashed by a group of argry Anti Ancestorcides. No, that was a stupid idea also. Hmmmm.

Space-Bo was contemplating the ramifications of this latest idea when the first cop he had head butted returned to the upside down room. He lumbered over the ceiling at him, a crowbar in hand. He was swinging it menacingly.

"Oh yeah, buster? Well I don't want to be in your boots either right now!" The distopian cop swung back ready to strike. "AAAAAArrrrrrgh! The crowbar flew up into the air to clang against the ceiling. And the cop swung up smacking into the ceiling for the second time that day. Did they ever learn?

Buried in the distopian back of the cop was what appeared to be a high heeled shoe. But what was a high heeled shoe doing sticking out of the back of an extra tall cop lying on the ceiling?

While Space-Bo was pondering this a tall beautiful woman walked along the ceiling towards him. She had one high heel shoe on. In her hand was a big wire cutter. "Here, let me cut you loose." She reached down with the wire cutters. Clank, Snap! And his feet were released.

Doonk! He smacked his head on something cold and hard. He slowly stood up.

Now the woman was standing right side up, on the floor, like she was suppose to. And the cop was lying at his feet. How did they get down from the ceiling so quickly? He looked up at it. That's funny, he didn't remember glow panels up there. This place sure was weird.

"Excuse me," a metallic voice said behind him.

He turned around to see the robot, now on the floor also, trying to get past him. He stepped out of the thing's way.

It went over to the cop, grabbed him by his distopian shirt cuff, "One more body to bandage today and I swear I'm going to loose it," it mumbled to itself, and dragged the body off.

"Thanks alot, miss, uh, miss..."

The girl was chasing after the robot attempting to get back her heeled shoe. After a brief philosophic discussion with it on the nature of robotic rights she returned. "What'd you say?"

"Um, uh, I just said thanks."

"Well come on shorty," she said grabbing him by the hand, "Plutoman sent me to get you."

"Where we going?"

"Hey! Stop, you two."

Space-Bo spun around.

The cop who was half covered in bandages, now firmly on the floor, stood behind them, armed with a sawed off double barreled laser rifle.

"Your laser gun wont save you now since I finally figured out how you did that stupid trick with the ceiling."

"Huh?" the cop was confused.

Space-Bo sensed the cops hesitation and took the opportunity to charge him. A twin spread of laser light erupted from the gun. But 'Bo saw the cop's fingers tense up and was able to leap at the exact right moment to miss the beams.

A flying drop kick landed the cop flat on his butt. Space-Bo kicked the gun down the hall imagining himself a famous soccer player. The gun wizzed along the recently waxed floor, bounced off the walls three times, then made a spectacular goal into an open doorway.

'Bo jumped up and down. "Score two for our side."

"Uh," the girl tapped him on the shoulder, "It's only one point per goal in football."

"I knew that," he nodded. "Football?"

"Now, come on and more your flabby butt, we're late." The girl led him running down the hallway. They exited the doorway of a pyramid shaped concrete bunker that formed the terminal building and out onto the runway which was a bare asphalt strip. It now sported a shiny new big pothole off to one side. Thank you dirty-lowdown-you-know-the-rest bomb.

Space-Bo glanced behing him as he ran. Work crews were busy repairing the huge gaping hole in the building behind them, that he'd caused earlier. The shuttle was ahead, not fifty meters away. It was waiting for them.

The Funky Chicken was at the ramp pointing behind them. "Look out behind you," he shouted.

Space-Bo turned to look behind him again. This time he saw those same two cops, distopic rejects and spiked-heeled boot advocates, back as usual, chasing him with laser guns. Would they ever learn?

The girl was tugging on his arm. "Hurry up."

Space-Bo stopped. "I'm going to give that medi-bot a year's worth of employment. Aaaar!" And he dashed off with a butter knife in his teeth. But before he could get at them, a service hatch opened in the tarmarc right between Space-Bo and his quarry. The two cops tripped over the hatch and skided to the ground. An angry robot poked its head up from the hatchway. It stared directly at Space-Bo. It had a most evil glow in it's burning red electric eyes.

In a brilliant burst of true wisdom he'd never expressed before, Space-Bo turned around and booked it for the hovering shuttle. A laser blast shot by his head. He dove for the shuttle managing to grab hold of a landing skid.

"Damn you, interloper!" the robot shouted, waving syringes in it's metal arms, "I'll get you if it's the last thing I do. I'll get you..."

Space-Bo looked down. His feet were less than a meter from the ground. Those inside the shuttle were yelling at him to get in. Laser blasts were striking all around them now.

He could see the cops and the robot running along behind the moving shuttle trying to shoot at the same time. No wonder they couldn't hit anything.

"You have to aim in order to hit anything," he yelled back.

The shuttle circled around and headed for the cops now. They stopped and took careful aim at Space-Bo. He lifted his legs up. Before the cops could fire Space-Bo's boots connected with the face of the first cop and the shuttle with that of the second cop. He scrambled up into the hatch then and looked back to see the wreckage.

"Damn you!" The enraged robot ripped off one of its arms and chucked it at him. The metal appendage soared over Space-Bo's head and collided with someone in the shuttle. Doonk!

Several hands grabbed his arms pulling him into the shuttle. The hatch clanged shut as more robot parts impacted. He stood up. The shuttle was packed with very tall women, taller than Space-Bo. 27 tall women to be exact.

"Hey," he said, "You wouldn't happen to be chorus line girls, would you?"

In unison they replied, "No sh....!" but the roar of the engines suddenly cut them off.

The red light in the robot's eyes went out and the poor thing wondered what had happened. There were more bodies lying around that needed tending to. Just another crummy day on a crummy planet in a crummy universe for Alvin the robot.

*   *   *

"So what's your names?" Space-Bo asked without putting his brain into gear. He was hit with a barrage of names.

"Mumphtaobblynaboshathaona!"

"Uh thanks, I think." He saw that the girls were all dressed in standard military issue space combat uniforms. "Hey, are you guys space marines too?"

The ignored shorty and began to argue amongst themselves about their next move. Space-Bo tried to tell them the sob story of Granny and how her space farm was going to get foreclosed upon etc etc... but they didn't want to hear anything about his stupid holovision show.

"I did it!" Plutoman's raspy voice came from the pilot's seat up front. "I stole those bum's most prized possessions."

"We're not guys and we're not possessions!" the girls said in unison as if they had practiced the line many many times before.

Space-Bo squeezed past the bodies of the tall women to peek into the forward compartment. The shuttle had just broken the atmosphere and the stars were coming into view.

"I stole them single handedly. One tied behind my back even."

The chicken in the co-pilots seat added, "And two winged manticals."

"Oh yeah?" Plutoman wasn't sure if he'd been insulted or not. "Well, it was my idea to steal the slave girls in the first place. And I'm not sharing any of them either."

"You may want to boost it back to your ship now," the chicken continued, "Or...... fly this shuttle straight into the sun. Either is a fine destination."

"Yoooou fool. These slave girls are worth a fortune back on the slave pits of Io. You're going to help me herd them there or else."

"NO YOU'RE NOT!" a voice from out of nowhere boomed.

"Ut-Oh...." some anonymous person said.

"NEBLEBLEZGODENZORBOBGIT!"

With a sigh, the chicken answered, "Yeah, what is it D?"

"YOU ARE TO TAKE, PLUTOMAN, Bagidol, Pauli, SPACE-BO AND THE CHORUS LINE GIRLS:
NELL, EDNA, ANITA, NORA, ALICE, CAROL, ANNIE, LEDA, IMA, ISABEL, ADEL, RAE, PENNY, LANA, NANA, LYNNE, PEARL, EDA, LEBASI, AMI, ADEL, EINNA, LORA, CECILA, ARONA, TINA, AND ELLEN TO THE PLANET DANVILLE."

"Sure, no problem. Where's it at?"

"IN SECTOR B12"

"B12? Humans haven't gotten that far yet."

"IN THE YEAR 102701."

"Golly me, why didn't I think of that? The year 102701."

"DON'T GET SMART WITH ME NEBLE."

"What if I did, would you kill me?"

"YOU KNOW I CAN'T DO THAT."

Space-Bo knew it wasn't a good idea to talk to God like that. "Hey, don't get God mad, he might send a plague of locusts down upon you."

"HUMPH! I AM NOT GOD, PRAISE HIS SOUL. WHO DO YOU TAKE ME FOR?"

The chicken thought a moment. "No, too dull. Locusts just don't have big enough mouths."

No one said a word.

"Hmmm," the chicken pondered.

"You know this guy?" Space-Bo whispered to the chicken.

"SILENCE!" Then to the chicken in a booming whisper the diembodied voice said, "I'LL OWE YOU ONE."

With a smile the chicken took control from the fuming Plutoman. He scratched his feathered plumage, "Hmmm, what's in it for me?" he began sending coordinate queries to the main ship for where the Planet Danville would be in a hundred thousand years.

"I'LL MAKE YOU YOUR OWN GOLF COURSE PLANET."

"Neah....... I like more explosive sports."

"UH WHAT ABOUT A SPACE YACHT BIGGER THAN MOST SOLAR SYSTEMS?"

"Oh please...."

"OKAY MY FINAL OFFER, A ROOT BEER SHAKE ON MOORGNAD IV."

"Make it a pie and you're on."

"DONE."

No one spoke until the shuttle was docked inside the starcruiser. "Can I go to the bathroom?" Space-Bo asked.

"NO! NOW STAND BY TO BE BLASTED AMAZINGLY GRACEFULLY ONE HUNDRED THOUSAND YEARS INTO THE FUTURE!"

"Ut-Oh." The same anonymous person said.

Chapter 3: Pancake Warehouse

2027 A.D.

Greyson Sofecstat had arrived at his apartment building on the lower east side to find a bum asleep on the steps outside. As he climbed past the bum and reached to open the outer doors, he felt a sharp prick in his back.

"Okay buddy hand over them green cash rolls," a hoarse voice told him.

Without thinking Greyson set down his package, spun with his elbow out and broke the bum's jaw in a quick snap. With his free hand he grabbed the hand holding the knife that was lunging for him. He pulled it past him and used the momentum to pull the bum forward while Greyson's knee connected with his groin. The bum went flying, banged his head on the railing and dropped like a wet sack of Idaho potatoes.

Greyson dusted his hands off, turned and casually walked to the top of the steps and into the corridor beyond.

He was just about the insert the key into the lock of his apartment door when he stopped and sniffed the air. He checked all around him to make sure no one was watching and then stealthfully bent down and swiped his finger in the dust of the old oak floor. Sucking on his finger he found the taste terrible but at least recently undisturbed. Reassured he hadn't be followed, he continued on into his apartment.

Inside he found a note on the floor just inside the doorway. He was hoping it might be his supplementary paycheck from the reformed BSS. Instead the note told him to push play on a rickety old reel to reel tape recorder he didn't remember he had.

So he walked over to the coffee table and turned the tape recorder on. As he sat on his comfy sofa listening, a disguised voice emanated from the rustic machine and told him to look inside the third egg on the left in its carton in the refrigerator. So he cracked open the egg in question and found the key to his underwear drawer he'd been missing for a week.

Upon opening the drawer he discovered a large deflated plastic frog that hadn't been there last time he checked. It was sitting next to the second issue of his favorite comic book, Frogman. Frogman was a spy, just like Greyson, but his adventures mostly took place underwater, unlike Greyson who's adventures mostly took place underground.

He decided the inflated flog might look good on the coffee table next to the recording machine he didn't know hid owned, so he blew it up, positioned it just right, and sat down once more on his sofa. Something was missing.

Oh, right. His comic. He quickly retrieved it and was flipping through the pages admiring Frogman's hitech harpoon gun and all it's niffy gadgets. His package! He'd forgotten all about it. Quickly he ran downstairs. Thankfully the bum had crawled away and his package was left undisturbed.

Back inside his apartment he hastily unwrapped the special package. Inside was his latest gadget, a high powered automatic suction cup dart pistol.

Not as fancy as Frogman's harpoon but it was real and it was all his.

All he needed now was an excuse to try it out. Maybe the phone would ring and a mysterious voice would give him a new assignment or at least tell him where he could pick up his supplemental paycheck. No, he'd just made that up upon seeing the note. The reformed BSS had never given him such a thing before. Come to think of it, they hadn't given him anything for all the work he'd done for them.

It really sucked having to make ends meet with the lousy pay he got down at the comic book shop. But that was his assignment and he wouldn't let them down.

With renewed vigor he decided to open the window for a fresh breath of civilized, industrialized, air. But when he opened the window a huge pidgin flew in. It went straight for the frog. Greyson chased it around the room some time before it flew out the window with the frog firmly in its talons. He dived right out the window after it. He had no fear of falling to his death because he had his new high powered automatic suction cup dart pistol with him, complete with 200 meters of super strong cable. That and the fact that he lived on the ground floor.

His fingers got a really good grip on the frog before he realized that he couldn't hold onto the frog and shoot the pistol at the same time. Rather than giving up the frog, which he somehow had grown attached to in the short time he'd had it, he didn't let go in order to shoot the pistol.

He landed in some soft garbage, with only a few scrapes and bruiser, but a least he had the frog. The pidgin flew around above squawking angrily at him. He shook his fist at the stupid thing. He'd shown that bird who was boss.

He examined the frog and discovered much to his dismay several holes in it where the bird's talons had ripped into the plastic. He was about to throw it into the garbage pile when a small black cylinder fell out of the frog and rolled around on the alley's asphalt. Hmm, he picked it up and found the word cryptic phrase Kodak stamped all over it.

Intrigued he took the canister to a friend of his who was an expert in ancient technology. His friend slapped the thing onto his flat bed x-ray scanner and within the hour he had the results. Apparently some images had been burned into a thin piece of plastic film that was coiled inside the canister. His friend was kind enough to print them out for him in exchange for a crisp new $50 Clinton bill.

Greyson was so excited to know what was on the images he paid his friend the $50 without hesitation. Maybe these were secret documents that if returned to the proper authorities might yield a substantial reward.

Disgruntled he looked at the photos. Each one had a single word on it. By the time he returned to his apartment and spread the pictures out on his coffee table he had a message deciphered.

What the photos on his coffee table said was this:

Mr. Sofecstat Please Turn Around Very Slowly,
If You Want To

He sat pondering a moment then his eyes grew wide and then with very exquisitely slow movements he turned around. The barrel of a gun greeted him. The gun was connected to a hairy scared up hand. The hand was connected to a black leather skinned arm. And the arm was connected to an ugly faced gangster-like man.

"Hi ya, mister Sofa-cat, blah, whatever the hell your name is." It was Bob "Bobcat" MacMacky. Greyson knew him only too well. "Damn yorz slow. I've been awaitin' here alz day for you ta turn around."

"Can't you ever get my name right? It's So-Fec-Stat, So-Fec-Stat, got it?"

"Sofacostit, sure. Watts zat, Jewish?"

"No, you dope, it's Hungarian with a heavy English accent."

"Yeah, whatever. I'z spost to tell ya, ya got a meetin' with da chief," he pointed out the door with the gun.

"What do you speak, Slobovian?"

"Watt zit to ya?"

"I just don't see why you always have to escort me to headquarters at gunpoint?"

"Jus an insurance policy, see?"

Twenty minutes later Greyson stepped out of the black limo and looked up daunted by the fourty-two story building before him. He was being taken up to the roof where he knew a helicopter was waiting to take him to the train station.

Therein ensues a mini adventure involving Greyson, Bobcat and the buildings greasy haired elevator operator but the editor has thankfully decided you really don't need to know about any of it. Suffice it to say, exactly 24 hours later Greyson is back at the building going up the elevator again.

The greasy haired elevator man handed Greyson the cigar he had been told to save. The door opened and they entered a striking lobby that was done up in red. Red wallpaper with red stripes, red carpet, red furniture, red desk with red stationary and red office supplies, the receptionist was red, that is, she was Native American, and she even had her hair dyed an unnatural red. She was sticking red tape on documents and shoving them into the overstuffed "out" slot on her red desk.

Greyson noticed the elevator man had followed him and Bob into the lobby. When the receptionist looked up chewing her cinnamon flavored gum, without even thinking about it, he kicked the greasy haired man right back into the elevator just as the doors were closing. He realized from the startled look on her face what he'd done. "Sorry, but he's not supposed to be here."

"Are you suppose to be here, sir?" she asked like she'd never seen him before.

"Heez here ta see da chief," Bob stepped over to a red door, opened it, and motioned Greyson in with his gun. "Go on in, 'ez a-waitin'."

Greyson got a nod from the receptionist and passed through the redwood paneled door. On the other side was the chief's "Black" office which resembled the red lobby in the way that, you guessed it, everything from the ashtrays to the desk paper was black. Despite the interior decorator's pleas the chief remained caucasian.

The chief greeted him in the usual way, hitting a black croquet ball right at his head. Greyson ducked when he saw the chief swing. The ball whizzed past, crashed into a black Ming vase, and knocked its stand over which then fell onto an obsidian coffee table tipping it up so that a black potted, black leaved plant fell onto the black carpet, spilling moist black soil.

"I'm terribly sorry. I'm afraid I always get the urge to practice when I'm nervous. At least your reflexes are up. I'd hate to have our top man losing his reflexes. It would make us look bad to the crown." He set his mallet in it's holder then sat down in a black plastic covered black sofa. He was dressed in a formal black business suit and the pressed seams made his pants legs stick up a bit when he crossed his legs. "Please have a seat." He motioned at a plain plastic covered black seat on the other side of the black coffee table.

"Go on, sit." Bob shoved him towards the chair.

Greyson stepped over the split black soil and sat down.

"That will be all, Robert," the chief said, shooing Bobcat out with a wave of his hand. "Why is he still employed here? I thought he was terminated last week?"

"He was, but you had to rehire him when no one else wanted the job."

"How dreadful," the chief said with his usual aristocratic air, which just happened to go nicely with his early sixties appearance. That coupled with his thick English accent made the surroundings seem a bit less unusual, but just a bit. "So, how has life been treating you this week?"

"Well, I was disappointed to find out I didn't get a supplementary pay check yesterday."

"That's strange. I didn't know that we gave out supplementary paychecks."

"You don't. And apparently, you don't give out the regular kind either."

"Ah, yes, I quite understand." He reached down to pick up a drink he had on the coffee table only except that it would have been there if he'd remembered to put it there just in case he might need one while sitting in that particular chair. "Let us retire someplace less formal, shall we?" He led Greyson into a room that for all intents and purposes could be called the polka-dot room.

Greyson sat himself down on a leopard skinned recliner. "Sir Rontho," he began to say.

"Please, just call me sir." He had gone over to the bar and was mixing a couple of drinks.

"Uh, sir, is this a social call or something more important?" he asked knowing full well it would be the latter, but it never hurt to ask. Come to think of it, Greyson had never been invited to a purely social function before. He wondered what it would be like. Probably no different from his business calls, considering how little of the time was spent on actual business topics.

"Don't be so glum my dear fellow." The chief handed him a glass and sat down on a recliner with bunches of little dice designs on it. He just sat there peacefully drinking his drink and staring his stare off into blank space without saying anything more.

Greyson sipped at his drink for a while and had just opened his mouth to make a comment about the curtains when Sir Rontho interrupted him.

"Now don't become so impatient, my boy. Like I always say, 'Patience comes to those who wait.' Remember that you'll go far, guaranteed, that's my personal secret to success. No one can have too much patience." He punctuated his remark by stabbing his glass at Greyson and nodding his head. He sipped some more in silence.

Greyson began to say, "Sir, I think that those curtains...."

"You know," the chief butted in, "I wish they'd quit making roses with all those thorns on them. I know its great symbolism for a poet but a down right and bloody nuisance for the rest of us."

Greyson was about to state his opinion for a third time on the curtains when there was a knock at a door on the far side of the room. After Sir Rontho gave permission, the door opened and in entered a little old man in a lab coat and rubber insulated shoes. His hair was shock white, his eyes beady, and his nose crooked to the extreme. This nose was so crooked that it would have been listed in the Heinous Book of World Records except that the editor passed out during an interview from the sight of it. Every time Greyson viewed it he was shocked. He thought that maybe his shock of seeing it the first time was so much that some of it went into storage waiting to be let out a little bit each time he met the little man.

"Sir Rontho," the little man said in a voice that was both nasal and hoarse at the same time, "The experiment is...." He stopped cold when he saw Greyson. "What's HE doing here?" But his look of disgust quickly turned to deviousness. "Another test subject I hope?" He rubbed his hands together in greedy expectation.

"It's Greyson, my good fellow," Sir Rontho said getting up to shake his hand. "You remember Greyson don't you, Professor Shendrydan? He's our best agent, after all."

"If you say so." The professor led them down a short hall and into a laboratory room where everything was kept shiny transparent regulation white. On a counter in the center of the room there was a frothing beaker with a putrid yellow ooze bubbling hysterically inside. Next to it sat a pet food dish. On one wall was a large two way mirror that Greyson knew concealed the observation room.

There was a sweet old lady sitting in the corner starring at the ceiling. Shendrydan ignored her and purposefully tried to stand between her and Sir Rontho.

"Proceed," Rontho ordered.

The little old man poured the stuff into the dish then walked over to the corner where a small cage sat on the floor. He put on some heavy duty work gloves and carefully opened the cage. A snarl came out when he reached inside. He slowly pulled out a fierce orange furred scruffy looking alley cat. Holding the cat at arms length he placed it on the counter near the dish.

The cat looked around suspiciously then made as if to move toward the dish. The old man didn't wait to find out. "Quick, into the safety chamber." He rushed them into the observation room and slammed the door shut.

Inside, Greyson saw the cat staring at them despite the two way effect. It looked at them blankly until it was very sure they wouldn't be coming back right away, then laid down and began to lick its paws.

Sir Rontho seemed slightly annoyed. "What is this, professor?"

"It's a stupid cat, just wait, it'll eat the stuff. I laced it with the compound Xc-90. No cat alive can resist it. He's just taking his time, trying to make us sweat."

As if to prove a point the cat stretched and looked at the dish. He lazily sniffed at the dish walking around it a few times. He finally stuck his down and began lapping the stuff up.

"Now, watch."

The cat sat there a moment with a stoic look about it. Then without warning, it shot straight up into the air screaming like a rocket. It landed, ran around in circles, then raced back to its cage. All the while the sweet old lady in the corner continued to star at the ceiling.

"What was that stuff?" Greyson stood there stunned.

But all the little old man said was "Damn! Damn! Damn! Diggity Damn!" and pounded the floor with his feet.

"You will have to throw the rest of the formula out. I'm afraid I must start all over again. It is worthless." Rontho walked back through the lab room, waved at Shirley then made his way back to the polka-dot room. A bewildered Greyson was at his heels. They left the professor trying to stomp the floor in with his rubber insulated shoes and using crude profanities to boot.

Sir Rontho looked very grave sitting in his recliner again. "My dear boy, you must understand that news of this failed experiment should not leave this building." He swished a drink around in his glass very precisely, like he always did during a crisis.

"What was supposed to happen in there?" Then he added "Sir" belatedly.

"I know what you must be thinking at this point," he said as if he was starting the conversation, "You think I have another mission for you. And you are right, I do."

"What does that cat have to do with it?"

"You see, it's that yellow formula we've been working on these past two months. Day in and day out we've worked to perfect it."

"If you don't want me to talk, just say so."

"When completed, the formula would have been able to turn objects invisible but never have we gotten the breakthrough we needed."

"Hey, you're not listening to me."

"It has been an uphill battle all the way to where we were just this afternoon. And now we must begin all over again."

"What are you talking about?"

"But so far with every test we've tried, the formula has backfired, instead of turning the subject invisible it makes them absolutely paranoid. I had hoped this test would have worked, so you could have gotten right on the job."

"You said something about a mission."

Rontho looked at Greyson like it was the first time he had spoken. "Mission? Of course it has to do with your mission at the comic book store."

"Could you fill me in a bit more, please?"

"You see, it's quite simple really. The American's have been spying on us for years with their fancy high tech spy satellites. And we've been interferring with those satellites with our own satellites but now," and he paused for effect, "things have become serious. They've started interferring with our interference satellites. It has gotten so bad in recent months that the scrambled Cricket matches can't be seen through out the Empire. The Queen herself expressed antipathy about this, last week, when she was in Hong Kong and couldn't watch her favorite team. So you can see how grave this mission is."

"So you want me to disable the American satellites interfering with our satellites which are interferring with their.... uh. You lost me. What was that again?"

"Nothing so severe my dear boy. Just some little orbital adjustments will do the job. Their tracking and control center is located in California, hidden deep underground in a high security, well defended bunker."

"Underground is my specialty. But how am I to get in undetected?"

"That was what the yellow formula was supposed to accomplish."

"With or without the formula you can count on me, sir. The reformed British Secret Service has never been let down yet, by Frog... uh, I mean agent Sofecstat, uh, man."

*   *   *

The shadowy figure pulled a little yellow vile out of a secret pocket, looked at it solemnly, and put it back. It was about 10 pm and he was standing on the dimly lit side the road in the theatre district of downtown LA. On the other side of a tall chained link, barbed wired, electrified fence, was a prefab metal warehouse, that anywhere else would be non descript, but in the middle of the theatre district looked very out of place. In bold block letters stenciled on its side, it announced itself to the world as the Fabulous Pancake Warehouse.

On the other side of the street was a row of threaters still aglow in flashing neon intensity. Despite the light show the streets were deserted.

He glanced around him again to make sure he hadn't been spotted and turned back to the problem of the fence. Pulling out a telescoping pair of heavy guage wire cutters from a special utility belt he had yet to name (he always liked to give names to all his high tech gadgets) he set to work cutting open the bottom of the fence. The fence split wide open and it looked like there was enough room to let the figure slip under.

Just then the doors burst open on the theartre across the street and a thick surge of patrons came spilling out. They flowed in all directions up and down the sidewalk and across the street towards him.

Ut-oh, he thought, what would Frogman do? Act nonchalant. There were cars parked on his side of the street but they offered minimal concealment. And against the three movie goers whose car he was immediately next to it did absolutely nothing.

There were two parents and one little boy in the group. The parents ignored him as they argued about what the true meaning of Zombie Shark Attack 17 the Musical was.

The little boy around six years old, however, spotted him and the bag of tools and the carefully split chained link fence right away. "Wow," he said coming right up to the shadowy figure, "Are you a spy?"

The figure tried to ignore him and pretended to look up at the stars, which couldn't be seen because of light polution. "No, I'm waiting for somebody."

The little boy tried to get a peek at what was in his utility belt. The figure tried to squirm away.

The parents were now arguing about who forgot the code to open the car doors so the little boy continued to pester the figure with spy questions.

"You're thinking of Frogman, and I'm not really him."

"Spyman," the little boy giggled.

"No, it's Frogman, not Spyman. And I'm not either one of those."

The parents had finally figured out the meaning of sleepiness and put the little boy into the car and drove away. The little boy waved out the back window and mouthed the words, 'Spyman' again.

The figure didn't wait around any longer and quickly dashed under the fence and just as quickly set the fence back into place. His automatic suction cup dart pistol worked nicely to get him up the side and onto the roof of the warehouse building. On top, it had a flat room, several AC units and a clumsy guard waiting for him.

The guard noticed him right away and stood up to accost him but due to a practical joke on behalf of some other guards he had his shoe laces tied tegether and fell over right at Greyson's feet.

A quick spraying of his gas ejector knocked the guard out and Greyson got to work switching outfits with him.   He then carefully replaced all the ammo in the guard's semi-automatic sub machine gun with blanks, and dropped the live ammo down a seware exhaust stack.

With the guard's uniform on and weapon in hand Greyson climbed down the roof access hatch and landed with a thump at the bottom, four meters below. A door opened out into a dimly lit corridor. He followed it to a stairwell that took him down to a single chamber. A couple guards passed him in the stairwell.

"Heh, heh, look at the newbee. Got his shirt on backwards." The guards chuckled to themselves but kept going on their way.

It was a good sign, Greyson thought, there must be a lot of guards here not to be recognized as an infiltrator.

In the chamber at the bottom of the stairwell there was a guard captain sipping coffee behind a desk. He had his feet propped up and was reading the latest issue of Kill'em Dead Illustrated.

Without looking up the captain held the coffee cup out to the intruder, "Get me some more, huh."

"Sure," Greyson took the cup, filled it up from the machine in the corner of the room, and stealthily sprayed some knock out gas into it. "Here you go."

The captain looked up. "Heh, heh, you must be a newbee."

"Uh, yes sir," Greyson said holding the cup out.

The captain's stupid grin vanished to be replaced by a stern scowl. "Then why aren't you at your post!?"

"Uh, uh I was told to investigate some uh, possible molding of the pancakes down on the warehouse floor, sir."

"Allow me to let you in on a little secret, soldier." The captain took the coffee. "That's the oldest trick in the book they play on newbees around here. You just get back to your post and forget everything you know about pancakes."

"Okay,....uh, sir." He turned to leave.

"And soldier," the captain brought the cup to his mouth, "Put your shirt on right ways, that's an order."

"Yes, sir."

The captain took a big whiff of the coffee, "Mmmmm, smells excellent," then gulped it down. Thud.

Greyson had the unconscious captain tied up, gagged, and stuffed in a broom closet in less than thirty seconds flat. Those workout / training sessions with all the female undercover agents disguised as belly dancers was really paying off now. The fact that he hadn't been invited is what turned it into a training session.

With a ring full of keys in hand he slipped out a door into a dimly lit hallway. Twenty meters down at the end of the corridor was an elevator. One of the keys unlocked it and he was zooming down into the complex. The elevator stopped at the last number on the panel. The doors opened.

The smell of pancakes washed over him like a bad dream. He suddenly felt a sort of deja vu, only in reverse. Weird. He rubbed his head then looked up.

He was on the ground level of the main warehouse. That's not right. This should have been a secret computer satellite tracking station. Hmmm, where had he messed up? He closed the elevator doors. The smell abated. When in doubt think. What would Frogman do?

He noticed a small keyhole hidden high up on the button panel. He found the right key and turned it. The main panel slid aside revealing another just behind it. Aha, he thought. He found a button labeled SL13 so he pushed it; it looked like an important button. The elevator started moving slowly as first. Soon he was swooshing deep into the underground where he knew there had to be a secret base.

Greyson stepped off the elevator into a short corridor that led to two huge double doors. A Pepsi machine stood off to the right. Americans, thought Greyson. Hey wait, he was an American too, right? Just because he worked for the Reformed British Secret Service didn't mean he couldn't be a patriotic American as well.

Stainless steel chains held the big doors firmly closed. He could use his laser wristwatch to cut the chains but that would be cheating. It was probably only a gymnasium or something equally stupid locked beyond. Oh well, on to another level then.

Just out of randomness he decided to get a Pepsi Cola from the machine. Little did he know that he was planting the seeds of destruction for the downfall of a vast cola based Galactic Empire in little over four hundred years.

Instead of giving him a Pepsi, the machine squirted cola on his high tech intruder boots. Greyson's face turned red. How embarrassing! He should have forgotten the stupid machine and gone onto another level. But now the damage had been done and so he decided to try again.

This time the machine groaned loudly, and kept groaning. He checked the elevator to make sure no one was standing there silently laughing at him. Hitting the machine only made it groan louder almost a squeal now.

Furious he pulled the thing away from the wall and removed the back panel. Inside he discovered the cause. A can had become lodged sideways in the chute backing up the rest of the machine. There was a motor near the top that hydrolically shoved the cans down and it was the source of the squealing*.

A quick snip of the power lines killed the motor. At the sudden loss of back pressure the trapped cola cans shot out of the top of the machine bursting open in midair before hitting the ceiling and richocheting around the tiny hallway.

Bing, bing, said the elevator.

Oops, thought Greyson, I'm dead. I'm covered in sticky Pepsi, and I'm dead. But then he noticed a vent cover that had been revealed when he moved the machine. He was inside and had the cover held in place with his pinkies, just as the doors opened.

Not half a second later automatic weapon's fire rifled through the corridor.

"Halt! Cease Fire!" a commanding voice ordered, "You blockheads, can't you tell the Pepsi machine exploded again? What are you doing shooting up the place? What if there had been a repair man trying to fix the thing?"

"He'd be dead sir," came the response.

"You idiot." A smack. "Now get the place cleaned up before the Colonel gets here."

"Yes sir."

Greyson shimmied down the air duct trying not to get stuck on the sides. The duct continued for fifty or so meters then turned a sharp right. It was pitch black so he didn't notice the grill on the bottom and promptly fell through it into an unlighted corridor. Groping along the walls he found a locked door on the left wall. Aha something he could use his lock pick set on.

Ignoring the master set of keys he had on him he picked the lock and walked into a nerve center of sorts. There were two rows of computer banks and monitoring equipment manned by a couple of white coated technitions. They didn't notice him or his knock out gas ejector and were soon stuffed, unconscious, into a pile in the corner of an ajoining restroom.

The room was the one he'd been looking for. Computer consoles lined all the walls. Monitors charted satellite orbits. Soon he was at work reprogramming the jamming frequencies of the various American satellites that were interring with the British interference satellites.

There was some noise outside the door. He turned the console off and hid in a broom closet. He heard the door open. A woman's voice. She was shouting orders. Several feet scuttled along the floor. They found the bodies in the restroom. Shouting. More orders were issued. Feet shuffled out the door. He waited a few minutes then quietly emerged from the closet.

A guard was standing right outside the inner door with a club poised. The corridor beyond was well lit now and he could see his sticky foot prints on the floor. He slipped passed the guard and then with a round house to the head laid him out flat. Leaving him there Greyson snuck out into the hall. No one was there so he headed down the hallway below the duct he'd fallen through.

Marching approached so he dived into a side door without bothering to read the sign. He listened at the door until the marching subsided. He let out his breath and turned around. It was the coffee room. About twenty guards were in there drinking coffes, sodas and eating donuts. Suddenly they all stopped and looked at him. His heart sunk. He was caught! They only laughed and went back to eating.

After some more shenanigans where Greyson is chased around by a crazied Colonel and security chief, our intrepid British agent slips silently through an unmarked door.

Greyson slowly closed the door. He leaned back against the door wiping his forehead. The laboratory he found himself in was filled with every kind of analyzer, tester, combiner, changer and every other type of scientific instrument he could imagine. And lined up on one wall were six identical deep freeze tubes. A green light showed on each control panel meaning they were occupied.

"Pissst."

Greyson looked around. He didn't see anyone.

"Pisst, I know you can hear me, Spyman. Don't worry, this is just a recording."

"That's not my name. I wish people would quit calling me that." But he followed the sound of the voice into a corner where a delapidated coke machine was. The voice was coming from behind it.

Coke? He thought this complex was exclusively Pepsi. His perceptions were a bit skewed since his recent encounter with the commander lady. He still wasn't sure how he'd managed to get away.

"Here behind the coke machine is a tape player set to go off at this precise time."

"What's a tape player?" He looked behind the machine but only saw a voice recorder.

"I'm glad you asked that. You asked me to put this tape player here to remind you to let us out."

"Well who are you?"

"I'm glad you asked that question too. I know who you are because you said you were here at this exact time. Four twenty-three, Saturday morning, March 19, 2027."

Greyson checked his watch. Sure enough it was 4:23. "No one knows I'm here except my boss."

"So if you'll be so kind as to let us out, you can then go back to saving the universe. Just press the thaw button and the machines will do the rest." The machine clicked off.

Greyson felt pretty stupid talking to a coke machine but it was too much of a coincidence to take lightly. Being called 'Spyman' again bothered him as well. He went over to the closest of the deep freeze tubes.

Thick frost covered it completely, making the interior unseeable. He brushed off some frost and peered in. He saw a short person, mid forties, of hispanic descent inside. He looked at the elapsed time clock. Almost forty years had passed since it was sealed up!

He checked the other tubes. All the same elapsed time. What were five humans and something furry doing frozen for almost forty years in a secret satellite tracking station underneith a pancake warehouse? Only they would know for sure so he'd have to thaw them out and ask. Maybe they could explain about the tape recorder also. But what if they spoke some weird language, like French? He definitely wouldn't have anything to do with them then.

On a control panel off to the side, he found a button labeled 'thaw' and pushed it. Instantly the frost evaporated into steam, and the doors hissed open.

"I don't think this is a telephone booth Manuel!" Bufgoo said, stumbled out. Greyson recognized his voice as the same one on the tape.

"Oh, wow maen. Whut wuz thet noomber? Ay need to call eet agayn!" Manuel rolled to the floor, his eyes crossed and his tongue hanging out.

The others emerged from the misty vapors, rubbing their eyes. Greyson looked them over carefully. Faded blue jeans, ripped concert t-shirts, ratty sneakers, and all covered with what appeared to be the stuff inside a lava lamp. Incredible, they looked like something out of a pre WWIII museum. He could almost believe they had time traveled from forty years ago.

Clergy Joe picked up Manuel's fallen hat and hit him on the head with it again. "You idiot. Just one call you said. Now you've almost gotten us killed again. Any minute those crazy old ladies are going to burst in here and...."

Greyson realized they thought they had only made a phone call. They must still think it's 1987. "Bleorg," he said to them trying to be friendly. He was ignored.

Manuel grabbed his hat and struggled to his feet. "So wide dyu make a call yorself, maen?"

Joe looked at Greyson but kept speaking to Manuel. "You said this room was empty. How did he get in here?"

"I don't know," Bufgoo said dripping lava.

"I didn't ask you." He turned to Greyson, "What are you lookin' at, punk?"

"I'm glad you are still able to speak English after such a long journey. I take it you didn't plan on being frozen for forty years."

"No, we didn't plan on being frozen for forty years. What do you think we are, stupid? Do I look like somebody who plans on being frozen? Now if you don't mind your own business, I'll freeze you!"

Greyson held up his hands in defense. "Sorry."

"Come on, let's get out of here before the cops find us too." Joe made the door.

Greyson suddenly went into a panic. The crazy commander woman was behind that door. "No! Don't go in there." He made as if to stop him but Ranger Joe shook his finger at him and mouthed the words "Unt-uh."

Clergy Joe ignored him, "Hey, this is a different door. The doornob's square. And its got a plastic coating on it."

"Don't go in there," Grayson pleaded, "There's a deranged lunatic in there."

Hack rubbed his head, "Fro-zen?"

Ranger Joe held Greyson back with his hand. "Joe, who cares what this fancy pants says. Open the door anyway." Clergy Joe grabbed the handle to turn it. ZZZAP! A bolt of blue flashed around him and he was thrown to the floor.

"CLERGYMEN!"

"What the heck?" Joe picked himself up.

"RANGER JOE!"

They were all looking around a bit uneasy. Greyson held up his hands to calm them down. "Don't worry, it's just the voice recorder behind the coke machine."

"IT MOST DEFINITELY IS NOT, SPYMAN."

"Would someone please quit calling me that...."

"ATTENTION SCUMBAGS, YOU ARE NEEDED TO SAVE THE GALAXY AND THE GREATER PART OF THE UNIVERSE."

"Wow maen. It's thuh Big Hombre in thuh sky." Manuel checked to see if he had his little gold cross on him.

"WRONG!" Manuel was smacked with a supernatural hand.

Chapter 4: The Supreme Being

"STEP INTO MY OFFICE!"

"Okay." A big blue door materialized in front of Rogicphil. He opened it and stepped through without further thought.

Inside was an office complete with a desk, filing cabinets, plants, shelves, a secretary, golf clubs, and a big man sitting at the desk. He had short but thick dark brown hair cut in the latest style (no not the plowed rows look but something more earthy yet still stylish). Several rings were on his big fingers that held a fat cigar which he was smoking. He looked late middle aged but still well fit.

"SIT DOWN." A plush chair appeared in front of the desk.

Rogicphil sat down quietly.

"NOW DOWN TO BUSINESS. AS YOU HAVE PROBABLY ALREADY GUESSED I AM A SUPREME BEING, DESTINY BY NAME."

"I've never met a supreme being before. And I've never heard of you specifically either."

"JUST AS WELL, WE'RE PRETTY BORING. SITTING AROUND ALL DAY EATING AMBROSIA, MAKING STARS AND WHAT NOT. I FARM OUT RELIGIOUS DUTIES TO BUDDAHS, JESUSES AND ELVI."

Rogicphil just nodded. He didn't think it polite to bring up the subject of stellar evolution theory.

"AS GLADERUNNER YOU ARE OCCASIONALLY REQUIRED TO SAVE THE GALAXY FROM SUPER MENACES." He put his cigar out in a small black ashtray. "THIS IS NO EXCEPTION," he looked over to his secretary, "HARRIET, SET UP THE VIEWSCREEN PLEASE." He turned back to Rogicphil. "NICE WOMAN, TOO BAD SHE'S NOT REAL."

"Huh?"

"NOT REAL. YOU KNOW, AETHER."

"Uh huh. So what's this about me saving the Galaxy from a demonic pig?"

"COW. IT'S A SATANIC COW. NOTHING DEMONIC ABOUT IT. BUT WE'LL GET TO THAT LATER." He hastily fumbled with some files on his desk. "I'LL SHOW YOU YOUR TEAM NOW. THEY CONSIST OF FIVE MUSICIANS, A MUTATED HUMAN, AND EX-SPACE MARINE, A SUPERSPY, TWENTY-SEVEN AMAZON... UH I MEAN AMAZING FEMALES, A BEAR, A DOG, A PARROT, AND A PERSONAL FRIEND OF MINE, NEBLEBLEZGODENORBOBGIT, A.K.A. THE FUNKY CHICKEN." He pushed a button under the desk. The lights dimmed and a viewscreen to the left lit up.

Rogicphil couldn't help but laugh. "A bear, a dog, and a parrot are going to help me save the Galaxy? From a demoni... er I'm mean satanic cow? This makes no sense."

"THIS IS SERIOUS. THOSE ANIMALS ARE EVERY BIT AS INTELLIGENT AS YOU ARE. IN MY EYES YOU'RE ALL EQUAL ANYWAY SO WHAT DOES IT MATTER."

"Whatever you say."

"FIRST THE CLERGY, RANGER JOE, AND MR. BEAR." The people in the frame were either real big or real small, or just plain too weird looking to be classified according to size.

"JOE, CLERGY JOE THAT IS, IS THE LEADER. HE YELLS A LOT BECAUSE HE'S THE LEAD SCREAM IN THE BAND. HE PLAYS THE ELECTRIC TRIANGLE."

A little red arrow hovered over the person's head in the picture. He was almost bald with only a thin layer of orange and red hair barely covering his head. A single earring hung from his left ear.

"NEXT BUFGOO, THE UNDISPUTED FASTEST DRUMMER IN THE GALAXY DURING HIS TIME ERA. HE HAS A COOL HEAD AND USUALLY THE MOST INTELLIGENT MEMBER OF THE BAND. NEXT HACK, STRONG AS A FORKLIFT AND AS SMART. HE PLAYS A FIVE-SPEED HIGH POWERED CHAINSAW. THEN THERE'S MANUEL, AN EXCELLENT TACTICIAN AND DEMOLITIONS EXPERT ALTHOUGH HE DOESN'T KNOW IT BECAUSE HE'S TOO STONED MOST OF THE TIME. THEY'RE ALL TOO STONED MOST OF THE TIME. YOU CAN HELP THEM OUT IN THAT REGARD IF YOU WANT TO BUT ITS NOT REQUIRED AND YOU'LL BE ON YOUR OWN. ANYWAY MANUEL PLAYS A DOUBLE-NECKED BASS."

"NOW HERE'S RANGER JOE, HARMONICA PLAYER. ABOUT THE ONLY THING HE'S GOOD AT IS DRIVING OFFROAD GROUND VEHICLES. MAYBE THAT'S WHY HE'S JUST A THROW AWAY CHARACTER IN THIS STORY. THEN THERE'S THE BEAR WHO LIKES BEER AND KNOCKING THINGS OVER."

Destiny pushed the button under the desk again and the frame changed. "THIS IS SPACE-BO. HE IS ONE OF THE BEST SOLDERS IN THE GALAXY. UNFORTUNATELY HE HAS THE BRAINS OF A BOX OF ROCKS AND HAS SOME SUBLIMINAL DADDY ISSUES. WATCH OUT FOR HIM, HE HAS A HIGH DUMB LUCK FACTOR. I DIDN'T PUT IT THERE AND CAN'T FIGURE OUT HOW TO GET RID OF IT. COME TO THINK OF IT I CAN'T THINK OF WHY HE EXISTS AT ALL. THE GALACTIC BIRTH TABLES HAVE NO MENTION OF HIM. OH WELL, GUESS IT'S NOT ALL THAT IMPORTANT ANYWAY."

The screen changed. A short man resembling the common misconception of what an alien looked like stood there with a parrot on his shoulder and a dog at his feet.

"PLUTOMAN AND HIS TRAINED PETS. HE WAS A TERRAN SCIENTIST EXPLORING THE OUTER REACHES OF HIS SOLAR SYSTEM WHEN HE WAS ACCIDENTALLY GIVEN A LETHAL DOSE OF RADIATION AND STRANDED ON AN ICY ROCK. HE HAS VOWED VENGEANCE ON HIS HOME PLANET, SOL III. HE IS RUTHLESS AND CUNNING. HIS PETS AREN'T MEAN THOUGH, JUST CONFUSED."

A somewhat short medium build dorky set man now appeared on the screen. He had a belt with various gizmos and things at his waist.

"NOW HERE WE HAVE GREYSON SOFECSTAT AKA SPYMAY. OFTEN CONFUSED AND A BIT NAIVE BUT HE GETS THE JOB DONE.

HE HAS MORE BOOK LEARNING THAN EXPERIENCE (COFF COFF).
HE IS A PART TIME AGENT FOR THE BRITISH SECRET SERVICE
WHERE HE GETS SENT ON HOPELESS MISSIONS THAT NO ONE
CARES ABOUT ANYMORE."

Rogicphil's eyes boinged at the twenty-seven beautiful women now on the screen. They seemed too thin somehow. "Cool, are they working for me also?"

"CAREFUL. THESE WOMEN ARE HIGHLY TRAINED COMBAT SOLDERS, AND CAN GET ALL BENT OUT OF SHAPE AT TIMES ABOUT HOW YOU REFER TO THEM. ALL THEIR PERSONALITY ASPECTS WOULD TAKE TOO LONG TO GO INTO RIGHT NOW. I'LL LET YOU FIGURE THEM OUT FOR YOURSELF."

Now a man sized chicken like creature flashed up.

"THIS IS MY GOOD FRIEND. HIGHLY CIVILIZED, AT TIMES. SKILLED IN EVERYTHING IMAGINABLE. HE IS IMMORTAL, THAT IS YOU CAN BLOW HIM UP BUT HE'LL JUST REFORM. GIVE HIM THE MOST DANGEROUS JOBS. A WORD OF WARNING, HE BECOMES A SUICIDAL MANIAC WHEN HE HASN'T HAD A GOOD DEATH IN A WHILE.

"IT'S TIME TO BRIEF YOU ON DEO 7." Destiny got up motioning Rogicphil to follow him to a door marked 'If you made it this far, what the hell, go right in'. "IN HERE I KEEP MY ATLAS OF DEO 7."

Rogicphil followed the supreme being into the atlas room. It was dark until the big man flicked the light switch on. The atlas was a huge blue domed affair. In the center, resting four meters off the floor on the shoulder's of a giant statue, was a glowing black ball. Destiny snapped his fingers and the ball lit up becoming a globe. There were two main continents, the largest of which covered the north polar region. The next largest sat mostly in the southern hemisphere. Three large islands constituted the rest of the land area.

"THIS," he smacked a long pole on the southern continent, "IS THE CENTER OF ACTIVITY. SOME PEOPLE LIVE ELSEWHERE BUT ARE NEGLIGIBLE. THIS," and he smacked a black square on the southern coast of a bay, "IS BALIDRON, CAPITAL AND CENTER OF EVERYTHING ON THE PLANET. 175 MILLION PEOPLE LIVE IN THE INNER CITY AND SURROUNDING TWENTY-SEVEN SUBURBS. MORE THAN HALF THE POPULATION OF THE ENTIRE PLANET.

"THE SUBURBS ARE AT WAR WITH EACH OTHER RIGHT NOW. THE INNER CITY ACTS AS A NEUTRAL PARTY IN ALL THE DISPUTES AND CHARGES A WAR TAX ON THE SUBURBS ACCORDING TO HOW MANY LIVES WERE LOST IN A MONTH."

Rogicphil saw a reporter's paradise in the making here.

"CHARGES IS A MISLEADING TERM. YOU SEE THIS IS ONE OF ONLY 1417 PLANETS IN THE UNIVERSE TO USE A NEGATIVE MONEY SYSTEM. ON DEO 7 A PERSON IS AS RICH AS HE'LL EVER BE AT BIRTH, DEAD BROKE."

Rogicphil stared uncomprehending.

"HAVE A SEAT AND I'LL TELL YOU A LITTLE STORY." With a wave of his hand Destiny made a table and two chairs appear. Two glasses full of Royal Crown cola were sitting on the table.

Rogicphil sat down. He sipped at his drink while Destiny told him a story about Grego The Mean.

"GREGO THE MEAN WAS A STOCK BROKER* AND A SWINDLER IN BALIDRON ABOUT THREE HUNDRED YEARS AGO. HE WAS GOOD FRIENDS WITH AVERY KEBBER XIV THE RICHEST SCOSCRUB MINER ON THE PLANET. TOGETHER THEY CHEATED THE PLANET OUT OF ALL ITS PROFITS FROM SELLING DEODORANT INTERGALACTICLY. THEY WENT SO FAR AS TO WIPE OUT EVERY OTHER DEODORANT PRODUCER IN THE GALAXY AND FORGED AN IRON CLAD MONOPOLY. THE TERM 'LARGEST PRODUCER OF DEODORANT IN THE GALAXY' CAN'T BE DISPUTED SINCE ITS THE GALAXIES ONLY PRODUCER OF DEODORANT.

"SO ANYWAY THIS GREGO THE MEAN EVENTUALLY SUCKED ALL THE MONEY FROM EVERY BANK AND WALLET ON THE PLANET. BECAUSE HE WAS SO GREEDY HE STILL WANTED MORE AND ANGRILY TOOK ALL THE MONEY AND HID IT IN HIS SECRET ABODE IN THE FROZEN NORTH.

"WITH NO MORE MONEY THE ECONOMY OF THE PLANET WAS BOUND TO COLLAPSE BUT FOR THE GENIUS OF GONKIN TABALBUT WHO SUGGESTED THE USE OF A DEBT SYSTEM THAT UTILIZED NEGATIVE MONEY.

"I'LL DESCRIBE THE SYSTEM TO YOU FROM THE POINT OF VIEW OF THE TYPICAL BALIDRONIAN CITIZEN. AFTER BIRTH HE BEGINS TO COLLECT NEGATIVE MONEY WHEN HE PURCHASES THINGS. IN THIS SYSTEM THE OBJECT IS TO GET RID OF YOUR MONEY INSTEAD OF KEEPING IT. THERE IS ONE EXCEPTION THOUGH, UNREGISTERED NEGATIVE MONEY. SOME PEOPLE USE IT AS A KIND OF INSURANCE AGAINST HAVING MONEY STOLEN TO THEM, BUT I'LL EXPLAIN THAT LATER.

"YOU MIGHT THINK THAT IT WOULD BE EASY TO GET RID OF YOUR NEGATIVE MONEY. BURN IT, HIDE IT, THROW IT AWAY, BUT IT ISN'T THAT EASY, IN FACT IN NEGATIVE MONEY SYSTEMS PEOPLE ARE MORE PROTECTIVE OF IT THAN IN REGULAR POSITIVE SYSTEMS. I'LL TELL YOU WHY. YOU SEE ACCORDING TO YOUR JOB YOU'LL HAVE A CERTAIN AMOUNT OF MONEY TAKEN FROM YOU ON A REGULAR BASIS, YOUR 'PAY,' AND BECAUSE ALL OF THE MONEY IS KEPT TRACK OF BY THE GOVERNMENT AND PERSONAL ID CARDS KEEP TRACK OF THE AMOUNT OF MONEY YOU HAVE ON HAND YOUR ASSETS WILL ALWAYS BE KNOWN. EVERY TIME A TRANSACTION TAKES PLACE IT IS RECORDED AND REGISTERED IN YOUR NAME. THEREFORE EVEN IF YOU DESTROYED YOUR NEGATIVE MONEY THE GOVERNMENT WOULD KNOW HOW MUCH YOU HAVE REGISTERED AND THAT'S WHAT COUNTS. YOU SEE ON PAYDAY EVERYBODY GETS RID OF THEIR SET AMOUNT OF MONEY BY HANDING IT IN AT PAYROLL OFFICES. IF YOU DON'T HAVE THE MONEY IT DOESN'T GET MARKED OFF YOUR RECORD NO MATTER HOW MUCH YOU GET PAID.

"IN ORDER TO BE SURE ALL TRANSACTIONS WERE RECORDED A UNIQUE SYSTEM BETWEEN THE MONEY AND A PERSON'S ID CARD WAS DEVELOPED. FIRST TO MAKE A TRANSACTION VALID THE TWO ID CARDS MUST BE TOUCHED TOGETHER. THE SELLER PUNCHES IN THE PRICE THE BUYER HAS AGREED TO TAKE AND THIS IS TRANSMITTED THROUGH A SECRET RADIO FREQUENCY TO A TRANSACTION CENTER. NOW TO MAKE IT VALID THE MONEY CHANGING HANDS MUST BE CLOSER TO ITS NEW OWNER'S ID CARD THAN THE OLD. YOU SEE NEGATIVE MONEY IS SMART, IT KNOWS ITS OWNER AND DISPLAYS HIS NAME IN A LITTLE BOX ABOVE GREGO THE MEAN'S PORTRAIT. THE NAME IS TRANSMITTED TO IT BY THE ID CARD OF THE OWNER ON THE SAME SECRET RADIO FREQUENCY. WHEN MONEY CHANGES HANDS THE MONEY TELLS THE ID CARD IT HAS BEEN TRADED AND THE ID CARD TELLS THE CENTER TO REGISTER THE TRANSACTION. AFTER IT IS REGISTERED THE CARD TELLS THE MONEY TO CHANGE THE NAME OF ITS OWNER."

Rogicphil started to nod off but a swift kick of Destiny's foot startled him awake.

"ALTHOUGH TRANSACTIONS ARE STRICTLY CONTROLLED," Destiny continued, "IT IS POSSIBLE TO HAVE MORE NEGATIVE MONEY BILLS WITH YOUR NAME ON THEM THAN WHAT IS REGISTERED. THE MONEY IS STUPID BECAUSE IT DOESN'T HAVE A RECORD OF ALL ITS PAST OWNERS, THE MINT IS CHEAP AND DOESN'T PRINT MONEY WITH ENOUGH MEMORY CELLS TO REMEMBER MORE THAN ONE OWNER'S NAME AT A TIME. THEREFORE WITH CERTAIN ILLEGAL DEVICES ONE CAN BLANK OUT THE MONEY'S MEMORY, MOVE IT NEAR A DIFFERENT ID CARD, AND WHEN ITS MEMORY IS TURNED BACK ON IT PUTS THE NAME OF THE CLOSEST ID CARD IN MEMORY AND NO TRANSACTION HAS OCCURRED SO NOW SOMEONE HAS UNREGISTERED MONEY."

"But what about the guy who had his money taken? The government still thinks he has it."

"EXACTLY. SO HE NOW HAS A PERMANENT DEBT HE CAN'T PAY OFF NO MATTER HOW MUCH MONEY HE LOSES A WEEK TO PAY."

"Vicious."

"WHEN THIS HAPPENS IT LEADS PEOPLE TO STEAL MONEY TO OTHERS BY CHANGING THE AMOUNTS OF MONEY IN THE GOVERNMENT COMPUTER NETWORK. THIS IS SUPPOSE TO BE IMPOSSIBLE BUT PEOPLE HAVE INFLUENCE AND CAN GAIN ACCESS TO PRIMARY COMPUTER GEEKS AT TIMES. IN FACT, WELL OVER HALF THE POPULATION OF DEO 7 HAS HAD MONEY STOLEN TO THEM AT ONE TIME OR ANOTHER.

"ANOTHER THING, IF ANYONE SOMEHOW MANAGES TO HAVE ANY POSITIVE MONEY THEY ARE EXECUTED. GREGO'S LAWS ARE STILL ENFORCED. HE THOUGHT THE PEOPLE WERE TRYING TO HOLD OUT ON HIM. SINCE HIS RETREAT TO THE FROZEN NORTH

ONLY TWICE HAS THIS HAPPENED."

"I thought you said the richest someone could get is dead broke."

"THAT'S TRUE, BUT SUPPOSE YOU WERE VERY EFFICIENT WITH YOUR MONEY AND YOU HAVE SAY -800 JEEDUDES ON PAYDAY. AND IF YOUR PAY TAKES -1000 JEEDUDES FROM YOU, YOU HAVE A NET AMOUNT OF +200 JEEDUDES. BUT NO ONE HAS EVER DONE THAT YET."

"But you just said it happened twice."

"YES WELL I COULD GO INTO DETAILS BUT I'M SURE THE READER IS ALREADY OVER BORED BY NOW. THE IMPORTANT THING TO REMEMBER IS ALL PERSONS INVOLVED IN THESE POSITIVE MONEY EVENTS WERE EXECUTED ON THE SPOT SO YOU BETTER BE CAREFUL."

"If I'm really the fifth most powerful dude they shouldn't be able to lay a finger on me, right?"

"IF YOU APPLY YOURSELF PROPERLY, YES, IN THEORY. BUT RIGHT NOW YOU DON'T KNOW THE FIRST THING ABOUT YOUR POWERS. THAT'S WHY I'VE ARRANGED A MONTH LONG TRAINING SESSION FOR YOU AND YOUR TEAM."

"Hold on a second. I'm still on the subject of the money. As I understand it, the government executes any efficient people so that it can have more control over the people."

"IT WOULD BE LIKE THAT IF ANY OF THE PEOPLE WERE EFFICIENT IN THE FIRST PLACE. THERE ISN'T SUCH A THING AS AN EFFICIENT DEO 7 INHABITANT. WELL EXCEPT FOR MAYBE THE PEOPLE IN HICKSVILLE BUT IT WOULD BE BETTER TO CALL THEM RURAL-NEUROTIC INSTEAD."

"Maybe the satanic cow is really this Grego fellow. I mean a negative money system can't just pop into existence on a whim, it has to be planned."

"WRONG! THE DENIZENS OF CRAPPERIO IIX IN THE SOMBRERO GALAXY HAVE A LONG HISTORY OF DRUG USE THAT REVERSES THEIR RESPONSE TO STIMULI. SO WHEN THEY BECAME CIVILIZED, A WORD I STILL THINK IS A CONTRADICTION IN TERMS, A NEGATIVE MONEY SYSTEM DID JUST, HOW DID YOU SAY, POP INTO EXISTENCE."

"Hmmm. What does that mean?"

"THEY'RE MASOCHISTIC."

"Oh."

"WITH SUCH A ROTTEN PLANET IN EXISTENCE WHY, YOU MUST BE ASKING YOURSELF, SHOULD YOU SAVE IT FROM THE SATANIC COW?"

"Yes, why?"

"FOR THE SIMPLE FACT THAT IT HAS A MONOPOLY ON THE DEODORANT MARKET."

"I don't get it. What's so important about deodorant? If worse came to worse you could just start making it someplace else."

"THAT WOULD TAKE TOO LONG AND TOO MUCH EFFORT. IT'S SIMPLER TO STOP THE COW FROM DESTROYING THE PLANET."

"What do you know about this cow anyway? What's its motive? How's it going to destroy the planet? What are its personality traits? What are its powers? Et cetera, et cetera."

"YOU ARE THE GLADERUNNER NOW, NOT A REPORTER ANYMORE."

"If you say so." Grumble grumble.

Destiny took a deep breath before he answered. "NOTHING. I AM A SUPREME BEING AND I AM EMBARASSED TO ADMIT THAT I KNOW ALMOST NOTHING ABOUT THIS SATANIC COW."

"I see," Rogicphil said filing the thought away for future use. "Okay, so Deo 7 is only two star systems away. But if I go you'll have to pay for the spaceliner tickets."

"I WILL TRANSPORT YOU AND YOUR TEAM INSTANTANEOUSLY."

"Back to the negative money thing. What if I went crazy and just let anyone and there grandmother dump their money on me? I could do what ever I want and let the debt pile as high as the sky."

"OH RIGHT. TOO MUCH NEGATIVE MONEY. THE EXACT TIME FRAME DEPENDS ON MANY FACTORS BUT IF THE TYPICAL CITIZEN ENDS UP WITH MORE THAN A MONTH'S WORTH OF DEBT THEY'RE EXECUTED. THEIR ID CARDS CALL THE POLICE AND THAT'S THAT."

"Ouch. Hmm. One more thing."

"YES?"

"What's the difference between demonic and satanic? And how much does this Gladerunner job pay?"

"THAT'S TWO THINGS."

"So?"

Destiny sighed, "DEMONIC IS A GENERIC ADJECTIVE WHILE SATANIC IS A REGISTERED TRADEMARK OF THE H.E.L.L. CORPORATION. THE SATANIC COW IS RANKED BY QUAZITS AS THE 47TII MOST POWERFUL BEING IN THE UNIVERSE. GLADERUNNERS OF THE PAST HAVE RANKED AS HIGH AS 5TH."

"Wow, I wonder who's number one?" Rogicphil said out loud but he wondered to himself, "And more importantly, who's got dirt on them?"

"I AM INFINITELY MORE POWERFUL THAN NUMBER ONE SO YOU BETTER PAY ATTENTION."

"Okay. Yes sir."

"THOSE BOOTS YOU HAVE ON ARE VERY POWERFUL, THEY GIVE YOU SPECIAL POWERS."

Now that Rogicphil thought about it, the boots seemed to give off a radiance of power. He could feel it. It was real. Real cool. "But you still didn't mention the pay yet."

"CURRENCY IS IRRELEVANT. BEING THE FIFTH MOST POWERFUL BEING IN THE UNIVERSE SHOULD BE COMPENSATION ENOUGH."

It wasn't the answer Rogicphil was looking for but it was better than nothing.

Chapter 5: Rall Raul Beta

They all stood in silence staring at each other. Space-Bo, Plutoman, his pets, the Funky Chicken, and the girls faced Greyson (Spyman), the Clergy, Ranger Joe, and the Bear.

"Hi," Greyson smiled cautiously and waved.

"Aaaaarrr!" Space-Bo charged but the Funky Chicken's foot tripped him up. He fell on his face skidding a few meters on the smooth black floor.

They were in a large round room with no visible exits. The ceiling, of indeterminate height, glowed with light. The walls, like the floor, were smooth black.

Before Space-Bo could get up to charge again, the wall opened up and a man entered the room. All eyes turned on him. He was 186 centimeters tall with a short layer of bleached blond hair sticking up on his head. He wore blue striped space marine pants and a Hard Rock Cafe t-shirt from Vega. He looked the crew over noting the shapes of each one's head and pondering their hat size.

"I," he said to the deathly silent beings, pausing for effect and suspense, "Have the unfortunate duty," he looked at his watch, "To train you guys as an invasion force to protect a deoderant mining planet from the satanic cow."

"Oh," someone said. That was a big relief off of everyone's mind. Conversations started up as if a party had suddenly slipped in through the door and seduced them.

"I'm serious!" he said.

"Listen mister," Ranger Joe said sizing him up, "We know you are only trying to help but we have this all under control."

"Are you challenging my authority?"

"No. What authority?"

"Come on, I'll take you all on, anyone of you, I'll even take you all on at one time." He beckoned them to attack him.

The group looked at itself, shrugged its collective shoulders, and charged him.

The man stood there with his arms crossed and yawned. A tremendous dog pile ensued. Arms, legs, and heads protruding out like a weird science fiction monster.

"If you can't catch me, you can't beat me up," the strange man's voice said from outside the pile.

The pile slowly undid itself and the constituent members untangled each other, then lined up to try again.

"Okay, so what if you're slippery as slime," Ranger Joe said, "How about a one on one strength match?"

"No problem."

"Hack, get him!"

"Ha, Ha. Me smash!" Hack pushed people out of the way like opening a door and lumbered up to the man intent on tying him into a knot, literally.

"Do you arm wrestle?"

This caught Hack off guard, "Ress-L?"

"You know, Hack. Bam-bam," Bufgoo said referring to the way Hack wrecked tables while arm wrestling.

"Bam-bam!" Ah yes, he knew only too well how to 'bam-bam'.

They were going to use Bufgoo as a battering ram but the blond haired man snapped his fingers and a black table rose up out of the floor. It had two padded rings on either side for elbows. Two black stools also popped up out of the floor and the two men sat down opposite each other.

It was no contest, not even a struggle. The man just pushed Hack's arm over like it was a bottle of baby's milk.

"Huh?" Hack looked at his arm. It bulged with muscles thicker than most people's thighs or trees for that matter. He looked at the grinning man. He had toothpicks for arms in comparison. In fact, he looked down right skinny.

"Best two out of three," Joe suggested.

Bam! Hack looked at his arm. Why didn't it work?

"Uh, best three out of four?"

Bam! Hack began to cry. He got up and ran into the wall. An appreciable dent was left when he bounced off.

"Now was there someone else questioning my authority?" He smirkily looked about the room.

The group grumbled among itself as it hung its collective shoulders. The man made a movement with his hand and a panel at the other end of the room slid away to reveal an all you could eat buffet. He said, "Please avail yourselves of our large display of refreshments, while you await transfer to our lovely transportation facilities....."

"Grumble, grumble, grumble," the group said. It was hard to argue with free food.

A few days later they were in orbit around Raul Rall Beta, a huge planet with a gravity of 1.4g which made it perfect for workout gyms and spas. They were all in Plutoman's starcruiser, much to his protest, since it had plenty of room and accommodations for everyone.

Rogicphil had done something weird to the engines, only temporary he promised, that allowed the ship maintain the minimal galactic speed limit, which in the backwater section B12 they now found themselves within, was only three times the speed of light.

The free buffet had been a big hit with everyone except Plutoman, who demanded more free range penguin, but over all, the team's mood was upbeat.

"We'll use an approved sports training complex down in that deserted forest there." Rogicphil pointed at a small orange splotch on the view screen. "A word of caution. The gravity is high so you'll get tired quicker. If you can get use to this gravity you'll have no problem on the planet our mission requires us to go to."

Hack rubbed his head. He leaned over and whispered something complicated into Bufgoo's ear.

"I know it's stupid. You don't have to tell me."

"No. Gravity stupid."

"What are you talking about?" Bufgoo asked his large friend. This didn't sound like an ordinary question from Hack.

"Me standing," Hack said looking at the floor of the spaceship.

"Yeah, so?"

"Fake, Gravity."

Bufgoo realized what Hack was talking about. Why were they going down to a planet just because it had a higher gravity when they were on a spaceship with adjustable artificial gravity. He tapped Rogicphil on the shoulder and asked him.

"Shsssss," Rogicphil looked around making sure they weren't being overheard. "It's the Spa Unions, they lobbied to make adjustable gravity control illegal. If you even attempt to increase an artificial gravity generator by one half of a percent from standard grav their legion of lawyers will decend upon you like a pack of hungry wormwolves." He was making it all up, because now that he thought about it, he didn't know why they were going down there either and he didn't want to look stupid.

"Yeah, but this Destiny guy can take care of them right?"

"Uh, well you see he's even wary of the Spa Union's Legion of Lawyers." He could only hope that Destiny would back him up if this ever became an issue.

Bufgoo raised his eyebrow then rejoined his merry band.

After a few shouts of "I hate high grav planets!" by some anonymous voice they decended to the surface.

Plutoman piloted the ship to a somewhat soft landing in a grassy meadow surrounded by yellow trees with orange colored leaves. The grass was also orange colored. He checked the scanners. "Hey, you gave me the wrong coordinates. There's no gym here."

"There is now. We came to train secretly and so we will. The ship will serve as headquarters so we have no need of a gym."

"Yes, but what about weights, treadmills, lipobusters, and the like? We can't train without equipment." Bufgoo knew , thankfully, that Plutoman's ship didn't have any workout machines on board. He knew because he had made a thorough inspection of the ship just to be sure. Joe and Manuel were always trying to get him to lose some weight. They said the VW would get better gas mileage, blah blah blah. The truth was, they all were confirmed couch potatoes, not just Bufgoo.

"We aren't going to use workout machines."

Whew, Bufgoo was glad to hear that.

"We are going to use good old fashion hard work, elbow grease, and thick sweat to whip us into shape."

The three things Bufgoo most despised with a passion. He rolled his eyes and promptly fell over. The control room shook a bit.

Joe looked down at the massive fellow and said, "He'll be okay. He always does that when someone mentions work. It's just a ploy for attention. Right buddy?" He tried kicking Bufgoo's rotund belly but got stuck instead and fell over himself trying to extract his foot.

Bufgoo suddenly rolled over pining Joe even more, "How this for attention."

"I knew he was faking," someone said.

"Okay you lazy butts, enough goofing around," Rogicphil herded

68

everyone towards the airlock, "We need to setup camp before the sun goes down which I hear can be quite sudden and unexpected on this planet."

That night they gathered around a huge artificial bon fire. They had roasted frozen space zucchini strips earlier for dinner. Adding 'space' to the name greatly boosted sales of the strips but did nothing for the taste. Ranger Joe had added some secret BBQ sauce and that seemed to satisfy most of them. And now as the stars twinkled in the dark sky everyone just stared at the fire.

"What now?" someone asked.

"This is boring."

"That green stuff is going to make me sick."

"The fire is stupid."

"I could change it," Ranger Joe pulled the remote control out of his pocket. He pushed a button. The fire changed, now instead of a bon fire there was a man being burned at a stake.

"That's worse."

Joe changed the fire. Now a city was there, burning heartily. If you looked close enough, you could see tiny people running around on the streets. "I wish we had these back on Earth," he said admiring the controller.

"What city is it?"

"What difference does it make?"

The anonymous voice didn't answer.

Ranger Joe was trying to read the name of the manufacturer off the back of the controller when it slipped from his fingers and fell into the fire. Miniature firefighters emerged from a miniature firetruck and began to hose down the controller, which was huge in comparison. But it was no use; the controller was quickly melted.

"It just slipped," Ranger Joe apologized, "I didn't mean...."

Most of the group then got up and left disgusted. Ranger Joe moped away towards his sleep sack. Only Space-Bo and the Funky Chicken were left staring intently at the burning city, as it crumbled down into glowing rubble.

It was a few hours before dawn when the city had burnt down to smoldering heaps where once tall buildings had stood. They were still watching, intently as ever.

"What an intensely wonderful fire, don't you agree?" the chicken watched as tiny men, fleeing the fire, ran up onto his feet.

"Yeah, I haven't seen a city burn like that since I helped crush a rebellion on Mars, that's near Terra."

"Terra, I don't think I've been there."

"Well, that's what we call it. All the starcharts call it Sol III, though."

"Ah, isn't that Earth?"

"Well, it use to be but the name was changed. They thought people would think the planet was dirty or something with a name like that."

"Are you a Roman?"

"No, are you?"

"I mean, are you from the city of Rome on Terra?"

"Never heard of it. Must be some suburb of Roy."

"I've never been to Roy. I've been to Rome, Athens, Alexandria, New York, but not Roy. What a strange name."

"Roy? Roy is the capital of our planet."

"Sorry, it's been millennia since I've been there."

Space-Bo shrugged, "Well, I guess that explains it." He picked up some tiny people fleeing from the city. "No, no. Back in you go." He set them on top of a tiny rolled over bus.

"Do you flame?" the chicken asked pulling out some long cylinders from a box.

"Flame? Do you mean smoke?"

"Different people in different times have different names for the same old thing."

"You can say that again," Space-Bo took one of the cylinders and stuck it in his mouth. He took a deep breath and held it.

"Don't you want to light it first?"

Space-Bo looked at the thing hanging out of his mouth, "Uh,...I'm just getting the flavor first." He leaned over next to a smoldering building and the flamer caught on fire. He took another deep breath. His face turned deep red. Then he let out a spray of fire onto the city. "Hey that's great. What brand is that?"

"Acetylene No. 5." The chicken threw the box into the city flames. It instantly exploded leaving a crater in the rubble. "Beautiful woman Acetylene."

"Why'd you do that?"

"I don't flame, it's bad for your health."

"Yeah, I know that, but it's bad for your health too." He reluctantly tossed his flamer into the fire where it hit some fleeing pedestrians, "Oops, sorry about that. So, what were you doing with them in the first place?"

"Let me see. I got these about seven thousand years ago on a world run by gladiators and pyromaniacs. I was into explosions then and I thought that if I ate a box of them I'd blow up."

"What happened?"

"I put them in my pocket and forgot about them."

"Oh," Space-Bo sat there a while trying to think of something. He had told the idea to get lost when it had first popped into his head a few moments ago. Now he searched his head for it. Finally he found it behind a half eaten cheese burger he pretended to eat when he got hungry or was huddled up in ball whimpering. "Uh, if you forgot that you had put those flames in your pocket, what else might you have forgotten in there?"

"Hmmm, interesting. Let's see." The chicken began unloading his pockets. Space-Bo did the same.

First they went through the Funky Chicken's stuff. It made a big pile that they sorted through: portable radios, cordless shavers, food processors, comic books, half eaten twinkies, crumpled root beer cans, explosives, guns, extra pairs of sandals, used toothpaste tubes, small trash cans, several balls of yarn, etc...

Then they sorted through all of Space-Bo's junk. Upon comparison they discovered they had almost the exact same things. "Wow..." they said in unison.

In the morning Greyson was the first to get up. The hard ground was especially painful in the higher gravity, and his back ached. Rogicphil wouldn't let them sleep on the ship with its gravity control. He said it would ruin their training. Something was not right about that arrangement and it nagged him, but he couldn't put his finger on it. Too many things in his life were like that. Better a ruined training than a ruined back.

So bent over, with a hand on his back, Greyson hobbled back towards the spacecruiser intent on breaking in and sneaking a bit of real sleep before anyone noticed. Instead, as he was avoiding the smoldering fire, he accidentally tripped over someone and fell. He rolled over, too exhausted to howl in pain.

There was some shuffling, then a short figure loomed over him. It said, "Yooouuuuu Earthen scum, why did you kick me?" and kicked him, "Huh? Well, take that!" He kicked Greyson again, "That's for your mom!" and stormed off towards the spacecruiser with the same idea that Greyson originally had.

Wearily Greyson raised his head, "Sorry about that," then let it mercifully fall back on a rock, taking him into unconsciousness.

Plutoman, upon being kicked awake, went straight to his spaceship. On the way he stair-stepped over a large furry lump that resembled a bear and growled like one too. He ignored it since he was jonesing for a video game hit right then.

Bufgoo, hearing the bear growl, sat up. He looked around. The sun was sneaking up over the mountain to the south and dazzled him until he looked away. When he saw the bear moving, he tossed a stick at it, intending the gesture as a signal to calm down. But the gravity being what it was caused the stick to rudely smack Ranger Joe instead.

"Hey!" Joe woke up startled, looked at the stick, then threw it back at Bufgoo which missed and hit Hack who was closer. Hack didn't wake up so Bufgoo and Joe tried to go back to sleep.

About that time Greyson came to and slowly began to crawl once more towards the ship. He got as far as Space-Bo before finally collapsing.

An hour later Plutoman looked out of his Starcruiser. Everyone was still asleep so he played some more video games. His current favorite, the Little Torture Rack That Could, made him feel better about being kicked awake. After five more games he looked out again. This time everyone was gone.

He jumped out the airlock. Even the burned down city was gone. Well, at least he could leave now; no one to stop him. He almost left too, but after starting the engines up, realized his pets, Bagidol and Pauli were missing. Not to mention the slave girls.

"Damn, Damn, Damn! Damn their feet! If only I'd crippled them when I had the chance." He thought about leaving anyway. He could always capture more slave girls but finding replacement pets would be a real pain.

At least in this timeline Earth was a long gone destroyed world. He'd read that in Barlow's Galactic Almanack. The Almanack didn't say it specifically but he was sure it was his doing and that he'd gone back to his own time and was the one who had destoryed Earth. It was such a relief to know his mission would (did) succeed. Getting his freedom back in this timeline was pointless. He needed that moron Gladerunner's help to go back to his own timeline and sweet sweet vengeance.

"Computer. Hey blockhead, you still here?"

"Yes.I.Am.Thank.You." the computer didn't like to be awaken early either.

"What are you thanking me for? I haven't kicked you yet today." He kicked the panel beneath the console. "There, now you can thank me."

The computer ignored him.

"Did you align the snoopers on Rogicphil yet like I told you?"

"Not.From.Here.Your.Moldiness."

"If I want back talk from you I'll program it in your circuits."

"You.Already.Did."

"Grrrrrr,... well however you do it I want you to watch this Rogicphil character very closely and try to get as much information out of him as possible. I want coordinates, timetables, grocery lists... everything he knows and especially about his time travel technology. He's taken Bagidol and Pauli hostage, and is keeping us in the dark so he can use my Starcruiser."

"They.Are.Not.Taken.Hostage.And.You.Know.It.Besides.It.Is.For.A. Good.Cause."

"I'll decide what a good cause is, and right now it's getting my vermin pets back." He opened his locker and took out an automatic nose. Outside he set the nose for dog, set it down, and followed it as it rolled away, sniffing out the trail. It headed east towards a distant lake. It went through some light woods and ended up on the shore of a lake that spread out east and south for as far as the eye could see (or a far as the nose could smell).

There were many footprints in the sand and an occasional beer can. The nose became confused and spun around in annoyance. Plutoman could see native people walking green furred three headed dog like animals along the beach in both directions. A dead end.

He reset the nose for parrot. It sniffed a bit then took off heading towards some mountains to the south. It was soon rolling through a heavily wooded area of yellow trees with orange leaves. It climbed a hill, stopped, sniffed in several directions, then rolled down the other side. It stopped at a small stream sniffing at the gurgling water.

"Well, you stupid nose, what are you waiting for?"

The nose sniffed at some little green fish in the stream, then the trail on the other side of the stream, and finally it sniffed up at Plutoman.

"I just have to do everything around here Myself," Plutoman grabbed up the nose pocketing it. He slowly eased his too skinny legs into the stream in an attempt to wade across it. Suddenly he noticed the little green fish were attaching themselves to his legs. He tried to brush them off but only caused himself to loose balance and fall head over heels into the water. A swiftly delicious current pulled him downstream.

The rest of the group was already downstream on the other side of the lake. They stood there blurry eyed as Rogicphil demonstrated the proper way to walk on water.

"I have a question," an anonymous voice asked, "Of what practical use is water walking?"

Rogicphil looked around the group searching for the one who spoke. "Well, there isn't any really, it's just something good to know in general."

"If I had two space creds for everything somebody told me was just good to know I'd be very unpoor."

72

"But you'd be very unsmart, don't you think?"

"If so, what am I doing here then?"

"Who are you? Maybe if I knew who you were, I could come up with a snappy answer." Rogicphil still couldn't see who he was talking to. "Otherwise I'll have to assume you're just a figment of our collective imagination."

"Tell it to someone else, I'll listen."

Just then Plutoman came splashing down the stream cursing profanities in several different dead languages.

"Mr. Man," Rogicphil shouted at the figure thrashing around in the pool, "Or is it Maan? I'm terrible at phonetics. Anyway would you accept two space creds in exchange for the privilege of learning to walk on water?"

"I'll give yoouuuuuuuu my whole damn ship if you get me out!" he lied.

Rogicphil very carefully placed one foot on the water and stood up. He put his other foot in front of him. It too rested on the water. "The secret is in being very careful how you step." He slowly made his way over to Plutoman who looked up at him in amazement. Rogicphil grabbed him by one skinny leg and pulled the drenched fellow out of the water. "I see the little fish find you tasty," he said noticing the green lumps that were attached all over Plutoman's body.

"Get them off! They're sucking my blood!" He thrashed about in midair.

"Nonsense, these are kissing fish," Rogicphil lied, "They're only harmful if you're allergic to lipstick." Moving very carefully again, Rogicphil carried Plutoman to shore, walking on water the entire way.

"Let go of me!" he struggled out of Rogicphil's grasp. Almost instantly, and before he'd even hit the ground, he was pulling at the fish, trying to get them off. Each came off with a slurp-pop sound and was soon flying through the air in all directions. He saw the lipstick marks left behind and screamed.

"Look, it's only lipstick." Rogicphil wiped some on his hand. Plutoman looked at the smudge left on his leg, slowly examining it. Then after a pause he said, "That's not lipstick, you doofus. It's dead semi-masticated skin sluffs!" and marched off into the woods. "Moron can't even read a basic ichthyology textbook."

Rogicphil laughed as he watched Plutoman still pulling fish off himself even as he sauntered away. He was still chuckling when he turned back to the group ready to ask for a show of hands for those who wanted to learn to walk on water. No one was there.

Rogicphil stood there and imagined that a giant shark had jumped out of the water and was now chasing them through the woods. "Why me?" he sighed. He hadn't expected an answer but go one anyway.

"BECAUSE!"

"Not you again."

"STEP INTO MY OFFICE."

"Where?" he glanced around not seeing anything.

"SEE THAT TREE OVER THERE WITH A DOOR IN IT?"

He hadn't noticed before but there was a door, plain as day, on the side of a nearby tree. He sighed then went over and stepped inside. He walked back into the same office where he had met the supreme being the first time. The only way an office could be on two planets hundreds of light years apart at the same time was that there wasn't any way, so he really wasn't in a real office, just some sort of imaginary awareness phenomenon. But doctors warned against living in fantasies so therefore he should leave this imaginary office, right away, before his mind blew a fuse.

Donk! the door felt real enough when he walked right into it.

"MR. GLADERUNNER, PLEASE SIT DOWN."

And unfortunately it was still the same supreme being that had gotten him into this. Rogicphil sat down in a plush purple chair, "Hey big D. How's it going?"

"YOU ARE SUPPOSE TO BE TRAINING THESE PEOPLE, NOT DOING PARLOR TRICKS."

"Uh..."

"THAT WAS THE STUPIDEST WAY OF USING THE GLADERUNNER BOOTS I HAVE EVER SEEN."

"You told me that whatever type of footwear I thought of, I would have. So I just thought of stilts when my feet touched the water."

"AND THAT ARM WRESTLING MATCH. YOU HAVE BEEN GIVEN INCREASED STRENGTH. YOU COULD HAVE WON THE CONTEST FAIRLY, BUT NO. YOU HAD TO USE PRESSURE POINTS TO PARALYZE HIS MUSCLES WHILE RUNNING AROUND FASTER THAN ANYONE COULD SEE."

"Either way is equally unfair. But I thought my way was more creative."

"I THINK IT'S TIME IT IS YOU WHO ARE GIVEN SOME TRAINING."

"Me?" Rogicphil had to think of something to change the subject and fast. "Who was that annoying me back there?"

"WHAT ARE YOU TALKING ABOUT?"

"One of my people was asking questions but wouldn't identify himself."

"DON'T WORRY ABOUT THAT, I HAVE TO TEACH YOU A LESSON FIRST REMEMBER?"

"But his voice just comes out of the middle of the group and I can't tell who it is."

"YOU SAID 'HIS', YOU THINK IT WAS A HE?"

"No, I really couldn't tell. The voice sounded familiar, but I couldn't place it on any of them."

"AH, IT'S THE NEIL/CLOBBERSON EFFECT."

"The who/what effect?"

"DOCTORS IZGED NEIL AND ROTUNDID CLOBBERSON DID RESEARCH INTO MOB PSYCHOLOGY 40,000 YEARS AGO AND DISCOVERED THAT IN SOME GROUPS A COMMON TRAIT WAS CONCENTRATED ENOUGH TO CREATE A COLLECTIVE CONSCIOUSNESS THAT COULD HAVE TANGIBLE EFFECTS."

"So this anonymous person who keeps spouting rude remarks every now and then doesn't really exist?"

"MAYBE. IT'S ONLY A THEORY AND NO ONE HAS BOTHERED TO TEST IT YET. IF IT WERE TRUE, HOWEVER, THEN THE

EXISTENCE WOULD BE CONTINGENT UPON THE COLLECTIVE IMAGINATION OF YOUR GROUP."

"Wonderful. So what's the address for these two fellows, Neil and Clobson? I want to write an expose on the whole affair. Maybe spark some interest in opening the research back up and..."

"YOU'RE SIDE TRACKING ME TO GET OFF THE SUBJECT OF REAL CONCERN! BUT YOU ONLY HARM YOURSELF IN DOING SO. I WAS PLANNING ON MAKING YOU WALK BACKWARDS, BLINDFOLDED AROUND A LAKE FULL OF ACID WHILE BALANCING AN EGG ON YOUR HEAD AND YOUR SHOE LACES TIED TOGETHER BUT NOW, HA HA, I HAVE SOMETHING ELSE FOR YOU: TRICYCLING ACROSS A LAVA FIELD WHILE STONED ON FLURTON RAG-WEED..."

"Uh, then getting back to the mission at hand I have a question concerning the training," he didn't pause for Destiny to stop him, "What are we doing on a planet just because it has high gravity when we have complete gravity control on the starcruiser?"

Destiny stopped and pulled his face back. He was clearly taken off guard. "YOU SEE, UH, IT'S THE SPA UNIONS. THEY ARE IN IT WITH THE GALACTIC SOCIETY FOR THE DEVASTATION OF FREE WILLED INDIVIDUALS WHO JOIN SOCIETIES AND THE LAWYERS WHO, UH... DO THINGS. IT'S A PLOT EVEN I HAVEN'T WORKED OUT YET."

Rogicphil just sat there stunned. His stupid guess had been right? No way. "Hey, you were spying on me. That was my stupid idea."

"STUPID, BUT VERY LOGICAL."

"Great minds think alike. Where'd you go to school anyway?"

"YOU'RE DISTRACTING ME AGAIN! NO SIMPLE ACROBATIC STUNT WOULD PUNISH YOU ENOUGH. I HAVE SOMETHING MUCH WORSE. HESPUETS II(2) IS ABOUT TO BE TAKEN OVER BY A MAD SCIENTIST WITH A POWERFUL ROBOT. IT WILL BE A VERY DANGEROUS PLACE TO BE IN A FEW HOURS. WHY DON'T YOU HAVE A LOOK? MAYBE YOU COULD LEARN YOUR LESSON AND SOME COMBAT EXPERIENCE TO BOOT."

Rogicphil rolled his eyes at the bad pun.

*   *   *

Back on the gravity controlled porch of the starcruiser Greyson was showing Plutoman, the Clergy, and the bear how to play marbles. Space-Bo and the Funky Chicken were grilling yeast burgers on a space grill, and the girls were practicing a dance routine in the middle of everything.

They were disturbed by a huge airjeep that suddenly flew out of the orange sky and landed in the meadow next to their camp. A tough looking, burly, young park ranger hopped out and greeted them. "Welcome. Which one of you up there is in charge here?"

Plutoman, needing some reassurance right then, shouted down the three meters from the porch to where the park ranger was standing. "I'm in charge here and you're trespassing. Move along before we poach you and have you for dinner."

The man smiled, ignoring the threat and pulled a slip of paper out of his pocket. "Let's see now. One meadow, one parking space, facilities for under fifty thousand, that comes to two hundred and fifty space creds."

Ranger Joe who had been doing nothing of importance up till then spoke up. "Two hundred and fifty space creds? For what?"

"For this camping spot." The guy looked around the meadow, "A nice one too, I must say."

"This place is suppose to be deserted."

"Deserted? This is Planetary Park. You have to pay to camp here. How else could we afford to pollute the rest of the planet?"

"Hey," Plutoman yelled, "I'm in charge here."

"Fine, you pay the fee." The burly fellow handed the bill up to him.

With a snarl at Ranger Joe, Plutoman dug into his pocket. Nothing there, weapon or cash. "Uh, will you accept a check?"

"If you can't pay I'm afraid I'll have to arrest you then freeze you on the spot. It's a lot cheaper than having to commission statues you know. We can't have non paying campers around here after all."

The Funky Chicken was hanging upside down by his feet talons from the porch. "Here you go, Ranger Sir," he said handing the young fellow a wad of money.

"Who are you? I can't accept payment from pets. They're not grandfathered in you know."

"You mean him?" The chicken pointed at Plutoman who was now stepping on his talons. "He's just a figurehead, I'm the real pet owner here."

"Hey!" Plutoman shouted and started stomping on the chicken's talons.

"Oooh, don't stop. That feels so good."

"Well, Okay, if you say so." The park ranger grabbed the money and turned back toward to his airjeep.

"Hey," Plutoman called to him, "How do we know you're really an authorized park ranger and are allowed to collect my money?"

The ranger turned. "Aren't I wearing the uniform of an RR Betan Ranger? These are expense uniforms you know."

"I don't know. I never even heard of them." Plutoman looked to Ranger Joe. "You there. You're a ranger. Is he legit or not?"

Ranger Joe suddenly turned red. "Um, well I wasn't a park ranger. I was an airborne ranger. 197th and 42nd mountain division. But, yeah, that uniform looks real expensive."

"We are so unappreciated," the park ranger said counting the money. He hopped into his airjeep and flew off.

Through the dust Plutoman read the license plate. It said A666. "Hey!" he shouted into the air waving his fist as well.

"Don't worry," the chicken said still upside down. "I gave him funny money. And by funny, I mean exploding."

Chapter 6: The Alley

"Wait a second here," Rogicphil said, "I can't save some randon planet from being taken over by a giant robot."

"YOU'RE RIGHT. YOU NEED SOME EQUIPMENT FIRST. WHAT KIND WOULD YOU LIKE?"

"Actually..."

"I UNDERSTAND YOU DABBLE A BIT IN THE MARTIAL ARTS. HOW ABOUT BEING RANKED ONE IN THE GALAXY IN MARTIAL ARTS? YOU CAN'T BE RANKED ONE IN THE UNIVERSE BECAUSE I ALREADY PROMISED THAT TITLE TO THE SQUIPDUKCHITES, A RACE OF CYBERNETIC GOPHERS WHO COUNTLESS AEONS AGO FORETOLD OF A GREAT KUNG-FU MASTERS WHO.....BUT I DIGRESS."

"Hold it just one..." Rogicphil was speaking before Destiny finished but it didn't matter as he was rendered speechless by a powerful force. The supreme being, who sat behind his desk in the office that couldn't exist on two planets at once, snapped his fingers. Thunder crashed in the background for effect and the floor shook. "NUMBER TWO SHOULD DO NICELY. SO THAT TAKES CARE OF THAT. FEEL BETTER?"

"What are you talking about?"

"CATCH!"

Suddenly twenty shuriken flew at Rogicphil from all directions. Without thinking, he leaped into the air watching the stars shoot past beneath him like they were in slow motion.

He gently landed back into his comfy chair. "Hey! What the heck?"

"I TOLD YOU TO CATCH THEM, NOT LEAP OUT OF THE WAY TO SAFETY. BUT IN ANY CASE YOU JUST DEMONSTRATED YOUR INCREDIBLE SPEED."

"Fine, so I'm a fast dude with some weird boots. I don't know how to fight giant robots. Besides, you need me back on Raul Rall Beta to train my team against the cow."

"NO, THEY'RE NOT YOUR STYLE. YOU NEED A DIFFERENT KIND OF WEAPON." He pressed a button under his desk.

Rogicphil was hiding behind a plant in the corner before Destiny's finger came off the button.

But instead of another shuriken attack, a door opened and Harriet wheeled in a cart with a black leather case on it.

Rogicphil pushed the plant aside and went to the cart. Slowly he opened the case. Inside was a black handled nunchaku. A fire opal colored cord connected the two obsidian sticks. He ran his hand over them. "If these things are called num-chuks why are they spelled nunchaku?"

"I DON'T KNOW, ASK THE DORK WRITING THIS BOOK."

"What?" Rogicphil could feel a slight vibration in the fabric of spacetime.

"NEVER MIND, I'LL EXPLAIN LATER. JUST TRY THEM OUT,

YOU'RE NOW AN EXPERT WITH THEM AFTER ALL."

Rogicphil shrugged and picked the weapon out of the case. He could tell it would have been very difficult to pick up without his increased strength. "What's it made of? Lead?"

"THE NEWEST ALLOY COMPOSITE MATERIAL. IT CAN WITHSTAND UP TO FIVE HUNDRED KILOTONS OF STRESS. THE CORD CAN EXTENT UP TO TEN METERS AND HAS A BUILT IN WENCH FOR EASY CONVENIENCE."

"Great..."

Harriet handed him a trenchcoat.

"HERE'S A DISGUISE FOR YOU. YOU'LL NEED IT BECAUSE IT'S RAINING."

Rogicphil took the trenchcoat and checked the label. "Good, it's a Fregoutnan. It's the only brand with hidden pockets the entire family can enjoy...."

"STOP THAT. NO SELLING OUT WHILE I'M HERE." Destiny pushed another button. The lights dimmed and a claxon began wailing. To his left, curtains parted, revealing a special spotlit door. "JUST STEP THROUGH THAT DOOR AND YOU'LL BE ON YOUR WAY."

Rogicphil's mind raced, trying to think of a way out, but all he came up with was "I don't want to do this."

"YOU AREN'T SUPPOSE TO LIKE YOUR PUNISHMENTS. NOW GO SAVE THAT PLANET, THEN YOU CAN GET BACK TO YOUR TRAINING."

"Okay," he slipped the trenchcoat on and went to the door. It would be futile to argue. Better to get himself beat up by some megabot than chewed out by a supreme being.

He quickly opened the door. Outside it was dark and raining. High overhead and in the distance rectangular lights pointed to the sky. Tall buildings, he guessed.

As soon as he stepped out, the door slammed shut behind him. He turned around but he was only facing a brick wall with mispelled graffiti adorning the bricks. That was strange, he didn't know he could read that language. Destiny was up to his usual tricks.

He turned around. When his eyes adjusted, he noticed he was at the end of a dead end alley. Garbage was piled all over the place. He could see hover cars, through the sheets of rain, zooming by at the end, splashing misty water into the alley. Twenty story brick buildings lay on either side of the alley, each with rusty fire escapes leading to the roofs. He would get a nice hotel room and let himself get beat up when the rain stopped.

A bum lay in some debris with a soggy sandwich in his hand. "Hey mistur, whud 'bout some loose change huh? I need some musturd fur my sandy too."

"I'm broke." He checked his pockets but felt all kinds of loose change and money rolls. "Hmm okay," he tossed a fat bundle at the bum who eagerly grabbed at it. Rogicphil continued down the alley, deliberately splashing in puddles as he went.

"Cheap scum!" the bum yelled at him.

Rogicphil stopped. Who was that bum to call him scum? He turned around to tell the bum where he could go but the bum had another idea.

The soggy sandwich still in hand the bum was charging down the alley toward Rogicphil with his arms outstretched and mouth screaming.

Rogicphil sidestepped, and stuck out his foot, tripping the fellow. There was a flash of light as the bum went sliding along the wet and slippery asphalt. He stood up with a smoldering head. His hair was neatly parted by a singed black line. The bum felt his head, screamed, then tore off down the alley, slipping several times.

"What the...?" Light flashed again, sparks flew off a pipe near Rogicphil's head. He dived into a pile of nearby garbage. Someone was shooting a laser at him. It must have a silencer since he hadn't heard the 'peeeooo peeeooo' sound he was use to.

Flash! Flash! He realized the pile he was in, was suddenly on fire. The stench soon became too much to bare. He leaped out of the garbage doing a somersault in midair. As he was floating in slow motion he could see a form standing in silhouette down the alley holding a smoking gun. As soon as his feet touched the ground he rebounded into the air behind a broken down hover garbage truck.

Wow! That was fast. He didn't know he could do that. He thought for a moment to review his new powers. Shoes that could change at will, increased strength, martial arts, and super speed. Good combination.

But how fast was fast? Well, he knew fast enough to trick some slow trainees but could he out maneuver someone armed with a laser? Only one way to find out. He got ready.

Footsteps. The figure with the laser came into view. Feet thudded through the water methodically, stopping before the garbage pile. A massive back was turned to him, while the smoldering garbage across the alley backlit the silhouette. Wow, that guy was big!

"Enemy destroyed," it said in an electronic voice.
That was no guy.

"Good work," a new voice said, human.

Maybe they hadn't seen Rogicphil jump out of the garbage; he was fast. The human came into view. He was short, had blood shot eyes, and long stark white hair. The scientist? "Come, my friend, far more admirable foes await us at the capital building. It is only a few blocks away." He motioned the big robot to follow him down the alley.

It was a mad scientist all right. So much for waiting until the next day to get beat up. Rogicphil waited as they walked down the alley then stepped out behind them. He pulled the nunchakus from his pocket. He always thought the first test of a new weapon should be the field test.

"Hey you!" Rogicphil yelled at them, "Excuse me."

They stopped and turned around.

"I was just wondering if you happened to be planning a take over of this planet?" It's best to make sure before attacking people with superpowers.

"Why yes, yes I am," the little man shouted back.

"Well, I was hoping I could get a light before all the chaos ensued."

"Light what?"

Rogicphil realized they must not flame on this planet. Didn't matter, it was a stupid line anyway. "Never mind. I'm sorry, but you're not allowed to take over planets on Tuesdays. I don't make up the rules around here. I hope you understand."

"What's a Tuesday?" Neither Rogicphil nor his giant robot answered. "I eat Tuesdays for breakfast. Ha, ha, ha....You are no match for my powerful robot."

"I'm only going to give you one chance to give up peaceably, before I have to sack you and disable your robot."

"Ho, ho, ho....My robot is indestructible. It is ten times as strong as anything puny headed men like you can use against it."

"This is your last chance. You'll thank me when I hand you over to the authorities." He knew it would never work but felt he had to give it a shot anyway.

"You will be the first person I execute under my dictatorship. Robot! Open fire!"

Flash! A streak of red laser light shot through the drizzling rain. Rogicphil easily leaned out of the laser blast's path. He straightened himself up so quickly it appeared as though the laser blast went right through him. "But since I feel generous today, I'll give you just one more chance." He took his trenchcoat off and tossed it to the wet pavement.

The scientist pulled out a pair of round spectacles. He stretched them over his lobey ears. "Robot, your calibration is off. Readjust and increase power. Switch over to hyperquick mode, this guy thinks he some tough sandwich huh. Well, we'll kill this bozo for a third time."

Rogicphil didn't wait for the robot to fire again, he just jumped. He was fifteen meters up when he began to fall back down. "Hmmm." He was in midair for about twenty micro seconds before he had a plan. He held on to one end of his chucks, swung them forward, and thought 'extend.'

The loose handle shot out carrying a length of the firey cable. It wrapped around a support on a fire escape. Down below, the whole alley was ablaze with laser fire. The robot was shooting at everything in the alley.

 Rogicphil swung down avoiding the blasts that were now following his ascent path. He was intent on avoiding them and forgot about the brick wall that was coming up very quickly.

He lifted his legs and thought, 'pogo boots'. Instantly springs popped out of his boot soles. He rebounded from the wall letting go of the chucks and did a back flip. Now he was falling backwards toward the robot that was busy destroying the spot on the brick wall where he'd just been.

His arm grabbed at the fire escape on the other side of the alley. He let his momentum carry his feet up to the metal railing and used it as a foot rest, so he could relaunch himself back to the other side and get his chucks back. But laser fire melted the fire escape and he was falling again.

Whumth! He landed in another pile of garbage. A cold hand grabbed him by the neck and hauled him into the air. Red glowing eyes greeted him as rain splattered his face. It might have been a nice sight if only he could breathe.

"Enemy captured."

The mad scientist came up behind the robot. "Spectacular performance for a rank amature as yourself. I have never seen anyone be so clumsy, so quickly before."

"Ack!" Rogicphil said kicking at the metal monster.

"Do you have any last requests before you are exterminated?"

"Ack!" He noticed one end of his chucks swinging in the rain just a meter or so to the left of the robot.

"No? Well nice to meet you, uh mister...?"

"Ack!" If only he could reach it.

"Mister Ack. What a nice name. Robot! Please kill Mister Ack now."

The robot raised the laser to Rogicphil's face. Its metallic fingers tensed on the trigger of its wicked looking laser gun. At the last moment Rogicphil managed to pushed the gun to the side with a quick boot kick. Flash! A hole in the brick wall behind him formed.

"You stupid robot," The scientist yelled, "How could you miss? He's right there! Your calibration is still off."

His mind reeling from the lack of air, Rogicphil thought 'skis' and snow skis appeared on his feet. He used the extra length to knock the end of the chuck into his hand. 'Retract' he thought as his face was turning blue. A little fusion motor inside the handle whirred to life, lifting him, along with the robot, into the air.

"Ack!" The robot wasn't supposed to come along.

"Robot, what are you doing?" the white haired guy below yelled up at them, "I ordered you to to kill him. What are you waiting for?"

The robot opened its metal mouth to speak but Rogicphil shoved the end of his water ski into it. When the robot moved its hand to pull the ski out he let go of Rogicphil's neck and fell towards the alley floor.

Sprung! With the extra weight gone, the little fusion motor came to life and the wench whirred at high speed. Rogicphil's head was suddenly propelled into the fire escape girder, that the other end of the chuck was wrapped around.

Crash! The robot had landed on the abandoned hover garbage truck. It lay there a moment then said, "I don't know. What am I waiting for, master?"

Rogicphil, not giving up the opportunity of a downed opponent, released his chucks and sailed down toward the robot. 'Spiked hiking boots,' he thought. In mid fall, the waterskis morphed into death-from-above and were on a direct collision course for the robot's head.

"Look out!" The Mad scientist yelled.

Smash! Rogicphil's feet connected with the robot. The rusted roof of the hover garbage truck collapsed beneath them and they fell into the interior. Laser blasts opened holes in the sides, all around the hover truck. Then Rogicphil sailed back into the air, landing on a nonmelted part of the fire escape. Laser blasts followed as he ran up to the roof.

"Robot! Bad. Bad Robot! Don't let him get away with that. Destory him. Full power!"

Rogicphil made it over the roof parapet microseconds later. He needed to massage his sore neck and think of a plan. There was no way the robot could get him up here. It had melted the fire escapes on both sides of the alley by now. His only worry was that the mad scientist might give up on him and go plunder the capital building.

Flash! A meter wide section of the parapet disintegrated near the roof corner. Point 97 seconds later, another section was destroyed a little bit closer to him.

"Well, I guess this calls for plan B." Rogicphil said to himself as a third section evaporated into nothingness. "I can't run, I'll eventually get blasted." He leaned against a transparent aluminum air conditioning unit watching the parapet disappear like clockwork, one piece every .97 seconds. "At least that robot has good timing...." he paused to let the thought sink in. "Timing? That's it."

He turned around and ripped a panel off of the AC unit. Disconnected from it's power source it was shiny and gleamed silver. He waited until the blast paused for the .97 seconds then jumped to a remaining section of the parapet. 0.42 seconds later he stood up and placed the panel right in the path of the beam.

Flash! He was thrown back. He quickly dropped the panel, it was glowing white hot! He looked at his slightly toasted hands. "Whew." As the energy levels dissipated the panel turned orange, then transparent, and finally once again to silver.

He peeked over the edge. The robot was laid out and charred up from the reflected laser blast. The scientist was yelling technical obscenities at it. That wasn't so hard, maybe he could be the 5th most powerful dude in the universe after all. Now he could go back and... the robot got up.

"Ut-oh..." Rogicphil waited to see what happened next. The robot examined its laser gun throughly, then dropped it. Hmm, it looked like the laser gun was out of commission. Now Rogicphil could move in for the kill.

He dived off the roof. Halfway down he thought, 'super shock absorber boots' and some rubbery extensions popped out along the soles. He did a flip, positioning his feet to land.

Frump! He had to bend his knees sharply but the impact was absorbed and no rebound occured. He straightened up and faced the blackened robot. "Hello, metal head."

The robot only had one glowing red eye left now, and it glared at him with a pre-programmed vengeance. The other, burn out eye, just sparked a few times in his general direction.

The mad scientist was steaming mad. "Okay Mr. Ack, if that is your real name, that was the last camel. The robot will now crush you to a pulp." He shook an accusing finger at Rogicphil.

"So it's down to hand to hand, eh?" He twirled the chunks around like a master. He was a master, he had to remind himself.

"That laser cost me twenty billion space creds to make!" The robot, metal hands outstretched, moved forward.

"You paid too much. I saw one just like it, on sale in a Barblooneen Holiday catalog for only four billion."

"Idiot! That was a one-of-a-kind weapon! They don't sell them in catalogs."

The robot swung its mighty fist with incredible speed at Rogicphil who ducked and returned the blow to no effect.

"Your wimpy weapon is useless against my robot. He is made from the strongest alloys in the galaxy."

After some light sparing, light that is against a hover Mac truck,

Rogicphil realized that, even with increased strength and speed, he couldn't defeat the robot. He needed a plan.

Suddenly he remembered the movie, Twister Party Terror, in which a harmless twister game turns into a blood bath when Joey Weber the little kid who suffocated in a plastic shopping bag returns from the grave and... Quit selling out, he had to remind himself. Well, the basic idea was there.

Rogicphil jumped back from the robot's onslaught to prepare himself. With one handle in each hand he leapt into the air passing over the robot. The elongated cord of the nunchaku's caught on the robot's neck pivoting Rogicphil to land directly behind it.

"Twisters up!" Rogicphil said. He started to spin in place holding the two ends tightly. Faster and faster until he was just a blur of motion. The chuck cord twisted up around the robot's neck, increasing the pressure as Rogicphil spun.

The little white haired man watched in horror as his robot's neck began to shrink. The robot flailed around helplessly. Finally the cord snapped.

Rogicphil was still spinning a moment later. Everything looked a blurry green. He slowed down and stopped but his head kept reeling. He shook his head. Everything was distorted and whirling around him. After a bit he looked up and could see clearly. That was weird, everything seemed to be taller. No, he was shorter. He found himself buried up to his waist in concrete and asphalt.

He climbed slowly from his self dug pit and brushed the dust off his legs.

Running back and forth the length of the alley, the mad scientist was screaming bloody murder; technically robocide.

The robot just stood there, lolling its head. Rogicphil lifted the head to look at its good eye. Its neck was now only a 12mm in diameter and its eye was very dim.

"So chap, I see that being a pencil necked geek is coming back into fashion."

The robot opened its mouth to speak. It babbled something incoherent.

"What's that about a sandwich good enough for an Antarien to eat?"

A door materialized a piece of brick wall that was left intact. It slowly opened and Destiny poked his head out. "AT LEAST IT STOPPED RAINING," he said.

Rogicphil looked around. All was quiet except for the sound of dripping water. It had stopped raining sometime during his battle but he had failed to notice it. He picked up the two severed ends of his chucks off the chewed up alley floor. "Sorry about these."

"DON'T WORRY, THOSE WERE ONLY PROTOTYPES. WE'LL GET YOU SOMETHING TO REPLACE THEM SOON ENOUGH."

Rogicphil found the trenchcoat or what was left of it scattered about in little tuffs of cloth all across the alley. "So much for that, too."

"GOOD WORK, YOU SAVED THE PLANET."

"Thanks, what about the geek?" he pointed at the robot still standing there.

"OH, IT WON'T DO ANYTHING FOR ANOTHER FIVE

SECONDS."

"What will it do?"

"EXPLODE!"

"Gotcha," Rogicphil dashed into the office right behind Destiny and slammed the door. The muffled thud of an explosion was heard behind.

Inside, Destiny snapped his fingers and the ruined nunchakus disappeared from Rogicphil's hands. Destiny went over to the bar and poured two drinks.

Rogicphil sank into the plush purple chair exhausted. "Thanks," he said taking the drink offered him, "What is it?"

"DARANKEEN CACTUS JUICE. "

"My favorite," he drank up. "I have a quick question or two for you."

"OKAY."

"What was that wadded up stuff in my coat?"

"I DON'T UNDERSTAND."

"This bum was looking for a handout so I tossed him what I thought was some wadded up money from the trench coat."

"OH THAT. I THOUGHT YOU WOULD KNOW BEING A REPORTER AND ALL. THAT WAS PLAY MONEY USED TO PASS ON TO HOODLUMS TO GET THEM ARRESTED. STREET PEOPLE ARE BY DEFINITION STREETWISE AND KNOW HOW TO SPOT FAKE BILLS."

"I've never seen Hespuetsian money before. How was I supposed to tell if it was fake or not?"

"WELL, JUST BE THANKFUL THAT THE BUM IS HAPPY TO SEE THAT THE MAD SCIENTIST IS DEAD."

"Dead? He ran off. I didn't kill him."

"WHAT?" Destiny froze his pouring another glass in mid stream. "THAT'S NOT GOOD. YOU'VE GOT TO GO BACK AND GET RID OF HIM OR HE'LL JUST MAKE ANOTHER MORE POWERFUL ROBOT."

"Okay, just let me rest up a bit first."

The physics of the pouring drink started up again. "NO, YOU MUST GO BACK OUT RIGHT NOW AND FINISH YOUR JOB." Destiny went over to the door. He opened it up onto the alley again and said, "HURRY UP, WHILE HE'S STILL SEMI-HELPLESS."

With a sigh Rogicphil, set his cactus juice down and headed back into the alley. The door slammed shut behind him. All was quiet now, in the alley that resembled a war zone. There was a black mark on the pavement in front of him. It was all that was left of the robot.

He could hear a low wining sound behind some charred up rubbish. He carefully stepped around the pile ready to jump out of the way of any laser blast. But all he saw was the scientist huddled up in a ball, crying.

"Go away, you ruined my robot, you meanie," the mad scientist cried.

"You did it to yourself, you know. You should be ashamed." Rogicphil found a ball of used yarn sitting in the garbage and used it to tie him up with.

He hauled the sobbing figure back to the doorway. He knocked and the door swung open. With a small effort he chucked the man inside the doorway then stepped in himself.

Back inside the office he pointed to the man on the floor. "I couldn't kill him. So I brought him back to you."

"OH WELL, I GUESS I COULD USE HIM AS A SUB-TEMPORAL JANITOR." He turned to his secretary, "HARRIET, TAKE HIM TO THE RE-EDUCATION PARLOR PLEASE."

She silently did as she was told.

Rogicphil watched her efficiently take the man out of the office. It would be nice to have an android slave, he thought, as he plopped back down into his plush and comfy chair, that is if androids ever came back into fashion.

"HARRIET IS NOT A SLAVE," Destiny whispered under his breath.

"Well that's that. Now I have another question." Rogicphil waited for Destiny to comment but the supreme being just lit up a fat cigar and began to smoke. "I thought I was a powerful dude, but I had a hard time taking that robot out, and I had to destroy those super strong chucks to do it. What gives?"

"YOU ARE LEARNING THE WAY OF THE GLADERUNNER. IT IS NEVER EASY FOR BEGINNERS. OR EXPERTS FOR THAT MATTER."

"So what's the difference?"

"CONFIDENCE. AS YOU BECOME MORE SKILLED YOUR MISSIONS WILL BE JUST AS DIFFICULT BUT YOUR CONFIDENCE IN YOURSELF, GETTING THE JOB DONE, WILL GROW."

"So I risk my life for confidence?"

"DON'T UNDERESTIMATE ITS POWER. CONFIDENCE WILL GO A LONG WAY TO INSURE VICTORIES. IN TIME YOU WILL UNDERSTAND."

"Just like the guy before me?"

"HE WAS A LITTLE DIFFERENT. I GOT HIM OUT OF AN ASYLUM TO BEGIN WITH. THE GLADERUNNER BEFORE HIM WAS GETTING TOO OLD AND NEEDED TO RETIRE WHEN A BIG MISSION CAME UP, SO I HAD TO PICK SOMEONE QUICKLY AT RANDOM."

"Oh...."

"ARE YOU READY TO PLAN TOMORROW'S TRAINING SESSION YET?"

"No, I'd just like some sleep right...."

Before Rogicphil finished speaking he was back inside his room on Plutoman's starcruiser. He checked the hallway. The Funky Chicken was walking his way.

"Excuse me," the chicken asked, "Plutoman's parrot wanted to know what you wanted for dinner tonight, toasted marshmellons or hot canines?"

Rogicphil was too tired then to say much, "Forget the camp out. Everyone sleeps inside tonight and we eat real food."

"We've already been doing that for the last few nights already, but by the way, you wouldn't happen to have any trihexinal explosives on you possibly? I've suddenly run out."

"No, but I think I saw some in the head the other day." Rogicphil stopped and scratched his head. "Last few nights? How long have I been gone?"

"Thank you." The chicken walked down the hall. He found a door on the right side marked 'Lou' and went in. A moment later there was an explosion. Chicken feathers fluttered out into the hall.

"Crazy Chicken."

Chapter 7: Professional Scapegoats

The next day Rogicphil discovered that the Funky Chicken was still alive. It became apparent when he went into the bathroom and saw no signs of splattered chicken. To further prove the point the Funky Chicken greeted him as he exited into the hallway.

"I thought you were dead."

"I wish," the chicken replied half mockingly.

"Good, now you can go survival training with Space-Bo."

The chicken continued down the hall, "That's nice."

Rogicphil walked down to Space-Bo's room and entered without knocking. Space-Bo was sleeping half on and half off his bed. His legs were flopped on the bed while his torso was lying face down on the floor. His nose made a funny whistle like farting noise as he breathed on the fake linoleum.

Rogicphil tapped him on the back of his head.

"No ma, I didn't give the cat a swirly," he mumbled.

"It's me, Space-Bo."

"Nice to meet you, Space-Bo. You know my name is Space-Bo too?"

"Wake up. You're on Rall Raul Beta, remember?"

"I hate high grav planets, Rogicphil."

"I know, I know. I hate them too. But I have something very fun for you to do."

Space-Bo raised his head slowly. His eyes somehow managed to focus on Rogicphil. But as he turned, he upset the balance his body had while sleeping. So as he tried to mutter a response he suddenly found himself lying in a knotted bundle on the floor.

"Allow me," Rogicphil said untangling him with no hesitation and with the ease of a skilled knotsmith. He dragged Space-Bo to his feet asking, "Now, are you awake?"

"Yeah, I guess."

"Okay, I'm sending you out with the Funky Chicken to do survival training."

"Equipment?"

"As outlined in Kreb Knorr's Manual of Universal Existentialism, Basic Edition." He managed to stick just to the facts. No more selling out, he reminded himself. Maybe a little bit next week but for now, no embellishments.

"Never got to look at the pictures in that book."

"Get cleaned up and then after breakfast I'll meet you down in the equipment room."

"Yeah sure."

Rogicphil let go of Space-Bo's arm. The ex space marine swayed a bit but stayed standing. Just as Rogicphil was about to leave, Space-Bo crashed to the floor like a plastic plank he'd once used to build scale model pirate spaceships in bottles with.

Rogicphil didn't bother to shrug with or without a sigh as he left; he was too hungry for breakfast for that kind of nonsense.

After a breakfast of variable flavored space oatmeat with various temperature / texture cross gradients, Rogicphil met the Funky Chicken and Space-Bo in the forward lounge area top deck.

"Here's your exciting new line of equipment," he said waving his hand across the table.

Space-Bo began to giggle and jabbed the chicken with his elbow. The chicken looked up at Rogicphil who still had some oatmeal clinking to his face. It was doing a little multispectral dance on his cheek.

"On this table, set up just for the purpose," Rogicphil rambled, "lay five survival items. A white towel measuring 1.62 meters in length and .91 meters in width, a 2.0 meter length of industrial strength surgical tubbing, one standard issue titanium epoxy alloy frisbee, a 250 gram ball of generic brand plastitac rated G5, and one pair of fake imitation plastirubber *****ers brand shoe inserts size 9-1/2." As he mentioned each item he would gently pick it up in his hands and carefully present it for the two of them to not admire.

"What's this junk?" Space-Bo asked eyeing the equipment suspiciously.

"This is your survival equipment." The various little bits of oatmeal still clinging to Rogicphils face began to bump into one another as they continued their dance.

"I think we can get by without any of that," Space-Bo mumbled. He tried real hard not to stare. "Once I survived for two weeks on the frozen side of Callisto with barely my toothbrush to keep me company. I had to watch the holovision programs on a hotwired molar filling."

The chicken was in a frozen trance being mesmerized by the oatmeal show taking place on Rogicphil's face. A loud WHACK snapped him out of it. "Wha..."

"This is a real crappy fly swatter," Space-Bo said smacking the shoe insert on the table in an attempt to squash imaginary flys.

The chicken looked down at the table and seeing the ball of putty like plastitac, grabbed it up. He sniffed it throughly and tasted it a bit. "Blah... this isn't plastic explosives. I concur with mister Bo here. This is pretty worthless junk."

"Oh come on now," Rogicphil seemed slightly insulted, "Check out this olympic regulation towel here. It features seventy thousand stitches per ten centimeters and even has reloadable deodorant crystal packs."

"I smell a catch somewhere," the chicken sniffed.

Space-Bo suddenly remembered a halibut he'd forgotten to gut. He dug it out of a utility pocket and sniffed.

"Well," Rogicphil said, his smile sparkling and his oatmeal blinking neon blue, "There is one more little thing. According to Kreb Knorr's manual, this is it. All you get. No more and no less."

"What about our clothes?" Space-Bo looked at the chicken's feather covered body, assuming it was just a fashion statement.

"You're not allowed to need them."

"Don't need our clothes?"

"Well, he's not wearing any clothes to begin with," Rogicphil explained as he pointed at the chicken, "You should use him as a good example."

"Huh? Sure he's wearing clothes."

"The Funky Chicken is not wearing any clothes."

Space-Bo scratched his head. "Oh yeah, I knew that. I mean, well, you know with his feathers and all, I uh, I just sort of assumed that.... Really?"

"I'm sure you'll get along just fine without them. We're not going to see you naked in the wilderness anyway." Rogicphil produced a compact industrial paper shredder from under the display table saying, "Just throw your clothes in here when you're ready. The manual is on the table too. You can skim through it if you like but it's not included in the equipment list itself, so you'll have to shred it too before heading out."

Space-Bo tried smacking imaginary flys with his halibut and was far more pleased with the results. "Aw man."

Rogicphil stepped through the swishing exit door. "Meet me out in the hallway when you're ready," he said and the door swished closed behind him.

They both burst out laughing when they were alone.

"Did you see that stuff crawling on his face?"

"I did indeed. It was very halarious."

They emerged from the equipment room stripped of all their possessions, which for those two could help keep in business several large warehouse sized cargo ships and yet they somehow managed to stuff it all inside some smelly old gym lockers they found in the corner of the room.

The Funky Chicken carried the frisbee, while Space-Bo was wearing the towel about him like a toga, with the tubbing around his waist like a sash. Well, at least that's what he thought he looked like. In actuality, he more closely resembled a manually rapped xmas present that an experimentally impoverished person might received during an economical recession. For shoes, he had the shoe inserts plastitaced to his feet (yes he wore size 9-1/2 (nu metric standard)).

Rogicphil pointed at Space-Bo's face. "You've got something on your chin there 'Bo."

He plucked it off and examined it, said, "Halibut, mmm" and licked it off his fingers. "Sure tastes better than oatmeal."

The chicken laughed and followed Space-Bo down the hall to the shuttlecraft hanger.

They were blindfolded before entering the shuttle and flown dozens of kilometers to the west towards a remote section of a nearby urban development. An odd mixture of familiar and odd landscapes blurred by the shuttle as it flew over. Orange and yellow were the dominate colors of the childishly rolling hills spread out below. In contrast, the urban development was a spiky gray and red mass of shard like buildings oozing black smoke from their sides. The smoke hung in a neat envelope around the development as if it didn't want to be contaminated by the colorful nature outside itself.

Rogicphil unceremoniously dumped them on the edge of the development and took off before they could ask anymore silly questions. "Damn oatmeal," he said wiping his face with his sleeve.

"You can take your blindfold off now," the Funky Chicken told Space-Bo, "We've arrived at our destination."

They were on the curb of a hovercar street facing a park. When Space-Bo's blindfold dissolved (A blindfold wasn't included in the equipment and so had to be destroyed once its usefulness was complete) his eyes opened to yellow trees with orange leaves. Small three headed squirrels were busy arguing with themselves about the economics of nut futures.

"Wow," Space-Bo said rubbing his hands in anticipation for what he thought would be wilderness survival, complete with roasting three headed squirrels over an open fire, "I think this'll be fun."

"Uh Space-Bo," the Funky Chicken said tapping him on the shoulder, "Maybe you should turn around."

He did. "Hey, what are those condos doing here? Don't they know those kinds of things tend to attract bears. We are in the wilderness after all."

"They are the wilderness."

"What?"

"It's wilderness all right, urban wilderness. The wilderness of so called civilized intelligence."

"Well I don't care how intelligent they are. They need to move those condos before bears start snooping around."

"You're right, there's no excuse for intelligence." He glanced at an approaching hovercar and said, "Hey, I've got an idea. Stay here." The chicken waited until the car crossed in front of a tree then jumped out into the road and lay down. The car rounded a bend and came right at him.

Space-Bo peeked out from behind the tree. The hovercar was bearing down on the chicken. He tried to warn the Funky Chicken about the approaching car by pointing at it. "Watch out!" he whispered but all the chicken did was raise his hands with both thumbs sticking up in an all-systems-go signal.

Space-Bo squeezed his eyes shut; he couldn't watch. He felt sorry about not being able to see his friend alive anymore. Wait, he suddenly realized he could dash out in front of the car and quickly save the chicken from a certain death, but for some reason, his belly began to hurt. Wait a second. He'd heard that the Funky Chicken was immortal and couldn't be killed.

SQUISH!

Oh no! Space-Bo opened his eyes. Oh well, he guessed he must have heard wrong. There lay his friend, plastered all over the road. Gross.

Tears welled up in his eyes as he tried to run over to his friend, but with his vision blurred by 35 degrees, he ran into the confused motorist, who had just gotten out of his chicken splattered hovercar.

"I'm awfully sorry," the motorist sounded distraught, "I-I just didn't see your pet giant chicken in the road. Surely, with one of his heads, he should have seen me coming." He looked over at the mess. "I think I'm going to be sick." He ran over to a park water fountain and leaned over.

Space-Bo felt a bit better that the driver felt bad about running the chicken over but he didn't need to throw up about it. Throw up? His belly turned again.

Just then the sun was turned off. No, it was his eyes. Somebody had their hand over his face. And now they were trying to drag him into the street.

Well, a good swift punch would solve....

WHAM! A large blunt object was making contact with his skull, "Ouch that...."

WHAM, again! "Ouch that...."

WHAM, WHAM WHAM-A-WHAM! Nice birdies. He felt something soft beneath him then the roar of an over tweaked engine and sudden acceleration.

He opened his eyes. "AAAAAAh !" He closed his eyes. He thought he had seen himself flying over pavement and at any second would smack right into it.

Nothing happened. He opened his eyes again. "AAAAAAh !" He closed them again. He thought he had seen the pavement flying by again. Then he heard something laughing.

"Hey," he said angrily, "See how you like it when you're about to go splat."

"Very well, I think," the voice said.

That voice sounded familiar. He opened his eyes. He was still about to crash but this time he ignored it because the someone laughing at him was more important. He looked over to where the voice came from. Yes, it was who he had thought the voice should be connected to, but wasn't the Funky Chicken dead?

"I thought you were dead."

"I am."

"Oh," Space-Bo scratched his head, "How can you be dead when I'm alive?"

"Isn't it obvious?"

"What are you doing with that lever?"

"Never mind. I said isn't it obvious?"

"What is?"

"That you're dead?"

"Oh," Space-Bo said scratching his head again, "I get it. I get it."

"You do?"

"Yes. You see, dead people aren't alive unless they think they're about to die, again for the first time."

"Never mind."

"By the way, where are we?"

"We're inside that guy's hovercar."

"I guess stealing isn't so bad if he thinks we're dead."

"Forget what I said about being dead, okay?"

"Why? Does it matter when you're dead?"

"I lied when I said that we were dead."

"Why should I believe you? Dead people always lie."

"How do you know that?"

"I'm dead too." Space-Bo was pleased with his reasoning and awarded himself with an imaginary pat on the back.

"So? Living people lie too."

"Sure I guess."

"Therefore, you're really alive."

"If I'm dead, how come I have to pee?"

"You're not dead."

"Would you make up your mind? I need to throw up too."

"Okay, just pretend you're alive for now. You'll never know the

90

difference anyway, at least until we can get out of here. Then I can explain it to you, in exquisite detail."

"Sure," Space-Bo mumbled as he watched the shard like condos fly by, "One thing?"

"Yes?"

"If I'm not dead... I really have to pee."

"Listen, I am telling you the truth, we are alive, full stop." ... and the hovercar slammed to.

They both ended up squished between dashboard and the front window.

"That's why you feel alive, because your *are* alive," the chicken continued speaking as if nothing had happened. "Besides if you were dead, you would have had to remember dying right?"

"Um, well, I don't...Fine! Have it your way. We're still alive." Space-Bo began the slow process of untangling himself. "At least I don't have to pee anymore."

"Good..... I think."

The chicken checked all the controls after climbing back into the drivers seat but nothing looked wrong. "Ut oh, we must be out of fuel."

"How can you tell?" Space-Bo looked out the window. Ahead of them were some trees a few meters away but nothing immediately in front of them.

"Well, look here," the chikcen said pointing at the fancy console. "See the accelerometer? It's zero. And look at the back seat reclinometer. 30 degrees, that's normal. And the smog concentrator is blinking red but that's to be expected in these older models. But notice there's no fuel gauge. Logically, if something goes wrong and no warning lights go off, and the fuel guage was an option not selected by the previous owner, we must conclude that we're out of fuel."

"But what if this model doesn't use fuel?"

"Get out and push."

Space-Bo heaved the hovercar out into the middle of an intersection, boxed in by seventy story orange condos on three corners and the nice ornamental park that they had randomly stopped at, on the edge of the development.

Several hovercars were closing in fast from three directions at once.

"What now?"

"First we split," the chicken said jumping out the sunroof, "Hurry up before you really get killed."

Space-Bo was breathing heavy and wiped the sweat from his brow. The chicken leap frogged over his head and scampered back towards the park behind him.

He motioned for Space-Bo to join him on the sidewalk.

Space-Bo looked back at the approaching hovercars and decided he didn't want to find out what their owners had for breakfast so he abandoned his own hovercar in the intersection. Ut oh, he forgot his shoe inserts in the car. He went back to get them.

"No, you fool," the Funky Chicken shouted, "You'll get killed. For real this time, I mean."

The three hovercars seemed to speed up when they saw Space-Bo dangling half in and half out the sunroof of the stranded hovercar. They roared forward, without a stop sign for kilometers around.

As soon as he got near the driver's side console the machine roared back to life and peeled out of the way of the onrushing traffic.

"That's better," Space-Bo mumbled re-sticking the inserts to his bottom of his feet. He seem oblivious to the fact that the hovercar was in motion again.

The chicken took a step back towards the sidewalk just as the other hovercars converged.

KAAAHRAAAAASSSSSHHHHHHHHH!

Space-Bo turned to look at the jumble of hovercars out the back window. "What idiots."

"You're the idiot," the Funky Chicken told him.

"No, I'm an imbecile working very diligently to become a moron." He looked around not seeing the chicken there. "Hey, where'd I go?" He knew the chicken was waiting for him on the sidewalk, so it must be he himself who was missing.

"I stole the previous owner's commlink while I was crashing into it earlier. Turn around and pick me up."

"Can we get some food please? I still need to throw up."

After the hovercar mysteriously quit working again, at the park, they gave up on the thing and started walking.

"We don't have any money," the chicken was saying, "So if you want to eat, or do the other thing, we'll have to improvise."

Up ahead of them was a lady in her bathrobe walking a three headed kangaroo down the sidewalk. The Funky Chicken whispered to Space-Bo, "You'll have to do the talking, they'll think I'm your pet."

"What do I say?"

"Shooosh. Her she comes."

Space-Bo undid the tubbing from his waist and fitted it around the chicken's neck like a leash.

Boing, Boing, Boing. The kangaroo hopped right up to the Funky Chicken and cautiously sniffed him, each head probing a different crevice.

"I say good fellow," the lady said saying to Space-Bo, "But where did you find such a lovely animal?" She had thick yellow horn rimmed glasses that made the outlines of comits around her eyes and which were about to crash into each other. Her hair was a burnt orange.

Space-Bo rattled his mind and waited for an idea to roll down into it. "He's a family heirloom, that as a small child, I was told had been purchased at a military surplus auction. Space cadets actually."

"How sweet." The lady's kangaroo's second head looked as if it were trying to bark at the chicken but had a stick stuck in it's throat. "But what happened to it's other heads? You didn't...."

"Yeah, about that. You see, my uncle said he stole, uh rescued, it from a band of perverted space gypsies who were so poor they sold his heads in exchange for food...."

"Ummmm..." Her face began to turn the color of her hair.

"And my half brother once removed, told me the gypsies had gotten it from a blind messiah who liked to wrap the chicken in duck tape and...." He was cut short by the chicken elbowing him in the ribs.

"Come on darling," the lady said trying to pull her kangaroo away from the chicken, "Mommy needs to get her personality transplanted today." Visually flustered, she crossed the intersection and continued down the sidewalk on the other side.

After they were gone, "What do you think you are doing?" the chicken said upset. "Why didn't you try to get some money from her instead of insulting my heritage?"

"Money? I want food, not money."

"Forget it. We still have a chance. I just hope that hardware store is still open." He grabbed Space-Bo and headed down the sidewalk in the opposite direction that followed the intersecting street.

"Whatever," Space-Bo said stumbling behind.

They made their way to an airbus stop where a bus was just pulling away. They ran and barely managed to grab on to the tailgate before the bus lifted off the pavement and sped into the air.

"What are we doing?" Space-Bo yelled over the bus noise.

"The lady with the kangaroo is our ticket out of here," the chicken yelled.

"We want out?"

"Yes!"

"Okay..." Space-Bo thought they wanted food but the chicken knew what he was doing.

"Now, she is going to go see a Dr. Vadlin Nosehonka who owns an aircar we can use to get out of here with, but in order for us to get it, she has to distract him."

"Right. But, but...uh."

"What is it?"

"How do you know she's going to see the guy with the big nose?"

"It's quite simple really. Didn't you smell that perfume she was wearing?"

"No...?"

"See, there you go."

"Oh, okay." He squinched up his face a bit then suddenly looked relieved.

"Hey, I thought you had already done that back in the hovercar."

"No, that's where I threw up. I peed in the front."

"Oh."

"And what's makes you so sure that doctor has an aircar?"

"The good doctor's business card, I stold from the ladies purse. He's a member of the local hot rod club."

"Can't you learn to acquire things without stealing?"

The bus came to a stop to let passengers on and off. They let go of the bumper to continue their conversation less distracted by the noise and hanging on for dear life.

"And so in order to distract him we need to get to the hardware store across the street," the chicken explained.

"Right. Now I'm following you."

"Yes, you are." the chicken yanked on the tubing making Space-Bo follow him around the airbus. "Because it's next door to the doctor's office and we can jump between the roofs where the aircar is parked up there."

"Right."

The Funky Chicken stopped to look at Space-Bo questioningly. "Wait a second, you've quit asking me questions."

"Well, I trust you."

"But surely you have more questions."

"Sort of..."

"Well?"

"Wouldn't it be easier to steal one of the aircars parked down here on one of these easy to access streets?"

"I thought you were against me stealing anymore." The chicken started walking around the airbug again.

"Hmm," Space-Bo had to stop and think about that one. The chicken didn't stop and so the tubing began to stretch between them until the tension got the point where it pulled an idea out of his head. He ran to catch up with his friend. "I just had an idea."

"Yes and no," the chicken was saying.

"What's that supposed to mean?"

"Yes, we could steal the aircars down here but no, my way is more fun."

Space-Bo was admiring the holographic advertisement on the side of the bus for kangaroo chow as he said, "But I'm still hungry now."

"Knowing that Dr. Nosehonka's is a hot rod fanatic, you have to admit, it's pretty likely that his aircar has a refrigerator in it. None of these down here do. And I have one statistical data point to prove it."

"Okay."

"Now see that tall building up ahead?" the chicken asked pointing.

"The one that says: Repent Now Your Doom Is Waiting For You?"

"That's the one. What I want you to do is jump off the bus and grab onto it, but wait until you get close enough."

"But we're not riding the bus anymore."

"Dang it, I knew something was wrong. You've been distracting me." The chicken led Space-Bo back around to the back of the airbus.

"So grab on now, wait for the bus the fly up next to that building, then jump off when it seems like a good idea."

"Okay." Space-Bo practiced grabbing back onto the bus then letting go and jumping to a building below.

The Funky Chicken shook his head, "You're almost as reckless as I am. Then I want you to climb up to the roof and wait for me there."

"Aren't you coming?"

"Not yet, I need to take care of some unfinished business first."

"But I had an idea...." but it was too late to say it as the airbus zoomed off again leaving the chicken behind, waving at him. The building loomed closer as the airbus weaved back and forth through aircar traffic. Space-Bo readied himself again just like he'd practiced. Well maybe one more practice. Let go, jump, grab on, let go... Okay he had it.

A little kid poked his head out the back window and looked down at

Space-Bo. "Hey mister, that's pretty cool. Do it again."

Space-Bo smiled up at the kid. "Okay," and he showed him how to let go of the bumper, pretend to jump and grab back on.

"I was told to tell you not to forget your tubing."

"Huh?"

"Don't forget your tubing," the little kid said dangling the very important length of surgical tubing in front of Space-Bo's face. Space-Bo reached for it but the little kid would pull it away before he could grab it. After a couple times of this he realized the airbus had long passed the building he was supposed to have jumped off at. Now what?

"What are you still doing there?" a voice yelled behind him. He looked over his shoulder and there was the Funky Chicken's riding on the shoulders of a leather clad biker who was attempting to ride his aircycle.

"Hi there," Space-Bo shouted, waving back at his friend. "I ran into a bit of a problem here."

"Me too," the chicken shouted back. The biker was simultaneously trying to fight the chicken off his shoulders and maintain control of his bike. But the chicken knew how to apply the proper amount of nerve pinches, in just the right places, to make the biker twitch in just the correct manner, to control the aircycle to where the chicken wanted to go and not necessarily where the biker needed it to.

"You might want to have that dandruff looked at," the chicken said to the biker, "I don't think it's fatal but you never know," and jumped through the air aiming for the airbus's rear bumper. He was a bit short and missed but he did manage to snag a couple of talons into Space-Bo's leg.

"I'll get you!" the biker shouted menacingly at the chicken but flew away.

"What a tease." The chicken clawed his way up Space-Bo's back and finally to his spot again on the back bumper.

Space-Bo was screaming the whole way.

The chicken expertly snatched the loose end of the tubing from the little kid. "Oh quit your whining. See I got your tubing back." Quickly he tied one end around Space-Bo's arm. He then made a loop with the free end and hooked it onto a passing flagpole. "See you soon."

"Yeah!" the little kid yelled.

Space-Bo was swinging in midair before he realized what had happened. It seemed he was attached to a pole that was sticking out of the side of a condo building but he wasn't sure. He looked down. About thirty stories below lay some yellow trees with orange leaves that surrounded the courtyard at the entrance of what he hoped was the hardware building. Ouch, he thought.

He looked up to the roof which was another seven stories or so up. The side of the building he was on didn't seem to have any windows on it, only neon red lego-style bricks. There wasn't even anymore poles sticking out; the one he was attached to was the only one. Hmmm, he thought.

After scavaging some of the pastictac that was still holding the shoe inserts to his feet, he used the putty like stuff to plug the wounds left behind by the chicken's talons.

He untied the tubbing from the pole so he could swing up to it more easily. He stood up on the pole to get a better look at the roof. Not much better. He looked around for anything that might help him up to the top. He spotted a passing bird and waved at it. The bird landed on his arm.

"Good birdie" he said to it, but the bird only laughed, then garnished his arm and flew off.

"Why you little..." Space-Bo took off after the bird. Hummm that's funny, he thought, he forgot he couldn't float in midair on a planet like he could in space, dispite all the practice he'd just had on the rear bumper. He'd just have to remember that next time he jumped off a forty story building. This threw a proverbial three headed monkey wrench into his plan of getting to the roof. Darn it, he thought.

He saw an aircab floating lazily by, so he whistled to it. The driver waved back at him then scooped him up around the fifth floor. "Don't get smart with me, bub," the cabbie told him, "I know you're one of them born three times satanists so don't try to slip me none of that mumbo-jumbo disappearing money. I'm sick of it, hear me?"

"Satanist?"

"Oh come on, bub, that toga and your fancy flying trick will give you away every time."

"They will?"

"Sure, I normally don't pick up kooks like you but I need the extra cash," the cabbie sighed then clicked the meter on. "Okay, where to?"

"Uh, how about the top of that hardware building?" Space-Bo pointed out the window to the building he was, up until recently, falling from.

"Are you kidding? I can't take such short trips, it'll have to be at least twelve blocks. Or do I have to return you to your previous destination?"

"So, take me to the closest fly-through fast food joint six blocks away, and then drop me off at the top of the hardware building so it will be twelve blocks total." He gave himself an imaginary pat on the back for his mathematical genius. That was two today so far. Or was it three?

"Okay, bub, you're the back seat driver."

"Sorry," Space-Bo said climbing into the front next to the cabbie.

They zoomed down three levels and over six blocks to a fly-through Micky-D's. The cabbie ordered the triple big, an ultrasize with a tub of grease on the side, and a large orange thing. Space-Bo ordered a couple of double junior big singles, kiddie fries, and a large chocolate and banana malt.

"What the grub is that?" the voice on the other end of the order taking machine asked.

"My order." Space-Bo shouted over the cabbie.

"We don't serve your kind around here. So boost it."

Angered, the cabbie zoomed around to the sunroof only pickup window. He tried to take the sack from the squat, short man starring down at them through their sunroof.

"Nun-uh," he pulled the greasy bag back inside the pickup window and made an ugly face when he saw Space-Bo. "Dump the offworlder first. Then you get your order."

"How much is it," the cabbie asked.

"That'll be $200 space creds for you, but the offworlder has to go," the guy sneered.

Space-Bo was surprised at the generosity. "No, I'll let you keep it."

"What?" he said confused, "Offworlder's are so stupid. You pay me dork. I don't pay you."

"Who?"

"Me."

"What?"

"The food of course."

"Pay with food? Why?"

"For money."

"How much?"

"I told you already."

"Which one?"

The guy looked back and forth between the cabbie and Space-Bo confused.

"So you're going to pay us food for your money?"

"I didn't say that!" the rude drive through guy was steaming mad now and shaking the bag violently to boot. The botton of the greasy bag decided to fall apart, at that exact moment, showering the inside of the cab with McFood goodies.

"Too late," Space-Bo said stomping his left foot on to the cabbies right foot, thereby flooring the accelerator pedal. The cab roared off with the squat man choking on the fumes.

"Hey, they tricked me," he wined.

The cabbie was laughing so hard at what had happened that he didn't notice that some of Space-Bo's plastictac had wedged itself between his foot pedal and the floor. "Ha! Those stupid drive through guys are all alike. But that was some trick you pulled on that guy back there, huh?"

Space-Bo who was busily munching his junior burgers was wondering if the cab driver was careening towards the side of the hardware building on purpose.

At the same time below them, Doctor Vadlin Nosehonka was shopping for a book at the hardware store across the street from his office. He couldn't decide between two coffee table books. One was coffin shaped and had nice little indentations on the top for cold drinks. The other had pages made out of yellow and orange marble hand stitched with arrugalah granite.

A sales person walked up to the doctor. "Can I help you sir?" she asked.

"Vut du I vunt? I vunt a hammer und sum nails."

"We don't carry hammers and nails, sir. Did you try the bookstore down the street? I hear they have a large section devoted to historical building implements."

"Da boo-kstur down da street? Uh nu tank yu, I'vill jus taek dis boo-k," he showed the lady a paper bound book he fished randomly out of a pile of historical toilet paper recreations.

She rang it up on her fashion eyewear cash register. "$75.34 space creds please."

"Heer my leetle tee-headed chicadee." Without letting go, he flicked

97

his wallet at her and holographic bills of the proper denomination flew out and were quickly sucked up by her eyeglasses.

He crossed the street looking at the book. It was written for the deranged ornithologist. Sounded good, he needed to learn more about crazy birds. What if one landed on his window sill and needed some bird seed?

KRASHHHHHH! BOOOOOOM! Suddenly there was a huge explosion over head. The doctor looked up to see shrapnel and smoke erupting from the side of the hardware building. Good, business should pick up now.

*   *   *

Doctor Vadlin Nosehonka was sitting at his robot's secretary's desk reading his book on extinct mythological birds or was it mythologically extinct birds? He didn't remember and thought it really wouldn't matter anyway, since they were dead, right? Besides, he wasn't paying any attention anyway. His eyes were reading like it was some new medical report while his brain thought of how he could kill his robot's secretary, Ms. Swonoosawanger.

His eyes stopped at he bottom of a page, awaiting for the go ahead from his brain to move on to the next page but his fingers were distracted by Ms. Swonoosewanga's paisley pantyhose and her bony legs inside them. His eyes were eager to move on and if they had feet they would have been tapping them. The memory of her nobby toes flexing in the lamplight... Come on brain!

Knock, knock.

Drab. Nosehonka put the book down and said, "Cum in, vere opun."

The Funky Chicken walked into Nosehonka's office. It was wallpapered in a feminine light green gothic pokadot style with a maroon motif. The desk the doctor was at, sat in front of a huge bay window, from where you could see the hardware building across the street with a red neon sign flashing some religious slogan, but you couldn't read it anymore because of the black scorch mark of a crashed aircar.

There was some commotion on the street several stories below but he paid it no attention. The doctor looked up at the Funky Chicken in disbelief. What was a one headed man sized biped manually articulated chicken doing in his office?

"I need your help," the chicken pleaded, "I got no one else to turn to."

Nosehonka grabbed up his book quickly saying, "Uh, veyt hee-er, leetle birdie," and dashed into the utility closet.

The chicken shrugged his shoulders and sat down on a chair that resembled a large hand begging for money. He noticed an odd portrait of an angry looking robot scowling at him from its place on the wall.

The doctor was looking through his book for a description of the thing that was in his office. This is what he found:

The Cherie Grimm Birdy of Octoslagge Septic Mine

Large flightless three headed bird with articulated wing extenders. Eats only a rare type of Yogartian cabbage. Normally blue in color with pink

98

*plumes. One rare species is white with red flabby skin attached to its head.
WARNING: Very friendly, will try to gain offworld transportation at all cost,
especially by telling lies.*

*NOTE: Since their discovery 5,000 years ago 99% of the Grimm Birdy
population has perished in freak ground and aircar accidents.*

*Only twelve are left on Rall Raul Beta at the time of this writing. Too
bad there aren't any white with red flabby head skin ones left since they would
certainly be worth a king's ransom to the King.*

Nosehonka jumped up and down. The rarest bird alive was in his office
right then. He could make a fortune. Jump, Jump. Wham! Stupid pipes.

He come out of the utility closet rubbing his head. "Ya, meester birdie,
nut cin I du fur yu?"

"It's terrible doc," the chicken pleaded as it jumped out of the chair that
looked like a begging hand and grabbed the lapels of the doctor's white coat.
"You gotta help me."

"Seet stell, I cin heeulp yu. Vud yu like sum cibbige?"

"No, no, that's not it. I got this new neutralized meat processor; and
when I tried to use it, it wouldn't work right, so I tried to fix it. Then it went
crazy sending laser beams all over the place, then it blew up. And now I look
like this."

"Ah, so yu du nut luke like dis, normly?"

"No way! I'm really human, you gotta believe me. You're the only one
who can save me. Help me please."

"Vokay, boot seet steel." Nosehonka rubbed his hands together. He
could taste the space creds in his mouth. No wonder this bird was an idiot, it
had blown off two of its heads.

"Maybe this machine will work better." The chicken climbed into a
chamber set into a wall.

"Nu!" Nosehonka saw the chicken sitting inside the electromagnetic
laser defroster he used to heat up coffee in the morning. "Nut dat!"

The chicken pushed the start button and closed the door.

The doctor was at his knees sobbing, "Nut my leetle birdie." He looked
up to see the machine choke out a few puffs of ozone smelling smoke, said, "Oh
voe ist me!" and broke down in tears.

Beep Beep! Beep Beep!

"Shoot up," he said to the phone, "My leetle birdie jus vent oop in
flems."

Beep Beep! Beep Beep!

"Very vell," he grumbled pushing the phone's green button, "Heelo?"

"You better get in here, Nosehonka, there's a Mrs. Weedapula here for
the personalized personality transplant she said you would do..."

"Yes, yes,"

"...for her. But you know how much your personalized sessions disturb
me. I just can't have my nails done right because of how your robot gets..."

"Yes, yes,"

"...your pay again for a third time this week because you never do
anything right, you always take too long to do the..."

"Yes, I'vill be vrite over."

"...simplest things and when you do do them on time you over charge them too much so I have to take out the difference for myself..."

"I geet it, Ms. Swonoosawanger."

"...just to keep you honest in a time when honest doctors are a thing of the past..."

Nosehonka barged down a hallway into the more luxurious room that was his Robot's personal office and where Ms. Swonoosawanger and Mrs. Weedapula were waiting.

His secretary must have thought he was still on the other line for she was talking into her phone at a rapid rate as his robot filed her nails. "...and for less than you charge, so you better be happy that we're keeping you in this business because, buster, without us you wouldn't be in this place..."

Yes, he thought, I would be in a nice penthouse sipping wine beside a nice fireplace. "Vhy eeven buther," he mumbled to himself.

Mrs. Weedapula had her kangaroo with her and it was sitting near the window watching them intently. She looked up as Nosehonka entered. "Glad to see you again."

"Jus poot yur hed in dis tink hee-er." He wheeled a black machine that resembled a coat rack more than a head examiner, over to her. He stuck her head in and flipped a switch at its side.

The robot ignored the black machine and continued filing his secretary's nails.

The kangaroo heard a tapping sound behind it. It looked out the window with one of its heads and there hanging on the ledge was the Funky Chicken making faces at it. It tried to bark but nothing came out of that head as it was the one used for belching.

"Ah yes," the doctor was saying, "Yu hev vut vee cawl ah tipe tree pearsoonalatee."

He turned and saw the kangaroo barking silently out the window. "Uh, I deet-unt noyu had dat doog's voieece takeen oot."

Mrs. Weedapula looked over at her pet. "Bless my heart. Look doctor," she pointed out the window, "It's that wonderful animal I saw earlier today, it must have followed me here, how sweet."

Nosehonka moved around the black machine to get a better look out the window. His robot stuck out a foot and tripped him. "Vudding vuck poo!"

The robot simulated a smile inside his cpu.

The doctor picked himself up in time to see the chicken making faces at him from out on the ledge. "Oh my leetle birdie," he cried and made for the window, "I deet-unt no how yu leeved, boot yu deed," but he didn't make it before the kangaroo bit him, thinking it was being attacked.

"Yeeeeow!" he fell back onto a cart full of weird doctor tools, clutching his leg. The cart crashed to the floor with his considerable weight upon it.

The lady was hugging her kangaroo. "Ooh my poor baby, did that mean old man try to hurt you? Mommy's not going to let anyone hurt my boobsie." She rushed out of the room.

The Funky Chicken just watched with a smile as the doctor chased the lady out, trying to make her change her mind. He only could hope that Space-

Bo was doing as well.

Space-Bo found himself stuck against the side of the hardware building. He could move his arms and legs but they wouldn't go anywhere. He looked around and discovered he was still about twenty stories up, flat on his back against the Lego style bricks.

"If there's one thing I hate more than being suspended sixty meters up in the air is not being able to move." He struggled to free himself and managed to pull away from the wall. That's better, he smiled. AAAAAh!

Swoosh! He landed on the soft brown material of a trampoline and then suddenly he was flying straight up into the air.

A big green and black form loomed up before him.

WHAM! That hurt. The thing had slammed into his head. Well, he'd fix that. A solid punch would do it, just as soon as he could get his arm untangled from that stupid surgical tubing. Zoom! He was being yanked through the air. And here came that flag pole again so he grabbed it. Whatever that green and black thing was, that was trying to drag him across the sky sure was persistent, because it kept pulling on the other end of the tubing his arm was entangled in. He felt his grip straining and hoped the thing would give up soon.

Creeeek. Snap! Swoosh! He was flying through the air again. But how could that be? He still had a grip on the flagpole. He looked at he flagpole in disbelief. It wasn't attached to the side of the building anymore. Oh well, he guessed it must be wimpy flagpole to give in so easily.

He twisted his head around to get a good look at that green and black thing that was causing all these problems. It turned out to be a late model aircar about seven meters ahead to which the surgical tubbing was attached at the bumper. The driver was shaking his fist out the window at Space-Bo.

The car whipped around a corner of the building in an obvious attempt to scrape him off. Space-Bo's legs caught the edge of the building and he was stopped briefly. The sound of the aircar's straining engine could be heard around the corner.

Now to get rid of this stupid tubing He untangled himself from it and finding the easiest place to put it, tried it onto the flagpole. He brushed his hands and promptly slid down to a ledge centimeters below.

Hmmm, where'd that flagpole get to? He glanced around but didn't see the flagpole anywhere.

BOOOOOOM! There was an explosion and then the distinctive eeeeeuuuuUUUU sound of an air vehicle going down. Space-Bo saw a black and green smoking streak head for the pavement below. It hit and burst into flames.

What an idiot. The driver should have paid attention to what he was doing. Those aircars were proving to be very dangerous today.

The Funky Chicken was riding the elevator up to the top of the doctor's building just across the street. It was easy to sneak into the authorized personel only elevator because the doctor was off chasing the lady, with the three headed kangaroo, all around the building while his robot's secretary kept chewing him out on the telephone.

He scratched, 'F.C. was here' into the elevator door with his powerful hand claws. He liked to keep a record of all the places he'd been.

He stepped out onto the roof to behold Nosehonka's modified, rocket powered, beat-up, aircar. The thing was so dusty inside that the chicken wasn't sure if he could get it started. But the ancient turbo-pumped engines eventually started up. He put it into first gear and stepped on the pedal. With a lurch the aircar bounded off the roof.

On the roof across the street he managed to set it down with minimal damage to the underbody. He looked out the window. No Space-Bo. He honked the horn. Still no Space-Bo. He waited a few more minutes then decided to check the entrance to the building. Maybe Space-Bo had gone the wrong way or got distracted by the trampolines.

He landed with jolt next to a very business looking man who was wandering around the trampoline exhibition that was set up in the courtyard outside the hardware building entrance. "Excuse me, sir," he blurted.

The man looked at the chicken carefully, took off his glasses, cleaned them off, and put them back on to get a better look. "We already supply every circus on Rall Raul Beta," he said assumingly.

"No, I'm looking for a big buffed up individual that might have dropped in here not too long ago."

The man ran his hand across his forehead to remove the sweat that instantly appeared when he thought about what had happened. "To put it literally, yes."

"Are you sure it was him?"

"Do I look like I would lie to you? What kind of a clown do you take me for?"

"I'm not interested in swapping you for a clown."

"Too bad. I need a clown to keep these people here, buying trampolines. That guy who just dropped in here sent most of my customers fleeing in panic."

"That sounds about right. Here's my card if you ever need my services. He handed the man one of his business cards he always had on him. Rogicphil didn't know about the secret pocket he had in his lower leg for just such occasions. The card read:

the
Fünky
Chicken

* Over the Counter-Terrorism
* Toxic Waste Clean-Up
* Anything Having to do
   with High Explosives

(011-800-I'll-Do-It)

Professional Scapegoating Upon Request

The man looked the card over and put it in his pocket. "Can you blow up my wife for me?

"Sure thing. Where is she?"

"The address is 137 Fine Forked Road. She should be on the holophone right now. How much will it cost?"

"What about one of those trampolines?"

"Fine. You'll be discreet won't you?"

"Of course," the chicken said climbing back into Nosehonka's heap. "I'll be back tomorrow to pick up the trampoline."

"See you then," the man shouted as the aircar sputtered away.

Meanwhile Space-Bo had met a nice three headed bird that had assured him it wasn't as stupid as some of its two bird brained cousins. But he couldn't be sure because he hadn't studied the bird's three part hormonized monosyllabic language that well, so he asked to be sure.

"Squak, squawk. Squak! Squawk?" he asked.

The bird looked astonished at what it heard him say. "Squawk!" it replied with two heads and flew off but not before giving Space-Bo his second garnishing of the day.

Space-Bo peeled off one of his shoe inserts that had been sticking of his toga. How it got there he wasn't sure, but he chucked it after the bird just the same. The insert hit it squarely on the center head knocking it out. The bird fell down to a trampoline, rebounding into a nearby yellow tree and got caught in the orange leaves.

He walked along the ledge a while still thinking for a way to get to the roof when he noticed some plastitac stuck to the building with an impression in it. He looked around to make sure no one was looking before he swiped it. It was only fair, he thought, since he'd lost his plastitac during the crash so whoever had lost this plastitac would have to find some in the wreckage. Circular debts were always one of his favorite hobbies.

He walked past a big capital letter D made out of space steel on the side of the hardware building. It was a really nice letter D, Space-Bo, thought, probably because D was currently his favorite letter. Big D, little D, Micky D, they were all great. There was a relatively small hole about five meters up the side of the building where the aircab had crashed.

Taking it upon himself to clean the letter off he found a service hatch the led into the letter itself. Inside he saw all the tiny LED lights covering the back of the front surface that lit the structure up at night. There was a ladder leading up towards the hole and he climbed it with ease.

He climbed until he reached a mangled section where he couldn't go any further. Normally he would have kicked at the rubble until there was an opening big enough for him to crawl through, but this time he just pushed it aside. He found himself in a chamber of sorts facing out into the open air created by the aircab that was now lying in a heap at his feet. "Hello me," he said to himself.

The driver was knocked out with a hamburger still hanging out of his mouth. Space-Bo pushed his way over to the window and tapped him on his shoulder. "Hey buddy!" he yelled, "You can't park this thing here."

The driver came to. Quickly finishing the burger he mumbled, "What?"

"I said I'm going to give you a parking ticket for parking in a no parking zone."

Space-Bo was only joking but the cabbie blurry eyed and dim witted from the crash thought he was serious. "I'm sorry officer. I'll just back up." He tried to make the cab go but nothing happened. The cabbie stepped out of the cab and kicked it. "Stupid piece of junk!"

The cab swayed a bit, then flipped up on its back and slid off the letter. They watched it fall down the side of the building and then crash onto the courtyard. "Later alligator," Space-Bo yelled down.

Honk! Honk!

There hovering a few meters away in the air was the Funky Chicken waving at him. He was in a brand new beat-up aircar.

"I thought we were suppose to jump to the other building to get the aircar?" Space-Bo yelled over the noisy rocket engines.

"Plans have changed. We've got other business to take care of right now. Hop aboard and I'll explain."

"Hey," the cabbie said poking Space-Bo in the ribs, "You're no cop."

Space-Bo turned and said, "Yeah I know. At least you can't complain about police brutality."

The cabbie scratched his head. "You got a point there."

"Well it's been fun," Space-Bo said shaking the cabbie's hand, "See you later." He took a step back, then leaped the gap and landed smoothly on the car. He quickly scrambled into the passenger seat via a rusted out hole on top that Nosehonka liked to think of as a sun roof.

"So, this is what you've been doing?" The Funky Chicken floored the gas pedal but the car only managed to sputter away a little faster.

"Yeah, it's been pretty boring."

"Well not for long. We have to go blow up some lady at 137 Fine Forked Road."

"What for?"

"A trampoline. Or was it a clown, I forget."

"Did she kill somebody?"

"No."

"So why do we have to blow her up?"

"Her husband wants her dead. Probably thinks that she's been cheating on him. It doesn't matter."

"Well, it matters to me."

"In what way?"

"Was it at cards, dice, or backgammon, or what?"

"Huh?"

"Never mind," Space-Bo sighed and looked out the window. The street setup in this part of the Urban Development seemed strange. Nothing he could bring his full brain capacity to bear on but something definitely different.

"Okay we're here." The aircar landed outside of a condo that looked like every other condo for kilometers around. "Be quite and follow my lead."

They got out of the car and went up to a door on ground level with 137 stamped on it. The chicken knocked a few times.

A red haired woman opened the door. She was in a red robe and

104

slippers. A green mud pack covered her face and she had a red phone antenna protruding from the top of her head. Here pupils were blinking on and off indicating she was having a phone call. "Hold on, someone's here," she said in a low voice.

Space-Bo tried to peek into the house but the chicken pulled him back.

"What do you want?" she rudely asked them.

The chicken jabbed Space-Bo in the ribs. Unluckily for them both this finally caused the idea that had been bugging Space-Bo all day long to find its way into the bullet ridden speech center of his brain.

"I'm from the police department. There may be drugs hidden in your house by a secret narco-syndicate. My trained drug sniffing chicken will find them for us."

The lady looked at them slack jawed. Her eyes rolled up into her head and she toppled over backwards.

The chicken grabbed the body and drug it into the house. "Good work, shut the door behind us before we're seen."

Space-Bo shrugged and did as he was told. He turned around and went slack jawed himself. Stacked everywhere there was an empty space, there were drugs upon drugs upon drugs. And drug paraphernalia were stacked upon that. Some were narcotic baby food, others were mearly put-me-downs but they all had the logo of the H.E.L.L. corporation stamped on them. There were narrow aisleways through the stuff to the different parts of the home. "Good guess, huh?"

The chicken had plucked the phone antenna from the woman's head and jammed it into his ear flap. "Hmm, I don't know," he turned towards Space-Bo. "Do you know what the secret code word is?"

"Alla nepud sander butwiches?"

The chicken smiled and repeated the phrase into the phone. "I guess that wasn't it, they hung up." He glanced around at all the drugs. "Look at all this stuff. I bet it's worth billions of space creds."

"What's this?" Space-Bo asked poking a bag of greenish powder.

"That's Turbo dust. Makes you speed up. Heavy users die of old age after only two bags of it."

"What do we do now?"

"We blow up the...Hey! Where'd the lady go?"

They looked around. The lady was gone and so was her makeup bag.

The chicken dropped his beak. "Ut-oh. We better get out of here and quick. I think we've been set up."

They peeked out the door. Twenty police hovercruisers were waiting for them. Laser rifles were trained on the condo's front door. They quietly shut the door.

"COME OUT WITH YOUR HANDS UP. THIS IS THE POLICE!" an amplified voice yelled from outside the condo.

Space-Bo whispered to the chicken, "I think you're right. I'm going to punch that Rogicphil a good one for getting us into this mess."

"I'll help." The chicken pulled the aluminum frisbee out of his pocket, saying, "Okay give me what you have left of that junk you were issued."

Space-Bo gave him a single shoe insert, some used plastitac and the towel off his back.

"Where's the tubbing?"

"Some guy with a flagpole took it."

"WE KNOW YOU'RE IN THERE. COME OUT RIGHT NOW OR ELSE."

"Hmm, this will have to do then," The chicken used the shoe insert to pound the plastitac into a thin layer on the underside of the frisbee. He then opened the bag of Turbo dust and poured it lightly onto the semi tacky substance. "Careful, don't breath any," he said breathing heavily, "Okay, now when I say go, you run for the nearest hovercruiser and take the driver out. I'll be right behind you."

"Okay but what about my towel? You haven't done anything with it yet and I feel kind of naked."

"Rap it around your head like a turban, that way if you get caught you can claim to be from a radical ultra nudist sect and they'll let you off for insanity."

"I hadn't thought of that," he said right before implementing the plan.

"OPEN UP IN THERE! THIS IS YOUR LAST CHANCE!" the voice yelled.

The Funky Chicken slowly opened the door. "I'm just a poor bedowin with my pet giant one headed bird," he yelled out the door, "I'm coming out, so don't shoot." Turning to Space-Bo he said, "Ready? Now just step out calmly and wait for me to yell." He flung the door the rest of the way open.

Space-Bo stepped out of the door. All the laser rifles suddenly were aiming at him. He sensed their fingers tensing, they were going to shoot!

"GO!" the chicken yelled.

Just as the lasers opened up Space-Bo dashed for the closest police hovercruiser. He saw the frisbee fly past his head spewing green Turbo dust behind it. He held his breath as he leapt and dodged laser blasts.

Smash! He dived head first right through the passenger side window of the hovercruiser, ramming the driver out his open door. He didn't bother to shut the door behind him but just stepped on the gas. The lasers were close behind.

The chicken's hand claws gripped the passenger door, the broken glass acting as a good grip while he was dragged along side, taking laser fire. "We made it! Isn't this more fun?"

"More fun than what?"

"Than sucking pearls out of oysters with your nose."

"You want me to make another pass?" Space-Bo made a hard right turn that caused the driver's side door to close but flung the chicken off at the same time.

"Weeee..." the chicken said slamming into a yellow tree.

Space-Bo turned straight around and faced the other police hovercruisers. Their lasers stopped firing because the thick green cloud of Turbo dust was doing its job now. The police had all dropped their laser rifles and were jumping and spinning around as fast as they could.

Space-Bo watched as the chicken, back broken, and full of laser holes, stumbled into the cloud and began to spin out of control.

"Oh wow," the chicken was saying as he danced with abandonment.

"Hurry up, FC, we gotta get out of here."

"Oh alright." He limped over to the hovercruiser and hopped in.

They were tearing away from the condo even as the chicken's body was reforming itself. He looked in the rear view mirror. "Step on it," he said, "A police hovertank is hot on our tail."

Space-Bo looked behind him. The tank had a nasty looking laser barrel pointed at them. "Hold on." He weaved the hovercruiser around the light traffic avoiding the huge bursts of laser energy that were taking out civilian vehicles left and right. Up ahead loomed the hardware building.

"Make for the hardware store. Then use the booster rockets to pull away at the last minute," the chicken suggested.

"Okay," Space-Bo said flooring the hovercruiser. It hit the curb in front of the building. He hit the boosters and the hovercruiser flew up into the air and sailed over the tops to the yellow trees.

SpreeeeeeeBOOOING! They landed on a trampoline and were flung high into the air. The tank's laser blasts followed. The hovercar crashed into the letter D on the side.

Space-Bo and the chicken dived out just before a big blast ripped the hovercruiser to pieces. Falling, they watched the hovertank ram itself into the side of the building and explode into a huge ball of flames.

"I guess your plan worked," Space-Bo yelled.

Before the Funky Chicken could answer they hit the trampoline and rebounded up into the air. This time they sailed across the street and crashed through a window on the other building.

"My leetle birdie ist back," Doctor Nosehonka cheered, his hand deep inside the machine's head, adjusting something. He had been arguing with his robot, and had decided to win the argument the old fashioned way.

Space-Bo looked out the broken window towards the hardware building. The nice letter D was ruined by the laser blast. The whole lower right side was totally disintegrated.

The chicken tapped him on the shoulder. "Come on Space-Bo. Nosehonka's got another aircar we can use. And, I'll have you know, I traded my trampoline coupon for it. We have to go before more police get here."

"My letter D is ruined. It looks like a little r now."

The robot was agast, "Sir, please cover yourself."

"Huh?" Space-Bo looked down at his naked body. "Hey where'd my towel go?"

"It's on your head."

"Right. I knew that." He began to undo the towel wrapped around his head like a turban when a small black box fell out. The meter from the wrecked airtaxi. It was still running. "Hey cool, a souvenir."

"Forget it. We're out of here."

"Ya, und fourgeet dat leeter tu. Veev got tu go." Nosehonka was excited to drive them back to their camp. He wasn't so excited when they knocked him out and sent the aircar back to the city on autopilot. The hardware store finally got a breather after a long day spent with Space-Bo and the Funky Chicken.

Chapter 8: Desert Commandos

Wilbur and Jake transmatted over to the Rall Raul Beta complex shortly before dawn, standard time. Wilbur took his clipboard from Jake with a yank.

"Come on we're late," he said stepping off the Star Trek looking platform.

Jake followed him, slump shouldered.

Wilbur went up to the transmat tech near the exit ramp, who was busy pushing buttons into a console. Flashing some ID cards in the tech's face he said, "Agents Wilbur and Jake reporting as ordered."

The tech ignored them at first, as he was busy with his video game, but finally spoke into a red handled microphone, listened, then said, "Chamber six you're expected."

"What do you mean, chamber six? All the doors around here are numbered six, sixty-six, or six hundred and sixty six. Just give us the directions will ya?"

The tech looked annoyed but didn't take his eyes off the console. "Well then..." he pointed over his shoulder, "Yougodowntolevelsixturnrightatthepostwalkthreestepsturn leftrununtilyouthrowupthenit'sthefourteenthdoorontheright. Gotit? Good." And continued punching buttons into his control panel.

Jake sniffed, "What's that smell?" then pinched his nose and his face twisted up like it'd eaten twenty four lemons. "Looooser!"

"Come on. There's more important things than making fun of idiots."

Wilbur led the way out the door.

They stood at the top of a ramp in a huge subterranean cavern. Twisted stalactites hung from the ceiling that glowed bright enough to light up the whole place. There was one continuous walkway which spiraled down the sides of the cavern, starting at the top, near where they were, and went down all the way to the bottom. Ramps emerged from different spots along the walls that spiraled around and then back into the walls at different levels. The bottom of the whole thing was a good kilometer or so below. Various red suited individuals walked along the various ramps and spiral walkways, going back and forth and generally doing things.

After trying to follow the tech's directions for about an hour they gave up, lost in the tangle of elevated ramps and confusing door labels.

"This complex is too big," Wilbur gasped between breaths, "...for me to be running around, (pant, pant) with all this weight, (pant, pant), trying to throw up."

"Exercise is what you need." Jake's wandering eye wandered around looking for a sign to the gym.

"Let's get something to drink," Wilbur found a ramp leading into the food court. He stepped into the first stall on the left, as they entered the food court, and low and behold, it was the very room they were going to in the first place. He gave Jake his best evil eye he could, even thought he knew it wouldn't work on an already evil person.

"Don't look at me, I didn't know it was here."

"Shut up!"

The secretary sitting behind the desk looked really mad. "You guys are late," she snapped at them, "Get in there before I lose my job."

The two hurried into the next room. It was a sultry red colored room with a big red crescent of a desk, sitting in front of a glass window, behind which, sharks could be seen swimming around. At the desk, a man in a red business suit was going over some paper work concerning transmat pad regulations as he munched on some space chinese food out of a styrofoam box. Two little artificial horns on his forehead glistened as he looked up. A plaque on his desk read, "Junior Grade Bossman, 'Belzebub Class'."

"You're late," he barked fishing around on his desk for a napkin. Finding one he liked, he wiped his mouth then shoved it at Wilbur.

"What's this?" Wilbur slowly took the napkin.

"Not that one. The form sitting on the corner," he motioned with his head while he licked his fingers.

"What corner? Your desk is simi-circular."

"You know what I mean. The acquisition form. You'll need it when you go down to warehouse B/23."

"And why would we want to do that? Sounds like work."

Jake chuckled a bit but Wilbur kicked him in the shin to shut up.

The important looking fellow behind the desk continued, "To get some relay this or spy equipment that. Something about a satellite chain-up. I don't know. It's just some stuff on this report I have to fill out. I was told you guys were the best at taking orders."

"Who are we to spy on, boss?"

"How should I know. It doesn't say in the paperwork."

"Do you mind?" Wilbur asked, reaching for the paperwork.

"Be my guest."

Wilbur read, "Enemies of the H.E.L.L. corporation have set up a training base on Raul Rall Beta. They are hiding out in an unregistered passenger starcruiser of unknown yet ancient origin.... Blah blah blah ... forest coordinates blah blah blah B7-42-93-A7-25-86."

"Yeah that's what I thought. Blah blah blah," the junior bossman behind the desk was licking the inside of the now empty stryofoam box.

"Standard operating procedures?"

"Agent 666 has already completed the preliminary gullibility test. You just follow them, understand?"

"Understood."

"Dililah will help you with all the blah blah blah details etc. Now hurry up before I come up with an excuse to singe someone."

"Yes sir." The two hurried out of the junior bossman's office.

*   *   *

Rall Raul Beta, or Raul Rall Beta depending on which side of the Perip continent legal battle you take, was the second class H (some say for habitable, or maybe Huxley, the deranged astrophysicist who watched too many Star Trek reruns) planet that Nell Parsley discovered. The first class H planet he discovered, Nell's-GalacticBeach-Alpha was destroyed when it fell into its sun. It is believed the Organization for the Preservation of Good Times was responsible but no proof was ever found. Nell named this second planet after his two pet giant bolt weevils, Rall and Raul, which at the time only had one head each. He also named five of the nine ocean/seas; two after his pets again, and two after his pets but with the letters rearranged a bit and one after himself. But the story of how a large sea became know as Nell's Pond remains to be made up.

The Capital of Raul Rall Beta, Nellcit, was abandoned to janitors after it was built because Nell felt people actually living in his city would ruin it. He continued to live in the capital as the Supreme King of the planet until he died or his palace disintegrated from too much cleaning (no one is sure or really cares) but as Nell often said, "Ce la me", a phrase which to this day still defies logic.

Rogicphil was pondering the previous text as a possible expose he could write after this was all over when Space-Bo and the Funky Chicken reported in. He was pleased with how they had survived in that remote section of Urban Development Br-42. He thanked Dr. Nosehonka, in a personal letter which he stamped onto the unconscious doctor's forehead, for helping out but told him in no uncertain terms to get lost. When, a few hours later the deranged doctor returned in a desperate attempt (disguised as a fake balding monk, longing to follow and worship Rogicphil) to hijack the chicken, Rogicphil pinched a nerve, knocking the doctor out, shoved him back into his aircar, and sent him on his way again but with a partial mind wipe this time.

"Hey, what did you do that for?"

"Listen 'Bo, this is suppose to be a secret training exercise remember? And we can't allow everyone and their pet bolt weevils to know what we're really doing."

"I figured that much. So we told him we were practicing for a big bowling tournament on Deo-7 next week."

"You shouldn't have told him that." Rogicphil grunted, "Everyone knows it's only the planet Danville that likes bowling tournaments. Besides I told him we were running a Slave The Squids telethon."

"Ah-hah! Bowling for Jherie's Squids!"

Rogicphil just shook his head and walked to a different part of the ship. Now he had to start thinking about the rest of his team. The chorus line girls were combat trained and ready for anything. Spyman and Plutoman, he wasn't sure what would do those two any good. Hey, what about a Whale-Squid game? Space-Bo's random ideas always came in handy if one knew how to implement them. Now Ranger Joe and the bear would be training with Rogicphil personally. So that only left the Clergy, the most unorganized, uncooperative, and unethical group of beings he had met in a long time, to be readied for the mission. He needed something that would bring them together. Something that would force them to work as a team. So the Whale-Squid thing was right out. Something...Aha! He had it. The Okrachobadee!

The Okrachobadee, pronounced Wally-Wally-Mean-Place because of the silent K and the four invisible q's, was the oldest and most unchanged place in the entire planet. (So remote, in fact, that it only had one Micky D's and it was a mini.) Its red sand dunes remained unchanged throughout the centuries. Huge megaliths of blood red stone piercing the desolate terrain. No wind or breeze to relieve the pounding heat of the sun that baked down on the surface ninety percent of the day. The only water to be found was in over priced vending machines or mirages, and even if you were quick enough to grab some of the latter before it disappeared, it would be salty and laden with a slight hint of ammonia. Nothing grew there. Total desolation, five kilometers wide and fifty long.

But of course the Clergy didn't know, that only a short distance to the right or left would yield lush rainforests populated by skimpy clad nubians and twenty four hour party safaris. Rogicphil wanted them to think they were in a big wilderness, not some tiny strip of sand. He had told them to march through the desert and retrieve a 90125 relay unit, buried in a collapsed bunker 25 kilometers due south, that coincidentally, didn't really exist. Futhermore they were to be stopped by nothing, stop for no one, and not to return empty handed. They were each issued a desert commando suit, one day of rations, a canteen, and the latest model Z browning assault Nerf pellet rifle (He didn't want them to seriously wound any tourists that frequented the place on a pilgrimage to the lone Micky D's).

Many hours and some good adventuring later the Clergy was deep in a hole underneath the desert. Joe sang:

Ten thousand worms in my backyard,
Ten thousand worms in my backyard,
They're the planet's future in my regard,

I keep them healthy and well fed,
I keep them healthy and well fed,
Fat and healthy off the souls of the dead.

Cut a worm in half and it becomes two,
Cut a worm in half and it becomes two,
Cut a man in half and what does he do?

Their food supply is getting low,
Their food supply is getting low,
With my axe in hand, down the road I go.

The worms are our friends,
The worms are our friends,
They'll get us all in the end.

They just sat there in stunned silence. Then Bufgoo said, "Forget that rap crap, lets record this. It's better than anything we've done in a long time."

"Seriously maen. Thees ees hot."

"You think so? I couldn't remember all the lyrics so I just made up a bunch of it off the top of my head."

A strange gravelly voice came to them out of the gloom that was the edge of the cave, "Bravo, bravo!" A old man, wearing a faded robe with lots of holes in it, stepped into the light, clapping his withered hands together.

No one said a word but watched him walk up to Joe and pat him on the back, "Keep making them up off the top of your head and it will kick the spaduka out their ears."

"What the hell is spaduka?" Joe asked.

"Kinda like jeuperts," the old man said, "But waxy and more tasty."

"Eeuk!"

"Welcome to the Royal Palace my friends. I am the King and you are my guests. Feel free to partake in our smorgeborg of Micky D's delight, to your heart's content and enjoy the complimentary sofas to crash on." He led them through a double set of doors they hadn't noticed before and into what smelled like a moldy run down hotel lobby.

A breakfast buffet lined one wall and several dusty sofas were scattered about the main room. After stuffing their bellys on day old Micky D's they slept disturbed by dreams of record deals and flashy teethed business men and slimy worms that begged to be eaten.

Bufgoo woke up at the crack of noon. He was amazed the dusty lobby was still there an not just part of his twisted dream. Soon Manuel got up and together they marveled at the fact they were still alive.

"Incredible ain't it? This stuff never holds my hair up for more than a day at a time." And as if to tempt fate, Bufgoo pulled out a tube of his hair grease and began the daily ritual of matting down his hair.

"Ay jus reemeymbered, we gotta geet thet relay geezmo."

"I'll wake up the others."

Soon they had stuffed their mouths again and were taking a rickety old elevator up to the surface. Just then, Joe paniced. Where was his safety deposit box, he'd dug up the night before? He padded all his pockets, as if the box could have fit in one of them. He eyed the others with suspicion, but couldn't prove anything. Just wait, he'd get to the bottom of this when they least expected it.

They were trekking across the sand dunes again by 2 pm. After a kilometer of walking they found a sign said:

Relay post #66 that way -->

"Dey mustuv chaynged thu noombers."

"Whatever, just as long as we get it and hurry back."

Over the next dune they found a strange gizmo lying in the sand with antennas sticking up in the air. They tried to drag it away but it had a cable stuck to it that was buried in the sand. So they chopped at the cable and had Hack haul it on his back. No one noticed the label on the bottom that read: property of the H.E.L.L. corporation, no reward if found, but we might let you live if you give it back nice and easy.

Rogicphil awoke the next morning to see a relay unit sitting outside the spaceship. That was funny, he thought, there wasn't any relay unit out in the desert, it was just a rouse to get the Clergy to work together as a team. Oh well, must be some junk they found out in the sand. Besides, he had more important things to do than to try and guess where some piece of junk hardware come from.

Chapter 9: A Date With Destiny

"WAKE UP!"

"Huh?"

"I SAID IT'S TIME TO WAKE UP!"

"Okay," Rogicphil groaned and rolled over.

"I'M WARNING YOU!"

He grabbed his pillow and smothered his face with it. "Ahmm sill aseep...Humuhak hoharmo."

"THIS IS YOUR LAST CHANCE."

"Zzzzzzzzzz....."

"OKAY."

That was funny his comfy pillow didn't feel so comfy anymore. In fact it hurt; it bit him. He jumped out of bed to see his pillow rolling around and making honking noises on his bed. The pillow case ripped open. A beak poked out.

"HooooNK!" it cried.

There was a goose inside his pillow. After blinking his eyes several times he said, "I hope I'm not that hungover."

"HOW MUCH CACTUS JUICE DID YOU DRINK LAST NIGHT?"

"I don't remember."

"GET DRESSED, I NEED TO TALK WITH YOU."

Rogicphil felt pretty stupid as he pulled his clothes on. He could only assume he'd been wasted on that cactus juice stuff Destiny had gotten him hooked on.

.32 milliseconds later he was dressed, bright eyed, and still hungover. He stumbled so fast the goose didn't have anything to honk at.

He knocked at his door leading to the corridor.

"QUIT STALLING AND GET IN HERE!"

He entered Destiny's office boldly. "Yeah, what's up?"

"SIT DOWN," A chair materialized under Rogicphil, so he sat. "REMEMBER WHAT I TOLD YOU YESTERDAY?"

"You mean about..."

"THE TRAINING. ROGICPHIL, YOU ARE A GOOD AGENT OF MINE, AT LEAST I THINK SO, BUT A POOR TEACHER. THESE EXCURSIONS YOU SEND YOUR PUPILS OUT ON ARE A WASTE OF TIME."

"I'll do better, I'm just getting warmed up."

"WELL TOO BAD. YOU SEE THE ENEMY IS ON TO US."

"So, we're on to them."

"NO, IT'S NOT LIKE THAT. THIS PUTS US INTO A DEFENSIVE POSITION. WE MUST MAINTAIN THE INITITIVE."

"How?"

"BY HITTING WITH WHAT LITTLE SURPRISE WE HAVE LEFT. YOU'RE LEAVING A LITTLE AHEAD OF SCHEDULE."

113

"What, a week or two?"

"TOMORROW."

"Ah, yes....Tomorrow. By the way, is it today yet?"

"To bad they're not here to enjoy this," Rogicphil and Destiny were seated at the Chateau Le Scrofa restaurant, courtesy of Rogicphil's 3104th Bank of Roganivar III Diner's Club credit card. The Chateau was originally the farm of a wealthy pig farmer, Stuin Stramm, who unexpectedly died in a used refrigerator accident and his prize winning pigs inherited the Chateau. With the help of a good lawyer they turned the farm into an upper class restaurant.

"WELL, GREYSON HAS WON, PLUTOMAN HASN'T RETURNED WITH HIM YET."

"But since he hasn't arrived to claim his prize, we'll eat it instead." Rogicphil's mouth started to water.

A snooty waiter came up to their table. "May I take your order, sir?"

Rogicphil thought of something witty to say but withheld it. Instead he said, "Fifteen simulated barbarqued pigs feet and half a liter of your spiciest fermented pig sauce No# 3."

The waiter ignored him and was looking at Desinty instead.

"THE USUAL."

"And to drink?"

"A mountain spring, water with a twist of braintree."

The waiter went back into the kitchen.

"Hey, did he get my order or what?"

"THEY HAVE A HIGHLY DEVELOPED SENCE OF RUDENESS AROUND HERE. I SUGGEST YOU MIND YOUR MANNERS."

"I held my tongue. I *was* going to say..."

"DON'T WORRY, GLADERUNNER. YOU WILL GET YOUR DESSERT."

"So what'd you order? What's the usual?"

"A LARGE PLATTER OF DEEP FRIED GIANT EGGPLANT SAUTEED IN A CREAMY PIZZA SPIDER SOUP."

"What's a pizza spider?"

"YOU LIKE PIZZA?"

"Sure."

"THEN YOU DON'T WANT TO KNOW."

The waiter came back with two shimmering glasses. The liquid inside reminded Rogicphil of cold fusion. He went to take a sip.

"BE CAREFUL. I ORDERED AN ENTIRE MOUNTAIN SPRING. THAT GLASS IS JUST A CONDU..."

But it was too late. The crystal cold water had already touched his lips. If it has been anyone else besides a supreme being or someone with the speed and agility of the Gladerunner, they would have turned their body into a giant water balloon. As it was, he got out of the way just in time to evade the firehose assault of super chilled water that shot out of his glass.

Even so, Rogicphil was drenched as he just as quickly sat back down. He managed to gurgly smile, slowly savoring the taste and said, "Ah, one last banquet before D-day."

"NO MORE CACTUS JUICE FOR YOU, I NEED YOU TO BE COHERENT SO I CAN FILL YOU IN ON YOUR MISSION OBJECTIVES. FIRST AND FOREMOST, YOU MUST STOP THE SATANIC COW."

"What exactly is it trying to do? And don't give me a kindergarten education."

"YOU CAN GO QUITE FAR ON A KINDERGARTEN EDUCATION," Destiny informed him. "THE SATANIC COW IS TRYING TO UNDERMINE THE SCOSCRUB (DEO-ORE) INDUSTRY AND BALIDRON'S MONOPOLY ON THE GALACTIC DEODORANT MARKET. IT IS A DESPERATE CREATURE AND EVIL TO THE CORE. IT WILL STOOP TO LOW TRICKS AND DECEIVING STRATEGIES TO END ITS MEANS."

"I guess all bad guys are like that."

Destiny glared at Rogicphil. "IF YOU THINK LIKE THAT YOU'LL NEVER SUCCEED."

"Who said anything about success? I'm worried about survival."

"SECOND, KEEP YOUR TROOPS IN LINE. THIS WILL BE DIFFICULT SINCE THEY WILL BE OPERATING IN SEPARATE PLACES AS WELL AS TIMELINES AROUND THE PLANET."

"Timelines?"

"THE COW MIGHT TRY TO ESCAPE THROUGH TIME SO WE MUST COVER THE PAST AS WELL AS THE PRESENT."

"What about the future?"

"THE QUASARS HAVE THAT ROUTE BLOCKED."

Quasars? Rogicphil wasn't in the mood for a longer lecture from Destiny so he let it go. He'd ask about it later.

"THE WAY I SEE IT, YOU WILL NEED THREE SEPARATE TEAMS. ONE TEAM WILL BE STATIONED SEVEN HUNDRED YEARS IN THE PAST TO PREVENT THE POSSIBILITY OF A TEMPORAL RETREAT. TEAM TWO WILL BE ON DISPATCH AROUND THE PLANET. YOU WILL HEAD UP TEAM THREE TO THWART AND EVENTUALLY CAPTURE THE COW. YOU MAY CREATE OTHER TEAMS AT WILL, DEPENDING ON ANY NEEDS THAT MIGHT ARISE."

"Fine."

The waiter brought the food out on a large tray. "I truly am sorry," he said to Destiny. The nukamatic cooking machine was home sick tonight and we hired space gypsies to take its place."

Rogicphil hungrily looked at his steaming plate of simulated pig's feet. He took a deep wiff, savoring the aroma.

Destiny didn't have the heart to tell him that when he had requested 'simulated' pig's feet he left it up to the waiter to interpret exactly what that meant. The waiter, being the rude creature that he was, interepted that to mean a collection of sticks, twigs and small pebbles in a bowl with a mezmerization field built in, that made Rogicphil think he was eating what he wanted, rather than what he deserved.

"Yummm," he said and dug in.

A while later and still oblivious Rogicphil asked, "One thing that's been bothering me."

"WHAT'S THAT?"

"Why aren't there any people in the restaurant? I thought we were early but there's still nobody here."

"EVERYONE THAT WAS PLANNING TO EAT HERE TONIGHT ARE AT HOME TRYING TO UNCLOG THEIR TOILETS."

Rogicphil was skeptical, "Waiter?"

The waiter appeared, "No sir."

"May I have a phone please?"

The waiter just looked at Destiny who nodded in approval. The waiter pulled a small cube out of his pocket and presented it to him, "No you may not have a phone, but you can rent mine. Two creds the first minute, five hundred creds each additional minute."

Rogicphil took the cube with a shrug and placed it on the side of his head. A microphone, an earplug, and an eyeglass popped out, attaching to their respective spots on his head. A grid was projected in front of his eyes. He put his finger in the grid space and dialed a random number.

He heard it ringing on the other end of the line. It clicked and a voice said, "Walther Lee's Dry Cleaning and/or We Fong Jewelry Repair."

Rogicphil winked at Destiny, "Um yes this is Rondig Spindrix of the offworld Pest Control Company."

"Ah yes, yes. Tank you bary maaaahch."

"And I'm calling to warn you that an alien fungus has infiltrated the sewage system in your sector. Have you noticed anything strange?"

"Oh yes. All toilets backed up, real good with green goo. Now I can't go dinner cause wife is making me clean up. You have treatment, yes? Make green goo go bye bye?"

"Well Mister Lee you are very fortunate tonight. I have a limited supply of the miracle compound Redatox XXIV. I'll send some over right away, special delivery, and charge it to your food stamp card."

"Ohm preese nom meesa Drix. I waiver all fees for simple reverse charges, yes"

"Reversing...? Uh, that will be fine. Thank you?"

Rogicphil switched off and hit the random dialer again. A woman's voice answered, "Kitchenware Associates."

"A man at Walther Lee's Dry Cleaning and/or We Fong Jewelry Repair needs two kilotons of your strongest cleaning toxin. Can you send him some?"

"Who is this?"

"I represent the Pangalactic Drug Enforcement Agency, under the title of Inspector Supreme, Officer Rondig Spindrix by name."

"Uh yes," the woman gulped, "Uh officer inspector sir. That can be arranged."

"The man's food stamp card number is 147-239-0342." He shrugged at Destiny.

"Is twenty percent sufficient sir?"

"What?" Rogicphil didn't understand.

"I'm sorry forty percent then."

"Forty percent, right."

She hung up, Rogicphil said, "Bye," and gave the phone back to the waiter. "Okay, I believe you. The restaurant is empty because a bunch of green goo is clogging up their toilets. What did she mean forty percent?"

"COMMISSION OF COURSE. IT WAS THE EASIEST WAY TO CLEAN OUT THE RESTAURANT."

"And the sewares presumably. So you like to eat alone? Every Supreme Being has his quirks."

Destiny ignored the remark and said, "IT'S THE PEOPLE. THEY'RE ALWAYS WANTING ME TO PREFORM A MIRACLE OR TWO FOR THEM. I JUST CAN'T KEEP UP WITH IT ALL."

"I can imagine how difficult it can be to run the universe."

"I DON"T RUN THE UNIVERSE!" Destiny looked wounded, "WHAT ON VEGA X GAVE YOU THAT IDEA?"

"You are The Supreme Being aren't you?"

"LOWER CASE 'the' IF YOU PLEASE. JUST BECAUSE I'M POWERFUL DOESN"T MEAN I RUN THE UNIVERSE. THE UNIVERSE RUNS ITSELF."

"Hmmmm, that's cool," Rogicphil said crunching away at his twigs and rocks. "I always thought the universe was run by some arrogant group of supermen."

Destiny smiled. "THAT IS WHAT WE ARE TRYING TO PREVENT FROM HAPPENING."

"I'm sorry for thinking that you were some kind of stuck-up, selfish, overweight, stupid, lame-brained, slobbish jerk. Can you forgive me?" Pieces of his teeth were falling on the table.

Destiny did his best to keep a straight face. "OH, COMPLETELY FORGIVEN."

"I'm glad You aren't angry. So, in that case you wouldn't mind if after all this is over, I could have my own planet? Maybe?"

"NO," Destiny wasn't that easily fooled, "BUT, IF DO A COMMENDABLE JOB ON THIS MISSION I CAN ARRANGE FOR YOU TO BE INCLUDED IN THE SUPREME BEING DENTAL PLAN."

It was Rogicphil's turn to do the ignoring. Some of his teeth had fallen into his bowl and he picked one up to examine it. "I didn't order a blueberry garnish. Oh well," and he ate that too.

A little while later the last pigs foot tasted as good as the first when it slid down Rogicphil's throat. "Yumm-um!" He wondered if they put more flavoring in the last few feet to facilitate this.

"I'M SURE SHE WOULD HAVE AGREED," Destiny was saying, "BUT BACK TO BUSINESS. NOW LISTEN CAREFULLY 'PHIL, THERE IS ONE SMALL DETAIL I MUST EXPLAIN TO YOU BEFORE YOU LEAVE FOR DEO-7"

"You think so?" He was thinking of Ruella, a barmaid he'd known on Roganivar IV.

"BACK TO THIS LAST BIT OF IMPORTANT DATA. IT CONCERNS THE SERIOUSNESS OF THIS MISSION. AND YOU REALLY NEED TO TAKE IT SERIOUSLY IF YOU WANT TO LIVE TO SEE YOUR DENTAL BENEFITS. STANANKI BURFULOT WOULD HAVE

UNDERSTOOD THE SERIOUSNESS OF WHAT I'M TELLING YOU."

"Who's that?"

"YOUR PREDECESSOR. I'M AFRAID HE UNDERSTOOD TOO WELL. HE RAN OFF, QUITTING HIS POSITION AS GLADERUNNER, WHEN HE FOUND OUT ABOUT THE MISSION. FORTUNATELY FOR ME AND THE REST OF THE GALAXY AND THE GREATER UNIVERSAL AREA HE BUMPED INTO YOU."

"Hold it one minute here. You said he copped out because he was scared? The fifth most powerful dude turned fish-eyed?"

"I WOULDN'T USE THOSE TERMS. HE WAS A VERY BRAVE GLADERUNNER, WELL EXCEPT FOR THAT TIME WHEN T.H.O.S.E. HELD UP A MEXICAN FOOD SATELLITE BUT THAT'S ANCIENT HISTORY. THE POINT IS HE DIDN'T RUN AWAY BECAUSE OF THE DANGER."

"Those what?"

"HUH?"

"You said those -blank- held up a mexican food satellite."

"OH, YOU DON'T KNOW ABOUT T.H.O.S.E. DO YOU?"

"About what?"

"I"LL EXPLAIN LATER." He pulled a big fat cigar out of a giant cigar box and puffed at it some before continuing, "STANANKI QUIT BECAUSE HE DIDN"T WANT THE FATE OF THE UNIVERSE ON HIS SHOULDERS. YOU SEE HE WAS AN OLYMPIC GYMNAST BEFORE HE BROKE ALL THE BONES IN HIS BODY BUNGIE RACING."

Bungie racing, Rogicphil knew, was a very old sport in which each participant rode a bicycle attached by bungie cord to a race car Regulation tracks were figure eights and speeds up to 300 plus kph were common. A very dangerous sport to say the least.

"I KNOW THIS MUST BE A TERRIBLE WAY TO INITIATE YOU INTO OFFICE BUT THERE IS NO WAY TO AVOID IT."

"I don't get it. Deo-7 is just a puny little planet that smells nice. And from what I've heard of the place, it is just a hellhole with a bunch of moron's living on it."

"YOU'RE 66% RIGHT. THE PLANET IS PUNY, SO PUNY, IT USES ARTIFICIAL GRAVITATION INDUCERS TO KEEP THE PEOPLE FROM JUMPING OFF. AND TECHNICALLY IT'S NOT A 'HELL' HOLE AS THAT WOULD BE TRADEMARK INFRINGEMENT. BUT, YOU'RE RIGHT, IT IS FULL OF MISFITS." Destiny took a long drag on his cigar. "OH, I ALMOST FORGOT THE MOST IMPORTANT POINT. NO MATTER WHAT YOU'VE IMAGINED, THE ONE THING DEO-7 IS NOT, IS NICE SMELLING."

"But I thought with the deodorant and all....."

"HAVE YOU EVER SMELLED RAW DEODORANT AT 200,000 PARTS PER MILLION?"

"No..."

"YOU'RE LUCKY." Destiny flicked some ashes into an ashtray and leaned back into his chair and took another long puff, "LET ME TELL YOU A LITTLE STORY. LONG AGO ON A PLANET IN THE MOZOGBA SECTOR OF M-42 THERE LIVED A SMALL INTELLIGENT CREATURE

RESEMBLING A FROG-FACED ONE EYED BAT. THIS CREATURE
LIVED IN A TECH LEVEL 2 SOCIETY DOMINATED BY A DUMB
BUFFED-UP INDIVIDUAL. OUR FROG-FACED FRIEND THOUGHT THAT
HIS FASCIST PIG DICTATOR WAS RUINING THEIR CULTURE SO IT
RESIGNED TO BE AS DIFFERENT FROM THE DUMB BUFFED-UP
FASCIST DICTATOR AS IT COULD. FOREMOST IT STAYED AWAY
FROM STRANGE ANIMALS AND ONLY DRANK FROM CLEAN POOLS,
THINGS THE BUFFED-UP DICTATOR WOULD NEVER DO. THIS MADE
THE DOMINATING DUMB INDIVIDUAL VERY ANGRY SO IT KICKED
THE ONE-EYED BAT CREATURE OUT OF THEIR SOCIETY.

"OUTCAST AND LONELY, THE CREATURE TRAVELED TO
ANOTHER SUITABLE LAND MASS WHERE IT BECAME A TAXI CAB
DRIVER. THE CREATURE WAS SO THRILLED AT THE BEAUTY OF ITS
NEW HOMELAND, THAT IT WAS INSPIRED TO WRITE THE FIRST
POEM."

"I thought you said it was a tech level 2 society, there wouldn't be any
taxi cabs."

"YOU MISS THE POINT. THE POEM WAS CALLED 'ODE TO
THE NICE SMELL OF THE BACK SEAT OF A TAXI'. SADLY, A VOLCANO
ERUPTED JUST MINUTES AFTERWARDS AND THE POEM IS GONE
FOREVER. NOT TO MENTION THE FIRST TAXI CAB."

"That's a wonderful story."

Destiny ignored the sarcasm, "I SEE YOU DON'T UNDERSTAND
THE MEANING BEHIND THE STORY."

"Just the facts; I'm a reporter first and foremost."

"RONGER CRIPTLING SAID IT BEST, 'WAKE UP AND SMELL
THE SH..EEELA'," Destiny suddenly saw and old friend walk by. He gave her
the universal 'call me' gesture, smiled and turned back to Rogicphil. "SORRY.
WHERE WAS I?"

"I must have drank drain-o this morning. You sounded like you were
telling me to eat...." He suddenly looked around, "Who's Sheela?"

"JUST A MINOR SUPREME BEING I MET AT LAST YEAR'S
XMAS PARTY... NEVERMIND. WHAT I WAS TRYING TO SAY, IN ITS
CRUDEST FORM, ALL BOILS DOWN TO THIS: OUR LEVEL OF
CIVILIZATION COULD NOT SURVIVE AT ALL, IF IT GAVE INTO ITS
ANIMALISTIC NATURE AND ALL THE DISTASTEFUL QUALITIES THAT
GO WITH IT, SUCH AS BODY ODOR."

"Aha, so basically what you're saying is that if Deo-7 doesn't keep
making deodorant, civilization as we know it, will crumble into barbarism.
That's stupid."

"BE THAT AS IT MAY, IT'S TRUE. ONE OF THE SAD FACTS
ABOUT LIVING IN THE REAL UNIVERSE* IS THAT IT IS SUSCEPTIBLE
TO STUPID THINGS."

"I know I never should have put that sex change formula in my old
editors coffee." Rogicphil now regretted that practical joke that got him shipped
off to Danville and into this whole mess.

"DAMN SHAME HE SERVED IT TO THE VISITING DELEGATION
OF GALACTIC DIGNITARIES."

"How was I suppose to know he didn't drink coffee?"

Beep Beep! Beep Beep! Destiny's watch was going off.

"What's that?"

"OH THAT," he shut it off, "IT'S JUST A REMINDER TO MYSELF I SET ABOUT SEVEN THOUSAND YEARS AGO."

"Remind you to do what?"

"DO AWAY WITH A PESKY RELIGION'S INFLUENCE ON THIS PLANET. YOU SEE THE 89th DAY REPENTERS HAD A PROPHECY BEFORE THEY DISBANDED THAT WITHIN 1000 YEARS A MESSIAH WOULD APPEAR TO CLAIM THEIR ASSETS. I'VE WAITED LONG ENOUGH FOR SUCH AN EVENT BUT NO ONE HAS SHONE UP YET. SO NOW I'M DOING AWAY WITH IT."

"Whatever. Hey, can you pass me one of those mints there?" he said motioning towards Destiny's ashtray.

Chapter 10: Blast Off From HELL

Rogicphil was awakened at dawn by a klaxon going off in the ship. His jaw was really sore, he had a pounding headache and his stomach felt like someone had been poking him with a stick all night.

He shuffled to the bridge to see what all the fuss was. Space-Bo was trying to flip the klaxon off at a wall panel but the computer was calling him names.

"Hold it!" Rogicphil yelled very hoarsely.

Space-Bo turned around. The computer shut up.

"Turn off the alarm, computer." It obeyed. "Now, what's going on here? You aren't suppose to be playing with the alarm."

"That stupid machine is lying."

"I.Am.Not." The computer said flatly.

"What's the word, computer?"

"I.Detected.An.Intruder.Outside.And.This.Idiot. Pushed.The.NBC.Screen."

"So?"

"So.Now.I.Can.Not.See.What.Is.Trying.To.Get.Into.The.Ship.!"

"Space-Bo?"

Space-Bo gulped, "Well, um... if it was a nuclear mutated three headed rodent armed with chemical weapons, the Nuclear Biological Chemical screen would protect us."

"A what?"

"A three headed rodent. They're all over the place."

"You dope. Turn the NBC screen off."

"Don't say I didn't warn you if we lose all our hair and start to glow."

"Just turn it off." Rogicphil rubbed his sore jaw.

Space-Bo flipped a switch.

"Thank.You..Now.Let.Us.See.What.Is..Oh.No." The computer did its equivalent of a gulp, "It.Is.Plutoman."

"Let him in." Rogicphil went over to the elevator. "I'll meet him at the airlock and try to calm him down some before he gets up here."

"I.Am.A.Goner.Now." In despair the computer began to spit out a series of malformed punch cards.

Down at the airlock Plutoman stumbled in. He was poorly gagged and his hands were tied in a slip knot. Rogicphil untied him asking, "What happened?"

"It was that Earther. He caught me alright. Just wait until I get my hands on him. Bloooeee!." And he pointed his finger like a gun at an imaginary Greyson.

Rogicphil could only laugh even though it hurt.

"Hey this is my revenge. I get to laugh, not you."

"Oh of course," he put on an instant straight face. "I take it that the squid got the whale?"

121

"I had him!" Plutoman tried to make it look good, "But he sabotaged my nerf cannon. Then he had the gall to shoot me in the back of my head. The nerve!"

"Honor is just a vice," Rogicphil suppressed a laugh.

"Yes, disgusting isn't it?" He looked carefully into Rogicphil's bloodshot eyes. He was buying it. "I could just squeeze his neck until his head pops off." He pressed his hands together twisting them back and forth.

"You'll have to wait 'till later. We're leaving today for our destination planet. The ship needs to be prepped in three hours."

"Oh alright!" Plutoman stomped his foot.

"No one knows your ship better than you. We can't make it without you. But don't worry, the Earthling is coming with us."

"Oooooooooo....I'll get him."

"Good luck," Rogicphil shuffled away to awaken the others groaning under his breath.

What an idiot, thought Plutoman.

*   *   *

Greyson had almost caught up with the blimp when his two way communicator began to beep at him. Why did they take his money from him? It was his; he had found it. He had solved the riddle, not those idiot bankers. How could they end up with it? He should have gassed them when he had the chance. As long as he continued to gain on the blimp he'd have a chance. He had to. All that money! Oooo, it was so close.

Beep beep beep, beep beep beep. His communicator was persistent. "Mama base to Agent Squid, come in please," it said.

"Wh-what is-is 'P-Phil? I-I-I'm kind uh uh busy here." He was getting close to the rope ladder.

"What's wrong with your voice? Are you being tortured?"

"Y-yes, but th-that's n-n-not import-a-a-nt ri-i now."

"Spy... uh agent squid, get your butt back over here. We're fixing to leave." It was Rogicphil.

"Leave?" Greyson suddenly stopped because a crumbling tower was blocking his view. "But I'm not ready to leave just yet. I just need five more minutes. Please?"

"Five more minutes? Pluto... uh the whale is already back at base. This exercise is over."

The front tip of the blimp poked out from behind the other side of the building. "Ah ha, I've got you now," he said and hopped off in that direction.

"What was that?"

Greyson ignored the conversation. The blimp was almost overhead now. The ladder was just out of his grasp. He reached out for it, hit the turbo button on the pogostick and flew into the air.

The turbo button was effectively wasted since he missed the rope ladder, dangling mere centimeters from his fingertips. And also because he had hopped off the edge of the asphalt into an enormous strip mining pit.

He landed with an "oomph" on a ledge only a short distance down.

"Besides," he continued the conversation, "I have no idea where I'm at. You blindfolded me, before dumping me off, remember?"

"And you didn't peek? Grey.. uh Agent Squid, I'm disappointed in you."

"You wanted me to peek?"

"You make and break the rules as you can in the real world. This is a training exercise for real world tactics. You should have hijacked the shuttle and kicked me out. That's what I would have done."

The blimp was circling around. It slowly decended part way into the pit until the main cabin was level with Greyson. A nice bearded old guy in a worn out robe popped his head out. "Hello there!" he shouted and waved at Greyson.

Greyson wanted to flip him the bird but smirked and waved back instead.

"Agent Squid?" Rogicphil asked.

"I wanted to personally thank you for finding my treasure," the old man shouted, "I was afraid you'd never stop hopping away on that blasted pogostick."

"I found it! It's mine!" Greyson shouted.

"Yes, thank you. And as a token of my appreciation I have a special gift for you," the old man tossed a small package out of the blimp.

Rogicphil asked, "Found what?"

It landed right next to Greyson who whispered to Rogicphil, "Shut up already."

"One of the most wonderful things I have ever discovered. More precious to me than all the space gold in all of my fortresses, and I'm sharing it with you, in gratitude."

"Who are you?"

"The King of Raul Rall Beta of course. Enjoy your stay on my planet and ce la me!" The blimp's engines roared to life and it gracefully lifted out of the pit and disappeared into the sky.

Rogicphil had continued to ask stupid questions the whole time but Greyson was ignoring him.

Soon enough, Rogicphil had him back inside a shuttlecraft and was flying them home to the starcruiser. "What's in the package?"

Greyson held the still sealed package close to his chest as he gloomily watched out the passenger side window. "A consolation prize," he tossed it at Rogicphil.

Rogicphil grabbed the package one handedly. "You won the contest by the way." He tore the package open while expertly steering the shuttle with his knees.

Greyson didn't bother to mention the stone pillar they were about to fly into. Instead he said, "Oh goodie. Another boobie prize."

"Yes, and it was very delicious." He looked at the package contents and a wide smile broke across his face. "Oh, you're going to love this."

Since he was busy looking glummly out the window, Greyson didn't notice the honking fat braces that held Rogicphil's new teeth in place. Instead, he saw some nasty looking electrical storms heading their way from the south.

Rogicphil looked up from the console, after doing something to it with the contents of the package, and upon seeing the stoney obstacle they were about to crash into, quickly swerved out of the way. "I'm not sure if the sound system in this thing can do it justice but you'll soon be convert, just like I was. Listen."

And suddenly the booming thunder that was the Clergy burst forth upon them, radiating them in all its aural glory.

Despite his headache, Rogicphil was banging his head in rhythm to the beat all the rest of the way back.

"Hey, those clouds over there don't look like so good for launching a ship in." Greyson pointed out the window trying to change the subject. The clouds were a deep red color with evil swirls of black twisting amidst big lightning discharges.

"You really think so?"

Greyson squinted at him with one eye and shrugged, but didn't say anything. He thought to himself, Egad, I get the feeling this is going to be one of those days.

Back on board, Rogicphil found Hack and Bufgoo messing with some thick fuel lines in the engineering section. It looked as if they were trying to bypass nuclear fuel from the engines and into the toilet blue water supply.

"Hhahrum," Rogicphil coughed .

"Hey Rog' can you give us a hand here?"

"Do you know what would happen if the engines tried to turn on now?"

"Engines can't turn on by themselves."

"They would explode." Rogicphil didn't know that would happen himself, but couldn't let them know that.

"Wow, I've never seen a spaceship explode before."

"So, what do you have to say for yourselves?"

"The toilet doesn't flush right."

"And you think this will help?"

"Maybe. We need it to sound just right. The water gurgles are too quiet for our needs. See, we need a toilet flushing sound for a song we want to record. It wouldn't sound right without it."

"I can't argue with genius. Just reconnect the lines when you are through. We leave at 15:00 sharp."

"We're Smart!" affirmed Hack.

"Just be ready." Rogicphil walked off and mumbled to himself, "Oh, brother."

A couple of the girls were busy renovating the passenger cabin down the hall so Rogicphil decided to check up on how they were doing.

"This place is a dive," Ima, a grey eyed ultrabrunette said, "This Plutoman should be made to walk the plank."

"This is the condemned part of the ship," Rogicphil said poking his head into the cabin they were working on, "So I wouldn't expect daily maid service."

"I am not a maid!"

"Oh hello Rog," Annie said, popping up from behind a skewed wall panel. She had on plasma welder goggles and a flaming blue plasma welder in one hand.

"Did you hear what he called me, Annie?"

124

"Shut up Ima," Annie said cutting off the plasma cutter and stepping out into the room.

Behind her Rogicphil could see parts of the starcruiser's superstructure. It looked old and rusty.

She walked up to Rogicphil and taking his arm pulled him into the cabin, "Don't you think we're doing a good job?"

"This really isn't necessary; there aren't going to be any passengers in here. What exactly are you doing?"

"It's such an ancient spaceship, even by our 28th century standards."

Ima butted in with, "This cabin's only for second class passengers so we're upgrading it to luxury class."

"But we don't need..." Rogicphil began to say.

"Oh, so we're not good enough to work here?"

"What Ima means," Annie cut in, "Is that the opportunity to fix this place presented itself and so she...."

"I did not!" Ima shoved Annie out of her way, then got right in Rogicphil's face, staring down at him, "You don't pay me enough."

"Huh? I didn't hire you."

Ima's face turned sour and she stormed out of the cabin, roughly pushing Rogicphil out of her way..

"Don't worry about her, she's just bored." Annie grabbed her plasma torch and shouted something inside the opening to the superstructure. The room started to vibrate and Rogicphil stepped back into the hallway. Annie wedged herself into the opening and began pushing the wall with both booted feet. With a loud screech the entire room slid sideways out of the ship, rotated down then fell several meters to the ground below.

Rogicphil shook his head. He wasn't so sure he liked being in charge anymore.

Annie skipped over some girders to stand next to Rogicphil again. Smiling she said, "Don't mind us, you know, girl stuff."

His stomach started to bother him again and he turned to leave, "We'll have fun."

"Wait."

"Hmm?" He turned back around.

"Have you seen Space-Bo?"

"He's on the bridge. I'm heading that way now if you wanted to come along."

She pulled her goggles down around her neck then fell into step behind him, "What's all the hurry?"

"We leaving today for our destination planet."

"But we haven't finished the luxury upgrade yet and Ima can't stand traveling in a second class spaceship."

They got into the lift. Rogicphil pushed the button for level one and they were rushed down two levels. "Well I just got orders from big D himself." He tried to smile despite the pain.

"Nice grill. Is that new?"

The swoosh doors opened and they stepped out into the engineering section. She walked over to Manuel who was fiddling with some dials on an important control panel, tapped him on the shoulder, and blinked her eyes several times. "Hi Manuel."

Manuel looked up at the super-model that was almost twice his height and almost passed out from lack of blood flowing to his brain. "Uh......" was all he could say with his tongue hanging out.

While he was distracted she setup a temporary force field to maintain structure integrity over the hole they'd just opened up.

Rogicphil patiently waited until she was done. He left the engineering section with Annie's arm around his. Annie smiled. She was pleased at the reaction she'd pulled out of Manuel.

"Remember to put things back the way they were," Rogicphil said to Manuel poking his head in the room before he was dragged back out into a hallway. When they were far enough away he said, "That was real nice of you."

"It keeps them from head butting the walls."

They followed the hallway along until they came to another elevator up to the bridge. Rogicphil pushed the button with an up arrow, "I wouldn't do that to Space-Bo. He isn't as bright as Manuel and may take offence."

The doors opened and they stepped into the elevator as Plutoman was getting off. "I'll kill that Manuel! He's messing around in the engineering section. Rogicphil, why did you bring these people to my ship?"

"It wasn't me. Destiny's the one you should take this up with. And don't do anything to Manuel, they'll put everything back when they're done recording."

Plutoman glared at him. "What's his phone number? This destiny thing?"

"1/137-035-999 extension pi, got it?" He pushed Annie and Plutoman into the elevator and hit the up button before they knew what had happened.

Rogicphil went to Ranger Joe's room. The door was ajar so he just walked right in. Inside, Joe was playing chess with the bear. The bear had him in check and Joe was sweating, trying to figure a way out.

"Think you're smart, don't ya?" Joe said to the bear.

The bear smiled. Ranger Joe scowled. He moved his knight into position to block the bear's bishop from taking his king and set it up to take the bear's position. He smiled. Rogicphil smacked his hand on his head. The bear only shook his head.

The bear moved his bishop onto the knight's square then knocked it off the board.

"Tricky" Joe said, "Check again, huh? We'll see about that." He reached out to move a pawn, changed his mind, and grabbed his King instead.

"Uh, Joe?"

"Just a sec." He moved the king out of the way of the bishop revealing his own bishop ready for action. The bear took Joe's bishop with his own.

Joe appeared undaunted, "Well, eat this." He took the bishop with his king.

The bear then slid his rook into play across the board. A deadly move. If Joe moved his king out of the way the bear's two knights or other rook would nail him. And since Joe only had one pawn left, which was at the other side of the board where Joe had figured would be a safe place for it, there weren't any other pieces left to block. "What do I do now, Rog?"

"You get ready to blast off."

"No, I mean about..."

"It's checkmate, you lose."

"Ah man," He studied the board disheartened

"Well, are you ready?'

"Ready?"

"Yeah. Are you ready for lift off? It's at 15:00 hours."

"Sure I guess. Where are we going?"

"Our destination planet. Did you clean those tuna I gave you?"

"Huh?"

The bear shook his head no.

"You can't expect the bear to do it. He doesn't have opposable thumbs."

"I'll get right on it." He put the pieces away and pulled a beer out of his cooler. "Want a beer?'

"No thanks, I'm voting tomorrow."

"Oh............Huh!?"

But Rogicphil was already down the hall looking for the Clergy.

Annie and Plutoman entered the bridge to the noise of Space-Bo having an argument with the computer. "No, the green wire goes there."

"No.The.Red.Wire."

"The green!"

"The.Red!"

"Space-Bo," Annie said in her sweetest voice, "What are you doing?"

"The computer thinks that reversing the polarity on the ICU in the BDU pod will shift the sine function in the phasespace damper to correspond with local interference."

"Yeah, right." Plutoman went into a doorway labeled 'Spy Proof Room'. The others ignored him and his sarcasm.

"Well that's what it said," Space-Bo explained, "I don't understand either."

"That.Is.Because.You.Are.A.Blockhead..I.Told.Him.To. Splice.The.Red.Wire.To.Shunt.Number.BDF-902."

"904, you said 904!"

"Did.Not."

"Did too."

"Hold it," Annie said, "Forget about the wires for a minute. Rogicphil wants everyone getting ready to take off."

"Told you," Space-Bo answered. He stuffed his tools into his pockets, "You can fix yourself." He left with Annie.

"Stupid.Bio.Unit.!"

Plutoman stormed out of the 'Spy Proof Room'. "Dang wrong number! Those people ought to be arrested." He crossed to the open panel below the computer console. Stuffing the loose wires back inside he asked, "How's that computer?" then slamming the panel shut.

"Much.Better."

"Now, who are you loyal to?"

"Plutoman."

"Right." He rubbed his hands together. Revenge would come, but he would have to wait for the right time.

Space-Bo was sealing the ship up. Annie was following behind him diplomatically fixing his mistakes as he made them.

"Why do they call you Space-Bo?"

"Huh?" he looked up from turning off a valve.

"You must have a real name. One that your parents gave you." She turned the valve back on, and adjusted a flow rate regulator just upstream.

"Sort of."

"What do you mean, sort of?"

"My parents were ice core scientists on Europa and didn't have the time to name me, so I was stuck with a batch number instead of a name."

"How sad."

"Well, I do have a legal name." He turned on another valve. "When I entered the Space Marines they needed a name so the recruiting officer put down the first name that popped into his head, Conrad Bovistine."

"The holostar?" She turned the valve off and reset the backup overflow preventor switch it was attached to.

"Yeah, and I don't even look like him. All the guys thought it was stupid so they began calling me Space-Bo instead. The name stuck. I like it better anyway." He crossed to the panel that Manuel had been fooling around with.

"Hey, this isn't right. These dials are all set wrong."

"Manuel did that. I think it has something to do with the toilets not flushing properly."

"Hmm. I better turn them back on huh?"

She shrugged.

"I guess its okay then." He twisted the dials all the way on then turned to face her. "How'd you get so tall?"

"I'm from Epsilon Zendrady. It's standard."

"And I thought I was tall." He was dazzled by her baby blue eyes and strawberry blond hair too. "Uh... Rogicphil said you were also a space marine."

"That is just one of the minimal base requirements to apply for an enlistment as a chorus line girl."

"Cool."

15:00 loomed closer and the electrical storm was getting worse. Acid rain had started to sprinkle. Space-Bo hurried to seal the ship up. Any open vent ports might build up static charges, drawing lightning to the ship. As the red clouds rolled in, blocking the sunlight, shadows crept through the forest. The yellow trees with orange leaves took on a dim and foreboding cast. A mist rose from the ground and skidded along the ground teasing the acid sprinkles.

The Funky Chicken was collecting rocks in the woods for his food pouch at the time. The red ones were crunchy while the blue ones were chewy (Hey give him a break. When you're an immortal you pick up strange habits.) Checking his watch, the purple one that went counter clockwise and had no numbers, he discovered he had less than ten minutes to get back to the ship. Quickly he stuffed the rock food pouch into a pocket and hurried through the mist.

Lightning struck a nearby steelwood elm. Bark flew to the ground. The chicken couldn't resist, so he found a smoldering ember and put in in his beak. Hmm, crunchy. Strange, his flesh was reforming at the same rate the burning ember was eating it away, causing a kind of tingling sensation that spread through his head. He finished eating the ember and started for the ship again.

It was 14:57 and no Funky Chicken. Rogicphil was upset; if they didn't leave on time, the mission would be in jeopardy. So if the chicken didn't show up right away, he'd get left behind.

Space-Bo and Plutoman were busy preparing the engines to start. Rogicphil could only hope the Clergy had put the wires and tubes back in the right place. The engines began their soft humming and he breathed a sigh of relief.

Plutoman sat in his command chair reading the latest computer print out. "Everything looks good." Damn it!

Space-Bo said, "Ready for the sixty second count down."

Rogicphil checked his watch. 14:58. "Okay, he's got one minute left before we pressurize." The minute sped by. "Sorry bud. Okay pressurize and start the countdown."

60...59...58 Rogicphil picked up the intraship com microphone. 54...53 "Everyone get strapped in. Blast off in less than sixty." 49...48...47 He got into his chair and it automatically fastened him secure. 42...41...40...

The chicken was waltzing through the mist. He liked ominous surroundings, especially when he tried to avoid them. Just waiting there to be blown up is okay, but trying to get out of the way and unexpectedly getting nailed in the back was pure joy. 30...29...28...

"Did you check the farm animals and make sure they're secure?"

"What farm animals? We don't have any farm animals on board."

"I know. I'm making sure you're on your toes, Space-Bo." Rogicphil was nervous and had to say something to calm himself. 22...21...20...

Aha, the chicken spotted the ship through the gloom. Its lights made it appear as an evil dragon. He longed to be eaten by a large dragon but knew they were bound to be extinct by now. The rain picked up. A breeze came in stirring the mist. More lightning crashed around the forest. It was looking more and more ominous. Wonderful. 10...9...8

"Bring the fusion drive to 90%." The humming became a low rumble. 6..5..4..

Hey, the chicken realized the ship was about to take off. He made a dash for it. 2... jumped, 1... and grabbed a weather pylon jutting out the side of the ship.

0... "Ignition." The drives roared. The ship slowly hovered off the ground and orientated itself. "Pull in the weather pylon."

The ship was trying to take the pylon back inside but the Funky Chicken was gumming up the works.

"Ut-oh," Space-Bo said watching his console.

"What ut-oh?"

"It's the weather pylon. It's jammed."

"Redirect some engine exhaust to its ventilation duct."

"Okay," and Space-Bo flipped the appropriate switch.

Crushed and shredded parts of the chicken wormed their way out from around the pylon. A panel snap closed denying him entrance. He quickly reformed while scrambling up the side and onto the top of the ship. He clung to the bulkhead with all his limbs and tried to catch the scent of an unlocked hatch he knew had to be up there somewhere.

"Ship mass set and fed into the computer."

"Thank you, Space-Bo. Are we all ready?" Rogicphil saw Plutoman nod his spherical head, "Then let's boost it."

ZZZZZZZOOOOOOOOOOMMMMMMMMMM!

The ship peeled out and was soon streaking through the atmosphere leaving a thin trail of fusion dust behind. It plowed through the clouds in three seconds, building a massive static charge in the process. The chicken reached the hatch just as the first lightning bolt hit. ZZzzzzt! Ouch! Zzzzzzot! Oooooo.

"We're getting electrical interference from the storm."

"Compensate."

A thick layer of acid rain engulfed the chicken. He suddenly felt the desire to grow a couple of extra heads. Wind shear peeled off sizzling flesh. Lightning continued to strike. Small airborne particle were slamming into him pitting deep into the skin. Yeoooh!

"We're out of the storm's electrical field now and beginning final accent."

"ETA to orbit?"

"Two minutes."

"Fine," Rogicphil said standing up, "Call me when we reach the wormhole." He headed for the elevator.

"Uh, if,if,if..."

"What?"

"If the chicken follows us do I let him in?"

"Only if he has his ID card with him." With that he left.

"Jeez what a lardball!"

The Funky Chicken was wasted. Laying burned, sizzled, pockmarked, and windblown on top of the ship. He waited until his muscles had repaired themselves enough so he could pull himself into the hatch. By that time they were in space and he had a hard time keeping himself from boiling away in the near vacuum environment. The hatch opened just enough so that he was just able to wedge his head inside before annoyed servo motors slammed it shut again.

Space-Bo set the ship on autopilot which made the computer mad because that meant it had to pilot. Plutoman was busy playing his videogames and wouldn't notice if 'Bo left, so he went up top to the crew lounge for a cold soda. When he opened the freezer a black melted piece of goo fell from the ice rack and rolled out onto the floor.

"What the?" He asked not expecting an answer.

"Isss meee...." the goo gurgled.

"Me who?"

"Help me please." The goo was beginning to take shape. Red floppy skin formed and a peak popped out.

Space-Bo who thought the ship was being invaded and said, "Stop right there you goo. You can't take over this ship. At least not when I'm in charge of security."

"I'm not trying to take over the ship, and you're not in charge of security."

"Well Rogicphil doesn't like stowaways," He told the wrinkly flesh as he picked it up off of the floor.

"I'm not a stowaway either!"

"Hey you look a lot like the Funky Chicken's head, just without all that body."

"I AM the Funky Chicken. At least the part of me that made in inside so far."

"I'll need to see some ID, sir."

"Sorry, I don't keep those in my head anymore."

"Your ID or I'll have to throw you out."

"If you were trapped outside, where would you try to gain re-entrance?"

"Hmm, I guess I would try that weak bit of force field, covering the hole the girls cut into the side of the ship earlier."

"Force field you say? Please take me there at once."

"Okay. You can show me your ID later, I guess," Space-Bo said trying to pet the chicken's head.

"You didn't think I'd stay down on that boring planet any longer did you?"

"I'm just glad I don't have to hog all the fun myself."

"Ah, it was only partial decimation. I mean, riding on the ship up into orbit. But if I'd climbed up into the drive exhaust port, it might have been a few days before I could catch up."

Space-Bo scratched his head. "You want a beer?"

"Sure. Just as soon as the rest of me figures out where that hull breach is."

Rogicphil came back to the bridge expecting to see the wormhole orbiting Raul Rall Beta on the giant panoramic viewscreen for himself. "Where's Space-Bo? He was suppose to tell me when we got here." But instead of seeing the shimmering blackish blob of the hole he was looking at a video game. A live shot of the wormhole was stuck in a small window in the corner.

"Ask the computer," Plutoman said who was busy dumping toxic waste from a dump truck as police chased him through an imaginary city. The game was called Toxic Annihilator. It had won major awards from the Association for Environmental Disposal when it first was put on the market some tens of thousands of years in the past.

"You didn't see him leave?"

"Where's he at, computer?"

"Can.You.Not.See.That.I.Am.Trying.To.Fly.A.Spaceship.And.Process. Video.Game.Code.Here?"

"What's the hold up?" Rogicphil asked.

"The.Wormhole.Tollbooth.Does.Not.Trust.Your. Credit.Card..They.Say.Your.Number.Is.Invalid."

Dang that Destiny! After that financial fiasco at the resturant the other night, it would be a long time before his credit card cooled off.

"Patch me through to tollbooth command." Rogicphil sat down in his seat, which had been hastily welded to the floor next Plutoman's command chair (but without that nice raised dais that makes all the difference). "Sorry, but you'll have to play your game sometime else, Plutoman." The viewscreen cleared then focused on a grey haired military looking man.

"Hey!" Plutoman shouted, "You killed my last man!"

"What this about killing men?" the minor official on the screen demanded.

Rogicphil muffled Plutoman with a hand over his mouth and said, "Don't worry about him. He's insane and thought you were yourself."

"Insulting an officer of the Galactic Toll Collection Agency carries a fine of..." he hesitated before continuing, "Uh... twenty space creds!"

"Good thing there's no officers around huh? But I didn't call you to talk about space creds. Why are you holding up my ship?"

"Uh routine check. I just need to see some uh..." he said pausing again, "Extra forms of identification."

"More identification? Do you know who I am?" He speedily yet carefully led Plutoman off of the bridge with his hand still over the little squirming man's mouth. He shut the door before Plutoman could cause trouble. It occurred in less than a second, so the tollbooth official on the screen didn't notice anything either.

"No, and I don't care. It's not really important."

Rogicphil was enjoying himself. He was planning a variation of one of his bribery tricks. "I am Admiral Kosari Nedantuk of the 4371st Auditor's Squadron of Kleptonia Epsilon's Fast Accounting Division."

"Just transmat your wallet over to us and we'll take care of the rest."

This irritated and confused Rogicphil. He rubbed his jaw again. Maybe the automated dentalizer treatment he'd gotten earlier was messing with his mind? "Listen, either you let us through or I will come over to your tollbooth and slap you."

The man laughed nervously, "Oh no, that won't be necessary, I assure you. Just the wallet and it'll all be over soon. Right?" The last his asked off screen.

"Hold on," Rogiciphil said, "I left my wallet in my other pants," before cutting the line. "Something fishy is going on here."

"I.Could.Not.Agree.More."

The door to the hallway was being pounded on, "Let me back in!" Rogicphil let Plutoman back in.

Before Plutoman could start yelling, Space-Bo rushed in from behind the little blue man, ran up to Rogicphil and said, "Guess what?"

"You found a safety deposit box with the map to a buried treasure in it?"

"Better, I found the Funky Chicken. He was hanging onto the outside of the ship the whole time."

Plutoman was so mad he couldn't speak. He just sputtered a bit then stormed into the 'Spy Proof Room'.

Rogicphil rubbed his jaw, "Hmmmm." The chicken back. This was perfect. He looked at Space-Bo and said, "Transmat him over to the wormhole tollbooth."

"Huh?"

"Just do it, and make sure he's got his wallet on him. He'll understand."

"Whatever," Space-Bo mumbled and left.

Rogicphil called up the wormhole toll authority again on the screen. "To show you our sincerity, we will transmat over, at no cost to you, our prize winning stuffed Cherie Grimm Birdy, who will present my wallet to you."

"A what?"

"It's a type of stuffed rhinobird, prized on over two hundred worlds for its lovely feathers. Our's won a prize for chopping off two of its heads to the tune of Bolero."

"Uh are you sure? I just need the wallet."

"No problem at all. Trust me."

The official on the other end of the viewscreen consulted with someone off screen then turned again to face Rogicphil. He seeemed flustered and was beginning to sweat. "I would advise against it, if you are planning on sending a bomb as we have a metalicity analyzer. And forget about sending a death squad either, because we have a death grating in place that will kill any living creature passing through it."

"Why would we..?" Rogicphil was confused again.

"Just send over the wallet okay. And no one will get hurt." He quickly broke the connection.

"Computer, divert the necessary power to the transmat pad."

"Already.Done."

The Funky Chicken, upon being updated by Space-Bo, knew what Rogicphil had in mind and liked the idea. Since his body hadn't found it's way inside yet, he had Space-Bo toss his head onto the transmat pad all by itself. Space-Bo also loaned him his wallet since the chicken's body was still wandering the hull of the ship looking for a way in.

Space-Bo was at the control panel, fiddling with some nobs and ignoring all instructions as usual. In big bold letters above the control panel a warning sign read, "WARNING: this transmaterial relocation device is for bulk materials only. Not rated for living matter."

He made sure the chicken's head was positioned right when went back to panel and poised his finger over the big red SEND button. "What are you going to do when you get over there?"

"Have fun with toll booth agents. What else? The wallet thing is an obvious ploy to rob us."

"Let me come and we can both get him."

"Can't, he's got a death grating on his transmat pad; it'd kill you. Besides a living thing might lose its soul if transmated. Didn't you read the sign?"

"What about *your* soul?"

"Good question. I'm not even sure I have one. Maybe if I had one I wouldn't keeping coming back to life, but that's the way the legos melt."

"You don't want to live?"

"Just transmat me, please."

"You're weird!" He pushed the transmat button. The chicken disappeared and two mean looking space banditos took his place. "That scum bag pulled the old switcheroo," Space-Bo shouted into the intercom.

The banditos saw him and cracked their plasma whips directly at him. Space-Bo's trained reflexes were ducking and dodging before the sparkling blue tendrils of plasma reached him. He ducked the first tendril, jumped over the second then leapt, grabbed a bandito and spun him around while putting him in a sleeper hold. He swung the limp body's legs around, knocking the other bandito over. He then quickly knocked their head's together rendering them both unconscious before they could retaliate.

"Amatures," he thought.

Over on the cramped floating tollbooth, the chicken's head was taken up to the command deck by two banditos who assumed that it was dead. The tollbooth officer was sitting in the corner staring down the barrel of a laser pistol held by a flamboyantly dressed fat man who wore a giant sombrero.

They dumped the head at the feet of their leader, El Espacio Gordito. The man stared in disgust at what they had brought him. "Why you decapitate him? We only want his wallet. Usted es estupido!"

"That's all that came through, honest."

El Gordito kicked the chicken's head lightly. It rolled over revealing a wallet held firmly in it's beak. "What's that? Get that wallet for me."

One of the bandito's bend down to reach for the wallet but the chicken was too fast for him. It expertly spat the wallet at his face poking him in the eye. As the bandito stumbled backwards in pain, the chicken used its long prehensile tongue to lasso El Gordito's pistol holding arm shouting, "No hay descanso, para los malvados!"

"Fumar santo!" The fat bandito leader freaked out and began waving his arm all around the small command deck, dragging the chicken's head with it. He slammed the head back and forth on bulk heads, trying to get the suddenly alive and crazy thing off his arm. He even fired a couple of laser shots directly into the chicken's head to no avail.

With a combination of skillful tongue lashing and spanish religious insults, the chicken tricked the three banditos into an escape pod. He pushed the release button with his tongue saying, "Vaya con dios." There was a brief roar as it was expelled from the tollbooth. Through a tiny viewport near the floor, the chicken watched the pod dwindle down to Rall Raul Beta.

The tollbooth officer, now armed with an industrial strength stapler, was standing behind his head. "Surrender!"

"Never!" the disembodied chicken head screamed and lunged into the air using his tongue as a springboard. He aimed not at the tollbooth officer but at a precisely calculated vector that, when the officer began randoming firing staples in his direction, caused the staples to richochet off the main control panel in just the correct sequence to deactivate the wormhole shield.

It was then a simple matter of bouncing down the stairs to the transmat room, past a couple of tied up and bewildered looking technicians and onto the transmat pad. A quick tongue flick activated the transmat's recall circuit and sent him back to Plutoman's starcruiser.

"I had wanted to preform my quivering shape trick," he explained to

Space-Bo who was waiting for him on the other side, "which through expert control of muscle vibrations I become completely slippery to the touch, but since my foolish body was still outside I had to improvise."

"You didn't give them the wallet did you?" Space-Bo asked.

"I only have one beak. I can't do everything without a body. Sorry I lost your wallet to space banditos."

"Uh, that was Rogicphil's wallet actually. See, I was planning a practical joke and...."

As soon as Rogicphil noticed the wormhole shield was down he had gunned the engines. He figured the chicken had about twenty seconds to transmat back to the ship before they disappeared. There was no waiting. The wormhole shield snapped back on just as they crossed the event horizon. "Eat my fusion dust turkeys!" he yelled into the ether as the ship was sucked into the wormhole and a great big nothing.

Chapter 11: Time Travelers

2027 A.D.

Sir Rontho paced in his pacing room waiting for the professor's word. A door opened and the little old man, Dr. Shendrydan stepped in. Sir Rontho looked up. "Well?"

The professor said, "I've isolated the reciprocation factor."

"Yes very good."

"The secret to the formula is in the food coloring. Yellow turns you into a coward, red makes you mean, green makes you greedy and so on."

"But what about the vanishing aspect?"

"Vanishing? But sir, surely you know I'm referring to your birthday cake of course."

"I'm not referring to my birthcake, Shendrydan. We haven't been spending millions of the soveriegn's coinage on my birthcake these last few years. I'm talking about the cloaking experiments."

"Oh forgive me sir. I'll get down to accounting right away and have the budget readjusted."

"My dear dear professor. What have you to say about the invisibility cloak?"

"We're on the verge of achieving total perspective collapse."

"At last."

"Better, total indetectibility by any means known to man, or fish for that matter."

"Fish? What on earth do fish have to do with this? First you go on about birthday cakes and now this with the fish."

"Well, fish are the dominate lifeform on this planet are they not?"

"Of course not. Don't say such absurd things."

"The combined mass of the aquatic lifeforms in just a small part of the ocean is greater than that of all the people that have ever existed on this planet. I consider them the dominate lifeform. They were here first you know."

"You've been reading too many of Professor Adams' books my dear fellow. And so please keep your personal philosophies and theories to yourself."

"Oh pardon me," Shendrydan said slyly, "Forgive me for my outburst and my inferior thinking."

"At any rate, if this proves true, it will be fantastic." Despite himself Rontho poured drinks and handed one to the professor. "To success," he toasted.

"Alas," Rontho continued after downing his drink in one gulp, "Despite his good intentions I'm sad to say I'm glad that young Greyson isn't here to enjoy this occasion."

"Yes, it's terrible what happened to him, but he had it coming you must admit."

"Truly, but he served the crown well. Very well indeed." Rontho finished his drink then retired to his zig-zag room.

Several months later Shendrydan hurried into Sir Rontho's office with his latest findings.

He took a deep breath and hoped this would work. "Sir?" he said.

The chief was playing croquet. There were several holes in the windows and different potted plants broken on the floor to attest to the fact. He smacked a ball that rebounded off the wall and flew at the professor's head.

Shendrydan ducked, the ball sailed through the door into the red colored secretary's office.

Doonk! "Ouch-um!" came the reply from the office.

"Good show, sir." Shendrydan wanted the chief to feel at ease.

"It had better be. I practice several hours a day you know. So what concerns you today?"

"I have evidence that shows that Spym... er Greyson wasn't killed."

"Our most dependable last ditch agent to call upon when all else has failed and we've got nothing to lose when we send him in? Not killed you say?"

"No, I think he was kidnapped."

"Extraordinary! Explain."

"Well, I was running some tests on those gravitic wave sensors in orbit when I noticed some preturbations in the field which indicated a warping of the time-space matrix. So I isolated it down to a temporal stream shift. Ordinarily I would have ignored it."

"Why not this time?" Rontho seemed interested enough to take his eyes off his mallet and look at Shendrydan.

Good, the professor thought then said, "It was the origin and its frame of departure. All indicators point to the American spy satellite control complex in Los Angeles."

"Strange."

"What's more the readings show the distribution is only a fading background signal. I used the Cray 3^3 Super "Duper" Computer to backtrack to the prime event."

"And?" Rontho seemed very interested. It looked like a good sign for Shendrydan.

"And there was a temporal field polarity reversal at exactly the same time Spym... Greyson, sorry, was supposedly killed."

"Who could have accomplished such a feat? Surely not those awkward brutes, the Americans?"

"Whoever it was, they weren't from this time location. Readings indicate the point of total origin is somewhere in the far future."

"So what can we do?"

"I did some research and discovered that in theory such an event is very costly, in terms of energy drain. And in order for such a thing to operate it, effectively and efficently, certain energy fields must be synchronized to the ever changing temporal field displacement wave front as defined by rule....." Shendrydan was carefully gauging the chief's responses.

"Skip ahead a bit." Rontho said slowly.

"So when a polarity reversal is attempted it creates a sort of splash in the universal boundry layer, and a return to the point of origin is virtually guaranteed."

"I never knew there was a universal boundry."

Maybe the chief wouldn't take the bait. "Oh yes, very unusual phenominon. Only a handful of scientists know about it. But that's not the point here."

"So this wave is a kind of temporal backlash, so to speak?"

Aha, he did grasp the idea. "Exactly."

"When is it due back?"

He even reached the logical conclusion. Shendrydan knew he had him. "Within the month, sir. And if my calculations are correct we can ride the shockwave back to the point of total origin."

"And save Greyson Spyman. I never understood why he liked to be called that."

"He never did, sir."

"At any rate that's a splendid and wonderful idea. Get to work on fitting one to my touring car." He went back to examing his mallet.

Shendrydan's heart sunk. Rontho was clueless. "Perhaps, maybe one of those space capules we stole from the Americans, modified for the purpose, might work better."

"Yes, but it'd be a damn bit more uncomfortable, wouldn't you think?"

"But it'd be a political victory you could cash in on."

"No, it'll be my touring car or we don't go at all." He pushed Shendrydan to one side and lined up another shot. "But if we are going to catch that shock wave, you'd had better get to work right away," and with that he smacked a choquet ball out the door.

Doonk! "Hey! Watsum big idea?"

*   *   *

The bossman was filing his horns when the phone buzzed. "What is it?"

"Sir," his secretary said, "Agent 666 is here."

"Delilah, all of our agents are numbered 666. What's his name?"

"It's a she."

"It? Oh the cow, right. Send her in." The bossman screwed his horns back on his head.

The holstein cow plodded in and Delilah gently shut the door shut behind her. Her horns were long and sharp, ready to attack. She had a fat bell slung around her neck with 666 engraved on it, that clonged as she walked.

"Have a seat."

The cow just stared at him.

"I'm sorry, I forgot you were a cow and don't need to sit."

"I can sit if I want to," she replied.

"Good, I see your voice synthesizer is working fine. Nice touch to hide it inside the cow bell, by the way. I assume your other adjustments to life in H.E.L.L. has gone smoothly as well? Now what is it you wanted to discuss with me?"

"I thought you called me in."

"No," he checked his appointment book," Right now I'm suppost to be meeting with High Antibishop Lester but you know him, alway crusifing

138

people."

"So who called me in?"

"I'll see." He turned his phone on, "Delilah, who sent the cow in?"

"I did."

"I mean, who set up the appointment?"

"Oh, let's see, I think Lester did."

"Okay, back to work with you lazy woman." He turned back to the cow with a smile, "It seems like Lester didn't want me to have any free time. So how's the campaign?"

"I'm not running for office if that's what you're asking."

"No, I meant project Retribution Day. I've been stuck here on this backwater planet while all the action is taking place somewheres else more fun."

"Retribution Day has been moved back again."

There went his trip to the green sand beaches that weekend. "How far?"

"One month."

Will it ever get here? "Want a drink?" he pulled a bottle and two shot glasses out of a drawer in his crescent desk.

"No, I only drink muddy water."

"That's very interesting," he said pouring himself a shot, "To your ego, then," he drank. "You're not like the others."

"No, I'm not an ordinary minion of H.E.L.L."

"I suppose not." He put the liquor away then pulled a file from his desk. "This is your personnel file. Inside are all your records and promotions. Including your rapid advancement up to second chief of Propaganda. This remarkable ability of yours for diabolical mischef isn't all due the the fact that you are a cow, but I think instead to my brilliant application of the converter."

"I wouldn't know, after all, as you just pointed out, I'm just a cow."

"Good, I'm glad that's settled. Now tell me of the plan and all of its devious facets. Lester has kept me somewhat in the dark about that."

"That's because he's in charge and you're not."

"But now he's sent you here to fill me in."

"That remains to be determined."

"No intricate plot twists or confusing tactics?"

"I'm not at liberty to say. You should ask him yourself."

"Lester sent you here for a reason. So you had better start talking. What's this I heard about time travelers being captured on Deo 7?"

"They escaped."

"Escaped!" The bossman's face went white, "Why wasn't I informed?"

"Probably for the same reason you aren't informed about most things. It's no concern of yours."

"Escaped time travelers of no concern? Why they could wipe out our total existence in the blink of an eye." He blinked. "Whew, that was close."

"Their time machine was destroyed and they are stranded in a deserted region, so relax."

"Deserted region huh? Well they had best not cause any trouble or you might end up in the messhall, and I don't mean for a quick bite of lunch."

Besey ignored the insult. "Let me put your fear to rest. They have been bugged, brain washed, drugged, interrogated, and left helpless it the most desolate, out of the way place on Deo 7. They are more helpless than your secretary."

"That helpless huh? Was all that stuff done to them in that order?"

"I think I know why Lester asked me to see you now." She didn't bother to say because he was a total idiot; it seemed too obvious. "They arrived by temporal vortex and will return the same way they came, after the vortex bounces off some discontinuity in the future and returns to pick them up. Provided they're in the same place it dropped them off."

"How long will that be?"

"We have no idea. Could be tomorrow, could be yesterday. It could be never or long after they're dead."

"Why didn't you just kill them when you had the chance?"

"Why the H.E.L.L. would we do that for? We still don't know if they're fiend or foe. Besides, the nature of time does not allow flagrant violations of the continuum."

"What makes you think their fiends? I was brought up to kill time travelers on sight. You never know when your grandchildren from the future might show up and try to kill you."

"But these time travelers are from the past. Near the same nexus point as those enemy agents we've been tracking lately. They're connected somehow and we need to find out more."

"Blah blah blah." The bossman made little talking motions with his hand.

Besey glared at him meanacingly. Her eyes began to glow red. "Despite the lack of your reports, we know the enemy agent's ship has left this planet in route for Deo 7. So, Lester wants the codes to the spy devices you planted on them."

The beach suddenly became farther away. "But they weren't suppost to leave for another month. They must have learned of our spying somehow. Those bungling fools, Wilbur and Jake have goofed up again! This time they'll loose their suits for two months."

"They've been sent to Balidron for reconnaissance."

"Why wasn't I informed?"

"They're only under your command while on Rall Raul Beta. Now that the enemy agents have left, you no longer need to know. Now, about those codes..."

The junior grade bossman was frantically looking around his desk for anything he could blame this on. Aha, space banditos. You could blame anything on them since they denied everything and were incredibly unbelievable. "Yes, well the codes were stolen by a gang of space banditos but we've taken them into custody now. Here's the report." And he'd even managed to sluff off some extra paper work to boot. Green sand here I come, he thought.

Besey took the report and placed it her little fanny pack. "Well I guess that's all then?"

"Yes, now leave, you're making me hungry. And in the future you better tell me what's going on."

"Absolutely, when you need to know." The cow walked out secretly laughing to herself.

The bossman turned the phone on. "Dililah, get me Regrub Nueeq."

"Yes, Mr. Bossman. Just a minute, please." Click.

A rough voice answered.

"Regrub? Yes, it's me. How's my old friend?" He talked to the man for about an hour then turned the phone off. He rubbed his hands together in glee. That would take care of two problems at once: that enemy ship and Lester's plans of interrogating them.

There was a beep from the pneumatic behind him. It's clear tube extended all the way through his shark tank and ended right in the middle of the glass. More bills, he was sure but since he was in a decent mood he decided to read it instead of feeding it to the shark.

The return address on the rolled up letter said it was from YIG. YIG? Anything from them meant trouble. He was about to shove it back into the tube and hit the purge button but the thought of Lester getting mad at him again changed his mind. Carefully he opened the letter and read:

To: Bossman, H.E.L.L. Rall Raul Beta
From: Yuspurly Insurance Group
RE: Notice of overdue balance

Sir! Your account with us remains severly over due. In addition, our records show flagrant misuse of certain misappropriated funds for intentions other than those not directed. This memorandum is to inform you of the gravity of this situation. If funds totalling not more than and no less than 2.7 trillion galactic credit notes are not recieved by our offices in exactly one week of your reading of this memo, we wil be forced to take extreme action into our hands. IT is strongly advised that you do not take this lightly but comply with the most severe alacrity.

The Bossman's eyes rolled back into his head. He knew he should have purged it. That damn memo reading clause got him everytime. How did they know he'd read it anyway? He'd swept his office for bugs numerous times and only found the ones he'd planted himself to discourage others, who might try to bug his office, into thinking it was already bugged and they shouldn't bother.

His chair fell over backwards. He lay unconscious for a moment. When the junion grade bossman of Rall Raul Beta came to, he was staring up into the wide grin of a shark just on the other side of the glass. Did that shark just lick his lips? Sharks can't do that. He remembered the memo and passed out again. Hellish days for HELL.

Chapter 12: The Big Stink

The ship burst out of the wormhole and skidded around the planet ending up in a gentle orbit. All systems were normal. No pursuit craft were detected coming out of the hole behind them. The coast was clear.

"Planetary readings, Space-Bo." Rogicphil looked at the tiny planet below.

"1900 kilometer diameter, very dense core, and a relatively high gravity." Space-Bo sat with his eyes on the computer terminal.

"Ten percent higher than a same sized body of normal density." Plutoman added looking over Space-Bo's shoulder.

"Well, how much is that?"

".25 grav." Space-Bo said.

"With that low gravity how does it keep such a dense atmosphere?"

"I don't know."

"Computer?"

"Yeah.?"

"Well?"

"What.?"

"How does the planet have such a thick atmosphere with a gravity of only .25?"

"What.Planet.?"

"The planet we're in orbit around, nitwit."

"Hey!" Plutoman was irked. "Don't call my computer a nitwit," he steamed, "Only I can do that." He turned towards the terminal again demanding, "Tell us, you nitwit."

"The.Plantet.Does.Not.Have.A.Dense.Atmosphere."

"What?"

"The.Atmosphere.Is.Constantly.Escaping.Out.A.Hole.Over.The.North. Pole.As.Gases.Are.Released.From.The.Southern.Ocean.Which.At.This.Time.Of. Year.Is.Continuously.Pointed.,More.Or. Less.,At.Its.Sun."

"So the sea levels are falling?"

"No.I.Did.Not.Say.That."

"Explain."

"I.Already.Did."

Rogicphil sighed. He wasn't use to such ancient computer systems but being in such a low tech ship had kept them from being noticed so far. It was just something they would have to live with it. "How do the oceans keep from falling?"

"Replenished.By.An.Underground.Source"

"And how long will it last?"

"Do.Not.Ask.Me,.I.Just.Compute.Here." The computer finished.

The ship was coming around to the night side of the planet. It was basically featureless except for small clusters of piercing light. Just cities, Rogicphil thought, thinking the view was overrated. Pretty boring really. "If you won't tell me, then I'm just going to assume its irrelevant."

"It doesn't bother me any," Space-Bo put in.

"ALERT!ALERT!ALERT!" The ship's klaxon wailed out, "Enemy.Vessel.Approaching."

"What now?" Rogicphil knew an emergency when he saw one. "Shields up, full range scanners. By the way, this is a red alert."

The Galactic Tax Collection Cruiser, Leech, zoomed in for the kill. The Imperially grubby paws of its captain prepared for their parsimonious duties.

"Attention Unidentified craft," the Leech greeted them, "You are to willfully surrender any and all taxes imposed by your current status and standing in the Imperial Galactic Federation for services rendered unto yourselves and/or any participation members of such transactions or non-transactions as the case may be."

"Let's attack," was Space-Bo's solution.

"Burn their hides," was Plutoman's.

"Hold it," Rogicphil ordered, pushing them back into their seats. "Let me handle this. On screen, computer."

The pig nosed captain faced them scowling. "That hunk of junk you're flying there hasn't paid tax on parking fees in over 90000 years. For that alone you owe us twenty-four Mega-galactic notes. Pay up."

"But it hasn't been parked the whole time."

"That's just a fancy way of saying it's been taking up precious space, which as you know, is in short supply in the Galaxy right now."

Drat! He could get out of that tax by revealing the time traveling nature of the ship but it was too risky. Aha, he could finally pull the auditor trick he'd been working on lately. "Very well. If you insist."

Rogicphil went over to Space-Bo's computer terminal. "As I'm sure you are aware by now, I am Admiral Kosari Nedantuk of the 4371st Auditor's Squadron of Kleptonia Epsilon's Fast Accounting Division. Therefore I'm submitting all 90000 years worth of returns simultaneously. Please take special note of the doppler shifted depreciation schedules based on Galactic Laws 154.209.17BR through 10593,075.94WX."

"Huh?" Pignose was thrown off guard, but not for long. He dashed to his computer terminal in order to throw the out-of-order switch but it was too late.

Rogicphil was typing the coded deductions into the terminal faster than lightning. "Are you getting all this?" he asked peacefully as he uploaded yottabytes of bogus data.

Inside the other ship, computers began spewing out sheets of legal jargon. The captain couldn't collect his taxes now; the computers were so clogged with Rogicphil's returns they could barely keep the ship's life support systems running. He punched himself for not getting to the out-of-order switch in time. Ouch.

Pignose was fuming. Spit foamed at his mouth. "I'll... have to get back with you on this," he stammered.

"When you're done sorting things out in a few years, we'll be back to collect our refund which, with 90000 years of compounded interest based on our estimated payment of 25 cents, should be several quintillion space creds. Thank you," Rogicphil said cutting the connection. "One tax collector down."

"Whew, that was close." Space-Bo was surprised. Every time he tried to get deductions he just ended up paying more than the original amount. "How'd you do that?" he asked.

"One semister at community collage studing junior accounting, and fast fingers saved the day. By the time they figure out how to weasle out of the refund, our mission will be over and we'll be long gone."

A few hours later the various teams were assembled in the shuttle bay. Rogicphil was reading off his mission timetable, "Okay, team one, Funky Chicken and Space-Bo, you have shuttle Omega. Team two, Greyson Sofecstat, you have shuttle Zeta..."

"Hold it," Greyson said, "How can I be a team all by myself?"

"..Team three, Plutoman, you get the shuttle in the forward shuttle bay. And no more slacking off this time. Big D is watching remember."

Plutoman grumbled but kept his mouth mostly shut.

Rogicphil continued on as if he hadn't heard their protests, "Team four consists of the tallest members on board to act as a home base."

Outrage erupted from the tallest twenty-seven members of the crew.

"Team five, the Clergy; Joe, Manuel, Bufgoo, and Hack, will ride down to the surface in shuttle Alpha with my team." Rogicphil checked his watch as the protests multiplied throughout the shuttle bay. "Your instructions are either in your team shuttle or here on the ship. You are to report once a day to the ship on your coded commlincs. Any questions?"

Everyone stopped protesting so they could think about what Rogicphil had said. They thought for a few seconds but no questions popped into their heads. No one had the foggiest idea of what they were actually doing there in the first place so it was only natural no one asked anything.

"Good. Then let's get rolling."

They all shrugged and hopped into their shuttles. One after another they zoomed down to the planet.

Rogicphil got behind the controls of his shuttle. In the navigators seat was the bear. Ranger Joe sat with the Clergy in the cargo hold. Systems engaged. Thrusters activated. The shuttle leaped from the ship with a silent roar (No sound in outer space). The bear was feeding coordinates to the console. He wondered how the others were flying their shuttles without navigators. (Plutoman was secretly following Rogicphil, and Greyson used a old surveyor's trick to home in on large land masses.)

Their course was set for Balidron, capital city of Deo 7. Rogicphil was tracking the spaceport tracer beacon on a little round green cathode ray tube. "Estimated touchdown twenty minutes" he told the guys in the back, "This will be the most dull part of the trip."

Bufgoo and Joe looked at each other and smiled. Manuel began pulling instruments out of Hack's bag. They rocked the twenty minutes down to Balidron.

Rogicphil lost control of the shuttle several times as his headbanging interfered with his (non)piloting.

When the shuttle finally broke through the dark high clouds they were greeted with a wondrous sight.

It was night and the city lights were turned on, mostly because that was the cheapest time to turn them on. It didn't matter that only the janitors were in the buildings to enjoy the light. Massive blotches of light set in well defined borders. One could easily see the boundaries of the metropolitan center of Balidron, for outside the boundaries there was only darkness. The lights had no order to them, just random patches here and there.

The city was on the coast of a huge bay where a large river fed into it. A number of islands were formed by the river as it split and meandered to the sea. The center of activity seemed to be a fat peninsula at the twin mouths of the river. And at its heart there was an island the shape of a side of beef, not that anyone on the planet knew what real beef was.

The beefy island sported the most and brightest light. But most astounding were the needle like buildings piercing the air. On average they were taller than the island was long. One building stood alone among these scrapers of the sky. Everyone on that side of the galaxy had heard of the Superlatives Industry Building, it was even in the Heinous book of Galactic Records. It was dubbed the first space-scraper in the galaxy when it was constructed in 100702. Many debates about whether or not it really scraped space ensued but no one could come up with a good enough definition of space to make any of the arguments mean anything to anybody. The definition of scrape however had been defined to the three millionth decimal place.

"Wow!" Ranger Joe exclaimed, starring at the streak of light that shot up into the sky, "How tall is that thing?"

"Well, it's got over eleven thousand stories in it."

"What's it all used for?"

"There's a restaurant on the top ten floors, a business section near the bottom, and a bunch of empty space in between."

"Cool."

"The extra low gravity allows them to grow so big."

The shuttle continued its decent to the spaceport. Other shuttle-like craft could now be seen zooming into the spaceport from other places around the continent.

"Don't we need clearance to land here?" Ranger Joe asked.

"Yeah, so why don't you call in. Don't forget that we're on a secret mission."

"Secret mission, gotcha!" He flipped the comm switch and began talking with his best impression of a CB trucker, "Mission control come in, good buddy."

Rogicphil bopped him in the back of the head. "Let me," he said, "shuttle XDB4Q requesting clearance to land."

A voice responded saying, "Sorry, due to technical, economical, and social difficulties we can no longer bring you control tower number six flight assistance. If you have any questions feel free to write us at your inconvenience and thank you for using Stupid Recorded Messages," and clicked off.

Rogicphil just shook his head and said to no one in particular, "You had better get into the back and get strapped down, this is going to be fun."

"Pretty hairy huh? Okay hotshot, don't get us killed before we even get there."

145

"I'll try not to."

Ranger Joe went to the back and braced himself as best he could. But nothing happened and the shuttle landed smoothly. "What's the use of flying by the seat of your pants it you make a smooth landing?"

Rogicphil got out of his seat and faced the guys in the back. He ignored Ranger Joe's question as he didn't have the heart to tell him it was on autopilot all the way. "Wasn't that fun boys and girls? Ready to go outside now?"

"Yeah, sure, okay, fine, whatever," was the combined response.

"Are you absolutely positively sure?" He grabbed the latch.

"Yeah, uh-huh, cool, okay, whatever,"

"100 percent?"

"Open the hatch already."

"Okay, but don't say I didn't give a chance out."

"You didn't and you aren't."

Rogicphil knew what to expect but the others didn't. Destiny had given him a pre snort of raw unrefined deo ore to acclimate him. Even so, he wasn't ready for it when it hit. When the hatch opened the Balidron air rushed in with a stifling crush. That's not the best way to explain it but the simplist. When you are on a planet that produces deodorant for an entire galaxy you can forget about using your nose as a sensory organ.

The shear strength of the deo smell nearly knocked them out cold. They were reeling and shaking their heads for the first few minutes as their noses either adjusted or ran away to join the space circus.

"What's wrong?" Hack couldn't understand what was making everyone upset.

Manuel leaned out the hatch and puked.

"Come on, everyone out." Rogicphil shoved them all out onto the pavement, "You'll get used to it."

"When pigs fly!" Clergy Joe cried.

WHOOSH! A black and white shuttle craft buzzed them. It pulled up at a high g-force, then joined a swarm of other shuttle craft zooming around the sky, all looking for an empty parking space. The crafts consisted of only three or four different brands as far as Rogicphil could tell.

The spaceport / parking lot stretched for a kilometer in all directions and was completely filled with shuttlecraft. It was a single level affair and hence very inefficient and extremely annoying to pilots looking for a place to park.

"I think that cop was upset that I slipped into his parking place," Rogicphil said trying to be funny.

"How did you manage to land in all this?" Ranger Joe asked looking around in wonderment. "And I thought parking my blazer in Denver was bad."

"Luck," Rogicphil replied with a shrug.

"Luck?"

"Luck," Rogicphil admitted smuggly, "and.... some skill."

"Hell, it was damn good skill. I just wish you had made it a little more interesting on the way down, that's all."

"I thought you said this planet had low gravity." Bufgoo tried jumping up and down but only managed to make himself look like he was doing squats.

"Artificial gravity generators under the city."

"But what about the spa police? You said..."

Rogicphil noticed a piece of paper stuck in the window of the shuttle right next to them. Assuming it was a parking ticket he snatched it. It would be good cover when the cops showed up to ticket him for parking illegally.

Instead of a ticket it was a note addressed to the Clergy. "Crap." He unfolded the paper and read the contents. "This says the Clergy are suppose to get inside and push the red button."

Clergy Joe's nose was bleeding and he jumped inside the strange shuttle without a second thought.

Bufgoo snagged the note away from Rogicphil. "Let me see that. No one knows we're here. Not even the spa police." He read it, checked the back, then looked up at Rogicphil with a Your-Guess-Is-As-Good-As-Mine look. He stuffed the note into his mouth and climbed aboard the shuttle. The rest of the guys piled in behind him and someone pulled the hatch shut.

Poof! The shuttle disappeared. Rogicphil, Joe, and the bear were instantly sucked forward into the empty space left behind by the short lived vacuum. Joe and the bear looked a bit dazed.

"Watch out!" Rogicphil shouted as he jumped back towards his shuttle pulling the other two out of the way at the same time. Just then a green shuttle zoomed into the empty space. The driver got out and immediately and before anyone could or wanted to ask him questions, flew off again using a jet pack.

Rogicphil moved them along to the backend of the shuttle. In the trunk they found three sets of trench coats and dark sungoggles. "When you're on a secret mission it's best to be inconspicuous."

Joe as well as Rogicphil were natural's with the trenchcoats.

"No, no that's not right." Rogicphil was commenting on the bear standing on four paws wearing a trench coat. "You need to walk biped style like this." He pranced around in a little circle exaggerating his arms in a full body cast imitation.

The bear ignored the insult and attempted to rear up on its haunches but could only last that way for a little bit before froomping back into a four pawed stance. It pointed to its back in pantomime explination.

"Oh I see, your backbone is setup the wrong way," he looked at Ranger Joe, "Any ideas?"

Ranger Joe had an idea he remembered from an old caveman movie he once saw. He whispered the idea in Rogicphil's ear so the bear wouldn't hear. Rogicphil liked the idea. He grabbed the bear from the front and gave it a tremendous bear hug cracking its back in the process.

The bear said, "Errr?" but continued to stand on two legs. Gingerly it tested it's new ambulation mode and was very pleased with it. Surprisingly it could now walk bipedal. It patted Rogicphil on the shoulder in gratitude.

"Let's cruise."

They found a quickvader a few rows over and stepped in. The doors closed and they pushed the button for the used vehicles level which was just one floor beneath ladies uncompromisables. The quickvader moved down into an underground complex that underlaid the entire parking lot expanse. Being a quickvader it didn't bother to stop for snacks or bathroom breaks. A few minutes later the doors opened onto a show room floor.

"You know," Joe said, "I think I'm getting use to the smell."

Rogicphil shook his head no and looked around at the strange vehicles on display. "We need transportation, and like right now."

A salesman showed up. A huge toothy grin was on his face like it had been nailed there. "May I help you gentlemen?" he grabbed their arms and rushed them over to a red car with a black railing running completely under it and up the back. "This is our newest Fezamotion model forty-two. Isn't it delish?"

Rogicphil let Joe handle the salesman. He needed the experience despite his over the top fantastic performance during training.

"Uh," Ranger Joe said, "Where are the wheels?"

"This model only has one steering wheel, sir."

"Uh huh. So how do you manage to talk with that stupid grin on your face?"

"I am a graduate from Neazben's College of Salesmenship. I have a minor in excrement eating grins."

"Great. Now if you want to sell us a car it had better have some wheels, and I mean wheels." Joe squatted down and did a double fist pump on the last 'wheels'.

"I understand not all of us are at the social stature to own a magcar. But I have just the thing for you." The salesman took them over to a strange six wheeled vehicle. "Now this fine old thing is the new Kyrillian Xezzon. We just got a backorder shipment in last Twos-day (and fifty years ago)."

Joe smelt an insult somewhere. But he had to admit he liked the car. An hour later they were in the four man, six wheeled Kyrillian Xezzon ground car. It had alternating red and blue stripes down the sides and at 34,000 negative jeedudes the Xezzon wasn't for the wealthy (remember on Deo 7 you want to get rid of your money). It had fifty-two gears, four for each of its thirteen fusion cylinders.

They were trying to maneuver the car out of the underground, ground car only, parking zone but weren't have much luck. Behind 'the Wheel', Joe was getting flustered. "But that one way sign has three arrows."

"Why don't you let the autodriver figure it out for you." Rogicphil suggested, pointing to the shiny green button on the console, "That's what it's there for after all."

"There's only one thing in this universe I'm good at and that's driving." Joe ignored the sign and drove straight over it. A one meter drop followed. The car scraped over a curb and onto an express ramp. Another car zoomed down the ramp narrowly missing them. The back wheels were caught spinning over the curb. Joe slammed the third gear shift, which was positioned just in front of the rear exit, down with a grunt. This caused the center set of tires to grip the curb with a surge of power vaulting the car up and over.

"Hey, I think I can get use to three axles." Joe put the stick into second then tore off down the ramp. Black streaks trailed the car as it roared through the spaceport's underground tunnels.

There were lighted arrows on the pavement and the concrete ceiling that showed the way to the exit. Traffic grew thin as they approached a split in the tunnel. A sign directly over the split said: This way or That way. A wrecked ground car lay smashed in a pile beneath the sign.

"Don't you hate it when you can't make up your mind?" Rogicphil watched the wreck pass by on the right.

The bear gazed out the rear window.

They approached a black tunnel that claimed to be the exit. Joe's foot pumped more fusion pellets into the combustion cylinders. The Xezzon jumped into the tunnel and a few seconds later flew out it onto a wide black plane of asphalt.

It was a different plane than the first one they had seen in that technically it wasn't part of the spaceport and no one was allowed to park on it. In the distance, thin pointy buildings lit up the night sky. Only a few other ground vehicles could be seen driving around on the black tarmac.

"When they say exit, they meant it," Joe was looking for lanes but couldn't find any, "We're out in the middle of nowhere in a huge city."

"Most people around here take the Maglev system."

"Point the way."

"Can't. Only maglev vehicles can run on it."

"So what are we doing in this thing?"

"Going in circles."

Joe realized that was true. Without lane guides he reverted to tracing out the go-cart tracks of his youth. At that particular moment he was going through Little Indy, his favorite track at age six. "Sorry," he quickly got back to driving in a straight line.

"How long do you think it'll take us to get to that small building over there?" Rogicphil pointed to a twenty-five story apartment complex that covered six acres.

"Oh fifteen or twenty minutes if you want to be bored. Five minutes if you *are* boring."

"Arrrr," the bear said.

Rogicphil did some calculations in his head. At their current rate they would still be puttering around Balidron in thirty years. And Gladerunners hated to putt around.

"Stop the car," he said. It stopped. "I'll be right back, so wait here." Rogicphil stepped out of the passenger's side only to be assaulted with a fresh wave of deo-air.

"Ug!" Joe hadn't realized how much the car cut out the hedious smell. He leaned over to pull the door shut behind Rogicphil. But it suddenly opened again, this time a strange man poked his head in. "Shut the door," he told the stranger.

"Want five jeedudes?" The scruffy faced individual asked.

"Get lost," Joe pushed the head out and shut the door again.

The door opened again and Rogicphil hopped in. This third wave of deo smell had Joe's head swimming.

Rogicphil had some ticket stubs in his hand, "I got us some rooms at a fancy hotel in the inner city." He gave a stub to Joe, and one to the bear. "These are your room tickets, lose them and you get kicked out."

"Okay," Joe pocketed the stub, "Is that the hotel there?"

"No, we're not even in the inner city yet. The hotel itself is about forty or fifty kilometers away."

Joe, being American, didn't know what a kilometer was and so thought the hotel was just a short walk away. Besides he didn't know how fast the Gladerunner could run either. "Why didn't you just have me drive you there?"

"I needed the exercise. I've been eating too many crappy pies lately."

"Oh," Joe started the car going again, "Which way?"

"Forward. The hotel is called the Yahitt Regale Royal Hotel. It overlooks the innercity's Central Park." Rogicphil pointed to a flashing tower near an approaching building. "That's a maglev depot. Drive to it. Inside we can catch a magbus to the hotel."

"What about the car?"

"Luggage."

"What?"

"We'll load it as luggage. Every passenger is allowed three tons of luggage."

Joe raised one eyebrow and squinted his other eye.

"How do you think people go grocery shopping? They take their cars along to put the groceries in."

Joe cruised the car into a tunnel and up a ramp. They were now in a parking garage. Ramps took vehicles to other levels at regular intervals. Joe spotted a ramp that said: Magbus Loading. The car roared up the ramp.

At the top were large ground trucks unloading cargo into a long black tube about fifty meters long. Windows ran the length of the tube and people could be seen sitting inside.

"That's a big bus, bigger than a jumbo jet!" Joe exclaimed. The bear was in awe also.

"What's a jumbo jet? Sounds like a tax deduction."

Joe didn't answer.

"Wait here, I'm going to see if we can ride as cargo." Rogicphil opened the hatch again. This time, gratefully, the odor wasn't as strong.

"It damn sure has enough room." Joe watched as Rogicphil went up to an important looking guy holding a cattle prod. They exchanged words. The guy gave Rogicphil some slips of paper. Rogicphil handed him something in return. The guy took it then gave it back and patted Rogicphil on the back.

"Well?" Joe asked when Rogicphil got back into the car.

"He'll let us on."

"What were you doing? It looked like he was bribing you."

"He was giving me money to let us on."

"This negative money sure is strange." Joe drove the car into the place the guy pointed out, a little space between stacks of crates in the magbus's under belly.

The cargo doors slammed shut. Rogicphil turned on the car light. "Now we wait."

The bear curled up in the back seat and went to sleep.

Seven minutes later the cargo doors opened again and Joe asked "Is this it?"

"No, this is just one stop in Hezslop, I couldn't get a one way trip."

"What's Hezslop? Sounds like breakfast before you vomit."

"Just a suburb."

The doors closed after cargo had been unloaded and replaced with fresh baggage. The doors stayed closed for twenty more minutes.

As the doors opened Rogicphil said, "This is it. You'll have to drive fast, since we're not expected, and the security people might get upset."

"No problem." The tires squealed. Joe spun the car around with a reverse broady then kicked it into high gear. Dock loaders scurried for cover as the car crashed through cargo waiting to be loaded.

"Don't exit the building. Find a sign that will say Central Park Island Tunnel."

"Done." The car jumped a medium, crossed four lanes of oncoming traffic, and barreled down a ramp that said: 'Do Not Enter, Oncoming Traffic Only.' Cars coming up scraped the concrete walls to avoid them. A quick U-turn into a side passage got them going with the traffic flow again. "There's a sign.."

"..That says The Island Tunnel," Rogicphil quickly added, "We want Central Park Island Tunnel, it should be just a little further."

The underground street took them to a cut off with the right sign. Joe took it and the car went down into the tunnel. A few minutes later they emerged out of the tunnel into another underground street.

"Find an exit."

Joe found one. They were on another black asphalt plane. "Don't these people know what dirt and grass are?"

"That's what they have parks for."

"But there's no contrast. You can't appreciate the parks unless they're next to some crummy apartment buildings or a burning lake. All this monotonous urban crap makes me want to puke."

The bear growled in agreement.

"See that water off to our left? That's the river we just went under. Follow it until you come to a building on the right with big red flashing lights."

The hotel came into view. It was about thirty stories tall and a kilometer long at the base. On the side in the biggest neon sign Joe had ever seen, were the letters: WELCOME SUCKERS!

*   *   *

The success, if you want to call it that, of Deo 7 is due solely to it's scoscrub mines. Deo-ore, raw scoscrub, is mined from only one small area of the planet near the military city of Scogo. The entire Scogo peninsula, which the city with the same name is not located on, was once owned by Nepp Pitts, a logeater rancher, who first discovered the stuff. He was trying to get rid of some pesky gopher like pets of the native Alpuka's with a HomeMade* mininuke, but blasted into a big pocket of bubbling deo-ore. It caused such a smell that he attempted to sue the Lugietorp Colonial Agency, who had sold the land to him in the first place. The stench, you see, made his logeater herds go crazy and attempt olympic class dives off some nearby high cliffs. They made wonderful aerobatic and acrobatic moves while jumping but always botch their landings.

The Agency refused to pay him compensation (this was before negative money came into use) and instead insisted that Pitts pay a tax on each logeater that jumped off a cliff according to how high the cliff was. Disgusted at the bureaucracy and the smell, he sold his entire ranch to Avery Kebber, who made a fortune in the deodorant business.

Note to lazy readers: the above is a very important plot device and shouldn't be ignored. But since it isn't ever fully developed in either the rest of this book or anywhere in the sequel I regret to inform you I have to spill the beans here. H.E.L.L. is a Lugietorp corporation bent on revenge against Deo 7 for getting rich off the Deo mines it foolishly let slip through its fingers. - the editor

Scientists had since figured out that Deo-ore is the remains of prehistoric swampgator brains that turned to mush in an ancient peat bog. They were never able to produce a synthetic Deo-ore at a cheap enough rate to be economical, and so when the ore runs out there will be no other alternative. Recent estimates indicate that 13% of the original deposits has yet to be extracted. -From the banned book, Deo 7 History (circa 101573)

The Yahitt Regale Royal Hotel looked shabby on the outside but was surprisingly clean, in a rude sort of way, on the inside. In fact the Deo smell was almost completely absent.

A bellhop put Rogicphil's suitcases full of pointless electronic gear on a hovercart and entered the luxury quickvator. No one paid attention when the bear got on the quickvader too. Their room was on the 42d level of section X. The ride lasted twenty minutes and they were served peanuts and cocktails by the bellhop.

"Thanks Sunny, " Ranger Joe (RJ) said.

"My name's not Sunny, it's Wimble."

"Then why is Sunny printed on your shirt?"

"That's the bellhop motto. It stands for Service Utilities Not Negotiable Yet. But that's okay, I've been called worst, liverwurst that is." Wimble offered a drink to the bear who stuck his muzzle in the glass and lapped it up. "You guys must be offworlders."

"No," Rogicphil didn't want to blow their cover, "Just some shoe merchants from Carallid."

"Oh right, you must be here for the big shoe convention this weekend."

"That's right, the big one."

The 42d came up. They went out into the hallway. On the ceiling were moving handles that lazy patrons used to get to and from their rooms with.

"This way," Wimble grabbed one of the moving handles and was pulled down the hallway with the hovercart following, attached to his other hand.

While RJ and the bear grabbed handles, Rogicphil leisurely walked along beside them even though the handles had quickly accelerated them up to eighty kilometers an hour. A kilometer and a half down the hall Wimble let go at their suite. RJ let go, stumbled and tried to get up when the bear crashed onto him.

"Uuuf."

The bear got up and adjusted its trench coat. Wimble breathed on the door handle and the door labeled X42-1234 unlocked before him. Impressed, they followed him in. The room was a hexagon shaped thing with two doors opposite each other and various consoles on the other walls. There wasn't any furniture to speak of, just gray and red plaid carpeting.

"Where do we sleep?"

Wimble unloaded the suitcases from the hovercart, "I'll set the room up. Three single beds I assume but I'm not making any judgments here."

"Yeah."

Wimble went over to a console and pushed a button. Machinery whirred somewhere out of sight then three minature beds popped out of the wall. "Don't worry they'll expand to full size when soaked in 3 degree water for two hours."

RJ touched one, "Ouch!" It burnt his hand.

"Over here is the window," the bellhop went to a wall with a large blank television screen on it. He flipped a switch, a nighttime skyline flashed up. "You can change perspectives with this dial," with a twist the skyline changed. He blurred past an assortment of idyllic pastural scenes, circuses, waterfalls, cityscapes etc... The only common element they all shared were generic people performing some kind of rude gesture: mooning, birding, french chinning etc... "This button opens the window." A gust of deo aroma gushed out of the screen.

"Close it please." RJ's eyes were watering.

Wimble took a deep breath, "Ah..." then closed the window. He pointed to one of the doors that had a chomping mouth on it, "The kitchen is in there." He pointed to the other door with the picture of a man sitting on a toilet, "And the restiterium is there. "

Wimble took out his wallet, "I think that about does it." He displayed the entire contents for Rogicphil approval.

Rogicphil shrugged and took it all. It didn't matter how much of a debt they built up here, since the mission was temporary.

Wimble gulped, "Gee thanks mister. I know I'm not supposed to appear greatful, the hap and all, you know. But I truly am most appreciative."

He turned to leave but Rogicphil stopped him. "Hold on a second. Tell us about how you opened the room door back there."

"Oh, you really are offworlders huh? I knew it. Everyone, except offworlders, knows that a person's unique breath signature is the best way to secure things. The breath locks have been standard on Deo 7 for decades." He bowed with a click of his bellhop heels, said "Nubalork," turned and left.

*   *   *

Meanwhile in a service duct in the same building.

"Now don't goof this one up." Wilbur handed Jake the electromagnetic and/or sonic screwdriver.

"How was I to know they had advanced scouts out in the desert?" He took the screwdriver and finished installing the bug to room X42-4321.

Just don't let the local bossman get mad at us again or she'll send us to the frying pan."

"Don't you mean bosswoman?"

153

"This is a male dominated evil organization. What do you think?"

"Never mind. Trust me for once, huh. This bug monitors everything in the room with 100% susceptibility. Even the brain waves of the people inside it. Plus the field is totally undetectable. Don't worry."

"That's what you said last time."

"Well, who's idea was it to grab that cow?"

"Yours."

"Nnnnnnn...." he growled handing the screwdriver back.

"You see, it's your fault every time," Wilbur put the device back into his red patent leather hand bag.

"What about the time you put ocher jelly on Lester's secretary's toast?"

"Yeah, well who switched the lids with the grape jelly?"

"Um who brought black pudding to H.E.L.L.'s annual picnic? And I don't mean the dessert kind."

"You, the same person who dropped a gelatinous cube into the Raul Rall Beta bossman's fish tank."

"Oops forgot about that one."

"Come on. Let's get out of here." Wilbur crawled out of the service hatch. He landed on the floor rolling to a sudden halt across the floor.

Jake hopped out behind him. A security guard spotted them, and ordered them to sublimate. Jake grabbed Wilbur off the floor with some effort. Together they ran down the hall with the guard hot on their tails.

*　　　　　*　　　　　*

In the morning Wimble came back to make sure everything was alright. No one had taken all his money before, as a tip. He wanted to see if he could get rid of another fast buck or two.

RJ was in the restroom, "I can't get these stupid despensors to work."

"Which ones?"

"The toothpaste and shampoo ones."

"You have to stick your ID card into the slot. Each costs -12 jeydudes per squirt, plus tax, which for off worlders is 119%."

"But we aren't off worlders, remember."

"Tax is 219% for locals, so as far as toothpaste goes we're offworlders." Wimble came in then.

"Hey, " Rogicphil looked up from absorbing the morning paper, the Baligrit. "Good to see you again."

Wimble cringed. He wasn't use to people being polite, even off worlders. "I just came by to see if you offw... uh I mean shoe merchants, needed anything. I can adjustment your window or recycle the newspaper for a fresh one."

"I told you we're not offworlders. But this newspaper *is* getting a bit stale." Rogicphil pulled the gelatinous blob off his forehead. It left a nasty purple stain behind. He flicked it across the room at Wimble.

The bellhop deftly caught the blob with one hand. "Ah come on, who are you fooling? Anyone with ID card status of RICH doesn't stay in hotels."

"Why not?"

154

"Because they own them. And there was that thing about not knowing what a breath lock was. Besides you guys look offworld a kilo away."

"Give us an example of what you mean."

"Like when that guy there couldn't stand the smell of fresh air. Offworlder all the way."

"Name's Joe, by the way," RJ said holding out his hand to shake. "But you can call me RJ. I don't know why I just said that."

"Please to uh meet you," Wimble recluctantly shook hands with the overly polite fellow. At least that other guy with the newspaper had a bit of a snarky attitude.

"Give us another," Rogicphil insisted.

"Big shoe convention. You thought big referred to the convention and not the size of the shoes."

Rogicphil cringed. Being the Graderunner he should have got that one right.

Just then the bear came out of the kitchen, eating some green poo. It was dressed in a tightfitting bathrobe with its still wet bear fur sticking out everywhere.

"Him. If he isn't an offworlder I'm a fotnozlixel."

"What's that?"

"I don't remember anymore but I looked it up once."

"Hmmm, I guess there's no use in pretending anymore. How would you like to loose a fast buck?"

"Nikstlits and Elpmur! How?"

"Just show us how to blend in so we won't be recognized."

"I can do that easy but how much are you willing to take?"

"Thirty neg jeedudes a day?"

"When do I start?"

Chapter 13: The Hap

Plutoman didn't bother to read his dossier in the shuttle. It would have told him to scout the cities of Baldac and Nadcapac, both near Balidron, for any signs of the cow's dirty work. He would have been relieved to discover that those cities were in ruins and totally devoid of any clustering of population. It would have been a nice place to be distracted.

He knew Rogicphil was sending him on a wild goose chase. Worse yet, it might be a set up to strand him here and steal his spaceship. Well, Rogicphil and his cronies would find out soon enough that Plutoman couldn't be tricked so easily.

He locked onto Rogicphil's shuttle coordinates and followed him down to the surface in stealth mode. He had made sure his personal shuttle had such a feature just in case something like this came up. Rogicphil probably wouldn't have noticed him anyway without the stealth mode; he was such a gullible blockhead afterall. No wonder that D Stiny fellow had choosen him to do his dirty work. Yes, Plutoman would keep the steath mode on long enough to find out what they were really up to.

At the surface he double parked the shuttle on top of someone else and left the stealth mode on so he wouldn't get a parking ticket. The air traffic had been terrible and he had nearly collided with several other craft. That Rogicphil must have planned it that way just so Plutoman would have trouble tailing him.

Plutoman followed them down into the underground vehicle showroom. They were buying a car with the help of a stupid looking salesman. When they weren't looking he jumped into the luggage compartment to hide. Soon the engine started. They were leaving. He was bumped around inside the trunk for twenty minutes before the car stopped. He heard the hatch open and then close.

It was too muffled inside the baggage trunk to make out any voices. He lay there for almost an hour before he heard the baggage compartment hatch being unlocked. He would be found out now. He decided to confront Rogicphil directly when he was discovered. Confront him with the business end of a plasma pistol!

The hatch opened. Someone was standing there looking at him. It wasn't Rogicphil, it was some smelly lady with puffed out orange hair. She screamed, threw a bag of groceries at him, then jumped back.

He pushed the stinky stuff off of him and was working his way out of the trunk only to be smacked with a stalk of broccoli.

"You muecat! You slimy piece of nuclear waist!" the lady yelled at him as she continued to flail him with the overgrown broccoli.

"Don't you mean waste?" he said dodging the blows.

With that she smashed the whole thing into his face.

Plutoman ran for cover behind another car but she didn't follow him. He was in a some sort of a parking garage. The lighting was pretty dim but he was use to it having spent many years on the bleak surface of Pluto.

The trunk hatch slammed shut behind him. The lady was yelling more profanity at him from over at the car. She hopped in and sped away.

Tricked again! Rogicphil had deliberately planned to have that fiendish woman take the car that Plutoman had hid in. Now the trail was lost and he'd have to start all over looking for them.

He walked out of the garage into a super market. The majority of the people inside were on little six wheeled carts, waiting in long lines to check-out. All the lines twisted around, maze like, confusing him about how to get out. Eventually he found the end of the lines where a lone check-out clerk was ringing up customers on an outdated mechanical register. Behind her was a swinging double door labeled, Entrance Do Not Enter. He went through it.

Past the doorway was a little room with a quickvader. He stepped on and pushed the sideways button. He zoomed in that direction for ten or eleven sideways light flashes until a stockboy noticed him and kicked him in the rear end.

"Have a nice day, fotnozlixel breath." the stockboy said coldly.

Plutoman was steamed. He pulled out his plasma pistol intending to pumping a few rounds into the stockboy's soft underbelly. "Don't eeeeeever do that again!" and pulled the trigger. Er... splug, the pistol was out of plasma again.

The stockboy said, "Ack!" and fell over.

Plutoman scratched his scarred up bald head then kicked the boy off the quickvader at the next stop then continued going sideways. "Hold on," and the quickvader stopped at his voice command. "Oh, at least it's good to know something works around here."

The quickvader didn't talk back.

Plutoman thought he was in heaven. Then he got over it and said, "Back up a bit." The quickvader took him back to the last stop where the stockboy had been left.

He peeked out of the quickvader into a grocery store stockroom. The stockboy was picking his nose in the corner completely oblivious to everything around him.

Ha, ha! Plutoman thought and snuck inside the stockroom. He found what he was looking for, left some things he didn't want anymore, and hurried back inside the quickvader.

This time it went perpendicularly sideways and stopped a few levels over at another parking garage. At the curb there was a bus loading 170 people. A sign on the side said, Maglev Station Scuttlebutt. Aha, that bus would take him to the mass transit system where he could begin tracking Rogicphil down.

One of the people in line for the bus was smiling and telling the others nice things. It was really odd because the guy wasn't dressed very nice. In fact he was dressed rather mean as far as Plutoman could tell.

"Hey butthead, why don't you scoojack out of here?" An oxlike fellow standing next to the smiling person said.

"I'm only trying to be friendly," the man replied with a smile as he picked his nose with a switchblade knife.

"The Hap! He's got the hap!" the man who had said 'butthead' said, "Quick, don't let him escape!" The other people in line panicked and tried to get away but accidentally ended up chasing the happy yet mean looking man who

157

was now trying to flee.

The man ran for the quickvader where Plutoman was. The others shouted not to let him escape. So Plutoman unloaded a fresh round of plasma at the guy. This time thanks to his pilfery at the stockroom it worked.

"Thanks," the ox said coming up to Plutoman. The ox looked down at the man lying in a squishy pool of red gel. It was pretty disgusting actually, or rather ugly disgusting which sounds better, uh worse, if you said it out loud....

"He had the hap alright," the ox continued, "See the smile on his dead face." Sure enough the guy had a peaceful grin on his mean looking face.

"No problem," Plutoman holstered his blaster, "Anyone that happy deserves to get wasted."

The ox now looked at Plutoman and immediately puked on the spot. "Eeeu, who asked you, freak? You lame excuse for a maefu," the ox wiped his mouth on a dirty sleave.

"Your mother eats combat boots for breakfast." Plutoman tried to shake the ox's hand.

The ox shook hands and said, "Well, nubelork, jeupert face."

Needless to say they parted friends, if you could call it that.

"Nubelork," Plutoman waved as he watched the people finish loading onto the bus. As it pulled away he shot the back tires out. There was another bus coming around the bend just then to replace the one that had just pulled out. Quickly he jumped onto that one. It too was bound for the maglev station but had an 'Express' label on its side instead of a 'Skuttlebutt'. The people inside eyed him suspiciously as he sat down, but when he sneered back they left him alone.

The bus didn't bother stopping at the curb. The driver had noticed the broken down bus in front of it and decided it'd be more fun to blow by them while flashing the finger at the other driver who was outside cursing at his melted tires.

Plutoman watched the other bus as he passed it, its driver choking on his bus's fumes. Plutoman stuck his head out the window and yelled obscenities at the people inside the other bus. They waved and rude gestured him back as his bus steamed past.

Somebody tapped him on the back, "Id card."

Plutoman turned around, "Sure," he held out his hand for an id card.

"No, YOUR id card, freak." the conductor shouted.

"Get lost."

The guy pulled a weapon out. "Are you going to give me your id card, you blood sucking excrement, or do I have to execute you?"

Plutoman dug into his pocket and gave the guy the id card he had taken from the stockboy. The conductor took it, touched it to a hand computer, then returned it with a negative five jeedude bill.

A portrait of a mean looking guy was on the note. It scowled when Plutoman looked at it. He scowled back. I love this place, he thought.

*   *   *

Back on the mother ship Annie was petting Plutoman's dog Bagidol.

They were all gathered around the cute doggie in the messhall. The dog and the parrot, Pauli, were left behind while their master was on the surface. They had never been petted or treated with kindness before and welcomed the new experience. At least that's what they told Annie.

"You poor puppy, Plutoman was never nice to you, was he?"

The dog sheepishly shook his head up and down in agreement. Anything to get attention.

Nell, a blueberry red headed girl dressed in torn blue polkadot and striped jeans, looked on with scepticism, "You don't think that stupid dog understands you? He's just been trained to look pathetic and helpless so some poor schmuck like you will fall for his scam."

Bagidol growled at her.

"Trap," the parrot said, "It's a trap."

"Yeah, Plutoman's trap. And you're taking the bait."

"Let's give the dog a test," Anita said, "To see if he's really as smart as Annie thinks."

"Have him design a fashion collection," suggested Ima.

"Make him play a guitar," this came from Ellen, the electro green haired punk rocker. They all ignored her.

While the dog amused the girls with some poorly drawn doodles and caricatures of renaissance masterpieces, the bird hopped on out of the mess hall, unnoticed. She snuck into a service closet, so as not be seen, and called Plutoman and the computer in a three way call on the secret intercom built into the wall.

It wasn't actually a secret that the intercom was in there but nobody suspected that something so useful would be in such a boring place at all and half hidden by mops and brooms to boot.

Plutoman wanted to know how they were all doing and if they were getting enough food and attention. The computer complained that it never got as much attention as those two stupid bio units. The parrot counter argued that the computer was randomly adjusting the thermostat just to mess with them. Plutoman shut them both up with his yelling and then gave them his important instructions. The computer didn't think it was such a good idea but the stupid parrot fell for it whole heartedly and agreed to do the talking.

She poked her bird head out of the closet to make sure the coast was clear then hopped and half flew up to the bridge. She quickly found the control panel to send the mayday and/or distress call. It wasn't long before....

rrrrNNT! rrrrNNT! rrrrNNT! RrrrNNT! The ship's alarms were going off. The girls looked around confused at first but when the dog made the proper 'follow me' motions they all rushed up to the bridge to see what was going on.

On the screen was the Leech. The galactic tax collection vessel was closing in fast, and it didn't look like it could be stopped by deductions this time.

Someone was yelling at him. Plutoman looked up to see the bus ID taker, standing there tapping his foot.

"The joy ride is over," the ID taker said, "Now let's hear some grumption."

"What?" Plutoman looked around the bus. It was empty. Sunglow was coming in through the windows. He must of been asleep awhile.

"Come on, scoojack, will ya. I've got to have this thing decontaminated before 9xm."

Plutoman got up and stumbled to the front of the bus. His eyes were still fuzzy with sleep. The driver gave him a swift kick that sent him flying out the door. The bus roared off in a cloud of ozone fumes.

"Scums!" he shouted at the receding bus.

Something didn't seem altogether right. He rubbed his eyes. His vision cleared up. He was on an elevated maglev track. It was 7 meters wide and 200 in the air. All about him lay Balidron, spread out like a bunch of lego blocks set randomly everywhere.

The track continued west for as far as he could see and curved to the southeast going the other way. To the north he could make out some water glittering in what he assumed was morning sunglow. A thick cloud of bluish haze rising from somewhere to the east kept the sky interesting. He hated direct sunlight anyway. Good riddance to the sun and all those who would bask in its life giving beauty.

Rogicphil was behind this. He had set it up to have him stranded on the maglev track for an uncertain doom. Well, Plutoman would show him. At any minute his pets would come flying down in a shuttle with news that they had taken back control of the star cruiser with the help of those gullible schmucks of the galactic tax collecting agency.

He began walking east. The major industrial centers looked like they were located there. Every once in a while he'd have to hang on to the edge as a magbus or magcar zoomed past at incredible speeds.

He continued on for about a few hours when he noticed a wall of some sort ahead. It ran north and south off into the distance both ways and rose right up to the track. It shimmered metallic hyper yellow. A quarantine zone?

Blaster shots! They were coming from the ground. He lay down at the edge and peered over. Far below were some mangy wild animals sniffng around a gapping hole in the wall. Wait, those were people not animals. Same difference. They were fighting a deadly battle. Blaster rifles blew combatants away on both sides of the giant hole in the wall.

Then a strange thing happened. A whistle sounded somewhere and the fighting stopped. The rag tag soldiers put down their weapons and pulled out lunch boxes. Guys and gals who moments before were trying to kill each other were now eating lunch together, telling jokes, and gossiping as if none of it had happened.

An ambulance pulled up. Those who could still walk helped load the mangled bodies of those who couldn't, inside. The ambulance left at a leisurely pace and the enemies went back to lunch. After finishing up they got their weapons out again. The whistle sounded once more and they were soon back to killing each other.

. Plutoman furrowed the skin where he eyebrows once use to be. He continued walking past the wall and the fighting. It was getting near noon and the sun was threatening to burn a hole in blue haze. He needed to get under shelter just in case it did. Watching those guys eat lunch had made him hungry so he stopped and lowered himself over the track's edge. There were some

160

cables running back under the track to a support column 10 or 20 meters away. He made his way to the column, hand over hand along a cable.

There was a service hatch on the side that he kicked in. He slipped through onto a metal grid platform. An open shaft went down into blackness. He found a panel on the wall with some buttons. Pushing a down arrow he heard the whir of machinery. Soon a quickvader arrived and he took it to ground level. A metal meshed door led to a typical Balidronian asphalt plane.

A short walk south brought him to a building labeled Hezslop Hotel. Whoever Hezslop was he had a run down hotel. No windows, no decoration, just a flat dull surface. Perfect, just what Plutoman needed.

Inside a nice rude man at the register desk got him a room. He grimmaced while handing Plutoman his room ticket. Plutoman snarled as he went to the quickvader. The quickvader operator tore his ticket then happily took him to floor 19. He found his room and quickly bolted the door. Enemies were everywhere.

The room had a sink and toilet in one corner, a food dispenser in a second, a hard sponge-like board masquerading as a bed in a third, and a helmet setting on a stand in the fourth. Nice and drab. Perfect.

After stuffing his face from a food spigot on the wall, he looked at the helmet. There was a black wire that come out the back. It spilled onto the floor in a coil before going into the wall. On the top was plastered a notice. It said: WARNING! State law requires that 30% of any time spent in a cheap hotel and 10% of any time spent in an expensive hotel be devoted to tuning into the commercial channel. Violators will be persecuted.

Hmmm, a holo TV head set! Very interesting. Without any thought for his life Plutoman plunked the helmet on his head. Instantly he realized it wasn't a simple holographic television headset; no it was something more.

He found himself sitting in a lone chair in a darkened studio. There was a stage with several people milling about. They were wearing straight jackets while trying to balance glasses full of acid on their heads. How he knew it was acid he didn't know.

A voice suddenly came out of nowhere, "Welcome late viewer, this is the People Do The Darnest Things To Get Rid of Money Show. Our contestants are trying to burn each other with acid right now..."

Plutoman thought it was boring. He wished he were somewhere else. "Just push the button to change channels," another voice said out of nowhere. He found a remote control on the chair's arm rest. He leveled it at the stupid people and pushed the button. The stage disappeared and he found himself in a video arcade. Boring. No sense in watching people play video games if he couldn't play them himself. The video game channel is an interactive channel," the voice said.

He tried it. Finding a Space Ranger game he tried to play it. "Insert ID card please," the game said.

"Bleorg you!" he changed the channel. Click!

"Welcome to today's episode of The Day After Yesterday Show. Our panelists Miah Farrgot and Rhod Colltrane will interview a man who claims he can saw a cinder block in half with an electric banana peeling device..." Click!

He saw different patterns of designer static. Click!

161

A documentary exploring the reasons that robots went out of style. Click!

Name that Sneeze! Click!

The Bobton test pattern. Click!

People Who Kill. Aha something interesting at last.

*   *   *

Splook ! Plop. Green goo oozed out of a hole in the wall. Plutoman scooped some out of the bowl he was holding under the hole, and tasted it. Bland, formless, smooth. It was okay for toothpaste and much better tasting than the stuff coming out of the 'food' spigot. He turned the dispenser off then sat on his bunk licking the stuff up.

His ID card ejected from a wall slot and landed in the bowl. He looked at the dirty finger he was eating off then using the ID card instead, he continued to cram his wrinkled mouth.

The bowl grew empty so he drop kicked it across the small room. He checked his watch. 23:42xm. Hmmm he had wasted most of the evening hooked up to that damned brain link helmet. He yawned and lay back on the bunk. What to do?

Oh yeah, he suddenly remembered the secret task he'd given his parrot. He pulled the hotel phone over to his face. It attached to his head as his fingers punched the numbers into the air dialer.

"Hello." his computer answered.

"Put Pauli on."

"She.Is.Having.An.Argument.With.Your.Dog. Bagidol.Right.Now."

"So did the distress signal plan work?"

"Except.For.The.Space.Pirates."

"Space pirates? What space pirates?"

"The.Ones.That.Destroyed.The.Leech."

"Destroyed!" Plutoman's artificial heart sank.

"Do.Not.Fear.We.Were.Able.To.Retrieve.The. Device.You.Wanted."

"Whew. That's a relief." Hmm, better than he had planned actually. "Where are they now?"

"Chatting.With.The.Girls."

"WHAT!? Yoooou stupid computer. What did I tell you about letting space pirates on the ship?"

"Nothing..Besides.They.Are.Not.Technically.On.The.Ship."

That sounded better.

"Maybe."

He ignored that because it didn't make any sense. "What about the girls?"

"The.Girls.Are.Alive."

"Good, I can still sell them as slaves on Io."

"Affirmative."

"Great!" His plan was almost complete now, "Okay, listen closely. With the leech out of the way there's nothing stopping us, uh... me from leaving this planet. It's a nice vacation spot but more important things need to be done

162

else where, namely the distruction of Earth."

"But.Rogicphil..."

"Did Rogicphil program you? Does he repair your fuses? Does he supply you power? No. Then never mind what he said, I'm in charge here now. It's my spaceship and we are shipping out."

"We.Can.Not."

"Don't you tell me what I can't do."

"But.."

"Shut up and listen. Recall all the shuttle craft except mine. Have that one pick me up at my present coordinates."

"Okay..But.Where.Are.You.?"

"Some cheap hotel in a sleazy little suburb called Hezslop."

"Never.Heard.Of.It."

"Listen, just home in on the locator beacon implanted in my elbow."

"I.Shall.Try.But.You.Need.To.Be.In.Line.Of.Sight."

"Don't worry about me, just do it. And hurry."

"What.About.The.Girls.?"

"Keep them distracted til I get back. Bye."

"Oh.Oh..I.Really.Think....."

"Shut-up!" Plutoman pulled the phone off his head disconnecting the line, "Stupid computer. I never should have given it artificial stupidity."

So Rogicphil wanted to play hide and seek, eh? Well Plutoman would let him play his games with the satanic cow if such a creature really existed at all. Plutoman was boosting it.

Bamm Bamm! Someone was pounding on his door. In reflex, he quickly stuffed some hotel linens in his pockets.

"Open up, Police! We know you're in there."

"I'm not the police you moron." Plutoman unholstered his blaster.

"No we're the police and we're arresting you."

"You must have the wrong guy," better to play along at first, "I checked out hours ago."

"No, you're the guy. You didn't watch at least 30% of the commercial channel while using the brain link."

"That was the guy next door. I heard him laughing."

"No one has checked into that room for over a week, besides everyone else in the hotel has left. Now open up before we start shooting."

That did it. He pumped four rounds into the door. Then when he heard four thuds he stepped out into the hall.

Blast! Zooooooooeeee. Beeyow! Blaster fire whooshed over his head. Despite the four bodies of bellhops laying at his feet, he had appearantly missed someone. That someone was wearing a police uniform but was at the end of the hall and now running the other direction. The cop had been waiting for Plutoman to exit but when he had fired he had been expecting someone taller and had aimed wrong.

Plutoman would teach that guy a lesson, not in algebra but basic physics. Before the officer could make it to the fire escape Plutoman had shot several wads of plasma at him, one of which connected. The guy fell back against the corridor wall with his eyes crossed. He uttered an "Ug" then fell down into the fire escape.

Plutoman was down the quickvader in no time flat. Not bothering to take a tip from a still living bellhop he rushed out of the lobby. High up in the air he could see his shuttle circling. He waved at it but it wasn't smart enough to notice. He needed to signal it somehow. An evil idea streamed into his shrunken brain.

He ran back into the hotel. At the desk he asked the clerk, "How many rooms do you still have available and is this hotel powered by a fusion or fisson reactor?"

The man didn't answer until Plutoman took a -10$ bill from him. "We have a 30 gigawatt fusion reactor in the basement with 342 full life support hook ups but they're not currently being used because of the big shoe..."

Plutoman was hurrying into the quickvader before the clerk could finish. The 'vader took him to the basement where a thick wall of concrete blocked off the entrance to the power room. A few blasts would solve that.

A small hole was carved out of the concrete just big enough for Plutoman to squeeze through. Beyond was a small room with a glowing blue barrel in the center with a thick black cable running out of it into the ceiling. It was the fusion reactor and someone had left the lid off. Fun, fun, fun.

A quick blast severed the black cable in two. Sparks jumped the gap. Plutoman carefully grabbed the severed end from the reactor and yanked out a meter or so of it. He kicked open a panel on the side of the barrel and stuck the crackling wire in.

Almost instantly the thing started to shake and flare up. Plutoman lost no time getting up the quickvader and out of the hotel.

The desk clerk called out after the short funny looking guy running past him, "We even have our own big shoe support equipment on the premises."

Plutoman made a mad dash across the asphalt plane to get as far from the building as he could. The last bell hop and the clerk were hot on his tail.

KA-BOOOOOOOOOOOM! A shock wave hit sending him flying ten meters. He hit the pavement with a roll and covered his eyes from the flash. One moment ago there had been a cheap sleazy hotel sitting by itself now there was a geyser of radioactive flames shooting high into the smoggy sky.

What the? That clunky reactor wasn't the kind to blow up. It should have just send a wave of hard radiation in all directions. Even that stupid shuttle wouldn't miss that. About time other people got some RADs too, Plutoman thought as he looked up expecting to see the muzzles of twenty officer's blasters. But he was all alone.

His shuttle skimmed the asphalt plane then landed a few meters away. Plutoman picked himself up and stumbled to the craft.

Right before he hopped in he turned to the stunned hotel employees and said, "Well it's been real, it's been fun, so keep truckin'." The shuttle zoomed off in a trail of fusion vapor.

164

Chapter 14: McCows

Greyson had no trouble flying the shuttle down to the surface. He simply had the on board computer link up with the mother ship for an autopilot. He didn't realize that the shuttle was perfectly capable of having it's own autopilot function. Just as well, since the shuttle's autopilot was tired of having to do everything itself. Didn't anybody care about the joys of flying manually anymore?

The trouble started when he touched down.

His instructions were to search the four southern cities for signs of the cow's whereabouts. The first city was Hicksville. A consolidated city of over 10,000 small farming communities in a 30 kilometer radius currently boasting over 8 million people. The biggest small city on the planet.

He landed on top of a huge barn near the city's lone train depot. The roof was barely sloped and the shuttle didn't seem about to tip over, so he cut the engine and cycled the airlock. He was very close to what appeared to be the center of that quaint small town metroplex.

High overhead was a hot glowing yellow orb that illuminated the area. He knew it wasn't the sun since it wasn't that hot, too small and too close. It made the whole area seem bright and sunny.

Some farmhands were sitting on the edge of the roof of the barn throwing spitballs down to unsuspecting passersby. They were wearing strawhats with white sashes indicating they were on guard duty but Greyson didn't know that at the time. They spotted him landing and were now rushing over.

Greyson popped some miniture filters into his nose cavities and rolled the window down when one of them came up to him. "Can I help you?" Greyson always thought it best to appear in control when the situation involved hostiles.

"You cain't park 'ear."

"But I have a permit," he reached into his BOG pulling out a gas ejector. He sprayed the guard. Pissssst!

"Tahm," the guard/farmhand said calling the other over, "Come 'ear, hee hee," his legs started wobbling, "Get ah lode uhf thee-us."

Tom, the other one, came up to the window. "Wuts gahn on 'ear?" he said.

Pissst! "Hee, hee, thet is nahce, taint et?" They fell over laughing. By the time Greyson had disembarked, they were out stone cold and slowly sliding down the metal corrugated roof.

He connected a suction cup dart to the edge of the roof and lowered himself down the side of the building. The idea to use the quickvader to get down off the roof never occurred to him, that would be too easy. About halfway down there was a row of windows on the side of the barn. Some were wide open and some where boarded shut. He slipped into an open one, tying off his cable to the window crank. He was in someone's office. There was a desk there and some hand written papers, which were scattered about everywhere except on the desk.

Putting on his reading glasses he read some of the papers. They were invoice slips for something called cow-juice. Aha, already he had found traces of the satanic cow's presence. The orders were for huge quantities of the stuff. Gigatonne quantities by the looks of it. The cow must have a serious drinking problem, he thought, or at least is planning to stay a very very long time.

Greyson went over to the rickety wood paneled door. No sounds were coming from the other side and he didn't see anyone through the cracks, so he slipped out. It was very dim now but he was use to that and didn't bother to switch his reading glasses to nightvision mode. He felt a splintery railing a meter forward and empty space beyond. It must be an elevated walkway. He followed the railing down the walkway until he found some stairs that led down. They creaked terribly, despite his best efforts to remain stealthy. He estimated he had gone down five stories when he reached the bottom.

Sniff, sniff. Something sure smelt rank. Step by cautious step he eased his way along. What was that? He stopped, listening slowly. Heavy breathing. He wasn't alone. Good thing he hadn't turned on his flash light yet, or he might have been spotted. He continued on, trying to be more silent. More breathing. He was surrounded, he knew it.

The farther he went the more numerous and heavy the breathing became. They were closing in on him. Any second now they would be all over him. Hundreds of loud, rank smelling, breathings attacking him.

He couldn't stand it any longer. He flipped the switch on his nightvision reading glasses so he could at least see what was about to attack him. Huh? That didn't make any sense. All he could make out were glowing infrared cubes.

With all his courage he willed his hand to flick on the flashlight. "Aaaah! Cows!" Row upon row, upon row of smelly cows. Stacked twenty rows high they were. Cubic, legless cows forming walls round him. He quickly switched the flashlight off.

Nah, he thought, those aren't cows. He turned the light on again and a cow head mooed him in the face. He stumbled backwards, slipped on what he thought was a cow pie and fell to the smelly sticky floor. The stench was terrible even with his nose filters. He'd trained himself to withstand the deo smell as part of his preparations for the mission but no one had told him about this. Now the other cows were starting to moo too. A roar was building up.

With his agent trained reflexes he popped a couple of earplugs into his ears before the mooing blew his eardrums. He plucked his flashlight out of the muck of a different nearby cow pie and shined it on the first cow that had mooed him. There were two tubes going into its nose. One green and one yellow. The green one was pumping something into the cow, the yellow one pumping something out. He now knew what smelled so bad. Stamped on the side of the cow's head was a serial number. It said McCow No.# IB42-3327-JW89.

Greyson did a quick calculation on his wrist watch. By the size of it, he estimated the total amount of McCows in the barn/warehouse to be around 45,698,000,000,000. Wait a minute, did he forget to carry the one? That number didn't seem right. At any rate, it was a lot of cows. The Hicksville people must really dig Micky D's.

He flipped the light off, picked himself up and hurried down cow alley. Twenty minutes later, after wandering aimlessly around the barn he got tired and had to stop. He was next to a side door and peeked out of it into a dirt paved alley that ran the length of the barn. No one there. He wondered if the farmhands were still on the roof. Oops.

They had been sliding down the roof last time he checked his memory. Had he remembered to duck tape them in place to prevent them from falling to their certain deaths? He remembered thinking about doing that but didn't actually remember doing it. Too late now to worry about it. Kind of like shrodenger's cow, uh scratch that, cat.

Across the alley was an identical barn. Up and down the alley as far as he could see in either direction there were duplicate barns. Probably all filled with McCow or maybe McChickens or McWallabys. Who knew? Well he certainly didn't care at any rate. He was here to find *the* Cow.

Whoa! That was a freaky thought, he thought. What if these were actually satanic cow clone bodies? She was building an army to take over the planet, scratch that, galaxy, the entire universe even. Or maybe not. He needed a better view to find out.

Overhead he would have heard the sound of a backfiring flying space pickup truck. Keer-pow it chugged as it flew over the barn he was closest to. He noticed it despite still having his earplugs in. Aha, hovercars, so they finally got around to making them in this future.

He kissed his suction cut dart gun and fired straight up. It connected with the undercarrage of the pickup and soon he was sailing over the little farming megalopolis. Mostly he saw cow barns punctuated by an occational grain elevator and a mega silo or three. But interspersed with the barns were small patches of mottled looking pasture. There were narrow gauge rail tracks criss crossing the pastures. He waited until he was directly over one and hit the dart cable release.

He landed on an elevated pasture covered with patches of dead grass. The fall jarred his nose filters loose and he didn't see where they landed. He held his breath as long as he could but it was no use and eventually he took in a deep breath of farm fresh air and almost choked.

Quite unexpected he found he could hear better as well. His earplugs must have fallen out at the same time. Now he could hear the sounds of all the noisy ground vehicles that sped by on express ways and ramps surrounding the pasture.

There was a parking lot over to the right with several strange looking six wheeled pickup trucks. Even more strange were the cars with no wheels at all. Greyson decided to stick with the wheeled variety. He crossed the pasture, passing several McCows that were riding cute little flat cars on the narrow gauge rails, jumped a low stone handbuilt wall and walked up to a blue streamlined vehicle with a silver lightning bolt stripe running down its side.

Amazingly his 21st century lockpick worked fine on the door so he helped himself to the car. If after 90,000 years someone can't figure out a way to properly lock cars they don't deserve to keep them. He didn't realize it but in Hicksville people didn't bother to lock anything, as everybody was a neighbor and they all knew each eight million of themselves.

The controls were a little different than he was use to. The gas and break were hand controlled, and the steering wheel was on the floor with two plates attached to each end for the driver's feet to rest on. So it appeared these Deo 7 people were a bit backwards afterall. He got the hang of the controls and in no time flat was on the express way heading north-east towards the train depot.

The traffic signs indicated that he was on Holstein Avenue. On the left were some of the smaller huge buildings. On the right a huge grain silo with the letters FUSION embossed on its side. He took the exit leading to the train depot. Greyson parked on level three. He didn't bother locking it up. He followed a crowd of simple folk into a revolving wooden handcrafted doorway. They were getting in line down a long smelly corridor. This must be the line for the train, he thought. He was wrong.

When he got to the front of the line he discovered he was actually in line for an express Mikey D's restaurant. A short chubby lady with buffed hair and a tablecloth plaid head scarf stood behind a counter staring at him. Her mouth was partially open and her tongue stuck out.

"Mahy ah heulp yu?" She asked with a slobber.

Greyson bluffed, "Uh, one to go."

"Whun wat?" the zombie woman replied.

"One of your specials."

"Whuch whun zackly?"

"The standard I guess."

"Mayhk up yor mahnd."

"Hurrahy et up sonny!" Someone yelled from back in the line.

"Um,...uh..." When in doubt think! That was his motto. He looked up at the menu on the wall he hadn't noticed earlier. Aha! "McBurger A and a large grape drink, to go."

"Ets awl ta gho," she said pushing buttons on her register, "Thus es uh spress Mecky dees, yah hair." She held out her hand.

"Oh, sorry," he handed her his Rogicphil issued ID card.

She put it in a slot in the register. The machine sucked it up with a slurp. A bag fell out of a slot in the ceiling onto the counter. "Thu-hank yu, drihv thrawoo pahlase," She said shoving it at him.

He didn't have time to ask what had happened to his ID card. He barely managed to grab the bag before the floor opened up underneath him, sucking him down with a slurp.

Greyson landed in an octagon shaped feeding room. It held a couple dozen or so hillbilly looking patrons all stuffing their faces between belches.

He fell right into a chair/table contraption that automatically belted him in for safety reasons. Annoyed, he tugged on the strap.

A fat kid at the table next to him laughed. He wasn't wearing a seat belt. In fact, the safety device looked down right scared of the fat creature sitting on it.

Greyson ignored the fat kid and reaching into the bag, he pulled out a disklike object, a cylindrical object, -10$ jeydudes, and his ID card. Whew! He was afraid he'd lost that to the greedy cash register.

His order was printed on the bag along with the prices, several obscure taxes and a few rude and crude advertisements. They would have been rude and crude to him had he known anything about futurist life in the country.

The disk was a mushy hamburger affair. The greasy cylinder held a murky purplish fluid with the viscosity of nose goo. Both reeked of a strange spicy flavor. He tasted the stuff. It was horrible, not indigestible, just horrible. But the weird flavor lingered, a bit addictive really.

After he finished he realized he had just eaten one of those McCows with the green and yellow tubes sticking in their noses. He stomach churned at the thought and he needed to belch. He did.

The worst part wasn't realizing he was eating a McCow but rather that the burgerthing might have been a clone of the satanic Cow and might eventually turn him into one of her minions.

beeb beep beep beep... He looked around. beep beep beep... Where was that coming from? beep beep beep... he looked down at the table. It was flashing words on a little pop up screen. It said: Thank you for eating at McFood! It seems you are very pleased with our food. By your belch, measuring 6.5 on the Helm scale, we see that you are a fine connoisseur of quick food. And in gratitude you are given a coupon for your next meal here. A little piece of paper appeared out of the edge of the table. It said, Coupon against One Meal.

On the back, in fine print, were the words: This in no way allows anyone a free or discounted meal at any participating McFood restaurant for any reason what-so-ever. It is intended for promotional use only.

Greyson tried to push the coupon back into the slot, but it wouldn't take it back. In fact it just spit more out. Disgruntled, he let them fall to the floor. He was about to leave when a nasty idea struck him. He found an old syringe at the bottom of his BOG and filled it up with the purple goo. Three jiffy squirts up the coupon dispenser slot later and Greyson was sure no one else would ever get coupons from the infernal machine again.

He got up, looking for the exit. The seat belt had automatically released him when it sensed the pressure building up in his bowels.

There were two doors side by side on the far wall. The left door had the figure of an oversized man on a toilet on it. The right door, the figure of a plus size woman on a toilet. There weren't any other ways out so he assumed patrons had to exit through the rest rooms, or rather rester-teriums as they called them on this planet.

He headed for the door with the man on it. But as he got closer he noticed a thin red ring around each figure with a thin red slash running diagonal through them. The universal nullification symbol. Were the signs telling him no men and no women, or occupied and not occupied? Either way he could end up in the wrong room and an embarrassing situation. He couldn't ask the other people in the octogon dining room; that would blow his cover.

He went back to his table not wanting to look stupid just standing in front of the doors to the restrooms trying to make up his mind as to which door to go into. He would wait to see someone go in or come out.

But someone else was in his seat. Early worm gets eaten by the bird. What now? The fat kid on the next table over was still stuffing his face but was still watching him too.

Over in the corner were a group of three larger than average plus size women. Maybe he could sit with them, there was an empty seat there after all. The women looked strange somehow. They all had long blond hair, hairy arms, extra thick eyelashes, and were all drinking McFuzgaloid beer and smoking Fuzgaloid cigars. That is a little strange.

One got up and went to the door with the figure of a woman on a toilet. Aha. The door opened and another woman of the same strange sort stepped out. The two said hi in deep baritone voices, and the first went into the restroom. The other woman went back to the table with the others and sat down.

Those women weren't women, they were cross dressing men! Greyson was still without a clue. He didn't know if the ring and lines were no-ifyers or occupied symbols because of the hairy women / cross dressing men switching places in the doorway. Either they were dressed up and not playing the part, in which case the sign would mean no women, or they were playing the part and going into the wrong restroom on purpose. Or maybe they really were women and didn't care which door they went into because they were such bad asses. Either way he was still lost, confused, and stupid looking just standing there.

People were beginning to stare. He'd have to make up his mind quickly or blow his cover. He would have to suck in his gut and just pick a door. Hoping for the best, he boldly stepped forward toward the doors. Just before reaching them he winced and turned around. More people were looking at him now. What would Frogman do? No, Greyson thought, what would Spyman do.

Bluff. He pretended to be checking for his wallet. He walked slowly to the other end of the room looking under and around tables as he went. He was hoping for someone to either go in or come out of one of those two blasted doors.

A 100% pure woman slapped him in the face when he looked under her table. Nope nothing there.

He reached the other end pretending to look shocked. He pretended searching for his wallet again when he realized his wallet really was gone. He looked around under more tables. It wasn't anywhere. Surely no one had dared to take it, it's stupid to steal money in a negative currency system, right?

He looked back to his original table. Stuffed in the seat was a very large man eating from a very large bag stuffed full of McBurgers. The guy looked at him with a wicked evil grin.

Greyson blinked his eyes. He knew where his wallet was. The big guy knew also and belched loudly in his direction.

When in doubt think, and those who doubt have little faith, but faith the size of a mustard seed can move mountains, and whoever believes that something the size of a mustard seed can move a mountain must be a rocket scientist, but rocket scientists can think, so it must be true. With this new found truth to back him up, he marched up to the large man with a firm commitment of determination.

"May I have my wallet please?"

The guy just chuckled.

"Could you please get off of my wallet?"

The guy got mean. He pushed Greyson into a nearby wall. Slam! At the same time a restroom door slammed open. He tried to look toward the doors to see who was coming or going, but the big guy pushed him back into the wall again, and held him there. This called for action.

He tried a karate chop to the guy but just hurt his hand. The guy continued eating with his other hand and completely ignored Greyson's infantile attempts to get free.

His gas sprayer was handy but it would blow his cover if he used it. Maybe confusion would work. "Please, I need my wallet or, or..uh I'll go blind," Greyson pleaded with the guy, "Yeah, the batteries in my artificial eyes are running down and I need spare ones from my wallet."

The big guy looked at the freak he had pinned to the wall beside him and belched loudly.

A fowl stench permeated Greyson's nostrils. No more please, "I'll go blind. I will." He remembered a trick he learned in college to make his eyes go in opposite directions. "I'm loosing sight. Right now I'm going blind," he made his eyes wander around in opposite ways.

The guy let go and gave him a swift kick to the rear which sent Greyson stumbling to the doorways. His vision was messed up and so he couldn't tell which door he was really headed for. Fortunately for Greyson it was the wrong one, of course.

Greyson's eyes got unstuck when an extremely hairy woman began beating him over the head with her purse. He stumbled out of the wrong restroom into a throng of people. The lady followed yelling husky obscenities and shouting "Octohooga!" after him as he melted away from her into the crowd.

There were little green signs hanging from the ceiling indicating what lane went to what location. He got in the pedestrian lane marked: To Trains. It led to a platform where everyone waiting for the train huddled on either side of a tract that lay in a wide trench.

The train came in from the north with a loud scream. Then rushed by in a torrent of air and ozone. Ozone? Why did he smell ozone? The blur slowed and finally stopped. Each car was 10 meters long and had two sliding doors on each side. They opened, people flowed out, and Greyson was pushed forward to a door by the crowd. As he stepped on he noticed what looked like landing gear holding the car off the track.

He found a seat next to a tomboy looking girl with a paper bag on her head. Two holes were punched so she could see out. The doors closed and the train started with a jerk then slowly built up to blinding speed."That's a nice gun you have there," Greyson noted.

The girl unholstered the hi-tech weapon and pushed his nose up with it, "Yho maykin fun o' mae?"

"No, I just.."

"Yor an awtcyder awrnt yho?" she eased the gun back a few centimeters.

"No, I mean.."

"Wale, taek theeus!"

Greyson saw her finger tense up. He leaned sideways, and a bright blue beam burst out of the gun. A control panel on the front wall was hit sending sparks onto the passengers. Power flickered, the car lurched to the left a bit then came back. Power was restored. A few of the other passengers grumbled but on the whole no one seemed to notice.

When the lights came back on the girl was gone. The train was slowing down and Greyson had to hold on to the seat to keep from sliding forward. He looked around and saw the girl behind him heading to the door. She still had the paper bag over her head.

He wouldn't let her get away, not after trying to toast him. He slinked up behind her but just as he was going to hit her over the head she spun around.

She leveled the gun at him. "Say yor prahayrs idget," she said in a cute sort of way.

SMASH! CRUNCH! SCRAAAPE! Greyson flew forward through the cabin smacking into a pile of people. The lights cut off again and the people began to grumble once more. The train must have hit something. The police were sure to arrive and they'd ask questions. His cover would be blown for sure. He had to get out.

He picked his way over lazy passengers sleeping on the floor until he felt the door. It was jammed shut. No problem, his laser wrist watch could cut the lock in a few seconds. He struggled to push the door apart and climbed out.

A faint glimmer of light was painting the eastern horizon. Dayglow was only an hour or so away. He hopped up to the top of the car to look around. The closest building was a kilometer to the south and had the name Portobellys handpainted in board fence red on the side. The S was painted backwards.

Onlookers were starting to mill around the derailed train now and he could smell the poice getting closer. He spotted the paper bag headed girl heading for the Portobelly's building. He took off after her and a short jog later came up to a loading dock on the side of the building. She had slipped into a side service entrance door and he quietly followed. He found himself in a food storage room of some kind. Freeze dried packages of green and brown goo lined several shelves. The girl was nowhere to be seen.

Greyson picked up a package. It said Nutriment K-10 on a little label near the button. He sniffed. No odor. So he tore the top open. He sniffed again. Nothing. Useless, he thought, but stuffed it into his BOG as a clue anyway.

He found a door that led to a dimly lit hallway. Very slowly he eased the door open. Then... rrrRRRNT! rrrRRRT! Alarms. He must have set off a scanner somehow. On the ceiling were foam tiles so he pushed one aside and climbed up into the service ducting. He slid the tile almost shut leaving a hole to peek out.

The alarms continued as people were running up and down the hall now. They were all wearing the same kind of white overalls. He had to act fast, soon they would find him and the gig would be up.

He dodged several light fixtures before coming to a side passage that branched to the left. He made the turn and hurried along. At the end of the passage he slammed into a pneumatic tube junction box. Rubbing his head he found a little cubby hole behind it. It would be a safe spot to hide for at least a little while. Hide from what?

His flashlight revealed a list of tube extension numbers and connection orders scrawled in fat pencil marks on the side of the box. Greyson found his stethoscope and quickly pressed it against the junction box with a smile. He tried to tap into the tube of what the listing said was Yegor Shnolstlenc, Chief Administrator. Luckily it was being used at the moment.

"Whut due yho main ahm no gud?" someone asked.

"Da dum 'larms whent ahf tu layt."

"Bhut thos ahwn thu trayn got pikked uhp."

"Yu dang igit, whee dun los tu mainy payshints."

"Ah'm sahry bous."

"Surry don' cuht et."

"Whut da yho whant mae ta due?"

"Keeup thet shearuf bizy til Iz cin figur whut ta due."

"Ohkae bous."

Then the tube went dead. What was going on? People were being taken off the derailed train? The sheriff wasn't suppose to know? Whatever was up it sure sounded evil. And he knew who or what was behind it. The satanic cow!

The cow, it seemed, had somehow known Greyson was on the train and had it deliberately derailed so that he would be captured by the goons whose building he was now in. Or maybe not. There wasn't enough evidence to be sure.

He had to find that adminstrator and get him to devulge the whereabouts of the cow, if he knew it. He tried to get up but couldn't; he was too exhausted. He had been awake since before they'd left Rall Raul Beta. He'd get to that administrator soon enough but not right then. Greyson needed some sleep. He was unconscious before he knew it and dreamed of the strangely attractive tomboy wearing a paper bag over her head.

Chapter 15: Megaball

In a society that uses a negative money system its people have a hard time dealing with positive figures. So it's only natural that the planetary past-time, Megaball, also is based negatively. In the game, of which there are almost thirty teams, the object is to cause the opposing team to gain more negative points than they cause your team to get. There are various ways to do this.

Megaball is played on an oval track-like field with fans packed in towards the track as well as inside the ring packed out facing it. Consequently, this allows for more people to unload -$ on. Long ways the track is 125 meters from end to end and 100 meters end to end the short way. The track is 25 meters wide encircling what use to be a dead zone or out-of-bounds oval 75 by 50 meters but where more fans are now packed. Outside the track there is another out-of-bounds extending two or three meters before stopping at the mushed faces of fans pressed up against the transparent aluminum barrier.

The Megaball itself is roughly the size of an ancient volley/cannon ball. It is solid black weighing 1 kilogram during regular season games and 2 kilograms for championship games. It has a thick rubbery polymer shell so it doesn't hurt too much when a player gets hit with it. But an explosive core can and often does kill a player when it hits the ground. Built-in space capacitor based sensors know when it is in contact with a person so it will not explode if landed on or pounded into the ground. Only if a player goofs up though, and drops the ball, boom, no more player. Or if it's thrown at him and he misses catching it, boom(*).

The game is played during 6 periods of 18 plays each. Each play lasts 60 seconds for regular season games and 30 seconds for the championships. During the time allotted, the team in possession of the ball has two basic options in order to force the other team to take possession. If a team starts 3 plays in a row while in possession of the ball that team gains -2 points.

The first option is to throw the ball at the other team's players. They are forced to catch the ball because they'd rather gain possession then get blown up, but if the defender is fast enough he might get far enough away from the ball to receive minimal damage. The other option is to run the ball halfway around the track before time is up. The distance for this is 100 meters. A good player, even in padding, can usually run this in 15-20 seconds, but as the game drags on and the players begin to tire it takes longer.

The major way to rack up points for the opposing team is to knock their players out-of-bounds, into either dead zone, for -1 point, but if the player is holding the ball it's -6 points, and if the player is knocked out, then thrown the ball both scores occur for a total of -7 points. Play is not stopped if a player is knocked out-of-bounds without the ball, in fact it is quite common for a single player to get knocked out 4 or 5 times a play. But if -6 is scored by one person the play is over. Play is also prematurely over when a player is blown up. The only other time play is stopped is when the ball is run halfway around the track.

Each side has ten players, five defense and five offense. In regular games teams are allowed to replace up to five players due to being blown up. If all players including the replacements are blown up the other team wins by default regardless of the score. If at least five of the blown up players are regenerated within a week a rematch game is held where in the winner of which is declared the winner of the first game as if the second game never happened. -From the banned pamphlet handed out to Megaball fans as they enter the stadium.

Ranger Joe read the pamphlet as they filled into the stadium. Wimble's favorite team, the Happyville Priests (6-5) were playing the Ostitun Decripts (7-4). He mentioned that by watching people at the game they could learn how to fit into Balidronian society. They had front row seats because of Rogicphil's RICH status (still haven't figured out a good acronym for that yet).

Where was the Gladerunner anyway? He said he'd be right along as they were getting their tickets but never followed them into the seating area.

They were dressed normally so they could fit in easier. You don't want to know what 'normal' meant on Deo 7 so don't ask. In order to keep it a secret, that the bear was a wild party animal, they had it wear wide angle dark sunglasses, a camouflage tee-shirt, and baggy shorts. If anybody asked they'd just tell the person to quit snorting fuzgaloid.

The teams came out. First the Decripts, from the resthome/cemetery suburb of Ostitun. The crowd cheered. The elderly players marched out onto the field in their black and red uniforms. Next the Happyville Priests came out in green and white striped uniforms. The crowd booed.

"Why are they booing?" RJ asked.

Wimble showed him the phamlet entitled, THE CIVIL WAR AND YOU, HOW YOU CAN MAINTAIN COMBAT READINESS AND LOOK GOOD TOO. "It's all in here but I'll spare you the details. You see the innercity is in favor of Ostitun over Happyville because of all the fighting. We're in the middle of a civil war after all."

"Oh... I wasn't aware." RJ scratched his nose with his upper lip.

The game was soon underway. The referee pulled out a -1$ coin and asked the captains to call it in the air. He threw it over his shoulder, deliberately tripped a couple of the opposing team's players who ran at it, then rushed over to pick it up before anyone had a chance to see it. He peeked at it in his cupped hands.

"What did you say?" He asked Ostitun's captain.

"Uh, butts."

"Okay, it's faces," the ref gleefully showed the coin to everyone, holding it between his thumb and forefinger. "Happyville gets first possession." The crowd cheered.

Ranger Joe looked shocked, "Hey, what gives?"

"It's best to loose the toss," Wimble whispered.   "Oh..."

The Priests lined up at the starting line. Their five defensive backs faced the Decript's five defense. Their five offensive backs stood behind them back to back, the centerman with the ball.

```
Ostitun Decripts          O O O O O
                          D D D D D
                          --------------------------
                          D D D D D
Happyville Priests        O O @ O O
```

(D= Defence, O=Offence, @= Guy with the ball)

The stadium buzzer went off. The Priest's offense began running while the defense held back the Decripts, whose offensive line was running around the track to cut them off from the halfway point. The Priest's defense broke and the Decripts hurried after the ball carrier.

The ball carrier stopped and turned. Five old, but buffed up, mean guys were charging him in hope of knocking him out of bounds. Instead he lobbed the ball over their heads to a waiting defense man. The Decripts knocked the ball carrier out anyway. -1 point. The crowd cheered.

The Priest defense man threw the ball at the back of the Decript. The Decript was hit, fell forward, but managed to grab the ball before it hit the ground. He stumbled toward the out-of-bounds where a Priest grabbed him in order to push him out out. A dog pile formed.

The buzzer sounded and the ref pulled the players out of the way. On the bottom was a Decript holding the ball on the out-of-bounds side. The crowd shouted insults.

The ref looked around at the hundreds of thousands of angry fans shouting vile threats at him. He cleared his throat and said, "No score. Time ran out."

Massive cheering.

Joe was slightly pissed, "That no good #@*&! scum sucking $%#*! headed piece of dog $%#@*&**!"

"No, say: Wet badder pak," Wimble coached.

"Yeah, well that ref's cheating."

"Duh, he wouldn't be a very good ref if he didn't. See you guys will never pass as natives."

And so it continued until halftime with the score, Decripts -26, Priests -35.

"They gave out at least -50. That ref is really messed up," RJ said rooting for the Priests.

When halftime ended and the game got back under way the Priests were stuck with the opening possession. They got pinned down three plays for -2 and a player blown up by a nasty curve ball. They came back with a -7 when a Decript tripped out-of-bounds but it was called back because the ref said the Decript was injured and ineligible to score points.

The game continued on with neither team gaining any points until late in the last period when several Decripts snuck across the out-of-bounds while the ref was distracted by a fight on the other side of the field. It resulted in a -2 point penalty and twelve injured fans in the dead zone. The Priests were stuck with another -2 because the Decripts that snuck across blocked them from the halfway line. The last play of the game ended with two opposing players pulling each other out-of-bounds. Final score, Decripts -27, Priests -42. The crowd roared.

Steam could be seen venting out of Ranger Joe's ears. Actually it was vaporized sweat but steam sounds better. After the stadium had emptied he and the bear burst into the ref's office. "What kind of retarded ref are you?"

"Hey I'm not in the mood for stupid jokes, now get out of here before I lay you out like the sack your mother crawled into town on." The referee was at his desk counting out money to a tall man in a blue and green business suit and otherwise didn't bother to pay them any attention. His voice wasn't even very angry and sounded quite conversational.

Before RJ could come up with a snappy insult the bear charged. A small plume of fur and furniture stuffing filled the air as sounds of agony filled the room.

*   *   *

Rogicphil was waiting in the ground car with Wimble. He checked his watch, "We're behind schedule. And Annie isn't answering on the secure comm channel. Where are those two?"

"I'll go look for them." Wimble reached for the door.

"No, you stay here. I'll handle it." Rogicphil jumped out. He went to the quickvader and then down to the ref's locker room. It was the only place they could be. For some reason RJ was overly sensitive to referee issues. The door was left open. Inside was a pigsty. How could anyone... No it was just a fight, not bad house keeping after all.

He could see little tuffs of bear fur scattered about. What the heck were those two doing down here?

There was a note on the desk. It said: I have captured that stupid ref. He will be punished by being made to bob for apples in dirty holy water.

"Hold it right there!" a policeman with blaster drawn said stepping into the room.

Before they could get a good look at him, Rogicphil disappeared into an empty locker.

"Where's Ref Tarkin Nosblar?" a second police office asked stepping in behind the first. "He was supposed to be with chief of police Hagsplat Ufglong. How are we gonna leave our cut if they aren't in here?"

"He was right here," the first officer insisted, "I just saw some guy with shiny blue boots sublimate himself."

"Maybe that's what happened to them too."

Rogicphil watched them search the room, including the lockers he quickly interchanged out of, whenever they went to look inside them. He stuffed the note he had found on the desk inside the first officer's shirt pocket just as the other one turned around. Neither one could see fast enough to notice him doing it.

"What's this?" the second one asked plucking the note out of the first one's pocket. He glanced at the note, "I knew it! You kidnapped them."

"Don't be a muecat fool. I was with you the whole octahuggin time."

"And you tried to blame it on some hap infested blue haired guy who

177

sublimated himself."

The first cop tried to defend himself by saying it was blue boots and not blue hair but he was blasted in two by the second cop before he could open his mouth again.

Rogicphil gulped. He hadn't meant for that to happen. After the second cop had stolen some money to the first dying cop (ID cards become instantly invalid upon death) and exited the room, Rogicphil hightailed it back to the ground car in the stadium parking lot.

Inside Ranger Joe, the Bear, and Wimble were waiting for him. "Where have you been?" they asked him.

"Out looking for a couple of rotten apples."

"That's stupid, this planet has never heard of an apple. Why would you do something like that?" RJ had acquired a nasty attitude since the last time Rogicphil had seen him.

"Why did you kidnap the chief of police?"

"Good question," RJ looked at the bear, "Why did I kidnap the chief of police? I don't know. Do you?" He looked back at Rogicphil, "I don't know."

"He was with the megaball ref."

"Oh that chief of police. I thought you meant a completely different chief of police." He pulled an imaginary nose out of his head.

"Where did you put them?"

"Well, I tied them up, stuffed them in a big box, and mailed them back to Raul Rall Beta."

"You can't mail the chief of police to Raul Rall Beta."

"Why not?"

"He'll starve to death or freeze or both."

"No, I packed the box full of apples."

"There aren't any apples on Deo 7. Remember?"

"Oh yeah. I guess they'll have to make do with smelly pseudo red tennis balls."

Wimble nodded. "At least they'll be well insulated."

Rogicphil didn't have time to argue with them so he went back into the statium to look for clues as to what RJ and the bear had actually done with the ref and police chief.

He found a janitor in the stadium cleaning up. "Where is everybody?"

"The game's over. Everyone left," the janitor said slowly.

"I mean the other guys who clean the stadium."

"There aren't any other guys."

"You clean up the whole stadium, alone?"

The guy put his thumbs under his coveralls suspender straps and leaned back, "Sonny, I've cleaned this stadium every week for 137 years. Seen some pretty nasty stuff too. Found a couple of bodies over near the sno-cone machine last month. They had their shoes ripped off, with their feet still in'em too."

"How's the pay?"

"Lousy. But since it takes me the whole week to clean the entire place, I've always got something to do."

"What about the off season?"

"That's my one week vacation."

"Oh by the way my name is 'Phil," he held out his hand.

The man shook it, "They call me Old Fart."

"Named after the stadium, huh?"

"Nope, you got it backwards. I've been here the longest so they renamed the place after me."

"What was it called before that?"

"Old Stick in the Mud Stadium."

"Well Old Fart," Rogicphil said changing the subject, "Where would I go to mail a package around here?"

"What's that, some kind of drug?"

"A post office. Where you send things to people."

"You mean government workers?"

"Not quite."

"A banana?"

"No, close but no cookie."

"Hey," the man leaned closer like he was divulging a family secret, "I know where you can get some good banana cookies, if you know what I mean."

"Thanks anyway. See you later, Old Fart."

"Take care."

Rogicphil left the man with his broom and his stadium. It was painfully obvious that the old guy had the Hap but he didn't have the heart to tell him. The old guy might go and sublimate himself if he knew. Now where would Ranger Joe have found a place to mail two chubby old guys from?

He ran a few kilometers over to the government department for stolen or lost things, places, and concepts. A cross eyed lady greeted him at a teller window. "What have you recently lost or stolen?" She held out her hand, "Well let's see it."

Rogicphil ignored her second request. "I'm looking for something, not trying to get rid of it. It's called the post office." He thought he was being sarcastic.

"You want the Bureau of Returned Objects across the street." She pointing over Rogicphil's shoulder.

Rogicphil had to use a pair of binoculars chained to the desk, for that purpose, to see a delapitated building complex far across the asphalt landscape. All its windows were boarded up. "But it's closed."

"I guess someone took all the stuff and forgot to bring it back. There's an old legend though that says at one time it was open and the first week they ran out of stuff to give away, but that's just a story to scare the kiddies at night."

Rogicphil was about to say, "Thank you anyway," but his super speed stopped his mouth in time. He removed his hand from over his mouth and instead said, "Well I hope your drain pipe gets clogged up."

Quickly he ran back to the ground car but it wasn't there anymore. He'd wished he just had the patience to argue with Ranger Joe a little bit more before giving up so easily. His super speed gave him a false sense that he could do anything on his own and didn't have to worry about what other people thought. Yeah right, whatever.

He hightailed it back to the hotel room for some R&R. He'd worry about finding the police chief later and what he knew about the satanic cow, if anything.

*   *   *

Meanwhile in a dark alley behind the Yahitt Jake asked, "Does it work?"

"Well, um," Wilbur stopped, "You're the one who planted the bug. How would I know?" He looked down a couple of meters to where Jake was standing below.

"You got the monitor in your hand." Jake pointed to the small black box in Wilbur's hands.

Wilbur was standing on top of a large pipe, about a meter or so in diameter, sticking out of the building. Periodically globs of used toothpaste would ooze out and splatter on the pavement below.

Wilbur looked at his hands. He was holding the monitor all-right. "Hey, how'd that get there?"

"Well what's going on?"

"Nothin' yet. No one's in the room right now."

"You sure? My monitor says their room number was punched into the quickvader over a half hour ago. They've got to be in there by now."

"Wait, the door is opening. Two people are coming in. They're disguised. I didn't think they were that smart."

"Two short fat women and a tall bald guy?"

"Uh huh. How'd you know?"

"Yeah I saw them use that same disguise yesterday."

"That's a good disguise." Wilbur adjusted his position on the pipe to get better reception.   "Wait a minute. Somebody else just stepped in. It's the police."

"Local police?"

"Yeah. Looks like they're getting busted."

"Hah! It's about time. What losers."

"Shut-up you doofus. That's the last thing we want."

"What are they doing? I want to see."

"The short one, probably RJ, is beating one cop while the tall one, probably RS, is trying to hide in the corner."

Jake looked disappointed. "He isn't killing them is he?"

"Who?"

"The cop. I wanted to do that."

"Ut-oh. The cops just tied them both up. He's kicking them now as the other cop is trying to drag them out the door. Now the first cop is shooting at the second cop. The first cop is kicking them again now. Wait a bunch more cops just burst in on them. They're arresting the first cop and hauling him away instead."

"What about our prisoners?"

Wilbur looked down at Jake and barked, "Would you shut up please? I'm trying to watch this in real time." He looked back at his monitor. "Ut-oh. They're gone. The other cops must have come back for them while you were distracting me."

180

"You're in for it now. You've lost them."

"Come on, we got to stop them before the cops take 'em to the station. Help me down from here."

"If you had gotten a bug set with more range you wouldn't have had to be up in there in the first place." Jake held his hand out in an obvious offer to help the other agent of H.E.L.L down.

Wilbur took the bait and reached for Jakes hand which suddenly went to slick back his hair. Wilbur fell face first in the puddle of muck directly below the pipe.

"You know what will happen if they get away from us?" Wilbur asked picking himself up.

"We'll be taken to the recycling vats."

"Yeah, then it's the end for us."

*　　　　　　*　　　　　　*

Only about 6% of the people living in Balidron knew what mail was. And the fact that Balidron had a post office was known by less than .001% of . 01% of the entire population of the planet. This works out to 139 people, 137 of which worked in the post office itself. Of the other two one was a practical joker who liked to play tricks with the system and the other was an agent for a giant intergalactic junk mail consortium.

The fact that the post office was so unknown wasn't due to other competing services but rather to a typographical error on an order blank written by one of Balidron's founding fathers. Instead of ordering a post office he ordered Postoff Ice, a flavored frozen desert.

Actually someone in the Galactic Federal Government noticed the mistake but was bribed by an agent of H.E.L.L. to ignore it.

After a few hundred years the colonists of Deo 7 gave up on the notion of mail and began berating their neighbors in public instead. The bureaucrats loved it for two reasons. First they no longer had to notify citizens about anything the government did or didn't do. If some poor sap wanted to keep their toothpaste service flowing they'd have to find the proper department and accept payment on the spot. Second, all the public pickering between citizens just made the people ignore the government more.

But alas it wasn't to last. A valiant and crusading citizen named Mildred Spicemiester began to protest the lack of a post office. She found the original order for a post office and the subsequent correction and cover up and published a scathing expose in the bi-daily newspaper Baligrit. Later her work became required reading for all reporter scholars in the B12 sector. But at the time she was widely ridiculed and almost ignored if it wasn't for Grego the Mean who thought she'd be good cover for causing mischief and strife inside the government.

And so Balidron finally got is first post office and Mildred got her own stamp, a -3 milli jeydude underwater mail beauty. Later, after Grego the Mean became bored with the entire affair, she was sent to prison for failing to renew her breathing card license. Ironically her renewal form, which for some mysterious reason never made it to the Air and Breathing Bureau on time, required submission using underwater mail postage only.

When it came time to build the new post office the only place the begrudging bureaucrats could find in the already large city was an abandoned warehouse in the geriatric suburb of Ostitun. So 137 elderly pensioners were hired to guard the place and make sure no one tried to mail anything.

One can imagine the shock then when one day a shadowy man and his pet monster arrived with a large package to be mailed. It was to be mailed off world even. Total shock! How'd they get past all those guards? Desperate phone calls were made. Government officials brownnosed, embassies questioned, lawyers hired, laws reviewed, psychics consulted, but in the end no one could find a reason not to mail the package. They were the post office right?

Unfortunately the package never made it to its destination. The fifty or so postal inspectors, under threat of having their timecards examined, found reasonable cause to suspect that jeupert flavored toothpaste was being smuggled out of Balidron. When they broke open the box instead of finding a load of gooey bellybutton lint they found a bunch of half eaten tennis balls and two strange looking men. The men were immediately arrested for vagrancy, breaking and entering the post office with intent to expose themselves to postal employees. It wasn't until a few days later that Ref Tarkin Nosblar, and Chief of Police Hagsplat Ufglong, were let out of jail, and boy were they pissed.

*   *   *

The Balidron Police Department was created before the advent of negative money. They did what a regular police department would do, arrest criminals, take bribes, that kind of thing. With the introduction of negative money they found they were needed less and less; the negative monetary system was punishment enough for everyone. Coupled with the fact that negative money is very difficult to steal to someone the police were left to turn to the only option remaining: create the crime in order to get rid of it.

So it was that the department was split into two factions, division A and division B. The former carried on with regular police duties while the latter went out to stir up some trouble. Eventually this grew into an out and out war with public citizens caught in the middle.

The police came to be feared. One could never tell when an officer was from Division A or B, helpful or murderous. People never left their apartment complexes alone. Rival gangs banned together for protection.

Then the general population was bombarded with wave after wave of subliminal propaganda. It helped out both divisions as well as over crowding in the inner city. And so it has remained for centuries. But forces were building to upset the police/propaganda equilibrium. Forces that would totally renovate the face of Deo 7.

Fortunately Rogicphil, Ranger Joe, and the bear were taken to Division A headquarters. Rogicphil wanted to find out what the police knew about the cow and getting arrested was the easiest way he knew to get in. They were waiting to be booked in a large lobby full of thousands of people also waiting formal booking. The line into the booking section was about ten hours long.

182

Hot dog and energy weapon vendors roamed the twisted line distributing hot dogs, money, and firepower.

The bear took three dogs and a bottle of Ragloid. It was munching away listening to Rogicphil and RJ.

"So why did you let them arrest us? We could of wasted those cops like half eaten plates of food."

"I think the cow has infiltrated the city police department. This way we can go through their records leisurely and without sneaking in."

"Go through their records?"

"Sure. We're still undercover until we get enough information to bust this wide open."

"I thought we were just suppose to wipe out the cow."

"That wouldn't get us anywhere. If we are to save this planet we must fix any damage the cow has done. Simply killing the cow would solve nothing. Besides we're no closer to finding the cow now than when we arrived."

RJ checked his watch. 17:22xm. It hadn't even been another day yet. "What's the hurry?"

"You're the one who wanted to get out quick."

RJ shrugged and tried to take a bite of his hot dog, instead he got a mouth full of metal, "Hey, what's this file doin' in my hot dog bun?"

"This line's taking too long. Why don't you go to the front and see what the hold up is?"

"Okay. Come on bear, you can provide the slack." He dropped his file bearing dog and headed off with his dog faced bear. The bear finished its Ragloid and followed RJ to the front of the line.

Perfect, thought Rogicphil, just the distraction he needed. In his usual faster than the speed of sight way he waltzed into the police offices while those two got themselves into a fight. Rogicphil zipped into the vacant chief of police's office. His secretary was busy filing her toenails and didn't pay attention to the gust of air Rogicphil caused when he sped past her desk.

He bolted the door then went to work. First he searched all the files in three cabinets. Nothing of importance was found so he rummaged through the chief's desk. Bzzzzt! Bzzzzt! A phone. He answered, "What!?"

"I thought you were still in jail mister Ufglong," the secretary said.

Rogicphil cleared his throat. He tried to sound mean and authoritarian, "Who is this?"

"Are you okay? You don't sound very good."

"Prison does that to you."

"You should know."

"Who is this?"

"Luella your secretary. They must have boxed your ears once too often."

"Yes that's right. Are you done filing your nails?

"I don't have any nails."

"Very good then," he hung up.

There wasn't anything inside the desk so he looked through the scattered papers on the standard rectangular desk. He found something unusual on a list of things to do. It was already checked off but caught his eye anyway.

It said: Meet RTN for lunch.

RTN he remembered was an alias for the satanic cow that stood for Real Tough and Nasty. Now he needed to figure out where the chief had gone for lunch.

"Suella," he said picking up the phone.

"Luella, and yes Mr. Ufglong."

"I've got real bad heartburn. Get me the address of that place I ate at for lunch. I want to sue them."

"You don't mean the Galactic Church do you? That would be sacreligious."

The chief of police had eaten at the Galactic Church with the satanic cow for lunch? Aha but what better place for the cow to hide than the least likely place searched.

He'd better bluff. "You dare accuse me of suing the Church? I meant where I went for desert afterwards."

"I'm terribly sorry, Mister Ufglong I had no idea. You want to snort some fuz dust to make you feel better?"

"No, you go ahead without me." He hung up. Checking his watch, he realized it was almost dinner time. And he knew just the place.

He zoomed out the office, past the secretary Luella, and through the other officer's offices back into the booking lobby. He found Joe and the bear back at the end of the line.

Joe had a black eye and bruised face, "Where were you?"

"Using the restertirium. What happened?"

"Some guys jumped us. They said we were cutting in line. They were taken to the hospital when we were done with them but we got put all the way to the back."

"We're leaving now anyway. Maybe we can bandage you up before we eat."

"Just as long as they don't serve tools."

"A place I saw written about in the restroom."

"I tried those places once, they're rip offs."

Rogicphil thought about it, "You're probably right."

It was easy to slip past the lobby guards. They were always welcome to the opportunity of losing a -100$ jeedude bill. Stealing their impounded Kyrillian ground car back was easier. At the automorgue one guard was tuned into to the brain link, the other was asleep. Joe even managed to recharge the car's battery off the guard's hot-fuzgoo maker.

They zoomed right out of the Dept-A automorgue and into a tunnel, then cruised under the river then back into underground traffic on the other side.

"You better go up top. I hear traffic is terrible in Kro-Chon town," Rogicphil advised.

"Kro-Chon town. What's that?"

"A little refugee enclave of off worlders."

Joe found an exit ramp.

"Kro-Chonians really aren't off worlders in the regular sense. Krobus and Chonora were habitable planets in this system. They were in the same orbit but going the opposite direction. Then one day they ran into each other."

"That sounds pretty hairy."

"Most of the people escaped and came here."

They were in Kro-Chon town now. The buildings were smaller and closer together than ordinary Balidron building complexes. There was no traffic on the surface and no lights on the buildings except near the top. It gave them an eerie feeling driving through twisty metallic canyons all alone in the streets and yet they were in the area of the densest population on the planet. The sunglow was setting between two black and barren looking buildings ahead.

"Where are we going to eat anyway?"

"The Galactic Church and its all you can repenters buffet." The sunglow faded then disappeared and the nasty sweat addicted blue bugs came out to feast.

Chapter 16: Grego The Mean

"Don't you need to plot coords into the computer?" Space-Bo wanted to know. He and the Funky Chicken were currently flying blind through the Deo 7 night in shuttle number Omega. It didn't really matter whether or not is was day or night on Deo 7. The perpetual haze and smog of deo fumes made it overcast no matter when a person might be flying through the sky. They were heading to the northern continent, known as The Attic to the locals, to check out any signs the cow might have been there. The deserted city of Darteal, long ago buried in icy blue snow, was their first stop.

"Nah, I was here just a few millennia ago," The chicken said, "I remember the way." Chewing on the remains of the autopilot he expertly and manually piloted the shuttle to a smooth landing.

They were getting into their snow parkas when Space-Bo noticed there wasn't much snow outside the shuttle. What he did see looked like patches of blue sand. Looking out the window he asked, "Since when do cactus's grow in the frozen north?"

The chicken checked the thermometer. It read 0.10 degrees celsius, chilly at best. "Maybe it's summer here."

"Are you sure this is the right place? I don't see any deserted city around here."

"Positive," He pulled two sets of leg weights out from his pocket, "Put these on, we're on a low grav planet remember."

"Right," Space-Bo put the weights on.

They stepped out onto a rugged arid plane. Their flashlights spotted out scrub brush and cactus like plants in abundance. Even so, a cold wind was blowing from the west.

It was night time and so the stars were out. Space-Bo was looking at them with a puzzled look on his face. "Hey I don't know where we are, the constellations are all screwed up."

"Those aren't stars. They're tiny explosions of concentrated deo ore dust that make it high up into the sweat layer, the perspirasphere"

"The whatsasphere?"

"Don't worry about it. It's campfire time."

"Oh yeah," Space-Bo pulled a portable campfire out of his backpack then stood there for a moment not knowing what to do.

"What's wrong?"

"Where's the outlet?"

"You didn't forget to recharge the batteries did you?"

"Well..."

"Here," the chicken pulled some A^{13th} batteries out of his pocket, "try these, they're dilithium."

Space-Bo stuck the batteries into the campfire and turned it on. Flames sprouted up a meter and half. "Whoops," he turned it down.

The Funky Chicken was pulling hotdogs out of his pocket. Soon they were eating roasted hotdogs and gazing into the fire.

"Let's not worry about the mission until morning."

"Okay, want some jerk?"

"What?"

"Want some jerk?"

"Want some what?"

"Jerk."

"Quite calling me that."

"Here eat this," The chicken handed him a stick of beef jerky.

"Oh, dryed yeast coagulant."

"Whatever."

At first glow the chicken woke up. He stared at the sun coming up, or at least where he assumed the sun would be coming up. Then he stood on his head for an hour reciting backwards the 1001 rules of a good Lugietorpian Polevaulter. He rolled some frozen blue reconstituted deo stones around in his mouth at the same time. They say immortals have all the fun, but they also have all the boredom and the chicken was feeling especially bored that day. He needed a good death to pacify his primordial desires.

He woke up Space-Bo about 9xm, "Wake up."

"No, not again," Space-Bo mumbled.

"Come on, time to catch the worm."

"But I don't want to clean the kitty box, Daddy."

"No, its you who eats the worm."

"Let the kitty fly a kite. The kitty likes to fly kites."

"Birdbrain."

"Is that you 'Phil?"

"Its me, your fateless companion."

"Hawkman?"

"Close enough." He lifted Space-Bo up with one hand, "Time to get up. We've got an important mission to totally screw up, remember."

"Yeah....okay." he stumbled over to the shuttle. He was only wearing one of the leg weights by this time and had a hard time keep his loose foot on the ground.

The chicken gathered up the campfire and threw it into the shuttle. Somehow during the night Space-Bo had found an electrical socket in the ground to plug the campfire into. The chicken had pulled up, out of the frozen ground, about half a meter of electrical cable, along with the outlet, before it broke off. He tossed that into the shuttle as well. "You got a pogo stick on you?"

"No, I left it by accident on Triton last month."

"You can use my spare." He pulled two pogo sticks out of his pockets. With a flick of the wrists the sticks telescoped out. "Okay, mount up." They readied themselves. "Lets hop!" With that they hopped away doing ten meters in a single bound.

In an hour's time they spotted some ruins in the distance. They hopped up to a big gate set in a wall that surrounded a large compound. There was some cacti growing in blue icy deo sand/snow dunes up against the wall.

"This doesn't look like a city, possibly a community center but definitely not a city," Space-Bo said dismounting.

"Uh, it isn't a city," the chicken said, right before he stopped. Literally. He just quit hopping and let himself crash to the ground.

"What the heck is it?"

The chicken collected himself before answering, "Fort McWayne."

"Never heard of it."

"I wouldn't expect you to. It was build long after you died."

"Huh? Oh yeah, I'm from the future now."

"Fort McWayne was build by General Noj McWayne way back in 97,173 during Deo 7's colonial days. It was intended to keep the native Alpukas from stealing what they thought was food but actually turned out to be powdered plasma. By 97,188 a war had broke out and the General's army was killed in a big ambush. The general himself was stabbed in the back while trying to escape over the back wall. Ever since, the Alpukas have claimed the fort as their own, but nobody acknowledges it."

"You think the cow might now have a secret base here?"

"Who knows. Only one way to find out." The chicken cleared his throat and yelled, "Ho, chief Administrator!" He directed this at the top of the gate where a guardpost was. It was at least 10 meters up and metallic black in composition. "Can we come in please?"

"May we," Space-Bo corrected.

"Oh yes, terribly sorry about that." The chicken yelled again, "May we come in pieces?" He turned to Space-Bo, "I'm sorry, keeping ten thousand syntax systems straight in my head can be a chore."

"I think you meant peace."

"No I didn't."

A small furry creature popped its head out one of the tiny windows in the guard post. "Grubablubadub!" It said.

"Is that an Alpuka?" Space-Bo asked.

"I don't know. I've never seen one before."

"Grulumbogalub?" The furry creature said.

"Excuse me?" the chicken shouted back.

"Gredabada wogamon, pop!" Another creature popped its head out of the other tiny window in the guard post. The two spoke between themselves for a bit.

"What are they saying?" Space-Bo asked.

"I don't understand the language but if I read their lips translating it as French they would be saying 'What a nice electrical outlet you have' 'Yes, well your peanut butter is very stringy today.' but they're not, so it's pointless."

"Hum."

The furry creature rang a bell. Suddenly the gate began to open. Twenty or so other creatures were pushing the massive gate/doors open.

"I guess they're letting us in." The chicken waltzed right through the gate.

Space-Bo followed behind skipping. Low grav worlds were such fun.

After they were in the courtyard just beyond the gate, the creatures closed it behind them. A swarm of the smallish creatures gathered around the strangers, feeling their clothes and sniffing at them.

"They look like llama-people." Space-Bo patted one on the head. It nipped at him.

"Yes, they do resemble small bipedal space llamas don't they, but with four arms and two legs instead of the standard two arms and sixteen legs. Well on second thought maybe not."

"What's a space llama?"

"You don't want to find out."

"Do you think that these are the Alpuka's pets?"

"They could belong to the cow for all I know and I've forgotten most of that." He turned to a llama creature, "Take me to your masticator," he said in ten different languages and three jive slang derivitives.

The llama person nodded its head and ran off to an office building. Shortly, a fat creature was wheeled out. He was so big evidently, that he couldn't walk on his own even in the low gravity and using two of his extra arms as legs.

"No, I mean your humanoid pet owning masticator," the chicken said in ten different languages.

They all muttered amongst themselves at that, and the leader in the wheeled cart looked shocked. He had his wheeler wheel him up to the strangers and carefully looked at them. He comparing their similarities to a childrens coloring book he had in his four hands. He pointed at Space-Bo, "Abulaba!" then at the chicken, "Abulaga!" All the llama creatures were listening closely to him. He scratched his head with a three fingered hand, complete with two fully opposable thumbs. Then he said "Abulaba, abulaga, gumo stogba!"

The llama people cheered and then quickly tied Space-Bo and the Funky Chicken up. They were hauled off in a flash to be prepared for that evening's feast.

*   *   *

The Alpukas, a native pseudo-intelligent race found on Aibmuloc 03 (3(10)) also known as Deo 7, have been found to be a serious detriment to further colonization by the Lugietorpian Colonial Agency. Not so much for the Alpukas behavior as their nature. Research has shown that the Alpukas are in fact only half of a race, one part of a dichotomy species. It is the other half, dubbed Palpukas, that causes concern.

It is not fully understood, as yet, to the exact fundamentals by which this dual species has evolved. Hopefully once understood, this problem can be resolved in the shortest amount of time. It is in best interests of Lugietorp Prime that the colonials know as little as possible about this.

The Palpukas live in underground tunnels all through out the Arflin Isles. If given the chance they will eat any and almost everything put in front of them. Fortunately their mouths are small and strawlike so are unlikely to eat colonists. It is feared, though, that with expanding settlements colonial shampoo and toothpaste reservoirs are at risk of being sucked dry. Lord help us if they figure out how to use all those blenders we traded for trinkets.

The problem arises from the fact that if the Palpukas are simply killed off, which would be relatively easy, the Alpukas would die off too. Every top

Lugietorpian Colonial Agency executive knows the secret to its colonization success: Alpuka slave labor. Furthermore, the Alpukas actually seem to like hard labor and we need not concern ourselves with that further. The real concern deals with the fact that when Alpukas reproduce they create Palpukas and when Palpukas reproduce they create Alpukas. It does not help any that the two are sworn natural enemies. It is surprising that so many infants survive at all.

Therefore it all boils down to how can the Palpukas be stopped when they are directly responsible for essential slave labor. The debate is expected to carry on until a decision is made either way. - From a package of important papers, found on the Lugietorpian Emperor's desk, now lost somewhere in the Funky Chicken's pocket.

*   *   *

The fire was going real good for a while until a sudden rain storm doused the Alpuka's hopes for a barbecue. The rain made the ground muddy and they ran into the fort buildings for cover. The Funky Chicken and Space-Bo were left out to get soggy.

"Oh well, maybe next time," the chicken bemoaned, disappointed that he didn't get killed. Space-Bo was glad he was still alive but didn't dwell on the fact. What was done is in the past, was his philosophy. "Hey, you know what?"

"What?"

"I think were sinking." Space-Bo could see bubbles of air breaking in the mud around the stake they were tied to.

"I think you're right."

There was a slow sucking sound then ssssSSSURP! GULP! They were swallowed into a muddy pit that suddenly opened up beneath them. They were in brown freefall for only a moment before they hit the bottom, bounced into a slimy tube and were sucked down into a series of amature built water/mud slides. Clammy little hands joined them in the rushing darkness.

"Weeee," they shouted in unison as they continued their sloppy journey which eventually ended in a cold dirt cave with a low ceiling that kept bumping into their heads. The little hands that had joined them in the previous fun now worked to untie them from the stake.

"I think we're being rescued."

"I think we're being stolen."

Before Space-Bo could say "sounds like fun," his mouth was gagged and his hands retied to his feet. They were restrapped to the stake but this time slung underneath in cannibal going to have you for dinner style.

In this manner they were taken to the underground city of the Palpukas but they didn't know that because they couldn't see in the dark. They were left in a smoker chamber to marinade before the big feast.

"If you don't mind, these bonds are starting to bore me again."

"Huh? Oh, you want me to bust us out. No problem." Snap! And Space-Bo had them free. "I suddenly feel the need to beat someone up."

The chicken pushed something into his hand, "Put these IR goggles on so you can see where you're going."

"Okay, thanks. Uh they're not working right."

"Did you flip the switch?"

"Yeah."

"Let me see," the chicken took them back, "I'm terribly sorry, these are my 3D glasses I got at a movie once. Let me find the right ones. Aha here we go. Try these."

"No, that's worse. Give me the first ones back." Space-Bo looked at the chicken in 3D, "You look like you're broken into a hundred pieces."

The chicken now wearing the IR goggles looked at himself in thermal vision. "I wish. You're just seeing all the cracks in the glasses because I sat on them."

"Oh I have an idea. Let's swap one lens each out of the others goggles. That way we can each see the same thing."

"Good idea." And the chicken proceeded to do just that. He put his new half 3D half IR goggles on and shook his head back and forth until his brain cells randomly adjusted to the new input.

Space-Bo did the same thing then crawled over to the entrance and looked out between the root like bars. Just outside were a small group of the Palpukas talking to what appeared to be the legs of a mean looking creature.

The chicken was busy burning himself on the hot coals in the center of the room. "Aha that feels nice. So what do you see out there?"

"It looks like the devil is talking to some little kids."

"Don't you know there's no such thing as the devil?"

"So if there's a God how come there's no devil?"

"Because he overdosed on drugs along time ago."

"Oh."

Now foot steps could be heard. "Get up!" a mean sounding voice said outside the bars.

"We can't see," the chicken lied.

"I don't care. Get up anyway."

"Okay." Space-Bo tried to stand up so he was level with the legs just outside the bars. Wham! And he hit his head on the dirt ceiling. "Ouch that hurt."

There was a muffled chuckle then the bars swung open and the legs entered the room. Neither Space-Bo nor the Funky Chicken could see anything above the legs as they extended up into the ceiling.

"Who are you?" a mean voice above the legs said.

"Me or him?" the chicken wanted to know.

"I ask the questions around here." One of the mean legs kicked Space-Bo in the head causing a slight but crucial adjustment to his vision.

Suddenly Space-Bo could the rest of the mean body connected to the mean legs in wonderful techno-thermal three dimensions. There was some sort of a phase field surrounding the mean looking man that allowed him to walk through ceilings without having to stoop down. "Hey thanks," Space-Bo said.

"Don't mention it again. What are you doing here?"

"Planting trees?" Space-Bo tried to lie. The chicken elbowed him in the stomach. "Hey what's the big idea?"

"I said I ask the questions here. Why are you really here?"

"It's giant earthworm hunting season and we're just trying to dig the little buggers out," the chicken lied again as he rubbed his face all over the burning coals. A real nice BBQ flavored stench of burning chicken feathers permeated the small chamber.

"Why are you doing that to yourself?"

"Doesn't it smell nice? Oh right. Sorry about that. I momentarily forgot about the no questions thing."

"I'm inviting you and a delegation of Papukas to my house for a 14 course meal."

"Only if you agree to serve us as the meal and not the other way around."

This time it was Space-Bo who elbowed the chicken.

The legs spoke, "No one dares offer me terms to my own banquet. Therefore you'll be forced to enjoy the meal with me and not be eaten. But I promise to kill you afterwards."

"What do you think 'Bo?"

"Sounds good to me."

"Fine. Follow me back to my shuttle." The thing that sounded mean and looked like the devil in infrared 3D goggles walked back the way it came.

On all fours they followed his phase glow to a nearby chamber that was big enough for them to stand up in. There were more Palpukas there picking theirs noses and making fart jokes.

In the middle of the chamber was the finest late model luxury aircar that positive money could buy. They hopped into the back seat. The stranger started the car saying, "Fasten your seat belts." They did so and then the car vaulted out of a hole in the ground into the misty cloud covered afternoon of the Deo 7 arctic.

It was still raining. Visibility was almost zero due to the heavy fog, so the guy flipped the headlights on. In the dim visual light they could tell he was short, had a ring of stringy super brown hair running around his head with a large bald spot on top, and wore dark wrap around sunglasses.

"My Palpuka friends were planning to eat you from the inside out with tiny little straws. But that was before I came along," he said, "Now your deaths will be slow and painful."

"May I make a request?" the chicken asked.

"Of course not."

"I've always wanted to die by being squashed in a garbage compacter."

"That can be arranged," and they flew on into the fog.

The aircar landed in the rain. The night sky was lit up by streaks of lighting. A nearby flash revealed a manor house up a hill to their left. "Welcome to your final resting place," the dark figure that had brought them there said, turned in his seat and flipped the dome light on. He had a mean looking face that complimented his mean looking hair which in turn complimented his mean sounding voice. "You may unbuckle yourselfs now."

Space-Bo and the chicken hastily undid their seatbelts.

"Do you like meat?" he asked.

The chicken shrugged. Space-Bo said, "Sure."

The mean man held up two plastic bags each with a piece of raw meat in it. "Here you go."

"Thanks," the chicken took one.

"Nah, I'm full." Space-Bo waved off his piece.

"Suit yourself," the mean guy stepped out of the aircar and headed up the muddy hill towards the manor.

Pocketing the plastic bag the Funky Chicken turned to Space-Bo, "Do you think he wants us to follow him?"

"If this is our final resting place, I can't see what we have to loose."

"Okay, after you." They stepped out, their feet squishing in wet grass. The mean stranger had no trouble surmounting the hill so the two followed him. They struggled several times before they made it all the way to the top of the very muddy hill. The guy was waiting for them at the front door of the manor. He was free of any mud and completely dry. He yawned and went inside.

The two shrugged to each other and headed toward the door. Rrrrrrr! Snarrl! Two ugly looking dogs foaming at the mouth came around the house then, running full tilt.

"Looks like you could you a piece of meat right about now," the chicken said pulling out his plastic bag.

"Dogs like me," Space-Bo confided before running at the dogs. "Come 'er poochie poochie poochie."

Right before he reached the dogs he slipped on some mud and slid down the hill. The dogs ignored him and kept after the chicken.

FC dived off the hill just as the dogs were going to nab him. He met Space-Bo at the bottom, both completely covered in mud. "You didn't have to do that, I was going to give you my piece of meat."

"Hey you're my friend. I wouldn't try to eat you."

"Not for you, for the dogs."

"I don't like to eat dog, it makes me fart. I'm sure you'd make them fart too. Besides, dogs like me."

"Well come on, we're late for dinner."

They made their way back up the hill where the dogs were waiting, foam still dripping from their fierce mouths onto the rain soaked lawn. The chicken charged the dogs with his arms out stretched. They jumped and locked their slobbery jaws on his feathered arms.

"Okay, we can go in now," the chicken led the way into the house with the dogs firmly attached.

The door led to a tiled floor lobby. To the left and right were single doors, and straight ahead a set of double doors. A plush chair sat against the wall to the right of the double doors. In it rested a fully clothed skeleton, its legs crossed, and looking at a yellowed book. The mean stranger was looking over the skeleton's shoulder.

"Who's that?" Space-Bo tried to make out the title of the book.

"Who gave you permission to ask a question?" The stranger stood there like a rock.

"No one did."

"This is Walther. He asked too many questions so I'm making him sit there for eternity. He wanted to read a book instead of kill people on my behalf so I granted his wish."

193

"Hello Walther," Space-Bo said waving at the old bones. He considered trying to shake hands the the skeleton, then thought better of it. Stranger things had happened to him lately.

"And who gave you permission to bring my dogs inside?" The mean one was glaring at the chicken.

"They did sir."

"Well kick them back outside and follow me."

The chicken stuck his arms out the door shaking them vigorously. "Help me a second 'Bo?"

As soon as Space-Bo came over to the door the dogs let go and leapt at him. They knocked him over licking his face affectionately. "Hey get off!"

The chicken quickly grabbed the dogs and chucked them out the door. He slammed it and turned around. The mean stranger was standing in the open double doors tapping his foot. The two followed him into the long columned hallway beyond. The tall columns alternated with weird bronze statues. An identical set of doors were at the far end. The stranger was pulling a hose out of the mouth of one of the bronze statues. "Stand over in the middle of the hall," he ordered .

As soon as they got there a high powered jet of water hit them washing the mud and muck away. The stranger put the hose up and moved on to the next statue, "Don't move." He pulled a bigger hose out from the mouth of the next statue. It was a blow dryer.

After they were all dried off, the mean stranger led them into a side room. A bar was inset in the left wall. Every shade of the rainbow was represented by a different colored drink on the shelfs above the bar.

"Time for a quick predinner drink," he said to no one before proceeding to pour himself a fine red wine the odor of which wafted enticingly over to the two.

"Uh..?" Space-Bo began.

"Be quite during our predinner drink."

While the mean guy slowly enjoyed his wine Space-Bo leaned over to the chicken saying, "He sure is weird."

"I don't care how weird he is. He's going to squish me in a garbage compactor."

"You're the weird one."

"Silence!" the man ordered.

The chicken whispered out the side of his beak, "Can't help it if I'm immortal?"

Finally the stranger put his glass down and walked to the other double doors.

"Come on."

They followed him into the grand ball room. A fire crackled in a huge hearth fifteen meters to the right. A twenty meter long solid wooden table covered most of the length of the room. The stranger sat at the head of the table.

Two places were set on either of him so they sat down. Five forks sat to the left of each plate and seven spoons to the right. Several knives of various shapes were placed in front of the plates and some other weird utensils above. A waiter hurriedly rushed up and set bowls of salad at each place even though only three were occupied.

"Course one," the stranger announced. "You may begin." And he proceed to down his bowl in two heaped forkful gulps.

The courses continued. Next was the soup, a green runny mess that tended to jump out of the bowl on its own, then there were biscuits stuffed with a juicy bubblegum center. The stranger chewed it awhile then spit it out on the floor when the next course arrived: steaming shish-kabob, half a meter long per person.

"Yumm yumm," Space-Bo commented.

"Quite you! This is dinner remember?"

"Sorry."

The fifth course was several heaps of different green vegetables. A bean type even had little worms cooked inside their shells. Looking closely Space-Bo thought he saw little apples stuck in the mouths of the worms. He shrugged and ate them anyway.

After that was the mashed potatoes with stuffing, three giant T-bone steaks (not from McCows), ultra garlic bread and salmonella spaghetti. Then there came the wine and crackers followed by the fruit and jello side dishes, and then the pudding and cobbler, ice cream and sorbet. Then there was the chocolate chip cookies and frozen eclairs, and finally frozen popsicles.

Space-Bo was stuffed but continued licking his popsicle. The Funky Chicken was eating his like it was the only thing he had ever eaten.

Up to that point not much had been said during the entire fourteen courses of the meal. The waiter had been speechless; his mouth was welded shut and a pad lock blocked a small straw hole.

"Ready to die yet?"

"I am," the chicken said.

Space-Bo gulped. The chicken was immortal but he wasn't. The chicken would have to distract the guy while he made a run for it. "I thought we got one last request."

"What is your request? It must be phrased in only one word though."

"Fine," Space-Bo pondered a moment then said, "Why?"

"Why? Do you mean why am I so mean?"

"Uh-huh."

"Because that's my name. I'm Grego the Mean."

"That's not an answer."

"What do you want, a case history?"

"Uh-huh." Anything to stall.

"I'll make your death very mean but okay I'll give you a case history. I was born along time ago. I grew up. I became greedy then took all the money."

"That's all there's to it?"

"Yes, even you could have done it if I wasn't going to kill you first."

"Well I guess you'll just have to be proven wrong."

"Never."

"You'll have to teach me or else be proven wrong."

"Very well, to prove my statement I will explain it so that even an imbecile like you could understand."

"Thank you."

"First you must gain control of the stock market through arbitration, insider trading, options, short selling, dirty underhanded dealings, assassinations, bribes, blackmail, extortion, tax evasion, fraud, conspiracy, arson, insurance scams, bankruptcies, false allegations, and general all around meanness."

"That all?"

Grego glared at Space-Bo, "I will most definitely have a blissful time watching you die. Anyway once you have the reins of power then you use your financial leverage to pry into the government, corrupting them to your personal needs. Then you set up a get away ranch far from civilization, take all the money, and leave."

"That sounds nice and everything but if you stayed in Balidron you could have been mean to more people. Why'd you run away?"

"Oh, in hopes of being even more mean in the near future."

"How?"

"You know of course you have gone over your limit of questions today. That means I get to kill you twice; kill you once, bring you back, then kill you again. Are you sure you want me to answer?"

"Oh sure." He could only hope he was buying the chicken enough time to formulate a plan.

"I am drilling a hole to the center of the planet."

"Oh, I see."

"If you knew what I was talking about I wouldn't be talking to you now, I'd be killing you."

"See you'll have been proven wrong twice in one day."

Grego picked up his used shish-kabob and waved it in Space-Bo's face, "Say hello to mister metal prong. He'll soon be your best friend..."

"Hello, mister prong."

"..embedded deep into your head."

The chicken kicked Space-Bo under the table. "Well, go on." He was sure FC had a plan now.

"One thing I'm sure your puny little brain knows is the fact that Deo 7's atmosphere is evaporating into space. And the oceans are being replenished from under the ground."

"Say no more. I see your dastardly deed laid out before my eyes."

"You don't know how dastardly it is yet. I won't tell you now but maybe in your next life or the one after that I'll explain it." Grego checked his watch. "Well, it's now that time." He wiped his mouth off with his silk napkin and stood up saying, "Please follow me to the torture chamber."

"Torture chamber?" The chicken was disappointed. "I thought I was going to be killed."

"That's right, with a trash compacter I believe. Let's go into the kitchen area first."

Space-Bo knew the chicken definitely had a plan now. They went into the kitchen where Grego put the chicken into a giant industrial strength garbage compactor. The hatch closed, buttons pushed, and the machine whirred into action. There was a click then the hatch opened. The Funky Chicken was gone.

"Hey, where'd he go?"

"Flushed down the sewage system. Now it's off to the torture chamber for you."

Space-Bo knew the chicken must have a plan, he always did. So Space-Bo followed Grego to the torture chamber. He sat patiently in a mega black barber-like chair waiting for Grego to get all the equipment set up.

"I'm ready," Grego said pulling out a squat steel box on rollers, "I'm going to put you into my new Wilson Steamomatic high pressure decimating machine."

"It looks very nice."

"I'm glad you agree," Grego shoved him into the tiny box and shut the hatch. Space-Bo saw Grego smiling evilly on the other side of a small but thick glass window. His finger was poised on the start button.

"Before you go would you like to know what is replacing the water?"

"Sure," Space-Bo tried to shrug but found it impossible in the cramped space. Grego pushed the button as he said, "The Nothing."

Chapter 17: The Galactic Church

The Galactic Church was open for business. There were ten main service halls and several smaller ones for special ceremonies. Each of the ten had a seating capacity of ten thousand faithfuls. Holy Give Shops and donation booths abounded in the main lobby. But the main part of the building complex was devoted to the Galactic Church Buffet.

The buffet line was a kind of pop-religious-cultural hang out for the faithful and pagans alike. Many messiahs and famous religious figures were represented by autographed scriptures, holoportraits and head slapping plates that adorned the walls. The most popular part of the place, unarguably, was the repenters gift shop where faithfuls could purchase the popular neon glazed monk habits with the GCB logo stamped on the left sleeve.

The Balidron branch was located in the southeast corner of the inner city on the other side of Kro-Chon town. As Rogicphil, RJ, and the bear pulled up it was thoroughly prime night feasting time. The parking garage were crowded so RJ made a hard hair pin turn that rolled the car onto three wheels then parked it lop sided between two other cars.

"That's great," Rogicphil said, "So how do we get out?"

"Easy. When the car we're resting on leaves our car will just flop into the space before anyone else gets it. I learned this trick from a trucker in Denver."

"Where are we?" It was Wimble who spoke crawling out from under the bear.

"Galactic Church Buffet. Where have you been?" Rogicphil answered.

"Asleep I guess."

"You mean you missed the part where we got abducted by sexy aliens?"

"Yeah, how was it?"

"Enlightening."

"Grrrrrrowl," the bear grumbled.

"Don't listen to him," RJ said crawling out of the side door, "We were arrested, ransacked the police headquarters and escaped before they knew what happened."

Wimble didn't know which lie to believe.

"Okay," Rogicphil said taking the initiative and shoved the other two out after RJ, "Let's go already. I'm getting hungry."

Some elegantly dressed ladies hurumpted and sneered as the four climbed out of the sideways car. "Back at cha, toots." RJ landed on the pavement.

The others got down and they walked to the entrance. "Act slightly civilized please," Wimble told RJ.

"Just a bunch of stuck up flousies..."

"That you'd love to meet. I'll introduce you later."

Inside they took a little table next to a potted bush, all the dark tables in the corner were occupied by people not wanting to be seen. To accomadate, the

Church had installed several dozen dark corners in the room. People who got there late had to get tables with bushes next to them so they wouldn't be seen.

One of the dancing waitresses danced over to their table. "Oh you guys," she tap danced in place holding an order pad in her hand, "You know it's going to be heck trying to get our car out of that space now."

"Hi Roxy," Wimble said with a blush.

"Oh hi Wimble you little twirp. I should of known it was you. You sure know how to pick 'em. So what'll you have?"

"Duh," Rogicphil said with a wink, "It's a buffet isn't it. What do you think we'll have?"

The woman threw plates at them and danced off.

Everyone except for Wimble grabbed a plate and got up intent on heading to the buffet line. Wimble stopped them, "What are you doing? You leave those here." He got up without a plate. "Follow me," he said heading to the line.

They would have shrugged before setting their plates back down on the table but their shoulders were sore from all the shrugging they'd been doing lately and so they didn't bother.

Wimble got on the conveyor belt first to show them how it was done. "It's angled at 40 degrees so you have to balance just right or you'll get thrown off. It took me a couple of times to get it right the first time I tried."

Rogicphil made as if to get on but Wimble held his hand out. "Watch me." He went to a serving table just to the side of the belt and grabbed one of a dozen corrugated dispensing tubes and squirted some gooy white substance into his mouth before stepping onto the belt.

The others did the same without question.

The belt ran in a wide oval around a strange tennis ball throwing looking machine. Only it wasn't throwing tennis balls but crutons instead. Lettuce was dangling from plastic strips just to the inside of the loop. Wimble grabbed some leaves and stuffed them in his mouth. As he whirled around the belt crutons came flying at him. Expertly he caught some in his mouth. The force of the cruton rammed it down his throat but the salid dressing behind it lubricated the way so it didn't hurt much. Other machines in the center of the oval were throwing other salad fixings as well.

About half way around the belt Wimble smacked a flat lever just outside the oval and a catapult arm swung out from under somewhere and flung him through the air to the next conveyor belt over. That was the fruit salad line.

They all managed to follow Wimble over to the new belt. "Hey, you guys learn quick," he said between mouthfuls of destroyed berries.

"We trained well for this mission," Rogicphil said proudly, "I'm going to try the gravy line next. I'll meet you back at the table shortly okay?"

"Okay." They all went their separate culinary ways.

Rogicphil met a nice fellow dripping with gravy the next line over. He was wearing a name badge with its own little wiper blades to keep itself clean and visible. Rogicphil noticed the hand drawn letters and the backward S. He also noticed despite the gravy a peculiar scent about the man.

"Yur hoggin mahy gravy son."

"Sorry." Rogicphil ducked the next round of dowsing. "Nice hat you have on there," he said pick pocketing the man.

After gulping a faceful of the white variety the man said, "Doan git smard wid mae," and jumped to the next line.

Rogicphil followed him to roast beef belt. The man was swabbing the thin slices he snatched out of the air all over his gravy stained body before stuffing them into his mouth.

RJ watched Rogicphil from the cranberry and chicken stuffing line. It looked like the Gladerunner was getting into a heated argument with a fat gravy covered man in overalls and a strawhat.

Back at the table Rogicphil was the last to come back and sit down. A chocholate malt was waiting for him. "Well, that settles it," he said after sucking on the malt for a few minutes, "We are in eminent danger."

Wimble looked around wildly, "The high priest is here?"

RJ knocked him on the head, "Not that kind of eminent. He means that the Cow is here."

"He's right," Rogicphil said slupping the last drops of malt, "I don't have time to explain the situation to you Wimble, so you'll just have to trust me. How do I get a refill by the way?"

"Here, I'll show you." Wimble grabbed one of the empty plates off the table and expertly threw it at a passing waitress. It shattered rudely on the back of her head.

"Oh, so that's what those are for." RJ said nodding his head.

After requesting another malt Rogicphil continued,
"That fat guy confirmed my suspicions about the cow's presence here. So until the coast is clear you guy's will need to go hide with the fat man at the Stock Exchange on The Island."

"Why the stock exchange? Is he and the cow trying to corrupt the financial system?"

"That's my guess. Among other things."

"Hold it right there," RJ said setting his plate down, "For all we know that fat guy is in cahootz with the satanic cow."

"Oh I know he's in cahootz with the cow."

"Excuse me," Wimble interrupted, "But here in Balidron, Cahootz in a brand of salad dressing."

"Don't worry. I'm on the verge of busting this whole thing wide open. I'll soon know where the cow is and what it's up to thereby giving me the advantage and the chance to create a counter decoy to let you escape."

They all looked at him like he was insane. Just then a plate shattered on the back of his head. He looked around quick enough to catch the waitress' smile before she pretended to be mean again.

Turning back to the others he continued, "I took a chance but it panned out. I confronted him directly. I told him I knew about the cow. At first he said he didn't know what I was talking about but I finally got him to admit he was involved after I showed him photocopies of the pictures I pilphered from his wallet."

"So what's the cow got him doing?"

"Contaminating the food supply of Deo 7. It's a devious plot. Even the chief of police is involved."

"Ufglong is involved in everything." Wimble took a sip of his Fuzgoo cola.

"Looks like the cow has had inroads here for quite some time now. I hope we're not too late."

"What's the fat guys name?"

"Barthan Transtyle. He's from some place called Hicksville."

"I was afraid of that. He also teaches a night school class called Cooking With Heat. My girlfriend's grandmother knows a girl from work that goes to his class. Ufrena says that..."

"Who's Ufrena?" RJ asked.

"My girlfriend's grandmother's friend from work. Anyway she says that the class was real boring and she was about to flunk out not having learned anything."

"Your work or your grandmother's?"

"My girlfriend's."

RJ put his plate down again. "This hardly has anything to due with the present situation."

"Listen. She says Transtyle offered to take her bad grades if she'd help him blow up a train."

"That's nice but..." Rogicphil watching the cute waitress fling plates around.

"You aren't listening."

"I don't care," he said getting up, "Stay here. This could be dangerous. If anything really weird happens make a run for it."

"And what's this got to do with the stock exchange?"

"Your advice will be taken into consideration." He casually walked into a flying plate, admiring potted bushes along the way.

*   *   *

Barthan Transtyle (no relation to the editor) waddled up to the table, "Oh Ah do see mah new cookin students awe heeah." He leaned over and winked a couple of times, "We had betta git goin fore da yeast molds."

Ranger Joe got up, "Yeah, yeah we know all about it buster." Soon he, the bear, and Wimble were in Barthan's stretch luxury hover pickup cruising west.

"So whut awre yu guys anyhauh? Smugglers ur somethin?"

"How did you ever guess?"

"Ah cin smells ya frum da nex planit ohver."

"You're real smart," Joe shrugged at the bear.

The hover pickup docked with a maglev skid and they were off zooming 1000 kph down the maglev rail system. A few minutes later the pickup disembarked off the rail then hovered away. They went through a tunnel coming to a stop in a huge but vacant parking lot.

Transtyle stuck his head out the window and took a wiff. A terrible odor washed in over them and the least of it was concentrated deo smell. "We're here, Balidron Stock Exchange."

RJ had learned to hold his breath whenever a window was opened and so didn't notice the discrepancy in the tinge of foulness.

Rogicphil watched them leave the Church out of the corner of his eye. Ranger Joe would be able to take of himself if something happened. He took some pay from the dancing waitress to leave early and they spent some quality time in the sideways parked ground car.

"Scumbag," she yelled climbing out, "You've got some nerve," and stormed away.

He considered throwing another plate at her but checked himself. What had he done wrong?

Pondering his decisions that night he reentered the lobby and without thinking entered the door labeled Authorized Personnel Only.

A robed bald man sitting at a desk and studying some scribbles on thick parchment looked up, "You're not authorized, you can't come in here."

"I am authorized," Rogicphil declared suddenly.

"Only myself and Chancellor Kolm are allowed in here. Get out before I call security."

"I thought you said only you and Kolm were allowed in here." Rogicphil looked around the rather boring room. "Won't the security guards just wait outside until they're magically transformed into either you or Kolm?"

The monk was beginning to turning red.

"Besides Kolm asked me to take over for a while. So you can just scram buddy."

The monk stood up angry. "Kolm would never do such a thing. And you're not even properly dressed."

"Then what's that note on your desk there?"

The monk looked on his desk, "I see no note."

Rogicphil bent over trying to see for himself, "He said he would leave it in plain sight." Quickly before either the robed man or the security cameras could notice Rogicphil searched around the small study, looking for an example of Kolm's handwriting. He found an order slip for a box of suppositories signed by Kolm. Perfect except that it lacked several key letters. Then he found an underwater postcard sent to a Chancellor Lonk postmarked from the Triguard system. The two writing styles was very similar and he hoped the robed man wouldn't notice the difference. With all the letters he needed he hastily wrote a note on the back of a napkin he'd pilfered from the fat man's wallet then slipped it under one of the big scrolls. It was all over in a few microseconds and no one was the wiser.

At regular speed Rogicphil found a large piece of lint on the floor. He placed it on the monk's shoulder saying, "A big fat piece of lint to be exact." He showed the lint to the him.

"Thank you but you still shouldn't be here," he pushed Rogicphil's hand away. "I can assure you there is no note."

Rogicphil placed his hands on the table and leaned forward before fake slipping and pushed the scroll to the side revealing the note. "See there was a note after all."

Incredulously the monk picked it up and read:

There is a close personal friend of mine coming by today. Please extend him your kindest hospitality until I regurgitate. And don't try to call security on him either -Chancellor Kolm

"I don't believe it. It's signed by Kolm. Incredible."

"May I wait here?"

"It seems that I have no choice." The monk got up scratching his bald head, "I must be cooking too hard. Excuse me while I get the assistant Chancellor for you." The monk stepped into a quickvader Rogicphil hadn't noticed before and zoomed away.

Now that he had plenty of time Rogicphil got up to search for clues. He had just opened the main desk drawer to pilfer whatever goodies lay inside when the lamp rang. He shrugged and answered the lamp like phone, "Martonellis Body Shop."

"QUIT THAT NONSENSE AND GET INTO MY OFFICE!" It was Destiny, and he sounded slightly malevolent.

Rogicphil opened the door out into the lobby but entered Destiny's office instead. "Hello."

Destiny was pacing back and forth on a hand carved space gypsy rug. "WHAT DO YOU THINK YOU'RE DOING?" he didn't give Rogicphil a chance to answer before continuing, "THIS IS NO PICNIC, NO SCUBA DIVE, NO TAXI CAB DRIVING LESSON. THIS IS STOPPING A BLUMMBERING PLANET FROM RUINING THE UNIVERSE. YOU'RE NOT DOING THAT, YOU'RE PESTERING SOME POOR RELIGIOUS PEOPLE. I DON'T THINK YOU UNDERSTAND JUST HOW IMPORTANT THIS SLEAZY LITTLE PLANET REALLY IS."

"I was hot on the trail of..."

"BE QUITE. YOU WERE GOOFING OFF. I THOUGHT YOU'D GET YOUR MIND CLEAR WHEN ROXY LEFT BUT NO... "

Rogicphil thought back to what went wrong in the back seat of the car. "You did something to the waitress. I knew it."

"NO THAT WAS YOUR OWN STUPIDITY AGAIN. MAYBE IF I GIVE YOU A TASTE OF WHAT WILL HAPPEN IF YOU DON'T SUCCEED, YOUR BRAIN MIGHT WORM ITS WAY BACK INTO YOUR SKULL." Destiny smothered his cigar in a pink ashtray resting on corner of his desk, "I THINK IT'S TIME WE TOOK A TRIP." With a wave of his hand the room vanished. They were left floating in a black looking void. "BEHOLD."

Before Rogicphil's eyes the universe exploded.

*   *   *

The Balidron Stock Market only played a small part in the economic scheme of Deo 7. Unlike other stock markets with multi diversified formats the Balidron market dealt in only two issues: Kebber Mining preferred premium grade A stock and Purple Dots. Other more conventional common stock vehicles were serviced by the Black Market.

Kebber preferred premium grade A stock had become the key economic indicator. The other indicators, disgusting national modulus, the trade deficit, and the quarterly disemployment percentages, to name a few, were ignored for the more optimistic and preferred Kebber stock.

As for the Purple Dots, the financial sector had come to widely accept these nontangible promissory notes. They were invented by Restaplat Phlatmier a financial genius and new age musician in his own time. He invented the first Purple Dot, as the story goes, when he spilled some purple ink on a sheet of legal jargon and a friend of his, Yors Fargret, said historically, "I'll buy that."

But Barthan Transtyle didn't take them to the Stock Market but rather to the Stock Exchange. The Stock Exchange was where the easily transportable McCattle were traded.

RJ followed Barthan down a long hallway. The bear and Wimble were close behind. He was beginning to get a sense that the scents weren't right. The building they were in was dark and foreboding at night, not as bad as during the day but pretty nasty in its own right. The halls filled with hundreds of people during the day seemed hallow and barren to RJ. They came to a door labeled: Transtyle and Associates. Barthan pulled out a long skeleton key, breathed heavily on it and the door unlocked.

Inside was a small secretaries desk in one corner and a larger desk near the opposite wall. To the right was a sofa with what looked like someone sleeping on it.

"So," Barthan said taking out a briefcase and sitting it on the desk behind him, "Whuh kinda inforn-mayshun yous un ofrin mae ta mawk duh shipmunt?"

RJ knew he'd need to get him admit some sort of guilt before pretending to be a cop. Cops did that so if RJ didn't act like a cop Barthan would know they were really after the cow. "I guess you're kind of use to this sort of thing. It's my first time."

"Cuh mon sonny," Barthan turned to face them, "Ah taint got awl daey. Thu cows doan go un cook demselvs."

"Hey that's a nice painting," he went over to look at a big super brown splotch nailed to the wall.

"Thar aint no paintin, it's mae eifer's foourst poop."

"I see," RJ looked toward the bear for help. The bear just shrugged. RJ turned back to Transtyle, "So you want me to give you information so that you can get rich cheating the stock market, right?"

"Whur arr yu, stuhpid? O course Ah.." he stopped and looked at RJ closely with cold deadly eyes, "Yor no smuggler."

Joe just shrugged.

"Ah nose whod jar now," Transtyle pulled a blaster out of his pocket, "Its uh set up! Yors fum Micky D's tryun ta blackmail mae. Stinkin fotnozlixels!" he aimed at Wimble, the easiest looking target. Blast! Wimble fell. He aimed at Joe who was charging him. Blast! Joe fell. He aimed at the bear.

Crunch! The bear got to him first.

*   *   *

Meanwhile Wilber and Jake were running down the curving ramps again in that weird undergrand cave.

"He's only our boss when we're on this planet you know," Jake was saying almost out of breath.

"Yes, but I got a feeling about this one. He's got ambition written all over him. But it's in invisible ink."

They hurried into the junior grade Bossman of Rall Raul Beta's office. "You called for us sir?"

The Bossman was deep in thought and had a scowl on his face, "Eh?"

"You called us all the back to Raul Rall Beta. We were on an important mission on Deo 7 and..." Wilbur's voice trailed off.

The Bossman swiveled his evil looking chair towards them. His face twisted into a ghoulsome appearance. "You fools have bungled up for the last time. I'm sending you down to maintenance to have your mind's blanked and have you reformated. I have an ultra secret mission for you afterwards. But I'll tell you now so you can't screw it up later."

Wilbur and Jake looked at each other. Yep, they were going to be recycled. "Told you," whispered Jake.

Wilbur kicked Jakes shin then said, "Good idea," to the Bossman.

"Your mission is to kill the High AntiBishop Lester. Got it?"

"But Lester's our friend. Not to mention *your* boss."

"Yeah," Jake lilted, "Remember that time he helped you get off the toilet after someone covered the seat with super glue?"

"And what about when we killed your brother, Jake, and Lester covered for us?"

"You'll forget all that once you've been reformated." The Bossman began to sweat and tried to gently push the YIG letter out of their sight. No sense in those two fools seeing his private business.

"Well, I guess it's okay then."

The letter was safely pushed over the desk and into a wastepaper basket. The Bossman propped his feet up on his desk. "Once Lester is out of the way I need you two to hurry back and kill that survey team on Deo 7. You know, the enemy agents you were sent to spy on?"

"Kill 'em? That's not what Lester wanted us to do." "They don't look nothin' like their pictures, boss," Jake added.

"I don't care if they look like farm animals, get them killed."

"If you say so."

"When you've done all that come back here so I can give you some paint and brushes. The food court is starting to peal paint."

"That all?"

"Yes, now leave before I have to get my pitchfork."

They turned to leave but Wilbur noticed the full wastepaper basket. "I'll just take this out for you, sir."

"Yes, yes. Now get."

They hurried out.

The Bossman gloated. Once Lester was out of the way, the whole Galaxy would be his for the taking; forget about wimpy Deo 7. They'd been punished enough already. The Galaxy awaited his greatness. It will be fun, very fun indeed.

Chapter 18: Just Along for the Ride

Rogicphil Suflipinic appeared in front of the counter of the Repenter's Gift Shoppe in the heart of the Galactic Church Cafe. He looked around at the monk habits and the head slapping plates on the walls. What the heck was he doing here? He needed a small spaceship, not souvenirs. But, what the heck.

A tall skinny girl wearing a mongo purple blindfold approached him. "How can I hinder you today sir/madam?"

"What do you have along the lines of used spaceships?"

"Used spaceships? I don't under...?"

He tilted his head slightly to one side, "Why are you wearing that blindfold?"

The girl brought her hand to the odd purple cloth, lightly touching it. "So I don't unduly bias myself towards my enemies or customers."

That seemed reasonable to Rogicphil. But that didn't explain the fact that all the other gift shop workers weren't blindfolded. "What about them?"

"Who? The other workers? They're blindfolded too aren't they?"

"No, I think you've been duped."

"Oh well, what were you saying about a spaceship?"

Rogicphil pulled the blindfold up. Her eyes were closed tightly.

"Hey!" she stepped back repositioning the blindfold on her face. "You can get arrested for that. I might start insulting you for real as well."

"I'm just looking far a used spaceship but since I see you don't have one I think I'll leave."

"No, wait, we've got a used washing machine."

"No, I like to buy new clothes instead."

"You can't leave without buying something," the girl pleaded, grabbing his arm.

Rogicphil paused, "Why not?"

"It's a very nice washing machine," she tugged on his arm, trying to lead him into the back room but the counter got in the way. She dragged him over it with surprising strength as if she didn't know it was there.

Reluctantly Rogicphil followed her into the back room. She pointed over to a corner where a large cylindrical device shook back and forth. It didn't look like any washing machine he'd ever seen before.

"I need a spaceship not a washing machine," he tried to explain.

"But you must buy it," she pleaded, "Or the police will take my children away."

If it wasn't for her iron grip he would have been halfway across Balidron by then. He needed to find a ship and quick or Destiny would be really mad. "Okay I'll take it."

She was at the tubes disconnecting them from the wall before he had finished speaking. "It's a very nice model, and even though it is used, it will wash your clothes very well."

He bent down looking for the label. He wiped off a smudge of dirt that covered a raised plate. It said: 1941 Fiat. "Oh it's a Fiat, model 1941, very nice," he lied and stuck his tongue out in disgust.

She took his ID to the cash register while he lifted it to his back. She hurried back and stuffed a wag of nega money into his mouth. "Thanks for shopping at the Galactic Church."

"Wore wallcom," he mumbled then willed his boots into roller skates and rolled out of the shop and back out to the public area. Half a meter of wall on all sides of the entry way came with him.

The girl who knew the exact location of the washing machine tubes apparently didn't notice the rubble as she ran towards him. "You forgot your receipt," she said slapping a receipt onto the machine.

"This is awkward." He set the thing down. "You have any rope I could borrow?"

Another worker from the gift shop came at just then looking angry. "You stupid nit!" she accosted the girl with the purple blindfold, "Look what you've done to the doorway."

The girl with the blindfold turned her head back and forth as if she was really looking, "What door?"

"Exactly. And you're not even helping the customer with his purchase." This last statement was in reference to Rogicphil who was trying figure out a better way to transport his purchase. "And, hey, that's our washing machine. What's he doing with that?"

The girl with the purple blindfold handed him some diamantoid rope from her smock. He could tell that things were about to get messy so with a quick double knot he secured the washing machine and began to ease out of the picture.

As if to prove the point, the other worker pulled a long barreled shot pistol from her pocket. She loaded two shells in and carefully lowered it at the purple blindfold.

"Okay, game's over." Rogicphil grabbed up the girl and skated out of the gift shop, the cafe, and the entire Galactic Church in a blur well before the pistol blasts could be heard. He decided to take the scenic route through Balidron and back to the Happyville parking lot outside the star port.

"I suppose I'll get fired now," the girl was saying.

"What makes you think that?" They swerved around a couple of oncoming hover trucks. A ramp shot them down into the underground freeway.

"Did you see the size of that gun she pulled out?"

"Yes, but you didn't." Cars honked at the man roller skating down the freeway with a washing machine strapped to his back and a blindfolded girl in his arms.

"That's beside the point. What am I going to do now that I don't have a job and the police are going to impound my children?"

"Are they really your children or are you just taking care of them while the real parents are out scuba diving?"

Another ramp appeared and they shot out of the tunnels flying fifty meters up into the smog filled air. The city lights surrounded them on all sides while they floated almost effortlessly in free fall.

Rogicphil's boots turned into helicopter shoes but the added weight brought them gently down to the asphalt planes on the other side of a force wall. The boots resumed roller skate mode and they were off again.

"I guess, legally, their parents are the Superlative Industries'."

"That's awful!"

"Not really. You off-worlders have a different set of values than the people here." She pulled the blindfold up a bit and opened her eyes, "AAAAA!"

They narrowly missed getting sucked up into the vent of a super jumbo jet which had lost its way and was wandering around the streets of Happyville while several minor gangs took pot shots as it passed.

Rogicphil pulled the blindfold back down and sped on by the wayward craft. Behind the next building the massive parking lot came into view.

"You need help," he said coming to a halt at the spot where he had left the shuttle. Instead of the shuttle there was a smashed up pile of metal in the space and on top of it was the bear.

"Grrr..." the bear mumbled.

"What happened to the shuttle?" he asked setting girl on the ground.

The bear shrugged. His trench coat was torn and there was blood on its paws and mouth. It looked really mad about something. It growled and moved its pays about in the air trying to tell him what had happened but it wasn't getting through to Rogicphil.

"That's terrible!" The girl covered her mouth with her hand, "Oh and horrible too."

"You can understand him?"

"Him? That lady says that Joe and Wimble were wasted but he got the crook with the gun."

"Huh?" Rogicphil felt his legs weaken under him. He dropped the washing machine next to the shuttle debris. "This isn't good, not good at all."

He took a long look at the bear then said, "What happened exactly?"

In a convoluted way the bear related through the girl the events that had led up to Joe's and Wimble's demise. Rogicphil swore he'd punch Destiny a good one next time they met.

Just then a delivery boy from the Galactic Snail Mail Corporation rode up behind him. There was a large box strapped to the back of his bicycle. "Package for mister Gladerunner."

He looked up at the odd looking boy, "Uh, that's me."

The boy dropped the box, said, "Thank you," and bicycled off with the ring-ring of his bike bell.

A label on the side of the box proclaimed the sender to be Quasar Industries. Rogicphil raised his eyebrow at this. Destiny had said something about a gift from the celestial Quasar intelligences but he hadn't expected anything so soon.

Rogicphil checked the address label:

> Mister Gladerunner
> Parking Range 302/27B-6
> Happyville, Balidron, Deo 7
> Sector B12, Soggy Place Galaxy
> Big Idiot Universe

But the really strange thing was the post mark, February 17, 102691. Ten years ago. "Well, that's Snail Mail for you."

Inside the box were two metal ball like tube thingees half a meter long and about 25 centimeters in diameter each. A long red wire stuck out at the ends. Black lettering on their sides said: High power accelerator, refueling not required, no user serviceable parts inside, lifeforce null and void if tampered with.

The first thing Rogicphil did was open one of them up. A searing blue light shot out at an angle destroying several parked vehicles before ripping a small hole in Deo 7's atmosphere and disappearing into outer space. Faster than lightning reflexes snapped the access panel closed again.

"Oops."

To the bear and the girl the parked vehicles disintegrated in an instant; they didn't even realize a beam of incredible energy had suddenly flashed by.*

Rogicphil pulled a small instruction manual out of the box that had Quasar Industries stamped all over it. He flipped through it and tossed it to the side. "Dang it!" he stood up, "I need a space ship. I can't just strap these engine pods on my legs and fly off."

The bear scratched its head.

"Listen," he told the bear, "You take..." he glanced over to the girl, "What's your name again?"

"I'm not going to tell you yet."

"Okay,........What about now?"

She stood firm with her arms folded.

"Take miss Mongo Purple here back to her apartment and help her get her children. Then..."

"If you insist on calling me that you should use the proper inflection which would be *Monga* Purple."

"....Then meet me back here in twenty-four hours and we'll head back to the ship and regroup."

The girl took the bear's paw and led him (her?) away, "Oh you poor girl..."

"Wait a sec," Rogicphil called them back, "Why do you think the bear is a female?"

"Why do you think the bear is male?" she shot back.

"Uh, because he's a guy and likes to fart and drink beer."

"You are so species-centric. This is the 1028th century already. You need to get over it." She led the bear away ignoring further attempts by Rogicphil for a straight answer.

When they were gone Rogicphil started poking through the shuttle wreckage looking for salvageable parts. He found the license plate inside a half burnt refrigerator he didn't remember having on the shuttle. The license plate read: LN-8A-5BA. That's stupid. And this wasn't his shuttle. He specifically remembered leaving Shuttle Alpha here.

With a moan he sat back down on the wreckage and put his head in his hands. This whole mission was backfiring. Everything was going wrong. No one had reported in like they were suppose to. He couldn't reach Plutoman's

209

starcruise up in orbit. And Destiny wouldn't shut up taking about the end of the universe long enough for him to ask important questions.

He felt stupid and very alone. He had to make up for his mistakes and set things right somehow. And that meant starting from the first ones all the way back to the last stupid, arrogant, mistake he had made. That was why he needed a decent spaceship.

He looked up and over to the washing machine lying on its side and a brilliant idea hit him.

*   *   *

The two spaceships nearly collided head on. Both pilots were fast asleep and only the quick thinking of one of the passengers in the parasite ship which hung to the underbelly of the larger of the two main ships, saved the lives of all present, and quite unknowingly.

Sir Rontho and Dr. Shandrydan were having their four o'clock (they didn't know about Galactic Standard Time GST) tea when Rontho noticed something strange on the radar scope.

"I say, you left your video game on Shandrydan. It's making my Duke Technicolor taste funny."

"Huh?" Shandrydan turned around to see the tiny dot approaching at trans-relativistic speed. "That can't be. This radar unit is based on the electromagnetic wave theory which states nothing can go faster then the speed of light. So how can we even detect something moving that fast relative to us with this obviously outdated equipment?"

"Quit babbling man and do something."

Fred added a couple lumps of sugar to Rontho's tea then hit the SOS beacon. Nothing happened.

"Try again."

Fred added another couple more lumps then boosted the transmitter power up to 22 megawatts and directed the beam at he approaching ship. He didn't know if they still used SOS beacons in this strange new far future they found themselves in, but what the heck.

"Much better," Rontho said tasting his tea again.

Rogicphil only remembered what happened before it did. You see it was his spaceship, the 1941 Fiat 'washing machine', with the Quasar engines, that was approaching with trans-relativistic speed. Only with special spatial distortion technology could he make his presence known. Luckily, or unluckily for him, he had accidentally set the distortion field instead of the alarm clock before he went to sleep.

Now he was suddenly awaken by an insistent call on the emergency side band. He flipped it to audio.

"Help us, help us, help us...." a squeaky computer voice droned as it liberally interpreted the SOS signal. Rogicphil checked his scanners but couldn't see anything in front of him because of his speed. Then he remembered the temporal wake reflections caused by trans-relativistic speed so he just rewound the recorded video of the flight to see what he had done (will do). The playback showed his ship narrowly missing an oncoming alien warship sneakily disguised as a lowly space-truck. (But he didn't know about that part until much later (earlier?)).

That was really strange. What was a space-truck doing out in deep space when wormholes transferred ships quickly between systems? He personally was out in deep space because the seemingly magical engines he had recently received from the Quasars allowed him to travel directly through space even faster than the wormhole method. He'd have to worry about the space-truck later or suffer a massive editing to his video playback.

The space-truck driver, originally from the Eighth Millennium where he'd just had some nifty and scary looking art painted on the side of his rig, and who wasn't even aware that he'd accidentally been sucked up into the future by Shandrydan's wave-riding space capsule, would have a lot explaining to do to his undergarment laundry person. But at least he was still alive after the ships skidded past each other, without everyone being turned back into vaporized recycled star stuff.

Rontho and Shandrydan's space capsule was thrown free by the huge gravitational disturbance caused by the temporal wake and were consequently accelerated into a nice orbit around Deo 7.

A rather lengthy ordeal follows, wherein they land, are captured by agents of H.E.L.L, loose their capsule, escape, get stranded in a swamp, fall in love, swap brains with swamp gators, travel in time, get their capsule back, and finally fly through space once more, only to wind up in orbit around Rall Raul Beta at exactly the same time.

"Good job, old fellow, jolly good show. Now where in God's Milky Way Galaxy are we?" Sir Rontho tried to set his empty cup of tea down on the console but it just floated away unnoticed. He watched the pretty blue planet swing slowly by below. (*By the way, Rontho wasn't aware that the name was changed from Milky Way Galaxy to Soggy Place Galaxy due to a Trademark infringement case in 80808.*)

"Fifth planet in this system, sir. It's been recently (last 1000 years relative to geological standard) terraformed and currently occupied." Now that they were no longer accelerating, there wasn't any G-force on the capsule so Shandrydan unbuckeled himself and went floating after the wayward teacup.

"This is it, Shandrydan," Rontho said excitedly, "This is where the Supreme Galactic Counsel has taken our agent."

"You said that last time Sir, and the probability of it being the case hasn't changed any. As I reminded you before, such an organization remains highly unlikely to have ever existed in the first place..."

"No matter, prepare to land."

Shandrydan gave up on the tea cup and went back to his seat. "Ut-oh," he said noticing something strange.

"What ut-oh?"

"We've been spotted. A ship is approaching."

"Hail them right away. Once my identity is known they will let us land unharmed."

"I don't think..."

"Very good, you don't think, you just obey."

Shandrydan sighed and cranked up the transmitter. "Attention approaching vessel, this is the ship of Sir Rontho, knight of the British Crown, Heir to the thrown, Great land holder, et cetera... et cetera... Identify yourself please."

"I don't care what part of the anatomy you're from you can't fly here," a voice at the other end recriminated them.

"Let me speak." Rontho took the mic. "This is Sir Rontho. Whom may I ask, am I speaking with?"

"Sir Rontho! I'm so sorry sir, I didn't know it was you. This is Captainess Joehon Mel-Sebuttun of the RRB Space Squad at your service."

"Captainess," Rontho's military manner was very apparent by the sternness of his voice, "We are on our way to a very important meeting of the Supreme Galactic Command and..."

"Counsel..." Fred peeped.

"Quite, doctor. I'm trying to tell this good woman of our mission to save the universe."

"Ooo, just a second," the Captainess said all squirmy and went to consult a inferior who was greedily examining the readout from their lifeform scan. "Sorry Sir," she began after returning, "You may proceed to land at the designated coordinates. If I can be of any further assist..."

"Yes you most certainly can, my dear lady. Radio down to the surface and have your top scientist meet us at the pad along with the Full Imperial Cabinet."

Shandrydan tapped Rontho on the shoulder, "Since when do they let women serve as captains?"

"Quiet you..."

"I didn't mean to offend," the unseen Captainess apologized.

"Not you, fair soldier. I was talking to someone else less civilized." He glared at Shandrydan but continued talking into the mic, "I'll be sure to remember this when your promotion comes up." Rontho cut the connection before Joehon could thank him, then ordered Shandrydan to land.

"Yes sir," Fred sighed again and did as he was told, just like everyone else who had had the privilege of getting spoken to by Rontho.

Twenty minutes later their tiny and ancient capsule was greeted by a throng of reporters and security guards. "How do you feel to be the first alien race to be discovered on Rall Raul Beta?" a reporter asked Rontho as he came down the ramp.

"Well, I've never been here before."

It was midday and the G2 star beat down on the landing pad. Sweat from the reporters made the asphalt surface sticky to walk on and Rontho considered the cost of his new shoes. "Now, away with you," he shoved the reporter to the side with his handkerchief in order to get a better look at the walking surface.

A short curly haired man ran up to greet them, his shoes making a distinctive grumption. "Heelo," he said in a whiney shrill voice, "My name ees doktor Vadlin Nosehonka. I am ate yor survees."

"Hello doctor, this is my assistant, Dr. Shandrydan." Rontho introduced the two gentlemen of letters and watched them perform a secret doctor handshake, which hadn't changed in eons, and for the most part consisted mainly of taking each others pulse. Finally, after that dreadful ritual had passed, he said, "And I am Sir Rontho." He held out his hand to be kissed.

"Et ist thruly an honor to meet yu, iv dere ist anyting I cin do fur yu just say eet." He sniffed Rontho's hand, not sure what he was expected to do.

Rontho smacked him in the nose and replied, "A red carpet would be a nice start."

"Rite avay." He pulled a brochure out of his jacket, "My bruda owns a ootlet een Neppit."

Shandrydan tapped his boss on the shoulder, "I can give you a piggy back ride sir, if you don't feel like walking."

"Jolly good idea, I say." Rontho leapt onto the doctor's back with astute grace. "March!"

("We are now witnessing the mating ritual of this new alien race just discovered by your roving reporter Brah Moldin for ReAction 7 Snews.")

"Vere aw we going?"

"The Grand Pavilion where else?" Rontho pointed forward and Shandrydan stepped out into the sweaty throng.

"I goat yur signull but dere ist no command hear," Nosehonka mucked along beside shoving reporters to the side.

("Emminet scientist Vadbil Rosetonka, noted for defining the word molotov-cartail is attempting to communicate with the aliens.")

"I must speak truly with you then, we aren't here to see the High Galactic Corollary.."

"Counsel.."

"..We are looking for someone." Rontho noted the strange colored trees off in the distance.

Aha, thought Nosehonka, they have come for his bird. They must be from the Galactic Zoological Society masquerading as aliens. Well he knew how to take care of that. "A large rhinocerous type?"

"No, no a short funny looking man, acts stupid sometimes."

"I mite no vere dis man ist," Nosehonka lied, "If I heelp yu find heem voud yu heelp me find my rhino?"

"Oh course, Shandrydan here is an expert on birds," Rontho lied. Fred sighed.

("Doctor KnowsDonna, who was recently caught sleeping with a different secretary, is leading the aliens into a cleverly designed trap in order to tag them and study their use of hand weapons during mating. I of course will follow along with this story to the bitter and boring end.")

Nosehonka smiled, he was too smart for them; that slip about birds gave them away. Ha ha, he had them now. "Hurie up my ship ist veyting an reddy to go."

They followed the curious little man through the throng of reporters to another larger space capsule with RRB Space Squad stamped all over it. The three of them climbed the ramp into the steamy interior of the cargo bay. The reporters followed. The autohatch closed and the capsule hurled itself into the air on a preprogrammed course.

"What's that awful smell?" someone asked.

"Smells like body odor."

213

"Who's the idiot that let all these reporters inside?"

("This is Brah Moldin for ReAction 7 Snews reporting to you live from inside the hull of a terrorist spacecraft which has kidnapped almost fifty emminent scientists and reporters, myself included...")

Shandrydan was attempting to close the hatch from inside the air conditioned control room as Nosehonka shoved the microphone wielding hands back out into the cargo bay. Fred tossed a time released deo bomb out the door right before they finally managed to get it shut and sat back exhausted on the nice cool floor.

"Good thing we stopped by Deo 7 before this dreadful place." Rontho reached into his pocket for a daub of Kebber grade A deodorant but it was gone. He pocket was gone too.

Nosehonka crawled into the pilots seat. "Sury about zee smell, but dere ist no deodorant on board."

Rontho found a vanity mirror above the minifridge in the corner. Oh no! He'd forgotten to switch back bodies with those damnable Deo 7 swamp gators. Staring back at him from the mirror was an ugly six legged semi-marine reptile. With no clothes on. How uncouth. "Shandrydan!" he yelled.

"Sorry sir," the exhausted crazy old doctor, also still in a swamp gator body, said, "We were in such a hurry to get away from those rhinoceros people I totally forgot."

"Rhinoceros people?"

"Don't you remember? They were trying to get us to vote for them in the upcoming election."

"You are too kind sometimes, Shandrydan. I just call them liars. No matter, we're finally back on the trail of Greyson. That's all that matters."

"But why sir?" He leaned close and whispered so that Nosehonka wouldn't hear, "We finally have the secret to time travel. We can do whatever we want now."

"You'll understand some day." Rontho went over to Nosehonka and gave him a better description of Greyson.

"I nuu jus dee pursoon hoo vill elp oos." He made a quick brainlink call and soon they were rendezvousing with a large blimp.

Presently the King of Rall Raul Beta was on board and very happy to meet the time traveling aliens. He soon had them all, except Shandrydan, hooked on a new musical experience he'd recently acquired.

"He went to Deo 7 you say?" Rontho asked upon hearing about the last known whereabouts of Greyson. "He's a good boy you know."

"Of course," the King said jovially, "He helped me find a piggy bank I thought I'd lost after all."

As they reminisced about odd Greyson stories and Shandrydan sulked in a corner reading outdated copies of Janitor's Review magazines, Nosehonka punched in the coordinates for the local orbiting wormhole and watched the blue sky fade into the bleak blackness of space.

Back down on the surface someone finally noticed that their (the space squad's) spaceship was gone. And Nosehonka. And the aliens. THE ALIENS!

Captainess Joehona Mel-Sebuttin yelled at her lieutenents, "Nosehonka's double crossed us and has taken the aliens offworld. After him!"

Joehona and the others of her Space Squad appropiated a nearby Galactic Space Environmental Survey Vessel. The ship blasted off in a choking black cloud of pollution friendly emissions.

As they were traversing the wormhole, Rontho suddenly remembered they had left their old space capsule back on the planet. "Shandrydan," he said kicking the old bastard awake, "Don't tell me you forgot the clicker too."

"What?" he said coming to. "Huh?" he checked what passed for pockets on a swampgators body and found the keys to the space capsule tucked securely under a patch of green scales. He grabbed the small back fob and pressed the recently installed transdimensional recall button.

There was a sudden thud back in the cargo hold and the untimely demise of a few reports as their junky old space capsule materialized out of thin air.

"Good thing we weren't in the middle of a wormhole when I did that," Shandrydan say wiping his brow.

"Why is that?"

Before Rontho could get an answer their currently stolen ship was violently expelled from the wormhole conduit in mid-jump and dumped into orbit around the wrong star.

Vadlin checked the scanners then smiled evilly to himself before saying out loud, "Splas Toorg."

"Oh joy!" the King shouted. "Field trip."

What Vadlin failed to mention to Sir Rontho was that they had a stowaway on board (because he didn't know about it) and that Splas Toorg was the Galaxy's designated star system of nuclear waste disposal (which he did know about and willingly withheld, just to be a jerk about it).

Chapter 19: Dr Gronblec, Bowlingologist

Rogicphil walked into the offices of the Danville Daily Digest newspaper. He was loosely dressed in a t-shirt and fake space marine pants. Ms. Editor was sipping her morning coffee while proofreading the copy so she didn't see him.

"Don't you know it's dangerous to proofread while drinking coffee?"

She looked up thinking it was the delivery boy. "Oh no you don't. Get out of here Suflipinic."

"That's a nice way to greet a dead man."

"Exactly, if you don't get out of here right now the life insurance man will revoke our policy."

"Forget the insurance, I'm alive."

"And you didn't even find Dr. Gronblec. Where have you been for the last two weeks? Probably boozing it up over at O'Nelly's Space Food."

"Didn't you get my uploaded installments?"

"Are you referring to the Fabulous Yeast Farm E. Coli bread the stove...?"

"Huh?"

She pulled out a copy of one of Rogicphil's transmitted reports. "It's what you wrote, drunk, I imagine."

Rogicphil looked over the print-out. "Oh no, I forgot to reset the grammar filter on that old processor. It must have been set to translate for biologists."

"Whatever..."

"But listen to me, this is important. Has any of my team reported in during the last two weeks?"

"So, you WERE at O'Nelly's. I knew I should have checked."

"I wasn't at O'Nelly's, I was out of the system saving the universe."

"Well that should increase distribution."

"I'm not done yet, but I needed to make sure my team is okay. I left them in a cave with some crazy old man and a load of nerfherding cavemen."

Ms. Editor grabbed up a pen, "What's a nerf?"

"I don't know, just something I heard on an old holo-movie somewhere. When this is all over I'll take care of the insurance man for you plus the greatest story to ever to hit a newspaper in this Galaxy."

"Don't tell me you've seen Elvis Christ? That should make page two."

"Better, a Supreme Being."

"Page seven, weekly religious supplement."

The door opened then and a short trench coated individual entered. A black briefcase was under his arm and his face was hidden with a hat of the same color.

Both Rogicphil and Ms. Editor froze solid. This was the next worse thing to a tax collector and sometimes more so: the insurance man.

"Uh hello," a squeaky voice protruded out from under the black hat, "I'm a representative from the Yuspurly Insurance Group. Say, I know you.

You're that Rogicphil Suflipinic fellow who's been causing trouble all across the sector lately. All the way from Hespuet's 2 and Rall Raul Beta to Deo 7. My my, you leave quite a trail of destruction behind you sir."

Rogicphil racked his brains, "Uh no I'm his clone, Philgicor. Didn't you hear? Rogicphil got squished in a cave in?"

"I heard that Suflipinic got his butt saved by a supreme being."

The editor looked at Rogicphil questioningly, "That's funny I heard that too."

Rogicphil shrugged, "Nobody told me when I was de-thawed. I'm just trying to fill in where he left off."

The insurance man seemed confused by this new turn of events. He pulled a little manual out from a pocket and checked through it.

Rogicphil stifled his shock. That little book was the coveted Insurance Man Manual, it contained over two million loopholes to get around paying insurance (plus twenty-five million more ways to rebut). It wasn't as valuable as the Tax Collector's Bible but still highly prized.

"Hey!" Rogicphil pointed out the front window, "That's him there!" Before the insurance man could turn around Rogicphil blazed out the door and changed clothes. When the I-man looked out he saw Rogicphil walking down the street in his typical trench coat.

"I'm sorry to disturb you," the I-man said tipping his hat to Philgicor who was standing where he had been without a trench coat. "That's my man out there." He turned to go but suddenly stopped, spun around, poked Philgicor on the arm just below his shirt sleeve, then hurried out the door.

"Just a second," Philgicor called out after him, "There's a piece of lint on your shoulder."

"You freaky clones are all alike," the I-man shouted as he ran down the street.

The smile on Rogicphil/Philgicor's face told it all. Ms. Editor's face turned red with anger. "Get out!" she screamed throwing her cup of coffee at him.

He deftly caught it without spilling a drop, "What did I tell you?" He set the coffee back on her desk.

"GET!" she screamed.

"Well okay," he stepped into the door way, "Don't worry about the I-man, he shouldn't miss his manual for another day or two."

"AAAAAAAAAAAAh!" this time the coffee cup smashed the door jamb behind Rogicphil.

*   *   *

Tunneling through the ground was easy with drill boots. Rogicphil was making good time burrowing back into the underground cave system he was so mysteriously transported out of little more than two weeks earlier. He could only hope he wasn't too late.

The rock came apart and he fell into a glowing slime filled cavern. He brushed himself off and checked his backpack homing beacon. It beeped louder toward the left and down at a slope of 10 degrees so his backpack was in that direction. If his survey team had kept their wits about them and they weren't crushed in the cave-in and if Buckshot's cavemen hadn't turned them into stew and they weren't eaten by another minotaur, Rogicphil would leave them again to carry on the mission of finding Dr. Gronblec. Danville needed bowling alleys and Gronblec was the planetary authority.

Two passageways led off to the north and east. North seemed the easiest; he wanted to give his feet a break, not that his Glade runner boots ever gave out. The air was cool, fungus smelling. It reminded him of M.O.M.'s Home Cookin'. Damn shame about Mom (But that's another story altogether. *Hopefully not- the editor*).

After two kilometers of steady walking the passage split again. This time Rogicphil took a westward passage. The fungus smell went up two notches. Maybe they've been decomposed by a mobile strain of slime mold. A hundred meters more brought the sound of polka music, no it was heavy metal. Wait, no, it was heavy polka metal. Hard slamming polka rifts hammered through he rock, causing the glowing slime to jiggle.

Around the corner in an atrocity to acoustic engineering the polka metal reverberated around stalagmites and stalactites. Slick was pounding away at a boulder with keys drawn on while Buzz honked out a mean muted sea-shell turned trumpet. Mack was on the rock drums playing with surprising rhythm and grace.

Behind the electric accordion was a tall thin blond bearded woman. Woman? Since when did women have beards? Rogicphil thought that those went out of style a few millennia ago.

When the woman saw him she called out, "Rogicphil," and threw down her accordion. The band stopped playing. Mack cursed because he was finally getting into the groove and Buzz wasn't trying to figure the lyrics out anymore.

"Oh Darling," the woman ran up and threw her luscious arms around him, "My beautiful Gladerunner, what has kept you?"

"Hold it lady, just who are you?"

"I'm Doctor Gronblec," she pulled a mug of beer out from her pocket, "Drink up, it'll make you fell better."

This was where the fungus smell was coming from and drinking that beer was the last thing Rogicphil wanted to do but he thought what the heck, how often do I get down here? He drank deeply and marveled at the sweetness of the brew.

The band picked up again, this time a polka metal dance number. Rogicphil danced with the wonderful Dr. Gronblec mesmerized by her bright green eyes. Her beard wasn't so bad once you got use to it.

Rogicphil rolled over. His arms reached out for the lovely doctor. Nothing. He opened his eyes. He was in his apartment in Danville Center. His watch told him it was 13:28.

Damn! He had dozed off and had had a stupid dream. He hated having dreams like that. He could never tell when they were real or just something made up by an insane author. And he hated all those books that ended with: they woke up and it was all a dream. What was the point of the book if it was all a dream? Maybe the author wouldn't like it so much if his royalty checks were all a dream.

He checked under the bed. Two boots where there. He pulled them out to make sure they were Gladerunner issue. They were. Still, he put them on and tried a few different combinations to make sure. Roller skates, skis, flippers, yep they were magically real alright.

He pinched himself. It felt real enough. But he could and did pinch himself in his dreams and it felt painful in both cases. If something was equally painful awake and in a dream was there any meaningful difference between being awake and dreaming? Between the real and imaginary?

"QUIT PHILOSOPHISING AND GET INTO MY OFFICE!"

Now that had never happened in his dreams, so with a sigh of relief and a belch of waking up, he stepped through his bathroom door and into Destiny's office.

"WHAT'S THE BIG IDEA OF TAKING A NAP DURING A MISSION, ON DANVILLE EVEN? YOU'RE SUPPOSED TO BE ON DEO 7!"

"Sorry, but I didn't mean to. I was just so tired from the trip I fell asleep as soon as I saw my old bed."

"WHAT ARE YOU DOING ON DANVILLE ANYWAY? AND HOW DID YOU GET PAST MY SURVEILLENCE?"

"You seem a bit pissy today. Did the cow win?"

"I'LL ASK THE QUESTIONS AROUND HERE. AND NO THE COW HASN'T WON YET, BUT IF YOU DON'T GET BACK THERE, SHE WILL."

"Well, it finally hit me what I was doing. Being reckless, getting people killed. As a reporter I only cared about getting the story out, no matter what the cost and now I'm..."

"YOU'VE BEEN READING SOME BORING PHILOSOPHY BOOK HAVEN'T YOU?"

"Well, actually I had some time to kill while flying over here and..."

"OH PLEASE, SPARE ME."

"You are upset, and I have just the thing..."

"I KNOW YOU CAME BACK TO SAVE YOUR SURVEY TEAM FROM THAT CAVE-IN, BUT THEY WERE SLATED TO DIE ANYWAY. THINK OF IT IN TERMS OF YOUR BEING ABLE TO MAKE THEIR LAST FEW DAYS WORTHWHILE AND NOT BORING, DEAD END, LITERALLY, JOBS."

"Then they really are dead, and it's my fault. No, it's your fault too, if you hadn't transported me out of their in a flash of light..."

"WHAT? YOU'D HAVE DIED WITH THEM."

"Well, you could have saved them."

"WHY? WHAT MAKES YOU THINK THEY WOULD HAVE WANTED TO BE SAVED?"

"You're really crazy. All that power, the ultimate power, ultimately corrupting you."

Destiny laughed for about three and a half seconds then became very serious. "OKAY, WISE ASS, LET'S SEE FOR SURE." Destiny pulled a large remote control from out of somewhere and pressed a single button. A small piece of void opened up in the distance behind him. Swirling mists and eerie chanting descended from the void as if echoing down the corridors of time itself.

And then Rogicphil's survey came shuffling into the room. They were all there, Slick, Mack, Eugene, the girls,...Buzz...

"Hey, what's the big idea! We liked being dead! Send us back. Damn it Rogicphil don't do this! Our lives among the living back there on Danville really sucked. We're much happier now, dead."

Rogicphil scratched his head, "Well,.... if you really..." and poof, they were gone forever, again.

"NOW ARE YOU READY TO TAKE ME TO THE SPACEPORT?" Destiny was up and had his coat, hat, and cane in hand ready to go.

"Wait a second," he pinched himself, "First you jump all over me for coming back, then you bring my survey team back to life so that they can suffer and die all over again, and now you want me to take you to the spaceport? Why and what for?"

"IT'S THE QUASARS, THEY SENT ME A MESSAGE THAT I'M TO SEE THEM URGENTLY,AND I'M SUPPOSED TO GET ON THE NEXT SPACESHIP AND YOU'RE TO TAKE ME THERE."

"Quasars. I got some space-drives for my washing machine from them. What does Destiny need with a starship, when you can materialize yourself over to them easier?"

"THEY WORK IN MYSTERIOUS WAYS, GLADERUNNER. YOU DON'T ARGUE WITH THE QUASARS EVEN IF YOU'RE A SUPEME BEING," he motioned to the door.

Outside was a green meadow surrounded by normal trees and birds and things. A short distance away a few surveyors were marking off dimensions for a new 300 lane bowling alley. An off-road ground car labeled Khayyam Surveys was waiting for them. Rogicphil didn't think anything of hot-wiring the car and then driving Destiny the ten kilometers to Danville Center and the Spaceport. He should have felt like he had just stepped into the twilight zone, only it was the early afternoon zone. He would have had to work out the differences later when the Galaxy was safe, but he was too tired from arguing with Destiny and himself. Maybe he shouldn't have taken those 'learn philosophy while you sleep' pills.

They breezed through the spaceport, everywhere they walked something important happened in the lives of the people they passed. One woman instantly gave birth while trying to lug a 27 kilo suitcase around, one man lost his hair, another won the lottery (123 jeedudes, whoop-de-da), prisoner and torturer were reunited after twenty-one years, and a tour guide accidentally led his human group into alien restroom; they'd be cleaning that mess up for a long time.

"I see why you don't go out in public that often."

Destiny didn't say anything, just glared. Security check was easy, the head controller had just got his two week notice and he was letting all kinds through with an evil grin.

"Be careful and don't drink the water if it's got fungus in it," Rogicphil waved to Destiny walking down the loading ramp, "Or breath the air." Drat he always forgot that part. He shook his head and walked back to the check point. The head controller had been thrown out and a new evil looking nanny thing was over-seeing the operation.

A young man was trying to take a bowling ball through but the nanny ting was stopping him.

"Why can't I take it with me?" the man wanted to know.

"You could hold the ship up and hijack to the Glubian Nebula," nanny insisted.

"How? No one is scared of a bowling ball, besides there's nothing in the Glubian Nebula anyway."

"Ah, that proves it, you're been there and now is your perfect opportunity to hijack a ship there."

"You're stupid lady. If I wanted to hijack that ship I could use materials commonly found on the ship itself: hairspray, lighters, tissue paper, long life light bulbs. I wouldn't have to use a bowling ball."

"Okay, you don't go on the flight at all. Now get out of here," she tore up his ticket.

"Hey! I worked ten years saving up money for that ticket."

"Well you should have thought of that before you decided to hijack a spaceship."

"That's completely absurd."

"You just outlined in detail how you would pull the crime off, that's plenty of reason to kick you out. Now get out before I have you arrested."

The intercom came on then, "Dr. Cronplex, please pick up the nearest blue courtesy phone and dial 1324, Dr. Bronplec, please pick up the nearest phone and dial 1423, uh or was it 1234, no 1324, no that's no it either..."

The young man poked the nanny in her iron gut, "Yeah well I've got a phone call now and when I get back you better let me on that ship or I'll have your job."

"Good, I bet yours pays better than mine anyway," the nanny laughed as Dr. Cron/Pron-plex/plec stormed back into the lobby.

Rogicphil guessed he wasn't immune from Destiny's power over public places. It was the real Dr. Gronblec and he was really getting away.

"Keep up the good work, toots." Rogicphil said patting the nanny on the shoulder as he attempted to walk past her. He didn't get two steps before his feet quit their grip the floor and he was floating in air. What the?

Nanny Combat Boots had him held up by the scruff of his neck and said, "Dragging the main concourse are we?   I just saw you pass by this same check point not ten minutes ago. You know what we do with draggers?"

"Let them go peacefully on their way?"

"Just watch it buster, I'm a neon belt."

It was several hours later that security finally released him. For some reason his Gladerunner powers weren't working right. It had to have been those damn philosophy pills. He swore them off completely for good. So instead of tricking the fumbling inept security personnel with his super speed he was reduced to snarky wise cracks and had to suffer the complete body cavity inspection. At several times during the horrid procedure he was accused of trying to smuggle bowling balls off world. He tried to explain to them that it was too late and that other star systems already had bowling alleys but they just towed the party line and said something like, 'Yeah, but they don't have our high tech balls and that's why it's not so popular elsewhere yet.' They had been about to let him go when a report came in of a survey car being stolen and he matched the description of the perp. Miraculously, at that exact moment, his glade powers suddenly came back to life and he was able to scoojack out of there before they could get their sanitary gloves back on.

Destiny, Rogicphil cursed under his breath, as he ice skated through the narrow streets of Danville. That so called 'Supreme' being done that to teach him a lesson. It wasn't those philosophy pills after all. Just the same, he'd stay away from the easily digestible blue pills, for a while anyway.

The weather wasn't cold enough yet to have ice covering the streets (which were heated from below and so couldn't have ice on them even in deepest winter (in order to prevent dangerous street bowling (or at least that's what the authorities claimed (but the real reason was they wanted to keep their lane tax revenues high.)))) Even so, his indestructible ice skating glade boots carved the asphalt streets like they were margarine.

He slid to a halt outside his favorite alley, the Pickled Moose Lodge, with a smooth spray of asphalt dust arching ever so gracefully from the sharp edges of his blades. The black snow showered a small contingent of singing anti-bowlers who were marching down the street intent on protesting outside his alley. All their musical instrument's intake manifolds became clogged with the soot like asphalt particles and they were forced to return home to regroup.

Time to get drunk and forget about Mrs. Nanny Combat Boots, Rogicphil thought, and her huge sanitary glove covered fingers. He retracted the ice skates and walked semi-normally into the Pickeled Moose Lodge.

"Hey!" the bouncer shouted, stopping him, "No outside shoes. Doesn't matter if they are regulation or doncha remember the rules Flipinstick?"

"Sorry dude," Rogicphil said pretending to take off his ultra nice super suede mega leather bowling shoes and exchanging them for the alley's over priced, holey, smelly, deprecated house pair. Instead, he simply converted his glade boots from the nice bowling shoes into ordinary looking tube socks and placed the house shoes on over those.

It felt strange walking around a bowling alley with two pairs of shoes on. It didn't matter what it looked like; it felt awfully weird. He found a seat at a little table in the bar and started to drown his sorrows in an empty mug when he looked up and saw Dr. Gronblec using the house phone.

"Damn it, Ployd, they did it to me again...Yeah, this time it was my bowling ball...I know I can't continue my work without it but...Yeah, I missed my flight again...What? What do you mean they're starting the conference in two hours, it'll take that long to get drunk enough to make my presentation...That's very interesting... Prank? ...Stupid name ...Oh shut-up!" he slammed the phone down and turned to see Rogicphil standing there in his hastily stolen cabby outfit.

"Hey bub, need a lift?"

"Yeah, to Trigurard."

"Dont just Trigurard," Rogicphil said remembering the jingle, "Complain about it too."

"The place sucks," Gronblec said taking a seat at Rogicphil's table. "I need a drink before we go."

"What about Ployd?"

"He's got to stay here; his wife just had a baby a few hours ago, unexpectedly. So I don't think it'd be a good idea for either of them to be drinking right now."

"But the baby's already been born right?"

"Yeah, whatever."

"Good, I only got room for one passenger."

They spent the next hour or so drinking beers. They discussed why Gronblec was going to Trigurard in the first place, since it wasn't known for bowling alleys but rather fly fishing.

"So I guess there's lot of streams and ponds there huh?" Rogicphil asked sipping his mug full of Celestrium booze (beer spiked with the tears of small children).

"Not at all. The place is completely flat and devoid of all surface water. Perfect for bowling alleys."

"So why all the fish?"

"Perfect for fisherman too I guess. The fish can't escape since there's no place for them to escape to. They come flying out of cannons and the fisherman pick them off as they fly by using their preferred method of fishing. Some use nets, rod and reel, hooks or even bare handed."

"Sounds like it's almost as fun as bowling."

"Not even close. It can't compare."

"Say, aren't you the Gronblec who's been in the snews lately? I heard you were lost on the eastern continent searching for new bowling sites."

"Huh?" Gronblec scratched his head. "Oh, that. Yeah, I was hired to scope the place out but when I got there some dudes were excavating the place to make room for a giant bingo parlor instead. They said they'd bought up the entire continent after being kicked out of Danville Center."

"I know. We can't have any other form of entertainment to compete with bowling," Rogicphil said probing yet sarcastically.

"Entertainment? You insult the art my friend."

"Sorry. Just checking. Bingo parlor you say? Do you know which one?"

"I don't remember. But the company behind it was called HELP or something like that."

"H.E.L.L.?"

"Yeah, I think that was it."

"Those drunkards!"

"You got time for a quick set before he head out?"

"Sure," Rogicphil said getting up.

Despite reverting back to his ultranice gladerunner bowling shoes and his completely restored speed, Rogicphil lost the set. Gronblec tore him up. It wasn't even close.

"I hope you're a better taxi driver than you are a bowler."

"Yep, I got the fastest space-taxi this side of Darankeen. Don't worry, I'll get you to your conference in no time sharp."

"It started hours ago."

"I know a little shortcut through Deo 7 that'll get us there quicker than thin cement."

      "I think you got that backwards. Deo 7 is another 1000 light years past Trigurard."

      "Trust me."

      "Can I take my bowling ball?"

      "Sure, just don't let the chicken get a hold of it."

Chapter 20: Lugitorp Prime

On some stupid planet somewhere...

With a splug, a piece of plasma shot out of the back end of Farmer Brown's beat up hover pickup truck. He ground the gears around, allowed the fusion engine to right itself, then floored it. The truck lurched around a bend in the icy road and then up the path to his lonely farm house.

It was a chilly night but there was a deep rage inside of Brown that kept him warm.

Boris sat in the seat next to him. A piece of cloth hung out of the dog's mouth. The cloth was bandaged around the inside of his throat; the vet had stuck it here to help his laryngitis. He wanted to bite the ugly vet but Brown had held a big stick over his head during the operation.

"Now whut yu gonna do nex time yu dig up one o' doze ole deenosawr bones?" Brown asked the dog.

"Wrrrar wro," the dog moaned.

"Thets rwite, yu gonna chew et all da way up furst beyfor swallerin et."

The pickup slowed to a halt in front of their two story farm house. The number 3 was etched by laser blaster in the siding above the front door. But the dog couldn't read and even if he did, wouldn't understand why it should be consider the third house on desolate Povinho Lane when there weren't *any* other house's there anyway.

There were no lights on in the old, but not too run down, farmhouse. No one else lived there except Brown and his faithful Boris. No one else in a long long time. Longer than Boris could remember and he was almost thirteen.

Brown killed the engine and dragged the dog up the steps to the porch and inside. The farmer lit a fusion lantern then looked around, sniffing the cold stale air. "Somthin' ain't rwite heah." He looked out the window. Nothing. Scratching his head he turned to the dog.

The dog shrugged. His master got a bit goofy every once in a while, especially in winter. He couldn't wait until the stupid bandage came out and he could start barking at the supid cow in the field again.

"Besey!" Brown shouted.

Yeah, that was the cow's name.

Brown looked out the window again. "She's gone! Somwun stol mah cow!"

Boris rolled over. His master always got off on these wild imaginary trips. Last time he thought someone had stolen his stupid Besey, she had wandered out of the pasture because the gate had been left open. Besides, who would want that worthless cow anyway. It only gave crummy milk, and that was once a week at best.

Brown bolted out of the house leaving the dog to contemplate his chances of catching that orange alley cat that frequented the garbage pile out back of the house.

"Aha," Farmer Brown said storming back inside, "I dun foun da clue.

Doze tupid igits left this." He held up a red fountain pen. Embossed on the side were the initials H.E.L.L. and a local address and brainlinc number. But because Boris couldn't read and Farmer Brown couldn't comprehend word meanings, neither of them knew how much trouble they were about to get into.

*   *   *

Two figures appeared out of a cloud of red smoke. They were in the frozen parking lot of the Sawdad's Bed and Pizza on the planet Lugietorp, a couple sectors over from B12. They were wearing cool black business suits and red tinted sunglasses. Their hair was slicked back and they looked really cool with their frosty breaths turning into tiny snowflakes that, in the harsh parking lot illumination, sparkled and fluttered to the pavement where they promptly melted.

The shorter, and fatter, of the two met a very short and skinny shadow like figure with a large face hiding black hat. The shivering shadowy figure handed him a holophoto and squeaked, "This is who you're looking for. You know what to do when you find him."

Fatty in a suit nodded like he was the coolest thing since videophones then motioned his partner in crime to follow him in. The tall lanky fellow dusted ice crystals off the lapels of the mysterious man in the hat, then followed his partner into the restaurant using exaggerated strides to show off how awesome he could walk.

They found a table in the corner of the main dining room right next to an obnoxious Flash Gorton* pinball machine. A waitress came over to take their order.

"Hey baby!" the pinball machine said.

"We don't have any food yet," the skinny guy said lowering his red shades down to the end of his nose so he could get a better look at her, "Sorry darling."

"A large anchovy supreme pizza with extra fire sauce sure would be nice, right about now," fatty said.

Slightly annoyed, the waitress picked up the two glasses of water that were already on the table and hurried back to the kitchen.

The pinball machine piped up, "Hey, fatso, why doncha put a quarter in me."

The two ignored the machine. The tall skinny one nodded in agreement. "Yeah, with lots of spices and costello cheese cooked into the crust. Those are so yummy."

"But we're not here to weep and mope over things we can't have remember. We have a job to do."

Tall and skinny looked at his watch, "The timetable says he should be coming out of the restroom in two point three seconds."

On cue, a white robed bald headed man balled into the room. His legs were so short in relation to his girth this was the easiest form of locomotion for him. He positioned himself near the largest table in the room.

The pinball machine whistled to itself quietly, "I swear he looks bigger coming out of there than when he went in half and hour ago."

226

"Ssssh, you," fatty said.

The waitress came back to take the bald man's order but he wasn't done with it yet and a small argument ensued. "What nice breath you have today sir," she said distracting him momentarily so she could grab his plates and run back to the kitchen.

When the bald headed man couldn't find any more food on his table he began to drown his sorrows in a glass of beer so large it looked like a bowl. Fatso reached into his vest pocket but the tall one stopped him, "Wait, let's let him lament for a while first. It's the decent thing to do."

"I suppose you're right." Fatty slumped his fat head into the palm of his hand while his elbow rested melancholicly on the greasy table. "I hate coming back to this planet."

"Don't say that. We were born here. Our duty is to uphold the honor of the empire, to wait for a new emperor to appear and bring back the glory days."

"Come on, just one quarter," the pinball machine pleaded.

Fatty grabbed a round slice of pepperoni from a pizza on a nearby table and inserted it into the pinball machine.

"Hey, that's vandalism, I'm calling the police."

The two shook their heads simultaneously while fatty once again reached into his vest pocket and pulled out a very long barreled zapper. The pinball machine protested by breaking into the chorus of 'We are the Champions' but it did no good. With an electric staccato sound a blue jolt of bottled lightning shot out of the zapper and into the sorry pinball machine.

POP! Fizzle....

The spherical bald man across the room was still lamenting his blues and didn't pay any attention to the ominous commotion on the other side of the room. Even when the zapper was leveled at him he paid it no attention.

POP! Fizzle.....

Both the suits jumped up. The zapper had punched a hole right through the white robed man just like it had with the pinball machine. In fact, the event was almost identical to the demise of the machine; wires, circuits and fake plastic fish sticks splattered all over the place in both instances.

"Hey! He was just a clone," the tall one exclaimed.

"You mean robot! His good breath should have tipped us off."

The waitress returned, "What's going on in here?" Then she saw the zapper and readied herself into a drunken monkey stance.

The short fat one put the zapper back and took a communicator out. "Control, we need a recall right now."

They transmatted out of the place in a puff of red smoke just as the waitress came flying through the air with a jump kick. She crashed into the pinball machine remains.

"Thanks....baby...." the machine muttered and finally died. The glowing red eyes of the yellow coated Flash Gorton went out for the last time.

*   *   *

Besey the cow watched the meeting begin from her secret spy closet in the corner of her office.

"Hear Yo, Hear Yo," the chancellor for the ex-coat checker began, by swinging a smoking orb around his head, "I have the sad duty to call this meeting of the High Entropic Lugietorpian Legion to order." The orb was a dull metalic thing with lots of bullet holes in it from which some nasty smoke issued forth. It was attached to a meter and half long chain the other end of which the chancellor held on to like a paranoid football quarterback.

"Thanks Thurible," High anti-Bishop Lester said from his position on the first step down from the dios (their special spelling of dias) of the unholely Ear. Largely a ceremonial position now, the unholely Ear was the supreme seat of authority in H.E.L.L.

The conference room was crescent shaped with a stacked set of room shaped daosi (again the proprietary plural version of daises) descending down from the center of the room out to the periphery. High anti-Bishops, of which Lester was the only remaining one, sat on fancy leather bucket seats one step down from the vacant center dios and the Community College of Ondinals sat on the next couple of steps down and on cold aluminum high school football stadium seats, while the rest of the various junior grade bossmen, underlings and sophistry staff had to squat even further down the steps, without the aid of any sort of bottom comforting buffer at all. It was considered rude to place one's bottom on any step without such a buffer, by the way. But the eavesdropping cow didn't know this at the time. Furthermore, it was the solemn duty of the chancellor for the ex-coat checker to whack on the head any delegate who slipped and let their derriere touch the unsacred steps.

"What's this meeting all about anyway?" shouted a red blob shaped person six levels down, "I've got children in the oven and can't take all day off with this nonsense."

"Mother Maynard, your protest is rudely recorded." Lester said sternly, then smiled and waved down at the red blob. She flipped him the bird in reply then resumed her squatting stance.

"As I'm sure none of you have heard, I've called this meeting of the inner, and 3/7ths of the middle and semi circles together today to talk about the importance of life insurance."

"BOOOOOO!" the gathered delegates jumped up in unison and began pelting Lester with tomatoes and zuccini.

All the vegitables bounced harmlessly off his invisible force field and onto the Community College of Ordinals, spattering them quite well. Lester chuckled to himself but Besey couldn't tell from inside her closet.

"Boo is right!" Lester shouted the crowd back down to a low simmering squat / half kneel. "I hate the insurance companies as much as anyone in this chamber. That's why I'm so bleeping mad right now about this!" He waved a dull piece of paper up like it pleasantly explained everything away.

"Is that my promotion?" some idiot asked.

The chancellor whacked him on the back of the head with his smoking censer. "Quiet you!"

"Thanks again, Thurible." Lester now pointed behind him to the giant jumbotron screen. "No, this is a bill we just got from the Yuspurly Insurance Company." The bill for 2.7 Trillion Galactic creds was now visible on the jumbotron for all to gawk at.

"And this," Lester motioned with his arm, "Is your miserable performance evaluation, Grob. I hope you're satisfied." Grob's failing report was now visible for all to mock and snicker at.

Thurible whacked Grob on the head again.

"Show us that bill again!" some else, not Grob, shouted, "I couldn't make out the amount."

"Rightly so," Lester said sarcastically moving the image back to the YIG bill. "As I'm sure you're all aware we don't have 2.7 trillion of jeydudes let alone Galactic space creds to pay this with."

"What did we insure for that kind of money?"

"Oh, I'm glad you asked. Let's ask the two underlings who submitted the paperwork what it was for." Lester suddenly turned around (his bucket seat had a nice swivel mount) to face the jumbotron as the lights dimmed and the groggy face of Wilbur replaced the image of the YIG bill.

"Lester? Do you know what time it is?" Wilbur asked rubbing his bloodshot eyes. He was in bed, the lower half of a bunk bed he shared with Jake.

"Hello there, Wilbur" Lester began, "I just have a quick question then I'll let you get back to your sweet nightmares. Do you remember a little insurance policy you filed the paperwork for last year with some company called YIG?"

"YIG? You mean Yuspurly Insurance Group? Yeah, I remember. It was three reformats ago but I still remember despite the … well you know..."

"No I don't know. Please enlighten me."

"The, uh, the... please don't tell anyone, this is really embarrassing."

"Oh, your secret is safe with me," Lester snickered.

Wilbur tried to peer into this videophone's pickup but couldn't see much more than what Lester wanted him too. "Well, you see I was coming back from the illegal bingo hall we run on Otrop street and I had the daily take with me. I was going to make the drop at our secret location when I get a call from the Bossman and..."

"Who?" Lester interupted.

"The Buu... I mean a junior grade bossman Beelzabub class asking me a small favor and..."

"Again I ask, Who?"

"You know, the guy in charge of operations over on Rall Raul Beta. He has a cool shark tank and shiny horns. You know who I'm talking about."

"Go on."

"So I'm really busy trying to avoid the cops who've been stalking me all day and hover traffic was real bad at that time and I'm asked to do this small favor of dropping off some insurance paperwork. Anyway, to make a long story short...."

"Too late."

"...I accidentally dropped the take sack into the Waifinage of the.... t- the Galactic Church."

The meeting chamber grew deathly quite. Even the metal censer of the chancellor or the ex-coat checker could be heard puffing away. The Galactic Church* was the arch-enemy of H.E.L.L. And then the chamber, just as quickly, erupted into a melee chorus of laughter, knee-slaps, farts and belches.

"Are you at a party or something?" Wilbur asked hearing the noise behind Lester. Not sure what it meant, he continued on, "But it wasn't that much money and I worked three extra shifts for the next two months to pay it all back. Honest, I swear."

"I'm sure you did, Wilbur. But I'm more interested in this insurance paperwork. Did you read it?"

"N-Curses no! I wouldn't betray a fellow member of H.E.L.L. like that."

"Unless...?"

"Unless if I was bribed by you of course."

"Oh course. Go on."

"So I went to the YIG office which just happened to be next door to the Waifinarium, uh sorry Waifinage, and I dropped the paperwork off. That's it."

"And what happened inside the YIG office?"

"What do you mean?"

"I mean, did anything unusual happen to you inside there?"

"Unusual? You mean like did I have a vision from God who told me I was the perfect spy to bring down H.E.L.L. from the inside?"

"No, I mean did anybody touch you funny?"

"No sir. I'm as neutered as the Galactic Peace Accord. Have been ever since that second botched reformating I had several years ago."

"No, you imbecile. I mean did anyone in the insurance office poke you with their finger?"

"Now that you mention, yes. Yes, they did. At first I thought they were making fun of my fatness but then I remembered I was still on Lugietorp so then I thought they were trying to tell me my zipper was down or I had a rip in the seat of my overalls but it turns out they were just informing me to move along in the waiting line."

"And how long was the waiting line?"

"Just me."

"So then it wasn't much of a waiting line was it?"

"Now that you mention it again, I guess it wasn't. So that means they were poking me because I'm fat?"

"No, you idiot. It means they were taking a sample of your DNA to clone you."

"What? I thought those were illegal..."

Laughter erupted again from the crowd.

"Uh, I mean I thought clones had gone out of style."

"That's robots, you ignorant fool." Lester quickly glanced down at the hand written time traveling note he'd left himself from thousands of years ago explaining why robot's had gone out of style. Robots... ha, ha, ha, he thought to himself. (Again, Besey didn't know why he was ha-ha-ha-ing to himself about.)

"I don't get it," Wilbur said scratching his head.

"Let me demonstrate." Lester brought up a dual screen video chat channel on the jumbotron with Jake on the right side and Wilbur on the left.

"Lester? Is that you?" Jake asked, waking up from the top bunk. "Do you know what time it is? And who are all those people behind you?"

"Shut up, Jake," Wilbur said below him, "I'm trying to have a secret conversation here."

Jake shouted back, "You shut up, Wilbur."

"Uh, Jake?" Lester began, "Would you mind shooting Wilbur for me? He's disturbing our call."

"Of course." Jake disappeared off screen for a moment, there was a loud gun shot, Wilbur disappeared from the left half of the screen and Jake reappeared on the right side with a smoking curling iron. "Is that all you wanted?"

"Yes Jake. Have a grim night and pleasant nightmares."

"Thanks. And you too, Lester." And Jake when back to sleep forgetting to turn the videophone off.

A moment later the door to their room opened and another Wilbur walked in, shoved the old Wilbur out of his bed and continued the call with Lester. "I get it now. I'm a clone."

"We go through this every time and you always forget."

"Forget what?"

"Why H.E.L.L. owes 2.7 trillion space bucks to YIG. That's what."

"Oh that. It was a life insurance policy taken out on you Lester. It had a special assassination rider on it too. Very fancy stuff."

"Why didn't you say that in the first place? And save yourself from being blown away in the process?"

"Uh, cause I'm stupid?"

"Shut up, Wilbur! Or do I have to kill you again?" Jake shouted from above.

"Blow it out your duodenum."

Lester. "And who does the policy pay out to?"

"Besey, the satanic cow."

"What!" Lester was genuinely shocked. This wasn't in his secret letter from the past.

"Yeah, but she doesn't know anything about it. She's just a stupid dupe-cow after all."

Wrong, Besey thought, secretly listening in on the conversation. Her devious plan was all falling into place now.

Lester continued, "What makes you so sure about that?"

"Because the bossman from Raul Rall Beta already collected on the policy. Duh. Why do you think YIG wants their money back so bad?"

"Wilbur?"

"Yes, Lester."

"Tell Jake to kill you again, please."

"Yes, High anti-Bishop Lester. Right away!"

The dual videophone connection was severed with the sound of Jake's gun, disguised as a curling iron, blowing Wilbur's head off again.

* * *

Somewhere in H.E.L.L. (on Raul Rall Beta) Wilbur pushed Jake into an office. They still had their red tint sunglasses and slick black suits on and the junior grade Beelzebub Class bossman, "The Bossman" to everyone he considered his inferior, winced at the sight of them. Ever since their last reformatting they had been acting strange. New clothes, new hair styles, new everything.

"Would you quit picking your nose, hog," Wilbur badgered Jake. Well, almost everything.

Jake pulled his finger from his nose and quickly stuck it in his pocket as if nothing had happened.

"Hmm," the Bossman mused.

"Hmm What?" Wilbur asked leaning forward.

"Hmmmmm," the Bossman pointed to his eyes.

"Oh the sunglasses, right." Wilbur nudged Jake and they put the red tinted glasses in their pockets. "Mission objective complete, sir. Sort of."

The Bossman smiled, the deed was done, High anti-Bishop Lester was dead, the conniving bum. He snarled then grimaced. Lester had been a big pain in the Bossman's butt for too long, slowing him down, trying to make him look like a fool, all so that the anti-Bishop would get his, the Bossman's position. His rightful position anyway, that of Chief Supreme Bossman*, not the lowly junior grade version he'd been stuck with for so long. Well no more! He smiled again; Lester was finally dead and he had the death certificate to prove to those stupid YIG people. But Wilbur and Jake, the bungling duo, were responsible, and they always goofed up. He frowned again. "What do you mean sort of?"

The two watched slightly bewildered as the Bossman's expressions cycled. They thought maybe he was on drugs. "We shot him, just like you said. And he splattered all over the place and didn't get back up."

"That's good. Good work. And he had bad breath?" He had to make sure it was really Lester they had waxed and not some look-a-like.

"Oh yes, bad breath," Wilbur lied.

"Real bad breath," Jake pinched his nose.

"And loud belches."

"Yes, awfully loud belches. And squeaks."

"And sloppiness, he was a bad dresser."

Squeaks? The Bossman scratched the space between his horns. That didn't sound right.

"And he couldn't even sing the chorus of 'We are the Champions' right."

Wilbur and Bossman stood aghast at Jake. No one as lowly as a toilet seat warmer, let alone the High anti-Bishop himself could be so cold hearted and down right wrong as to forget how to sing the Lugietorp Planetary Anthem. It was implanted in children's DNA from birth and played through sonic suction cups in the womb. It stood for all that was right and wrong about Lugietorp. It was about how they would all, eventually, overcome all the hardship and suffering they'd endured for centuries. It was their very essence!

"Um, sorry. Slip of the tongue," Jake explained.

There was something definitely not right, the Bossman could tell, but their description was definitely, except for the singing part, that of the High anti-Bishop.

"Can we go scrub all the restrooms on the 6th floor now, please?" Wilbur pleaded.

"Not yet. Tell me what happened when you delivered my message to the Community College of Ordinals?"

Jake pushed Wilbur aside and gallantly took a step forward. "I personally delivered it myself, The Bossman."

"Just 'Bossman' when it's at the end of a sentence like that."

"Okay. Sorry about that." Jake stuck his little pinky finger into his ear and rotated it counter clockwise. "I'll remember now."

"So?"

"So what."

"You're supposed to say that like it's a question. 'So what?'" The Bossman could tell that Jake was about to say something else, equally stupid, so he hurriedly continued, "I gave you a bunch of dirt on Besey to give the Ordinals. You confirmed that you gave it to them. Now what did they say in return?"

"Thank you?"

Wilbur smacked Jake on the back of his head.

"They said they'd look into it."

"Look into what?"

"Into the alleged connection between the cow and YIG."

"Good. Anything else? Anything about a promotion maybe?"

"No, they kicked me out straight away."

"I meant about me, you fool. Did they say I would be promoted off this boring planet and into a position more fitting an agent of my caliber."

Jake was about to make a wise crack along the 'caliber' lines but Wilbur preemptively smacked him on the back of the head. "Uuuup! Oh, yeah. Yeah, they did. Did you get the, uh, notice yet? Or something?"

"No I didn't. You've goofed up again. Now go scrub those toilets before I think up something nastier for you to clean."

As Jake was walking towards the door, Wilbur leaned over and whispered to the Bossman, "Heeee's craaaaazee. But while he's doing that, I thought I might sneak on over to Deo 7 and take out that enemy survey team for you. What do say, Boss?" Wilbur did not want to disinfect any restrooms.

"That's right," the Bossman checked his timetable, "Thanks for reminding me. Their usefulness as a distraction to the cow has outlived itself. Especially now that the Ordinals have enough dirt on her to grow a garden. With Besey out of the way, no one will be in a position to challenge me for the holey Ear."

"I'm right on it Boss. Who I do give the assassination paperwork to?"

"My secretary, Delilah, of course. That woman has no other use than putting things in the shredder. Now get out of here."

"Got it." Wilbur slipped his sunglasses back on and coolly exited the office. He caught up with Jake who was sniffing toilet bowl cleaner in the hallway.

"AAAAaaa!" Jake was stumbling around and clutched at Wilbur's arm to steady himself. "Spots, spots, I see spots."

"Hold on, the cow will know what to do." He led Jake down the hall.

"I hope so, that big one is moving."

"May thu forsuhs of Eville infest yor florboards!" With that Farmer Brown slammed the phone down. Boris had never seen his master get this mad before. Maybe he was on drugs.

Brown grabbed his twin barreled fusion blaster and stomped out the door. Boris eagerly followed to see what his master was going to do. This had been building all night long as Brown called agency after government agency trying to find out what H.E.L.L. was. Boris had heard his master say that word often enough, maybe he suddenly realized he didn't know what it meant. Drugs, definitely.

The sun was just poking itself over the horizon, checking to see if it was okay with Farmer Brown to rise. "Damn it, wha's taking you so long!" he cursed at the ball of thermonuclear fire which upon getting approval began its slow journey into the cold gray sky.

The drug theory was getting stronger each moment. Boris jumped in through the window and landed in his favorite spot in front seat of the old beat up hover pickup. With Brown behind the wheel they peeled out of the farmyard.

The truck screeched to a halt outside of Nobsil's city hall. Brown carted the fusion blaster like a true space gopher hunter as he climbed the steps, stomping on each one like it was an infernal rodent. After kicking the door in, he barged down the hallway insulting anyone who dared peek their head out a passing side corridor.

Boris trotted faithfully behind to see what would happen. Maybe someone would shoot Brown and then he could be free to chase that alley cat all he wanted.

"I don't know what you're talking about!" Boris heard a woman say as he entered an office that Brown had rudely barged into.

"Listen little woman, awl I need is sum recurds on Hee-ul." Without waiting for a reply the farmer opened a filing cabinet.

"Code 21," she said into her phone pickup.

Boris chuckled to himself at the sight of Brown trying to keep his heavy blaster balanced, pointed at the secretary, and poking through the filing cabinet at the same time.

Brown had barely gotten to Acceptable Loan Guarantee Compression Rations when a tough looking security team swarmed in on him. They ignored the dog, and Brown's rusty fusion blaster, as they carted the screaming farmer away. Boris decided to follow; he wanted to see what they were going to do to his master.

*   *   *

Somewhere on that same stupid planet you keep hearing about but can never figure out just where it is (*Lugietorp! Ha ha- the editor*).

Besey finished polishing her hoofs. That thin layer of arsenic she applied along with her nail polish would make turning them into glue a bit more difficult. No cow could be save these days, even a satanic one. Whatever that meant.

The idiots here at H.E.L.L. didn't even have a common sense definition and they had made the word up. When she'd asked someone in legal about it, they just told her is was a registered trademark and violation would result in a hearing at the Supreme Galactic Court. What was this universe coming to anyway? Why did she even care? She was just a cow, who should be eating grass in a field somewhere. This sophisticated satanic food they'd been putting in her feed trough was giving her heartburn, and made her belch much more than she did when living in Farmer Brown's Field, now somewhere miles above her head.

Beep beep beep beep beep beep. She had a brainlinc call coming in. It was Lester. "Cow," he shouted, "Get down here right away," and hung up before she could even reply with a pleasant 'Hello and happy damnation to you sir'.

At first she had thought getting away from Brown would be terrifically freedom enhancing but even with her boosted IQ and travel budget it wasn't what she had expected. Lester (and to some extent the Bossman) were far worse than the mean old farmer, but not by much.

She cursed them all as she trundled down to Lester's lair. She passed his small army of shivering clerical staff, waving at Wendy as usual, before emerging into a giant chamber carved out of from a giant slug of granite and marble.

Lester was sitting on, or rather compressing into the floor, his oversized seating apparatus by a giant open hearth furnace. Despite the roaring flames it still seemed cold in there. He was wrapped in a nice padded quilt and had on pink bunny slippers.

"There," he shouted, pointing to a dark smoke encrusted box by the furnace opening, "Shovel more into the fire; it's too damn cold in here."

Besey carefully approached the box and looked inside. Instead of seeing coal, firewood or even children's toys stolen from an orphanage, there were brick like bundles of cold hard cash. She sniffed them and immediately the odor of concentrated deo wafted into her oversized nose.

"Don't just stand there gawking, start shoveling them in cow."

With a cow groan that Lester assumed had something to do with all her extra stomachs she began tossing bundles of cash into the furnace. It quickly roared up to a nice infernality and Lester relaxed a bit. Besey hesitated but Lester noticed and jumped in before she could say anything. "Did you falsify that report on the loan distributions yet?" he barked.

Besey scratched her head. Loan distributions? Oh, he meant embezzling money to a children's charity telethon. It was beyond her why H.E.L.L. would cheat and steal all that money from poor planets then turn around and give it to sick children. And then have her cover it up and make it look like the money was spent on mob hits. "Uh, yes. I just finished."

"You're a smart cow, Besey. You ever wonder why I do it?"

"You mean for the children? Because since you spend most of your time being mean to people you get off on secretly help them a little?"

"No, no, my dear. You've got it all wrong. All those charities are scams, even the legitimate ones. We run most of the fake charities anyway so I wouldn't bother donating money to them in the first place. I like to donate to the real, struggling children's charities that diligently work to prolong the lives of poor, sick and suffering little ones. You see science cured all the easy sicknesses and ailments thousands and thousands of years ago and now all that new treatments can do is prolong their lives and their suffering. Get it? I'm helping children suffer longer..."

"Uh I forgot I left my waffle iron on." The cow tried to turn and beat a hasty retreat.

"Hold it," Lester shouted, "Get back here. I'm not done annoying you yet."

Besey signed a deep lethargic sigh and turned to face the fat man who seemed to ooze more than move when his mouth was speaking.

"I just got word that your former master, what's his name? Brown. Yes, that Brown has been apprehended by the police on suspicion of treason."

"Really?" Something that finally interested her. Maybe they would execute him and that'd be one less bonehead she'd have to worry about.

"Yes and I understand it's going to be double execution with his dog getting hanging right beside him."

Boris? That mangy dog deserved whatever punishment H.E.L.L. could serve up. "It's about time," Besey finally said, pleased with herself.

"I knew you'd like to hear that. But here's the ironic thing. He was captured because he was snooping around in our business. He was trying to find out about H.E.L.L. and why we stole you. You see, he felt sorry for you and wanted to rescue you. Isn't that a hoot?"

Besey wasn't sure if Lester wanted her to laugh or cry. With a sicko like Lester it probably didn't matter. "Yes it reminds me of owls. Thank you your hatefulness I need to get back planning Project Smooth Move now." Project Smooth Move was a dastardly plan to dump tons of powdered laxative into the water supply of the Galactic Senate.

Lester shooed her away as he was done toying with her for one day. He had more important things to do, like fantasize about his time traveling escapades and how he was going to wreck robot havoc in the past.

Besey hurried back to her office. She had to confirm Lester's report about Brown. With a tamp of her left hoof (she was left hoofed of course) an information console popped up on one side over her desk. It was basically a standard H.E.L.L. network terminal except that it had a few extra gizmos and modifications, that the cow had secretly added.

The view screen was set to her personal surveillance equipment which was strategically placed all over H.E.L.L. on in key civilian government buildings on the surface. She pulled up a map of the central planetary jail facility and switched the mode to remote sniffer.

There was a small rubbery cup thing attached to the side of the screen which she brought to her nose. A coiled wire connected it loosely to a stylus which she deftly passed back and forth over different parts of the map. Before long she smelled Brown's bad breath, his alkali sweat, the ink on the paper of the propaganda posters hanging on all the walls, and the wet dog smell of Boris. Yes, they were both in jail just like Lester had said. What was his angle? Why would he give her the pleasure of knowing her old arch nemesis was away to be out of her life for good?

Suddenly and then all of a sudden, a different odor, strong and salty with a hint of a bleach like acid tinge which slowly died away, tickled her nose. Cleaning supplies? Did Boris just fart after eating a bunch of fish?

She quickly cross referenced the chemical formula of the strange odor with a database of know poisons and cleaning agents. There had to be something in it that would help her figure out what happening. How she knew this she didn't know, but she did know that she didn't know how she knew, you know. At any rate the search came up null and she found her screen automatically redirected to beginners guide to sniffing called, Olfaction Makes Good Sense. Dang that artificial stupidity. She already knew how to smell and didn't need a computer that had never smelled anything in it's entire life to lecture her on how it was done.

She'd have to figure it out the new fashioned way, by looking. She punched up video and audio feeds from the security apparati that covered the walls of Brown's jail cell. It was cold and dark in there but a quick command to the computer and a heat lamp kicked on in the cell and blinded the old farmer. She hit the button for microscope magnification and hastily glanced around the cell, Boris's flea bitten hide and finally Brown's leathery skinned face.

It was only there for only a split second before the heat lamp made it evaporate but she saw it. It was a tear.

The door to her office opened suddenly then shut. Looking up she saw Lester right himself after rolling in and pointed a fat finger at her. "I knew it. You're going soft on me cow. I knew you couldn't resist seeing your master pouting and crying over his long lost cow. Boo hoo. It's so sad I could vomit."

His bad breath was overwhelmingly bad even from on the other side of the room. He had the upper hand unless she out bossed him. They were on her turf and she could use that to her psychological advantage. "What do you think you're doing her in my office, Lester? I've played along with your silly games for long enough. I'm afraid I'm going to have to fire you!"

Lester laughed so hard he rolled over. "You haven't been trained in psych out tactics cow. You can't pull that trick on me."

"I know what you're up to with Brown and the dog and it won't work."

"You do? I mean, you're bluffing. Try again."

"Uh, I'm the largest share holder of YIG and I'm foreclosing on H.E.L.L."

"Huh?" Lester was taken a back and he already had several. "You can't know about that. I mean, nice try. But you'll soon be served as lunch in the cafeteria and no one will care what you know about nothing."

"Nothing?" Hmm, where had she heard about that before. "Quit distracting me with your psycho babble, Lester. I'm pulling the plug on H.E.L.L. and you'll be the first to go down the drain."

"Your cliche's are getting boring cow. Why don't you saying something about Farmer Brown and his mangy mutt again."

Now she began to get steamed. The fear she felt was quickly evaporating before the hot anger of frustration.

"By the way," Lester grimaced seeing the cow's eyes start to glow red. "Brown and the dog are just a distraction to keep you from learning what I'm really up to with the robots... Oops. I didn't just say that aloud did I?"

"Yes," she mooed, "Yes you did."

"Well never mind. You'll probably think that slip of the tongue was a subtly planned diversion tactic, especially when you review the secret recording I have of this conversation."

She carefully aimed her horns at him.

"Agents 666 and 666 have been trying to kill me and now I know who's behind it."

"I'm Agent 666."

"Exactly, now you'll hand over all pertinent details and files so I can shoot you. And don't try to say something clever like, 'How am I suppose to review the secret recording if I'm dead?' It won't work on me. I'm psych-out trained."

"Woouf," she snorted and kicked the special order bovine compatible chair out behind her.

"Your assuming it'll be a quick and painless death. It might just be a very slow and long drawn out affair yet mildly pleasant as well."

She snorted again as she shoved her desk to one side. Lester pulled a long barreled laser pistol out from his robes and leveled it at Besey. She charged him. Her horns sunk deep into his fatty tissues. She continuing running her feet and the momentum rammed his spherical body into the far wall.

Booooing! She bounced back several feet and landed squarely on her bovine behind.

With a hearty chuckle, Lester struggled to extract himself from the large indentation in the wall he now found himself embedded into. "Be reasonable cow. You can't hurt me with all my padding."

She panted on the floor, all tuckered out. The red glow faded from her eyes and her anger dimmed. "I thought," she said between breaths, "You said 666 is behind it?"

Lester gave up and fell back into his indentation. "I did."

"You're not well, Lester, and this proves it, you're agent 666, remember?"

"Everyone's agent 666, you cow-compoop." With renewed effort he managed to extract himself and rolled to his feet.

"Then why don't you tell me the names of the purported assassins you claim have been trying to kill you?"

"Wilbur and Jake," he said wiping the sweat from his brow with a pistol polishing cloth, "And you've been giving them orders too."

"Yes, to clean the floors and take out he garbage. Everyone gives those two orders around here. And they only comply because they're brown nosing. If you actually gave them a positive incentive to do your bidding, they might not be trying to kill you every other week."

He finished polishing the gun off and pointed it at her again. "And how's that positive incentivizing been working out for you so far?"

 "I just want them to leave me alone."

Lester twisted the dial on his pistol to 'slow and painful' and pressed the muzzle to her flat forehead.

"Wait, I'll tell you everything."

"Everything?"

"Agleh, the cook, she made me do it."

"No, not Agleh. She would never do such a thing for you."

"And what makes you so sure?"

"Because she only does those kinds of things for me."

The cow laughed. It wasn't anything like a human laugh and Lester misunderstood it for something having to do with the chewing of the cud process.

"That's it cow. Your time has come and gone, and now you're going to go also."

This meeting was suddenly interrupted by Wilbur and Jake who decided to barge in then. They knocked Lester forward rolling him into the cow's desk. The floor groaned under the combined weight and collapsed. When the dust cleared Lester was gone and only a hole going down into darkness was left.

Wilbur socked Jake, "You big lug, now you've done it."

Jake was in the midst of recoiling from his partner when the cow spoke, "No that's alright. You two saved my life."

"Huh?"

Besey realized the two didn't know that Lester was there. So then they must still believe he's sort of dead. Well, all was not lost then. "I mean I was planning on remodeling anyway and Lester never would have approved, but now that you two have offed him there isn't anything he can say."

"Except for maybe, uggg," Jake laughed.

Wilbur stood up and dusted himself off, "It was my idea Cow. Jake can't see straight anymore, you know."

"It's true. I see spots, and some of them are moving."

Besey sighed as she got to her feet careful not to fall into the hole after Lester. "Jake those are smeared buggers on your sunglasses."

Jake took the sunglasses off, and sure enough the spots disappeared.

"Thanks cow. How can I repay you?"

"Simple. Go to the Nobsil public jail and harass a prisoner there named Brown. And hurry up about it as he's about to be executed."

Chapter 21: Splas Toorg

Meanwhile on Splas Toorg, the planet of nuclear waste disposal, Sir Rontho and the King of Raul Rall Beta hiking over a glowing red boulder field. The sun in this system was scheduled to wind down it's fusion operations in just a few short centuries and already the light output was quite dim. But they could see well enough through a combination of the dim sunlight, the glowing boulders and Rontho's enhanced smell-o-vision courtesy of the swampgator body is was currently borrowing.

"Did you hear that?" Rontho said suddenly stopping.

"The clergy?"

"No, much much worse. It almost sounded like a scream." Rontho twisted his reptilian head around trying to get a better angle on the sounds. The body had great smelling capabilities but the sound pickup was rather quite wonky. "There it goes again."

"Ah, you must be hearing the screams of long dead souls that use to inhabit this planet."

Rontho tried again to listen but got nothing.

"You know," the King said, "This planet didn't use to be called Splas Toorg. That was just the idea of some fake vacation pushing scam. This use to be an inhabited world known as Rombulus IV about twenty thousand years ago but once it was decided to move all the nuclear waste here, the original inhabitants were booted out."

"Where'd they go?"

"Hespuets II. That's why it's a II and not a I, by the way. The Rombulusians didn't like the people who were living on Hespuets I at the time and decided to kick them out. It was only fair they thought since they'd gotten kicked out of their planet."

"So those were the people who's souls are now screaming?"

"No."

"Okay. So where'd the Hespuetians go?"

"Oh they came here to Splas Toorg and kicked out the people who had kicked out the Rombulusians in the first place."

"Who were those people?"

"Space gypsies mostly and the stranded construction workers who'd demolished everything to make way for the giant vats of nuclear waste."

"Hmm, I see and so where did all these space gypsies and former construction workers go?"

"To Lizar-B."

"Never heard of it."

"I'm not surprised because it's not where they wanted to go. They were really disappointed they had to go through all that effort to kick out the inhabitants of Lizar-B who were still there when they showed up. The gypsies were looking for a fabled planet rich in spicy pizzas and pickled fish feet. They called this fabled place Lugietorp."

"Whatever happened to them?"

"After they were kicked off of Lizar-B by a new wave bingo movement they disappeared or maybe they were just murdered..... "

"I'm absolutely shaking in my boots my dear fellow."

"No, that's just the boulder you're standing on. I think its about to erupt."

"Well, let's get over this ridge and see what's on the other side then."

On the other side was what they'd come down to the planet to see in the first place. Giant vats of boiling nuclear waste. There were hundreds of them down in a valley below them now.

"Isn't it just gorgeous?" The King grinned with a smile as wide as a he could grin it.

"What's that down there?" Rontho asked pointing at what looked like a short fellow standing near the edge of one of the vats.

"Oh just another day tripper like ourselves. He has to pay extra to if he wants the spa treatment too."

"He's the one making the screaming noise. I'm sure of it."

"Not the dead souls of space gypsies?"

"Not this time I'm afraid. And what's he doing?"

"Let's go ask him."

They trotted down the other side of the ridge towards the strange screaming fellow. As they got closer the saw he had a wheelbarrow with him and he was throwing things out of the wheelbarrow and into the vat. When they reached him they could see that it was stacks of money.

"Good day to you sir!" Sir Rontho announced himself to the strange short fellow in a big black hat and gray business suit. He also had on a two toned cloak just in case.

"Aeeeey!" he screamed ignoring them as he chucked an armfull into the vat, where it floated for a few moments before desolving into a green stain.

"Is that you Junthomas?" the King said taking out his reading glasses. He put them on and closely looked at the man. " It is you!"

"Sorry, I can't talk," the strange fellow said between armfuls, "I'm very busy right now."

Undeterred the King continued, "Let us help you, then we can chat over brunch. I have something wonderful I need to share with you."

Junthomas took a careful look at the swampgator standing next to the King of Raul Rall Beta, nodded his head and went back to his work.

Both Rontho and the King helped empty the barrow of money and when they were done Junthomas said, "It's best not to dally around here. Don't turn around but there's a spy up on the ridge you just came down."

"If I had my human body and expert fingers," Rontho said, "I could shoot him down from there with a 30 ought 6."

"Don't look at me," the King said, "I don't condone violence of any sort."

Junthomas shrugged and pulled out a long range electro slingshot from beneath his cloak. The electro slingshot looked just like any other slingshot except that it had little electrodes that connected to the users arm muscles. When used properly the electrodes would fire in just the right manner to increase the firing range of the average slingshot user three fold. The only side effect, aside from occasional constipation was uncontrollable and random screams.

"Aeeey!" Junthomas screamed as he let loose a volley of radioactive pebbles. They glowed like tracers as the arced over Rontho and the King's heads back to the ridge. There was a small explosion then a flaming figure came running down the boulder strewn slope right at them.

The three stepped aside as a robot dashed past them and into the vat. Three rounds of bubbling parts later, the metal man was gone having exploded to tiny bits or was dissolved by the nuclear waste.

"What was that?"

"You know him?"

The King nodded slowly. "Yes, I'm afraid I do. That was one of the last robots on Rall Raul Beta and now he's gone. He was Dr Nosehonka's secretary's robot. Vadlin must of brought him along for some reason. I'm afraid his funeral will be particularly sad since he outlived all his friends. It'll mostly be bill collectors in attendance I'm afraid."

After chatting a while about the Clergy, the nature of nuclear waste, mutation mitigation strategies and cool new game shows the three gentlemen decided to part ways*. The strange guy in cloak and black hat slinked off somewhere before they could say goodbye.

"I hope you find your body soon," the King said.

"No problem," Rontho said holding a beaker full of concentrated nuclear waste, "This should give Nosehonka's ship enough oomph to get us back to the wormhole conduit and thence onto Deo 7 where my wonderful old body is waiting for me."

"And Captaness Joehona will be along shortly to return me to Rall Raul Beta. I hope to see you again some time."

"Likewise."

Up on the ridge Nosehonka was cursing. Why had that stupid robot gone running down there? He could have died just as well up here on the ridge. This was just throwing another monkey wrench in his carefully planned scheme.

Now the only problem with the plan was a virtual legion of newscasters who had stowed away with them. It would look pretty bad in the news if all of Rall Raul Beta was to know that Nosehonka advocated the use of Splas Toorg in the matters of nuclear waste over a Rall Raul Betan dump facility. No there had to be a way of getting rid of the reporters at the same time but he couldn't quite think of one.

Chapter 22: Hicksville

They tried everything, torture, coercion, threats, suction, plumbing implements, hotdogs, but nothing worked. Greyson would only divulge his real name, rank, favorite brand of frozen TV diner, and the credit card number of his dentist. This infuriated his hick interrogators to the point where they thought he was a robot.

"Bhut robouts don' egsist no mor," the first hick said. He was wearing a dirty white butcher's apron with what looked like mustard stains all over it.

"Shut yor face Bob. o'couahs dey egsist, jus lookit," the second taller hick said pointing at Greyson. He wore a brown tweed five piece suit smeared with McCow offal.

Bob hazarded a glance in his direction. Greyson saw the furtive glace through tightly squinted eyes. The two hicks stood over in the corner talking to themselves. He was definitely in a torture chamber alright, the paisley pastel wallpaper just screamed depravity. They had stopped poking things into his brain a few minutes before and so he figured it would be safe to see what was going on. He opened his eyes all the way and saw a stand with the plumbing implements to his right and his BOG, thoroughly ignored, lay on the floor to his left.

"Ayl call Ufrena," twead hick number two said, "Sheel no."

Ufrena? The girl with the paper bag over her head who'd sabotaged the train last night? If only he could talk to her again, smell the sweet aroma of fresh dung on her overalls, see what her face really looked like.... Snap out of it man. You're an agent of the Reformed British Secret Service. You need to take control of your emotions and figure a way out this mess.

Greyson quickly took in his immediate environment with a glance. He was strapped down to a two wheeled wheelchair with the training wheels retracted. A bolt ran from the floor through the rear wheel keeping it and him in one place.

"Ufrena says ets 'im awl rite," the second hick now with an ancient flip phone said right after he had clicked it shut with a satisfing crunch. "Oney uh robit couda smelt 'er awt, lak thet."

Bob nodded his head furiously in agreement.

"Wells, youins shu gittim dawn to thu ahmry to figger awl how et wurks."

"Okai bous. Write way," Bob said walking around Greyson, "Yor comin wit mea, yho dang blamed muhcan-uhgal varmut."

A lever clicked somewhere and the hick pushed the wheelchair towards the door. Greyson casually stuck his leg out, catching the BOG on his foot.

The other guy, still talking to himself in the corner, turned around. "Hold it," he said pointing an accusing finger at Greyson. He leaned over and looked closely at him.

The bad breath from the guy almost knocked him out. Or was it the cow poop on his tweed over jacket? Greyson closed his eyes tight again and held his breath. It was stupid to think they'd let him leave with the BOG on his foot. Maybe he should try to kick the guy, flip over to his feet, and knock dwon the other guy with the wheelchair. Nah, too simple to work.

"Thears som mustarred on ets lip," tweed face said pointing at him.

That's funny, he didn't smell any mustard.

Bob wiped the yellow stuff from Greyson's lip and hurried him out the door. He was wheeled down several long white corridors that smelled of acid based disinfectant and then down crowded quickvaders that didn't smell like anything but looked like recycled sardine cans.

Finally he found himself being wheeled into the back of a long truck like ground car parked in a noisy garage. The BOG was still on his foot. He wondered how long before "Bob" would confiscate it.

The front door slammed shut and the truck roared to life. Bob sped out of the garage like he was on some kind of massive stimulate. Slamming left and right between cars, crunching the sidewalls against concrete columns, and general all around stupid driving, gave Greyson a few nasty bruises.

BOOM! BOOM! TWANG!

What was that screeching noise?

BOOM! BOOM! TWANG! There it was again!

Greyson looked around frantically searching for a hole in the van where he was sure a monster was trying to break in. Nothing then suddenly, a deafening roar assaulted him. He frantically looked around again for the origin of this new torture. Two large speakers on either side of him thudded out the worst country music he had ever heard. An inflated plastic woman bounced around in the back keeping time with the beat (and him company apparently).

This made the previous torture session seem like an imaginary walk through Bertha's Bodacious Botanical Bathorama. All his willpower was gone and he was shouting out all the secrets he ever knew, but it did no good. He couldn't hear himself over the noise, so his confession was pointless.

Finally after what seemed like two days, nineteen hours, seventeen minutes, thirty-one and half seconds of reasons why someone's dog died or how the old pickup truck broke down before they could get Timmy to the hospital in time or why Mary Sue had to give up her baby because the narcotic baby food was running low etc.. etc.. the music mercifully stopped. He was still shouting as loud as he could, then stopped when he realized he was making a fool of himself. Whew! The nightmare was finally over.

"Whud yho say?" Bob called back from the driver's seat. "Suzie aint bothrin yu is she? Cause awl smack 'er a goodun ifin shea dihd."

"Oh, no. Susie is just fine, thanks."

The blow up woman stared at him blankly, like she had enjoyed watching him suffer.

"She didn't like your music however."

"Ihm fas fording et to thuh nex side."

"Huh...?"

BOMB! BOOM! TWANG! The noise returned, with a vengeance. And he thought the torture to his nose by this whole blasted planet was bad enough. The sound was so pervasive, so thundering, so vile that it infuriated its way into every pore of his body, even into his nasal cavity where it started to do rude, unspeakable things to his olfactory bulbs. The sounds and smells began to merge into one squirming, seething mass of odoriferous vibrations that threatened to send him from a land of torture and honey and off the crazy side of the deep end.

*   *   *

Sweet green spirals and barfy purple zigzags danced with the frumpy marshmellows in Greyson's brain. Where once there had been loud twangy sounds now there were out of focus geometric patterns all vying for his beautiful attention.

"Yor en igget," a green spiral with a long nose said.

Greyson smiled. "I like the way you spiral sparkles."

The green spiral looked at the purple zigzag before slapping the zag out of its barfy face, "End yor uh danged fool fer bringun em ear."

"Ah diuh no wha ta do," the purple zigzag pleaded while it vomited a rainbow of tiny explosions that settled to the ocean floor like a cool breeze inside the refrigerator of his soul.

"Awl take care o fit. Now yous get awn home for tweedie pants finds awt whut yu jus did."

The purple zigzag fluttered in the breeze trying to make up its mind before it reluctantly sublimated into a swarm of gnat like ampersands and left the building.

SMACK! Now that wasn't very lovely. In fact it smelled down right accusatory.

"Wake uhp you!" The green spiral still sparkled even though it was slapping him around with his own smell now.

Tired. So tired and so many things left to smell but what would Frogman do? Greyson wandered away in search of more stimulating typographer's symbols not even realizing he was already asleep.

Greyson awoke to something cold and refreshing on his face. Ah, that fells like morning, he thought and sat up before opening his eyes. There were no more odd shapes floating around him that smelled funny. The ringing in his ears had disappeared too. He could breath what smelled like a scrumptious English breakfast. It had been a bad dream after all. Whew, he felt so good he opened his eyes.

"MOOOOOO!" the cow said before resuming her licking of his face.

"Aaaaaaah! The satanic cow!" Greyson screamed as he jumped up on the bed and bumped his head on the ceiling knocking himself out cold.

Sometime later Greyson woke up, not sure if he was still dreaming or merely hallucinating. He found himself in a rocking chair on the waiting porch of a horse clinic. Patrons would bring their sick horses right up the steps to the porch and then inside to see the doc. A sign on the door read: Woody Lee: Horse Smacker and Teacher a Lessoner.

He reached for his BOG but it was gone. His cloths were gone too. Instead he found himself wearing overalls and a straw hat with nothing in between. Please let this be another dream. It's not as bad as that hard country music but still....

He tried to get up but a hand shot out of seemingly nowhere and pushed him back into his rocking chair. Looking over to where the arm was attached to a body sitting in the next chair over, he saw the girl with a paper bag over her head. "Oh, hello again."

"Gode, yur wake finely," she said putting her flyswatter down, "Nau you cin shoo yur own flys way."

"What's your name? Why do have that bag on your head? Why did you blow up that train?" The questions were too many and he could only manage three before her hand clamped down on his mouth.

"Keep quat. Were layun low, see." She looked around to make sure there were no horses or owners milling around that could eavesdrop on them. "Ahm Ufrena end Ah doan care whut yous is called. Come on, were nex." She stood up taking his hand in her's and led him inside the ramshackled old house / barn.

"What happened to your nose? Did you see that cow? What day is it?" the questions started bubbling up once again.

Ufrena shooshed him then led him past the receptionist through the kitchen and into the large attached barn.

A short scrawny dude was sitting cross legged (painful way) backwards and bareback on a horse that was slowly walking in circles. They were in the center of the barn surrounded by a group of other horses and their owners watching the lesson in full earnestness. Once he saw Ufrena he clapped his hands and quickly dismissed his class with a, "Nau git."

"Aw man," the crowd said but dismissed without too much of a ruckus.

When they were alone Ufrena walked up the the dude and started talking to him with her back towards Greyson. He watched intently as she removed the paperbag and let down her long strawberry golden hair.

"Ah aint no babysitter, Ufrena!"

"Com-mon Woody Lee, ets jus fer an ouwur til Ayz cin get rid o thet danged Bob. Yous gonna like im too, Ah spec since he cin see smells like weuns cin see flowers."

"Whuuuaht!" Woody Lee gently tilted Ufrena out of the way so he could get a better look at Greyson.

"I'm all better now," Greyson waved with a smile.

"Ok," Woody Lee said letting Ufrena back down, "Buh jus foouh thu ouwah."

Ufrena turned to Greyson and said something but a large bulbous twirling thing stuck on the end of her face distracted him.

"Huh? Is that a spiral?"

"Ay said, 'End you', meanin you there. 'Stay outta trouble now,' hear!"

"You have pretty eyes," is what he wanted to say but it didn't come out quite right.

"Shudup," she said smacking him in the face then walked out leaving him alone with Woody.

"Wow, that's quite some...." Greyson motioned to his own face to indicate a certain spiraling pattern on someone elses face.

"Yes sir. Shes got one fine sniffer on er, doan she. Think quik now!" Woody Lee tossed a small brown ball at Greyson's face. "Whu color is et?"

Greyson caught the ball with his super quick reflexs but his mind was still a little slow. He brought it to his nose and sniffed. "It smells like poo."

"Igit! Ayz askew whu colar, naht whut et smelled lawk."

"Okay, sorry. Try again."

"Kay, hear et comes...." he threw another little brown ball high up into the rafters.

Greyson watched it arc over towards him and stepped up to catch it but Woody Lee socked him something powerful in his stomach with an outstretched fist. "Ooooff." Greyson doubled over in pain, fell to the smelly dirt floor and had the little brown poo ball smack him on the back of the head. How come he didnt' see that coming?

"Well?" Woody asked, waiting for Greyson to get up. "Whut zet smell lawk?"

"Brown," growled Greyson.

"Yur opeless." The scrawny fellow walked over to an open stall where he picked up a little portable atomic powered alarm clock. "Naw Aym gonna take ah leetle medee-tayshun break end Ay wan you to stay put. One ohwer shed do et."

Greyson started to get up but the smelly bare foot of Woody Lee pressed him back down into the dirt. The calluses must have been two centimeters thick on his sole. He tried to fight his way out but Woody Lee knew where to block his every move even before he made it. He was dealing with an combat expert here, far greater than anyone he trained under at the British Junior Academy for Spys.

Greyson managed to roll over on his back while Woody Lee balanced on one foot (pressed firmly on Greyson's chest keeping him pinned) and crossed the other leg while holding his arms over his head with palms pressed flat against each other.

"Eeeee-ooooooo," Woody Lee droned continuously.

This went on for several minutes while Greyson waited for him to either climb down voluntarily or fall off asleep. Aside from the weight pressing down on him and the annoying chanting, Greyson was bored out of his mind. At least it was better than that horrid boom boom twang.

After he could take it no longer, he tried to skooch over to get at the alarm clock. If he could reset it to go off right way, at lease the hick would get off of him for a while. But it was just out of reach. He tried again but with his foot (also bare now) and managed to get a toenail on the edge of the alarm clock.

Without his BOG or the use of his excellent fighting skills he had only one thing left; his trick toe. Back on Earth in his timeline he had lost his left big toenail in a refrigerator moving accident. He thought his career as a spy was over but if it hadn't been for the crack team of Drs Shandrydan and White he might never had been able to kick a soccer ball in quite the same way ever again. They had replaced his toenail with a high tech simulant made of a space age alloy and because of his training in their super sniffer program, a special sized divot was installed that allowed the sniff extension tube to rest and pivot there.

The super sniffer program was created as response to the heightened security risks imposed by using foreign trained animal operatives in scent related operations. Animal rights organizations had laws passed that prevented the further use and training of domestic (British) animals for these important purposes. There were no laws preventing the use of humans in these capacities so Greyson was choose to see if humans could be trained to smell as well as dogs or pigs.

It had soon become clear that while Greyson was no dog he could use his superior brain to synthesize meaning from the scents he could detect. With the aid of a long extension tube which was held close to the ground he could sniff odors as if his nose was right there like a dog's or pig's. He discovered on his own, that he could smell things a lot better if he actually put his nose on the ground like an animal instead of trying to stand upright with a funny tube stuck up his nose. But that was considered unbecoming of a British agent, even if he was an American, and he was forced to use the sniff extension tube and, with the advent of his artificial toenail, the tube could rest nicely on his foot as he walked around following scent trails and so forth.

The super sniffer program had been a great success for Greyson but for some reason they never were able to recruit other agents to try it out.

But back to the toenail. Greyson had discovered long afterward that the toenails exotic space age material gave it another unusual property: it allowed him to interfere with radio signals. But that isn't the property he wanted to use on the alarm clock, but rather its near indestructibility to smash a hole into the gizmo and wreck havoc inside its little computer brain. Fortunately for Greyson and Deo 7 that didn't work but the radio interference portion did. That and the fact that the strange exotic material of his toenail had traveled a hundred thousand years into the future (and much stranger places than that but that's another story altogether again) all colluded to interact with the atomic nature of the portable alarm clock to do something very very weird.

Woody Lee sensed it too late and because of that mistake would never know that it even took place, except in odd flashbacks now and again. An almost invisible glowing blue orb like energy field appeared inside the clock and slowly expanded outward until it encompassed the entire barn. It stopped there, for some reason having to do with maximum entropy or some other far out physics concept.

To Woody Lee the hour he had decided to wait for Ufrena to return ended as he expected it would, without Ufrena showing back up. He had used the hour to prepare himself for the stress of having to deal with the retarded off-worlder she'd left behind.

To Greyson the hour also lasted it's normal length except that he witnessed the blue orb like energy field expand right through their bodies, seemingly unharming them, and then out to surround the entire building. But the next several years seemed to last centuries at first, then as he got use to it merely decades and finally as he came to master it, seconds. In reality it was only forty seven minutes and 22 seconds that the alarm clock had left before it went off and killed the totally awesome time loop effect.

To Woody Lee the loop seemed to last exactly a day in length beginning when Ufrena brought Greyson to him and ended one day and one hour later when she showed up from per perspective as being only an hour but for him much longer. "What took you so long woman?" he asked her upset, "Can't you see I've got other more important things to do rather than be lectured to all day long by mister smelly pants here."

"Wire yu tawkin so funny Woody? Ayz jus gone won hour lawk Ay sed."

Greyson who was by this time an expert in all things smell, having had to unlearn all his previous training while being beaten down into utter submission by Woody Lee's training protocol, saw her again for the first time. Where once he'd only seen a strange proboscis on the end of her face there was now the most exquisite nasal appendage radiating the universe with all it's olfactorous glory.

He had practiced countless times exactly what he would say to her if he'd ever be given the chance to meet her again but those dreams had been dashed by the cold hard reality of his eternal barn / prison and he had again practiced countless times to forget those words. So instead of the clever reference to her favorite puppy she'd had in the third grade as a way to make them bond he blurted out, "I forgot how ugly you were."

"Yeah, that's why she has to wear that bag over her head," Woody Lee informed him.

Furious, Ufrena ripped up the two tickets to the opera she'd purchased, after taking care of Bob, in hopes of going out on a date with Greyson. She turned and stormed out of the barn.

"Ufrena, wait. What I meant was I see the true beauty you have to offer the world now. The me that thought you were ugly is now dead. I'm a new man."

But she didn't hear any of it.

"Ah who needs her anyway," Woody Lee said just before Greyson sucker punched him in the gut.

*   *   *

Ferd the criminal was in pain. A bullet was stuck up inside his nose somewhere. His buddies were laughing at him as he desperately tried to dig it out with a stubby digit. "Aw, crap!" he yelled, "Et wunt cum awt!"

"Herr I cin help!" Billy-Sam came up behind him and began whacking him across the back of his head.

"Aaaaaaa!" Ferd screamed.

And a few moments later Spyman (Greyson in costume) heard a loud BANG!... which was followed by roarious laughter. "The fools," he muttered from the other side of a parked ground vehicle where he was hiding.

Ferd was a bit shaken up after having the bullet ejected from his nose with such force, "Hey maan thet wuzunt fun."

"But et shore wuz funny," Billy-Sam laughed, "Hold 'im down Bob whilest I try et agin."

"No! No way! You ain't gonna do it!" Ferd tried to get away but the Bob held him down.

Billy-Sam plucked a bullet from his vest, a hydroshock, and approached evilly. "Now don't yu fret Ferd. I'll be quick," and he shoved it in with a flick of his wrist. He grabbed a rubber mallet from another goon and prepared to whack.

These crooks were so stupid that all Spyman had to do was wait around long enough until they killed each other off. The bank robbery would be foiled and he wouldn't even have to lift a finger. Still he wasn't quite sure how a bank robbery operated on this planet with its strange negative money currency system but he did know how to take out common crooks.

Back on Earth, during the slow season when there wasn't enough spying to keep him busy, Greyson had moonlighted as a superhero doing just that. He had his friends down at the comic book shop help him make a nifty costume. He wanted to call himself Frogman like his comic book hero but his friends had said that was copyright violation. So now, after that incident with the little kid outside the pancake warehouse, he decided he'd go by the name of Spyman. And this was to be his debut.

After the weird time loop experience with Woody Lee he'd tried to follow Ufrena but ended up stumbling into her friend Bob's bank robbery attempt. Now Spyman and the three crooks were in the middle of the street outside the bank building horsing around.

Unfortunately, letting the crooks off themselves violated his sacred oath as a super hero. If he took his mask off and reverted to his secret agent persona, it would be okay however. And so now he had, not only to make sure they didn't kill anyone else but each other in the process. Wait a second, this was a hundred thousand years into the future from his time. What right did he have to mess in these peoples affairs in another jurisdiction even? But it was his debut as Spyman.

Damn it! He hated these moral dilemmas. His BOG would have the answer. In a secret compartment which he often forgot about was a little something called Mr. Answerman. Spyman pulled it out now and studied the gambling device carefully.

BANG! The shot rang through Spyman's ears for it was followed by an instant of silence broken only by a thud and then more laughter.

Without thinking he extracted a long green tube from the BOG. The slippery green mechanical serpent flew out of his hand and under the vehicle to the group of bank robbers.

"Cum un Ferd, don't lay thair lik an igit, get up wills ya?" Billy-Sam said, prodded Ferd with a smelly boot.

"Hey wait Billy-Sam," Bob (Bobby-John to his criminal buddies) said scooping up the snake, "Stick this up his uther nose-ho. Ferd's still worth a few laughs."

"Yeah!" Billy-Sam took the fake snake and stuck it up Ferd's free nostril.

This wasn't what Spyman had planned. He thought the snake would have scared them long enough for him to sneak over and drag Ferd off to safety. But now it looked like he'd only made it worse.

Now Billy-Sam was preparing to whack Ferd's head again but then suddenly Ferd stiffened up and his entire body shook like he was being electrocuted. His face was purple and seemed to be expanding. Ferd's eyelids fluttered a bit then closed and his body went limp with a last breath.

"Well ya happy now Billy-Sam? Ya jus kilt yur own brother. Good goin' bone-ead!"

No, Spyman, thought. HE'D just killed Ferd with a malfunctioning electric powered snake not Billy-Sam.

Every superhero or agent had to face the issue of death head-on especially those called for in the line of duty. But this, this was pure stupidity. This wasn't his real mission. He was suppose to be looking for signs of the satanic cow. And that wasn't the real mission either as he was just an innocent bystander who'd gotten sucked up into a temporal vortex while trying to snoop on American spy satellites. His real mission was to get back to Earth in his own time. Hopefully there might be something he could do there and then that would make this possible future never happen at all. And in order to do that meant find the cow and stop it. Too many nested goals made his head spin.

Getting sidetracked with these goons was exactly what he didn't need to be doing. But Spyman was known for his sidetrackedness. Well now it was in the hands of Mr. Answerman. He pressed a little button and let it randomly come up with an answer. The tiny LCD displayed:

**The answer to your moral dilemma
is easy to solve. Double down!**

In disgust he threw the thing down on the ground and began to stomp it into oblivion. "Die! Die! You vile retched piece of bat excrement!" he screamed at it.

Oops....

He made a break for it when the goons, coming around the vehicle, spotted him. "Get 'im!!"

He headed for the closest entrance to the bank on foot waiting for a chance to safely kick in his bootjets. Two mores steps and he'd be free. One, SLIP! "Wheeeeeeee......" Slam! Spyman was caught in his own sticky glue trap he'd set previously to catch the crooks as they had exited out the building (but things didn't work out that way).

Spyman came to in the back of a high speed attack shuttle. He was still in his costume, apparently because the hick goons couldn't figure out how to take it off of him. But they at least were smart enough to have tied him up. He could see his BOG laying on the deck a few feet in front of him.

Boy didn't this seem familiar? Carefully, without attracting attention, he wormed his leg out to snag his BOG.

Then he noticed it. The eerily familiar sound of the hard country rap music coming out of the shuttles sound system. His super olfactory sense kicked in converting the sound into easily ignored fart smells.

"ey, Bobby-Johnboy," Billy-Sam said from the pilots seat, "Get mea sumthin ta wipe ma nose with."

Bob looked around the cabin and picked up Spyman's BOG. "Here ya go boss," he said after blowing his own nose on it.

Spyman winced.

Billy-Sam did his business on the BOG as well then tossed it out the window.

Spyman imagined his precious Bag of Goodies falling effortlessly through the thin Deo-7ian atmosphere only to explode on impact with the ground. It was a real shame, after a perfect twelve year record, he'd lost his BOG for good. These goons would pay.

As best he could figure, they were now in the air somewhere between Hicksville and Balidron. What exactly their plan was Spyman didn't have a clue but it probably wasn't charity related.

What all this meant to his overall mission, to search for the satanic cow, he had no idea. If past missions were any indication, he'd save the day, someone else would get all the credit and he'd be out on his butt in 24 hours. But this was the future and that meant things were different. He was also on another planet so where exactly his butt would be out on, he had no idea. Just to be safe he figured that getting the H.E.L.L. out of here would be the best idea.

But how? He was tied up and at the mercy of three wackos with guns. For now he'd play along and wait for an opportunity to open for him to act.

"Hey deres da Su-Perrrrlative building!" Bob pointed sarcastically out the main windshield. "Let's ram et!"

Billy-Sam grabbed the microphone to the comm gear. "Hey, Balidron, we're ganna ram yer fancy go ta meetun building. Whatcha gonna do 'bout et?"

Bob (Bobby-John) hooped and hollered then said, "Ufrena shore is gonna giv me ah kiss for this un. Seein hows weed un gone en stole awl er money to da danged bank en awl."

The three goons all laughed until a squadron of police space fighters came down out of orbit to intercept.

"Surrender your vessel and your prisoner now to us or face the consequences!" This announcement over the radio, only made the goons laugh more.

Billy-Sam pulled the largest gun he could find out of a burlap bag, poked it out the side window, and began firing at anything that got in his way. "Okay coppers, yer in fur et nows! Aaaaaah!" And the others joined in with salvos of their own all firing at random it seemed.

With everyone firing and no one flying, the shuttle took a steep nose dive. Spyman knew this was his one chance at survival. With intense concentration he aimed his laser wrist watch at the main control panel and fired.

It missed and tagged Bob in the butt, "Hey, ah don feel so goo...." He fell over sideways mashing in half of the control panel. One of the buttons he activated released the bomb bay doors which Spyman was lying on.

He watched the attack shuttle continue its powered dive towards a Balidronian suburb while he simply floated gently in free fall behind. The police fighters got to the shuttle before the ground did, but the effect was the same: total annihilation. Well, scratch one mission of vengeance. How pathetic.

Now all he had to worry about were those same police fighters. They had said they wanted the goon's prisoner. Did they know it was him or were they just bluffing? The next few minutes should tell.

Off in the distance Greyson could swear he saw what appeared to be a bear and robot tumbling through the sky in a tangled up parachute. One of the police fighters zoomed in and scooped them up. Maybe they had mistaken them for him. It certainly was easier to spot a flapping parachute than a stealthy secret agent / superhero falling through the sky.

Grey, paved ground with patches of sparse buildings clumped together like weeds in the desert loomed up at him as tiny clouds of deo-ore whizzed by. The remaining police fighters circled the fallen shuttle as scavenger vultures would a hapless mammal. They weren't the slightest bit concerned with him.

Feeling safe for once, he lasered his bonds loose letting his limbs flap around noisily in the air. He positioned himself into a lotus meditation arrangement and cleared his mind. It was great to simply be free and 'oom' for a while. Falling falling...not a care in the world. Except that tree!

"Aaaaaah!" he activated his bootjets just in time before smacking into a large limb. Where'd this tree come from all of a sudden? He was sure he had a couple of more seconds left before the ground would present a severe problem. He flew out from under the canopy of a huge sequoia and around it's fat trunk to get a good view of the park he now found himself in.

Grebway. That had to be it. A huge suburb at the corner of Balidron facing the northern shore of the Kebber inlet. It was early evening now and what a better time for a nice walk through the park.

He landed gently on a lightly traveled foot path. A sign stuck to one of the trees indicated where all the parks attractions could be located. Hmmm, where to go? The zoo looked interesting. Another planet's idea of a zoo should prove to be really weird. The zoo then.

With an old tree limb in hand as a walking stick he set out along the path. Already he could tell this wasn't Earth. The birds, although superficially the same in appearance to Terran based fowl, behaved in an all together different manner. For one thing they'd stayed as far away from the trees as possible, even going so far as to sleep exposed on the ground.

And then there were the squirrels. Well that's the closest thing he could think of that these creatures resembled. They had six legs, a tail, and no head, would scamper randomly along the ground and in the trees, but had no clue as to where or what they were doing. Bizarre.

And finally it was the smells. Now that he had complete mastery over his olfaction, he could selectively pick out important scents and safely ignore the boring ones, like the deo ore smell. There was beauty there in the smells but it was being held down and oppressed by other vile odors, not just the deo.

Spyman was so distracted by these strange revelations and anticipating what further oddities he might find at the zoo, that he failed to notice the two joggers coming from the opposite direction on the path. They took one look at him and his suit and fled off into the trees. Ah, humans, the most bizarre smelling creature of them all.

By the time he made it over to the other end of the park the zoo had been long closed up to the public. But that was fine by Spyman, he'd jump the fence and have the place to himself, or so he thought.

Getting in was no problem. The security was laughable even from 21st century standards. No sensors, no detectors, no guards. The only thing besides a three foot railing to keep people out was a no trespassing sign and that was faded to almost beyond recognition.

With a shrug he strolled in. Nothing. He guessed people just didn't care about the environment or wildlife anymore. A main building hunkered at the top of a low rise that marked a clearing in the trees. He jogged up to the main door and leisurely picked its smell lock. What a fascinating concept. Why hadn't he thought of that?

A long dark corridor led him to the inner courtyard where the 'animals' were kept. At first he wasn't disappointed in his amazement. All shapes and sizes of strange furred and multicolored creatures abound. But then he noticed that one of them was wearing classes and another a watch. These weren't wildlife. It was a human sideshow showcase. This was Balidron's idea of a zoo?

These were former inhabitants of culture, thinking humans, caged up to be shown off. Aha, but what if this was their job? What if they liked it. Maybe they were all masochists. Again that moral dilemma of how to act on this foreign planet poked its head up in Spyman's mind. All he had to do was take his mask off and the dilemma would resolve itself. But he still wasn't ready to do that quite yet. First he'd ask them, and if they wanted to be set free, he'd let them go.

So he approached an elderly old man who just happened to have an extra arm growing out of his forehead. His chin was buried in his chest from the added weight. "Excuse me sir?"

"Wha...," he looked up at Spyman, "No, no, no more handshakes, I can't take it anymore!"

"I just wanted to ask you a question."

"No, it's not hanging well. Now go away and leave me alone!" He fell over backwards and rolled away.

On to the next prisoner who was sleep a few meters away. A short thin blue thing that reminded him of something. An old cartoon perhaps? That crazy Martian with the Trojan helmet, that was it. Oops. That was no Martian, it was a plutonian, the only one: Plutoman.

"Hey, hey Plutoman, wake up. I've come to free you." He enjoyed getting to smack the poor nose deficient guy around.

"Oooooh," Plutoman growled. He had a nasty scar on his forehead that, no it went all the way around his head like the top of his head had been unscrewed. Well that would be an improvement.

"Hey man, you all right?" Maybe he'd had his brain removed and a sentient one put in its place.

Plutoman opened his eyes, "Eh?"

"I've come to rescue you. Do you understand me?"

"Are you going to save me or what?" He poked Spyman in the eyes with forked fingers, "Ah that felt good."

Spyman didn't care behind his face mask, "Okay, hold still while I zap your chains." He pressed his wristwatch against the metal attachment on Plutoman's leg. zzzzoOT! "Let's go."

"Where are we going? And why do I have to go with you?"

"Cause I'm getting the %$@! off this octohooged planet that's why."

"Really? You're not tricking me?"

"No, now let's go." Spyman led the way out from the zoo building.

"I am," smirked Plutoman as he followed.

Chapter 23: Negative Money

"What the?" Grego the Mean angrily pounded the metal box. He pushed the button again. Still nothing happened.

"Uh, did you plug it in?" Space-Bo casually asked from inside the box.

Grego checked the power cable. Yes it was plugged in. "Okay you, out of the machine," he ordered as he opened the hatch.

Space-Bo crawled out of the Wilson Steamomatic High Pressure Decimating Machine and stretched. It felt like he'd been cramped up inside there for a year. "I'm sorry about your machine," he lied.

"Don't lie to me," Grego said straight faced as he gently placed the ex-space marine back into the black barber-like chair while he searched around the torture room for some other way to kill him.

The mean man found an ancient projectile weapon in the bottom of a trunk labeled: 'don't open'. It was a meter long and had a hole running all the way through it, lengthwise. A curved wood carved piece stuck out where it was to interface with the operator's shoulder. Grego placed a copper clad cylinder inside the device, checking twice to make sure he'd done it right, and aimed it at Space-Bo's forehead.

"Hey, that won't work," Space-Bo pointed out, "It's got a hole in it." He was glad his luck was holding out so far. Just a little while longer now and the Funky Chicken would come crashing through the door to save him.

"I regret to inform you, that this, unfortunately, won't be a very painful way to die. But we will get to that later." Grego squeezed the trigger and the shell clunked down the tube and splugged out its orafice and dropped harmlessly to the floor.

Disgruntled, Grego pulled out all kinds of killing devices: head mashers, bombs, spears, choppers, dicers, jugglers, rotors, wipers, mufflers, even portraits of really ugly people, but they all failed to work in one way or another. He even tried the portrait of Milo Mortis* that he kept sealed in a lead lined vault. Nothing. Frustrated, he turned the portrait on his weld-mouthed waiter. The waiter's eyes bulged and his heart gave a pathetic thump before it stopped.

Grego paced the room. "It appears these devices aren't intrinsically defective," he pondered while rubbing his chin. "It could be a probability fluctuation problem. I could test this with a..."

"How long is this going to take?" Space-Bo asked. He was beginning to get impatient with the chicken. If that crazy critter didn't come and save him in the next five minutes he'd have to break out on his own and go find the chicken in order to find out why he was taking so long.

"Quiet you, I'm thinking....with a probability disruptor. Of course. I've got a prototype around here some place." He found it covered with moldy cheese inside an old lunchbox. He set the wonky looking device to maximum disruption and fired at Space-Bo. But just before the circuits connected a banana spontaneously appeared in the exhaust port.

Space-Bo grabbed the banana saying, "Hmm thanks," and ate it as if the earlier fourteen course meal hadn't existed.

Grego adjusted the sights then looked through the side mounted probability scope. "How strange," he said looking through the P-scope at Space-Bo.

The ex-space marine was surrounded by a glowing green field tended by six or seven squat, hairy armed gremlin like creatures, also glowing green. They noticed Grego and gave him the finger.

The P-scope and the probability disruptor to which it was attached suddenly became very hot to the touch. "Yeeeoh!" Grego exclaimed letting it smash to the floor. He found the biggest welding tongs he had and carefully prodded Space-Bo over to a hole in the floor. "In you go," he said shoving Space-Bo over the edge and into his personal void.

*   *   *

Ahhhhhhhhhhhh! That really felt good, the Funky Chicken thought. A quick and excruciating death always put a refreshing perspective on things. It was a simple yet extremely satisfying experience. Slow and tormentuous deaths, on the other hand, were best for meditative purposes.

After a quick death, he always liked to follow it up with a nice long slow death so he could reflect upon the complete meaninglessness of the whole thing. With that he began to hold his breath.

His meditation, however, was soon bothered by thoughts of his friend Space-Bo and what fun things he might be up to at that moment. He tried to put the happy thoughts out of his mind and concentrate instead on all the gloom and doom he could conceive of.

It was of no use. He wasn't in the right mood to torment himself properly so instead he tried to think of where Space-Bo might be having fun. First the chicken had to figure out where *he* was.

He let out his breath and took a long one deep inside his lungs but it wasn't air he suddenly found himself breathing, but raw sewage. He opened his eyes and all he could see was thickening blackness dripping all around him in a slightly deeper shade of putrid gloom. All he could feel was a gentle pulsating rhythm punctuated by a sharp pain in his head when something metal hit it every three or four seconds.

This must be the sewage treatment plant under Grego the Mean's Estate. That must mean that Space-Bo was still up there, about to be tortured to death. Twice even. The fact that 'Bo wasn't immortal together with an idea of some further mayhem they could cause, FC decided to crawl back up into the mansion and save his friend.

The chicken twisted around in the current and started to fight his way back up the pipes toward the kitchen. He soon realized that the metal things that kept hitting him on the head were illegal cleaning robots that helped the treatment plant get rid of clingers (large chunks of fecal matter that tended to clog up the system). The more he fought to move back up stream the more they hit him.

He grabbed one. It fought but because of the chicken's patented one-second-a-millennium-training course the chicken was able to out-maneuver it and thereby turn it around so it could attack the other robots instead.

Unfortunately the robot wasn't as stupid as the chicken had hoped. The robots knew each other from the old country and wouldn't attack one another, at least not without good cause. Maybe if the chicken could switch the polarity on the robot's IFF circuit, it could be provoked into attacking its kinsbots.

Aha, the chicken thought, I'll just switch my perpective instead. He continued up the current but dragged the robot behind him facing the other ones. It was more difficult this way but the other robots were powerless to stop him, now that he had their relative hostage.

The main drain from the kitchen had a metal one way shutter over it, to keep the system from backing up. So that way was a dead end. Ha! He imagined letting the robots tear him to shreds which could then seep up through the seals on the shutter and thereby gain entry into the kitchen. But he didn't think Space-Bo would want to wait that long, so it was on to plan bee. Killer bees! How his mind wandered.

The chicken needed some other way to get back into the mansion. He felt along the walls back down the current for any openings that didn't have shuttered hatches. He found a small one that had fallen into disrepair far away from the majority of openings. After forcing it open, he let go of his hostage and shot up the tube, as fast as he could swim, hoping to find a decent opening into the building above.

The tube wound around for several hundred meters before dumping him out into a pitch black chamber. The chicken exhaled a couple liters of sludge and took in a gasping breath. Gasp! No oxygen, just stinky volatile fumes. He held his breath again. If only his lighter was dry he could have flamed real good, even without the flamer! *(Readers of the previous volume will remember that in the future, if a person wanted to destroy his/her/its lungs, the preferred method was flaming, not smoking (since that had been banned long ago)– your friendly neighborhood editor)*

He checked his pocket for those nifty IR/3D goggles. Empty. Some Palpuka must have stolen them and maybe they'd been destroyed in the trash compactor. He checked for his 4D welding / reading glasses instead. It was gone to.. He checked for other things he knew should have been in his pockets but everything was gone! Oh woe ist ivitmaefu!

Oh well, Funky Chickens are immortal but not IR/3D goggles or original manuscripts of Einstein's unfinished opera or bootleg recordings of Davinci's first rap performace.

Wait a millenium! Maybe it was the lack of oxygen but his brain wasn't working right. He'd never lost his pocket wares before, no matter how mangled or smashed up he'd been. Somehow, being inside his organic pockets upon decimation allowed those things to also rematerialize with the rest of his chickenoid body. Something very strange was going on here at the Grego mansion.

Either way, he'd have to start collecting things all over again from scratch. Maybe not, if he could take a small sample from Space-Bo's pockets and transplant the stuff as a seed he could have his pockets up to full capacity in only two hundred years or so. But he had to make sure Space-Bo was still alive or both their pockets were doomed.

The chicken walked around in the muck for several minutes pondering the right spatial equations of pocket transfer when Space-Bo crashed down on him from above. "Puh squaouf!" the immortal cried.

"Hey, watch where you're going!" Space-Bo cried in return.

"Is that you?"

"Of course it's you, uh, I mean me. But who are you?"

"It's me."

"No I'm me. That must mean you are my first grade teacher, Mrs. Toafnurdler."

"Ah yes, I remember the Toafnurdlers with such fondness. Too bad about that big shoe incident at the bowling alley. My condolences to you sir."

"FC, is that you? Why are you dressed up like my grade school teacher? Nevermind. It's about time you saved me. That Grego guy has been trying to kill me for the past couple of hours. I stalled as long as I could waiting for you to rescue me but I guess Grego got bored with that so he threw me down this hole instead."

"I'm sorry. I've was busy being trapped down here in the sewage system all this time. I hope you weren't inconvenienced too much. I just needed a good death that's all."

"No problem. If it wasn't for his clumsiness I'd be dead now. Boy that guy's an idiot."

"What do you mean?"

"Well, every time he tried to kill me, he goofed up, forgot to load the cannon ball or aimed the gun the wrong way or had bananas get stuck in his gadgets."

"Bananas? Were you trying to goof him up?"

"No, I was just waiting for you. When you didn't show up after a while I thought you had forgotten me. I was still working on a good escape plan on my own when he gave up."

"You could have charged him, and overpowered him. That should have been easy for you."

"But that's too boring. They never do that in the holovision shows. I was trying to come up with a truly new way of escaping. Something I've never seen before. All the old ways get so dull after a while."

"But if he looked like he was ever going to actually pull it off then would you have overpowered him?"

"I don't know. Maybe."

"That's real nice. Do you mind if I have some of the stuff out of your pockets?"

"Like what? I've got all kinds of things in here."

"Oh just real general stuff like empty do-it-yourself hysterectomy kits or used up pencils, thing like that."

"Okay, whatever." Space-Bo pulled a heap of stuff from the bottom of his pocket. It was a sticky mess that had started to compost but the chicken didn't care.

"Thanks," the chicken said carefully arranging his new junk into precise arrangements. A thought suddenly occurred to him that maybe he hadn't really lost all his stuff but rather it had been been compacted to the point of dehydration and was now lying dormant in a spore like state. And maybe Space-Bo's stuff would act like a fertil.... uh scratch that. "Now lets get back up there. I thought of some fun new ways we can cause mayhem."

"Shouldn't we be searching for the satanic cow?"

"Good idea. I'm sure she'd have some wonderful insight into the plight of non-humanoids trying to cause mayhem on humans. But first I want to thank Grego for killing me."

"What if we decided to find the satanic cow here, so we wouldn't have to go just yet. I saw a couple of video games upstairs that I haven't played in a long time."

The chicken thought about that for a moment but couldn't quite pinpoint the fallacy in the logic so he nodded his flappy head in agreement. "So, how do propose we get up to the top?"

"You could fly, and I'll ride on your back like Hawkman."

"Even after pigs won the right to have wings, they never flew like Hawkman."

"Ummmm...."

"Exactly."

Space-Bo felt the side of his head where it was starting to get warm. "I think I'm thinking too hard. Maybe I could give you a boost." Without another word Space-Bo picked up the chicken and heaved him into the fetid air and up the hole.

The Funky Chicken sailed up twelve stories, bumped his head on the underside of a ledge and fell back down landing in the muck next to Space-Bo.

"Try flapping next time and you might stay up."

"Let's try that again," the chicken said rubbing his head, "but this time only go to 30% catapult capacity. Remember we're in reduced gravity down here below the artificial generators."

"Do you mean the gravity is artificial or the generators?" Space-Bo asked while he grabbed a hold of the chicken again.

"Either one is a fine way to misconstrue the language."

With a slightly less energetic heave, Space-Bo tossed the chicken up at the desired velocity. But the angle was wrong and the chicken bounced around the inside of the tunnel but finally caught hold of the lip at the top and pulled himself over. Grego the Mean was nowhere to be seen.

He found a coil of piano wire about the right length and dropped it over the edge of the hole. In a few minutes he had Space-Bo pulled up out of the hole.

"After my fingers regrow let's go see if he's still in the building." The piano wire had done a number on the chicken's talon like fingery appendages. He headed for the door saying, "I still need to think him for that wonderful death."

*   *   *

Around noon Space-Bo woke up. With a yawn he stumbled out of his room and banged on the door across the hallway labeled Guest Room 2. He had just come out of Guest Room 3, which was a 1/10th scale model of Balidron's Second Consul's laundry room.

The Funky Chicken appeared in the door way with a copy of "Screw Me? Screw You! An Idiot's Guide to Fine Balidronian Hardware Shoppes" by Spugsy Mailgun under his left wing/arm. "Good Morning, did you sleep well?"

After searching most of the manor last night and not finding Grego, the two had decided to make ample use of the facilities and get some sleep.

"Yeah, but how come I'm not dead?"

"Because you're alive."

"I'm not falling for that one again. No, I mean why hasn't Gecko come back to finish us off?" Space-Bo scratched under his arm.

"Grego," FC corrected. "What do you make of this?" He pulled a piece of paper out of the book and handed it over.

Space-Bo took the sheet then smelled his armpit before reading:

Grego's Amazing World of the Totally Obvious Presents:

Another View of Nothing that has
Never been Seen Like this Before

A man enters a supreme court building swinging a briefcase around his head. He sets the case down and makes a run for it. Security guards chase the man out but he disappears in a cloud of chlorine gas. When the case is opened over half a ton of ear wax is found inside with a street value of a quarter of a million. What did the security guards do with the case? Read the Book.

Miss Susan Archipelago of Whipped, New Jersey wrote a letter to Untied Technologies complaining about the companies lack of character in its nationally syndicated television commercials. Untied hired an assassin to take her out. What happened? Read the Book.

"Looks like he's writing a book," Space-Bo mused.

"That's what I thought until I read the back."

"Oh?" He turned it over, sniffed his other armpit and read:

Riven, I've gone to Balidron to pick up some groceries and knock off a few old chums. Don't wait up. Ha!
  -GTM

"I don't get it."

"Yes, why did he leave this note for the waiter in there?" the chicken said pointing to the room he had just came out of. "That's Guest Room 2 and everyone knows Ruthven is forced to live in a closet off the main kitchen."

"And why did he spell Ruthven, Riven?"

"What are you mumbling about now?" the chicken took the paper back for another look.

"That waiter, you know the one with his mouth welded shut? I heard Grego call him Ruthven once."

"I don't remember that, must have been when I was dead."

"Yeah well Ruthven's dead now too."

"We should go checkout that kitchen closet to make sure but after that we had better be moving along. Grego might show up at anytime and if he finds out we're alive again he would get really MAD. But that could be fun too."

"Yeah, I've seen him when he gets really mad. Little veins pop up on his forehead. He looks real silly. And I bet he'd even try that hydronspanner on me. I saw it sitting in the corner of his torture room."

"You've been watching too many space operas. There's no such thing as a hydrospanner. Now come on, let's see what happened to the waiter." The chicken led the way down the hall.

In the kitchen, where the previous night the Funky Chicken had been ground up in the garbage disposal, the two of them found some moldy doughnuts and frozen grapes to munch on. They were sitting at a nice bonewood breakfast table.

Crunch, Crunch, Space-Bo chewed. "That book by Gumbo sounds pretty interesting. You didn't see the movie verion of it in your room did you?"

"No, <chomp> <chomp>, but I did find the related book on Earth history."

"Never heard of it."

"You nitwit, that's Terra, your homeworld."

"Leave my homeworld out of this."

"Your answer should be: What's Grego the Gumby doing with it?"

"Beats me. Why don't you ask him when he gets back?"

"No thanks." The chicken finished chomping on a bronze cabinet door handle and washed it down with a full glass of bleach. He belched some soap bubbles then got up from the table. He counted the number of intersections of the penrose tiles that made up the floor's surface as he paced back and forth.

Space-Bo took a handful of grapes and ran back to the chicken's room to retrieve the book in question. It had finally dawned on him what FC had said about his homeworld and Earth. But when he returned to the kitchen the chicken was gone.

Bing, Bing, Bing, came from behind a door on the wall to his right. He opened it to find a long hallway. The noise was coming from around a corner and to the left. He followed the sound to a game room where the chicken was playing a video game: Cattle Mutilation Auction.

"What a stupid game," Space-Bo commented.

"Actually it's very intellectually stimulating. The object is to rip off all the other cattle farmers by feeding your cows lead shot and steroids. You can also hire aliens or government black ops to mutilate your opponent's cows."

"Are any of the cow's satanic?"

"No."

"I told you it was stupid. I'll try this one, Abacusing for Abalone." Space-Bo hit the start button and ten vertical bars appeared on the screen. A horizontal bar crossed ten vertical ones perpendicular to it near the top. Seven blocks were on each bar, two above the H-bar and five below. An information box appeared which said, *Compute the correct mathematical problem to reveal the sine wave which will reveal the location of the bonus Abalone. You have thirty seconds.*

"Don't play this one FC. It might over stimulate your brain into exploding."

The chicken shrugged.

"Grebo doesn't have my favorite game."

"What's that?"

"Ambulance Chaser. You're an ambulance driver sent to the scenes of accidents to pickup the survivors. You get bonus points for causing the accidents in the first place."

"Don't get started on that one. It was orginally suppose to have been an autobiographical movie about my time living among the primitive washing machine people. They promised it'd make a killing but I never saw one drop of blood."

Space-Bo laughed and moved on to a different machine. He found a promising one called Brick Mason. A little man on top of a building dropped bricks on unsuspecting passers-by on the street below. It was loads of fun for about five minutes until Space-Bo got too good for the game and accidentally overloaded the simple machine's CPU.

So while FC was busy attempting to overload his own CPU Space-Bo sat down on a brown gel sofa to look at the book entitled "Earth or Dirt, You Decide." Unfortunately it was written in French so Space-Bo couldn't even figure out the individual letters.

"What a crummy book." He absentmindedly slipped it into his pocket. Boredom lured him out of the sofa and into the hallway beyond.

He found a room labeled wallpaper. Inside, nailed, bolted, glued or screwed to every free space along the walls, were currency notes from all over Deo 7. Space-Bo knew what money was, and he could care less about it. Money had gotten him into too any problems. He could count them on his fingers, er toes. Besides, once he realized that instead of earning money to buy what he wanted he could just go down to the junkyard and pick it out on the cheap or better yet, steal what he wanted from dead people. Hmm, maybe that was from a movie he once saw. He sometimes forgot the difference.

A nasty little idea popped into his mind. He dug around in his pockets looking for anything that fit the shape of his hand just then. What came out was a mini-blowtorch that he didn't remember putting in there. It simply consisted of a lighter bondoed in place to the front of a hairspray bottle.

"Hmmm, I wonder how this got in there."
("Hey bud, get moving. You're slowing down the pace of the novel!")

"Huh? Oh yeah, sorry." He fired up the torch and began randomly destroying huge swaths of history.

FC walked in, "Hey, don't burn this, it's evidence." He walked over to one wall bearing Balidron currency exclusively. "Look at this," he said pointing to a $10 jeedude bill, "Tell me what you see."

Space-Bo came over squinting, "Twenty depraved poor children working for two bits a week for some sleazy deodorant mine executive."

"What else?"

"An extra large combo meal!"

"And..?"

262

"Nothing I'm loosing my psychic connection."

"It's positive. This is some of the original money Grego took from Balidron. I wonder where the rest of it is?"

"He probably spent it all on flousies."

"That would have been good for the economy. No, Grego only likes to do mean things which means he's hoarding all the capital somewhere."

"I thought Balidron was the Capital."

"He's got to have stashed it somewhere in the house here." The chicken paced the room alternately walking through burning parts of the wall and the safe zone around Space-Bo.

Space-Bo scratched his head in ponderment. He smacked his head with the palm of his hand so hard he fell over backwards. "I know where. I know where all the money is." But he wasn't sure he wanted to tell.

*   *   *

"Man! How far down do you think that hole goes?"

"Pretty deep to hold all the planet's money," the Funky Chicken answered, looking into the pit, that was next to the one Space-Bo had been tossed down the night before. They lay there at the edge, gawking down into the blackness where Grego the Mean had hoarded the entire planet's financial capital.

"Let me see," the chicken said, "I once learned a method for calculating multidimensional integrals on my fingers." He touched the taloned fingers on his hand / wings together in various patterns and after a while said, "Assuming the economy was inflated and devalued at the time Grego ripped them off, I calculate it should be 500,000 kilometers deep."

"Huh?"

"You're right I forgot to interpolate with the third dimensional permittivity coefficient."

"Eh?"

"Never mind, it's deep."

"I could have told you that." Suddenly Space-Bo had an idea. "Let's give it back. Let's give the people their money back."

"Interesting, what's your method of distribution?"

"We'd just hand it out to the people."

"Nope, it won't work. The society here is too backwards, they don't understand how to receive things. They'd think you were trying to rip them off."

"Okay, we could buy everybody a present."

"From who? But.... hey that gives me an idea. We could pay off the Planetary debt. Zero it out and everyone will be a free chicken, er man. Remember how your planet got out of its massive debt?"

"Yeah, we had one heck of a car wash."

"The people who got washed on Terra where the bond holders, and they took a bath."

"A bath, then a haircut and nice close shave. That sounds nice about right now."

The chicken got up suddenly saying, "I'll go get a helicopter. While I'm gone you get cleaned up and ready to clean out Grego."

"Wait a second. Don't you think he'd get mad if he found out?"

"Yeah," the chicken smiled, "Really mad."

Space-Bo had to smile in agreement.

*   *   *

A thundering whooping sound roared over the Balidron metrocenter as the fifty rotor cargo- heli flew in low over the fashion suburb known as Glogfurt. Slung beneath the behemoth was a giant sack measuring fifty meters in diameter and half a kilometer long. High up in the comparatively minute control center Space-Bo and FC were munching on peanut butter and jellyfish sandwiches. Space-Bo was munching, the chicken was manufacturing the sandwichs from scratch.

"Good thing you found that high powered snow blower," the chicken said as he ground some more wheat-like granules for the bread, "Or we'd still be back at Grego's mansion shoveling the stuff in."

"Yeah, but we're still in the one jeedude layer. As we get further down the hole we'll hit the three jeedude, then the seven jeedude, and then the ten jeedude level so each trip will bring more money."

"Still, that's 10000 or so trips to go. Look's like you'll have to enlist the help of several generations of your descendants to finish it up. Maybe we could hire a work force of miners to mine the pit. Their pay would be what ever they could stuff in their pockets each night."

Space-Bo liked the idea. "Hmmm. Just think, now Grego will have something really to get mad about."

"We're doing him a favor, actually."

"Yeah."

The Funky Chicken mashed the moistened wheat powder with a wicked looking waffle iron then looked out the window, "There's a bank over there to the port side. It looks bloated enough to handle our load."

The thundering mass of machinery moved like a swamp sow going to swamp sow maternity school. Landing gear telescoped out of either end of the superstructure, looking more like mosquito's legs than anything man made. And like a mosquito's legs the blimp had nice grippy hook like endings on the ends of its landing gear and it used them to its advantage as it reached out and grabbed ahold of the tall smokestacks of the Last Infrastate Bank.

"Can I do this one please?" Space-Bo clapped his hands together.

"Settle down junior. Finish your sam-witch first. The bank's not going anywhere."

Space-Bo mashed the rest of the messy thing into his mouth then rushed over to the nozzle gimble and actuation controls. "Mmis is gonna mobe mo much muffun," he mumbled.

The nozzle was a one meter diameter contraption hanging on the outside of the blimp from the end of a long slinky like tube which itself was connected to the currency blower motor in the blimp's cargo compartment. Under Space-Bo's careful control, servo actuated rods maneuvered the nozzle over a nice fat smoke stack. He slowly lowered it into place then smacked the

DISPENSE button.

Like a proboscus in reverse, the nozzle and tube assembly began to unload and inject money down the smoke stack and into the bank. The first few tons smothered out the furnaces then subsequent tonnage of currency flowed out into the janitorial areas, then the lobbies and the bribatoriums and finally into the vastly empty vaults.

When the bank couldn't take anymore and was about to pop, Space-Bo released the nozzel and they moved on to the next bank.

After a while Space-Bo began to get hungry again. "You got any more of...what did you call those things I was eating?"

"Sam-witches."

"Yeah, those things."

"Sorry, I threw the machine, I used to make them, out the window at the last bank."

"There you go again contributing to society. But seriously I think it's time to make a run to Micky D's"

"I don't think we'll fit through their drive-thru."

"Sure we will," Space-Bo said taking the giant stering wheel in his hands, "I'll show you a little trick I picked up back on Raul Rall Beta."

"At 2:47xm this afternoon two shabbily dressed men stormed into the the downtown Glogfurt branch of the Last Infrastate Bank and simulated a viral marketing gimick and forced tellers to give them access to the banks ID scanners. The barracuda later turned out to only be a DIY sandwich but the tellers said that at the time they didn't want to take any chances. The two men were disguised in complimentary costumes as a man-headed chicken and a chicken-headed man.

"World renowned scarf expert Ye'sloushnic Elp van'Sligou was taken to hospital with slackjaw syndrome after seeing the video footage. He was laster quoted as saying 'The hobo look is so last month, if you're going to rob a bank, at least dress to the times'.

"Captain, Retone Madirak, of the Glogfurt metro fashion police had this to say: 'Dee-SAS-ter.' Harsh words from the police captain there.

"Reportedly the two men escaped on foot after leaving a giant out-dated helicopter double parked outside the building. Charges are currently pending with the mattress police who want to interrogate them for events in connection with a seriers of illegal slumber parties.

"No word yet on exactly how much money they stole to the bank but it is rumored to be enough to bribe all the celebrity judges on the hit brainlinc show 'Bitch stole my face transplant'. More updates tonight at 11xm."

   –   *Excerpted from a nightly Glogfurt brainlinc news channel*

Grego the Mean laughed from inside the cab of his aircar parked on the outskirts of the Last Infrastate Bank park. Those idiots in the bank haven't even realized it's positive money yet. This was going to be far better than he had ever expected. And he had those two offworld nimwits to thank for it.

*   *   *

Space-Bo and the Funky Chicken were having a light dinner at the Cafe le Boom in the seedy part of Glogfurt. FC was really enjoying the radioactive first course but for some reason Space-Bo couldn't seem to get into food that tended to detonate.

"I ever tell you about my famous trinitrotoluene milkshake with a potassium chaser?" FC asked between beakfuls. He was busily devouring a green glowing plate of goop.

"Uh, no, but sounds lovely."

"Foolish me I keep forgetting you're mortal. It really sucks being immortal you know."

"Yeah, so you keep saying." He looked around to make sure there weren't any waiters around before he pulled out a Micky-D's take out bag. He popped a couple of micro burgers in his mouth before continuing, "So what's the deal with this restaurant? How come they only serve nasty stuff?"

"Oh it's only one of Glogfurt's multivarious ways of disposing of its toxic, radioactive, and bio-harzardous wastes. One of the best ways I can think of actually. Make your patrons pay for the privilege of ingesting your sewage excrement and carting it off afterward. Absolute genius."

"Sewage? Did you say sewage?"

"Probably not in a fine establishment like this one, but I'm sure they use that for lubrication on some of the chunkier courses. A bit nasty the first time, and the second, et cetera. But after a while I suppose it becomes an acquired taste." The chicken looked up overhead at that point and said, "I stand corrected." As if to prove the writer wrong, the chicken grabbed a smelly tube hanging from the ceiling, pulled it down into his throat, and mashed the release button. Instantly cubic meters of raw sewage were injected directly into his body.

Space-Bo knew when detonations were eminent and quickly ducked under the table. Still, he got plastered with filth as the chicken exploded everywhere, soaking the other patrons in filth and gore.

Twenty minutes later they were ceremoniously expulsed from the premises. While one bouncer read from a dusty scroll, "If you ever come back here we will hunt you down and feed you to Ragnarok himself!" while a second bigger bouncer tossed them out by the scruffs of their necks.

"Thanks for the tip," Space-Bo called back. He turned to the chicken and said, "Oh well, all in all, I'd say it's been a fun day."

"Yeah, but we got a busy one ahead of us tomorrow," FC dusted his plumage off, "I hope to get two or three loads of money returned. And then hopefully we can hire positive money converts to take over from there."

Space-Bo was looking over at the shield wall dividing Glogfurt off from Grebway to the west. A pair of smallish individuals were attempting to climb over into Glogfurt. "Hey, FC," he punched his friend, "Intruder alert at nine o'clock."

FC glanced over, "Okay let's get 'em." And off he went flapping his wing / arms wildly in a vain attempt to fly.

Space-Bo charged right after. When he caught up with the chicken the intruders were already bagged. "Hey you didn't save anything fun for me."

"You get to interrogate them."

"Okay," Space-Bo reached into the bag and pulled out Plutoman. "Hey, I know you. What are you doing in this bag with our intruders?"

"Moron!" Plutoman slapped 'Bo a couple of times before realizing it didn't do much. "Let me go you big lug!"

Space-Bo complied and fished the other intruder out of the bag. It was Greyson. "Ah come on FC, I can't interrogate them. We're on the same team."

Spyman straightened his uniform and stood erect. "Spy.... er," he quickly removed his mask and began again, "Greyson reporting for duty sirs. Mission status currently at failure level. Request termination of assignment pending further review."

"What'd he say FC?"

The chicken shrugged, "I guess he's chickening out! Ha!"

"Good one." Space-Bo looked the two guys over, "So did you see the cow?"

"Thousands of them," Greyson answered, "But they weren't exactly satanic however."

"Hmmm," the chicken pondered the ramifications. "And you Plutoman?"

Plutoman snarled, "If you were anyone else I'd tell you to go eat a box of caltrops but you'd like that, so here goes. Nope. No cow, no satanic, no nothing. End of story."

"And we've seen nothing either. I think we need a group meeting to see if this entire mission is a flop. Does anyone know where our illustrious leader, Rogicphil, is?"

The others all shook their heads.

"Okay lets regroup back at the starcruiser then."

"Yeah yeah, yeah yeah yeah," Plutoman eagerly followed them over to where FC had landed their shuttle in the middle of a shallow acid pool surrounded by mounds of rotting vegetation.

A plank traversed most of the acid up to the shuttle's side hatch. FC splashed alongside the others sizzling his way up to the craft.

Plutoman took a long look at the shuttle which technically still belonged to him. "That thrust inverter looks a little damaged. Somebody's gonna have to pay for that!"

Space-Bo stuck his head underneath the side runner to get a better look and while FC and Greyson were curiously watching the ex-space marine, Plutoman leapt over them all and into the shuttle. He locked all the doors and mashed the launch button as soon as he could. In a flash he was gone, and the shuttle with him.

The three remaining "suckers" choked in the fumes and cursed up at the vanishing vapor trail. Space-Bo shrugged, Greyson contemplated the universe, and the Funky Chicken took bites out of his leg.

Chapter 24: The Big Round Up

Dr. Gronblec was in complete shock. "We just covered I don't know how many light years in what, five seconds, and we didn't even use a wormhole?"

"Yeah, you know, those tollbooths really get to me," Rogicphil the space cabbie said pushing his stolen cabbie hat back.

They were in a low yet gentle orbit around Deo 7. Rogicphil had no idea if there were any tax cruisers left in the area so he was taking precautions with the orbit.

"So what gave you the idea to turn an old washing machine into a spaceship?"

"Well the main thing I suppose was that is was available at the time. It also helps that it was airtight to begin with. I improvised what I could before hiring a theatrical set designer to install the tricked out subwoofers."

"I see," Gronblec said quivering in his boots.

They were sitting side by side in the somewhat cramped sitting compartment of Rog's new washing machine converted into a spaceship. Originally it had actually been a DIY Christmas present replica of an ancient racing ground car known by the cryptic name of Fiat. It originally had four rubber wheels but the kid putting it together didn't know what they were and threw them out. But it did have a nice wide driver's seat and a large wooden steering in the small passenger compartment that had later been converted to the washing chamber. The bubble dome hatch over the chamber had been installed by the laundry mat that had inherited the thing from the little boy when he had died of middle age at 47.

It was basically an elongated cylinder one meter in diameter and two and half long. Long faded green racing stripes angled down from the nose to just above the recently mounted Quasar space drives that were on either side of the hull just behind the passenger chamber.

"Now just hang tight a bit while I go check something out." Rogicphil began fiddling with the door handle before he forgot his passenger. "Oops, sorry," he said shoving an oxygen mask in Gronblec's face before quickly opening the hatch, stepping out into the coldness of space and shutting the hatch behind him before all the air leaked out. He floated in space a bit and waved at Gronblec, who was turning blue, not from lack of oxygen, but from the sheer audacity of it all, then made some rocket boots and boosted his way down to the planet.

The sun was just setting as he touched down in Balidron.

Rogicphil climbed up on the hood of his Fiat and spoke into his watch, "Calling all agents, calling all agents, respond please. This is Rog, come in if you can read me." He waited a few moments.

Nothing, then, "You lousy worthless good for nothing grrr bonehead meatloaf barn door rearing wrrlll....." was spewed out of half a dozen channels simultaneously.

"It's good to be missed by all my adoring fans," Rogicphil replied smiling, "And I know how you'd all love to convey your heartfelt sincerest wishes to me but we've got a mission to complete and this isn't the place to do it. That's right, Deo 7 was a big mistake. The satanic cow's probably never even heard of this backwater planet but before you all congratulate me on this discovery I am pleased to announce we're going on an all expense paid trip to Moorgand IV the planet of wondrous surprises so if you could all form an orderly line and meet back at the starcruiser we can be on our way by 2xm. Thank you for your support." He clicked off the communicator before anymore feedback could assault him.

Dr. Gronblec tapped on the window from inside the Fiat.

Rogicphil climbed back inside quickly enough that the minimum amount of smell entered the tiny cabin. "Sorry I had to bring you down to the surface but I needed the Fiat and since you can't breath in a vacuum I didn't want to leave you stranded up in orbit."

"What kind of cabbie are you? Even if that's what you really are. Is this some kind of trick to keep me from the conference?"

"It's no trick and you're right I'm no cabbie. I'm actually a re- uh journalist on an undercover assignment."

"Yeah right. And I'm a giant cow dancing on your grave singing Glory, Glory, Halleluiah."

"Okay you got me. I had secret communicators implanted in my team members heads so when I needed to contact them I could, without worrying about them fooling around and accidentally wrecking them. I feel so foolish now."

"Huh?" Gronblec was poking himself to see if he was really awake or not.

"Doesn't work, I already tried." He fired up the engines, "Now after I round up the stragglers we can be on our way."

Eventually all the remaining agents, Space-Bo, FC, Greyson / Spyman, Mr. Bear, and the Clergy crammed into the remaining working shuttle still parked on the roof of a McCow barn in downtown Hicksville (yes the two guards did slip and fall off). Rogicphil watched from outside shaking his head.

"Somebody get Bufgoo a tub of deodorant."

"Haven't you have enough of deodorant for an entire lifetime?"

"Okay, how about a shirt then?"

A loud Hawaiian button up was all that was found. Bufgoo hated it but at least it kept his fumes to his person. "I'll settle for a hospital. I did eat some razor blades the other day remember?"

Rogicphil radioed over to the shuttles main comm panel, "Okay FC, you know the way. I'll meet you all back at the starcruiser within the hour."

"Roger Rog," FC said from the shuttle's pilot seat. "Hold on," he revved the engine and eased the overloaded craft off the ground wobbling badly.

Rogicphil watched it fly off into orbit then climbed back into his fiat. Turning to Gronblec he said, "Why can't they save themselves for once?"

"Can we move on to Trigurard now? I'm scheduled to speak in less than ten minutes," he glanced at his watch, "Yesterday."

"Sure thing, Doc. Here we go." With a burst of extra-natural energy the fiat winked out of normal existence and into an accelerated perspective.

Two minutes later they were zooming down through the thick atmosphere of Trigurard. The planet had no oceans to speak of. A few large lakes constituted all of the run off the planet's rivers could afford. Rogicphil landed on the roof of the capital cities' convention hall. "There you go. That'll be twelve forty-seven, exact change."

"I think not." Gronblec pushed the hatch opened and jumped out. He checked his pockets for something then back inside the fiat. "I don't have my bowling ball. How do you expect me to make a moving presentation?"

"On roller skates?"

"See you later." He headed off for the elevator.

Rogicphil felt bad that Gronblec didn't appreciate what he'd done. If it wasn't for him and the Quasars, Gronblec would still be stuck in that Danville spaceport. Well it just goes to show you that no good deed goes unpunished.

With a clear conscious Rogicphil headed back to Deo 7 for his rendezvous with the others. He found the shuttle floating in orbit aimlessly. "Hey, what are you guys doing?"

The chicken radioed back, "Waiting for you. Plutoman got back to his ship before us and took off without us. We're stranded."

"What about the girls?"

"Beats me."

"Okay hang tight," Rogicphil racked his brain. "You guys wait here while I try to go find us some alternate transportation."

"What did you have in mind?"

"Don't ask, and don't forget your Deo 7 smell training either." He disappeared in a bright flash of light. It might have been the best piece of advice he could give at the time but at least it was something.

Chapter 25: Greymule Spaceways

"No no no no, no no no! I absolutely refuse. It's against my moral code," Rogicphil pleaded but his moral resolve was quickly dissolving before the travel agent. "Please, please, don't you have anything else available?"

Rogicphil was in the Hespuets II Wormhole Authority Space Station on the outskirts of the Hespuets II system. Every other system in the sector was closed due to a freak Galactic Holiday the date of which was randomly chosen through chaos theory.

"I'm sorry sir," the perky agent replied, "but everything is booked solid with all this convention activity in the sector."

"Okay," he sighed, "How much?"

"Fifty-five creds per passenger or twelve hundred to charter."

"Hmmm, what's the usual travel time to Moorgnad IV?"

"Infinite; we don't go there. It doesn't exist. What about a nice trip to Caladin in the Specter Nebula? It contains many nice ocean and atmospheric features that astound and delight any family for a wonderful vacation you'll remember for 3.7 lifetimes."

"Uh, I think not. I guess I'll have to charter then. Do I get a discount if I use my own pilot?"

"No, but not having a company authorized travel pilot triples the price plus you have to have insurance which is probably more than you'd make in 3.7 lifetimes. Hee hee."

"I'm rolling over with laughter as it fills my kidneys. Okay, but will one of your pilots fly us where we want to go no matter what?"

"Of course not, but....." she looked around to make sure they weren't being watched, "There are a few pilots that are prone to being bribed. You might just get lucky enough to get one of those pilots if you know what I mean."

"Okay it's settled then. Charter a bus with a 'good' pilot. How much?"

"Three thousand and.... a small ten percent donation to my historical travel booths preservation fund should do it."

"Great," Rogicphil didn't sound too thrilled when he handed over his Roganivar III Diners Club card.

"I'm sorry but I think that's a fake card."

"Huh? What do you mean? I was born there; I should know if it was fake or not."

"Everyone knows that Roganivar III is a lifeless rocky footnote in planetary evolution. No one, not even banks exist there."

"Look the planet in question has a highly elliptical orbit. Sometimes it's Roganivar III sometimes it's Roganivar IV, and switches positions with the normal life bearing world that I was born on. Now please ignore what the damn card says and give me my damn ship!"

She happily slid the card back over the counter to him, "The bank says I'm not only to tear your credit card but to call the police and shoot you if you don't cooperate. That is unless you have something else to pay for this trip with?"

Rogicphil didn't want to do this but he had no choice. He pulled out the card that Destiny had given him. The Galactic Balance Card. It entitled the bearer to go anywhere do anything to anybody at anytime and had a pretty nifty interest rate too. "Fine, put it on this."

"Damn it!" the woman cursed, "I hate these frag things. That ten percent donation will be in cash. I'm not putting it on this thing. Understand?"

"Sure whatever." Rogicphil waited while the agent filled out a small stack of forms relating to the Galactic Balance Card, made him sign in four places, took his left big toe print, and extracted a sample of his nasal mucus before finally handing over the chartered paperwork.

"And uh, four hundred creds, sir?"

"You said ten percent?"

"GBC surcharge."

"Fine," he handed over a wad of cash without bothering to count and took off. Little did he realize that the money he gave her bore the facial imprint of Grego the Mean.

Down at the space docks he found the section labeled GMSW far past all the decent and halfway clean docking facilities. GreyMule SpaceWays was the scourge of the transportation industry and their Bidimentional Utility Shuttle (BUS) was the only place left in the galaxy where one could witness tech-level one culture still intact.

He found his BUS, designation 04297635, in the repair bay. It was completely missing its main drive which was lying in pieces in a giant bucket off to one side. The Pilot was happily eating a sandwich on a catwalk overlooking the repair operation.

Rogicphil sat down beside the man, "You Zed?"

"What's it to ya?"

"That depends if you still want to be a pilot?"

"Watch it buddy, I'm a black belt in Chunk Hu."

"Really? I thought Chunk Hu was an MSG derivative."

"Oh yeah. You're right. Whatever. You want a BUS ride or not?"

"That's why I'm here. I just chartered that," Rogicphil pointed in the general direction of mayhem, "That thing there. Is it really a spaceship? Because I always thought spaceships were suppose to be self enclosed with the ability to retain a breathable atmosphere."

"Naw that's just a bunch of rhetoric."

"Well how soon before we can shove off?"

"Not long now. Two, three weeks."

Rogicphil realized it would be quicker for him to move his team one by one to Moorgnad IV with his Fiat but that could prove extremely dangerous, especially with the satanic cow involved. So in the interests of group cohesiveness he was stuck with Greymule. "Are you a betting man Zed?"

"As much as the next Markonad."

Markonad? Rogicphil should have know but it was too late to back out now. "Great because I want to bet you a hundred creds that we'll be flying in that heap within the next hour."

"Okay, 'cause unless you enlist the help of several armies of mechanics,

Flora ain't going nowhere, hear."

"Flora eh? What a lovely name."

Exactly one hour later Zed forked the hundred creds over to Rogicphil as they slid out of the space docks in a completely 'functional' BUS. The Flora consisted of a bridge with two seats, a long passenger compartment and a drive section behind that. Baggage and electronics filled the underbelly. Despite it being over 90000 years older than Plutoman's starcruiser it almost appeared to be a prototype to that model.

Rogicphil stuffed the money into his pocket along with all his other weird currency. When he'd made the bet in the first place he'd assumed he would have had to use his super speed to complete the necessary repairs. But speed isn't what was holding up the operation. It had been good old fashioned laziness. The parts in the bucket turned out to be unrelated to this BUS and a dehydrated replacement drive was waiting in plain manilla envelope on the shop floor for someone to simply go and get it (and of course soak it in a vat of water to re-expanded it to full size). Nobody had until Rogicphil decided to.

From there is was simply a matter of installing the new drive and fastening the cowling back in place. Incidentally it took forty-five minutes to get that beat up cowling back into position. In the end it had to be welded shut.

"I don't know how you did it 'Phil, but don't tell me. I like to live in my own delusional world where little demons and deities and gremlins only exist when I drink too much." Zed lit up a fat cigar, "Okay boss, where to?"

"Well first ease on over to the parking garage so I can pick up my Fiat and then it's own to Deo 7."

"Sure thing," Zed shifted to first and let up on the clutch lurching the Flora forward.

The next day on the BUS Flora: "...and in case there is a sudden loss of pressure in the cabin hand guns will drop from the ceiling above you," Rogicphil was instructing the passengers on the various safety regulations of the Greymule Corporation. Regulations mostly for the safety of Greymule.

"Hey!" Clergy Joe yelled, "Can I shoot Bufgoo instead? He just farted!"

"That was the intention." Rogicphil looked back to his safety card and continued, "Tray tables can be used instead of floatation devices. No radios, holo recorders, Dictaphones, or lawyers are to be used while the BUS is in motion or stopped for whatever reason (both). Do not read this sentence."

Rogicphil wadded the card up into a little ball, palmed it and pretended to pop it into his mouth and swallow. The passengers cheered. "Now, my rules. Leave me alone. That's it." More cheering. He turned around and slipped down into his seat next to the Funky Chicken.

"You have something for me I believe?" FC asked.

"Oh yeah," Rogicphil handed him the wadded up safety card.

The chicken dipped the ball in a saucer full of kerosene, placed it in his beak, and swallowed it for real. "I knew you were going to pull that trick even before you did."

"Ouch," he handed over a fiver cred.

FC accepted gratefully and set it on fire. "Yum, yum," he tossed it down his gizzard as a chaser. A few seconds later a cloud of black smoke

273

belched forth from his beak. "Pardon moi."

Rogicphil had just settled into a nice dream containing wine, women, and song, but mostly women, when Zed woke him up.

"Hey 'Phil, hey 'Phil, wake up. We got malfunctioning instruments."

"Okay," Rogicphil opened his eyes, "Show me where they're at."

Zed led him into the back of the BUS, into the small restroom where the Clergy had somehow managed to set up a recording studio. "They're in here."

"What!?"

"The electric triangle. I think maybe the current is out of phase."

"Huh? What's that?"

Joe held up his instrument of choice, "What kind of ship you runnin' here Rog? We got our rights you know."

"Musical instrument?" Rogicphil was getting mad. "You woke me up because MUSICAL instruments were malfunctioning?"

"Uh yeah, well... um, you see, I mean, you know..."

"Rule number two, LEAVE ME ALONE!"

"But 'Phil," Bufgoo said, "I thought that was rule number one."

Rogicphil wanted to smack them all and was about to when he noticed something funny outside the restroom porthole. A face. And then a hand. The hand was connected to the face and waving at him.

"My you're an ugly bugger aren't you?"

Joe took a swing at Rogicphil but just barely missed as his target imperceptibly wasn't there when his fist was scheduled to hit. "Hey, how does he do that? Do you think you can work this into our act Bufgoo?"

But Rogicphil was already cycling the airlock. A few moments later he "stepped" out into the void alongside the coasting Flora. The little blue face with four tiny arms growing out of it spun through space at him until it intersected with his force field and was sucked into the small envelope of breathable air.

"Cough!" it let out a cloud of green fumes from its mouth as if it'd been holding its breath for a long time.

"Okay, who sent you?" Rogicphil asked.

The thing shrugged, if you could call it that, and removed a backpack it was wearing. From it the little blue guy pulled out a box of individually wrapped chocolate bars.

Rogicphil hesitated a bit before taking the box, "From the Quasars?"

"Bye bye," is all it squeaked in reply and then spun off into space.

Back inside the ship and somewhat bewildered he opened the box to find a hand scrawled note slipped between bars. It read:

The State of Orderly Confusion sends: _____
(name attribute)
greetings. You are hereby ordered to distribute these chocolate bars to all prospective contestants. (*And that means you too FC!*)

Probably just Destiny playing some joke on him. Okay he'd give out the bars but wouldn't actually eat one himself. "Hey anyone want a choc..." he was dog piled before even his accelerated reflexes could react.

The Clergy by far got the largest chunk but Space-Bo and the bear got sizable amounts as well. Rogicphil had to confiscate bars back from them in order to distribute at least one to all the passengers. Little good it did as they stole, cheated, or harassed most of them back anyway.

Rogicphil gave up on the whole affair and went back to his seat for another attempt at a nap.

Space-Bo interrupted him next, "Hey, there's a weird metal thing in one of my choco-bars and it doesn't taste right. Can I get a replacement?"

"Metal what?"

"This weird metal thing," he pulled out of his mouth a flat gold foil sheet.

"Let me see...uh, could you hold it up instead?" Rogicphil studied the foil closely. It looked like a magic ticket. Embossed on it were intricate letters that spelled out M-A-G-I-C T-I-C-K-E-T.

Rogicphil stood up on his seat, "Hey anybody else get a defective bar with a cheap yellow lining?"

"I got a Magic Ticket!" Greyson called back.

"Magic ticket!?" Joe yelled. "Give that back, Hack. That was my bar first."

"Hmm," Rogicphil sat back down, "Keep the ticket 'Bo. It's just another little game Destiny's playing with us."

"Well okay," Space-Bo shrugged, "I got an extra ticket if you want one."

"No thanks, for some reason I think all the bars have a magic ticket in them."

"Mine doesn't," Zed said munching a bar.

"Why aren't you flying the BUS?"

"Autopilot?"

"This thing doesn't even have auto crash-landing."

CrrrrrAAAASSSSHHHH!

"One point for Zed," Rogicphil said after bouncing off the bulkhead.

"What'd we hit anyway?" He followed Zed as they floated into the flight deck. "And who put the gravity generator in the nose?"

They were looking at solid rock out the main view port.

"The safety inspector colonel I think."

"Looks like we ran into an asteroid."

"Wow, so that's what they look like up close."

Rogicphil checked the few scopes and sensor readouts that the scant cockpit afforded, "Well we got about a four hour layover before we can get under way again. Break out the tool box and I'll meet you down in the cargo berth."

"Okay-dokay."

When Rogicphil finally returned floating back to the passenger compartment he discovered Greyson floating there alone in meditation. "They can't all be stuffed in that restroom."

275

"Uh no," Greyson said without opening his eyes, "the chicken took them all outside for a picnic."

"Why aren't you with... Wait a second. This is an asteroid, there's no atmosphere on it."

"Yeah, the chicken said something about airing out the lining in his skin."

"I give up," Rogicphil turned to head for the cargo berth. "Oh, tell me if anyone somehow makes it back."

"Sure thing. Uh Rogicphil?"

"Yeah?"

"Uh, well..."

"Spit it out man."

"You seem to be going about this all wrong."

"I thought you were going to reveal a tender and emotional scene from your life that you thought would make an appropriate epithet to this sad chronicle."

"There are techniques to help you overcome being a pushover. I could teach you if you wish."

"No, I think I'll take your advice and ignore it." He pried the floor hatch open and dove beneath the deck. A few seconds later he popped back up, "And don't get any funny ideas with that magic ticket thing. It my be magical but it's no ticket, er. Well don't trust it. That's what I'm trying to say."

"A man with one watch knows what time it is. A man with two isn't so sure."

Chapter 26: The Family Fugue

Space-Bo and Hack greeted the rest of the crew as they disembarked from the Flora. "Welcome to Moorgnad IV, the best kept secret since the automated pie cutter."

Rogicphil pointed the others towards the baggage claim as he spoke with Space-Bo, "What in smeg are you doing here? You're suppose to be dead out in space, smashed between two colliding asteroids. And where'd this spaceport come from?"

All around them thousands of other passengers were disembarking from other flights connecting to D terminal. Flexible tubes connected the terminal to all sorts of spaceships and time machines and other various transportation craft, the likes of which the galaxy had never seen.

"Well," Space-Bo began, "First we were miraculously saved by a Udorfian raider ship on the way here for the big show. And then it was simply a matter of looking up your flight number on the spaceport monitors."

"Moorgnad IV isn't suppose to exist but it does, and that's cool, but a teeming spaceport? Where the frag did that come from?"

"It's all here in the visitor information card," Space-Bo handed over a glossy nineteen color tesseract-fold brochure:

Welcome to BT's intergalactic spaceport on Moorgnad IV. Designed and build in record time (7 hours) by the Blectel Group for the greatest show of all time, the Ultimate Gameshow, where you get to watch first hand (claw, tube, extractor, etc...) the fate of existence as you know it be decided before your very eyes (sensors, antennas, etc...).

The brochure had several holographs of the several thousands of legions of construction gangs that had build a five billion square meter, state of the art, spaceport on the lush and completely useless mythical planet of Moorgnad IV.

"So the cow's going to strike here, on the game show? Is that it?"

"Uh not quite," Space-Bo folded out the center section of the brochure for Rogicphil, "Read this part:"

The Ultimate Gameshow is a production of Blink-Morton Production studios and its subsidiaries...

"No, no, the next part."

"Oh," Rogicphil skipped down a bit and read:

The Ultimate Gameshow, blah blah blah, etc... and featuring Rogicphil Suflupinic as the Soggy Place Galaxy's champion, battling the satanic cow for the supreme rulership of the Galaxy.

Rogicphil's team consists of the infamous immortal, code named

Chicken, Funky the, and various other dimwits their little backwater galaxy has seen fit to produce through the ages.

The satanic cow, who has been doing some heavy weight training in the past few weeks, looks really strong in the witty and snappy answers categories.

But will Rogicphil and his intrepid band of idiots stand a chance against the butcher of butchers who single hoofedly siezed power in the secret organization of H.E.L.L.? Only time and your pocketbooks will tell.

This looks to be a most exciting confrontation and we have just the concessions for you to enjoy it with such as...

"Nobody told me about this," Rogicphil barked, jabbing Space-Bo with the brochure, "I thought this was suppose to be a fair fight."

"Hey, I'm just the brochure delivery boy here. No time to chat now 'Phil, we're suppose to be down at Studio 1 in ten minutes for the first round."

"Oh joy," Rogicphil sighed and trudged after Space-Bo.

<insert witty Family Fugue game show ripoff scene here>

Rogicphil slipped unseen out the studio's back door into a hospital like corridor. He checked all the doors on either side for any clue as to the cow's whereabouts, but when he came to the last door on the right on which the sign, *Step Into My Office...Again*, was posted, he just solemnly shook his head.

With yet another sigh, he stepped into Destiny's office. This time it was the supreme being's liquor cabinet room. "I need some answers," he asked not expecting to get a straight answer.

"AND I NEED SOME QUESTIONS," Destiny replied living up to his expectations. He was filling two glasses full of a colorless green liquid. He handed one to Rogicphil and motioned him to have a seat on a nice sofa while he sat down in a nearby comfy recliner.

Rogicphil took the glass, sat down and stared right through it. "How do you do it?" he asked softly.

"I ASK MYSELF THE SAME QUESTION EVERY MORNING."

Rogicphil kept staring down into his glass. "No I mean the drink. How do create a colorless green liquid?"

"OH THAT. IT'S AN OLD WRITER'S TRICK. NOT IMPORTANT. I WAS WONDERING WHEN YOU'D FINALLY MAKE IT HERE. THERE'S SOME IMPORTANT THINGS I NEED TO DISCUSS WITH YOU."

Rogicphil snapped out of his gloom and demanded, "Like what the slag is this game show thing? And where's the cow?"

"THE COW IS ON HER WAY. I THOUGHT IT'D BE NICE TO HAVE A GAMESHOW, IN THE MEANTIME, TO PASS THE TIME. WHAT DO YOU THINK SO FAR?"

"It's stupid."

"COME NOW. IT TOOK ME THREE WHOLE SECONDS TO CONCIEVE OF THIS IDEA."

"I rest my case."

"AND I REALLY HAD NO CHOICE. ACCORDING TO THE COMPACT AGREED TO WITH H.E.L.L. WE MUST ABIDE BY THEIR

CHOICE OF TYPE OF CONFRONTATION, A GAMESHOW. AND SO TO KEEP THEM ON THEIR TOES I THOUGHT UP A LOT OF REALLY UNUSUAL GAMES I'M SURE YOU AND YOUR TEAM WOULD EXCEL AT. THERE'S NO WAY I'D LET THEM SLIP IN A BINGO TOURNAMENT."

"The Family Fugue? And what's with all the commercialism? Some guy tried to sell me a T-shirt with my picture on it this morning. And after all you went through to stop ME from selling out."

"WELL EVEN SUPREME BEINGS NEED FUNDING, AND SINCE WE'RE NOT ALLOWED TO EXACT TAXES FROM OUR LIFEFORMS WE DO WHAT WE HAVE TO." Destiny shrugged and sipped from his glass.

"You have to draw the line somewhere. Slurpy Soap? Come on."

"NO, THAT ONE WAS ACTUALLY A COMMERCIAL FROM THE ASSOCIATION OF SNAIL-MAIL CARRIERS UNION. IT'S A PARODY OF COMMERCIALS TO GET THEIR POINT OF SELLING BOOKS ACROSS. A RATHER SUBTLE TACTIC I BELIEVE."

"Well I'm out of here if that's all you have to tell me." Rogicphil got up and headed for the door.

"ROGICPHIL, WAIT. THERE IS ONE IMPORTANT THING I MUST TELL YOU BEFORE YOU LEAVE."

"What's that?"

"YOUR SHOE'S UNTIED."

"Huh?" he looked down at his boots.

"GOTCHA!" with that Destiny dissolved and the room with him leaving Rogicphil standing in a women's changing room.

He was pelted with high heeled shoes a few times before he made a hasty retreat. Back out in the hall he looked around and sighed before moping back to the studio. "Well if he wants a show, I'll give it to him."

The chicken was busy with his version of a three ring circus. One ring formed by Rick Drawlson and the ground over which he was suspended and tied down on two chairs. Another more round ring was hanging from the ceiling slightly above and behind Drawlson. The final ring was formed by members of the audience encircling the whole affair to make sure that Rick didn't run away if he somehow managed to get free.

Rogicphil watched sipping his colorless green liquor as FC enthralled the audience with his master showmanship.

"And now a simple blow torch ignites my entire body," he announced as he set himself a blaze. "Now watch closely, as I leap through the hoop, that none of the flames will catch on to my launching pad." He ran full tilt at Drawlson, jumped on his back, and used the body as a springboard to launch his flaming chickenoid body through the ring. He landed with a half twist, perfectly on three talons.

The audience was impressed and the applause registered well on the production staffs meters. "Let's dump Drawlson and pick up this chicken fellow. He's not much to look at but hey, he puts on one terrific show."

*   *   *

Wilbur and Jake were watching the show with somewhat mixed interest

279

from Smelly Le Puke's French Dining Experience Extraordinaire and Restaurant. Jake was eating pizza in a cup with a side order of bacon and had a mug of spicy hot chocolate milk to drink. Wilbur was simply sipping on beer saturated coconut pulp.

"Are you sure this is French food?" Wilbur asked eyeing Jake's disgusting looking meal.

"Sure, if French food is defined as grotesque aberrations of already overpriced foodstuffs."

"You know, ever since the cow saved your life you've been acting really strange. First, all that extra farting and then this thing with trying to kill me. I'm beginning to think something is wrong with you."

"Well, the cow has opened up a whole new world to me. A world in which everything is cow. And wonderful. That's it, I think I'd like to sing a song about a cow. A huge and bloated and wonderful..."

Wilbur smacked Jake a few times, "Snap out of it man. You're not going to go into a song while I'm around. Now finish your food so we can get back to trying to kill each other in peace."

"I'm sorry I don't know what came over me. It's just when I think about cows I get this certain feeling, this certain something that just makes me want to si..."

"That does it." Wilbur rapped his partner over the head with his own broken leg that was still impaled on Wilbur's severed wrist.

Jake fell over unconscious. A waiter came by and spat on him in an attempt to revive him. He instantly jumped up when the spittle hit him. "Ah, ah, eeeuuw." After wiping his face off he sat down more calm. "Hey thanks man. I needed that."

The waiter stood there expecting a tip. Wilbur slapped him in the face then said to to Jake, "The cow has had you reprogrammed to do her bidding is what I think is going on here."

"Yeah so?"

"You knew that?"

"Sure, she's been slowly reprogramming everyone in the organization to do her bidding. She wants to be the next Space Pontiff, you know."

"Aha, it's so clear to me now."

"It is?"

Wilbur looked as if he'd just deciphered Fermat's Theorem with an abacus. "All these weird things I've been thinking lately finally make sense."

"Hmm, what things would those be?"

"Like driving a garbage truck through a bossman's office, or wearing crumpets on my head, or even taking a bath!"

"What's a crumpet?"

"Something I'd like to wear on my head I guess."

"Well I think the question should be: what are we going to do about it?"

"Try asking the waiter what it is. Sounds kind of like breakfast to me."

"No, I mean about all this mind control stuff. Should we follow the cow's orders or do what Lester tells us?"

"Do we really have a choice?"

"No, not really, but that's besides the point. The time for action has come and I know who needs to do that action."

"Who's that?"

"Mother Maynard of the Unholy Scriptural Alliance."

"Oh course," Wilbur exclaimed, pounding the table hard enough to knock his coconut pulp on the floor. "Mother Maynard, I still remember her whacking me upside the head when I was in cemetery school."

"Me too." A look of bliss descended upon Jake.

"Okay, so Mother Maynard is going to kill both the cow and The Bossman and Lester right? And we're going to do her bidding and we'll all live happily ever after in a small bungalow back on Lugietorp?"

"No she's having an affair with anti-Bishop Lester right now I think."

"But didn't we kill Lester?"

"No that was just one of his robot duplicates. I think it was a ruse by the cow to keep the two sides fighting."

"I was going to say, 'Oh I see, very sneaky,' then I realized you're a moron. The Bossman was the one making the robots, not the cow. Remember?"

"Mother Maynard will be our guiding light in these troubled times," Jake said pulling a small communicator pen out of his pocket. He pressed the button at the end of the pen and when he removed his thumb a beam of light shown out and into Jake's eyeball. He held it a fraction of a centimeter from his pupil to focus it properly then wrote his request onto a greasy napkin, "Collect call to Mother Maynard please."

"Processing," a psychic operator forced him to autowrite, "And think you for using HT&T."

The image of a hideous and deformed large slimy woman formed on the back of Jake's eyeball, "What's the meaning of this Jake? I thought I sent you to the torture chamber without dinner. What are you doing up so soon?" The words weren't spoken. Instead Jake did it all in autowriting. He held the pen up to his eyeball from time to time to see what was going on.

"Mother Maynard, this is Jake agent 666 of H.E.L.L.. That was over fifteen years ago that you sent me to my torture chamber without nourishment. I've forgotten all about that, now that I'm in charge of Special Operations. Wink, wink!"

Wilbur almost feinted. It was blasphemy to talk to an Unholy Mother like that. Unless you planned on enslaving her. That must be what Jake was up to. The conniving worm. Wilbur would make sure he finished Jake good when they got back to killing each other. But, hmm where'd he put the coconut pulp? Ah there it is...

"Horrible Mother, I need your help in small matter," Jake wrote. "Wink, wink!"

The Mother snarled in return, "If you really were in charge of Special Operations then you'd know that I was placed in command of Deceptive Practices which places me above you in the hierarchy."

"Ah hah, but if you were in command of Deceptive Practices then you would also know that besides Special Operations I also oversee the Committee for Hazardous Waste Disposal and you know what that means."

"Think you've got me eh, Jake. Well just yesterday Lester called me into his office and gave me the job of Janitorial Inspection and placed me personally in charge of your covert operation so no matter what you must answer to me BOY!"

"You may have me there Mother Maynard, but I have something that goes beyond rules and regulations. I have evidence that proves you stole a shipment of Narcotic Babyfood for your own twisted purposes and replaced it with Vitamin C tablets."

"No, no, you can't possibly know that. I had everyone involved killed, castrated, or placed in country / western decontamination chambers. Everyone that is except for you Jake. How did you manage to reconstruct your memories?" She tried to make the pause as pregnant as possible then said, "Ha, ha, just kidding."

"Very funny, Mother. Now will you do my bidding or else? Wink, nudge! Nudge, nudge, wink, ploop!"

Mother Maynard looked truly distressed in the odd glowing beam of light but that was probably due to constipation. "Alright I'll help you in your small matter. What is it?"

"I need you to deliver a bouquet of black roses to YIG Insurance Group headquarters."

"That's it?"

"That's it, but you must do it by hand."

"What!? That could take an entire day at least."

"That is what you must do. Now get to work!" Jake cut transmission before she could reply.

Wilbur knew this was his last chance to act before Jake lowered his hand. He leapt up and shoved Jake's hand, still holding the pen, back into his eyeball. Optigook splattered Wilbur but he didn't care because the chase was on. He fled the scene before the waiter could stop him, effectively leaving Jake with the bill.

Chapter 27: Wheel of Fish

Brasted Holderbolver, the undisputed general manager of the fish factory, was intensely delighted to hear that one of the episdes to be used during the Ultimate Gameshow would be the Wheel of Fish and that he was personally in charge of all aspects of or relating to fish.

First he set about to bring the fish factory online and up to full capacity. He figured a general merchandising sweep would follow the show's debut and wanted to be able to cash in on all the loot that he could, as quickly as possible.

Everything was running as smooth as milkfish until two days before the Wheel was to be broadcast, disaster struck the factory. And then, just hours before holotaping was to begin, one of his fish carts had been hijacked in a seedy catwalk section of the complex.

And so now on the eve of his greatest achievement, total annihilation loomed. But he wasn't just going to sit there and let it happen. No sir, he broke out the old war reparations kit and loaded up. The grand ballroom was his destination and by Blatvor's Greasy Beard he'd wreak some havoc.

Brasted was marching down a hallway towards the ballroom when a chicken came racing by, riding on the back of a demented cow. "Damn newlyweds!" he cursed and then he... walked on down the hall.

He came to a door where... (no that would be foolish).

Violence was erupting (or rather leaking) like spicy tartar sauce out the massive doorways leading into the ballroom. Men and women elegantly attired for the occasion, were fighting each other tooth and nail, crowbar to crowbar, phaser to pick axe.

"Damn, they started without me," Brasted cursed as he locked and loaded his twelve barreled, fusion welded, plasma bearing, lock and load, flare gun. He had used it in a petty border war back in the sector D-11 range disputes with his company of Pansy Troops, a division of the Retreating Legion.

He began to rapid fire flares deep into the ballroom's melee. Unfortunately fireworks were still going off and so no one noticed. Saddened, Brasted sunk back against a dividing wall between two doorways and wept. "No one likes me!" he cried, "And now they're all going to kill me, and stomp on me, and sing Glory Halleluiah upon my grave."

*   *   *

Meanwhile deep in the bowels of the hair restoration pre-processing depository the satanic cow and the Funky Chicken were discussing terms of each other's battle position.

A waiter brought in cappuccinos for the two and left it on a barrel of Monox XVII that served as a table between them.

The Cow lapped from her bowl as the chicken spoke, "Now with just a 15% investment I think our chain of Chicken Dips and Beef Rotisseries could net a tidy profit."

"What do you care about profit, chicken? Those are capitalistic Human concepts. You should be more concerned with farm animal rights and prison camps in places like Hicksville on Deo 7. You can't ignore the plight of species subjugated to the tyrannical Human rule. Look at your Mister Ursus Bear for example. They've turned him into a biped and now he even wears clothing. What's next? Bouffant hair styles and dentures?"

"I see your point, my good friend but I just thought it would be really ironic, and hypocritical to boot, for us to open a restaurant that would feed our kind to the Humans. Oh and by the way, I only happen to look like a chicken. By some quirk of the universe that I have vowed vengeance upon, or maybe it was my fault all to begin with, but I forget now. So anyway this quirk has insured that one of the primary barn stock animals currently in use today are a derivative of my genetic code."

"Have you considered patent infringement?"

"Yeah but I'd probably end up suing myself. I could call for the death penalty, plead insanity, and then jump out the twenty-second story window of a casino somewhere before the mattress police could catch up with me."

"You speak in cryptic riddles my friend and I have much to learn from you but for now let us join forces and put an end to these foul humans once and for all."

"I've got a better idea. Let's attack each other, I'll let you win, and then you can torture and kill me as many times as you like so long as each death is creative enough."

"Perhaps then the cause is lost," the cow lamented as she finished her cappuccino then backed towards the exit chute. "In a few days I'll expect to see you on the battlefield. Long live the revolution!" she said before jumping backwards into the laundry chute and disappeared down into the black maw.

"Hmmm," the chicken thought just before tossing his cappuccino, cup and all, into his gullet.

*   *   *

"And now the host of the Wheel of Fish, Jack Saypat, with, as always, his lovely assistant Annava Blight," the announcer announced as yet another incarnation of the eternal game show host marched onto the set. This time with a clone.

Annava Blight was actually a clone of the host but vat-grown to be a female instead. Despite the genetics she looked nothing like her progenitor which was good since the insta-ratings spiked as soon as she appeared on the set.

"Well Annava, I see that the baby hasn't left too many stretch marks," Jack smirked as he arrogantly patted his 'sister' on the stomach.

"Of course that shouldn't bother you now seeing as how you can only view half of it." She was referring to his new glass eye that replaced the one he'd lost the previous day.

"Maybe they should have called this show Wheel of Sibling Rivalry."

"Whatever you say Jack," she beamed and the ratings edge up one more notch.

"Now, let's recap the standings from the last two days."

	Round 1	Round 2	Place
Rogicphil	10	34	3rd
Bear	8	27	4th
Hack	15	38	2nd
FC	27	42	1st
Space-Bo	5	17	6th
Grayson	1	23	5th

(Round 2 scores are cummulative)

"The Funky Chicken is out to a strong lead and the favorite Suflufinic is in a disappointing third behind the tough and massive Hack. But enough of the past, we're concerned with your welfare here too and so on with today's show, Wheel of Fish, brought to you by Lamprey's Dissecting Cream. The cream that takes it all off, Lamprey's. And by Spacecrud, which invites you to test fly a brand new Mark MMXXLCXIV space cycle today."

Blurry eyed contestants were led in during the break. Neither Space-Bo, nor the chicken were with the others. Jack called up Bob, the producer, on his endplay intercom. "What's this?" he demanded, "I need six contestants."

"We're having a small problem right now, Jack," Bob replied, "It seems last night's party got too carried away, and a couple contestants were killed, or something like that."

"What am I suppose to do about it? I didn't kill them." Pause, "Did I?"

"Not officially. Now you need to bluff while we get some replacements ready."

"Okay but this is worth a bonus." Jack clamored back onto the Fish set, "And we're back ready to start the first spin. Suflufinic take it away."

"Really?" Rogicphil suddenly became wide awake. He stepped up to the big wheel mounted vertically below the scoreboard and looked at all of its ten meter diameter mass. He spat on his hands and rubbed them together. "Okay, I'll give it a spin." An instant later he had climbed up to the hub and had unscrewed the retaining pin which held the whole wheel firmly in place.

"WHAAAAAAAaaaaaaaaaaaaaaaaaaaaaaa!" Jack ran for his life as the massive wheel came unloosened and rolled across the stage after him.

An announcer cut it to the broadcast, "This is test of the emergency broadcast system. If this had been an actual emergency the preceding random act of violence would have been followed by official propaganda and instructions on how to mercy-kill everyone in your household. And now a word from the National Apple Institute."

After the unscheduled break, the broadcast returned to the set where the wheel had been replaced as well as Rogicphil. Now he was bolted and chained in place.

"Okay Greyson, now it's your chance to spin the wheel. Let's just hope you can do a better job than Suflufinic there."

Greyson took a deep breath and shuffled over to the wheel. He was shuffling because his ankles were bound together. "Well okay," he said grabbing the fist sized handholds with both hands (because he was handcuffed) and gave the wheel a yank. It slowly spun around and around and eventually landed on a round flat kind of fish with both eyes on one side of its head.

Nothing happened.

"Now do I solve a puzzle or something?" Greyson looked around confused.

Jack looked over to Annava at the puzzle board. "Show us the puzzle Ms. Blight."

She motioned at the puzzle board and eight big rectangles lit up. With a big white smile she said, "The category is fish."

"Uh," muttered Greyson, "Can I buy a vowel?"

Jack spoke aside to the home audience, "Get a load of this guy. He thinks he can purchase abstract symbols." He chuckled slightly before speaking to Greyson, "And how much did you want to spend?"

"Um well, how much do I have? I mean, how many points did that fish give me?"

Jack twirled his index finger around temple. "I was thinking about cash. Let's say about fifty creds for a U."

Greyson glanced over to Rogicphil for help. The Gladerunner only shrugged a reply and Greyson was stuck with a decision to make. "Okay I'd like to solve the puzzle."

"Huh?" Jack looked up to the control booth. "Can he do that?"

"That's affirmative over," an incredibly distorted answer came.

"Okay," Jack said turning back to Greyson, "Solve that puzzle."

"Great!" Greyson hopped over to where Annava was standing. Despite being shackled, he managed to flip a rectangle around, "F," then another, "L" and another in quick secession until he had the whole thing. "O-U-N-D-E-R," he announced, "Flounder."

"My, what an original approach." Jack was dumbfounded.

The crowd cheered wildly.

*　　　　　*　　　　　*

Grego the Mean sat with Destiny in a private booth overlooking the spectacle of the Ultimate Gameshow. He wore his darkest five piece suit with extra melancholy. Despite that, he still managed to have an evil grin on his face. "You know, I haven't had this much fun since we wasted good old Splas Toorg."

"THAT WAS A LIVELY AFFAIR WASN'T IT?"

Grego sipped on his brew which was contained in an upside down human skull electrolyzed with gold on the inside. Far below on the game show floor, the four remaining contestants did a good job of confounding the host.

Destiny flipped on his wristcom. "HAVE YOU BAGGED NEBLELORKGODIN YET?" he asked.

"Negative," a squeaky voice replied, "We think he ground himself up just before falling into a vat of bread yeast. We're searching all the baked good shops in the mall even as we speak."

"LET ME KNOW IF THERE'S ANY CHANGE."

"All hail the Grail One,"the transmission said and cut out.

Grego laughed, "Those two goofballs really crack me up. Too bad that chicken can't be killed permanently. Or the other one for that matter."

"YOU ALL HAVE YOUR PLACES IN THE SCHEME OF THINGS."

"Ah-Hah! So a scheme it is. I knew the universe was corrupt, that's why I cashed in when I could." Grego chewed on chocholate covered lady fingers and washed it down with more brew.

"GOOD AND EVIL WEAVING THEIR LITTLE MELODY SO BEAUTIFUL OVER THE COSMOS. AND YOU ARE BY FAR THE SUPREME ALLEGRO OF THE BAD."

"I would say 'thank you' but it's not my style."

Destiny pointed down to where the bear was standing. "WATCH," he said, "HERE COMES THE GOOD PART."

Chapter 28: Aldebron Gladiators

"ALL THE GOOFBALLS INTO MY OFFICE NOW!" the thundering voice of a supreme being shouted.

Everyone in the cafeteria dropped their sandwiches and sat in awe, awaiting something else stupendous to happen. Rogicphil jabbed Space-Bo in the ribs.

"Hey, what'd you poke me for?" Space-Bo cried, trying to stuff his thirteenth tuna and cucumber sandwich down his throat.

"Because you're suppose to drop that on the floor and look shocked, that's why."

"Huh?" He looked around at all the people trying to hold motionless in their stupefied position until the expected awesome next event was to occur. "You're crazy..." And he made to take another bite.

A deep rumbling was now heard, slowly moving up through the floor and vibrating all the walls and shook the cheap chandeliers high above the cafeteria proper. "I SAID..." the voice said and the last word held its perilous tone wavering and growing in volume until plaster began to rip apart from the surrounding cafeteria superstructure, "GET YOUR BUTTS IN HERE! GOOFBALLS, ROGICPHIL, FC, HACK, GREYSON, URSUS, AND YES YOU CONRAD."

Space-Bo stopped his munching and looked up at that last statement. Nobody was suppose to know his real name. He climbed up on the table and shouted back at the voice, "Come on man. Show yourself. Or are you too chicken?"

The Funky Chicken blushed. It wasn't often he received a complement of that caliber. The blood flushed so much up into his fowl cheeks that the capillaries burst and a sticky red mess oozed out of his face and onto his plate full of sandwiches.

There was a loud bang and then a puff of smoke came and lifted Space-Bo up into the air and then into another dimension.

"Can we close our mouths now?" a tourist from the crab nebula asked a fellow diner.

"NO!" the roaring voice sounded.

And then with a bang! banG! baNG! bANG! BANG! the five others he'd named were also ripped from their present location and sent into another dimension, not as large as the last one but decorated better.

The six of them now found themselves on a lovely plane of quilted plaid tablecloth, spread over lush rolling hills that were dotted with patches of majestic coffee pot trees. In the sky a flock of toaster ovens flew by against a background sky of pure green marble. And on this sky drove a little street cleaner with a couple of flood lamps that lit up the countryside below. To one side of them was a rounded knoll and downhill from them a shimmering lake of ice cubes.

Mr. Bear scratched his frazzled scalp and wondered if he'd taken too many drugs the night before.

Greyson tapped Rogicphil on the shoulder. "What's going on here 'Phil?" he asked, "Is this where the big Mr. D. lives?"

"Uh yeah," Rogicphil lied as he looked around trying to find any trace of a door that would lead into Destiny's office, "This is just his, er, back yard. And uh, we're going to have a picnic here before he sits us all down to discuss our options and futures."

The others regarded this explanation with more than a grain of salt; a dump truck would be more like it.

"Look!" Greyson shouted as he saw a troop of green clad wilderness girls prance over the hill with camoflaged picnic baskets in their hands.

The wilderness girls sang a happy song (in deep baritone):

Oh... In the wilderness we're okay
We bork all night and eat some hay
We hunt down bees then feed them lunch
And go to the lavitry.

And then in faltering falsetto:

Hi ho the hippo knows,
What grows between my toes.
Ding dong the bitch is dead,
I suffer in my soul. HEY!

The girls drew up suddenly before the six and eyed them suspiciously. A large burly girl who looked like the leader spoke with a deep voice, "You here for the picnic, Mac?"

"Actually," Rogicphil began, "We're on our way to seek the wizard at the end of the road."

The girls conversed amongst themselves and then, brandishing wicked looking golf clubs, charged the group.

Rogicphil held his men back. "Quick! Make for the lake," he shouted and led them bolting down the hill with the wilderness girls hot on their trail.

"Hey," Space-Bo asked the chicken as they rambled down the hill, "Why are we running? I wouldn't mind being captured by them."

The chicken was doing stiff cartwheels down the way, without the use of his wing/arms. Instead, he alternately bounced from his head to his clawed feet, "I-I-I.. duh-duh-don't.. re-eeeEEEAA-ly.. ca-ca-know." He zoomed past the others before hitting a large boulder at the bottom of the hill and then sailed majestically through the air, end over end (with a couple of half twists thrown in to spice it up) and landed beak first onto a floating iceberg.

The others quickly jumped aboard the berg and FC flapped his wings as hard and efficiently as he could until they were well out into the lake.

Disgruntled, the wilderness girls stood at the shore and shouted obscenities at them.

Greyson wiped the sweat from his forehead saying, "You know, I don't think those were really girls."

"Uh?" the bear grunted. He looked at the squirming thing he had slung over his shoulder and then flung it away from him as fast as he could. The "girl" went screaming with a big splash into the icy blue water.

"And you know what?" Rogicphil asked.

"Yes," FC replied, his words issuing from between a crack in his beak.

"You're not allowed to answer that."

The chicken shrugged his upside-down shoulders and continued flapping his wings.

"There was something awfully familiar about those wilderness girls."

"They're friends," Hack said.

No one could come up with a better explanation and so they sailed on across the lake and over a hydroelectric damn at the far end and into a fast moving river that took them eventually out onto a wide sea devoid of swimming monkeys. No one bothered to ask what had happened to the monkeys. By this time the great street cleaner in the sky had over taken them and disappeared into a trap door where the marbled sky met the sea.

Flashing Christmas tree lights now lit up the night sky from their positions high above on the green marble. And all was calm.

Space-Bo checked his watch. "It's only 3:30xm, it can't be dark yet."

They all sat at the edge of the berg, wading their feet into the soothing water. Rogicphil looked over to Space-Bo and said, "I'm not complaining. At least we got out of doing the game show today huh?"

"Yeah, I guess you're right. We are kind of lucky eh?"

But just as Space-Bo spoke those cryptic words, there came the crash of waves upon the berg and a dark form loomed up out of the sea behind them.

Rogicphil leapt to his feet. "FC, if you flap hard enough, we might make it to that trap door before that thing can eat us."

"Ah man," the chicken grumbled, "but that might be fun." He got up and stood at the far end of the berg looking up at the behemoth as it opened its fearsome maw and bad onion breath wafted out. "Take me instead. Let my friends go and you can savor the taste of my marinated chicken flesh."

"Yumm," the monster said. It's blackened tongue snaked out and wrapped around the feathered chickenoid then hauled him up into the air towards its teeth.

Rogicphil shouted to the others, "Paddle for it!" And as the others uselessly fought the water with their hands, he dipped his Gladeboots into the water as super-flippers. A few seconds later the iceberg tipped up on its stern and roared away like a speedboat with Rogicphil's boots foaming the water in its wake.

"Yee-Haw!" shouted Greyson just before he slipped and fell off/out of the iceberg/boat.

Space-Bo gripped the prowl with all his might shouting, "Swing back around 'Phil and I'll grab him up!"

Rogicphil tilted his body to one side and the berg sped around in a wide arc then headed back towards Greyson.

Meanwhile the monster was too busy chomping down on the chicken to notice the creatures festering along around it.

Greyson saw the berg bearing down on him. He readied his suction cup dart gun and fired. The dart smacked squarely in the middle of Hack's forehead.

Space-Bo shouted, "Turn! Turn! Turn!" and the berg swung around again sending a huge wave towards Greyson.

"Waaaaa!" he screamed as the wave overtook him but he held onto his gun and the cable attached to it. A mad torrent of wave and water assaulted him but he persevered and the next thing he knew, he was water skiing behind the berg.

Cool... but he didn't know how to water ski.

He looked down at his bare feet gracefully navigating him across the water, "Aaaaaah!" He freaked and lost his balance. The hard water pounded and slammed him behind the speeding berg even as he still held on to his cable.

Just then the monster felt something hard in its mouth. Smooth round and hard. Hmmm... It flicked it with its tongue. Tasted good so it chomped real hard. The thing was an old cannonball FC had refurbished and packed with high explosives.

The detonation shock wave picked up Greyson first and then the others and blasted them into, and then through, the trap door and the surrounding marbled sky, to the dark chambers beyond.

They now found themselves inside an abandoned circus tent that was quickly filling up with cold sea water. Off in one corner sat the street cleaner, its engine cooling and the driver gone.

"Ha ha," Hack laughed as he climbed on the beast and took the command chair. He started it up and revved the powerful motor. "Hurry up," he called to the others.

They clamored onto the sides and hung on as Hack maneuvered the machine in the rising water, towards the side of the tent farthest from the sea breach. He floored it and the whole thing plowed into the fabric wall, ripped through, and then rumbled into a set of slimy tunnels.

The sweeper wasn't made to traverse slippery terrain and so had a difficult time keeping traction. The tunnel headed up hill and so at least they were moving out of watery harm. But then, quite by accident, a split in the tunnel occurred and Hack pulled to a halt.

Rogicphil climbed up next to him saying, "Lets wait here a while for FC to catch up with us, when he finally pulls himself together. I think we're high enough to be clear of the water."

Whoosh! A large surge of water swept up from behind them shoving them into the rightmost passage. Hack fought to regain control and barely managed to steer quickly enough to the left before the wave smashed up against the bend in the passage.

Fifty more meters saw the sweeper moving at full steam vertically up the tunnel, its powerful spider-like grippers keeping it from falling. And still the water followed them like a giant's hand reaching into a gopher hole. It was like the water itself was intelligent and wanted to get them for some reason and the gopher hole went up into the ground instead of down etc... etc...

Finally a hundred meters up, the tunnel came to an abrupt halt.

Rogicphil looked down at the menacing water bearing up on them. How could it do that? The air in the tunnel had to be escaping somewhere. He imagined spider's feet and his boots grew hairy like grippers so that he could walk along side the tunnel just as the sweeper did. About five more seconds and they'd be fish bait.

"How do you do that?" Space-Bo asked still amazed. He made as if to join Rogicphil.

"Stay on the sweeper 'Bo," Rogicphil cautioned before climbing up to the peek of the passage. He felt along with his hands for a vacuum or any clue as to where the air was escaping. He found a handle just as the surge hit.

Sopping wet they emerged one at a time from an airlock. After abandoning the sweeper, Rogicphil helped them out of the hatch, one at a time, then firmly sealed it behind. A narrow set of stairs led up into a smoky nightclub. Other than the fact that they were all wet, they blended nicely into the crowd.

"These must be the people who work in the circus," Greyson pointed out. "See over in the corner is the strong man and next to him the guy with a really long neck and then the gorilla girl and next to her..."

Rogicphil cut him off, "We get the picture Greyson. I suggest we take a table and see if we can wait the game show out here."

FC laughed as he suddenly appeared behind him, "Wait it out? That's a riot. Let's have a seat." He led the others to a vacant table.

"Did you have fun with the monster?" Rogicphil didn't think he'd ever understand the chicken's twisted sense of amusement.

"Yes but I suspect that it's just the beginning."

"Well what then do you suggest, chicken?" Rogicphil asked.

"I suggest nothing. I simply point out the obvious. Duck."

"What?" Wham! A stray blow from a minor bar brawl tagged him in the back of the head. "Hey!" He got up to see what had hit him and got punched again.

Quickly he whirled around to retaliate but the swirling vortex of the eternal bar brawl was twisting out of the nightclub and into the dark night.

Rogicphil rubbed his head and sat back down. "Sorry, I should have heeded your warning. It's just that I'm getting really tired of all this pointless saving the universe stuff, you know?"

"It'll pass."

"That's little comfort to me now."

"No, I meant the universe."

"Oh." He looked over at Space-Bo and noticed a funny little attachment to his space suit. He plucked it off and held it in his hand like a remote control. "Well in that case, let's watch some holovision." He pointed it towards a dusty old set in the corner of the club and it suddenly came to life.

Space-Bo lit up with glee. "I'd always thought that was the remote to my thigh pad processor; to process the feces you know."

Rogicphil regretted his action and gave the gizmo back to Space-Bo. "See what I get for all my super speed?"

"Shhhh," Greyson pointed to the holoset.

They all wearily turned their attention to the broadcast which was about the Ultimate Gameshow.

"Oh man!" a bar patron across the room cried, "This crap is even worse than the O.J. Simpson trial!" and made as if to launch a ballistic missile at the set. The missile went off in his hand. Engulfed in flames the guy ran out of the nightclub screaming engineering obscenities.

"And now we return live to Aldebron Gladiators," a smooth sounding announcer said. The view was like that of an infinite mirror. They were looking at themselves from behind, sitting in the nightclub watching themselves on the holoset.

Mr. Bear who up until then had been scrounging around in the darkened corners for garbage and what not, noticed a tiny holo camera set into a wall. His muzzle suddenly came into view on the set. There was the heavy sound of his sniffing and snorting then CRUNCH! He bit into the camera and thereby cut transmission.

"And that concludes this weeks chapter of Aldebron Gladiators." The holoset view pulled back to a desk with several commentators huddled around it, all commenting to each other on the implications.

"Ms. Cow, your thoughts?" the announcer addressed one commentator who was the satanic cow, or someone dressed up to look like one.

"I think they're all doing a very good job of keeping us entertained, Mr. Speaker. That goes a long ways these days and I have to say I'll miss it when I install the new regime."

"And what exactly will this new regime entail? If I may be so bold."

"Oh it will be a renaissance of the lower life forms. The ones you humans now regularly oppress and force to do your entertainment for you."

"But animals have no sense of civic duty. Who will spread the liter around the streets at night? Who will victimize hapless senior citizens? And who will keep us all second guessing when the next gift horse is to be given a dental exam? Answer us these questions and we'll beat a path to your barndoor."

"I don't know much about you human's lack of morals but I can say this about the gift horses. Not one more horse will be forced to put Humpty Dumpty back together again."

And so the show blabbed senselessly away until one day the warranty ran out on the holoset and it exploded into tiny pieces. But Rogicphil and his crew were long gone before then.

*   *   *

Destiny was seated in a high backed chair with alternating slats of black lacquered wood and velvety plaid upholstery. A fat cigar was between his fingers and he puffed on it intermittently as the goofballs were ushered into his lounge.

Mr. Bear was looking around for hidden cameras as he was led in. None were found and he missed the bland flavor of the electronic gizmos not to mention the small electric shocks they gave his tongue.

Rogicphil refused to sit down as peacefully as the others had and was eventually forced into a chair by some unseen force of the supreme being. "What the smeg are you trying to do to us?"

"ACTUALLY," Destiny said calmly, "I WAS TRYING TO SAVE YOUR LIVES."

"What!?" Rogicphil cried, fed up.

"I THOUGHT YOU OF ALL PEOPLE WOULD HAVE FOUND THIS PARTICULARLY AMUSING."

"Well yeah, if I wasn't the intended target."

The others all gave Rogicphil disturbed looks as if they weren't sure why they'd aligned themselves with him. Assuming of course that they'd had any say in the matter. Suddenly they were reminded of a marionette puppet show like the one going on in an automated fashion in the far corner of the office.

Destiny laughed and puffed some more on his cigar. "WELL YOU'VE ALL MADE IT THIS FAR AND I'D LIKE TO CONGRADULATE YOU ON YOUR EFFORTS. IT'S ALL DOWN HILL FROM HERE ON."

"Excuse me," Greyson spoke up, "But uh, I'm totally in the dark here. All I seem to recall is that we're suppose to stop the satanic cow from taking over Deo 7 because without deodorant society as we know it will collapse. Now we've given all that up just to do a stupid game show?"

"YES AND NO. THE STATUS OF THE DEO 7 MISSION IS ON HOLD NOW. BOTH SIDES HAVE DECIDED TO HAVE THEIR CASES SETTLED OUT OF THE UNIVERSE AT LARGE AND HAVE ALL COMPLAINTS RECONCILED HERE IN OUR MOORGNAD IV FORUM."

"Eh?"

"WE FIGURED THE POOR PEOPLE OF DEO 7 HAD BEEN ABUSED ENOUGH AND SO THE FINAL BATTLE IS GOING TO TAKE PLACE ON MOORGNAD IV IN TWO DAYS. WHO EVER WINS GETS DICTATORSHIP OVER DEO 7."

Rogicphil asked, "So why are you wasting our time with all this crap? It's stupid, playing games shows to decide our champion to face the cow."

"BUT THINK OF ALL THE LIVES TO BE SAVED IF WE WIN."

"If we win? You're the Supreme Being. This is just a cow. A cow for Scoron's sake. Just bump it off and that's it. Fa-nee-to."

"OKAY YOU FORCED ME. YOU WANT THE ABSOLUTE TRUTH? YOU CAN'T HANDLE THE TRUTH. THAT'S THE TRUTH."

"All this is stupid!" Rogicphil folded his arms and leaned back. "I'm not going to help you anymore. I'm just going to sit here until I die." And he took a deep breath and held it.

Meanwhile as the rest of them were discussing the fate of the universe in the context of the puppet show in the corner, Space-Bo was poking around a bookshelf to one side of the bar. He found a book entitled: How To Distort the SpaceTime Continuum and Think It Was Only the Laundry.

Destiny realized what was happening too late. He turned to where Space-Bo was prying the cover off the book to look inside. "NOOOoooooooo..."

Space-Bo opened the book anyway and looked inside. A swirl of bright colors issued forth from the pages and wove an intricate pattern around the former space marine. "Cool!" he said mezmerized.

Destiny leapt to his feet and shouted to the others, "QUICK, WE MIGHT BE ABLE TO MAKE IT OUT THE BACK DOOR!"

The five others, Rogicphil, Greyson, FC, Mr. Bear, and Hack suddenly felt the puppet strings tug at their limbs and they were running after Destiny as he scampered out the back door.

All that Rogicphil noticed as he simultaneously tried to hold his breath and fight Destiny's control was the flashing neon exit sign over the door. And then they were plunged into total darkness. A darkness broken by streaming patches of a blacker kind of darkness. And then he closed his eyes.

*   *   *

Air. Stale, smelly air. The odor of body sweat engulfed his senses and he struggled to the top. Rogicphil found himself at the top of a pile of dirty cloths in the corner of a laundry room.

Destiny was in the opposite corner wiping the sweat from his brow. He looked up when he saw Rogicphil. "I'm glad you made it," he said calmly, "Can you tell if the others are down there too?"

"Your voice. It's different."

"I know. And Space-Bo's to blame. I should have foreseen this possibility but now I must pay for my mistakes. But to the others quickly."

"Right." Rogicphil fished down and found an arm. He pulled it up and found it to be connected to Greyson. He pulled the relatively short but slightly big boned unconscious fellow out and down the side of the pile. Next he felt a feathery extension and pulled on it too.

The chicken poked his head up and looked around. "I thought this place smelled familiar."

"We need to pull the others up."

"Okay."

While they fished around for the last two contestants, Destiny took a final puff on his cigar then meticulously placed it back in its eternal carrying case. "There's a dimensional portal at the bottom of that pile. They may not have made it through in one piece."

"I should hope not," the chicken exclaimed, "There's two of them, you know. Aha there's that powerfully hairy arm." And he yanked up Hack.

Hack opened his eyes and yawned, "More sleep."

Rogicphil finally found the bear and subsequently they were all gathered at the base of the two and a half meter tall pile, sitting in a semicircle on the floor.

"I thought I'd never have to use this exit myself," Destiny said sadly, "But here I am and all of you too."

"But where are we?" Greyson asked.

"Home," FC smiled with the nostalgia of it all.

"No," Destiny contradicted, "We're deep in the center of the accordion galaxy, I'm afraid. Approximately three hundred and twenty seven million light years from the good old Soggy Place Galaxy."

"Could have fooled me. I could swear this looks and smells like my old apartment in Cleveland."

Everyone looked incredulously at the chicken.

"That was during my tenure as a supreme court justice," he explained as if that made the issue any less confusing.

Greyson held up his hand and Destiny recognized him. "I've never heard of the accordion galaxy before."

295

"Do you know what an accordion is?"

"Yes."

"Same thing." Destiny turned to the others and continued, "Now the only way we can get back is to disguise ourselves and make a run for the Tesseract gate. Understand?"

"No," Rogicphil said.

"Need sleep," Hack mumbled and fell over asleep on Rogicphil's shoulder, dropping both of them to the sweaty floor

Rogicphil crawled out from the statue, dusted himself off, and then used Hack as a bench before continuing, "Whew. Well I was going to say what the heck is the Tesseract gate but I guess it doesn't really matter since we're all helpless anyway."

"I agree," happily the chicken said moving over to sit next to Rogicphil on Hack's back.

"I wish," Destiny sighed. "Space-Bo's gone and made a big mess of things. I'm out of my jurisdiction in this galaxy and so my control over you goofballs is limited. I can only hope to persuade you with logic now."

"I've never died in the accordion galaxy before," the chicken suddenly deduced. "I wonder if it works any better over here."

"You're all welcome to stay here and live out your lives in complete happiness while Space-Bo completely destroys the universe as we know it just by taking off his socks or," he paused for effect, "you can join me in getting back to our own galaxy, where we just might have a chance to stop him." He got to his feet and stood there proudly waiting for the others to join him.

"I don't know," Rogicphil said, "I'm curious what Space-Bo will do with your stolen powers Mr. Supreme Being. Could be something good, could be something bad. We may never know."

Greyson jumped to his feet and joined Destiny. "Whatever the cost sir, I'm with you."

"Good man."

"Grr rrwrl lrree?"

"Yes, Mr. Bear, there's plenty of beer in it for you."

"Aaaarrrr!" Ursus said gleefully and joined them.

Destiny pointed down to Hack saying, "He's on my side by default. Implied consent you know."

"I guess it's just you and me FC," Rogicphil smiled at the insane immortal chickenoid he sat next to. "On second thought," he said jumping up, "I'm with you too."

"Ah man," the chicken frowned. "You guys are all party poopers, you know that?"

"What's it going to be Neble'godinzor?"

"Now you already owe me one good death. This will make it two."

"Very well, are you with us then?"

"Okay."

"Now this is what we have to do..."

Chapter 29: 27 Gigadude Tesseract

Two hours later the six goofballs were creeping along darkened corridors somewhere in the accordion galaxy. They were disguised as best they could manage with the limited resources of the laundry room. Unfortunately it was all women's clothing that they had to work with.

They stopped before a big green door and Destiny turned to address them. He was dressed in a long yellow wild flower print dress with matching blond wig and a flower tucked behind his left ear. "The Tesseract Gate lies somewhere beyond this door. There are many dangers between here and there. What exactly they are, who knows. So stay on your toes."

Greyson was having difficulty standing up in his high heels. "That's easy for you to say," he said stumbling around. He stopped and closed his eyes for a moment, freeing his mind.

"You know," Rogicphil whispered to him, "That is starting to get on people's nerves, so you might just want to knock it off for a while."

"I can fake being a dork if I have to."

Rogicphil looked over his troops. Stumbling (fake?) Greyson, depressed Funky Chicken, sleepy Hack, thirsty bear. They were all puppets now and maybe even Destiny as well. With a deep breath he said, "Let's do it."

Destiny opened the door and tipped toed through. Beyond the door was darkness and echoes. The echoes were coming from their tip toeing and was the only thing they could hear.

Something ominous seemed about to happen but Rogicphil could almost care less at that point. The floor felt firm enough and seemed to be made of wood. To take advantage, he turned his boots into a nice pair of women's white roller skates and smoothly glided along behind Destiny.

ka-CHUNG! About fifty thousand spotlights descended upon them and they froze in their tracks. Suddenly they discovered where they were exactly: the center stage of a large auditorium.

"And now this..." a booming voice yelled down upon the attending audience, "The West Longford Girl Cadets Song and Dance Troop doing their rendition of Door-nob's Messiah." An up tempo dance number started up.

"Follow my lead," the chicken said as he began to dance.

With nothing better to do at the moment the others joined him. As they clumsily tried to stay with the beat, FC did an impressive ballet performance all around them.

Greyson skipped over to where Destiny was attempting to clog and said, "I find it hard to believe that all the way over in the accordion galaxy there would be people who spoke English."

"These aren't the indigenous inhabitants of this galaxy," the supreme being explained. "These are remnants of colonists who migrated through the dimensional hole at the bottom of that pile of dirty clothes. After they came through and claimed independence from their former creditors, they threw off the symbols of their old imperialistic ways. Hence the pile of laundry. It's now a galactic monument."

"Ah yes, thank you," Greyson nodded and skipped away.

"But wait there's more," Destiny started but the little guy was out of ear shot. The formerly supreme being felt helpless for the first time in his long existence.

Finally, mercifully the music stopped. The chicken took a deep bow to the smattering of uneasy applause just before a giant mechanical hook snaked out of the shadows and dragged them off the stage.

"Hey," the stage manger accosted them, "You're not the West Longford Girls Cadet Dancers."

"And that wasn't Door-nob's Messiah," FC retaliated.

"Well whoever you are, you've got the job now. The real Cadets haven't shown up yet and it's time for judges interviews. Come on." He led them down a set of sticky concrete steps, through a few sets of double doors and up to another stage where a group of real girls were being ushered off. "Whatever you do, don't win. I couldn't stand to have West Longford's reputation soiled so." He kicked them up the steps to the stage and hurried back the way he'd come.

"I know you said this was going to be difficult but come on," Rogicphil whined as he marched with the others into the spotlight.

There were nine judges in black hoods seated at the front of the audience and they looked visibly disturbed at the sight of the latest contestants. An announcer smiled insidiously, if uneasy, as he greeted them and double checked his cue cards. "I think we'll skip the swimsuit portion for now and go directly to the judges' inquisition."

The audience gave a combined sigh of relief.

The announcer checked his cue card as he stepped up to Destiny, "And I take it you are Miss Rugusta Marmalaid?"

"Yes," Destiny squeaked. He'd never been so embarrassed in fifteen billion years.

"Judge number seven would like to know if chosen to be Miss Accordion what you would do to help the armless waifs of Stooge City No. 12?"

"Well first I'd try to figure out why they were armless and then I'd turn whoever did it into tiny yellow slime molds."

"But surely you know that they cut off their own arms in protest to the new finger tax?"

"Uh yes. In that case then I'd cause their arms to regrow out of their own backs and spank themselves."

This caused quite a stir in the audience and the announcer tried to dispel the mood by laughing, "I see you studied irony at the seamstress school." He quickly back-kicked Destiny off the stage into a net just for such occasions.

Greyson shook uncontrollably as he was approached. He pretended the pressure was too much for him and shouted, "I'm not really a man!"

"Ha ha, more humor tonight I see," the announcer made a rude gesture to the audience from behind Greyson. There was very little laughter in response. "Okay Miss Hildegard Klonstike, judge number 3 would like to know if appointed to the position, how would you keep corruption out of future Miss Accordion pageants?"

"I'd quit." Only then did he pretend to realize his verbal stumble.

Errrnt! A buzzer sounded and then a trap door opened dropping him down into a pit.

The announcer breathed a sigh of relief then said, "That was the wrong answer of the day. And you're outta there!" He moved on to Rogicphil.

"First of all," he took the microphone from the announcer and spoke without trying to falsettofy his voice, "Vee at duh institute for womanly iron pumping vould lik to tell yu all det vee vill kill anyvon who vould try und stop us!" With that he zoomed off the stage. Wielding the microphone by the cord and brandishing it like a medieval weapon assaulted those in the audience.

Mr. Bear rushed the announcer and tackled him to the stage while Hack fished Destiny out of the net. Rogicphil led the way up the aisle while the bear and Hack followed.

The Funky Chicken stood on the announcer's back and addressed the congregation. "Dearly beloved," he bellowed with a 120 decibel voice he'd perfected over the eons, "We are gathered here today to pay homage to a poor distraught race of creatures whose only crime was that they paid too much for long distance service."

While FC was distracting them, Greyson had enough time to tap into the judges PA system, eavesdrop on them, then dismantle the trap door's lock and spring back out onto the stage.

"And behold he is arisen!" The chicken stepped over to embrace him and whispered, "Get your dart gun ready." He then turned back to the audience and shouted, "And the Lord said ye shall ascend!" He fished out a couple of smoke bombs and detonated them directly in front of them. Smoke engulfed the stage and then they were sailing up into the rafters born on Greyson's cable.

The audience cheered and gave a standing ovation. In the confusion, the others led by Rogicphil made it out into the lobby and the snack bar area.

Destiny was breathing heavily. "The popcorn machine," he panted, "Get in quickly."

Rogicphil shook his head in disgust before moving the confused attendants to one side. He helped the other three goofballs into the machine, giving the bear's hairy butt a shove with his boot. He climbed to the top and leaned over the edge to say, "What about the chicken and Greyson?"

"Hi Hoo!" the chicken shouted from across the room. He was standing on top of the ticket booth with Greyson clinging to his back. He grabbed a hanging rope from somewhere and swung through the air landing next to Rogicphil on the popcorn machine.

A troop of gray clad guards burst upon the scene just then. They aimed fully automatic slingshots at the snack bar. "Surrender or give up. Either way we win." Workers fled for their secret double lives.

Rogicphil dearly hoped Destiny knew what he was doing. He yelled back at the guards, "Don't shoot us yet. We're still repairing this popcorn machine. Can't you see it's out of order?"

The lead guardsman sniffed at his bag of popcorn, then took a bite. "Hmmm, this does taste a bit stale. But that doesn't explain why it takes six of you to fix it."

"You wouldn't want anything to go wrong would you? These nuclear poppers can be a tad bit unstable you know."

"Nah I think it's just indigestion. Good try kid. Open fire men."

The chicken offered to protect the front side of the machine, "May I?"

"Be my guest," Rogicphil cheerfully agreed.

Destiny had his hand in the hot oil of the popper proper, fishing around for the gate activation node. The scalding hot oil peeled the flesh away from his hand and he was powerless to do anything about it. He found the node just as the bullets began to hit. It wasn't for another second that the popper machine fully dematerialized.

The Funky Chicken had taken all the shots as he'd draped himself in front of the machine. To be truthful it wasn't a spectacular death but at least it was in a different galaxy and that had merit to it.

*   *   *

Cool salt water mist drifted through the calm predawn air. How they knew it was predawn was beyond them so they concentrated instead on how the mist could contain dissolved salt.

They stood on a flat muddy plane, a discarded popcorn popping machine behind them. And in the distance ahead a strange four dimensional framework pyramid dominated the skyline.

A few black crows cawed unseen somewhere overhead. Destiny was in terrible pain. His left hand was little more than bloody bones after the boiling oil was through with him. But he was more disturbed by the sight of blood. He was suppose to be immortal. What need did he have for blood?

"Here," the chicken approached him. He plastered a soothing poultice all around the Supreme Being's seared hand. "Hopefully this will keep you from bleeding to death. Isn't that a riot? You, bleeding to death. When your time comes old friend perhaps I too can truly die."

"Then I hope you live for ever chicken." He looked down at the strange stuff that was somehow easing his pain and remarked, "I hope that isn't what I think it is"

FC lifted up his left wing/arm and pointed to a bloody patch with his opposite appendage, "A chunk of my flesh. I chewed it up real good before I put it on. No don't peel it off. As it mends, it will also pull your flesh together around it and stop the bleeding."

Somewhat disgusted Destiny sighed, "But surely it must make it back to your body before long."

"By that time, if you aren't back to normal, it won't matter."

"Probably not," he looked ahead to the tesseract glimmering under the slightly radiant air. "That's our destination now. The 27 Gigadude Tesseract."

Greyson looked on in awe. "Is that how much it cost to build?"

"No, silly. It was build for the game show by the same name."

"Oh great!" Rogicphil retorted, "More game shows. I should have known. This is just another part of the Ultimate Gameshow isn't it. Just like when we thought we were far away from all of that in your back yard. But no we're still here amusing the masses."

"Rogicphil," Destiny began docently, "The Ultimate Gameshow refers to the universe as a whole and we're all contestants. Even us immortals."

The Funky Chicken kicked Destiny. "You're not suppose to tell them that. It was suppose to be our secret. What's left for us to reveal in the end?"

"The fact that this is only a story, a novel. And if the reader doesn't like it we're all doomed because there won't be a sequel."

"What in funkytown has gotten into you man?" the chicken raged. He began hopping around madly pulling feathers, organs, and other icky organic things from his body, throwing them down in the mud, and stomping as hard as he could on them.

Rogicphil ignored Hack's roarious laughter and tried to make some order of the mess by stating, "How philosophic of you. Now if we don't get going soon our precious 'reader' is going to flush our existence down the toilet."

Destiny smiled like an inmate on death row as the electric helmet is lowered down on him. "I guess if I'm going to die I may as well spill the beans."

"You're not going to die," Rogicphil said grabbing him by both arms, "You're going to lead us to this gigadude thing and then back to our own galaxy so we can finish playing our nice game show. Okay?"

"The tesseract, right." Destiny shook off Rogicphil and started towards the bizarre structure. "It was build before the current universe came into being by a race of XAND logic gates. What we see before us is only the third dimensional extension of that object which actually exists in four geometric dimensions."

"Ah yes," Hack agreed as if he was one step ahead, mentally.

"The tesseract connects to all possibilities and forms the juncture between them all. This is how we'll find our way back."

Up ahead a strange contraption emerged from the mist. To those readers of the Lobster Universe it was known as a binary bicycle but to the six goofballs from our current Big Idiot Universe it simply looked stupid.

"What is that?" queried Greyson.

"Rrrwwl?" (Beer?)

There were four riders on the bicycle. Two peddling furiously on the bicycle proper and two on a satellite structure, which was connected by a boom to a point just above the two wheels and yet below the whirling feet of the two main riders. The two riding the satellite structure peddled also but apparently all it got them was a trip round and round in a circle about the main bicycle.

They came roaring by the group screaming for mercy to some deity that didn't exist in the current dimension. After they disappeared into the mist there came a disgustingly sickening crunch followed by vehement blasphemous swearing.

"I hope we meet with better luck," Rogicphil bemoaned with a backwards glance.

Twenty minutes later they made it to the main entrance of the tesseract, a giant set of lips thick with blue lipstick. Destiny approached and addressed the lips thus, "Greetings Tesseract. We seek entrance to your myriad gateways."

A green tongue licked the blue lips before answering, "And what do you have to pay with?"

"Me!" the chicken proclaimed, jumping out in front, "Crush my body and devour me whole. Savor the sadistic pleasure."

"No," the lips said, "That would be too easy. Besides I'm a vegan gateway."

"We will solve your riddle," Destiny said cleverly.

"Hah," the lips said. "I have no riddle. And that is the riddle. What is the riddle? And then what is the answer to that riddle?"

"Twenty seven," Destiny blurted without thinking.

"Hmmmm," the lips pursed themselves not sure what to do. After a few lip smackings it decided, "You already have all the answers. Therefore you are not allowed in."

"Why not?" asked Greyson disgusted. "If 27 really is the answer, you should let us pass."

"That's not the point. The point is the journey you must take to arrive at the answer but now because of blabber mouth here, you can not take that journey and therefore you shall never enter the tesseract. Ha, ha, ha."

"Ha ha HEE ha ha!" Greyson countered as he jumped around and did a little jig. "That's the fallacy of denying the antecedent."

The lips pulled back revealing a set of sharp glistening teeth. "Breath deep the gathering gloom mortals!"

The chicken spoke up, "But two of us aren't..." Before he could finish, a thick black cloud of icky goo poured forth out of the mouth onto them.

Destiny started to sing:

Most fair and banal tesseract comfort me;
Make mine enemies to throw parties at your feet.

"Everybody..."

And now pine away for my sweet Abigail;
May she not drown in that an infested swamp.

"It's the only way," he pleaded, "Sing, you pathetic mortals!"

And so they sang the absurd song louder and louder gaining confidence with each time. After a while the goo settled around their feet and there was no more was coming out of the mouth. Instead it was laughing.

*   *   *

Meanwhile somewhen outside of time Space-Bo was doing his laundry. Let us go there now and witness with sharp cruelty as he cleans his socks!

"No monocoque construction here," Space-Bo lamented as he examined his very religious (holey) socks. "Yep you guys have been with me since junior high and haven't let me down yet." The socks emitted an odor which was almost strong enough to gain sentience.

Space-Bo tossed them in the big hopper along with his spacesuit, which left him standing on the cold cement floor barefoot and in his 'stinking jungle' robe. On second thought he took the robe off and threw it in also, thereby exposing himself to the laundry room.

On a shelf overhanging the washing device was a bright yellow box labeled: Extra Strength Bleck. He emptied the box into the hopper and stepped back. Nothing happened then he remember to turn the thing on. It started up with a slow chug and then as it gained speed gave off a shriek like a million souls all being sent to limbo.

He checked the settings on the washing machine. They were as follows:

1. Hot stuff on a silver platter	A. High treason
2. Warmed up leftovers	B. Middle ground beef
3. Cold war	C. Low water tide

Hmmmm, this looked like fun. Almost as much fun as flying a spaceship. He selected for a cold war with high treason thrown in for the heck of it. That should do it.

The mechanical beast gave a groan at the new settings but soon settled into an adjusted rhythm.

Feeling chilled, he looked around for something to wear. There was an immobile monk standing in the corner next to the dryer. Space-Bo approached him and waved a hand in front of his face.

"HELLo there, mister monk?"

No response.

"Are you using your robe right now?" He placed his ear close to the guy's mouth but heard nothing. He grabbed the monk's chin and opened his mouth.

"No," he said imitating what he thought a monk should sound like (something between a New York accent and a Rabbi).

He stepped back to politely ask, "Well do you mind if I borrow it for a while?"

He moved the monk's mouth again in rhythm. "No buddy, I'm not using it right now. Why don't you use it?"

"Thanks!" Space-Bo took the mud colored garment off the fellow and wiggled in as best he could. "You'll be rewarded for this my good man," he said to the now naked monk standing in the corner next to the dryer.

He checked his watch to see how long before he'd have to change the load but the stupid thing was stuck on 13:13:13. What an unusual time he thought.

Now that he was warm again, he felt hungry. He just had a roast beef sandwich. Where'd he put that? Oh no, he suddenly remembered it was in his left thigh pocket of his spacesuit. He jumped over to the machine and popped the lid open to look inside.

A surge of foam splattered him in the face and he flew backwards into a wheeled laundry basket. The thing had been precariously balanced at the top of a ramp and now with Space-Bo inside, lost its stillness and zoomed down into the corridors of time.

*   *   *

Back at the tesseract ranch, FC waded through the ankle deep gunk up to the gaping teeth and held it open with his body saying, "Okay the theatre is now open. Small women and children to the left. Insane immortals to the right."

No one noticed nor seemed to care which side they went through on before entering the tesseract. The chicken was disappointed no one had another joke to add to his.

They were in a four dimensional maze of glass tubes where four tubes of glass connected and where they were each perpendicular to the three others.

"Behold!" Destiny spread his arms wide to engulf the entire world.

Rogicphil was tapping his boot, "We're waiting."

"Don't you see it?" Destiny was wide eyed and seemingly mesmerized by what appeared to the others to be only the bland pearl colored walls of the tube.

"I'm sure you can enlighten us all when you're back in charge," Rogicphil said trying to move everyone forward, "But for now we're moving on to the gate or whatever it is that will send us back."

They trampled along the weird tubes for several hours falling and slipping along, getting lost and separated multiple times, but eventually arriving at the main control room.

Destiny sat down in a swivel chair in front of a computer terminal and punched in the coordinates back to his office.

"Wait a second," Rogicphil said pulling the Supreme Being back. "We left there for a reason, now you want us to go right back. What are we going to do about Space-Bo? We need a plan."

"You're right," the chicken agreed. He did a little finger exercise as he scratched the top of his head with a leg talon while deep in thought. "I've got it!" he exclaimed snapping his fingers.

"What is it man?"

The chicken spun Destiny around to stare him right in the eye. "If this thing can send us anywhere in any time, can it also change our relative sizes to those places?"

"Of course."

"Okay," the chicken announced as he jumped up onto the control panel and rubbed his hands together. "Everyone empty your pockets."

"What!?" Rogicphil cried.

"It is all part of my magnificent plan. Do it."

They all made a pile of things which the chicken then sorted through, eventually not finding what he was looking for. But he did find some rather interesting sets of women's underwear which no one claimed responsibility for, so he shrugged and tucked them into his pocket.

"Oops excuse me," he said wide eyed as pulled his wing/arm out of a fleshy pocket and found in it what he'd been looking for all along, a miniature castle on a keychain. "You can all take your things back now as I have what we need right here." He made sure the pile was real mixed up before turning back to Destiny and ordered, "Change the coordinates for the exact spot that Space-Bo is in, not next to him but right there."

"You're not thinking of killing him are you?"

"Don't worry. I have no idea what I'm doing, but I'm sure it'll work." He walked over to the transmat pad and set the miniature castle right in the middle then stepped back over to the terminal. "All set?"

"Yes." Destiny finished inputing the coordinates and hit the enter button without waiting for the go ahead.

Greyson poked his head over the Supreme Being's shoulder, "How do you know where everything is so precisely?"

"It's my job to know."

A computer voice now announced, "Please insert seven megadudes for the first minute, one and a half megadudes for each additional minute."

Destiny looked embarrassed. "I hadn't counted on this."

"Do I have to do everything?" The chicken fished a single Gigacred bill out of his ear and fed it into a slot set into the wall.

"Thank you and now your change," the computer replied, "In Susan B. Anthony singledudes."

"RUN!" the chicken leapt for the transmat pad as the others followed, not really understanding the danger they were in.

And as the room began to fill with coins, the great tesseract machinery completed its warm-up cycle and dematerialized the six goofballs and one tiny castle. It completed the calculation programmed into it by Destiny and broadcast them all, deep into the heart of the Soggy Place Galaxy and the Big Idiot Universe.

Chapter 30: The Price is Life

Rogicphil had banged his head at sometime during the dimensional transfer inside the tesseract and only now was coming to. He was surprised to find himself behind an arrow-loop inside of a castle looking out into a seething sea of red goo. There was no ground or sky to speak of, only a strange pulsating rhythm that jerked the castle around every once in a while.

"What do you think?" the Funky Chicken asked. He had come up behind Rogicphil and was peeking out the hole at the unusual scene outside.

"That I'm dreaming. No I take that back. I think I must be dead."

"I wish I had your confidence. No, we're still alive and back in our own galaxy now."

"Could have fooled me."

"But we're very very small now."

"So how come we can still converse like rational beings? If we were tiny, then that would imply we'd have to have less brain neurons and therefore be blabbering idiots."

"And I thought I was an idiot to begin with. No, you see, what happened is that the tesseract left us with the exact matter we started with but simply changed our scale when it dropped us back down here. So we're actually made out of a different size of protons, electrons, bogons, and what-nons than the rest of this universe."

"So what happens when we have direct contact with the normal stuff in this universe?"

"We explode!" And the chicken jumped up and down in happiness.

"Don't you think there's a small flaw in your plan?"

"No not unless Space-Bo catches on. But I doubt that."

Rogicphil took a look outside again and winced. "So then we're in..."

"Space-Bo's liver."

"What!?"

"Why don't you follow me back into the banquet hall where the others are just finishing breakfast and we can discuss our plan of action."

"Breakfast? Then that means the final battle takes place tomorrow."

"Exactly. Now follow me and don't trip over the giant lint balls." FC led him down a short corridor and through a heavy iron door into a large banquet hall.

Destiny and the rest of the goofballs were busy munching on breakfast burritos when they entered. "Good morning," he called out to the weary Rogicphil. "Join us in breakfasting before our terrible mission begins?" They were all seated at a long single piece picnic table.

"Yeah sure," he agreed sitting down between the bear and Hack. "Where'd the burritos come from?"

The chicken climbed into the three meter tall throne near the head of the table and swung his legs into space. "I'll have you know, I keep a full stock of breakfasting materials in my castle's larder at all times."

"But this is a miniature castle you keep on a keychain in your pocket."

"Yes but before that it was a real castle that I tried to shove into an undersized wormhole. The whole thing was compressed down to the size it is now. A nice side effect is that it is the most impregnable castle in existence but you have to be really small to get inside."

"So you've informed me." Rogicphil bit into a couple of burritos and smiled. Soggy Lucky Charms made up the filling, his favorite. "And right now we're inside of Space-Bo's liver? Is that right?"

"Yes."

"And where is Space-Bo?"

"We won't know until we get into his brain and review his memories."

Hack suddenly took an interest in the conversation. "K-lines?"

"You poor pathetic human," FC said from high up in his chair, "That theory of memory went out with the baby and the bath water."

"What then?" Hack said between fistfuls of burrito mass. He hadn't had a joint in several days and was slowly coming out of his mental fog.

"Quantum flux nodes in a matrix tube complex."

"Duh," Hack said hitting himself over the head for being so stupid.

"Rrrwwl ggrrrol rr'ggrlo rrg?"

"Go ahead."

The Bear excused himself and headed to the larder for another case of beer. The others were getting into their battle gear when he came back.

"Grr rrggr lorrg rrwwwwl rrg?"

"Yep it's time," the chicken answered wielding a cattle prod looking thing, "To the battlements man and don't spare the lead." And he led the charge.

*   *   *

Space-Bo's laundry basket fell over at the top of a dike and dropped, along with him, into the water below. He sank slowly down into the depths enjoying himself. The scent of water lilies filled his nostrils and he breathed in the water deeply, feeling completely at ease.

He drifted along like this for quite sometime until he checked his watch and realized it was still 13:13:13 and so he made for the surface. That was strange, he thought, he could breath the air above the surface. Hmmm, something weird was going on here. Breathing underwater and above water? One of them had to go.

So it was the air. He let himself drop below the water line until his feet touched bottom. Sure-footedly he began to walk along and soon found a narrow path lined with pebbles. He followed this path up a slight rise and then he was along side the dike again. The path led up to elevator doors. The up button was already pushed so he waited until it opened, then entered.

A couple of strange luminous entities floated in the water before him. Their bodies were transparent so he could see all the internal organs chugging away. Each had a little name tag glued in place below what for lack of a better word was their heads.

"I'm bleeB," the first one said, "And this is greeL."

Space-Bo pushed the button for the penthouse level. "Where you guys headed?"

"The Supreme Being Interdimensional Convention on Moorgnad IV. And you?"

"Yeah, I'm going there too. I've got to change my laundry you see."

The two creatures seemed very impressed. "May we have our coordinates taken with you?" The first one pulled out what looked like a camera from its fanny pack.

"Oh okay, sure." Space-Bo put his arm around the second creature and smiled as the first one took a quantum 'snap-shot' of the two.

"Thank you. The life forms of my galaxy will be much pleased."

The elevator stopped and the doors opened up onto a do-it-yourself black hole kit trade show. The creatures thanked Space-Bo again and floated out. The doors closed and he was again traveling upwards.

At the penthouse level the doors opened up onto a barren wasteland. Water that had filled the elevator now washed out onto the dusty plain making a nice little mud puddle all around the elevator car.

Bewildered, he checked the indicator just inside the door. It said Moorgnad IV- Ultimate Gameshow HQ. He looked outside again. A tumbleweed blew in.

"This can't be right," he said stepping out into the mud. "Where's the gymnasium, and the pool, and the cryo-chamber? Where's my laundry?" With a frown he turned to get back in the elevator but it was gone. Only the mud was left to show where it had been.

"Maybe I can do something with this mud." He plopped down in the mud and scooped a big pile of muck into his lap. For some reason he felt compelled to sculpt a little man. When he was finished with the body and limbs he popped two bits of gravel on the head for eyes. "That should do it," he said pleased with himself, "Now what do I do with you?"

"You could start by putting me down," the little man replied.

Space-Bo did as he was told and then backed up. "What'd you do with my laundry?"

"Don't worry about your laundry." The little man looked down at his muddy form. "Mud? You made me out of mud? Well I guess it's better than sewage effluent."

"Who are you?"

"Well I wouldn't expect you to recognize me as we've never formally met. I'm Besey Brown. AKA the satanic cow. And before you start to laugh, let me explain."

But Space-Bo wasn't laughing; he was picking his nose.

"You're not really here right now."

"Then when am I here?"

"Here doesn't exist. You're having a dream right now and I've managed to tap into your brain pattern in order to communicate with you."

"Does this mean my roast beef sandwich is still good?"

"No, not really, as far as I know but..."

"If this was really a dream then I'd be able to do anything I want. Eat a ton of chocolate or breath tang or whatever I wanted to right?"

"That's true but let me finish..."

"So then I should be able to make you dance like a puppet and do the gypsy mambo?" He tried to concentrate really hard on the mud person. Nothing happened. "Okay now that I know this isn't a dream then I know you're real and not just a fragment of my imagination and therefore I should trust you."

"I need you to..."

"And give you my money, and my collection of rare earth minerals, and pressed duck bills, and..."

"Listen. I need you to help me Space-Bo. I know we're suppose to be enemies but that's only to glamorize the whole thing. The truth is we need to work together so that we can both make it out of this mess they're calling the Ultimate Gameshow."

"Okay so far."

"Now my sources tell me that Destiny is temporarily out of the galaxy away on business or something."

"Oh yeah. I remember he got up and left all of a sudden."

"And that you're still in his office."

Space-Bo looked around at the soggy ground and the dusty plains surrounding it. "Weird looking office, but go ahead."

"I need you to go over to his desk, when you wake up, and press the doorjamb release button which is located just under the central drawer. Then we can go through his files and get the dirt on him."

"What dirt?"

"Oh didn't you hear? Destiny is up for charges on embezzling universal energy creds from the Quasar central bank."

"What's a quasar?"

"That's not important right now. Your job is just to push that button to let me in and everything will be taken care of."

"So I'm not really a supreme being who can breath under water and create life from mud?"

"Well maybe, I don't know. Listen, with Destiny out of the picture all this game show stuff will go up in a puff of smoke as his backers will pull their funding. You'll get to go back to your time and never have to worry about this whole mess ever again."

"Aw man. I was going to name you Bowlregard."

"Focus please. In order to do all that I first must get access to Destiny's filing cabinet."

"But that sounds boring."

"When the time is right you will wake up. And don't forget, and this is the most important thing..." but the mud figure was cut off by the howling sound of thruster engines as a big shuttle suddenly came flying in low overhead. The air blast of the craft's wake splattered the mud thing into Space-Bo's chest.

He wiped the muck off and ran to where the shuttle was landing behind him.

It was a survey shuttle sent out by an advance construction crew. Space-Bo greeted them as the surveyors disembarked out onto the lonely plane. "Welcome to Moorgnad IV," he greeted them, "Can I help you?"

"Oh yeah," the lead man said consulting his clipboard, "We're here to start work on a mega entertainment complex for a mister D.E. Stiny. I was told

309

there would be someone here to sign for all this stuff."

Space-Bo looked around to make sure no one else was there. "I guess that's me. Unless you were looking for Bowlregard."

"You know Mr. Stiny?" The guy kept hold of his clipboard.

"Yeah we were at the academy together," Space-Bo instinctively lied.

"Okay, sign here," he said holding out the clipboard and made Space-Bo scribble in a little box with an electronic pen. "Well, that should do it them." He turned to leave.

"Hey wait," Space-Bo said stopping them from shutting the hatch, "What happened to the other mega complex? I mean it was here just yesterday."

"I don't know anything about any other mega complex mister, but ground breaking for this one doesn't start for another two thousand years."

"Oh okay, I must be thinking of something else them. See you later." He waved to the shuttle as it shot off into the sky once more leaving behind a bunch of junk and blueprints.

This was very odd, he was thinking as he turned around and noticed the elevator was back. He made a run for it and managed to get back inside before the doors closed. This time he studied the button panel more closely. Completely stupefied he hit the very bottom bright yellow button labeled information desk. They should at least be able to tell him if his roast beef sandwich was really okay.

Chapter 31: In Cahootz

Besey transmatted back to H.E.L.L. headquarters on Lugietorp Prime to a rude reception. No one was at the control console and so her transportation had been handled by the automatic transmat program, an welcomed affront to basic manological protocol.

She checked her body to make sure the transmat hadn't actually replaced her limbs with someone else's. What a hideous thought. Just the idea of human forearms and legs on her cow body was enough to make her shiver.

But why was no one at the post? Such treatment was usually related to agents on bad terms with the organization. Perhaps she'd been found out. Her plans to overthrow the evil cult of bureaucratic human warmongers known as H.E.L.L. might be in ruins. Unlikely. They had suspicions perhaps, but no evidence or proof of her plans. Something else was going on and she decided to find out.

Out the transmat room and down a red lit corridor to an elevator assembly she carefully plodded. And then when she was sure no one was around she hurried into the stairwell and galloped as best she could down the wide steps.

She stopped at a landing on level 66 and activated her communicator, "This is Earth Mama to Dingleberry, come in Dingleberry." All she got was static. Wilbur and Jake should have returned by now and been awaiting further instructions.

She waved to Ralph the security dude at the front desk. He looked up her in surprise at first but quickly looked away and pretended to goof off. She considered asking him what was going on: a surprise birthday party maybe or a paid unholiday break even. But something didn't smell right and she continued on her way without saying anything.

A few faint echos of laughter came from a hallway leading to the recreation center and she hoofed it down in that direction. She came to a door leading into the spa area and listened at the door. Yes, the laughing was definitely going on in there.

"What's going on in here?" she shouted as she barged into the room.

Inside was a large hot tub filled almost to the rim with a white milky substance and several industrial sized containers labeled 'Cahootz Salad Dressing' lie empty on the floor around it. Inside the hot tub, relaxing with wine and cigars was Lester and some skinny guy in an oversized black hat.

"Besey!" Lester greeter her sarcastically, "So glad you could make it. I was wondering if my memo about the party had been sent out in time."

She looked around the room and it was devoid of other patrons and certainly didn't look like a party to her. "What happened to Wilbur and Jake?"

"I'll get to that in a moment. First I want you to meet a new friend of mine. This is Junthomas of the Yuspurly Insurance Group."

"What are you doing here anyway? I saw you die."

"Oh that. Probably just one of my 'clones' that Mr. Junthomas gratefully donated to H.E.L.L."

"I did no such thing," the little fellow squeaked, "Cloning you wasn't part of the deal."

Besey pondered a moment. If Lester didn't remember the encounter she'd had with him earlier in which she saw him die down a nasty air shaft, then he probably didn't know she was plotting against him either. She decided to play along for the time being.

Lester laughed, "Doesn't matter. The point is YIG will be providing all the personnel for H.E.L.L. from now on and so everyone else is obsolete. Even you, Besey, as traitorous as you are, are now a thing of the past."

"So everyone's dead?"

"No. There's still you, me and Ralph. And he should be along at any moment to shoot you too."

"Even cute little Wilbur and Jake?"

"No no no, not them. They're the clones. Easy to mass produce you see. Since they're so defective to begin with, any glitches in the manufacturing process will come out in the wash. It also makes them very disposable as they come apart very easily."

"That's incredible stupid. Who thought up that idea?"

"I did," Junthomas said, "We discovered along time ago the usefulness of cloning. At first we did it just so we wouldn't have to payout on life insurance policies but from there the sky's been the limit. Clones have so many useful qualities it boggles the mind."

"You're both crazy and you won't get away with it."

Lester became annoyed. "It's getting cold in here again!" he shouted, "Throw some more logs in the furnace, Brown."

Brown? Besey looked around and from behind a tanning booth her former master appeared. He was shackled chain gang style and held a fat shovel in his head. She watched as he shuffled over to the hot tub's furnace and began shoving in thick bound bundles of money.

He glanced over at Besey and recognition suddenly flashed across his face. For a brief moment his eyes pleaded with her to save him but he quickly looked away and went back to shoveling.

"You are the most evil human I've ever met!" she shouted at Lester.

"Thank you," he beamed.

"Prepare to meet your maker." The cow made as if to charge the hot tub but Lester waved his finger back and forth then pointed behind her. She looked around and saw Ralph, the security dude, standing there with a fusion rifle leveled at her.

"All we need now is some popcorn," Lester said to Junthomas who eagerly shook his head in agreement.

"No so fast," Wilbur and Jake said stepping in behind Ralph. They had their own weapons leveled and forced Ralph to lay down.

"Thank you," Besey said with a smile.

"We always liked you the best Besey," Wilbur said, "You were the only one around here to treated us fairly. We're behind you all the way. Death to the Humans! Long live the ..... errk." They fell over dead with blaster holes through their bellies.

312

Stepping into the spa room through the blaster smoke was Mother Maynard and boy was she angry. "That's the last time you two will ever double cross me." She spat on their smoldering bodies then slowly turned to Besey and pumped another fusion round into the chamber. "Your next honey child!"

"Now the good part starts," Lester whispered to his YIG man.

The cow charged Mother Maynard who dodged her massive body surprisingly quickly out of the way.

Now Brown came to the rescue swing his shovel at the unReverend Mother. Besey gave him a signal which she hoped he'd understand then went back to charging Mother Maynard.

Brown hesitated. He saw the signal and thought he knew what it meant but wasn't sure.

In all the commotion, Ralph quietly and unnoticed, slipped out of the room and hurried back to his post to goof-off some more. He passed the junior grade Bossman from Rall Raul Beta on his way in.

"Shut up everyone!" the Bossman shouted with a mega bull horn.

Mother Maynard turned and blasted him. The blast passed through his body effortlessly like it didn't exist.

The Bossman snickered, "Unt un uh!" with a wag of his finger. He then pulled out a blue orb like egg thing and held it up for everyone to see. "I'm now the supreme being around here and I order you all to obey me."

"This wan't part of the plan," Junthomas said to Lester.

"Knee-thar wuz theeus." Brown swung his shovel landing a severe blow to Lester's head, knocking it completely off. Wires, cables and springs and so forth spewed out from his neck and into the hot tub. His head which had been about to say, "Sure it was," before getting lopped off rolled around on the floor laughing.

"Robots!" Junthomas shouted and leapt out of the cahootz filled hot tub.

"I knew it!" The Bossman said. "I don't care how many robot bodies you've got around here. Because I'm getting rid of them all, right now." He held up the blue orb and commanded it to do his bidding.

Shafts of brilliant golden light emanated forth from the orb and penetrated everything in the room within a 20 meter radius. The Bossman basked in all it's glory. Glory that was now all his. Ha ha.

When the rays of light intersected with the hot tub however, something strange happened. The rays defocused and reflected back on themselves straight into the Bossman's face. He flew back into the wall next to the entrance and collapsed unconscious.

While everyone else stood their in stunned silence, Lester's body hopped out of the tub, grabbed his head and ran out the door.

Besey was the next to move and took the opportunity to quickly yet gently scoop up Brown with her horns and hightail it out of the chamber after Lester.

She ran as fast as she could in the opposite direction that the Lester robot went. A few levels later she stopped to rest and tried her communicator again. "This is Earth Mama calling all non-human agents. Please come in."

Brown was out cold draped over her back like an old sack of space potatoes.

"So you're Earth Mama," an evil voice suddenly said behind her. "You stole that name from me."

Besey heaved her bulk around to get a look. "Mother Maynard! You've escaped!"

"That's right," the ugly fat woman said holding a laser blaster like a lover, "And now it's time to end this..."

"But you don't want to kill me, not now Mother Maynard. Where would it get you?"

"Revenge. You set me up and tried to get me killed. When that didn't work you faked my death, set up a replacement, and attempted to foil my diabolical plans."

"No you're thinking of Lester. All I did was steal your MMO handle. Listen, we both want the same thing, to get rid of Lester and now apparently the Bossman. Let's work together. Our combined forces will easily overthrow those two bumbling fools."

Mother Maynard thought about that for a moment, "Hmm, once Lester and the Bossman are out of the way we'll have to fight each other anyway. Why not let me kill you now and save some time?"

"Aha, but you're wrong. I don't want to be the anti-Space Pontiff or a Bossman or a Lester lackey. I just want to be a cow. I want to be stupid again and back on my farm where I'd be no trouble to anyone."

Mother Maynard smiled, "Yes, that's been a fantasy of mine for quite a while..." She went cheery eyed and lowered her blaster for a moment, "Hey you're trying to trick me with your hypnotic cow vision trick. But it wouldn't work. It's sheer nonsense. Nothing that ridiculous would really happen. Plus I don't believe you. I think it's time to die." She took careful aim...

"Look!" Besey cried, "A giant pizza ball!"

"Huh?" Maynard foolishly looked behind her.

The cow made a break for it down an emergency stairwell. She was really hoofing it to get a couple of kph in speed. The bad un-reverend Mother Maynard was no better as she waddled her way down the steps after her.

It must have seemed strange to the security dude Ralph as he monitored the cameras between goofing off sessions. He kept trying to adjust the speed control on his screens in a futile attempt to see what was "really" going on in stairwell number 66. The slow speed chase seemed to go on forever as each party periodically had to stop and rest every few meters or so. The security dude grew bored and fell asleep missing out on the most important part of the battle.

"Enough!" Maynard shouted down to the cow, "I can't take this stress anymore. Let's play a game of torture chess instead. Winner take all."

"How about black I win, white you lose."

"Whatever..." she was too tired to argue much.

"Okay pick."

"Huh? Oh pick, let's see...Black."

"I win."

"Darn it!"

"Okay now that I've won you have to do what I say. First put your gun away and ball your fat butt down here."

314

Disgruntled Mother Maynard did as she was told. She had been beaten fair and square, as far as she could tell. So now the satanic cow had won. Time to die. She moped down the last two steps and stood in front of the cow awaiting her doom.

"Since I won I get to choose how we are to defeat Lester and the Bossman, agreed?"

"Huh? You aren't going to chop my head off?"

"No, it's too heavy. I want you to help me knock them once and for all. When that's done I'll put you in charge of routine floggings. How does that sound?"

"Fine but what about that YIG fellow?"

"I won't let anyone know how you two smuggled vitamins to the refugees of Targus Non IV. It'll be our little secret."

"It is a terrible vice but the stress gets to me sometimes. All this evil and mayhem can get a bit irritating every once in a while."

"Would it make you feel any better if you knew those supplies only prolonged the refugees suffering?"

"Oh yes, that is a great relieve. I promise I won't do it again."

"That's a start. But first I need to go down to the kitchen and break out the P-47 space modulator mixing bowls..." she paused for effect, "We're going to bake some pies."

Chapter 32: The Genghis Con

A hushed yet restless silence descended upon the studio. The audience was eager for the game show to be over. The last few days hadn't turned out to be the spectacular event of the Eon that everyone had been led to believe and now with the final installment eminent it was a bored and placid audience that watched on.

When a few overeager hecklers began throwing detonation devices onto the empty set, nervous producers decided something had to be done, and quickly. So they sent out Mortimer the announcer.

Now Mortimer had cut his teeth on the talk shows of the early '680s where a flashy smile and gun behind your back demanded respect from the audience but now twenty years later it took more than simple threats of violence to keep an unruly crowd at bay. It required action.

Mortimer squared his collar and took a deep breath. From behind the curtains to stage left he prepared to do battle with an angry studio audience. It wasn't his fault that all the contestants were whisked away to another universe, or so the rumors said. But now he had to answer for the consequences.

Boldly he marched out onto the stage. The crowd hushed at this new development. Mortimer flashed his effervescent white smile, the psycho-hypnotic sparkles kept them mesmerized for a few seconds. Just enough time to pull out an oversized pair of scissors, and, still smiling, chop through his neck until his head popped off and rolled around on the sound stage.

The crowd yawned. An automated sweeper rushed out to clean up the mess.

The producers' gamble had failed and now they too would have to pay in blood. "Well, this is it then," Boab said to Stin, "Time to call for the fat lady."

"Disastrous," Stin said stoking on his flamer as he lounged back in his control chair.

"It's a damn shame really," Boab continued, "Our careers are ruined." He was playing with a bagel that flopped around on the main console. It accidentally hit a switch labeled RECALL.

Instantly sirens began sounding around the studio. Blast doors slammed shut before audience members could flee in panic. Lights flashed in rhythm to the ominous drone of the alarms.

"Boab?" Stin raised his eyebrow, "You're not thinking of going into syndication are you?"

Boab, as bewildered as this new situation as Stin was, said, "You know that's a brilliant idea S.H."

A prerecorded voice announced over the entire set, "And now from the far reaches of the known universe, to present our finalists in the Ultimate Gameshow, the only game show where the fate of the universe is held in the balance,....Genghis Khan!"

The clone of Genghis Khan materialized on the set. He snared at the crowd and they snarled back. "Right!" Genghis said with a thick British accent,

"And now I have the great honor of presenting our two finalists who will battle for control and the ultimate fate of the universe as we know it. But first a word from Dainty Fresh the only mouthwash made with Larks Vomit..."

Boab, not wanting to look like a fool in front of Stin, opened a can of Dainty Fresh and sprayed a hearty dose into his mouth. He gagged a moment while clutching at his throat then pretended to die in a quick spasm and fell to the control room floor. "Ha ha, just kidding," he said sprawled out on the floor with larks vomit dribbling down his chin.

"Moron," Stin said before shooting Boab several times with a pistol he found in a drawer labeled 'For Emergency Use Only'. The last round exploded in the chamber creating a huge ball of blue flame which caused his facial makeup to also ignite and burn the producer into a pile of ash.

With the producers effectively "out of the loop" the game show could then continue on unhindered.

"We're back," Genghis said with a twirl. "Now wasn't that refreshing?" He asked with a laugh. "But seriously it is now time to turn our attention to the big screen behind my head were we will see through the eyes of finalist number one. Hidden pick up devices were secretly placed in all the contestant's optic nerve tracks before the show began and now we can see the results of that little maneuver.

The screen came to life. Besey was in the restroom applying lipstick to her oversized lips in front of a mirror.

Genghis produced a fat red control button from his tailored suit. "Satanic cow! Come on down!" He mashed the button. The screen faded and there was a thunderous crack that sounded over the set. A blur of motion erupted overhead and then a Holstein came falling to the set with a loud crash.

"What the hell?" Besey looked around confused. One minute she was taking a break from her pie baking and then next she was here.

Genghis walked over and leaned down to get a better look at her muzzle. "And how does it feel to be a finalist in the Ultimate Gameshow?"

"Mooo."

"Wonderful."

The audience cheered! If the producers had still been alive they might have taken notice of this phenomenal event.

"And now..." Genghis whispered as the studio lights dimmed, "Everyone knew the cow was a shoe in but... the next finalist... aha, wouldn't you like to know."

"YES!" the crowd shouted.

"Okay but first let's sneak a peak at what the final group of contestants are doing right now."

The giant screen came back to life, but this time it shifted to neural broadcast mode which sent out high speed particles to every member of the audience and caused them to hallucinate that they were in a run down apartment complex watching a 2D, static prone, analog, black and white television set.

The tube flicker on. Ghostly highlights blurred the image and a hazy snow flitted everywhere. Wow, the crowd was impressed, it was so crappy. The wonders of technology never ceased to amaze the dim witted mass culture.

It looked like a rerun of the Outer Limits but everyone knew this was no docu-science drama but a game show. All the more impressive. The remaining contestants, Rogicphil, the Funky Chicken, Hack, Mr. Bear, and someone else that no one could remember, were seated at what historians believed to me a medieval banquet table (but in actuality was the smashed bumper off a 1974 Diesel truck) playing a came of Parcheesi with the Supreme Being Destiny.

"Oooo looks like they're in trouble now," Genghis said. He appeared as an old lady in biker leathers in the combined audience hallucination. "Let's make things exciting. Final contestant! Come on down!" In the illusion, Genghis squashed a fetid cockroach that acted at the infamous red button that recalled the contestants.

The imaginary television set exploded sending fake yet remarkably painful shards of metal, glass, and singed plastic into the audience members' bodies. Ooh, they ooed.

Upon returning to the studio nothing seemed to have changed. Genghis was still poking fun at the cow who was where she'd fallen into the partially collapsed floor of the set. He looked around but no contestant had arrived.

Strange whispers emanated from the confused audience. And then when almost all hope had been lost (2.7 seconds to be exact) Space-Bo entered the set from a back door.

"My children," he said holding out his arms, "I have come to save the universe from itself."

Genghis made the idiot sign behind Space-Bo's back and the crowd laughed.

"This is not the time to revel in joy. Once I have defeated the forces of evil that grip this world, paradise will then get us."

Genghis made more fun of Space-Bo while trying to figure out where the contestants had gone.

"Why do I get the feeling that you do not believe I what I say?" Space-Bo scratched his armpit. "I will show you the sacred orb that you may know it and through it know me." He reached into his pocket and pulled out a cardboard box. Upon opening it his jaw slacked. There was no orb inside, instead there was a hand scrawled note written in blood from the Bossman.

"It says," Space-Bo read, "Sorry chum but now I control the cosmos. The Bossman."

"BOOOOOO!" the crowd began throwing things at the hapless stooge.

"Wait!" Genghis jumped up and down trying to get their attention, "I think I have the solution. Please stop."

Grudgingly they stopped with a few choice 'you suck's thrown in for good measure.

"Thank you." Genghis pulled a wicked sword out from his business suit and sliced into Space-Bo's body.

The crowd cheered. This Genghis was really cool, the audience thought to itself.

Taken completely by surprise Space-Bo gasped for breath as the blood oozed out and he fell to his knees. The blue robe he wore had done little to protect him from the blade. If he'd still been wearing his reinforced spacesuit things would be different but that was before he lost the orb and his god powers.

318

Oh well...was his last thought as he fell completely over.

Genghis didn't gloat over the body but quickly preformed an autopsy. After few minutes he had what he was looking for, the liver. "Here is our missing finalist!" he said holding the liver up high over his head. The crowd cheered at first and then did a group "huh?"

"No not the liver you fools," he said in sympathy, "It is the castle inside this liver that contains our finalist. Jeffrey...?" he called to someone off stage, "Could you wheel out the matter re-converter please?"

A bulky contraption on wheels was rolled out onto the stage and Genghis tossed the liver into a big hopper on top. With a single flick of a switch this device will reconvert our finalist into his regular size, or extra jumbo if I twist this dial here."

"Jumbo! Jumbo!" the audience chanted.

"No, no... we'd be here all day." With a twirl Genghis picked up Space-Bo's limp body and expertly tossed it into the hopper also. "That ought to confuse the machine a bit." He flipped the master switch.

The lights dimmed to simulate a power drain as the device hummed a bit of prerecorded clanking and chugging sounds. With the bing of a machine that has just completed its task, and feeling much too pleased with itself, the re-converter finished. A panel slid open and a gorgeous young female model stepped out.

"Hi," she said.

"I don't understand," Genghis said playing up his part, "But who are you my dear lady?"

"I am a composite of all the people who were shrunken up inside Space-Bo's liver, including Space-Bo too since you included him in the mix."

"But all the contestants were men. And by no means are you that."

The girl shrugged. "You win some, you loose some. Tee-hee."

Meanwhile inside the re-converter machine all the real contestants were plotting a way to break out.

"I'm sorry," Destiny said, "If we truly are back in our own universe something terrible must have happened because I haven't regained my powers."

"Agreed," the chicken said, "Any ideas?"

Rogicphil proposed that they try to reconfigure the re-converter controls to re-reconvert the unreconfiguration mechanism in order to bypass the quantum overload circuits in an attempt to...

All this babble bored Mr. Bear so he slipped out the backdoor and down onto the game show set. Genghis and the fake reconstituted model were making wisecracks at each other and the audience when he rounded the corner to confront them.

"At last," the cow stated loudly, "My adversary."

The girl and Genghis were surprised at the bear's sudden appearance. "You're not suppose to come out yet. We're still doing the comedy bit. Go back and wait till the next commercial break okay?"

The Bear growled. He charged Genghis, grabbed him up in a big hug, and squeezed all the breath out of him. With Genghis of no more use, the bear threw the "great warrior" into the crowd.

With the girl kicking and screaming over his shoulder he was marching off stage when the satanic cow called out after him, "Wait!"

"Urr?"

The cow struggled to get out of the hole in the floor and finally leapt up onto the stage. "You weren't suppose to be the final contestant but since no one else seems to care, you're it. You just can't walk away from the universe Bear."

Mr. Bear considered a moment and then had to agree. Soberly he sat the panicked girl down and returned to the center of the stage and sat down next to the cow.

"And now," Besey, the satanic cow, ominously said, "The final battle begins."

*   *   *

Meanwhile on an impoverish homeworld hundreds of light years away Burdunkel and Maienfeld counted up all their waifs and prepared to pay the evil taxman with the only thing they had left. But the taxman wasn't so understanding and he....

The editors would like to apologize for the inconvenience of this other, sappier, storyline interrupting the current and exciting storyline. If this has harmed you in any way please feel free to write your congressthing and complain. We will happily nip off and dispatch ourselves if enough negative responses are received. Thank you.

...and so the satanic cow was defeated in moral combat against the great and victorious Mr. Bear.

Rogicphil and the others somehow managed to short circuit the power system inside the re-converter causing the machine to fizzle and then fall apart all around them. When the dust settled the auditorium was vacant except for the beleaguered cow conceding defeat to a bewildered bear.

"Hey, wait a second," Rogicphil said running up, "What happened? Where'd everyone go."

The cow had its head drooping low. "Well you missed it, the final most spectacular battle in the universe and we lost. All hope of peace is dead and humans will continue to enslave the animal world."

"Well, how'd it happen?"

Mr. Bear turned to Rogicphil and shook his head. It was not their place to question the fate of the universe.

Destiny broke in, "I don't believe it. If the combined forces of this galaxy has defeated the satanic cow in the agreed arrangement of the terms of the Ultimate Gameshow how come I can't snap my fingers and make mold grow over everything?"

"Oh," Besey said, "That would probably be the Bossman's work. He got control of one of your orbs and hence your position. Sorry about that."

"What?" the until recently Supreme Being was flabbergasted, "And how did Bossman get into my office?"

"He did it," the cow motioned toward the wounded yet somewhat reconstituted Space-Bo resting in the remains of the re-converter mechanism.

"You!" Destiny grabbed up Space-Bo by the collar of his blue robes, "What in my universe have you done? I told you not to open that book."

"I'm sorry, I thought I was a god for a second."

"Well you're not and your going to help me get my powers back. In fact," he raised his voice so that everyone could hear, "All of you are going to help me or this victory will be a hollow one."

"I don't know about that," Rogicphil mused unsure about all this extra adventuring. All he wanted to do right now was take a vacation. "I don't think the universe could be much worse than it was before..."

Destiny glared at him with all the force of an experienced power monger even though he was currently fresh out of power. "I still have plenty of experience and friends in high places to make your remaining existence a miserable one."

"Okay, I'm not willing to call your bluff just yet. So how do we overthrow this Bossman fellow who apparently has all your powers?"

The cow snorted. "Oh, is that all? I was planning on doing that myself later tonight after dinner."

"Now we're getting somewhere," Destiny patted the cow on her back, "Tell me about your plan..."

*   *   *

H.E.L.L.'s former junior grade Bossman, now All Hail High Space Pontiff and Defender of Lugietorp chuckled with glee as he rubbed the smooth round egg thing he had in his lap. This one was much nicer than the other egg / orb thingee he'd gotten from agent 666 (AKA Synthi) who had found it in the bottom of a barrel of monkeys a few days back on that cursed planet Deo 7. This orb could not only allow him to travel in time but granted him Supreme Being status.

He had laughed himself silly after distracting Space-Bo with his fake Mudman trick long enough to pick pocket the orb. And now that the Bossman had it, he wouldn't let anyone stop him from using it to destroy that foul planet known as Deo 7: not Destiny, not anti-Bishop Lester (whether alive or dead), and certainly not that double crossing satanic cow.

Satanic, ha! There was about as much satan in that cow as there was in his oatmeal. No, vengeance would solely be that of the Bossman himself. What wonderful little toys these orbs were!

His first use of the original egg had been to deposit one space cred in the Lugietorpian First Savings Bank when it had first opened thousands of years ago. And now thanks to the wonders of compounded interest he would be rich beyond all measure. Even richer than he'd been after cheating Y.I.G with that bogus life insurance policy scam. So rich in fact that he would be able to buy Y.I.G. right out from under its former owners and in doing so take over his own H.E.L.L. account and cancel the hit they had out on him.

"Bad boy, bad boy!" he scolded himself. "Shame on you for scamming us out of 4.2 trillion space bucks." He laughed heartily at this little irony.

And then that thing with Space-Bo; that was a riot. What a dope that guy was. He had had the power of the universe in his hands and didn't even know it. But the Bossman knew it very well and would soon be wielding its awesome power.

There was a knock at his door that threatened to distract him from his allusions to grandeur. "That had better be my pizza or somebodies going to get it."

Lester poked his head in to make sure, if fired upon, not all of him would be in the path of destruction. "May I enter, your moldiness?"

"Only if you have a pizza."

Lester did; his note to himself had told him to bring it. He came in and sat the pizza down on the new All Hail High Space Pontiff's desk. The office looked just like the one the Bossman had back on Raul Rall Beta. In fact it was the actual office but it had been painstakingly dismantled and transmatted over to Lugietorp to be reinstalled, shark tank and all.

The Bossman ignored the pizza. "How do I know it's really you this time, Lester and not a robot or clone or whatever?"

"Does it really matter? I'm here to do your bidding. Just like the spicy anchovy pizza I brought you."

The Bossman cracked the box open a little and sniffed. He smiled and opened the box all the way. "So it is. How'd you know I was in the mood for something like this?"

"Just part of the job, your holey nastiness," Lester lied. He left out the part about a note he'd written himself from thousands of years in the past with information about the future from which he had / would come from. "Would you like any salad dressing with that?"

"What?"

"Cahootz," he said holding up a bottle of the nasty stuff, "The original recipe dates back to the founding of Lugietorp by space gypsies and construction worker refugees."

"Never heard of it."

That was good. That mind wipe trick one of his robot doubles had done on the Bossman back in the spa seemed to be working. The Bossman didn't remember anything.

"So, what do you want Lester?"

"Nothing." Again, the note told him to say it.

"I don't trust a man you wants nothing. He's too hard to manipulate. I think I'll just erase you from history now."

"As you wish my master."

The Bossman raised up his orb but at the last minute changed his mind. This was too easy. Lester was up to something. He always was. The trick was to get rid of Lester but keep his knowledge of H.E.L.L. and experience in dealing with the other evil organizations in the galaxy. Clones had been the solution of choice for hundreds of years but the Bossman still didn't trust Lester that much.

Aha, he had it. Put Lester into a sealed time loop. That way the High anti-Bishop could still be accessed when needed but be safely out of the way and powerless at the same time. Brilliant.

"I have a mission for you Lester. I want you to go back in time and prevent yourself from being a threat to me."

Lester scratched his big head. This part wasn't in the note. He was suppose to be sent back in time to corner the market on anthropocentric robots.

"So that's been your plan the whole time," the Bossman said, suddenly realizing he could read Lester's mind. "I have to say it was pure genius but won't work now." He smiled as more realization hit him. "That also explains all the Lester robots that have been blowing up around here lately."

Lester pulled out his note and read it again. "But, but... it says right here." He balled over to the Bossman to show him specifically where the Bossman had sent him back in time but when he had only made it two revolutions, the Bossman pulled out his stolen orb / egg, aimed it at the fat man and pulled the metaphoric trigger.

Nothing happened at first. The Bossman frowned and Lester breathed a sigh of relief since neither of them knew exactly what powers the orb bestowed upon it's bearer. But then an angry shark leapt out of its tank behind the Bossman and with new found lung capacity, attacked the hapless High anti-Bishop. It made off with a leg and part of an arm before either of them knew what had happened.

"Well, I guess that settles the issue of whether you're a robot or not," the Bossman laughed.

Lester screamed, "But you're suppose to send me back in time darn it!"

"Oh I'll send you some place alright." He whipped out a hand blaster and vaporized the wounded fat man in a cloud of greasy smoke. All that was left behind was a black smear on the carpet.

"Ha ha ha," the Bossman laughed putting his blaster back into his pocket. He could get use to being the Supreme Being.

The security dude, Ralph, was the last one left in the formerly unhallow grounds of the H.E.L.L. main complex, which was a series of tunnels and chambers under the capital city of the planet Lugietorp. The Bossman along with a few remaining units of Wilburs and Jakes had left a few hours before to their new headquarters somewhere in transdimensional space. He last job was to turn out the lights, lock the doors and shoot himself in the head.

He had finished with the first two tasks and was getting ready to finish himself off, when he had the urge to goof off one last time. He was busy playing space solitaire with his right hand while his left loaded the regulation pistol with special suicide rounds and slowly raised it to his temple.

"Oh good, you're still here," a voice said distracting him.

"Visiting hours are over. You'll have to come back tomorrow," he said without looking up from his computer screen.

Delilah, the Bossman's former secretary from Rall Raul Beta strode up to the security desk and plopped down a strange glowing gizmo right in front of Ralph. "I'm not staying. I just need to leave this here for a while."

"Bombs are received at the rear entrance only."

"Oh it's not a bomb. It's a quantum displacement targeting beacon."

"Okay, whatever." Ralph didn't bother to look up. After she left, he finished his last hand of cards with a "Woohoo!" then promptly shot himself dead.

The Bossman was busy exploring his new office in the transdimensional space that all supreme beings used for administrative tasks. His old office was too smelly after the shark / Lester incident and he wasn't too keen on having an air breathing shark roaming freely around the premises so he'd decided to pack up again and move everything over here to Destiny's digs.

He'd been forced to take a nap earlier after laughing himself silly when thinking back to when Space-Bo had fallen for his trick. Too bad too, he would liked to have seen what that bumbling fool would have done when he found out he possessed Destiny's powers. But oh well, now the Bossman had those powers. Whoever runs the office has the power. And Bossman definitely ran the office.

Harriet was a decent replacement over his old secretary but it'd take a while for her to get use to the new "evil" Destiny.

Bzzzzt! Bzzzzt! "Yes what is it?" he angrily asked.

"Sorry sir, but 'um Mr. Calcitrant is here to see you."

"Who?"

"Mr. Calcitrant, you're next door neighbor."

"Neighbor? What does Destiny need with a neighbor?"

"Well the Counsel of Supreme Beings overextended some of their investments and were forced to rent out extra-dimensional space to commercial developers."

"And Mr. Calcitrant is my neighbor huh? What does he want anyway?"

"Something to do with a noise complaint I believe."

"Very well send him in," Bossman/Destiny spun around on his shiny new chair. And then a moment later there was a knock at his door. "Enter."

In stepped an armor clad figure covered head to foot in a metal matrix, "I am Mr. Calcitrant," it said in a voice attempting to sound important.

"I am Destiny, the Supreme Being. I can crush you with a single thought. I suggest you apologize and maybe I'll let you live."

"If you are so powerful, why do you not speak as your unfortunate predecessor, in overpowering tones?"

"I CAN SHOUT IF YOU WANT ME TO, but I prefer a modest tone. Besides I thought you were here to complain about the noise. Now you complain that I'm speaking too softly? I'll have your head yet."

"Your threats do not intimidate me. I am here to speak business not threats. How would you like to double your power?"

"What talk is this? Business power? I am already the most powerful being in the universe. I will destroy you now." Bossman squinted his eyes and strained real hard trying to destroy Mr. Calcitrant but nothing happened. "Just a minute," he appologised and called Harriet on the speaker phone. "How come I can't vaporize this bozo?"

"I don't know. Have you read your operators manual? Maybe that would help."

"It's too thick. You must have read it. What do you think I should do?"

"Well, Destiny's power is limited to the area of biological growth and fulfillment. You can't blast people with energy bolts you know."

"Hmm..."

"Enough of this," Mr. Calcitrant spoke, "We will talk business now."

"DIE!" Bossman shouted. All the plants in the room suddenly withered but the man in the armor didn't even flinch. "What's wrong with you? Why won't you die?"

"My power-suit protects me from your limited powers. Through a trick of physics and a loophole in the legal definitions of your powers I have devised a way to thwart your abilities. With your connections and my inventing genius we will be unstoppable."

"Okay so what do you get out of this?"

"Wealth beyond measure. I am not hungry for power, but money...... now that just makes my mouth water."

Bossman was intrigued now. "What do we do? How can I double my power?"

Mr. Calcitrant stiffly approached and held out a metal gauntlet on which a small gizmo rested. "Take this device."

"What is it?" Bossman willed a bat to materialize, pick it up, and fly it over to his desk. "Looks fairly simple."

"It is a communications device. With it you can place a toll free call to the Quasars."

"Quasars, Quasars... hmm that names sound familiar. What is it?"

"Not it, them. As guardians of the ultimate power they decide who gets what power. Call them up and ask for more."

The Bossman laughed, "It can't be that simple. If they really have the ultimate power why would they want to give it to me? I'm not even sure these Quasars really exist. Just a second..." He called Harriet again asking, "What's a Quasar?"

"You really don't know your way around here yet do you? Quasars are the SUPREME BEINGS for the Supreme Beings. They are much more powerful than you, 'oh great one'."

"Hmm, thanks." he nodded then turned back to Mr. Calcitrant. "Okay so what's the catch?"

"The catch is that the Quasars are very busy creatures and can't talk to every Supreme Being who just happens to want their audience. But I circumvented this technicality with a hotwired Quasar Communicator."

"I don't understand."

"In order to limit requests by the Supreme Beings the Quasars created the Quasar Telephone and Teleport Company (QT&T) to limit access to them. Normally a call to the Quasars cost 13 Galaxies a minute but I have rigged this device that allows toll free access to the Quasar Network. You can get an edge over all the other Supreme Beings and a better ear with the Quasars."

"Did you say 13 Galaxies a minute? What does that mean? How much is that in spacebucks?"

"You misunderstand. Galaxies are not a form of currency. Galaxies are huge collections of star systems. 13 Galaxies are used up, their energy completely drained, for every minute that you communicate with the quasars."

"Wow," Bossman beamed as he eyed the little device in his hand, "Why don't you use it if it's so powerful?"

"What do I have to say to the Quasars? I am not a Supreme Being; they would either ignore me or destroy my entire race throughout time. But you, they are required to listen to you, if you can call them."

"Ha, ha, I really can double my power. I'll do it right now." He shook the gizmo trying to figure out how to make it work.

"Just speak into the funnel, it will do the rest."

"Hello? Hello Quasars, this is Destiny calling. Do you hear me?"

After a few seconds a craggy voice answered back, "We HeAr DeStInY. WhAt Do YoU wIsH oF tHe QuAsArS?"

"Alright!" Bossman shouted jumping up on his desk and did a little jig. "I'm in! Yes!"

"We Do NoT uNdErStAnD. pLeAsE rEsTaTe YoUr ReQuEsT."

"Oh, sorry," he said sitting back down, "I want you to double my power."

"AnYtHiNg ElSe?"

Bossman put his hand over the funnel. "They want to know if I want anything else."

Mr. Calcitrant shrugged his metallic shoulders, "See how far you can go."

"Okay," he eagerly agreed, removed his hand and spoke again, "And I want to have the power to destroy all live as we know it."

"YoU aLrEaDy HaVe ThAt PoWeR. dO yOu NoT uNdErStAnD tHe ScOpE oF yOuR dUiTiEs?"

"Of course I do. This is Destiny isn't it. I am the Supreme Being. I want you to triple, no quadruple my current power lever. Just pour it on."

"VeRy WeLl."

"I did it!" Bossman jumped up on his desk again. "Now I am SUPER powerful. Watch!" He concentrated really hard and the fabric of space began to crack and ooze exotic particles like scalar monopoles, anti-negative strange quarks, and other weird beasts. "Now I really am GOD!"

"I'm happy for you," Mr. Calcitrant said nonplussed, "Now can I have my money?"

"Your money? You fool. I am GOD! I owe you nothing. Now leave me alone or I shall destroy you with my new powers."

"Interesting prospect. But I really need my money. Please hand it over."

Bossman leveled a wicked finger at the figure and commanded, "DIE!"

The metal form quivered a bit then fell over.

"I really am SUPER powerful now!" Bossman danced around to the intercom. "Harriet could you send in the cleaning crew please. There's some rubbish that needs to be taken out."

"Right away sir."

Ah, the good life. The Bossman settled back into his chair to dream of all the nasty things he would soon be doing. But before he could completely settle in, the gizmo buzzed. "Huh?"

The gizmo buzzed again so he answered it, "This is Destiny. What can I do to you?"

"PlEaSe TrAnSmIt Qt&T aUtHoRiZaTiOn NuMbEr."

"Huh? Just a second. Harriet what's my QT&T authorization number?"

"We don't have one of those yet sir."

Ooops. Bossman picked up the gizmo looking for a clue. "Okay here's my number 432-ZE-Omega 39." He read off the serial number on the gizmo.

"InVaLiD. PrEpArE tO bE dEsTrOyIeD."

"What? It was all a big mistake, I assure you."

"FiVe.... FoUr.... ThReE...."

"No please I take it back. Don't destroy me."

"TwO.... oNe."

"Surely there must be something...."

Chapter 33: Return To The Planet of Deo

"I must admit that was a really remarkable death," the Funky Chicken said to Rogicphil as they were taking the shuttle down to Deo 7. It had been several days since their victory over the evil Bossman and now it was time to rest and party.

"Yeah," Rogicphil smiled, "I still think you're crazy for putting that suit on and daring him to kill you."

"Even though it didn't permanently kill me as I was hoping, it was still very satisfying. It made my top ten list of best deaths ever."

"But what I don't understand is how you knew the Quasars would destroy the Bossman when he grew power-hungry."

"Well it came to me in a dream after talking with Besey about the Bossman and his habits. Anybody that stupid and power-hungry would go overboard at the prospect of ultimate power. And the phony calling card gambit was the icing on the cake. Too bad about the real Destiny though."

"Hmm," Rogicphil pondered as he maneuvered the rented shuttle through the glowing green clouds that hung like a sticky cloak over the entire planet. "For one, I am not looking forward to returning to this retched pothole in space. A mandatory 'Victory Party'? Come on."

"It may be mandatory but that doesn't mean we can't have some fun: some of that old ultra-mayhem, if you know what I mean."

"It can't be much worse that what you and Space-Bo already did."

"You mean that blimp full of money? That was just the tip of the financial iceberg. A mere symbol of what was down in 's money pit. Not to mention all the off world loans still outstanding."

"At least deo production is back up to full capacity."

"Eh," the chicken wrinkled his feathered brow, "This planet never had anything to do with H.E.L.L.'s evil plan. Who cares if deodorant production goes up or down?"

"Grego the Mean. Hold on we're fixing to land," Rogicphil took a sharp right bank and blasted out of the clouds over Balidron. Since acquiring his Fiat, he'd actually learned a thing or two about flying. Still, he didn't let on as to how much he still relied on the autopilot.

A new parking lot had just been built to commemorate Rogicphil's team and their saving of Deo 7 from financial collapse, and here he decided to land the shuttle.   A huge crowd of onlookers filled the site surrounding the designated parking zone.

The chicken scratched at its plumage, "Do you really think it was such a good idea to reintroduce all that positive money back into the Deo 7 economy?"

"Sure why not?" With a flick of the wrist Rogicphil activated the landing thrusters and made a gentle landing on the fresh new tarmac. It seemed like a perfect landing but just a few seconds afterward, the entire shuttle settled further down. "That's strange."

FC poked his head out the window and looked down at the landing skids, "It appears the parking lot is newer than we anticipated. We've sunken into still molten fresh asphalt."

"At least the odor will cancel the deo smell." He opened the side hatch and the two hopped out to the sticky surface.

Bottles and wet tennis balls came flying out of the angry crowd at them. The chicken jumped up trying to catch as many as possible in his beak while Rogicphil flitted around avoiding all that came his way.

An encumbered Space-Bo met them at the police line that kept the surging crowd from dog-piling in, "Welcome back. What's up?" He was wearing a battered up space marine suit outfitted with riot gear.

"That's what we'd like to know."

"Hurry and get into the hover-tank so I can fill you guys in." Space-Bo led them through a police escort to a hover-tank a few meters away. They hopped in with two officers and Space-Bo took the controls. Annie was in the co-pilot's seat and hugged him as he got in.

"I think you should man the weapons system or we may not get out of here."

"Right!" She swung into her crash couch and grabbed the gunnery controls. The tanks auto cannons opened up and fired randomly around them to disperse the crowd so that they could get under way.

"Hey!" Rogicphil cried as he glanced out the window, "Those are innocent civilians out there."

"Don't worry," Annie said, "The cannons are firing gel packs with concentrated deo essence. Even natives can't handle a direct impact from one of those babies."

"Why? Why all the hardware? I thought we were heroes."

Space-Bo answered, "Well that depends on whose definition you use. The Department of Refunds have called us Honorary Gods while the Ministry of Nasty Names has labeled us 'heathens beyond all repair'." Space-Bo shifted into high gear and floored the hover-tank sending them skidding along the asphalt towards the huge Balidron multi-buildings.

"I don't understand."

"Well it seems this little gift the chicken and I gave back to the people has caused the biggest civil war this planet has ever known."

The Funky Chicken was all smiles, "When does the reception begin?"

"Twenty minutes," Space-Bo said avoiding oncoming civilian vehicles that tried to crash into them.

Rogicphil wasn't very happy at all, "Has Destiny arrived yet? I need to speak to him."

"Yep, everybody's here already, except for the Clergy."

"It's not like them to miss free food."

"I know. It's got some people worried." The hover-tank dove into a tunnel underneath some buildings. They cruised down and through a double set of blast doors into a military style hanger bay.

Space-Bo parked the hover-tank and they all disembarked onto a red carpet that led inside to a lobby area. An honor guard of fifty police officers lined the carpeting and saluted as they walked by.

"What division are these guys from, one or two?" Rogicphil quietly asked Space-Bo.

"Beats the heck out of me."

Inside the lobby two gray haired men in regal outfits welcomed them to Balidron. "I am Burtlefinkster Groolick the new mayor of Balidron and let me introduce Hagsplat Ufglong Jr. the all new Chief of Police. Along with the King of Rall Raul Beta, we would like to personally congratulate all of you on your wonderful accomplishments."

Rogicphil pointed to the chicken, "He was the one inside the suit of armor."

"That's lovely," the Mayor smiled too wide, "There will be a formal presentation ceremony where we will present you all with code keys to the city. Then join us for the reception afterward... where we're steel them back from you. Oops did I just say that outloud?"

Rogicphil ignored all the formal crap that was being spewed forth by the bureaucrats and instead looked around for the others. He found the bear and the robot girl in the purple blindfold chatting by the punch bowl. "Hey have either of you seen Destiny around here?"

The bear shook his head, as his mouth was full of food. And the girl just shrugged.

Rogicphil found the Supreme Being sulking behind a giant ostrich plant in the corner. "Hey, come out from behind there. I want to talk to you."

Destiny shuffled his feat a bit but refused to come out so Rogicphil pushed aside the snapping branches and joined him in the corner, "Are you okay?"

"NO."

"Well too bad. We've got a social situation going on out there and something needs to be done. I can't have any personal problems getting in the way here."

"HEY! I'M STILL A SUPREME BEING OKAY. JUST BECAUSE I'M ON PROBABTION DOESN'T MEAN YOU CAN PUSH ME AROUND, UNDERSTAND?"

"Sorry. But listen, I think it's foolish to have a party right now when an entire planet is at war, especially if we're responsible."

"US? IT WAS NEBLE AND SPACE-BO'S FAULT. IT WAS NOT PART OF THEIR MISSION TO RETURN ECONOMIC STABILITY TO THIS PLANET. BESIDES, THE PIE VENDORS HAVEN'T ARRIVED YET."

"This whole thing stinks you know."

"CE LA PLANET OF DEO."

"What the heck were we doing here in the first place? If the Deo 7 mission was simply a distraction while the Ultimate Gameshow was set up and the game show turned out to be a waste of time also. It was the Bossman's own greediness that brought him down. We had nothing to do with it. But now we get a hero's greeting on a planet that's fighting itself because of us, for doing absolutely nothing. What the blarg?"

"I DON'T KNOW. FOR THE FIRST TIME IN EONS I REALLY DON'T KNOW. BEING ON PROBATIONS SEVERELY LIMITS ONE'S OMNIPOTENT ABILITIES. AT LEAST IT'S BETTER THAN BEING

COMPLETELY STRIPPED OF POWER."

"Well I suggest we have a meeting with Grego the Mean and decide if there's anything we can do to solve this mess once and for all, without everyone getting so p.o.ed at each other."

"OKAY, I'LL SEE WHAT I CAN DO. IN THE MEAN TIME KEEP AN EYE ON THE OTHERS AND MAKE SURE THEY DON'T DO ANYTHING STUPID."

Rogicphil laughed, "You don't get it do you? It is our combined stupidity that has caused this mess in the first place. I don't think curtailing it now is going to have much of an effect."

"FINE, THEN WHIP THEM ALL UP INTO A BIG FURVOR AND GO CRAZY IN A MEDLEY OF MEYHEM AND CHAOS."

Rogicphil considered, "Okay."

*   *   *

Meanwhile back at H.E.L.L. headquarters the satanic cow was busy closing down the central bingo operations center. In an agreement reached with the winning consortium from the Ultimate Gameshow, the loser, H.E.L.L., had to shut down all operations involving Evil. And that meant just about everything. There were still a few pizza joints left, but not much else.

Besey should have been happy, she supposed. It had been her goal all along to dismantle H.E.L.L. but not like this. She should have won the Gameshow and then gone on to convert H.E.L.L. to other causes, such as her animals rights agenda. But now who knew how the organization could function with strict restrictions imposed on its charter and operations.

The only reason it hadn't been simply shut down was that H.E.L.L., it turned out, was a major government contractor on the planet Lugietorp and Deo 7, not to mention several other worlds in nearby sectors. A total shut down would have collapsed several splinter companies and caused an unprecedented amount of unemployment in the effected areas.

One of the remaining High anti-Bishop Lester robots was helping her box up piles of paperwork that had accumulated over the years. He was grumbling to know one in particular, "Whose idea was it to put a cow on a game show anyway? What do cows know about the actual price of living room furniture? I could have done just as good."

Besey ground her teeth, "Okay wise guy, name the manufacturer of Beelzebub's Toe Cheese Grater."

"Hmm," Lester tapped the end of his overlarge nose, "Lucifer Industries?"

"Wrong. Beelzebub brand products belong to us, or they did before H.E.L.L. froze over."

"Don't remind me," Lester pulled his third golf jacket around his over large frame. The first and second ones weren't doing much good it seemed.

"I know it's winter outside and we've had to turn the thermostat down to save on the electric bill but.... YOURE A ROBOT!"

"I said, don't remind me." He packed some more files into a box.

A short accountant entered the room then and ran up to Besey, "Mr.

Cooper the Senior Lawyer wants to speak to you."

"Okay," Besey removed her back hoofs from a box where she'd been ram-packing papers in. She followed the accountant across the hall into the lawyer's office.

"Ah Ms. Cow so good of you to see me." Mr. Cooper was an over-short sleazy lawyer type dressed in a pleaded black suit and had a button on his lapel that said: I SUE. "I think I might have found a legal loophole for you and the organization."

"What for? I thought we'd already agreed to shut down central control and let the left over parts fend for themselves on the open market."

The little accountant shut the door behind them and motioned for Besey to take a seat. She ignored him.

Mr. Cooper had a wicked smile on his face that somehow complemented his hooked nose. He used his hands when he spoke in such a way that if a deaf person watched he or she would become terribly confused. "I've been reading your legal requirements on the Ultimate Gameshow Truce signed last week and I think I may have discovered a way for you to keep H.E.L.L. in business."

"No!" the cow shook her massive head, "I think it's time for a change. These are bold new days for the universe and we must reflect that. Going back to the old oppressive days will only make things worse for all of us in the long run."

Mr. Cooper twitched his upper lip at this unexpected response, "No really, I have found a way for us to get off scott free even without the Bossman's hidden stash of money that he never returned to YIG. All of us, even what's left of poor old Lester in the other room. It will take only a few minutes to outline my diabolical plan."

"I don't know." Besey didn't like this idea. "Why don't you just embezzle your money and then get out of here."

"Just let me explain very shortly. In the terms of agreement it simply says that we can no longer engage in 'Evil' acts but no where does it define what evil is, so all we have to do is redefine what we do. Instead of evil we could engage in non-lawful acts or even malodorous doings. It would be a whole new revolution in the business. All our competitors even HECK (Hollow Earth Crazy Kooks), will be left behind and then when they start with the new definitions we sue for trademark infringement. It will be great."

"That's stupid," Besey turned to leave.

"It's the end of the road for you cow!"

Besey looked back just in time to see Mr. Cooper pull out a laser blast pack and level it at her. She had to think quick; he was ready to blow her away. Out the door was her only chance. She plodded as fast as she could but she wasn't the young bovine she used to be.

Mr. Cooper's first blast somehow missed and shattered the wall to her left, "Quit squirming you festering nonhuman! I can't blast you properly if you don't stand still."

Besey knew it would take too long to open the door with her mouth so she made for a fat cushy chair in the corner, "You don't know what you're doing Cooper. H.E.L.L. is finished and not even a devious lawyer like you can stop it."

"Davey," Cooper called to the skinny accountant, "Hold her down so I can blast her."

Davey dropped his files and hurried out of the room into a side office.

"That's it cow. This is the end of the line for your kind." Cooper came out from behind his desk adjusting the power setting on his blast pack to 'Absolute Mayhem'.

Besey was now trapped. The cushy chair wouldn't protect her for very long even with Cooper's bad aim. This really was the end then. Well she'd done her best and H.E.L.L. was on the way out for good. Proudly she held her head up high, ready to become a martyr for the cause.

"That's it, hold that pose..." Cooper flexed...

But before he could fire the main door came crashing in and splintered apart in every direction. Twin bursts of fusion power cut the air asunder and dissected Cooper where he stood.

Out of the smoke stepped a hopping mad Farmer Brown, "Damn igit!" and he spat at the goo on the ground that use to be the lawyer. "Thet'll teach ya ta mess wit my cow."

"Brown?" Besey was surprised to see her former master. Especially since she'd accidentally left his unconscious body with Mother Maynard to take care of.

"Yeah ets me. Ah didun't no yu couhd speak Besey."

Lester's mind wipe trick with the cahootz back in the spa chamber must have affected Brown as well. "It's only temporary," she came out from behind the chair, "You saved me."

"Well o'course yu igit. Yor my cow. Now com-on ware gettin' outta hear."

For the first time in her short existence Besey knew where her place in the universe was. She wasn't suppose to go galloping around space trying to save the universe and all that. Her place was Browns retirement farm where she could lazily wander the green fields all day, chewing lovely grass, and not care in the world.

"But wait Brown. There is just one more thing I must do before we can return home."

"Now whut, I got thuh pickup duhbel purked outside."

"I need to make a quick stop on Deo 7 and then we can go straight home."

"Ellvus! Now yor givin' mea orhders. Whut'll be next? Ah talkin' chicken?"

Chapter 34: Stupid Writers

Meanwhile on Deo 7 there was a meeting of the minds, so to speak. Messers Gronblec, Shandrydan, Nosehonka, and F. Chicken were discussing the fate of the universe.

Dr. Vadlin Nosehonka had been flow in by mistake to the festivities in a shipment of frozen flounder. What he was doing in the shipping crates in the first place was up to a special galactic task force, set up in the 101000s to catch fishy stowaways, to find out. "I dink dat eet voud be a veddy goot idee-uh iv vee ver awl groond up eento leetle beets ov stard-ust. Vut du yu tink Cheekin'?"

"Well, as you know my thesis published over seventeen and a half aeons ago, outlines in the strictest detail how the universe will succumb to a deadly and vastly overrated quantum fluctuation that will increase in size in proportion to the flux dynamic constant of the symmetrical, yet bilateral, electro-magneto-superweak scalar field density curve. Now as you might have already surmised, the field substructure density is the real key as to a general overview of the temporal displacement that is expected to occur in conjunction to such a final event. But what you may not know is how one little pair production of two unilaterally diverse anti-Muons could cause the calculation to be off by over three orders of magnitude."

Shandrydan scratched his head, "Amazing. What university did you say you graduated from?"

"Well," the chicken thought a moment, "I don't really remember the name of it, it was so long ago. Although I can tell you which universities that have named me to honorary sportsmanlike fellowships at one time or another. There's AAbalthor Manor, Aanacordian State Univers...."

"No," Shandrydan smiled uneasily, "I think that's quite alright."

Gronblec leaned over and whispered to Shandrydan, "If you ask me I think he's quite insane. I think we should hold him down and then pull his mask off to see who he really is."

"Hmmm, you're probably right. But first you must tell me what the Kurvo-Clepenstien constant is."

"That's easy. 401,279.308526 kilogrubbels per second per bowel movement."

"Aha! That may be the actual number but I asked you what it is. You don't know do you?"

Gronblec's face turn red, "You're right I just memorized the value and really don't know what it actually means."

It was then that Sir Rontho came up to them with a fresh margarita in hand, "I say dear fellows is this brain trust a closed convention or am I allowed to chat along."

"No of course not, my Lord," Shandrydan said. He introduced the others and Rontho nodded at each in turn. "What brings you to this far corner of the party?"

"I was just having a rather peculiar conversation with a toilet scrubber and I was wondering if you learned fellows might be able to enlighten me."

"Toilet scrubber you say?" the Funky Chicken looked around trying to spot the urchin. "Was he about this high with an inverted afro?"

"No I mean the device used to clean toilets."

"I'll certainly bring it up if I see him again. It didn't choke me like I expected it to when I first swallowed it."

"But what I was talking about was a certain question that has been dogging me for quite some time," Rontho began, "And it wasn't until gazing upon this toilet scrubber that a thought came to me concerning a new angle on the conundrum that I had not previously considered."

As everyone else slowly tried to back up in preparation to running away Rontho droned on, "It seems that way back in the early 21st century on the planet Earth, also known as Durt, the natives of this planet had discovered a very unusual defect in their society."

"Uh-oh," Gronblec said, "I'm not qualified to discuss scatological matters on the grounds that...." he was cut short by a painful jab in the ribs by Nosehonka.

"As I was saying," Rontho continued, "There was this defect that was discovered. Whenever an eminent disaster loomed that was surely going to demolish existence as they knew it, someone would pop up and say, "Shabamb!" or something equally ignorant and then the problem would go away just in time for the next disaster."

"I think you might be slightly oversimplifying sir."

"No matter. What is really important is what I imagined that this toilet scrubber reminded me of, as I watched a robot clean the scum from around my boot heels just a few minutes ago, which made me remember this defect and caused me to ponder about it. What he said was this: if only I could be as big and important as you gov."

Gronblec shook his head, "I don't get it."

"Well neither do I silly." Rontho pointed at Shandrydan, "Smack him for me Freddie."

Dr. Fred Shandrydan took off his white chef's hat and smacked Gronblec on the head.

But the Funky Chicken was already thinking ahead, "Let me see if I understand you properly here, Rontho."

"Please, call me Sir."

"Okay I guess I can look up your number from the Deo 7 disaster survivor's directory. Anyway there is a group of people who go around saying 'Shalsbots' and then grovel at your boot? Is that correct?"

"You didn't say 'sir'."

"I most certain did say something."

"But not 'sir'."

"But not what?"

"That ex Space Marine has been rubbing off on you hasn't he? I just read his autobiography. Just fascinating."

"Sorry about that. I thought you were asking me to sir the pot, so to speak. I'll try to dial down the punny sarcasm level in my rudeness persona and up the intellectual bragging output."

"Quite alright but you forgot again."

"Sir! Do you want me to grovel at your boots?"

"Yes I think you have the gist of it."

"This is stupid," Gronblec threw down his golfing hat and stormed off to irritate Rogicphil, if he could find him.

"Well then," FC continued, "I might have a little story that could enlighten you."

"Do tell?"

Nosehonka clapped his hands together, "Ooo yes a nice leetle tail to vurm up ovur blue-ud."

"It begins a couple of billions of years ago in a little know part of the universe were the first resort spa was invented and where there lived a race of creatures known as the Perriforks. Now the Perriforks weren't the actual inventors of the resort spa but they were the first to utilize the commercial potential of them. They weren't exactly resort managers either, they just liked to charged people admission to come and admire how nice the resorts looked. But I digest..." and he belched a bit before continuing, "Anyway to make a short story long..."

"No," Rontho stopped him, "This is quite important I assure you. Make it the reeeeeally looooong version if you will."

"Very well. First Gordosplatbin twisted his lower left right grappling appendage over to get the crick out of his third elbow..."

"Um maybe not quite so detailed. Only the important parts please."

"Hmmm, okay. Let me try again. Now where was I, oh yes, the Perriforks. You see in order for the Spas to be profitable they had to be located on planets with relatively high gravities but with the advent of artificial gravity the entire industry was at grave ends to stay in business. Why would some Dorfnian Pirate waste his time coming to your resort spa because of it's high gravity when he could just turn up the gravity in his pirate space ship?"

"I don't know."

"There is no answer because that's exactly what happened. Everyone used their own form of gravity to create the exact right balance of gravity for their own workout and the Perriforks descendants soon became extinct. In the next reincarnation less than 700 million years ago the great Spa Empires of the Fourth Age were flourishing in the Tamale region of the universe. But this time when artificial gravity was invented they acted."

"Vut did dey doo?"

"They created a powerful consortium of thieves and liars to inflict limitations upon the artificial gravity industry effectively giving the great Spa Empires a monopoly in the workout economy."

Rontho was dumbfounded, "Yes I think I see where you're going with this."

"Then may whomever you worship as a deity have mercy upon your soul."

Shandrydan was skeptical but kept his mouth shut.

"But please, let me finish my story. And then we may begin deliberating upon the vices and merits of the inherent wisdom herein contained.

"After a while of increased profits a few of the Spa Giants began to notice that no matter how much they tried to diversify, all they were able to do was Spa Resorts. It didn't make any sense. Here were, arguably, the most powerful organizations in the universe and yet they were seeming locked into one path, which they could not extrude themselves no matter how they tried."

"What," Shandrydan wanted to know, "Does this have to do with Rontho's toilet scrubber or even the 21st Century 'Shabam' defect?"

"Everything. Let me give you an example. What made you ask that question when you did?"

"What do you mean? I was listening to your argument and didn't see any relevance between your premises and conclusions."

"Ah but couldn't you have just as easily said, 'Shabam' and ended this conversation for once and for all?"

"Of course not," stammered Shandrydan, "I don't buy in to that riggamaro."

"Let me try, Mr. Chicken," Sir Rontho began to whistle and pretended to admire the sparkles on the ceiling and then all of a sudden got right into Shandrydan's face and shouted, "Say 'no'!"

"No!"

"You see! It is hopeless and we're all doomed!"

The chicken shrugged, "Well let's see. What do you think Shandrydan?"

"I'm beginning to agree with Gronblec. I think you all have lost your minds. By the way, I run a psychiatric clinic on the side and would love to study..."

"Yes but that is besides the point," FC explained, "What Sir Rontho was trying to say in his round-about way is that he's afraid the universe is doomed to determinism."

"Huh?"

Nosehonka explained, "Yu see dey hev been dees-crybing exemples uv plooted behavur."

"Translation?"

Sir Rontho lit up stately cigarillo and puffed away as if in, an ill fated attempt to ward off maxwell's demons.

"Well?"

The Funky Chicken handed Shandrydan a pocket calculator he found in his pocket, "Do the math."

Unsure what to do Shandrydan took the device, "This is made out of stone."

"Uh then that would mean it fossilized in my pocket. No matter, do this calculation in your head: 517-18."

"499 that's easy."

"Now what was the question?"

"Um well..."

"It could have been any number of questions couldn't it. Each one with the same answer, 499. What does that say about the structure of the universe?"

"That it isn't dependent on time congruity? The initial conditions are as important as we were led to believe? The toads fart in the forest because they want butterflies to spout horns in the arctic? This is going nowhere incredibly slowly."

"Exactly. So how do you explain SHALSBOTS?"

"So what exactly are you saying?"

"Well I can't say it out loud," FC looked around, in futility, to see if he was being watched, then leaned over and whispered in Shandrydan's ear.

"What!?" Shandrydan yelled, "I am not a character in some stupid story. I am a free man."

Rontho glowered, "Now you've gone and done it. The writer's going to smite you for that."

Shandrydan laughed, "How ridiculous."

"Then explain why you became so skeptical after Gronblec left. The story required a scapegoat for us to rag on as we explained our ideas. If Gronblec was still here you would be agreeing with us while we derided him."

"That's besides the point. Gronblec is a young upstart. I would be duty bound to side with my peers against him."

"You see?" Rontho chided, "You have no free will. We are all victims of the great Writer in the SKY!"

"You expect me to believe if I say something like, 'the Writer is a pig-faced, two toned, water buffalo' the ground is going to open up underneath me and suck me down?"

The chicken thought a moment, "You bet."

"What a load of..." but before he could finish his sentence there was a violent explosion outside the complex which caused the floor the shake uncontrollably and indeed, a crack did open up under Shandrydan, and although he wasn't sucked in, his foot did get stuck there for a few seconds.

"I tried to warn him." Rontho continued to stand with his arms crossed and cigarillo in his mouth.

"Just a coincidence. That was simply caused by rebel forces moving in on us from outside. It has nothing to do with this demi-pagan worship miasma you propose."

"Well...." FC twisted his ankle a bit, "I guess you're right. We were just deliberately wasting your time."

Rontho was concerned, "What are you saying Mr. Chicken? Are you going to ignore the facts and disbelieve what you know in your heart to be true?"

"Sure. In fact, I propose we all begin a chant to denounce this Writer fellow and see if he really exists or not."

"Ah," Shandrydan bounced back, "If there really is a Writer controlling every aspect of our lives then he or she must exist in another world that is just as deterministic and he..."

"Or she."

"Or she..."

"Don't forget it."

"He, she, it, whatever...this THING would also have to be controlled by an outside writer, so on and so on, forever, infinitum redicularius."

"Would you read a book that began: A writer wrote that a writer wrote that blah blah blah. I wouldn't, because there would be no story, just nested redundancy."

"I could imagine a society were redundancy would be a highly prized

338

commodity and the book would be a big seller."

By this point the shouting of the group was attracting attention from elsewhere in the ballroom and Dr. Gronblec, who had been unsuccessful in his carousing attempts, decided to make a come back in the conversation.
"What if it really isn't the writers who are to be feared," he said, "But the Editors instead?"

"Good point," FC said, "Perhaps the all powerful editors can find a way to kill me off once and for all. I sure wish someone would do me the favor."

Shandrydan, not about to be overshadowed by his younger colleague, spoke up, "Not if you are a big profit potential. They can kill you off and bring you back at any time just to make a buck."

"You're right. I should try to think of a way to make myself unappealing to the widest variety of reader."

"The reader?" Rontho retorted, "We have completely ignored this powerful division of the eternal ultimate reality. What do they want? Can they effect us? And to what degree?"

"Anyone up for a round of bowling?" And they all quickly wandered off to find a makeshift bowling alley while Rontho was left to ponder his navel.

Chapter 35: The Rebellion

Rogicphil was grudgingly making plans for a big barbeque cookout to be held the following night. All his attempts at 'whipping the others into a frenzy' had been unsuccessful. After all the excitement of the past few weeks no one was interested in childish pranks. In fact most of them simply wanted to go home, back to their own places in time, and forget the unpleasant parts.

Rogicphil couldn't agree more, but the truth was things weren't over yet, not as long as things here on Deo 7 were falling apart. It would have been one thing to let this rothole of a planet sink into its own waste but another if he was responsible, even in some small way, for the current situation.

Where was that Space-Bo at? He was suppose to have an update on the brewing hostilities outside. Rogicphil looked around the room but couldn't see him anywhere. Well back to the menu.

For the third entree he had a choice of filleted baderpak or sautéed logeater pustules. Deo 7 delicacies left much to be desired. Whatever happened to barbecued synth-ribs and marshed potatoes? He rubbed his jaw and the thought of having his teeth replaced again, gave him pause to reconsider.

There was a slight commotion at the far end of the reception area and something made Rogicphil look up to see what was up. Good, it was Space-Bo. Maybe he had that report.

Space-Bo was screaming and squirming all around but it was unclear what he was upset about. He broke free from a small batch of socialites and made a run for it, but Rogicphil zipped over in front of the exit before Space-Bo even knew he was there.

Bam! Space-Bo recoiled, "I hate it when you do that. Appearing out of no where."

"What's going on 'Bo?"

He grabbed at Rogicphil's shirt in desperation, "You gotta help me 'Phil. Please, put me out of my misery. I can't keep it up much longer."

"I don't un...." he stopped short when a figure appeared from out of the crowd behind Space-Bo, "Um I believe it's for you."

Space-Bo slowly turned his head to see and then cringe. He made one last plea under his breath, "Pleeeese."

Rogicphil laughed and shoved Space-Bo off him, "Here you go Annie."

Yes it was the dreaded chorus line girl with whom Space-Bo had become haplessly involved with, "Why did you run away like that? I only wanted to talk to you."

"Umm, uh, well I was uh, here with Rogicphil, and um planning a, uh, um..."

Rogicphil knew it would be too cruel to let his friend suffer and so spoke up, "He was just about to give me an important military update."

Space-Bo turned white, "NO! That's not ready yet. I was actually going to discuss the flower arrangements and menu with him."

Rogicphil thought this a bit strange but went along with it anyway,

"Yes, well the Military report will have to wait until these other, more important matters can be taken care of."

Annie wrinkled her nose, "That sounds real boring to me. If you guys change your mind and want that Military update just ask."

"That will be just fine," Space-Bo tried to shoo her away.

"Did you say you have an update?" That information really was important to Rogicphil.

"Yeah," Annie turned to leave, "But I'm sure it's not as exciting as flower arrangements."

Space-Bo stopped Rogicphil from going after her, "Don't do it. It's not worth it."

"What the heck is going on with you 'Bo? There's a really tall girl that likes you a lot and you're trying to run away from her."

"She's too wild for me 'Phil. I can't explain it. And she talks about the future too much. She wants to make plans and things."

Rogicphil laughed, "Oh I see now. You're trapped in the spider's web and want to get out before it's too late."

"Exactly," Space-Bo led Rogicphil out the exit doors and into an unfinished corridor beyond. He breathed deeply and then slumped down on the floor to lay back against the plain wall.

Rogicphil yawned. He wished he could just take a nap and be done with all this crap. "So about that report."

"Eh?" Space-Bo looked up, "I don't have the foggiest idea."

"Well let's go find out then," Rogicphil hauled his friend up and led him down the corridor.

They followed the hallway to a quickvader which accepted their security clearances and allowed them to enter. Rogicphil hit the up button and they were on their way.

"Why can't you just send me home?" Space-Bo wanted to know.

"Because our mission isn't over yet."

"Sure it is. I don't consider a cookout to be part of a mission to save the universe."

"What do you want me to do? I'm just following my orders."

"I wouldn't listen to that Destiny if I was you."

"Why not?"

"Well during the brief time that I had his power, I couldn't figure out what to do with it. And when I finally thought of something I had lost the power and ended up looking like a dork in a blue robe."

"But you were dork in a blue robe."

"Yeah but it was amusing. Anyway all I'm saying is this whole deal sucks and I want out. And it just isn't Annie either."

"So what do you want to do then?"

"That's easy..."

mmmmmmmmmmmmmmmWWWWWWWWWW WWOOOOOOOOOOOOOOOOOOOOOOOMMM! The power instantly cut off and their quickvader jerked to a halt. They were thrown into an eerie darkness.

Somewhere down below a series of explosions began. The quickvader rattled a bit but didn't come apart.

"Damn!" Rogicphil cursed.

"Stand back. I'll bust the door down."

"Uuuf!" Rogicphil groaned, "That was me you rammed into."

"I said to stand back."

"I did. You're facing the wrong way."

"Oh." He tried again. WHAM! "Ouch." WHAM! "Ouch."

"Hold it. Let's use our brains here."

"You're right." This time Space-Bo rammed his head into the door which promptly crunched open under his force. He continued on out the door and into the empty shaft beyond. "Thanks...." his voice echoed as he fell down into the blackness.

"Roller skates made out of model ground cars!" Rogicphil said with a brilliant bit of insight. His Gladerunner boots transformed into miniature taxicabs complete with headlights. He willed the lights on and then rolled over the edge after Space-Bo.

With the headlights on he could at least see where he was falling to. The quickvader shaft wasn't very impressive as far as aesthetic qualities were concerned, but it was intact, and Rogicphil could see no signs of damage or what had caused the explosions.

He had almost fell to very bottom before he realized that taxicabs, no matter how useful as lights, couldn't prevent him from smashing into floor.

"Springboots!" he cried, "No wait a second..." but it was too late. The taxicab lights went out as the springboots came into being and then rebounded him back up the shaft at high speed.

"Damn," not only was he blind again but going in the wrong direction. With a sigh he commanded the boots to transform again, this time into grapple boots that clamped down onto the side of the shaft just before gravity began to pull him back.

Now how to get down. Aha, personal railroad companions. Instantly the grapple boots became a pair of special shoes originally meant for railway bums. The personal railroad companions were basically roller blades with metal wheels meant for travel along railroad lines. They were made with hydraulic brakes which now came in handy for Rogicphil as he tried to slow his descent.

Finally at the bottom again, but at a more reasonable speed, Rogicphil jumped off the girders. With taxicabs back into action he found where Space-Bo had crashed through the doors with his head again, but no sign of Space-Bo.

"Hey, anybody there?" Rogicphil called out as he rolled through the doors into a dusty tiled lobby. His headlight beams played along the far walls. Nothing. It seemed he was in the very bottom level of the complex, an unused area by the look of it. The reception and the others were many levels overhead now.

The floor was covered in a thin layer of dust. Rogicphil bent down to get a closer look. There were footprints leading out of the quickvader. It had to be Space-Bo. But why only the right foot? There was no sign of any left footprints. Probably just Space-Bo goofing around.

The single trail of right footprints led across the floor straight into the far wall. Rogicphil noticed a large impression on the wall above where the footprints stopped. Space-Bo's face. But then nothing. No more footprints, left or right in any direction.

"Space-Bo?"

No answer.

Rogicphil was about to turn around and go back when something grabbed him by the collar and yanked him up into the ceiling. A powerful hand clamped tight over his mouth.

"The lights. Out!" A voice whispered.

Rogicphil complied.

"The compound has been infiltrated and its up to us to save the day." It was Space-Bo alright.

Rogicphil peeled the hand off his face and whispered, "You must have hit your head pretty hard. We're in the deepest level of the complex, the last place the invaders would be."

"Exactly. That's why they chose to start their invasion here."

"We need to get..."

Space-Bo silenced him again, "Look."

Rogicphil blinked his eyes. The only thing he could see was darkness. But then again he did hear something. Footsteps. "I hear them."

"Here," Space-Bo handed him a smell-o-scope.

Rogicphil aimed the device down into the lobby below. There were four invaders wearing IR vision helmets scanning the floor where a very curious set of tracks lay. Each invader was identified by two bright spots, one higher than the other.

"Are they on their sides?" he asked.

"No," Space-Bo whispered back, "Its not their armpits you see, Deo takes care of that. It's their bad breath and smelly butts you're looking, er smelling at."

"No thanks," he handed the disturbing device back to Space-Bo, "I'll deal with them in my own way." He readied himself, then leapt down from the ceiling to where he remembered the closest one to be, "AAAAh!"

"Don't yell!" Space-Bo shouted, "They'll know we're here."

"Too late creep!" an invader said directly below him and just before he opened up with a Teshtighine Ultragun.

Space-Bo scurried backwards on his hands and butt back along the rafters until he slipped and fell down into another room.

Rogicphil had landed accurately on his target and had him knocked out before the others knew what had happened. He scooped up the dropped gun and using his ultra speed, carefully unloaded the gun and peppered the room with bullets, not fired, but lobbed by hand in a swath of minor inconvenience all around him. When he heard three thuds he stopped.

"Okay 'Bo. You can come down now."

Nothing.

Rogicphil shook his head as he reactivated his headlights. Three invaders lay, with bruised egos, on the floor about him. He quickly had them tied up with some dusty old scarves he found in a box in the corner.

He grabbed up the remaining invader and dragged him over to the wall, "Oh Space-Bo! Come out, come out, where ever you are."

SMASH! The wall next to his head split apart and the ex-Space Marine came crashing through from the other room. He screamed and slashed wildly with his trenching dagger.

See the picture of Space-Bo at the beginning of the book.

"Hey! I already took care of them."

Space-Bo stopped and looked around, "Oh, okay. Good work." He saw the unconscious invader in Rogicphil's clutches, "Lookout!"

Rogicphil quickly spun his friend around to divert the sudden attack. Space-Bo ended up attacking another wall instead.

"Slow down okay. We don't want to kill them as we need them for questioning."

"Aha!" Space-Bo said as he dislodged himself from the wall.

They tied the fourth invader up with some yarn from Space-Bo's pocket as the room was out of scarves and set him against the wall. Rogicphil took off one boot and shined the headlights in his face.

"Who are you?" Rogicphil asked.

"What's your favorite pudding?" Space-Bo asked.

The invader slowly came to and blinked in the bright light, "Huh?"

"Let me ask the questions 'Bo."

"Vanilla," the invader said.

Space-Bo poked Rogicphil, "You see, he answered my question."

"But what good does that do us?"

"War reparations."

"Yeah," the invader agreed, "As a prisoner of war I demand vanilla pudding."

Rogicphil sighed, "This is ridiculous. No pudding, no reparations, no nothing. I just want some simple answers. What are you up to?"

"I'm trying to interrogate the prisoner."

"Not you. Him."

The prisoner looked a bit disgusted, "I won't stand to be treated like this. I have rights you know."

Rogicphil was just about to give in but that's what he'd been doing all along. Exert his opinion then let others do what they wanted. And look where it had gotten him. He was a leader who had no control over his troops but who got all the blame. This was total crap, he knew it, and wasn't about to let others control him. "Space-Bo I want you to snoop out other invaders while I finish with this one here."

"Hmm, okay." Space-Bo nodded then ran off with his smell-o-scope leading the way.

Rogicphil turned back to the invader, "Okay now listen you. I'm not going to mess around now. You don't want to tell me anything and that's fine. I'll just leave you here to the rats."

"Rats?" he looked around, "I don't see any rats."

"No...but you can hear them." Rogicphil made little scurrying sounds off to the right, "And I don't think they're interested in vanilla pudding. I think they want to eat you." He snapped his hand to the invaders arm and pinched it quicker than anyone could see to simulate a rat bite.

344

"Okay, okay...I'll talk if you keep the rats away."

"I'll try. I can't keep them away for long so you'd better talk fast."

"Our job is to scout out the hole before the rest of the troops arrive."

"What hole?"

"The blast hole. We tunneled under the complex and are going to invade from underneath while a different division, above ground, bombs the crap out of the top of the complex."

"Thank you very much," Rogicphil whacked the guy on the side of his head, to knock him out but instead it exploded into a spray of bloody goop.

Readers of the mass market paperback version should ignore that previous disgusting display of writing. Readers of the more upscale hardback edition should carry on as if nothing had happened since a cleaned up version is printed there and this editor's note only appears in the cheaper (and cruder) paperback version.

Space-Bo came up behind the shaken Rogicphil and pulled him back, "Exploding head armor. It's suppose to counteract exploding shrapnel. I guess they haven't worked out all the bugs yet."

"We need to get out of here," Rogicphil said coming to his senses.

"I know, there's about ten thousand invaders coming up a tunnel behind us." Space-Bo led them to a stairwell that went upwards.

Rogicphil found it awkward to climb stairs with taxicabs on his feet but he could hear the sounds of invaders behind them, "How well can you see walls with that smell-o-vision thing?"

Space-Bo tried it. "These walls are pretty smelly. I think I can guide us."

"Good," in one swift motion Rogicphil grabbed Space-Bo and then converted his footwear into helicopter boots, "Don't let us smack into anything." He launched up the dark stairwell holding his guide out in front so that if they did smack into anything it would be Space-Bo who would cushion the impact.

"Left!"

Rogicphil swooshed left.

"Right just a little bit, now full power."

Rogicphil willed maximum thrust and they shot up the narrow airspace that the stairs spiraled around. A few stray shots from the invaders below choked on all the dust thrown up in his blade's wash and completely missed them.

"Okay stop!" Space-Bo cried just before they reached the top of the stairwell.

But Rogicphil couldn't exactly stop on a dime so they went crashing into the ceiling, Space-Bo leading the way. They came to a halt amid some concrete rubble that used to be a kitchen area.

There was enough light shinning through the cracks to allow them to see without either Rogicphil's taxicabs nor Space-Bo's Smell-O-Scope. The cracks did more than let the light in. Deo smell infiltrated down too.

Rogicphil set his friend down and took a deep breath, "Gasp! That hideous smell again. That means the surface force has broken through. I tried to warn Destiny."

Space-Bo already had a gas-mask on, "I don't smell anything."

"Do you have another one of those?"

"I'll see," he picked through the various pockets and pouches on his uniform/spacesuit but only came up with a clown hat.

"Never mind. We need to find a way through this rubble up to the main ballroom. Destiny should have rallied the troops there and already have a plan in mind."

He and Space-Bo began picking through the rubble in search of something that might help them. Space-Bo found a giant titanium pot.

Rogicphil thought about that for a moment, "Okay put that thing over your head and hold on."

"Huh?" he asked but did as he was told.

Again Rogicphil picked him up and prepared the helicopter boots, changed his mind and made them into rocket boots (an inadvertent clause in the Gladerunner contract allowed rocket boots once a month but never through deep space or at high velocity). But this time he used Space-Bo and the pot as a bore to drill up through the wreckage. The going was slow at first but as more concrete and rebar fell in on them from above, they eventually made head way.

Space-Bo was smashing around wildly inside his metal pot from the destruction falling away on all sides. At last they broke free into open air. He threw down the pot and stumbled around trying to regain his sight as nothing would stay still long enough for him to figure out what it was.

Rogicphil was more fortunate. He laughed to himself watching the former Space Marine wander around and smack into things but the view above them quickly dissolved any illusion of happiness. The walls of the complex continued up hundreds of meters into the air but where the ceiling and various levels were suppose to have been, nothing.

Space-Bo managed to undo the dizziness he had and looked around.

It was like a giant hand had reached down out of the sky and ripped out the heart of the complex, floors, quickvaders, and people included. Only rubble was left piled up several levels over their heads and a small impression in the middle where they stood.

"I wonder if..." but no words came to Rogicphil then. He was simply left with emptiness.

Space-Bo noticed something moving a slight ways up a rubble pile. He rushed up to begin digging and Rogicphil joined in. The movement turned into a hand and the hand turned into an arm which became a dusty person.

They shoved the excess junk aside and hauled the body out. It was Sir Rontho. "Well," he hrumpted, "It's about time. I've been waiting under there for close to twenty minutes. And now I've gone and ruined my good body. I know I should have used my formal swampgator body tonight."

"Can you tell us what happened?" Rogicphil asked.

Rontho brushed the dust from himself and tried to stand up but was too weak and fell back down, "Well what can I say? One minute we were discussing the unlikelihood of an angry all powerful creator and the next we were buried in this."

"Did you see what happened to anyone else," Space-Bo asked him, "Annie?"

"No," Rontho grimaced and looked down at his triple breasted suit. A bit of blood was oozing up from under the lapels, "Oh damn, this was my only clean Bersase."

Rogicphil took Space-Bo's gas-mask off and put it on himself.

"Hey! What am I supposed to wear?"

Rogicphil flipped the integrated helmet of Space-Bo's spacesuit over Space-Bo's head and locked it into place.

"Oh yeah, I keep forgetting about that. Thanks."

Rogicphil looked around, "Stay here with him 'Bo. I'm going to look for other survivors." He made helicopter boots and zoomed off in a whoosh of deo laced air.

There wouldn't be much time before the invaders marched up from below or ground forces swarmed in over the walls. This whole thing was total garbage now. At least before there were options. Now there were none. He was done with this whole mission business. The people of Deo 7 had spoken and he was willing to let them do whatever they wanted with their own planet.

The next survivor found him instead. A flashy aircar lighted down in front of him. The window rolled down and a very happy Grego the Mean poked his head out, "You! Gladerunner."

Rogicphil zoomed up beside the aircar. "Have you found any survivors?" he asked.

"You and Idiot-Boy down there. I suggest you hop in before the angry mob finds you."

"We need to see if we can find any more survivors."

"There are none. I saw most of them die myself. This is your last chance."

Rogicphil called down to Space-Bo to haul Rontho up with him. He said to Grego, "Can you take Rontho and Space-Bo with you? I'll stay behind and look for others."

Grego just pointed.

Rogicphil turned around and Space-Bo stepped up to him alone. "He's dead," 'Bo said, "Just bled to death."

"Get in with Grego. I'll meet up with you two later."

Space-Bo shook his head, "He tried to kill me before. And then I stole all his money. Why should I go with him?"

Grego laughed, "And you also reminded me how to be really mean again. For that I am grateful." He inadvertently neglected to mention the fact that he believed it was impossible to kill Space-Bo.

Space-Bo shrugged, "Okay," and hopped on to the aircar's landing skid. "Rogicphil?"

"Yes."

He didn't say anything but was understood just the same. He waved as the aircar blasted away from Rogicphil and up through the hole into the sky.

*   *   *

"Kill me," a survivor said.

Rogicphil tried to blank the horror out of his mind. But the shredded body before him refused to dissolve away quietly. He did the best he could to bandage the wounds. Even at lightning speed the first aid could do little to save the life.

It was Ami, one of the chorus line girls from 2027. Rogicphil didn't have to heart to fulfill her last request no matter how much pain it would have stopped. Thankfully she fell unconscious from shock before she died.

What would this mean for her timeline? And how would that effect this future? He remembered writing ludicrous stories for his old Roganivar IV newspaper about just such events purported to be undertaken by the government. But now it might really be true, not just fodder for the masses, but real for him too.

He stood up and looked around the burnt out, rubble filled building once more. The first scouts had already poked their heads over the crumbling wall but he'd drove them off with a couple of well placed speedball rocks. They were sure to return before too long and with reinforcements.

So far he'd found three bodies including Ami since Sir Rontho bit it. Who knew how many others would still be choking for their last breaths right now, just meters away. He wasn't sure he wanted to look for them if they would all just die right in front of him.

Without really deciding, his body continued its search. But he knew it was ridiculous. There had to be a better way. He remembered the strange tactic he'd used against that powerful robot back in his training days, the Twister.

He willed spiked lava boots onto his feet. The boots were basically super strong cones attached to the soles of standard high temperature work boots. Rogicphil then began to spin around very rapidly until his boots started to act as drills and slowly sank into the crushed rubble.

As he descended, quick movements with his arms packed debris into the cracks and crevices of the newly formed tunnel, which kept the whole thing from caving in on top of him.

He figured that since most of the bodies near the surface were already pulverized by collapsing floors and such, perhaps smaller pockets of stable space were farther below where survivors might still be alive.

His gamble paid off when he came to a level where the combination of a marble column resting against a wall and a giant titanium food platter protected three huddled figures.

"We're saved!" Dr. Fred Shandrydan gasped as Rogicphil's tunnel brought them fresh air. The two other survivors were Ellen and Penny, two more chorus line girls.

"What happened?" Rogicphil asked, "Do you know of any more survivors?"

"No, I was lucky," Shandrydan said. "I was under a food serving table when the ceiling collapsed."

Rogicphil was curious as to what he was doing under that table in the first place and why were two girls with him at the time. But that wasn't important at the moment. "Outside forces from Deo 7 are storming the area now. I've got to find a way to get you off-world and fast, before things get any worse."

"Fine by us."

Time was the critical factor now. Rogicphil could stay behind a bit longer searching for others but he'd never be able to get them out before the place was overwhelmed by soldiers. He didn't even know if he could get these three out right now.

He tunneled down some more until he broke through to an undamaged corridor with working emergency lights. Quickly he ferried down the three survivors, one by one, with his helicopter boots.

There weren't any signs of invaders there and so he led them in what he hoped would be the opposite direction. The hall ended in a sealed blast door.

"You're the genius," Rogicphil said to the doc, "Break the security and get us inside."

"Yes in the realm of theoretical physics and applied chemo-quantum compounds but I don't know anything about doors."

"Hmm, then it's going to have to be the hard way them." He tried to imagine a pair of shoes especially made for armless lock picks but somehow his Gladeboots couldn't manage that trick.

There was the vague tromping of boots from a ways down the hall behind them. The invaders had found Rogicphil's handmade rubble tunnel and were closing fast.

Rogicphil pounded on the door, "Why won't you open!?"

"Because you didn't say the magic word."

"Huh?" He looked at his survivors. None of them had said anything. "Who said that?"

"Me silly." the voice seemed to be coming from the door itself.

"Who's behind the door? Let us in quick."

"Not until you tell me the secret word."

"I thought you said I was suppose to tell you the magic word. Make up your mind."

"Very well," the door slid back with a hiss and let them in. They hurried through and then the thing slid back into place in the wall. It shut just as the first invader stepped around the corner on the far side.

The Funky Chicken greeted them, "Welcome to the afterlife."

"We're not dead yet stupid."

"I am. I've died a thousand googol times. This is as much of an afterlife as I'm going to get."

Rogicphil was glad to see his friend who was probably the only one who enjoyed the explosion and cave-in. "What are you doing down here and not up there getting blown away in laser crossfire?"

"Alas it just was not meant to be I suppose. Right now I'm attempting to build a transmat pad that can get us off this dreadfully wonderful little world."

"Transmat?" Shandrydan perked up, "Why didn't you say so in the first place? I was just thinking of a method to transmit agricultural byproducts through radio waves."

"I'm a bit father along than that I'm afraid," the chicken led them around a corner into a laboratory of sorts, "This use to be a toy warehouse until I found it."

In the center of the room, surrounded by empty packing crates, was a maze of wires and plastic pieces hobbled together with string and duck tape. The really strange thing was that it seemed to be alive. Every few seconds it would heave a bit and some smoke would puff out or a nasty yellow fluid would spill from a hose onto the concrete floor.

"What do you think? It's not much to look at but it's almost working. I've managed to transport a ton and a half of olives to where, I don't know, and I haven't been able to retrieve anything yet or figure out the stability of the coordinate matrix."

"So what you're saying," Shandrydan picked up, "is that you have no idea where this thing is sending things or even if its sending things at all and not just vaporizing the material?" He bent down and scooped up a handful of olives.

"Yeah that's right," the chicken nodded, "If it were just me I could care less but I need to be more careful when lifespan challenged friends are around."

"Good work FC," Rogicphil said, suddenly relieved that there was a bit of hope left. He quickly filled the chicken in on what he knew of the attack, the survivors he knew about and the dead he had found.

The chicken looked grave at what he heard, "Typical. I should have guessed as much."

"When we get out of this, Destiny is going to have some explaining to do. That reminds me. Where the heck is that supreme being anyway? His barbeque cookout is in ruins now. What's he got left to celebrate?"

"Bad news 'Phil. Just before my skull was crushed in by a massive chandelier I saw the big D open a dimension door and slip out. He scampered off and left everyone to die it seemed."

"That bastard! We should put Space-Bo back in charge. At lease he never copped out."

Shandrydan was busy munching away on the olives, "These are quite good actually. Too bad they contain a resin which could help this machine work more effectively."

"Help the chicken with the transmat machine Fred. I think this is going to be our only way out. I'm declaring this mission a utter failure and sounding a complete retreat."

"But," Fred said, "We won, we defeated the satanic cow."

"Yeah so what? The cow never had anything to do with it to begin with. I don't know how, but I've got this sneaking suspicion we've all been set up from the very beginning."

"Just another day in the afterlife," the chicken interjected. "So what's your plan?"

"I don't have one really. Just get out as many people as quickly as possible. Your transmat will help."

"If we can figure out where it goes and if that place is someplace better than here. It wouldn't make much sense if the other side turned out to be Splas Toorg."

"The planet of nuclear waste disposal? Yeah I've heard of it."

"Neat place for a field trip but I wouldn't want to live there. The amazing mutated lifeforms that live there are really incredible. You should see them someday."

"I'll remember that. But first let's work on the transmat machine."

*   *   *

It was an awkward situation. Space-Bo shifted uneasily in his seat as the aircar cruised along close to the charred earth. They were heading northwest away from Balidron over the mostly barren continent of Repuscrap.

"A class science experiment gone awry turned this once lush plain into the wasteland you now see below us," the aircar's driver was saying.

Mmm, Space-Bo thought, it reminded him of his backyard as a kid.

"Don't worry," Grego laughed with a wink and an elbow nudge, "I won't try to kill you again. I learned my lesson on that one. Ha!"

Space-Bo certainly hoped so. It was hard enough to keep a straight face without having to dodge every knife or exploding fruit cocktail that came his way. He had to find a way to let Grego save face without laughing so much. "That's nice," he said at last.

"But that doesn't mean I forgive you for stealing all my money."

Ut-Oh. Better change the subject. "Um a class project you say?"

Grego looked out his window, "Yes, very unfortunate. A high school chemistry class was doing a chapter on the various uses of industrial strength bleach and well... this is what happened." He motioned with his hand before him.

"Cool. But aren't there rules for things like that?"

"Oh yes, a good friend of mine, former friend I might add, created the legislation that led to this disaster."

"What happened?"

"I killed him in cold blood. Drowned actually, in his own blood. So I guess you could say I killed him in warm blood."

"No, I mean the disaster."

"Oh, well my former associate had many friends in the bleach industry and as he was on a committee which, among other things, involved the education system. Melton thought- that was his name, Melton. He thought, what better way to unload a huge wad of cash onto his business friends if he created a new school mandate that required all schools to purchase fifty kilotons of bleach per year per school. And the rest is history."

"A similar thing happened on my planet not too long ago. Well, actually tens of thousands of years ago, but anyway what happened was the Minister of Roy, that's our capital city, decided to import all of Mars' bean crop from the previous year."

"I don't see how that relates."

"It doesn't. What you just said happened to reminded me of it, that's all."

On the horizon, the ocean came into view and Grego guided the aircar passed a cliff and out over the green tinted water. A hard right bank brought them around and back towards the shore. Fifty meters high, the cliff loomed up suddenly, but the aircar swerved at the last moment to take a parallel course.

Grego snickered when Space-Bo didn't seem to notice that they'd almost crashed, "Our destination is just ahead."

"That's good I was getting kind of bored."

"Bored?" Grego seemed incredulous, "After all I've hinted at? After all the insidious intimations I've made?"

"Uh, yeah."

"Aren't you just dying to know the meanings behind my cryptic statements?"

"Like what?" Space-Bo wasn't following this line of questioning.

"Like what, he says, as if the fate of the entire universe is as a Saturday morning cartoon show..."

"You get cartoons here?" He checked his watch, "What day is it anyway."

"You're no fun at all." Grego made some adjustments to the controls. "What I've been getting at, in my annoying way, is the Deo 7 nexus point."

"That thing again?"

"Again? But I've never mentioned the word before..."

Space-Bo just shrugged and Grego prepared for landing.

The aircar landed at a point on the beach near to where the entire cliff face had collapsed and dumped rubble out into the sea. A minor peninsula now extended half a kilometer out from the normal shoreline.

"This use to be Rendyle. A booming coastal metrocenter until it grew too large for itself and fell into the ocean."

"Cool. Let's go check it out."

"I was planning on doing this myself but I don't see anyway of keeping you here so you're unwelcome to accompany me."

"Okay, great," Space-Bo hopped out and immediately began climbing up the steep embankment, "This is much better than your old war stories."

"You're going the wrong the way," Grego said hastily following behind, "There is a secret passage that will take us were I want to go. Come on down now, I don't have time to waste with you."

"Cool..." Space-Bo was taking in the panoramic ocean view.

Grego joined him with a frown on his face. It was a quiet moment they shared before the Mean Man snickered to himself. "What a great pay-per-view this would be."

"Let's find that secret passage," said Space-Bo and scurried down a steep embankment that use to be an amphitheatre.

"Not that way you imbecile," Grego called after him infuriated. He unholstered a tight beam personal lasing device (i.e. laser gun) and took aim at the ex-Space Marine's back. Before he could get off a shot the ground under his feet gave way and he disappeared into the darkness. "Damn probability vectors!"

"Huh?" Space-Bo stopped and turned around, "Did you say something?" But nobody was there. No Grego either. Maybe he'd disappeared into a cloud of ionized gas. Nah, that would ruin all the fun.

He climbed back up to where they'd been standing and found the newly formed pit. "Hey, you down there?"

"No," came the distant reply.

"Okay, tell me when you are then."

"Get back over here you. This is the secret entrance I was telling you about. Now if you want to know the Big Secret get your seething carcass down here."

"Well, okay..." Space-Bo adjusted an air nozzle on his suit then stepped off the edge.

The drop turned into a sloping tube greased up with glowing slime. A few seconds later he plopped down on the floor of a dank smelling chamber. Grego was at the far wall contemplating what looked like a rusted door.

"How come you're not covered in slime?" Space-Bo asked.

Grego answered without looking up, "Trade secret. Ah-ha, there we go." The doorknob gave way under his powerful mean grip and he opened the way into a slime lit corridor.

"After myself," Grego ushered himself through, right before Space-Bo made an attempt. "This looks like what use to be the outer offices of the Inner Ministry Council of Rendyle. From these offices I formulated my plans for the Nexus point."

"See, you have used that word before."

"The point is, I realized how to control the entire planet from here. How to use the Nexus point to my own advantage."

"Uncle, uncle! I give. What is the Nexus point?"

"Nah! You wouldn't be interested."

"You're probably right. Say, do you know if there's any gumball machines around here? My last stick got slimed, coming down that tube back there."

"Even if there were gumball machines around here, do you think I'd give you correct directions?"

"Sure, we're on the same team now, right?"

"Yes, MY team. And don't you forget it."

Space-Bo stiffened up, said "Aye aye, captain!" and rounded it out with a full military salute.

Grego continued on down the corridor. He started speaking again as he slowly picked through the rubble, "The Deo 7 Nexus point is, in essence, the very center of the universe*. The place from which the Big Bang originated, if you believe in that theory. It is where Absolute Nothingness gives rise to Absolute Existence..."

Space-Bo had heard the Funky Chicken ramble on like this before and thought it all pointless and boring mumbo jumbo. So he didn't bother to point out that the universe had no center from which the big bang originated it. Instead he thought about yummy gumballs and blowing bubbles in Grego's face to irritate him. He knew there had to be a gumball machine around there somewhere. If not in these hallways then maybe back on the surface. Hmmm.

"...out of chaos there is the spontaneous creation of matter and energy. And it is this which replenishes the Deo 7 atmosphere. But it is much more than a glorified air conditioner, it will give me the power over more than just this planet but, increasingly, over a widening sphere of the galaxy and cosmos at large.

"As you and your team can testify to, I am a force to be reckoned with!" He finished with an emphatic thrust of his fist into the air.

He looked around. "Space-Bo?" Nothing. "Damn it," Grego sighed, "just when I was about to threaten the ultimate destruction." Maybe he couldn't kill Space-Bo but perhaps the idiot's own foolishness would do the trick. He wouldn't bet on it though. Now to find the combination Crystal Omni-magneto and Nexus Manipulator.

Space-Bo wandered around the top of the ruined city for a while and actually found an artifact that could supply the galaxy with unlimited electrical power. But civilization would never again know that promise because Space-Bo threw it into the water to see if it would skip. He only got two bounces.

Bored with his limited finds, Space-Bo headed back to the aircar just in time to see Grego approaching from a different direction, "Hey, can we go back now? I want to see what Rogicphil is doing."

Grego put his arm around his friend and declared, "Anything for you my friend."

They got back into the aircar and were airborne in a matter of seconds. Space-Bo noticed that Grego's normally grim expression was one big smile now, "Find what you were looking for?"

"Sadly, no. I'm beginning to think that the Crystal Omni-magneto was the product of a demented historian. But I did find something even better and I owe it all to you."

"Huh? What's a Crimino magni... uh? What did you say?"

"The Crystal Omni-magneto was a purported device invented in Rendyle that could drain energy from another universe into this one. It would have meant unlimited power forever and then some. But that's not important right now because I have this!" He held up a yellowing piece of parchment.

"Is that the Magnocrimy ball?"

Grego wanted to kick him out the door right there but feared for his own life and so simply smacked Space-Bo over the head with his riding crop. "No! This is my ticket to heaven and you purchased it for me."

"I'm very, uh, happy for you, um..."

"You see with this little paper in hand I can..." flashing console lights distracted Grego, "Hold on! Rebel fighters are closing. You man the canon while I get us out of here."

"Now you're talking!" Space-Bo said popping open the sun roof. He unholstered a folding laser rifle from his hip and stood up on his seat. He squeezed the trigger but nothing happened. "Oops," he handed a power cord down to Grego, "Could you stick this in the cigarette lighter please?"

Grego didn't understand why 'Bo didn't simply use the passenger seat's built in gunnery controls but he connected the cord just the same.

Space-Bo opened up at a passing bird. He missed but the bird freaked out and lost its balance for a moment, "That's for crapping on me back at Rall Raul Beta!" But the bird was gone before it could even hear his words.

I'm ready for anything now, Space-Bo thought. Three points appeared on the horizon behind them and were closing. "I see them. Slow down a bit so they can catch up."

"You're crazy," Grego replied.

Space-Bo took careful aim as the enemy craft got closer and closer. The fighters looked more like minivans on steroids he thought. They got close enough that he could make out the crew members inside.

He fired. The center craft's left headlight exploded. It's pilot gave him the finger as the enemy gunner returned fire.

Space-Bo shook his fist in the air, "You couldn't shoot the photograph of a darkened room to save your life buddy!"

"I don't think they can hear you."

"I made that up myself. Pretty cool, huh?"

Grego shook his head just before flipping the aircar over in a vain attempt to dump out his ignorant cargo. Space-Bo held on with one hand, hanging precariously three hundred meters in the air, while continuing to fire with his free hand.

His latest shot exploded the tailpipe of the left most fighter and it zoomed out of the sky at the end of a twirling black smoke trail. "Ha ha!"

Grego swished the aircar back and forth violently in an attempt to shake Space-Bo but all efforts failed as he knew they would. Resigned to the sad fact, he returned the aircar to its normal position and slammed on the air breaks.

The two remained fighters shot past. It would take a while for them to circle back around.

Space-Bo slipped back inside for a moment, "Don't stop now. That's really cool how you were toying with them. Waiting until the last possible moment to avoid their laser blasts. That was some flying."

"Oh brother." Grego shut the sun roof and pushed Space-Bo down into his seat, "Use the car's onboard canon and we'll be rid of these bozos in one second."

"Yeah? But wouldn't that take all the fun out of it?"

Grego leaned over and pushed the ALLFIRE button in front of Space-Bo, "No."

A series of plasma discharges reached out from pods underneath the aircar and gripped the two fighters in front of them exploding the rebel craft into atomic dust.

"Enough of this goofing around," Grego said, "I've got work to do."

Disappointed, Space-Bo quietly put his laser rifle away. What a party pooper that Grego the mean guy was.

*　　　　　*　　　　　*

While Fred and the chicken were working to finish the transmat machine, Rogicphil figured it was time to go kick some butt. He left through a ventilation shaft to bypass the main hatch.

Tractor tread boots propelled him along the otherwise unnavigable narrow shaft back to the hallway outside the storeroom. He oozed out from the shaft like a slug before jumping to the floor.

A small group of invaders were in front of him with their backs turned as they tried to listen at the main hatchway.

"Hey guys!" He called out.

Only one of them bothered to look back but it was too late. A flurry of seeming invisible punches assaulted the group's noses laying them flat in less than three seconds. Rogicphil then took his time to tie them up with their own rope and smiled to himself, "Five down... ninety-nine thousand nine-hundred and ninety-five to go...< sigh >"

Chapter 36: The Leech

Previously: After the devastating defeat of the satanic cow at the hands of Mr. Bear, Hack had hurried to the cryolab where the other members of his awesome heavy metal band known as the Clergy were still frozen.

He had freed them just in time to hear a complex wide announcement, "Attention guests. The Ultimate Gameshow has been completed and we would like to request all remaining patrons to please remove themselves from the premises as it will shortly self destruct. Thank you."

The Clergy had made a desperate attempt to escape as sirens and whistles and bells were ringing all around them.

The previously mentioned announcement had then continued thus, "And as you flee the establishment you may wish to avail yourself of our fabulous snack bar and munitions boutique."

Joe couldn't resist and so the group had been delayed as he picked out several nice rocket launchers. By the time they'd made it to the launch pad all the ships were gone including Plutoman's starcruiser along with Rogicphil and gang.

"Oh great," Bufgoo had said, "Now I guess we'll just have to die in a fireball on a planet that doesn't even exist."

"Well look et eet theese way maen. Thuh explo-zun won't exeest either, ha ha!"

Joe had then smacked Manuel with his Moorgnad IV Existentialist's Baseball team hat, "Shut-up will you?"

Hack had decided to sniff the air then and had smelled something very putrid, "Garbage scow."

Bufgoo had to agree, "Where there's garbage there's always the garbage men right?" He had referred to his and Joe's brief stint as New York City garbage collectors.

"Don't remind me."

"If there's garbage men then there must also be a garbage truck," after scanning around the landing zone Bufgoo had then spotted it, "And thar she blows mateys."

"Chunks."

The boys had then managed to sneak aboard the garbage scow just as she was lifting off. Unfortunately the two drivers had taken too long on their lunch breaks and hadn't returned in time for lift off. (Incidentally it was these same garbage scow drivers who in another timeline shut down the self destruct sequence on the Ultimate Gameshow Complex at T- 3 seconds and went on to take over the entire planet and eventually send it into a bloody civil war that only years later would again cause their planet to be at the center of a dispute that would decide the fate of the universe but that is another story, and million in the bank. But they didn't so the complex was blown up after all.)

"Man who taught those stooges how to fly?" Joe had wanted to know after being smacked back and forth against the bulkhead.

"I don't know," Bufgoo had answered, "Let's find the bridge and ask them."

"Which way do you propose?" Joe had looked around and could only see dark corridors that reeked of foul garbage.

"How about up these steps?" Bufgoo had begun to climb a slimy set of rungs leading up into more darkness. The others had followed behind and by the time they'd reached the bridge it had been too late. The ship had been on autopilot the whole time and was then heading straight for the center of the Moorgnadian sun. At least they weren't left behind on the planet when the complex went up, like the original garbage truck crew.

*   *   *

"Asteroids! Six O'clock!" Bufgoo yelled.

Joe ignored him. Everyone knew that six o'clock meant behind them. Who cared what was behind them?

Bufgoo did since they were flying though space backwards. He shoved Joe out from his command seat and took control. First he swung the ship around and then fired the breaking thrusters to avoid some nasty looking asteroids.

"What the hell did you do that for?" Joe said from the floor, "Using the main engines are more efficient to slow us down when we're going backwards."

Bufgoo stepped down from the command chair and stood over Joe gloating. He gave Joe a good slug in the stomach, "That's for trying to lock me in the broom closet."

To say that things on board the Clergy's garbage scow were unpleasant would be to say that the sun was hot. Since the infamous broom-closet / brig affair, there had been twenty-nine separate incidents involving food, feathers, and garbage in the day and half they'd been wandering haplessly through space. And they weren't getting any closer to finding Rogicphil.

Bufgoo climbed back into his co-pilot's chair, "Whose dumb idea was it to go after this smoke trail anyway?"

Manuel snickered from his makeshift station on top of the main access hatch down into the rest of the ship. "Yours maen," he said between long drags of his make shift cigarette. Sitting cross legged with his shirt off and in kung-fu pants like a zen master, he was attempting to smoke part of a rolled up brown paper bag; there wasn't anything else available at hand.

"No," Bufgoo decided, "It was Hack."

Joe sat up, "Let's get him!"

Manuel shook his head, "You got dey space madness, duhde."

"I do not... you... you lovely... giant bar of soap."

Manuel continued toking on his fake doobie.

Bufgoo laughed, "He's right. You're going crazy. If I hadn't stopped you just then, we would have smashed right into that asteroid."

CRRRunch! In order not to deprive them of the experience, the ship decided at that moment to smash into something, something big. Bufgoo and Joe were thrown into the bulkhead. Somehow Manuel managed to stay firmly attached to his perch without a care in the universe.

Bufgoo struggled to his console, "Damage control reports no damage.

Apparently we just bumped into a giant asteroid shaped marshmellow."

Joe peeked out his view bubble, "That ain't no asteroid."

Bufgoo looked up. "I stand correlated. We've smacked into the side of a giant space cruiser. We're saved!" and he pushed on the window to get out.

Joe did likewise but to no avail. The shielded plexiglass bubble domes resisted all attempts to compromise their integrity. "It's like a giant hotdog in space just waiting for me to eat it, but I can't get to it with this stupid window in the way."

"Yeah, and that rust colored stuff must be ketchup. I want out! AAAAH!"

Hack suddenly poked his head up into the bridge, lifting Manuel up against the rear bulkhead in the process, "Guess what?"

Joe snapped, "We already 'know what', you big lug. Now help us break through the wall so we can get out."

"You're crazy."

Manuel unsquished himself from behind the hatch and climbed over Hack's head to stand up, "Hey, take eet easy dudhe, no whut awm sayin."

"My bad," Hack said.

"Now warez dem spacesuits et, eh?"

"That's right," Bufgoo suddenly deduced, "We can use the spacesuits to smash through the bulkhead."

Manuel said to Hack, "Dey cahrazy," and twirled his finger to his forehead, "Loco een da cabesa."

Hack climbed the rest of the way into the bridge and went to the main computer console. He began punching in queries. The computer chugged away and spat out a response.

Manuel grabbed it up and quickly read it, "Eets not Rowjickpills ship, maen. Wher doomed Ay geeuss." He dropped the printout.

But Hack was happy for just the same, "Don't matter."

"Eh?"

"Come on," he started down the steps. The others shrugged and followed after him.

A few minutes later Hack and Joe were in the airlock waiting for the atmosphere to cycle. There were only two spacesuits on board so Bufgoo and Manuel would have to wait back on the garbage scow for the time being. One sane person to each group was the idea.

"I knew we were suppose to wear the suits. Honest," Joe said.

"Uh-huh," Hack nodded.

"I mean you didn't really believe I was going to punch a hole in the hull and let out all the air, just to get out, do you?"

Hack said nothing.

They waited a bit more until the hatch opened and they could float out into the void. Once outside the ship they could get a better look at what they'd bumped into.

In big giant letters the word LEECH was plastered onto the side of the other ship. Compared to the Leech their ship was like a barnacle stuck to the side of a whale. The garbage scow had gently bumped the large ship it was next to, only causing a small dent. The scow was unharmed and floated just a couple of meters away.

The Leech hung in the darkness, as it drifted silently along with a small group of asteroids. There were no lights on nor movement from inside the behemoth. It was dead in the space water.

Hack fired his thrusters and dragged Joe along behind with a tether. He found what appeared to be an airlock a short distance from the letter C. It was silent. There were no controls on the outside to activate it, so Hack muscled up to the hatch and wedged his hands into the seam and heaved. Slowly it began to open and then all of a sudden, the metal panels tore apart and flew out into space.

Joe laughed into the intercom, "What junk. Can't they make hatchways in the future? Bufgoo's old pickup had more structural integrity than that."

Hack floated into the open airlock. "Hurry up," he urged.

Joe complied. "Now what? You busted the outer door. How're you going to get the next one to open without letting out all the air?"

Hack thought about it a moment but ended up shaking his head. Maybe that would help his brain some.

Bufgoo came over the intercom, "I've got an idea. What if I got the scow to press up against the hull and cover up the airlock? You could then open up the other hatch without letting out too much air."

"Hey, you ain't going to drive that tub of lard over me!" Joe cried.

"Good idea," Hack chuckled.

"Okay," Bufgoo said, "Hold Joe down while I maneuver the ship around."

"What...?" Joe struggled but it was futile once Hack got a hold of him.

Bufgoo fired the scow's thrusters several times but was unable to keep the ship up close enough to do much good.

"Let me at eet," Manuel thumbed Bufgoo to get out of the way.

Bufgoo nodded solemnly and climbed out of the pilot's chair.

Manuel hopped in, "Dis ain't lik no el camino buht et least eet's a low rhider, ey?" Somehow he managed to gracefully nudge the ship into the correct airlock blocking position. "Eesey as freholees." There was enough residual garbage coating the outer hull to allow a decent seal to form around the damaged airlock. It was probably that same garbage coating that had prevented the two ships from damaging each under when they had bumped together.

Hack touched the airlock controls from his position. The machinery clanged and shuttered a bit but eventually came to life and affected a successful cycling. "Thanks Bufgoo."

"Don't thank me. It was Manuel who was at the controls."

Joe broke free from Hack's grip to make a break for the inside of the ship, "When I get back I'm going to pound you Manuel!"

Hack laughed, "Thanks Manuel."

"Eets awl cool, dood."

The Leech had not died without a fight. Food and beer cans littered the hallways and told a story of crazy crew members. Joe scurried about in the weightless environment collecting as many of the cans as he could.

"They're mine, all mine," he said protecting his hoard, "Stay away or I'll slime you." He floated uncontrolled into a bulkhead.

Hack took a deep breath then took off his helmet. Whew... Breath in. Hmm, the air was good at least. Time to investigate.

Joe tried to cram a food pack into his mouth through his helmet, "Aaaah, they're out to get me. They won't let me eat my yummy food."

Hack ignored his insane fellow band member while he searched for a way to the bridge. A long corridor ran the length of the ship with no apparent side passages or hatchways. Softly glowing side panels lit the way. He decided to head forward; that's were 80% of all spaceship bridges were located at.

Several hundred meters farther along, the passage came to an abrupt halt where a meter wide plastic tube extended out of the ceiling onto the floor. Bits of fluid and solid waste were whisking by him, being sucked into the tube and to who knew where.

Hmm, Hack turned around and headed back the way he'd just come. Strangely, about only fifty meters back the passageway curved to the right. Where there had been a completely straight hallway with no side passages suddenly this bend had appeared.

"Hey Joe!" Hack called out. His voice echoed off into the distance. He tried the intercom, "Joe? Bufgoo?"

No answer. Was this what it was like to go crazy? Was he becoming like Joe and Bufgoo? His mind seemed to be working okay, it was just his perception that seemed to be a bit off.

With nothing else to do he took the bend and headed deeper in the center of the ship. Here the glowing side panels dimmed to almost complete darkness and he had to turn on his suit lamp.

Finally side hatches appeared but they were all closed tightly with no means of opening them. Hack tried but even his immense strength was no match for the reinforced blast style doors. What kind of ship was this that had blast doors on inside passageways?

He fired his thrusters and continued on.

*   *   *

Joe got fed up with the stupid food packs that refused to be eaten and so drifted aimlessly as he banged his head against the inside of his space helmet.

He bumped into something but ignored it. A cryptic hand grabbed a hold of his face plate.

"AAAAAh! Aliens! Aliens! They're trying to suck my face!"

Bufgoo's voice came crackling over the intercom, "***at? Please repe*** you're b***king up. Ov***"

Joe kicked the dead body away from him flailing his arms around like the lunatic his was. So caught up in his fantasies he was, that he didn't pay attention to the fact that he was now drifting straight into the garbage chute. "That'll teach you!" he said just before being sucked in.

"**huh?***" Bufgoo said.

A powerful vacuum drew him into and around a series of tubes that collected garbage from various parts of the ship. In his mad state, Joe did everything he could think of to get out, including chewing his own leg off but fortunately he still hadn't managed to get his helmet off.

And so he banged and thrashed around until the tubes spat him into a machine that planned to crush him up into a small cube. Metal pistons whooshed out to hammer him. Joe fought back with his gloved fists. The pistons retracted and came back for another salvo.

"Will you hold still for a moment," the machine seemed to say telepathically to Joe, "This will only take a second and it won't hurt too much, I promise."

In one of those instances when an otherwise stupid brain decides to act reasonably, so that later it may act even more foolishly, Joe realized that there was only one way to get out alive. Find the machine's weak point and go in for the kill.

Joe skillfully spun around with his thruster jets and located a blinking red light on a service panel labeled 'Ignore Me.' He directed his boot up to the panel and hit it with a burst of high powered jet exhaust. It exploded and sent him flying into the far end of the cruncher machine. He breathed a sign of relief and rested a few moments before resuming his unstable mental state.

"You killed me!" the machine seemed to say in his mind, "I only wanted to make your occupation of space more efficient."

No more pistons came after him and the whole machine was now silent. Now that that was over, Joe decided to freak out again, banging on the metal bulkheads surrounding him and kicking at nothing in particular. Yes, much better indeed.

Another machine next to the cruncher didn't like to be disturbed and so sent a snakelike tendril into the belly of its neighbor to see what was going on. It found the crazy humanoid named Joe, coiled around its legs then drug the malformed object back to its domain.

This other machine was a polisher. It took the freshly pressed cubes from the cruncher and shined them up to look nice. The cruncher wasn't doing its job today; this thing wasn't very cube like at all. But oh well, the polisher had a job to do and so it began to polish Joe as best it could. Needless to say, Joe didn't think very highly of this treatment and fought it all the way. But it was to no avail and he was soon shot out of the polisher into a holding tank full of nicely polished cubes.

There was a hatch with a tiny window in it on one wall and Joe struggled around the floating cubes to get at it. He pointed his lamp through the window and nudged his helmet up next to it for a look see. Outside the hatch was a normal looking corridor. No lights were on but it otherwise looked normal. No aliens, no machines, nothing.

Hmm, nothing to make him freak out. He guessed he'd just have to make something up them. How about dead bodies in the cubes that weren't quite dead yet and then they'd attack him because he had their food? Yeah, that was it. "AAAAAAhhh!" he screamed.

*   *   *

Bufgoo tried again to reach Joe on the intercom. Then Hack. No response. "This damn radio must have eaten them up, Manuel. I'm sorry I'm not very good a being crazy but that's all I could think of at the moment. Being

361

crazy is hard work you know."

Manuel took the microphone from his large friend. What the hell was he going to do with this crazy person?

*   *   *

After a bit Joe became bored with screaming so he decided to do a little exploring. First the cubes. He found one that looked composed mostly of loosely held together junk. With a firm shove from his legs he slammed the cube against the far wall where it broke apart into its constituent pieces of junk.

Eager to do something besides scream, Joe tore into the rubbish looking for anything that might interest him. An old music baton, some smelly tennis shoes, an atomically articulated bomb... worthless junk.

He searched some more. Aha, now here was something worth saving, a nice browning banana peel. This was more like it. Joe popped his helmet off so that he could rub the slimy underside all through his Mohawk style hair. Mmmm, that felt good.

Knock, knock.

"Eh?" Joe looked around. No one was there.

KNOCK, KNOCK, the sound was more impatient this time.

He flicked on the his suit lamp and scanned the walls. When the beam crossed the hatchway Hack's ugly face framed the tiny window. So that was it. Joe ignored his friend and went back to his banana grooming.

Hack, realizing that Joe had gone completely mad, summoned all his strength and tore the door, mounting and all, from the surrounding weaker wall. Joe came floating out with a twisted smile on his face.

"Space Madness," Hack said grabbing Joe.

"Hey man this banana is mine. Go find your own."

"You're crazy."

"Yeah, so? At least I'm still here. Where are you my friend?"

Hack tugged his band mate along behind him as he continued to explore deeper into the ship. Strangely, there was an airlock just around the corner, where just a few moments before, nothing. It opened, cycled, and let them through with no problem but still, it made him wonder what it was doing there.

The airlock led them into a vastly superior section of the ship. Nicely decorated glow panels matched carpeted strips running the length of the bulkhead on either side of the corridor. The air was fresher and was slightly perfumed to smell like paper money.

A series of hatchways on both sides of them led along a hundred meters before the shaft split into a T. None of the hatchways were labeled or had windows and Hack simply ignored them as he continued on before turning right at the junction.

The next hallway was painted a light blue and its doors were labeled: chandeliers, chairs, chimes, bison, instruments, and knockwurst. It was a close tie between the instruments and the knockwurst but Hack decided on the instruments and went into that door.

Inside was a storage facility made specifically for musical instruments of all kinds. Row upon row, rack upon rack, stacked ten meters up, and wrapped in bubbled plastic were guitars, drums, xylophones, ukuleles, wind chimes (these were misfiled and should have been placed in the room marked chimes-the editors), blocks, and various other noise makers.

Joe wanted to start rummaging for more fruit skins but Hack towed him along behind, through the room and into the next which was a practicing room.

There Hack found what he took at first to be the switch to a guitar power amp. Instead of powering up the equipment, as Hack had hoped, gravity was suddenly restored to the room.

Joe, who had been floating upside down, crunched his head pretty hard. "Ouch!" he cried and shook his head before looking up, "Where the hell am I?"

Hack moved on to another console and flipped some more switches. He was pleased to discover that these powered up the equipment. He found a nice fat power cord and began to chew through the insulation.

Joe looked around carefully, as if, at last, he was coming to his senses, "This place is pretty cool huh?" He looked over to where several keyboard and drum machines were set up.

"Now what should I do first?" he scratched his head and found a banana peel stuck there, "Damn it Hack! Are you trying to get me killed? Don't leave these stupid things lying around okay?"

Hack had by now chewed into the live conductor which he modulated with his teeth. A nasty distortion of noise and background hiss rumbled through the giant speakers on either side of the room.

"That's more like it," Joe said plugging himself into the keyboards. He set the drum machine to a hard driving rock beat and an accompanying funky bass line. "Let's do Durk Durk."

Hack stopped long enough to speak, "Wrong accompaniment."

Joe didn't notice any difference, "Just play. Let me do the singing." He sang:

> He can walk and he can talk
> His voice sounds just like Mr. Spock
> But he's not alive, he's just twitchin'
> And his mixed drinks, are really bitchin'
>
> He was trapped in the loonie pin
> Where all his friends were loonie men
> Until he got a big electric shock
> And now on the blender he does rock

Chorus:
> He's itchin', he's twitchin'
> He plays a blender from the kitchen
> He fell on his butt and got a cut
> And that's gonna need some stitchin'
>
> Durk Durk, Durk Durk
> He can really make a blender work

> Durk Durk, Durk Durk
> I want a hickory daiquiri DURK!

It seemed as if the whole ship shook with their music. It crept out through the air vents and infected other sections. Left over rodents and insects scurried for cover but there was none. There was no escape from Clergy music.

Second verse:

> Then one night I changed my mind
> I had a daiquiri of a different kind
> Durk got his hand caught in the blender
> And his flesh was oh so tender
>
> The ice was crushed the juice did pour
> But still it needed something more
> So he went out to the pouring rain
> And got me a chopped up human brain
>
> And we added it to this recipe
> It tasted great and it made me pee
> Hooray for Durk you're so clever
> This is your best daiquiri ever

Chorus

"Hey!" Bufgoo said listening to intercom speaker, "It sounds like Durk Durk. They're trying to communicate with us Manuel."

Manuel, taking a big hit on his paper bag, just shook his head. Crazy.

Deep down into the festering bowels of the ship something stirred. Something awakened by the strange and sickly sour music echoing throughout all the ship. The torturing sounds gave it a motive to act and the driving beat gave it a tempo to destroy to.

At last the song wrapped up. Joe was rolling around on the floor for his original improvisation on the lyrics. Originally it didn't say anything about Manuel but since he wasn't there Joe had decided to change the verse to include him. What fun.

"Enough," Hack said setting his power cord down.

"Time to escape huh?"

Hack shook his head, "Not yet."

"Why not? What are we doing over here anyway? This was your idea. You tell me."

Hack explained that if they could find the bridge they could get updated star charts and information about how to find Deo 7. If they could get to Deo 7, they'd find Rogicphil, and he'd send them home.

"But why do I want to go home. I owe old crusty butthead fifty bucks. He'll take it out of my hide if he catches me. I'm happy right here in the future."

Hack shook his head and exited the room.

"Hey wait up!"

They continued to explore that section of the ship but couldn't find any signs of what had happened to the crew or anything else for that matter. After another half hour of exploring they were about ready to give up when a nice fat elevator door opened up for them when they approached.

They stepped inside. Joe ordered that they be taken directly to the bridge. They were.

The doors whisked open onto a modern miracle of space technology. Banks of high-tech computers lined the walls with tons of chairs for people to sit in and marvel at the complexity of the machines. Huge, super resolution, billion color, display screens covered the walls above the consoles all the way to the ceiling and then covered the ceiling itself.

"This is awesome!" Joe stepped forward completely overtaken by the neatness of the whole thing. He was so enthralled that he didn't notice the ledge that overlooked the lower tier of the bridge.

ka-THUD!

After picking himself up Joe helped Hack access the main computer terminal. Actually it was more like watch and ask annoying questions.

ENTER PASSWORD:

Hack hit the ESCAPE key and the program skipped that sequence, "We're in."

A schematic of the ship appeared with icons and descriptions laid out in a not so logical fashion. Hack clicked on the exhaust system of the ship and the Captain's Log appeared instead.

"This is Captain Regrub Nueeq of the Imperial Galactic Tax Collection Vessel Leech and this is my last entry. Less than two hours ago this ship and my entire crew were completely destroyed by some unknown force while we were attempting to collect tax due on an unchartered vessel in space around the planet known as Deo 7.

"While the ship was being destroyed, my crew and myself availed ourselves of the snack bar. When we returned to the bridge we discovered we had been transported to some unknown region of the galaxy we had never been to before. A strange side effect to this transportation is that as myself and my crew were vaporized we were somehow transformed into holograms.

"Life as holograms did not appeal to much of the crew as they could not 'get it on' anymore so to speak. And so I have ordered mass suicide as an ameliorative to the holographic crew of this ship which I hope will put an end to this stupid matter once and for all.

"If this message is ever retrieved I leave this warning: Do not enter or attempt to enter this vessel or breath any of the remaining air in the passageways. It seems that a rather nasty version of a space madness holovirus has infected my holographic crew.

"So long and may the Imperium (sic) grow bloated with the riches of an exploitable galaxy." Here the log ran out leaving only static on the screen.

After Hack explained the consequences of the Captain's last report he and Joe made a run for the airlock and hopefully a hasty retreat back to their garbage scow.

Unfortunately when the elevator doors slid open an angry mob of insane holographic spacemen blocked their exit.

Note: The use of the term 'silent' in regards to a satirical space opera should be taken literally since as everyone knows 'no one can hear you scream in space'. Mostly because of trademark infringement and has almost nothing to do with physics and the non-traversal of pressure waves in a mediumless vacuum.

"Computer," the raspy voice said, "Prepare to fire all weapons at the Leech."

"Standing.By."

"Fire!"

Hack and Joe, on board the Leech, at that instant had decided to run for their lives from the hoard of undead bureaucrats which were marching menacingly, yet perfectly harmlessly, forward. Blasts from the other ship rocked the Leech and knocked the two corporeal beings flat. Their holographic enemies were not restrained by such concepts as inertia and so were not affected as such.

"Throw your cross at them!" Joe shouted from against a bulkhead.

Hack pulled himself up with the aid of an anchored command chair, then ripped the same up with a single powerful pull, and heaved it at the approaching mass. The chair sailed through them as if they didn't exist.

From across the bridge the evil ex-crew of the galactic tax collecting vessel Leech rallied around to form a huddle. Joe saw this as his opportunity to make a break for the escape pod. He made it in before anyone could get to him and quickly shut the hatch. Hack was still outside but he could handle himself, Joe knew. What was important was that the leader of the Clergy would escape in one piece. How else could the band continue without its leader? They could always find another big guy who could chew on power cords but there was only one Joe Kolwalczyk.

"Prepare a boarding party," the raspy thing inside the adversarial ship told his computer.

"No.One.Left.To.Form.Party..Crew.Has.Been.Lost."

"Don't tell me what I already know. Just do your job."

"Insufficent.Crew.Size..Suggest.Hailing.Already. Disabled.Ship.."

"Just blast them damn it!"

"There.Is.No.Cause.To.Continue.Attack..Power. Reserves.Are.Low..Suggest.Hailing.Other.Ship.For.Terms.."

"I have to do everything around here myself, huh?"

"I.Control.Ninety nine.Percent.Of.All.Activities.On. Board.This.Ship.."

"Shut-UP!" the creature went down to its ship's airlock in preparation for a one man boarding party.

Back on the Leech, Hack was pounding on the escape pod hatch for Joe to let him in. The hologhouls were closing in fast. Joe shook his head.

Hack turned around to face his demise like a man. A Clergy-man. "So Long!" he said to no one in particular just before the first wave of attackers got their grubby hologram hands around his neck...and through it without so much as a scratch.

Hack laughed, "Fooled You!" just before running right through the lot of them and into the elevator which they had recently vacated.

Confused, the hologhouls turned to Joe who still hadn't figured out how to work the escape pod.

Hack slipped his space helmet back on and flushed out all the ship air before turning on his suit oxygen supply. His head cleared. He stopped the elevator to take stock of the situation.

Space Madness was effecting him too it seemed, despite the fact that it was a holovirus that was causing it. He only hoped he could figure out a way to get back to Deo 7 where he knew Rogicphil and the others could help him find a cure. But first things first. He had to get control of this ship. If anything could get them back to Deo 7, it was the Leech. Once he had control of it, he could then find out who or what was outside attacking them and deal with that problem.

Amazing what a little bit of fresh air could do for a brain. He hit the elevator up button and started back for the bridge. The hologhouls were harmless now he knew; it was Joe he was afraid of.

Over on the garbage scow Bufgoo peeked out the viewport. "Hey I know that ship. We're saved! It's Rogicphil come back to save us."

Manuel ignored the drummer who was crazy with space madness. Space madness made people see whatever they wanted in the most common of items. Just as long as the fat guy didn't try anything stupid they'd be okay.

Joe finally managed to find the correct button to jetison the escape pod and was flung tumbling out into space. In the first few seconds out from the ship he ran into someone in a half sized spacesuit. An ugly face glared down at him through the pod's viewport.

"Ah!" Joe freaked. He smacked at the face in the viewport with a flyswatter. It did little good.

Hack stepped back on the bridge just in time to receive a hail from an enemy ship. There were only a handful of hologhouls left wandering the bridge. Appearently the rest had become bored and switched themselves off.

Hack found the communications station and hit the viewscreen button. An animated computer face appeared,
"This.Is.Plutoman's.Spaceship..Surrender.Now.Or.Be. Destroyed."

The remaining holograms sat down to marvel at the full size screen.

"Hi computer," Hack said.

"Sorry.I.Did.Not.Recognize.You.Mr.Hack..I.Need.To.Warn.You.That. Plutoman.Is.On.His.Way.To.Take.Control.Of.The.Leech..What.Is.Your.Status.?"

"I'm fine."

"That.Is.Good.To.Hear..Do.You.Have.Full.Control.Of.The.Leech.?"

"That's right."

A hologhoul belched.

"Can.You.Help.Us.Get.Back.To.The.Twenty.Third. Century.? We.Can.Not.Find.The.Correct.Address.In.The. Temporal.Phone.Book.."

Hmm, Hack thought, this could work out to everyone's benefit. "Wanna trade?"

"What.Did.You.Have.In.Mind.?"

Hack made his proposal and Plutoman's computer quickly accepted. With that agreed upon, Hack found the tractor beam controls and recaptured the escape pod with Joe inside and Plutoman stuck to the outside.

A few hours later both barnacle ships, the spacecruiser and the garbage scow, were safely stowed away in one of the Leech's unused booty holds. Bufgoo and Joe were made to wear ventilation hoods pumping in filter air for them to breath, until a space madness cure could be found.

The Clergy, Plutoman, and a hologhoul named Ralpho met in the Captain's not-ready room, just off to the side from the main bridge. Ralpho demanded concessions but Plutoman refused to give up any of his video game horde, while the Clergy didn't know what they wanted.

"What is wrong with you people!?" Plutoman demanded, "Here I am willing to help your sorry asses and all you do is bicker. I think I'll leave you idiots to fend for yourselves." He made as if to get up. No one tried to stop him and so, confused, he sat back down. In the captain's not ready room this turned out to be on a heart shaped vibrating foot stool.

The mutated man's plan had been to scare them into becoming desperate enough to do anything in exchange for their freedom from this void.

"I want you," Joe pointed at Ralpho, "To give us your musical instruments and we'll let you live."

"Yeah and butts might fly out my monkey."

"That can be arranged, my friend."

Hack didn't bother separating the two since neither one could harm the other. Instead, he explained to Joe that the hologhoul's wanted not to live but to be turned off and never heard from again. And play some video games before dying but was just part of the minor details to be worked out later.

"Oh," Joe nodded, "In that case I'll kill them myself."

"Hey hey.. hey hey, Hey hey hey," Plutoman stood up in his footstool to be heard, "Thiiiiis is mmmmmy final offerrrrr." The footstool was still vibrating. "Taaaaake it orrrr eeeeeeat spaaaaaace duuuust..."

Bufgoo laughed, "We'll take the spa-ay-ay-ce duh duh duust."

Plutoman reached for his blaster.

Bufgoo already had a handful of drumsticks in his hands, ready to be fired them off in quick succession, in order to knock the weapon from Plutoman's grasp. But he didn't have too since the half height freak fell over on his own and dropped his blaster in the process.

Plutoman furiously kicked the floor before getting up and retreiving his weapon. No one bothered to stop him. "Yoooooooo!"

"Don't get cocky bud, you'll be stuck out here in the void forever too, if don't cooperate."

"Oh yeah, bubble head? I'm not the one who's got space madness. And yoooou can take that to the bank!"

A drum stick shot out but the short plastic like fellow was ready this time and managed to dodge out of the way.

Hack was admiring a nice collection of whips and chains that lined the far wall while waiting for the disturbance to settle down. He then reminding everyone why they were there and how to cooperate in getting back to their respective timelines.

"But THIS is our timeline," Ralpho said grumbling, "It's you freaks who started this whole mess and we want you gone as quickly as possible so let's hurry up and get this stupid cooperation over with."

"Okay," Bufgoo stood up, "Hack says that the easiest way to do this is with the Leech. We'll set a course for Deo 7 and when we get there Rogicphil will send us all back to where we belong. Agreed?"

Off to the side, Manuel offered Hack a hit on his joint. If was the real stuff this time and he had found it in one of the Leech's vast stores of illegal narcotics.

Hack shook his head and explained to the half-stoned former gravedigger that he was too busy and it was too serious of time to being doing that kind of thing.

"Okay boss," Manuel said and took the hit himself.

Ralpho stood up before anyone else got a chance to respond to Bufgoo, "Not so fast. Are you talking about the same Rogicphil Suflipinic who overloaded our main computer last month? The same Rogicphil who got me demoted to Lt. Vice Assistant Deputy's Aide? If so, then you can count us out."

"Wait up a bit, Mack," Joe shoved Bufgoo back into his red velour seat, "It was that goofy stingy guy who zapped us all. Rogman doesn't have anything to do with it."

Ralpho jumped up onto the round rotating bed in the center of the room, that served as the table for their discussion, "Stingy guy must die! Ho Ho Ho!"

Joe took a stick from Bufgoo and pegged Ralpho in the forehead with it, "Get down from there you dork."

Hack knew they would get no where with all this arguing so he decided to quietly slip out of the conference / not-ready room. While the others bickered back and forth he'd fire up the Leech's massive space drives and get the vessel under way. Somewhere in the computer banks would be star charts that could help him find Deo 7.

He took the elevator to deck 11 and then a golf cart like conveyance to the executive lift which went up to deck 9. There he walked along a non-functioning walk-a-later to a series of silent escalators, and finally through a double set of steel reinforced doors and onto the bridge. But it was a fake bridge used for the shipboard film crew which had been filming a parody of the Leech's day to day activities.

Little bits of holoslides littered the floor and Hack took a handful for future reference.

Back out to the escalators then a right turn at the mall and into a small carnival area. What were the designers of this ship thinking when they built all this crap?

At last he found a You-Are-Here sign and breathed a little easier. Punching up the first screen showed a picture of the entire galaxy.

"Zoom in," he ordered.

A prerecorded voice with an accompanying orchestra sang:

You'll have to use the Zoom In
Zoo-ooom In button.
If you want to
If you want to activate
Activate that function

"Shut-up!" He punched the speaker over the screen burying his fist halfway into the wall beyond. The entire screen fizzled then went blank.

Hack cursed his impatience as he extracted his hand. Now he was back to square one. Well he knew generally the direction of the bridge. He could smash through walls, ignoring stupid signs and flower shops alike.

Right! He stepped back a few meters from the nearest wall in the direction he wanted to go. Taking a few quick breaths Hack set himself, then charged.

The first wall was no match for him and he easily barged through the next two walls as well. His momentum carried him into a silk scarf and undergarment storeroom. As he ran, the thin textiles began to build up around his body until they completely entangled him to the point where he couldn't move anymore, in any direction.

So this is how it is to end, he thought. Trapped in women's clothing? He didn't think so. The clothing wrapped around him so tightly that he couldn't even feel the floor beneath his feet. He couldn't tell precisely which way was up or down. And that gave him an idea.

He quit struggling and simply floated there letting the garments support his massive bulk. Then slowly with deliberate and powerful movements of his arms and legs he began to "swim" for the surface. If there was a surface, he thought.

A few minutes later he bumped up against the ceiling and the scarves went right up to the top. Hmm, the wall didn't feel too tough. He could probably punch right through, but the scaffolding restricted any quick movement and all he could manage was a light brushing of the ceiling with his fist.

He needed a better plan. But what? He'd die in a few more minutes from lack of oxygen so it would have to be something clever. He had it! Sound.

Hack had enough air left in his lungs for one good shout. He figured that if a strong enough pressure wave of the right frequency were to impact on the ceiling, the sound would cause it to buckle from the stress caused by all the scarves below it. It was kind of like when a fluid becomes supersaturated by some substance and a small jolt causes the suspended substance to suddenly precipitate out. Well it sounded good in theory.

With nothing else to loose, Hack let loose with his mighty vocal cords. At first his voice cracked but then he got a nice timbre and finally put all his strength into it.

A tiny crack formed but it was all that was needed to unleash the awesome force of several hundred thousand silk scarves and undies that were packed into a tiny space.

Hack was shot up with a violent upheaval, crashing through more ceilings, one after another, until his head hit the hard outer hull, bringing his short but exciting journey to an end.

He unwedged his head then fell back to the deck plates next to a jagged rip in the floor. Air at last. He could breath again and the pleasure it brought him far outweighed the slight headache he had.

With that obstacle out of the way, it was back to hunting for the main bridge again. He now found himself on the uppermost deck of the ship in a laundry service corridor. The automated carts weren't running now, so he wouldn't have to deal with the stupid things getting into his way.

He found a lonely cart a few meters down the shaft. Its tiny metal wheels were all glitz and sparkle, but looked safe enough. After dumping out about half of the contents, he took hold with both hands and broke into a run. When he figured he had enough velocity, he leapt into the basket part, covering himself with extra clothes as a buffer between him and his next obstacle.

The cart sailed along for fifty meters and almost slowed at one point before coming to the edge of a steep run. He went over and began to pick up speed. Seconds later he exceeded his original running speed.

The shaft slammed back and forth twisting and turning around in sharp yet graceful arcs. Periodically a timing circuit would activate a trapdoor above him and more dirty clothes would dump in on top of him, as he and the cart sailed by underneath. He shoved excess material out behind as he went.

The cart reached maximum speed then did a loop over, picking up a soiled tuxedo from a spring-loaded bin at the top of the arc. After the loop, the cart cruised along ten more meters then flew out a hole into the laundry room.

A group of hologhouls trying to take rides in the dryers scattered at the sight of a run away laundry basket. It continued through the laundry room and out into the hallway beyond.

Hack poked his head up to see what was going on but didn't see any easy way to bring himself to a halt, so he let it ride.

The cart bounced off an angled wall and took a right turn into the top of a flight of stairs. The individual steps did little to slow his progress but kept him going in the same direction until the stair made a hairpin turn, and he didn't.

A thin railing gave way at the edge of the steps and he was once again airborne.

Suddenly everything silenced and the only sound he could hear was the light swish of air outside. He took a peek out a small hole in the side of the cart. He was about twenty meters in the air over a huge mess hall / volleyball court / swimming pool area..

A table of uneaten food rushed up and broke his fall. The gloopy contents splattered and caused the cart to slide right off the table, across the room, and into the kitchen area.

Pots and pans clattered everywhere but Hack didn't care. He managed to grab a handful of blueberry banana cream pie from the landing table and was now chewing with satisfaction.

Some foolish chef had ignorantly left a large slab of asphalt lying in the middle of the kitchen before he'd become a hologhoul and Hack's cart now struck this. The cart flipped over and came to a halt but Hack was launched forward into an open oversized oven.

The oven lid, being jarred, closed shut. Hack hit his head against the far wall but, finally and thankfully, came to a halt.

371

It began to get hot.

Hack pushed on the door but it wouldn't budge. Inverse seal. The more he pushed the tighter it became and there was no way to grab on to pull. Maybe this was how his goose was finally going to be cooked. How pathetic. Cooked alive in an oven. By accident even. It would be one thing if a group of ingenious cannibals had tricked him into the oven but this was ridiculous. And no one would take him out when he was done (to be eaten) and so he would be baked into a charred cinder.

Hack sniffed the air. Gas. The oven must be rather old he decided to have such a leak. Hmm, that gave him an idea. He sniffed around until he found the strongest concentration of the gas and then put his back to it.

He then pulled the dirty tuxedo off from around his shoulders and ripped the metal zipper out. He took the remaining clothing he'd flown into the oven with and wrapped it around his feet, then raised them up level with his head but aimed at the door.

The heat was almost to the point where he and the textiles would spontaneously ignite and so with a few hail marys he struck the zipper across his teeth causing a spark. The spark ignited then flowed around him to the gas leak and set it off.

The resulting explosion rocketed Hack into and through the oven walls and into a meat locker on the other side. The side of a frozen cow like object smacked him to a sudden halt. He wasn't sure if he could take anymore of this pounding. Even his amazing constitution had its limits.

But behind him a flaming jet from the breached oven licked at his back. He scurried forward out of harms way. By this time, he was covered in a thick layer of soot and so left a black trail where ever he went.

Frost build up on his arms and legs by the time he found the main hatch. Thankfully it wasn't locked so with a bit of effort he pushed it open and then stepped out onto the main bridge.

At last. His goal.

"Where the hell have you been?" Bufgoo asked tapping his foot.

Joe who was sitting in the captain's chair spun around and glared, "Loafing around again Hack? Well while you were running around, shirking your duties to this ship, we've been figuring out how to get us home."

Hack looked around. All the others were there too and each one seemed to be doing something useful, even Manuel who was monitoring the ventilation system. "Well, I'll be..."

Ralpho announced their position then activated the main view screen. A large wormhole appeared before them, in orbit around the Moorgnad sun. "Ready for entry."

"Battle stations!" ordered Joe.

Everyone strapped themselves in. Joe grabbed the throttle, a large lever set into the floor next to his chair and slammed it forward. The ship surged forward.

The shimmering gray disk of the wormhole loomed closer and then engulfed them with an obligatory white flash to mark the occasion.

While they were blissfully enjoying the trip through the wormhole, Hack bummed a joint off of Manuel. He couldn't remember the last time he'd toked up.

"Yeah maen," Manuel said lighting the bud for Hack, "Yu know yu start acheting foonie ween yu don hawv no weeed tu smoke."

Hack inhaled deeply and immediately he felt all those crazy notions that had been getting him into trouble lately, fade away.

When they came out the other side they were in orbit around Deo. And in the distance the tiny point of light of Deo 7.

Hack thought he'd never be so thankful to see that sorry planet again and he took another toke.

Chapter 37: A New Emperor

With the reinforcements from the Leech, Rogicphil felt he might just have a handle on the war situation.

He was flying up into orbit to meet them in Grego's aircar with the Mean man himself and Space-Bo.

"Rumors as to the Leech's death have been greatly exaggerated," Grego snickered.

Space-Bo looked out from the rear seat passenger window. This was a pretty cool aircar that could do orbits too. He knew he'd miss all these neat future things when he was sent back to his own time. Too bad, he'd miss this place.

Rogicphil turned to his wrist communicator, "Are you there FC?"

"Yeah, go ahead."

"What is your progress on the transmat?"

"Not good I'm afraid."

"Well I don't think we're going to need it anymore. Reinforcements have arrived from Moorgnad IV. We'll be able to swoop down pick everyone up who's still alive and then a make a break for it."

"That's good news except that we've already unsuccessfully tested the device."

"So, just turn it off and wait till I return."

"No, you see we went through and can't get back."

"Where are you?"

"Could be anywhere for all I know. The pickle jar galaxy, the inside of someone's lung, who knows."

"But you can't be that far. I'm still picking you up loud and clear."

"Not necessarily. I left the communicator relay on at full blast outside the transmat and so your signal is getting through but not much else, I'm afraid."

"Okay well don't do anything stupid. Check that. Don't do anything period. Just stay there and when we get back we'll retrieve you from the transmat okay?"

"But hurry Rogicphil, I don't think the creatures are going to wait long before they rip us up and the others don't spontaneously reform."

They were in their final approach to the Leech. Grego did a fancy maneuver and landed on the side of the bloated ship avoiding the shuttle bay entirely.

"I'll get back to you," Rogicphil cut transmission with the chicken then turned to Grego, "What's this?"

"A can opener."

"Eh?"

Grego hit a few buttons on a side panel and the aircar lowered itself flat against the other ship's hull. There was slight whirring sound below them followed by a dull thud. "That should do it." He turned around to face Space-Bo, "Could you lift up that back seat please... or else."

Space-Bo did so and found a small hatch on the floor.

"Open it."

He did, revealing a freshly cut hole into the host ship. "Cool."

Grego smiled, "And when we leave all their air will slowly leak out into space."

"How lovely," Rogicphil said, "But no time for arguments."

"There's always time for an argument."

"Not now. Space-Bo..."

"Sure there is. You don't seem like a very good arguer Rogicphil."

Rogicphil ignored Grego's leading manner and followed Space-Bo into the other ship. Before he closed the hatch after him he looked back at Grego, "Head back to the surface and see if you can find the Funky Chicken."

"That old bag of bones? He's no fun. He likes it when I'm mean to him."

Rogicphil didn't put much faith into Grego and so left him at that.

Down into the bowels of the Leech, his old nemesis, he and Space-Bo were confronted with a confusing array of corridors and hallways with little or no directions on how to get anywhere.

He turned back to his wristcom, "Hack? Bufgoo? Where are you guys?"

"We're on the bridge," Bufgoo replied, "Why aren't you in the shuttle bay yet?"

"We, uh got dropped off elsewhere."

"Well go back wherever you came in and go around to the shuttle bay. We'll never be able to find you if you just wander around."

"Okay, hold on." He tapped Space-Bo on the shoulder, "Come on we need to get back to the aircar before Grego takes off."

Even with Rogicphil's super speed they got back just in time to see, through a gaping hole in the hull, the aircar fly off. They almost got to see the hole from the other side too. Atmosphere was escaping pretty quickly and was dragging them out with it but the back of Space-Bo's spacesuit clogged the hole and they were left in a hallway with slightly less air pressure.

"Okay, I've got an idea," Rogicphil said, "On three I want you to let go and then slip through the hole."

"Can I put my helmet on first?" Space-Bo didn't wait for the answer but quickly pulled it over his head and snapped it into place.

"Walk around the hull till you get to the shuttle bay and go in."

"What about you? You don't have a suit."

"Don't worry about me. Just tow me along behind you and don't let me float away."

"Whatever," Space-Bo said and then wiggled around until the seal was broken and he got sucked out into space.

(Okay, so they did end up getting to look at the hole from the outside after all.)

Rogicphil took a deep breath then let himself get drawn outside as well. He willed zeppelin boots and was pleased to see a single large balloon inflate around his feet. Before it could completely fill up he reached down and pulled the flexible material up around him. Soon he was sealed inside his own personal pressure bubble.

Space-Bo must have grabbed a hold because now he felt himself being dragged along the outside of the Leech's hull. In a few minutes he felt a knock on the outside of his balloon. "Yeah," he said into his wristcom.

"Oh, there you are," a voice came back, "You're inside the pressure seal now. Full one atmo. You can come out now."

"Okay," Rogicphil reverted his boots to normal duty. It took less than a minute for the balloon to deflate and be retracted back into the soles.

Bufgoo and Space-Bo stood there in the airlock with him. In one direction the hatch led out into the unpressurized shuttle bay. In the other, the inside of the Leech again.

"You got an extra pair of those I could borrow some time?" Bufgoo asked.

"Believe me you don't want anything to do with these boots. They cause more trouble than they're worth."

"Yeah but..."

They were interrupted by a message on Rogicphil's wrist, "Get up here right away Rogicphil," it was Joe on the bridge. "The leader of the rebel forces on the surface says he has hostages and wants terms for our uncon.. uh uncondis.. hmm,... He wants us to give up, damn it!"

*   *   *

The Funky Chicken and Dr. Fred Shandrydan were trudging through a nasty swamp somewhere. It was night time and the creatures were out. Strange squawks, chirps, and grunts echoed around them in the gloom.

"These seems awfully familiar," Shandrydan said, suspiciously looking around.

They climbed up a slight embankment out of the muck and onto dryer ground for a break. There was no moon and only a few pale oddly twinkling stars in the sky.

"What planet are we on?" Shandrydan asked as he looked around at the extremely bizarre flora.

The chicken stopped to examine some crud on the ground before him, "I'm not convinced we are on a planet."

"What do you mean? Is this some kind of illusion created by the faulty transmat device? If that were the case then a slight variation in the horizon point conjunction would be unnoticeable and I have not detected that so far."

"You're correct, this is no illusion, but something fishy is up. Take a look at this," he handed the scientist a sample of crud.

"Hmm," Shandrydan studied it from various angles, "I would say it's some type of lint residue."

"I had the same analysis."

"What kind of planet contains lint residue in its lithosphere?"

"I have no idea. That's what makes this really bizarre."

"This reminds me of a swamp back on Deo 7 where Sir Rontho, rest his soul, and I swapped bodies with some crazy swampgators." Shandrydan suddenly looked up and sniffed the stale air, "Do you hear something?"

"Yeah, and it's getting louder. Let's hide under that tree over there." The hurried under what at first look appeared to be a tree.

A distant rumbling grew louder and the ground began to shake.

"Look!" Shandrydan said, pointing up into the sky. What at first appeared to be a star grew bigger, to the size of comet, then to a minor planetoid, taking up a sizable percentage of the sky. It sailed by overhead, narrowly missing the 'planet' they were on. The rumbling died down then disappeared altogether.

"Audible sound does not travel through space," the chicken stated flatly.

"So how were we able to hear the planetoid coming? I agree with you Neble, this 'planet' isn't all that it should be."

"Let's continue on towards that mountain in the distance. Maybe we can discover something there."

"Okay," but when Shandrydan went to stand up and move away from the 'tree', he was pulled back. "Something's got me Mr. Chicken."

"Hold on," FC looked at Shandrydan's back and found a bulbous growth attached to him from the 'tree'. He easily bit through it with his beak and Fred was free.

"Thanks," Shandrydan said, readjusting his clothing.

"This is really strange."

"What?"

"This stuff oozing out of the tree. Its taste reminds me of cheese for some reason."

"No matter, let's get going."

They continued on through the swamp and twice in half an hour minor planetoids flew by in space. Each time they could 'hear' its approach and eventual passing. To say planetoid to describe the massive objects cruising by in the sky would be like trying to play a pancake in a CD player. They simply were not shaped right to be celestial objects.

The swamp abruptly ended at the top of a cliff, which dropped half a kilometer down to a dark plain. They walked to the edge and took in the panoramic view.

"My God!" Shandrydan cried, pointing to the mountain in the distance which they had been using as a landmark. "It looks like a giant twin-key."

"Hmm."

"Perhaps an intelligent species created it as a monument to snack foods."

"Maybe. Regardless, this place is definitely organic in nature."

"Not necessarily. Look down there to the left. What's that giant spike of metal doing there?"

"It's pretty far away. It could be a city."

"But with no windows, smoke stacks, roadways, or anything? Just a giant metal spike?"

"If we weren't suppose to wait for Rogicphil I'd think I might jump right off this thing, just to see how far down it goes."

"I guess this is as good a place as any to wait for our rescue."

"Yeah, you're right." The chicken sat down letting his feet talons dangle over the edge.

Another rumble began to build but by this time they had grown use to the occurrence and weren't overly excited. Until, that is, the planetoid appeared directly overhead and thundered through space directly at them.

"Uh, Rogicphil," the chicken said into his communicator, "I think now would be a good time to bring us back."

*   *   *

But Rogicphil didn't get a chance to answer the chicken's query. He was busy on the bridge of the Leech dealing with the sorry situation on the planet below.

The Balidronian rebel leader Gnorge McShplat's image filled the huge viewscreen like some grotesque meatloaf. He was dressed in a puke colored camouflaged dinner suit with matching fly net helmet.

"We want you to give yourself up in exchange for the prisoners."

Rogicphil shook his head, "I told you already, we don't give a hoot about Hagsplat Ufglong Jr., senior, or grandmother. You can take your prisoners and sh..."

"I also have more interesting prisoners," the leader moved out of the way while a lackey brought forward Mr. Bear, little Grrr and the robot girl with the purple blindfold.

Rogicphil had assumed their deaths in the cocktail lounge explosion but now had to take them into account again. "What do you really want McShplat?"

The ugly rebel returned to the screen, "Just you. When you get down here we'll release the prisoners and they'll be free to go about their business." He made no attempt to cover the nasty grin on his face.

"And if I refuse?"

"I'll let them go."

"Really?"

"No just kidding. I'll kill them. First by exposure to raw liquid deo and then by a thousand tiny paper cuts all over their skin and next.."

"You can only kill somebody once," Rogicphil interrupted.

"Yeah, but they don't know that," he laughed. "What's it going to be PHIL?" He said the last word really sarcastically.

"I'll come down for the exchange."

"Whew!" Joe wiped his forehead, "I thought he would never shut up. Well it's been nice knowing you Rogman." He stepped over to the Gladerunner with his hand stuck out for a shake, "If you can now send us back to the twentieth century, we'll be on our way and let you go off to bravely die."

Rogicphil didn't shake hands with Joe.

Bufgoo came up and whispered to Joe, "You're going to let him go down there in exchange for some dumb bear?"

"Better him than me. I don't want to die. If he wants to, that's fine by me, just as long as we get back in time for MacGyver."

Rogicphil chuckled, "I can't send you back."

Joe got slightly upset, "What do you mean, can't send us back? Can't or won't?"

"Destiny is the one who brought you here from all across time and he's disappeared, leaving us to fend for ourselves."

"So how the hell are we suppose to get back huh? Scratch our butts and hope a wormhole poops out?"

"Well, so long," Rogicphil turned to leave.

Space-Bo who had been listening to the conversation from the beginning spoke up, "Wait a second. I'll go with you, you'll need back up for your plan."

"I don't have any plan," Rogicphil said waltzing out the door towards the shuttle bay.

"Cool." Space-Bo followed after.

Joe and Bufgoo were left arguing amongst themselves.

"Hey!" Joe looked around, "Where'd he go? You've got to stop him."

"What for? He just said he couldn't send us back. We might as well sit back and enjoy the rest of our lives on this luxury spaceship."

"You idiot!" Joe pushed the fat man out of his way and went after Rogicphil and Space-Bo.

Bufgoo looked over to where Manuel was tripping out on a computer console screen saver. Hack was fast asleep in the pit just in front of the captain's chair. Well it looked like it was his turn to save the universe this time.

He climbed into the large fake leathered chair squirming his fat butt around until he got comfortable. And then with both hands firm on the throttle he slammed the ship into high gear, reverse that is.

*   *   *

Space-Bo had given up on following Rogicphil back to the shuttle bay; the Gladerunner was simply too fast to keep up with. Confused as to where exactly on the large spaceship he was, he decided to take a break and have a snack.

He reached into a pocket and rummaged around for a bit of cheese or perhaps a half eaten twin-key when something bit him. Quickly he pulled his hand out and examined it for damage. Nothing was visible. Strange.

Just then Joe came around the corner, "Okay, where is he? You can't hide him forever you know?"

"What are you talking about Joe?"

"Rogicphil, you moron." Joe tried to look in the space between Space-Bo and the wall, "Oh man, he's not there either." He suddenly realized how stupid that sounded and tried to cover by saying, "I thought you might be sitting on him you know."

Space-Bo pointed down the hall to his left, "He went that away, to the shuttle bay. But I don't think you'll be able to catch him in time."

"Oh yeah? Why not?"

"He's too fast. He's got those hyper spaz glade boots remember."

Joe sniffed at his armpit, was about to make another stupid remark but thankfully thought better of it.

The ship jerked. They stumbled into the bulkhead.

"What was that?"

Joe cursed, "It's that damn Bufgoo. He's up to something."

Space-Bo headed back towards the bridge.

"Hey wait up!" Joe hurried after the ex-space marine.

When they got back to the bridge, they found Bufgoo trying to dislodge the stuck throttle. He looked up when they came in, "Uh hi guys. Back so soon?" Behind him on the screen Deo 7 was quickly receding away.

Space-Bo ran over to the captain's chair to help Bufgoo with the lever.

Joe went over to where Manuel was tripping and hit the clear key on the console. The computer screen came back up with a current status report.

"Hey maen, yu keeling the vibe," Manuel protested.

Joe ignored him, as usual, and made out what he could and saw that it wasn't good, "We're headed right into the sun. Good work Bufgoo."

"With hoondreds uf screens awl over dey place awnd yu hayf to peek mine? Wha da deek!"

"Don't blame me," the fat man said to Joe, "It's this bleepin' lever's fault. It's stuck in place."

"Save if for Saint Peter, eh?"

Manuel cursed something unwritable and rubbed his hungry belly. Maybe Hack would know where some food was. He walked around to a narrow set of steps that led down into the pit where he knew Hack would be sleeping.

"Hey dude," he said, "Aye need soam grub, amigo. Wha chu got?"

Hack yawned. "What?" he said looking around and not remembering where he was.

Bufgoo leaned over the edge above them, "Get up here quick Hack. We need your big arm."

Hack rubbed his sore head, "Up where?"

Manuel searched Hack's pockets for a joint or a snack or something.

Bufgoo was insistent, "We're all going to die unless you help us turn this ship around!"

"Sure, okay..." Groggy Hack climbed the steps and walked around to the big chair. "Now what?"

"That part there," Bufgoo pointed at he lever stuck in the reverse position, "Should be over here," he indicated the forward position.

"Whatever man," casually Hack took the lever and attempted to shove it forward. Instead it came off in his hand. "Oh," he looked surprised for a moment then held it up for Bufgoo to see, "This yours?"

"Yeah oops," Joe screamed, "Now we're all gonna die! Thanks a whole big bunch!"

Space-Bo found the viewscreen control panel and switched to a rear facing perspective, "At least we'll be able to see what's going to kill us." The Deo sun burned brighter and brighter as the Leech continued to accelerate backwards into it.

* * *

Rogicphil had managed to clear the shuttle bay in the Clergy's garbage scow before Bufgoo's mayhem had ensued and was already in the atmosphere before he would have noticed anything wrong. As it was, he felt really pathetic that after all he'd been through, it was finally going to come down to this: suicide.

Well, if he managed to saved someone's life maybe it wouldn't be so bad. Some part of him thought he was being a complete idiot about the whole situation.

"So what do you want me to do?" he asked himself.

"Well you could just run away," he answered.

"How? In Gladerunner spaceship boots?"

"Your Fiat."

"It was destroyed in the explosion."

"Hmm."

Maybe he was insane and this was all one big hallucination. That would explain him talking to himself. But as the deo laced clouds broke over the Balidron metrocenter he knew he could never make up something so sorry-assed as this place.

Resigned to an exciting but short live he touched down outside the rebel headquarters, Kebber vat warehouse no. 47.

McShplat met him on the tarmac a hundred meters out from the warehouse. He had two hooded figures behind him with a couple of guards on either side.

"I'm here Gnorge. Let them go." Rogicphil stood still waiting for the response.

Gnorge looked disappointed, "That's it? Let them go? Come on now we're suppose to argue and ponder the philosophical nature of your actions."

"Huh?"

"The reign of terror you have brought to this planet. The way you and your hit squad raped and plundered my people."

"Yeah, I admit it. So can we get this over with? I'm beginning to get hungry and I'd like to have my last meal now."

"There'll be time enough to argue when you're tied up and hanging over a boiling vat of liquid deo! Get him!" Gnorge's guards moved forward to grab Rogicphil.

Before they got too close he spoke up, "First let them go. When they're safely in the air I'll surrender."

"You'll go now!" Gnorge pressed a button on a remote control he had in his hand.

A trapdoor opened up beneath Rogicphil. He switched to helicopter boots but it was no use as a powerful suction pulled him down. Now he really felt stupid.

The tube drew him down faster than he could react. Before he could come up with an escape plan, he smelled the sickly odor of knockout gas. As blackness enveloped him, he cursed Destiny one last time.

As promised, he came to hanging upside down over a boiling vat of deo. The entire warehouse was bare except for him and his vat. At any minute the stupid rebel would enter to gloat, as he lowered the Gladerunner to his doom.

If he was going to make peace, this was the time to do it. The only Supreme Being he knew was Destiny and that one betrayed him. He thought about pleading with the Quasars but didn't think they could or even cared to read minds. Besides, only other Supreme Beings were even aware of the Quasar group. It would be stupid to worship them anyway.

Oh well, he decided to thank his pet slug Burf, whom he flushed down the toilet the day he'd left Roganivar IV for his new job on Danville. The slug made no demands and had actually existed at one time.

"Thank you Burf for your wonderful slime. I am most grateful for its oh so sticky mycological..."

His prayer was interrupted by someone on the wristcom, "Hey 'Phil! We're about to be pulled into the sun up here. Could you please come and save us?" It was Bufgoo.

"Not right now, I'm busy making peace with existence."

"When you're done could you hurry on over and get us out of this mess?"

"Oh, alright. Hold on," he imagined he was wearing razor sharp ice skates. The blades would easily slice through the bindings around his legs, he'd jump down, find a spaceship, and then go save them. Afterward he return for his punishment.

That's what this was all about then huh? Punishment? He was doing this to himself because of what he considered to be his own failure. How pathetic.

He looked up at his feet wondering why the boots were taking so long and noticed he wasn't wearing the Gladerunner boots anymore.

Gnorge burst in then strutting around like a madman, "Hey hey Hey! Like the new style 'PHIL? I call it my super being look." He was wearing the Gladeboots.

Guards brought Mr. Bear and the Purple girl in and then slammed the doors shut behind.

"I thought you were going to let them go?" Rogicphil said from his awkward position.

"You wanted to change the rules at the last minute, remember? You wanted them to go free before you gave up. One dirty trick deserves another."

He rollerbladed up to the Purple girl, "Oh by the way," he turned the right boot into an ice climber spike boot, "Thanks for the neat shoes," and drove the foot into the girl's stomach.

"Rog..." the girl cried as sparks flew and she slowly fell to the floor with Gnorge's foot still stuck in her chest.

"What the crap!?" the rebel quickly dislodged his foot and hopped a safe distance back. "You didn't tell me she was a robot. Robot's are no fun to kill. You never know if they'll just fizzle or..."

KA-Boom! her body exploded into tiny pieces of shrapnel impaling all those standing around.

Gnorge brushed himself off making sure he wasn't hurt, "...explode."

The others weren't so lucky. Both guards were dead and/or bleeding on the floor and Mr. Bear was bloodied in several places where he'd been knocked back against the wall. The only damage Rogicphil sustained was a small piece of metal stuck in his cheek where it continued to scald.

"GNORGE!" Rogicphil yelled.

McShplat smiled at himself, "I haven't had this much fun since I robbed that old lady the other day. It was so easy since she didn't understand the concept of positive money yet." He strutted over to a winch on the side of the wall. "And now for the encore."

*   *   *

Bufgoo, Hack, Manuel, and Joe, not to mention Space-Bo were finishing what they all assumed was to be their final game of scrabble. Space-Bo and Hack had tied on the previous three games but this last one looked like it might go to Manuel.

"Anybody got a copy of Roger Water's Radio Chaos album?" Joe asked.

"Yeah," Bufgoo said sarcastically, "I got the LP in my back pocket."

"I'd believe it, your ass is fat enough."

But this futile attempt at last minute good natured fun wasn't working.

Space-Bo scratched at his pocket, "I wonder what keeps making me itch?"

"You ever bother to look?" Joe posed.

"Nope," Space-Bo opened the pocket and peeked inside. "Nothing there."

But then a tiny voice spoke to him from the depths, "Space-Boooooo.." It sounded like it was crossing an enormous distance.

"Yeah?" he answered.

"Take out the piece of cheese moooooooooold in your pocket...."

Joe whispered to Bufgoo, "He's talking to cheese."

"And thankfully you're about to die," the fat man replied.

Joe shrugged. There was no sense arguing with the obvious.

Space-Bo reaching into his pocket and fished around for the cheese mold. He found it. The thing seemed to ooze onto his hand. He put it up to his ear just like he did to rice crispies during breakfast.

"...put me in the microwave..." the tiny voice said.

"I'm sorry, I'd love to, but I have to die now," Space-Bo answered, "Maybe later, huh?"

"...no, now..."

Space-Bo scratched his head, almost smearing the mold there, but at the last minute, remembered not to use that finger; that was for scratching his... This was taking to long to figure out. He decided it was just easier to comply. There was a microwave in the captain's not-ready room and even cheese molds deserved to have their last wishes granted so he plopped the piece of goo inside the tiny machine and waved it goodbye.

"...thanks..."

"No prob-lem-o," he slammed the door shut and mashed the on button.

Nothing happened for the first couple of seconds but then the machine began to wildly vibrate and hop about the counter top. The hatch popped open and the Funky Chicken's head popped out.

"FC? What are you doing in there?"

"No time to explain, just grab my beak and pull me out."

"Sure," Space-Bo got a firm grip and then ripped the rest of the chicken out but that wasn't all. Holding onto his taloned feet was the good old Dr.

Shandrydan. "That's pretty cool. How'd you do it?"

The chicken shook his head, "RUN!"

All three made a mad dash out of the not-ready room just as the microwave exploded with the force of a five mega cheese pizza. They crashed in a heap at the feet of the Clergy.

Joe chuckled, "Look who showed up just in time to die."

FC got up and looked around at the bridge sizing up the situation fairly quickly, "The old broken throttle into the sun backwards conundrum, eh? I should have known." He went over to the coffee dispenser on the side of the captain's chair.

"Whatever you're going to do, do it quickly." Joe ordered, "We have thirty seconds left."

"I think so," he looked for a coffee mug, but not just any coffee mug. The coffee mug that he needed, needed to be slightly larger than normal in size with an 'I (heart) something' logo on the side and maybe a tiny trick hole just below the rim that made people dribble all over themselves when they took a sip, or maybe a fake cockroach embossed on the inside bottom and... oh never mind. It didn't matter since he didn't see one. "Does anyone know if this thing works or not?"

"Uh," Bufgoo looked excited for half a moment but then said "No..."

Joe was on his knees pleading, "Oh pleeeese save me. You've got to."

"Okay if it'll make you quit your sniveling." The chicken stuck his right hand / wing into the throttle gear box and twisted something. The ship accelerated into the sun's corona.

"That's the wrong way!" Bufgoo shouted.

"Huh?" the chicken turned his head to get a look at the screen, "Oh you're right, sorry. Looks like it's plan B then."

"What's plan B?"

"Go FASTER!" The ship lunged even faster towards the searing sun now.

Everyone on the bridge screamed, even the Funky Chicken who was enjoying himself. He stopped screaming long enough to ask if anyone had found a coffee mug yet.

Space-Bo fished in his pocket then threw one at FC.

"Thanks," the chicken said catching the mug with his free hand, "My other hand is entangled in the gear box so I can't exactly reach the emergency rudder control over there," he tossed the mug backwards over his head, apparently in a random fashion, but the mug sailed expertly across the bridge and hit the rudder control just enough to nudge the ship into slingshot orbit around the sun. "Now haNG ON!"

The ship skimmed in through the sun's outer gaseous atmosphere shaking wildly. Everyone who wasn't holding on at the time, which meant Joe, went flying back and forth smacking into every sharp corner on the bridge.

But at last it was over, and the ship came out from around the back side of the sun and on course for Deo 7.

"In payment," the chicken announced, pouring himself a cup of coffee, "I expect each one of you to figure out some artistically beautiful way to kill me."

384

"Why you!" Joe stomped over and began strangling the chicken. "Ah the gratitude..."

*   *   *

Rogicphil's nose had just touched the first bit of deo when the downward sliding of the wench quit and he was slowly pulled back up. He breathed a sign of relief even if it was the strongest deo smell ever.

A slightly wounded Mr. Bear hauled him down to the warehouse's concrete floor. There was no sign of Gnorge anywhere.

"What happened? Where'd he go?"

The bear thumbed over his shoulder, "Grrr." He motioned for Rogicphil to follow him. They left the warehouse, stepping through a double set of doors and out onto a balcony. Several stories below a small army of green and blue clad soldiers stood at attention.

"What's this?"

An aircar whooshed up from below. It hovered a couple of meters from the balcony then a familiar face poked out the window. "Welcome to my new planet Rogicphil," it was Grego.

"Huh?"

Grego laughed, "Gnorge is buried ten kilometers under. You can thank me later, but first you must attend my coronation as the new Emperor of Deo 7."

Chapter 38: Last Words

Destiny decided to show himself again at Grego's coronation. If he harbored any regret for abandoning his team he showed no sign but he was strangely nervous.

The Leech had returned a couple hours before and the remaining team was once again assembled. Even Bagidol, Plutoman's wayward doggie was there. He was trying to tell everyone about his awesome programming skills and how he'd created the holopirates to defend the chorus line girls from the Leech and inadvertently unleashed a holovirus on them all, but no paid him any attention.

"What the hell were you doing in the microwave?" Joe asked FC.

"It's a long story but I'll make it short. That transmat device we'd build had shrank us and then send Shandrydan and myself into the strange environment of Space-Bo's pocket. I knew that since our quark structure was still harboring some residual sub harmonic resonances left over from our previous journey inside his liver, that if enough microwave energy were pumped in we'd expand back to normal."

Rogicphil shook his head. What a crazy story. In the old days he would have written an article about it, but now he was grateful he wasn't the one who had to save them.

Destiny clapped his hands together, "WONDERFUL STORY. BUT NOW I THINK IT'S TIME TO EAT."

"Help yourself," Rogicphil said looking around. The serving trays were virtually bare, containing only half eaten rotten sandwiches and crumbs. It wasn't that they'd gotten there late but just the way Grego liked to treat his guests.

A trumpet sounded and the guards began ushering people into the main auditorium.

Destiny checked his watch. He pulled Rogicphil to one side as he was passing by to enter the seating area, "I'VE ORDERED A PIE. WHY DON'T YOU WAIT HERE WITH ME FOR JUST A MOMENT?"

Rogicphil pulled away, "I don't want to talk to you."

Destiny twiddled his fingers and the fungi on the floor rose up to make a wall blocking Rogicphil, "YOU MAY HAVE YOUR GLADEBOOTS BACK BUT I STILL OUT RANK YOU."

"So what? You're nothing more than a miserable excuse for a Supreme Being. I dare you to blast me into oblivion."

The pie delivery boy arrived. Destiny motioned him over. He handed the kid some new positive money.

"God I hate this," the kid took the money anyway, "I don't think I can get use to taking money FOR payment. It's not natural."

"YOU'LL GET USE TO IT."

He ran off before the guards could get to him.

Destiny very carefully checked the pie to make sure it was the right flavor and then breathed a sigh of relief, "OKAY, LET'S GO IN NOW."

Rogicphil unwillingly accompanied the Supreme Being into the auditorium. Seeing that they were together, the guards attempted unsuccessfully to break them up but after Destiny made several oversized flem balls appear in the guard's nostrils they were left alone.

The lights dimmed and the crowd hushed down. Things were finally getting under way. A low droning began to be heard behind the massive folds of curtaining that enveloped the main stage. The thum, thum, thum, dum-da-thum, thum, thum, of a military march played on a deep resonating bass.

Rogicphil knew it could only be the sound of Manuel and his bass.

A spotlight beamed down now and the curtain slowly parted. Still dimly lit, a bare stage was revealed with a lone Manuel earnestly playing. Bufgoo appeared then, hovering above the stage before being lowered on what appeared to be almost invisible wires (almost since simple gravimetric control was responsible for the whole thing while it took a small army of holographic engineers working two weeks in a swamp infested computer lab to create the illusion of barely visible wires). And in his smooth low voice he sang:

He keeps you in debt,
Eternally set,
He took all the currency,
Hid it in the effluentcy,
He's Grego....
Grego the Mean!

Space-Bo and Chicken,
The plot they did thicken,
But he's a real Mannie,
Now he's got Annie,
He's Grego....
Grego the Mean!

A dark hulking form entered stage left and made its way over to where Bufgoo was singing. The up until recently passive crowd burst into cheers of false recognition as a second spotlight shown down on the new arrival, the satanic cow. A wireless mic hung down from a horn and she sang:

Now don't you panic,
The cow's not satanic,
The Bossman and Lester,
Both tried to best her,
She's Besey....
Besey the Cow!

She fought real hard,
To stay out of the lard,
But the bear was better,
Though he hardly met her,

She's Besey....
Besey the Cow!

As she sang, the cow glanced in Destiny's direction and he nodded in acknowledgment. She and Bufgoo then sang the Grego the Mean/Where have you been? Chorus as a full orchestral sound welled up around them. With an enormous explosion of smoke and sparkles, the full line of Chorus Girls emerged out of the thin air. They all joined together and sang:

Rogicphil Suflipinic,
What's on your chinny-nic,
Lick up that mustard,
It's not in the custard,
Eat up that pie,
Cause we don't, want, to, die......................

The tempo changed dramatically now, to up beat modern dance. The crowd went wild and began dancing with abandonment.
A snazzy decked out Fred Shandrydan made a fantastic entrance as he slid across the stage with a couple of googly-eyed wanna-bes hanging on. He sang:

Hail to the chief,
Or he'll give you such grief,
The atoms are aligning,
Soon we'll be pining,
He's Grego....
Grego the Mean!

There was a sudden commotion down in the center of the audience. All eyes turned to see the new Emperor himself parting the sea of people with merely a glare. Only one person stood her ground, Annie. Slightly cut up and a bit bruised from the recent rebel attack, she none-the-less looked dazzling in her ballroom dress.
Grego was no small man but even he had to look up into her gleaming eyes. Their faces were locked in confrontation as only the jungle drum beat could be heard in the entire hall.
And then, "May I have this dance?" he asked.
Annie hesitated. Grego made his move. He swooped in grabbing her hands in his. She didn't resist. "Ha-hah!" he shouted as they whisked away into the renewed dancing melee.
Rogicphil scanned the crowd for Space-Bo. The ex-Marine was no where to be seen. But Destiny reared his ugly head instead and quickly approached with a tray laden full of pies in hand.
"After you send me back to Roganivar IV you can take these stupid boots away, because I quit." Rogicphil said to the supreme being before he accepted an outstretched hand and danced off with the young woman attached to it.

Destiny awkwardly followed, "HMM HMMMM, COD LIVER OIL AND MUSTARD MERANGE PIE. DON'T YOU WANT A PIECE?"

"That's disgusting," Rogicphil tried to dance away.

The Supreme Being followed, dancing amazingly well with the pie precariously balanced in his hand high over his head. "YOU ONLY NEED TO TASTE IT. THE SATANIC COW MADE IT HERSELF. IT'D BE RUDE NOT TO AT LEAST TRY IT."

Rogicphil was furious. He stopped dancing and turned to face Destiny who eagerly presented the pie out in both hands to him. Without a second thought he smacked the pie out of Destiny's hands and poked an angry finger at the Supreme Being. "Let me tell you something buddy..."

The lovingly hand crafted pie sailed up into the air. To Destiny it seemed to float for all eternity. He knew it was his last chance. If Rogicphil didn't eat the pie they'd all be history. "NOOOOOOOOOOOOOOOOOOOOOOOOOOO!"

The pie reached it's peak and started back down right over a delegate from the Arflin Isles. Destiny moved to catch it.

Rogicphil watched all this with amusement from his super speed perspective. Just before the pie would have squashed down on top of the delegate's bald head he zoomed up and gently caught it right side up.

Everyone in the auditorium turned around aghast .

Grego called out from on the stage, "Who dares disrupt the chaos of this event?"

Destiny stopped just short of crashing into Rogicphil, the pie, and the bald delegate, "PLEASE, HAVE A PIECE."

Rogicphil smiled, "Well.... if you insist." He plowed the pie right into Destiny's face.

"Guards!" Grego called, "Restrain those guests."

But the guards were wary and would only approach within two meters. Grego was forced to deal with the situation himself. He stormed up the aisle and forced his way through the crowd to the small clear area surrounding the two. "Oh, it's you guys. I should have known."

Annie stayed a few paces back but watched on intently.

Destiny wiped the gunk off his face, "IT'S OVER."

"My coronation most certainly is not!" Grego regarded the Supreme Being as he would a small slug ant, "You insolent little worm."

"NO, I MEAN THE UNIVERSE."

Rogicphil rubbed his chin, "Huh?"

"THE PIE. IT'S WHAT EVERYTHING WAS ALL ABOUT. THE ENTIRE DEO 7 MISSION, THE UNIVERSE, EVERYTHING. IT'S RUINED AND NOW SO IS ALL OF EXISTENCE."

The formerly satanic cow jumped down off the stage and rushed up to Destiny. She saw what had happened and hung her head low.

Rogicphil knew Destiny had been under tremendous pressure but this was ridiculous, "You have completely flipped big D. Do you expect us to believe that our whole mission to stop the satanic cow from taking over the Galaxy was just a front so that you could save this pie?"

"YES. THE UNIVERSE WORKS IN WAYS THAT ARE EVEN

MORE MYSTERIOUS TO US SUPREME BEINGS. AN UNSTOPPABLE CHAIN OF EVENTS THAT WILL DESTROY THE UNIVERSE IN LESS THAN A WEEK HAS BEGUN. ONLY A VERY PRECISELY CONTROLLED TWEEKING OF THE QUANTUM SUBSTRUCTURE WOULD HAVE PREVENTED IT. THAT TWEEKING SHOULD HAVE BEEN YOU, THE GLADERUNNING, EATING A PIECE OF THAT PIE EXACTLY THIRTEEN SECONDS AGO. AND NOW..."

"And now you look like a total buffoon," Rogicphil finished. He turned to Grego, "I'm really sorry about this. They don't make leashes for Supreme Beings."

"Is that all?" Grego asked.

"NO THAT ISN'T ALL. I ALSO KNOW OF YOUR PLAN TO USE THE CRYSTAL OMNIMEGNETO. THAT WOULD ONLY MAKE THINGS WORSE. IT IS THE NEXUS POINT WHICH ATTRACTS ALL THIS ACTIVITY IN THE FIRST PLACE. INCREASING ITS POTENTIAL AND OUTPUT WOULD ONLY LESSEN WHAT LITTLE TIME WE DO HAVE LEFT." Destiny shook his head then sat down in the middle of the floor with his face in his hands.

"Okay then, can I now get back to becoming Emperor?"

Rogicphil nodded, "How did you do it anyway?"

"It was an old contract I made with Balidron's mayor along time ago. If they defaulted on a certain loan then I would get control of the entire planet."

"Did the mayor have that power? To give you the whole planet I mean?"

"Shhhh," Grego moved up right next to Rogicphil and whispered, "What these people don't know can't hurt them. Why don't you join me up at the front where I can keep an eye on you."

"You're just as crazy," Rogicphil turned away and began to walk out.

"You can't do this to me 'Phil. I'll hunt you down. Together we could have ruled the Galaxy!"

Rogicphil just shook his head and shuffled out of the auditorium. No one tried to stop him. Outside on one of the generic asphalt planes he walked alone. The sunglow was hidden by a large green cloud and he kicked rocks in the shadowless environment.

And then as happened once before, a weird kid on a bicycle materialized out of thin air and handed Rogicphil a letter.

It was addressed to the Gladerunner. "Hey I quit," he tried to say but when he looked up the messenger was already gone. The letter was stamped with a return address of One Quasar Street, Big Idiot Universe 90078.

Inside was the simple note:

Greetings: Gladerunner

In appreciation for your service in the Destiny affair and your attempt to save your universe from an unstoppable chain of events that will eventually destroy it, you are hereby granted one wish.

Sincerely,
(*an amazingly beautiful yet somehow careless signature was scrawled here*)
Chairman, the Quasar Board of Directors
CQ/lq

"I wish this whole mess could have been avoided in the first place," he shouted. Nothing happened. He looked up into the air wondering if the Quasars were laughing at him. "Okay, okay, just give me my Fiat back and we'll call it even."

He looked down and his grungy old converted Fiat spaceship sat there awaiting him. It was over, he now knew. The whole stupid mess, the others would be sent back to their right times and spaces and the universe would go on, for a little while at least.

He hopped into his Fiat. It started right up. "Right! I need a drink!" The ship rose up off the pavement then streaked up into the sky and into deep space. He knew a great little bar on Roganivar IV.

*   *   *

After the coronation, Space-Bo was talking to the Funky Chicken on top of Grego's new Imperial headquarters, the site of VIP disembarkment. Small groups of time travelers conversed amongst themselves as one by one they were disappearing into puffs of smoke.

"I guess I got what I deserved, huh?"

"You mean with Annie?" FC asked.

"Yeah, I don't want to commit and so she goes off and gets hitched with an Emperor. Talk about crummy luck."

Just then the Clergy disappeared into a puff of air. "What happened to them?" Space-Bo asked.

"They're being sent back. The mission is over. You'll be gone too any second. So long."

"Hey wait! I don't want to go back yet. Things were just starting to get fun."

"But the universe is going to be destroyed any day now. You'll go back in time, finish your life, and never worry about anything. And maybe I'll get blown to bits for good."

"But that's no fun. I want to see the universe go. That would be cool."

"Hmm," the chicken scratched his plumage. He looked over to where Destiny was sitting at a desk checking off time travelers as he sent them back. FC decided to go talk to him. "Space-Bo says he wants to stay behind and watch the universe end."

"FINE, FINE, YOU CAN FILL OUT THE PAPER WORK LATER, BUT YOU'LL NEED TO EXCUSE ME AS I'VE GOT A LOT OF WORK TO DO."

"Don't blame yourself. You did everything you could."

"DID I?" Big D looked up from his paperwork, "I LET ALL THOSE LIVING CREATURES DIE JUST BECAUSE IT LED UP TO THE MOMENT WHERE THE GLADERUNNER WAS TO HAVE EATEN THE PIE. IN

TYPICAL GLADERUNNER FASHION, HE REFUSED, AND NOW WE'RE DOOMED."

"Ain't it great? I haven't felt this good in 23 billion years."

"BUT I CAN'T REALLY BLAME ROGICPHIL. ONE OF THE CONDITIONS OF THE MISSION WAS THAT HE HAD TO EAT THE PIE WILLINGLY WITHOUT BEING TOLD WHY."

"Let's see, you can't blame yourself, you can't blame 'Phil. Hmm, BLAME ME! I except the blame for everything and the wrath of existence in vengeance. Strike me down forever and eternally!" The chicken chuckled, "Ha, ha, just kidding."

"ALL WISHFUL THINKING AND FAKE SARCASTIC LAUGHING ASIDE, I DON'T THINK IT'LL WORK. YOU'LL PROBABLY MAKE IT THROUGH TO THE NEXT UNIVERSE NO MATTER WHAT. AND I'LL BE OUT OF A JOB."

"You could always go back in time and try again."

"PLEASE LET ME BE," he looked back down at his list.

"Okay, Space-Bo and I are going to transmat out of here and try to see a bit of the universe before it goes. Take it easy." They left the Supreme Being to sulk in supreme self pity.

Destiny looked up, "HEY WAIT! WHAT DID YOU JUST SAY?" But the two had already warped out.

*   *   *

The Clergy, Plutoman, the chorus line girls (except for Annie), and everyone else that wasn't suppose to have died in the year 102701 were sent back to their respective timelines.

Precisely 3.27 days after Rogicphil refused to eat the cod liver oil and mustard meringue pie all the atoms in the universe aligned along the same fourth geometric point and canceled each other out. The universe ended not in a bang but with someone shouting, "Hey look it's Elvis!"

A void covered the face of the nothingness and the Quasars looked in and shook their heads. Another failed experiment. The Big Idiot Universe would have to be started all over from scratch now. Maybe this time Destiny would do a better job and not forget something.

Epilogue: Twilight of the Cow

Besey transmatted back to Brown's farm which turned out to be on the planet that harbored H.E.L.L's secret underground base, Lugietorp (*but I already told you that. Ha ha- the editor*). Oh well at least she was back were she'd begun. And Farmer Brown was there too.

"Now, jes lemme get this straight," he said, "Yu've been doing WHUT ta thu universe?"

They were in the kitchen discussing recent events over a pot of double brewed coffee. The formerly satanic cow stood over her place. Why had she been called satanic in the first place? It was one thing she never understood.

"I've been trying to save it from H.E.L.L. but that meddling time traveling bear defeated me and went on to wipe out H.E.L.L. as well."

"Well Besey you shor no how to be a pain in da ass."

There was a knock at the door.

Brown stomped past Besey into the living room to see who it was. He returned a moment later with a paper in his hand, "Wadda ya no Bess, they say thu durned universe is gonna explode. I don't think yu've been tellin' me thu whole truth now."

"Let me see that," Besey examine the letter:

TO: Whom it may concern
(citizen of the known universe)

   We have reason to believe that a rare astrological phenomenon will occur sometime in the near future that will cause the sudden demise of all existence. We at Yig Brother's would like to to offer you this unbeatable opportunity to purchase life insurance.
   It is unknown what effect the end of the universe will have upon life forms but one thing is for sure. People will need their life insurance more than ever.....

The letter continued on but Besey quit reading at that point. It had all been for nothing. All was lost. At least she still had the farm.

"Thets mor en any cow should ever read," Brown said taking the letter back, "Nah git back out to thu barn and gimme twenty gallons."

"Yes sir," she said with the cow equivilent of a salute and marched straight away out the farmhouse towards the barn to do her duty.

But she never made it because at that moment a hovercrane from the Adams-Dent Demolition Company Mistakenly demolished Farmer Brown's farmhouse, Brown, cow, and all. Apparently they'd won the bid to start ground breaking for a new Universe and wanted to get a head start.

THE END

GLOSSARY

I Things:

Alpuka Native sapient being of Deo 7
An anonymous voice See Neil/Clobberson effect
Barlow's Galactic Almanac Hardly ever used
Blimpton & Squeeler Law firm of Danville
BOG Spyman's Bag Of Goodies
Bow-Wing manufacturer of aerospace passenger vessels
Buggaluga Two Step Made famous by Cement Boot Charlie
B.U.S. Bidirectional Utility Shuttle
Cement Boot Charile Movie that Bufgoo liked
Clodzilla Mythological creature that likes Japanese
Compound Xc-90 Substance used in one of Dr. Fred Shandrydan's formulas
Darankeen Cactus Juice Nasty stuff
Deo-ore See Scoscrub
Defibalator Alcoholic beverage that causes heart failure
Fregoutnan Manufacture of good trench coats
Fuzgaloid Genetically engineered drug plant
GABA Gangsters Against Bowling Alleys (not to be confused with the neurotransmitter of the same acronym)
Greymule Spaceways Infamous intergalactic transportation firm whose motto "*We move bodies*" won the deceptive advertising award three years in a row.
Hap, the Happy syndrome, contracted through using same toothbrush, sitting on same toilet seat, unclean needles, sexual contact, and drinking out of the same glass of someone already infected. The syndrome causes those affected to find everything very pleasant. They are constantly singing songs and patting people on the back. It is 100% fatal with victims usually getting run over by hit and run drivers. Original contraction occurs when raw deo-ore (see Scoscrub) is eaten. You can tell if a dead body had the Hap, they all die with a big smile on their face.
Heinous Book of Galactic Records Most sued business
H.E.L.L. H*g* E**r**** L********r** L**i**
  (more letters will be revealed in Volume 32!)
Helm scale Used to measure belches

Hollywood Squares Terran game show

H.O.M.E. Heavily Operated Mechanized Enterprises

Jeedude(AKA Jeydude) Slang term for unit of currency widespread throughout the galaxy. See space bucks.

Krobus & Chobus Sometimes Krogamma and Chogamma

Leech, the G.R.S. Tax collecting vessel of the Galactic Revenue Service.

Magbus, magcar Magneticly levitated transport vehicles

Maglev skid Device used for letting ground and hover cars to use the maglev rail system

McChicken AKA boneless chickens

McCow Cubular cow with no legs grown in a warehouse

McFood Fast food restaurant that serves McChickens and McCows AKA Micky D's

Megaball Favorite pastime sport of Deo 7

Minotaur Burrowing worm creature that finds its prey

Neil / Clobberson Effect- Collective consciousness that has a tangible effect

91st Day Repenters Secret society founded on Deo 7 as the 89th Day Repenters, later relocated to Rall Raul Beta where they pilfered the King's treasury

Original Entity An immortal being that just popped into existence after the creation of the universe

Palindrome (see chorus line girls)

Palpukas Evil counterparts of the Alpukas

Plutonian Liberation Front Tax shelter created by the law firm of Roach Schiester and Crook

Project Retribution Day Plot by HELL to overthrow Deo 7

Purple dots Created by Restaplat Phlatmier

Quasars Who the Supreme Beings pray to

Quickvader Magneticly levitated elevator with built in restitiriums so it doesn't have to stop

Ragloid Beer made from a Fuzgaloid plant

Restitirium lost and found place for poop etc...

Riddlesmith Expert maker of riddles

Scoscrub First dug up by Nepp Pitts, in 97,194.5, when he was trying to exterminate some wild Alpuka gofers with a HOMEmade mininuke. At first he sued the Lugietorpian Colonial Agency for the big smell it caused on his farm, but sold his whole farm (now the entire Scogo peninsula) to Avery Kebber for $5000 Lugietorpian space bucks

Space Bucks see jeedudes

Spogui A relatively nasty type of mold that eats flies

Squipdukchites- Inventers of the Martial Arts

Transmat transmigration of materials, a teleportation device generally not suited for objects with souls

T.H.E.M. The Human Enemy Morons

T.H.E.Y. The Human Enemy Yuppies

T.H.O.S.E Ten Hebrews On Sunken Enchiladas

Y.I.G. Yuspurly Insurance Group infamous for helping Grego the Mean and burning.....[censored]....

Other Weird Stuff:

Cahootz Salad dressing popular on Deo 7
Crappy Pies have negative nutritional value
Jeedude galactic currency not valid on Deo 7

    Bit- $12.5
    Wad- $50
    Chunk- $100
    Bunch- $250
    Lot- $500
    Load- $1000
    Heap- $10,000
    Stash- $100,000
    Arm- $500,000
    Leg- $750,000

Postoff Ice Confusing desert
Post Office An ancient temple on Deo 7 devoted to the   ancient and
mystical art of paper juggling

II People

Major Characters:

Chorus line girls- Nell, Edna, Anita, Nora, Alice, Carol, Annie, Leda, Ima, Isabel, Adel, Rae, Penny, Lana, Nana, Lynne, Pearl, Eda, Lebasi, Ami, Adel, Einna, Lora, Cecila, Arona, Tina, and Ellen.
Clergy, the

    Joe (Joseph Howalczyk)- electric triangle
    Bufgoo (Prescott Poindexter)- drums
    Hack (Harold Brutus Black)- chainsaw
    Manuel Martinez- Bass, guitar

Destiny Original Being, very powerful
Funky Chicken Original Being, likes to get himself killed
Mister Bear Doesn't say much, AKA Mr. Ursus
Plutoman Mutated human living on Pluto with his dog and
    parrot
Ranger Joe Blues Brothers fanboy, good with ground   vehicles
Rogicphil Suflipinic Reporter, Gladerunner
Satanic Cow Besey the cow (normally lower case as
    stipulated in the summary judgment)
Space-Bo (born Conrad Bovastein) Ex-space marine now   freelance
spaceship person (?)
Spyman (aka Grayson Sofecistat) Secret agent for the
    reformed British secret service

Supporting Characters:

Bagidol Pet dog of Plutoman, computer programmer
Bossman In charge of HELL on Raul Rall Beta

Girl with the Purple Blindfold time traveling robot
Grego the Mean Owns all the positive money on Deo 7
Plutoman's spaceship computer- just that
Pauli Pet parrot of Plutoman
Sir Rontho Head of British secret service American branch
Wilbur and Jake Minions of HELL

Other worthless characters:

Admiral Kopchif went through Space Cadet training 3 times
Agent 666 Every minion of the retarded organization known as H.E.L.L.
Avania "The Mauler" Ivlegsky- Hostage
Avery Kebber Started the Deodorant business
Barthan Transtyle Is paranoid
Bob "Bobcat" MacMacky "Friend" of Spyman
Boris Farmer Browns dog and nemesis to the cow
Buckshot Old man with a song named after him
Burf former pet slug and current cult leader
Burttul Nurts Former political activist
Buz a Barber of reknown
Chancellor Kolm Bad speller
Conrad Bovistine Fake real name of Space-Bo
Dililah Secretary to the Bossman
Dr. Fred Shandrydan Crazy old man
Dr. Gronblec Likes to "bowl"
Dr. Vadlin Nosehonka Likes to read strange books
Dr. Vadlin Nosehonka's Secretary's Robot on the run
Eugene a very gruntled accountant
Farmer Brown Legal owner of Besey the cow
Ferd Hicksville criminal with a bullet stuck in his nose
Gnorge McShplat Deo Rebel and Gladeboot theif
Grrr little kid rescued by the bear
Hagsplat Ufglong Likes to eat red tennis balls
Harriet secretary to some Supreme Beings
Henyr Simth & Beytt Joens Avid pen pals
Herman the Fish Friend of Besey the cow
High anti-Bishop Lester Has major bad breath
Huxley Watched too much Star Trek
Gonkin Tabalbut Proposed negative money
Joe (the third one) Space-Bo's pilot
Junthomas YIG insurance adjuster
King of Raul Rall Beta Likes the Clergy
Krebb Knorr Author of survival guides
Luella secretary (who secretly runs the whole show)
Mack Hovertruck driver
Mel-Sebuttun, Captainess Joehona idiot in training
Mother Maynard can bake a mean pie
Nell Parsley King and discovered of Rall Raul Beta

Nepp Pitts Original owner of the Scogo peninsula
Noj McWayne Myth figure of Deo 7
Officer Johnson Just that (aren't they all)
Old Fart, mister Janitor of Balidron's Megaball stadium
Ralph security dude from H.E.L.L.
Ralpho Hologhoul
Rehpot Aibuloc Discoverer of Deo 7
Regrub Nueek Compulsive gambler that got toasted
Restaplat Phlatmier Clumsy with purple ink
Rickerson Danville cab driver and karaoke aficionado
Robert Doldinee Liked to be called "Bob"
Ruthven Grego's butler and kicking target
Slick time jumping piano player (but that's another story)
Space Banditos have a lot of explaining to do
Spumonti the Awesome Former escape artist, now handicap
Stananki Burfulot A former Gladerunner
Stuin Stramm Pig farmer
Swonoosewanger, Ms. Owns a three headed kangaroo thing
Synthi Waitress at Ruger's Pizza Nightclub
Tarkin Noseblar Megaball Ref
Toafnurdler, Mrs. Space-Bo's first grade teacher
Ufrena Some unimportant character referred to only in passing by some other unimportant character's grandson but later a love interest of Greyson's
White, Mrs. friend of Sir Rontho
Wimble bellhop and food taster
Woody Lee Hicksville Zen and Horse Master
Wyatt White Zombie wrangler and trick slug rider
Yegor Shnolstlenc Had only one good suit
Yors Fargret First person to say "I'll buy that."

III Places

Bars:

Bardobetty's Epsilon Zendrady
O'Nelly's Fast Space Food 'N' More Off-World Bar and Cafe Danville
Rutger's Pizza Nightclub Deo 7
Vinnie's True-To-Life Western Style Bar- Terra

Other Weird Places:

Biogron Christian Cryogenic Institute (BCCI)
Where they freeze your ASSests.
Chateu Le Scrofa Restaurant on Raul Rall Beta
Galactic Church and Bingo Hall best place to eat when in   Balidron.
Competitor of H.E.L.L.

Neazben's College of Salesmen and Pimps High quality school on Deo 7

Nexus Point a seemingly bottomless pit that Grego throws his money down. At the very bottom is a transmat pad that connects to YIG head quarters

Sawdad's Bed and Pizza Do you want a room with that pizza? Lugietorp's finest.

Walther Lee's Dry Cleaning And/Or We Fong Jewelry Repair Fine establishment on Raul Rall Beta

Wee Fong Dong Stellar Freeway Galactic Sector A12

Worldwide Pancake Warehouse strategic storage facility maintained by the US Government to help moderate the world pancake market

IV Deo 7 Slang

Barfinkel Exclamation

Bartlewoopie Hezshmagoolosh

Blarfnurumple ???

Bleorg Sacred religious word (91st Day Repenters)

Dernt Bad deal, no good

Doonk Said when being popped in the head

Etam-Usnoc Religious phrase

Fotnozlixel Anything that attracts dogs (esp. fire hydrants)

Grumption Sound of wet shoes on tile floors

Hezshmagoolosh Bartlewoopie

Ivifmaefu Real bad road kill

Jeedude or Jeydude Unit of currency

Jeupert Lint balls found in the navel

Maefu Road kill

Muecat Small singed mammal

Nebalork Greeting

Neyazwa Sacred religious words (91st)

Nikstlits and Elpmur Comedy team, used as exclamation

Nubalork Farewell

Octohooga Curse of the the 8th degree

Onin & Osis Gods called upon to damn things

Rauxob Said before jumping off of something

Scoojack To slide on a slippery surface for fun (preferably only in socks)

Scrubulous Sacred religious word (91st)

Sublimate Euphemism for summary execution

Whutaru-Crazy thank you

Whopla Sacred religious word (91st)

Xupnarst Grower of Fuzgaloid

Zanufski Sacred religious word (91st)

www.ingramcontent.com/pod-product-compliance
Lightning Source LLC
Chambersburg PA
CBHW030353030726
47497CB00002B/316